P9-DBT-619

WIND WALKER

BOOKS BY TERRY C. JOHNSTON

Cry of the Hawk
Winter Rain
Dream Catcher

Carry the Wind
Borderlords
One-Eyed Dream

Dance on the Wind
Buffalo Palace
Crack in the Sky
Ride the Moon Down
Death Rattle

SONS OF THE PLAINS NOVELS

Long Winter Gone
Seize the Sky
Whisper of the Wolf

THE PLAINSMEN NOVELS

Sioux Dawn
Red Cloud's Revenge
The Stalkers
Black Sun
Devil's Backbone
Shadow Riders
Dying Thunder
Blood Song
Reap the Whirlwind
Trumpet on the Land
A Cold Day in Hell
Wolf Mountain Moon
Ashes of Heaven
Cries from the Earth
Lay the Mountains Low

BANTAM BOOKS

New York
Toronto
London
Sydney
Auckland

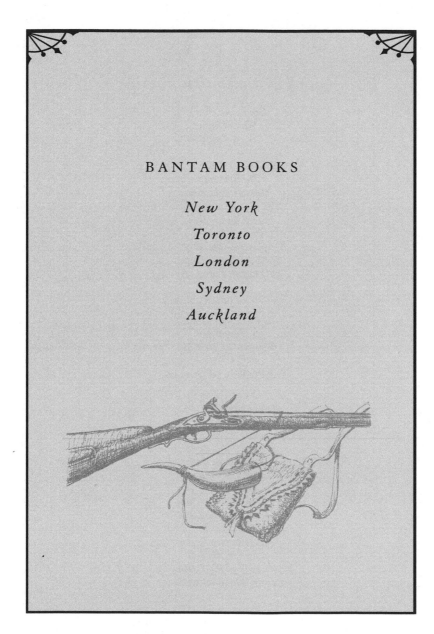

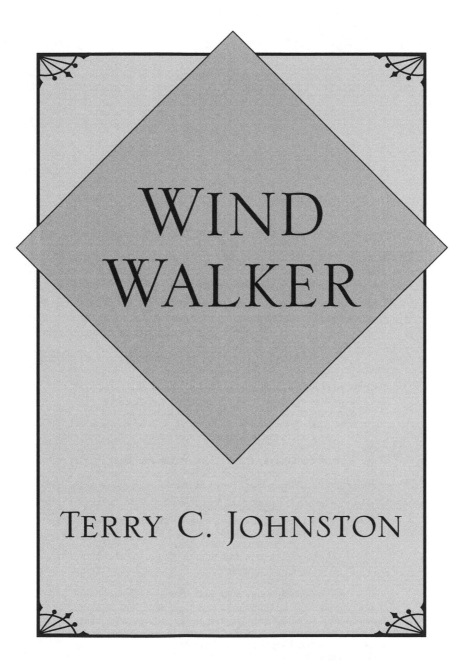

WIND WALKER

TERRY C. JOHNSTON

WIND WALKER

A Bantam Book / February 2001

Map by Jeffrey L. Ward

Library of Congress Cataloging-in-Publication Data
Johnston, Terry C., 1947-
Wind walker / Terry C. Johnston.
p. cm.
ISBN 0-553-09090-9
1. Bass, Titus (Fictitious character)—Fiction. 2. Ohio River Valley—
Fiction. 3. West (U.S.)—Fiction. I. Title.
PS3560.O392 W53 2001
813'.54—dc21
00-48570

Published simultaneously in the United States and Canada

Bantam Books are published by Bantam Books, a division of Random
House, Inc. Its trademark, consisting of the words "Bantam Books" and the
portrayal of a rooster, is Registered in U.S. Patent and Trademark Office and
in other countries. Marca Registrada. Bantam Books, 1540 Broadway, New
York, New York 10036.

PRINTED IN THE UNITED STATES OF AMERICA

BVG   10 9 8 7 6 5 4 3 2 1

For all that his steadfast friendship has meant to me
and my writing career across many, many seasons—
from the Rocky Mountain front to the grand Pacific Coast—
it is with honor that I dedicate this final novel in
the saga of Titus Bass
to my old and dear friend of Colorado's Front Range,
the one who has been braiding the rope
others will one day strive to climb,

Kent Havermann

a man who would do to ride the river with,
a friend who would stand at my back against Blackfoot . . .

A man Titus Bass himself is proud to call his friend!

The old man sang his death song then;
His voice rang clear and high:
"O Sun, thou endureth forever,
But we who are warriors must die!"

—STANLEY VESTAL
Fandango, Ballads of the Old West

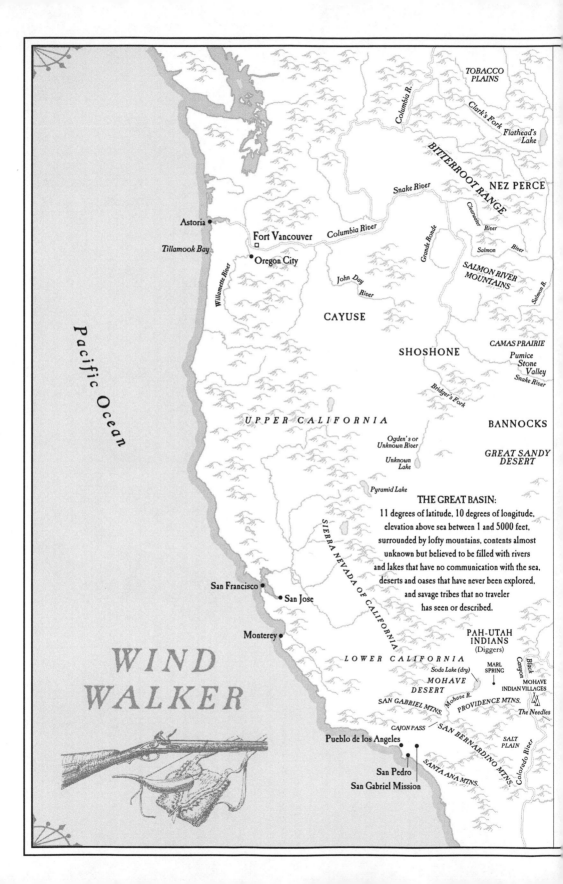

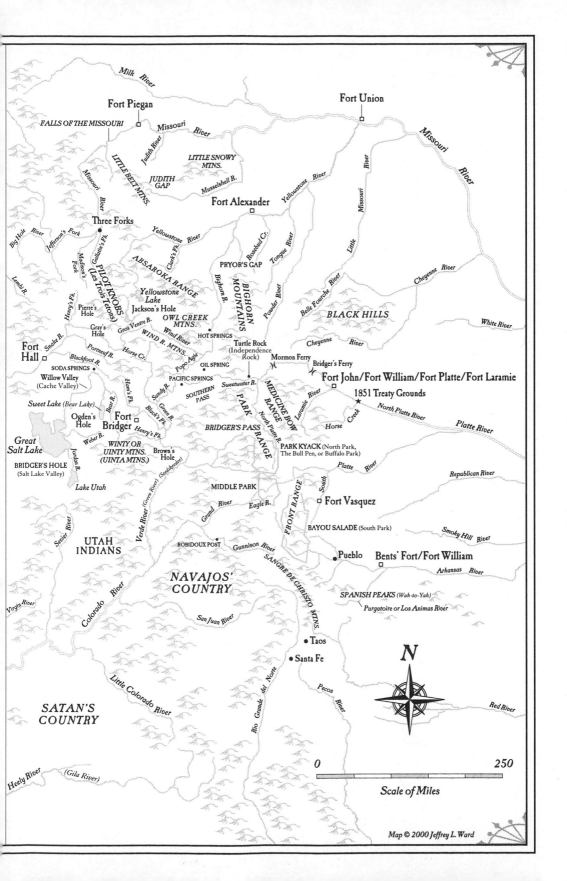

Milk River

Fort Piegan

FALLS OF THE MISSOURI
Judith River   Missouri   River

Fort Union

Missouri   River

LITTLE SNOWY MTNS.

Missouri   River

LITTLE BELT MTNS.

JUDITH GAP

Musselshell R.

Fort Alexander   Yellowstone   River

Missouri   River

Little   Missouri   River

Three Forks

Big Hole   River   Jefferson's Fork

Gallatin's Fk.

Madison Fork   Clark's Fk.

Lemhi R.

Henry's Fk.

PILOT KNOBS (Les Trois Tetons)

ABSAROKA RANGE   Yellowstone   River

PRYOR'S GAP

Rosebud Cr.   Tongue River

Yellowstone   River

Powder River

Cheyenne   River

White River

Pierre's Hole   Yellowstone Lake   Jackson's Hole

BIGHORN MOUNTAINS

Bighorn R.

Belle Fourche   River

BLACK HILLS

Gray's Hole   Gros Ventre R.   OWL CREEK MTNS.

Wind River   HOT SPRINGS

Fort Hall

Snake R.   Blackfoot R.

Horse Cr.   WIND R. MTNS.

Popo Agie   OIL SPRING

Turtle Rock (Independence Rock)

Mormon Ferry

Cheyenne   River

SODA SPRINGS

Willow Valley (Cache Valley)

Ham's Fk.   Sandy R.

PACIFIC SPRINGS

Sweetwater R.

Bridger's Ferry

Fort John/Fort William/Fort Platte/Fort Laramie

1851 Treaty Grounds   ★

Sweet Lake (Bear Lake)

Ogden's Hole   Bear R.

Black's Fk.   Green R.

SOUTHERN PASS

PARK RANGE

MEDICINE BOW RANGE

North Platte R.

Laramie River

North Platte River

Platte River

Fort Bridger   Henry's Fk.

Weber R.

Horse   Creek

Great Salt Lake

WINTY OR UINTY MTNS. (UINTA MTNS.)

Brown's Hole (Seedskeedee)

BRIDGER'S PASS

BRIDGER'S HOLE (Salt Lake Valley)

Jordan R.

Lake Utah

MIDDLE PARK

PARK KYACK (North Park, The Bull Pen, or Buffalo Park)

Platte   River   South

Republican River

Sevier   River

Verde River (Green River)

Grand   River   Eagle R.

FRONT RANGE

Fort Vasquez

BAYOU SALADE (South Park)

Smoky Hill   River

UTAH INDIANS

ROBIDOUX POST

Gunnison River

SANGRE DE CHRISTO MTNS.

Pueblo   Bents' Fort/Fort William

Virgin River

Colorado   River

NAVAJOS' COUNTRY

San Juan River

SPANISH PEAKS (Wah-to-Yah)

Purgatoire or Los Animas River

Arkansas   River

Little Colorado River

Rio Grande del Norte

Taos

Santa Fe

Pecos   River

Red River

N

SATAN'S COUNTRY

Heely River   (Gila River)

0   250

Scale of Miles

Map © 2000 Jeffrey L. Ward

WIND WALKER

ONE

"Strangers?"

Without looking at his young son, Titus Bass nodded and eventually whispered, "Yes, Flea. In this country, you must consider everyone a stranger."

His own words stabbed into the frozen air, hung frostily for but a heartbeat, then were ripped away by a sharp, sudden gust that stirred up skiffs of the dry, two-day-old snow around them, where they lay on a ledge of bare rock.

"Get me the far-seeing glass," the fifty-three-year-old trapper said, never tearing his eyes off the distant objects plodding like black-backed sow beetles across the everywhere-white ablaze beneath the brilliant winter sun in a far-reaching sky.

Without making a sound in reply, the boy of ten winters scooted backward into the stunted cedar, where he rose in a crouch and quietly padded away, the soft crunch of his thick winter moccasins fading in the utter, aching silence that made itself known each time the winter wind died here on the brow of the low ridge. It wasn't long before Titus heard his son returning. Flea went to his knees, then plopped onto his belly to cover those last few yards, crawling right up beside his father, their elbows brushing.

"You are a good son," he whispered to his oldest boy in the child's strongest language, Crow—the tongue of Flea's mother.

Brushing some of his long, gray hair out of his face, Titus again vowed that he should teach his children more, much more, of his own American tongue in the months and years to come. Down in the marrow of him he was growing more certain with time that they would need that American tongue before they became adults. His children would grow into maturity and give birth to children of their own in a world that Bass knew nothing of. A world very much unlike the world he had grown up in at the edge of the frontier, back there in Kentucky—essentially the same world his own father had grown up in, and to a great extent the very same life his grandfather had known before them. Right in the same place, on the same land both father and grandfather had tilled, sweated into, and prayed over. But . . . Magpie, Flea, and little Jackrabbit would soon enough confront a world their father knew nothing of.

He smiled as Flea held out the long, brass spyglass to him. "You are a good lad," he said, this time in American, slowly too, pulling out the three sections to the spyglass's full length.

"Lad." Flea tried the word out, then paused slightly as he strung more words together, "I—am—a—good—lad."

"You're about the best lad ever could be," Titus confirmed, again in American, then patted his son on the shoulder.

Poking his trigger finger through the small slot cut in his thick buffalo-hair mittens so he could fire his rifle with those mittens on, Bass swiveled the tiny brass protective plate away from the eyepiece and brought the spyglass to his one good eye. Blinked several times. Then peered through the long instrument as he slowly scanned the far ground below them until the image of the riders flashed across his view. Back he brought the spyglass, then slowly, slowly twisted the last of the three sections to bring the figures into better focus.

"Here, Flea—have a look for your own self," he said as he handed the boy the spyglass. When his son had it against one eye, Bass spoke in Crow. "Turn it slow, like this, to see the riders come up close in your eye."

The man rubbed the long, pale scar that angled downward from the outside corner of his left eye while he waited for the boy to scan the ground ahead with that strange, foreign instrument. He had worn that scar for some fifteen winters now, cut there in a last, desperate fight he had with an old friend whose right hand had been replaced with a crude iron hook.

As the youth panned across the landscape, Flea jerked to a halt and held the spyglass steady, breathless too.

Titus asked, "How many you count?"

Flea's lips moved slightly as he continued to concentrate his attention on the distant objects. "Two-times-ten, perhaps a little more."

"No, in American."

The boy took the spyglass from his eye and concentrated now on this new problem. Then he said in his father's tongue, "Ten."

"No," Titus prodded in a whisper, speaking his own native language. "That's the wrong American word. Two-times-ten. So in American, you say *twenty*."

"Why is this number more important than those riders down there?" Flea asked with a youth's irritation.

Bass sighed and said, "You are right. We must think on the riders. All those horsemen—do you think they are enemies?"

With a nod, the boy answered in Crow, "Just as you said, in this country there are many strangers . . . and strangers could be enemies."

For a moment he glanced at Wah-to-Yah, the Spanish Peaks, rising against the blue winter sky off to the west. Then he asked the boy, "Tell me what you think about those riders. Do you see the horses that don't carry any riders? The animals loaded down with packs? What of this bunch coming our way—should we hurry back to your mother and the rest of our family? Should we get them into hiding fast?"

For a long moment Flea regarded his father as if it might just be a trick question. Then he whispered, "They don't ride like Indians."

"Why do you say they don't ride like Indians, son?"

"Because, Popo," Flea said, using that affectionate name for his father, "the Indians I know—they ride in single file."

"So these horsemen, what are they?"

"White men?"

"Say it in American for me."

"White men," Flea said assuredly. He knew those words. His father was one. Half his blood and bone and muscle was white.

"You see the dog?" he asked his son.

"Dog?"

"Look carefully—and you'll spot him."

After some moments, Flea finally declared, "That dog is white—I did not see him for a long time because of the snow."

"Big dog, ain't it?" he asked in American.

"Yes."

"Injuns have dogs near big as that critter?"

The boy shook his head.

"That's right, son," Titus whispered. "Dog like that lopin' along them horses—it's a sign them are likely white men comin' our way."

Over the last few agonizing weeks Titus Bass had grown all the more certain that he would see that every one of his children knew everything he could teach them about the white man. Not just his language, but his ways. The good and the bad of the pale-skinned ones who were trickling out of the East. Titus would have to teach them everything he inherently knew about his own kind so that his half-blood children would not get eaten alive when the mountains grew crowded with strangers.

They knew of enemies. *Iskoochiia.* The Crow had always suffered the mighty enemies who surrounded their Absaroka homeland. But those forces still to come would be even mightier than the Sioux or Cheyenne, stronger still than the powerful Blackfoot too. Titus Bass had seen a glimpse of what was on its way to these mountains. That one meant more were sure to come—

wagons—every last one of them filled with corncrackers, sodbusters, settlers . . . farmers with their women and their young'uns along, bringing their
plows to dig up the ground and their Bibles to pacify the wildness out of this
land. Almost seven years ago he had watched that first wagon with its dingy-
gray canvas top wheel into their final rendezvous on the Green River, the fabled
Seedskeedee Agie, or Prairie Hen, River. It hadn't been a trader's wagon. No,
that wheeled contraption did not turn back for St. Louis when the annual trading fair was over. Instead, the sodbuster took his wagon and family on west . . .
making for Oregon country.*

A few more of their kind had already come at earlier rendezvous—but only
a string of preachers and their wives, missionaries come to the wilderness to
take the wildness out of this primal place and its Indians. Come to bring the
word of the Lord to the red man—to civilize these warriors and their squaws,
turn them into God-fearing, land-tilling white folk just like everyone back east.

Damn them, anyway! To make over this land into their own image instead of
leaving it just the way it had been when Titus Bass himself arrived back in
eighteen and twenty-five. This coming spring would make it twenty-two years
since he'd come to the mountains. He could count each and every season—
every summer and every winter—marked inside his soul the way a fella could
peer down and count each year of a tree's life.

"And those horses under their heavy packs—like a white man. Indians pull
travois. These are white men, Popo," Flea whispered now, in Crow, taking the
spyglass from his eye again. "Just like you."

"No," his father corrected patiently. "Don't you ever believe that just because a man has pale skin like me, that he is just like me, son. That thinking is
downright dangerous. Most white men aren't at all like me."

"Not the . . . the," and Flea sought for the word. "Greasers? They're not like
you?"

With a wag of his head, Titus explained. "No. Them greasers come to kill all
the white folks from America what come down to Mexico. Kill any women
married to them fellas. Greasers come to butcher their children—just because
them young'uns was like you and had some white blood in 'em."

"That why we ran away, Popo?"

Laying his hand on his boy's shoulder, Titus vowed, "I'll run anywhere I
have to, Flea—to save my family."

"We run away from these strangers?"

"Not just yet," Bass answered, considering the steel-gray, overcast sky.
"We'll have us a close look come sundown when they make camp."

As they slid backward on their bellies through the snow-dusted cedar and juniper, Titus did his best to pray that those horsemen weren't renegade Mexicans
or the Pueblo Indians who had thrown in together and let the wolf out to howl

---

* *Ride the Moon Down*

in Taos. They had prowled the streets for any American, even anyone who consorted with Americans, then hacked them apart with their machetes and farm implements. Titus Bass got his family out of the village and into the hills with no more than moments to spare. By the time they were approaching Turley's mill just north of town, the murderous mob was launching its attack on the mill's inhabitants. Titus struck out for the foothills with his family, and that of his long-ago partner, Josiah Paddock.*

But right from the beginning it was clear they couldn't hold out forever with their loved ones, hiding in the foothills, waiting for any roving bands of Mexicans or Pueblos to discover them as they went about hunting for something to eat, collecting wood to fight off the numbing cold one snowstorm after another. So Bass volunteered to push north alone, across the pass, pointing his nose for a trading settlement founded by former trappers, a place called the Pueblo. After losing his horse and subsequent days of foundering on foot, nearly starving and close to freezing, Titus had stumbled into a cluster of canvas tents—a camp of westbound sojourners who called themselves the chosen Saints of God, a party of religious pioneers wintering near the trading post until the spring thaw would allow them to continue west, on to their promised land reputed to lie somewhere beyond the high mountains.

After those Saints delivered the half-dead old trapper to the gates of the traders' stockade, Titus hurriedly delivered the terrible news of the Pueblo revolt. Wringing their hands in anger and frustration, the former mountain men argued over what to do. Although there weren't near enough of the old trappers to beat back the hordes of Mexicans and Pueblos on a rampage, the Americans nonetheless voted to start south immediately—if only to be close enough to keep an eye on the village of Taos and be ready when the army's dragoons marched up from Santa Fe to put an end to the riot and murder. But before their ragtag band marched out south early the following morning, they sent one of their own to carry word of the uprising and brutal murder of the American governor himself to Bents' Fort on down the Arkansas River.

Wasn't a man there in that cold, hushed, dimly lit room at the Pueblo where Titus had told his story could argue that William Bent didn't deserve to know how his older brother, Charles, had been hacked apart by the Taos mob—just as fast as a runner could get a horse on down the Arkansas to that big adobe fort with the news.

Louy Simmons volunteered to make that ride east while the rest turned their faces south for the valley of the San Fernandez and that tiny village of Taos where the icy streets had run red with the blood of Americans. Although weary and weak from his ordeal in bringing the horrible news, Titus turned right around and started south, leading Mathew Kinkead and the others who were setting off to right a terrible wrong. With his family and old friends hiding out

---

* *Death Rattle*

among the hills above Taos, he could do no less. Then somewhere along that trail, in those long, cold days spent racing back to his family, Bass had decided against joining in the retribution. Not that the Mexicans and Indians didn't have a judgment day coming—be it a dragoons' firing squad or a long drop at the end of a short rope noose tied by the hands of those American mountain men.

But this simply was not his fight.

By the time he had watched his half-blood children lunging toward him through the knee-deep snow, Titus Bass knew he would start his family north for the country where life was his fight. The others, like old friend Josiah Paddock—they had a decided stake in this land where the American army had come to conquer the Mexicans, this land where those chosen Saints of God had migrated to wrest their promised land from an unforgiving wilderness. As soon as he finally held his Crow wife tightly in his arms, rejoicing at their reunion, Titus realized if he did little else, he had to get his family far enough north that they would be in country the white man did not want. Only then would they be safe from those dangers he did not begin to understand.

Some dangers he could comprehend: the hatred between the Crow and their ancient adversaries to the north and east. Dangers such as the great white bears that could tear a man apart in heartbeats, or beasts that broke your leg so you could not move and slowly froze to death—those were the challenges and risks a man could fathom. They were a part of the life he had endured for more than two decades already. Such were the dangers that he reveled in, the very risks he had come west to conquer. Titus Bass could understand those challenges that had been an integral, and daily, part of his life for so long. But he did not care to make sense of armies coming to take away an old way of life from the Mexicans and Pueblo Indians, nor did he make sense of those Mexicans and Pueblos who staged a bloody revolt to drive out all those who were different. But what made him seek to hurry his family north even faster was his inability to make sense of those religious zealots who had come to the mountains to make a place only for their chosen few.

Ever since he had arrived here back in '25, this had always been a land where a man celebrated his freedom to do and be . . . but now there were armies and emigrants, murderers and zealots come to change the face of this wilderness, come to change the very nature of what had belonged to only the daring few for so long.

Putting the San Fernandez Valley at their backs, Titus and his family struck out for the snowy pass, then started down, angling off to the northeast for the Picketwire.* Near its mouth, on the north bank of the Arkansas, Titus promised them they would find the mud-walled fort where the Bent brothers traded with the likes of the Kiowa, Arapaho, and Cheyenne. But they hadn't escaped the foothills when they spotted those distant horsemen—dark figures crossing the

---

* Purgatoire (Purgatory) River

crusty snow. Turning his family and their animals into a juniper-cloaked draw, Bass took his eldest son and together they worked their way to the edge of a rocky overhang.

Through the spyglass the figures appeared to move like white men, at least by the way they rode spread out rather than strung back in a long column like a war party would ride on the march. But who could tell for sure, what with those horsemen bundled under layers of winter clothing—wrapped in wool blanket coats or thick fur hides as their hang-down animals plodded for the foothills while the sun continued its fall. He and the boy would watch from here until the horsemen made camp for the coming night . . . then leaving his loved ones back in the safety of that ravine, Titus alone would slip up on the strangers.

First off to learn the color of their skin, and then to discover the purpose of their journey south toward that land of revolt and bloodshed.

Titus didn't recognize a one of them.

Not that it was particularly easy for him to pick out a familiar face as the strangers hunkered around their fires, their faces obscured by furry hats or the hoods to their blanket coats, lit only with the flicker of low flames a dull red on the snow as they murmured to one another. He waited in the darkness, listening to a foreign tongue he knew was not Mexican, but a language he had heard plenty of during those years he languished in old St. Louis before striking out for the mountains. Some of these strangers were Frenchies, the laborers who had long played an important role in the fur trade across this wide, wild continent.

Silently he pushed back, sliding into the dark, and inched over closer to another fire, where he strained to listen to the quiet talk of those men rubbing frozen hands and warming icy feet near the flames. This bunch was Americans. Leastways, what he could hear of their few words.

Slowly rising to his feet, Bass called out, "Ho, the camp! I'm comin' in! Don't get no itchy fingers—this here's a white nigger!"

At his first cry the men around those half-dozen fires leaped to their feet, some snatching up guns and preparing to make a fight of it, others ducking behind what cover there was in their baggage. The huge white dog leaped up, a deep, menacing growl rumbling at the back of its throat. In their midst a man of middling height stepped forth, longrifle in hand, yelling orders at the rest as he seized hold of the wide collar buckled around the big dog's throat.

"Hold on there, you men!" he roared as he jerked the animal into a sitting position. "You heard him say he's a white man." Then he turned and flung his voice to that side of the camp where the shadow emerged from the brush at the base of the ridge. "How many are with you?"

Bass stopped and started to grin. With a shrug he held out his arms and replied, "Jus' me. Ain't no others."

Lowering his smoothbore, the leader said, "C'mon over here."

Less than two dozen men quickly surrounded Bass and the leader, who yanked the mitten off his right hand. "My name's Bill Bransford." The dog growled at the newcomer, so Bransford snapped, "Hush!" then peered at Bass. "We met before?"

"Not that I know of," Titus said, stuffing his right hand under his left armpit and yanking off his thick blanket mitten. They shook. "My name's Bass. Titus Bass."

"I heard tell of you," Bransford replied with a grin. "Sometime back, you was over to the big fort on the Arkansas with some other fellas and a big herd of horses you was sellin'."

"You're good at 'memberin', Mr. Bransford."

"Hell, I was a junior clerk back then. Brought my dog here out from St. Louis when I come to work at the fort years ago. So I well remember how you dickered on every last dollar for your horses, and ended up riding off with a couple of Charlotte's puppies too."

The remembrance of those fat, furry pups made him smile as another man stepped up. "Your name's Bass?"

Titus instantly turned on the speaker, intrigued at something naggingly familiar in the clip to the stranger's words, and replied, "Titus Bass."

"You're the one I heard who's called Scratch?"

"That's right. And what be your name?"

"Lewis Garrard."

"Ever you spend time on the Ohio River?"

"Born in Cincinnati," Garrard responded with a grin. "How'd you know?"

"I come from the Ohio River country my own self," Titus explained. "Boone County, Kentucky. Thort I heard the ring of that country in your words."

"I've come west looking for a little adventure," Garrard remarked.

He asked Garrard, "How you get hooked up with these pork-eaters?"

"I was with William Bent, trading out to the Big Timbers, when word of his brother's death reached us."

Bass looked at Bransford again, eyeing the man up and down. "Knowed Hudson's Bay had Fort Hall across the mountains, but I didn't think John Bull's boys ever come this far south. How come Hudson's Bay got hooked up with them Bent brothers?"

Bransford spoke up defensively, "We ain't no Hudson's Bay!"

"So you claim you ain't a John Bull* outfit?" Titus inquired.

"No," Bransford answered, looking mystified. "What made you think we was?"

"Laying out there in the dark, I was listening to them Frenchies palaver over yonder at that fire. Just figgered with them parley-voos along you was Hudson's Bay."

---

* Term used by Americans during this early time period to refer to anything English.

"William has him some Frenchmen working for him," Bransford explained. "A few of 'em are hard workers. Like this bunch."

"Where away you bound, headin' south for the pass?" Titus asked. "You know there's trouble south of here now."

Garrard rubbed his hands together eagerly. "Just the sort of adventure I came west to find."

Bransford motioned Bass to join them at the closest fire and said, "You'll soon get all of the adventure you're wanting, come the day we reach Taos, Garrard."

"Taos?" Bass echoed in surprise. "So your bunch is headed for Taos?"

The leader turned on his heel and glared at Bass. "Sounds to me you know something of the bloodbath down that way."

"I carried news of those doin's all the way north to the Pueblo," Titus declared sourly. "Kinkead and Fisher, the rest of 'em too, they set out with me the next day."

"What are you doing up here if you returned to Taos?" Garrard asked.

"Decided it ain't my fight."

Garrard snorted. "Isn't my fight either—but it's bound to be one helluva time!"

Bransford leaned forward. "Why you wandering around out here by your lonesome?"

"Taking my family to Bents' big lodge. Afore we push on north for Crow country."

"Your family with you?" Garrard asked.

"That's why I ain't making that scrap in Taos my fight." He pointed to the coffeepot at the edge of the fire pit. "You got something hot to drink?"

"Pour this cold man a cup," Bransford ordered. "We're on our way to Taos, maybeso to help the soldiers and those fellas from Fisher's fort put down this revolt."

Scratch watched the hot liquid hiss into a tin cup he held out, steam rising into the cold air. "Ain't much any of you can do," he explained quietly. "By now them murderers gone and butchered every white person in the area. They wiped out Turley's mill."

"Turley's mill too?" one of the strangers repeated.

He nodded as he took a first sip of the hot coffee. "I'll lay as how them greasers got their work done awready. No one left to save now."

"William Bent wanted us to try," Bransford declared.

"Bent hisself?" Bass echoed. "So Louy Simmons did make it after all."

"Like Garrard told you," Bransford nodded solemnly. "Simmons reached William when he was off trading at Big Timbers."

Then Garrard spoke up. "I was right there with William, and old John Smith too—when Simmons came riding in with word that Charles was murdered."

Titus turned back to Bransford and asked, "What's this Big Timbers?"

"Place on the Arkansas—lots of cottonwoods—where William Bent's wife's folks, Cheyenne they be, where them Cheyenne camp out of the wind of a winter," Bransford explained. "William rode right in the forty miles to the fort, 'thout stopping, soon as he heard tell of the revolt in Taos."

He tucked the long, slender braid he wore in front of the left side of his face behind his ear and took another sip of the scalding coffee, then asked, "Bent's gone an' rode on ahead of you fellas?"

The leader shook his head. "Lord knows he wanted to—if only to find out 'bout his brother, how Charlie died. But when Frank De Lisle came in with the company wagons from the company camp on the Picketwire, sure as hell that a greaser army was right behind him—Captain Jackson and his soldiers convinced William he should stay put at the fort to protect it against an invading mob. Jackson's got him a small company to begin with—and now there's a score or better of his soldiers too sick to stand for service. There's less'n a dozen able-bodied men to guard them walls now that we're marching for Taos."

"Protect the fort? Ain't no greasers gonna come this far north," Bass snorted and savored the warmth of the coffee tin between his hands. "How 'bout them Cheyennes he married into? Didn't them Injuns at the Big Timbers offer to whoop it on south and wipe out them greasers what kill't Charlie Bent?"

"Damn right, them chiefs volunteered their warriors to do just that," Bransford explained. "But William turned 'em down cold. Told the Cheyennes it was a white man's problem, and the white man'd put it right."

"Maybeso that's square thinkin'," Bass said quietly. "White folks caused the problem in Mexico—it's right that white folks should fix things down there."

"So you're going to find safety in Bents' Fort?" Garrard asked.

"I been there, twice't now," Titus said, turning to address the man. "But, my woman and our young'uns never been. I figger chances be a mite slim I'll ever make it back down this far south—so I decided to show 'em the fort while we're this close."

"You tell William you run onto us," Bransford said. "He could well use another good man while the rest of us is away."

Scratch peered over that motley collection of some two dozen former trappers, Frenchmen, half-bloods, and free men. "I ain't looking for to hire out to no man. Figgered we would camp nearby for a day or so before pushing on north for Crow country."

"What's the country like 'tween here and Taos?" Bransford asked.

"Snows blowed clear on most of the road," Bass declared. "You'll do well if'n you keep your stock watered and fed."

"Had only five horses when we started out," the leader said. "And they was owned by these five free men who decided to throw in with us. Got family down in Taos."

Bass quickly glanced at the stock they had picketed close by, then asked Bransford, "How'd you come on the rest of your horses?"

"When we left the fort, we put our bedding and supplies in a small company wagon. Figured we'd get our hands on some mounts at the Bent brothers' ranch aways up the Picketwire."

"We was hoping them greasers hadn't already raided and run off the horses afore we got to the ranch," a voice called out from the group.

"No greasers showed up at all," Bransford confided. "But a string of government teamsters was already holed up there, afraid to push on south for Taos until word reached 'em that the army had things under control down there."

"You took the wagon horses from them teamsters?" Titus asked.

"Just the ranch stock," Garrard said. "But them riding horses was what the teamsters wanted to hold on to, so they'd have something faster to make their escape than on those slow wagon teams."

"It nearly came to shots fired before those teamsters let us ride off on the ranch horses," Bransford snorted wryly. "Damn if they weren't a scared lot. Tried to hold on to horses what belonged to William and Charles Bent in case they had to gallop on outta there with the Mexicans comin' down on their asses!"

"But look around you, Mr. Bass," Garrard roared. "Do these men look like the sort to walk off without those horses?" Most of the half-breeds and hard-cases laughed heartily. "Not after what they had been through to get to the ranch on foot!"

Bransford went on to explain how his bunch had been hampered for more than a day when they were forced to take shelter during a howling snowstorm. Later, they hadn't found much water in the dried-up creekbed of the Timpas— and what little they scratched up was so laced with alkali that even coffee was undrinkable.

"For two nights we were without anything that would burn for firewood," Garrard explained. "Bill here offered to let me sleep with him and share our blankets—but first we had to convince his damn dog!"

"Back when we reached Hole in the Rock, we thought we had Injuns or Mexicans slipping up on us," Bransford said. "That's when my dog here set up a awful bark. Must've only been a coyote or some other critter."

"You fellas gonna find yourselves in greaser country soon enough," Bass sighed, then blew across the surface of his coffee again. "Keep your ears open and your eyes peeled back—ain't likely this bunch will lose their hair."

"Where you leave your family?" the group's leader asked.

"Back 'round the end of the ridge aways."

"Go fetch 'em and bring 'em here to spend the night."

"Naw," Titus replied, then took a long gulp of the coffee. As he tipped up the coffee tin to drain the last sip, the decorative beads suspended from his long ear wires clinked against the rim of the cup. "Time I get back, them young'uns gonna be sleeping."

"That's a shame," Garrard admitted.

Bass stood and held out his hand to the adventurer. "Grateful for the coffee, and the palaver too."

"Thanks for your news on Taos," Bransford said as he stood and they shook. "Maybeso we'll run onto you up to Bents' some day."

Scratch wagged his head and set his empty cup down near the fire ring, then tugged his coyote fur cap down so that it covered the earrings dangling from both lobes. "Don't figger that'll happen. Sure enough we'll stop by there to let my family have a look-see in the next few days, but I can't think of a thing ever gonna bring me this far south again."

As Titus Bass started out of the circle of strangers, Bransford called out, "Watch your topknot!"

He stopped, turned, and patted the back of his well-worn coyote fur cap. "I been skelped once't awready. Got more holes in this ol' hide than I care to callate. I aim to ride out for that north country, where this nigger won't have to worry 'bout them what wants to lift his topknot. I aim to live out all the rest of my days up where a man can die at peace, fellas. I reckon I'll die a old man wrapped up in my buffler robes."

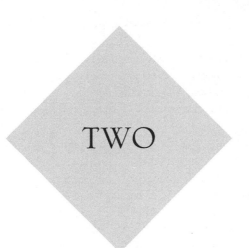

TWO

Like a great, golden pumpkin the adobe walls of the post glowed in a last glittering benediction of winter's late light that third afternoon after leaving Bill Bransford to press south with his avengers to put down the Taos rebellion.

Bass pulled back on the old horse's reins. As the rest of his family came to a halt on either side of the old trapper, he felt his wife's leg press against his as her pony snorted a gauzy mist.

Waits-by-the-Water tugged the thick woolen scarf below her chin so she could speak, exposing the cheeks scarred with the white man's pox. She asked, "This is where the seeing was taken from your eye so many winters ago?"*

Leaning off his horse, Scratch rubbed the small of her back a moment, then answered with a thick voice, "Yes. I come here to find Cooper, afore I finished my journey back to you and little Magpie."

With a flick of her eyes, Waits glanced at their oldest child. "She is not so much a child anymore. Look and you will see!"

He chuckled, then said, "Soon enough Magpie's father will have to sleep by the door of your lodge with his gun in his lap."

"Why would you sleep with a gun in your lap, Popo?" Magpie asked as she urged her pony closer.

Instead Waits answered, "To frighten off all the young men who will be strutting around you like noisy mosquitoes on a summer evening."

---

* *One-Eyed Dream*

The girl's eyes went to her father's face. "Do you . . . you really think the young men will find me . . . pretty?"

How he laughed at that, his face raised to the sky as he roared, "Magpie! You are as pretty as any woman I have ever seen, in either world I have lived in. Why—you are as pretty as your mother was when she was your age and her own father had to start beating the boys away from their lodge door with a long coup stick!"

"We will be safe here?" Waits asked, the sound of her words more solemn.

His eyes crinkled with reassurance when he recognized the worry on her face. "Yes, we will be safe here. The only reason there was danger here so many winters ago was that I came looking for it."

"These horses are tired, Popo," his oldest son reminded. "And they need water too."

"We'll take them down to the river and let them drink their fill," Titus suggested. "Then I'll take my family into the trader's mud lodge."

At the north bank of the Arkansas while Waits-by-the-Water sat with the other children, Scratch and Flea clambered out of their saddles and trudged to the river's edge with their short-handled camp axes. Together they chopped a long slot in the ice while Magpie and her mother dismounted and started the animals toward the bank.

As the horses drank, Titus laid his arm across his wife's shoulder and turned her to look at the distant golden walls. Softly he said, "It will be a good thing to get these children out of the cold for the night."

She gazed up at him, then laid her cheek against his chest as the noisy horses nuzzled the water behind them. "For these children of ours, this little cold does not bother them, Ti-tuzz. I have never heard them complain."

"You are right," he whispered with his chin resting atop her blanket hood. "The winter is much, much colder in our home country far to the north."

"But a fire will feel very good to my feet," Flea said as he brought their three Cheyenne packhorses up the bank to where his parents stood.

"Yes. It is time you show us this big mud lodge that shines red as a prairie paintbrush flower here at sunset!" Magpie goaded him with giddy excitement.

"You too, Jackrabbit?" Titus asked of his four-year-old son still sitting his saddle, his short legs swaddled inside a buffalo robe that was tucked under his arms.

"Go with Popo," the boy answered, a smile brightening his whole face. "My belly wants to eat!"

Squeezing his wife's shoulder, Bass turned to his red horse and said, "Woman, we best go feed this boy before he starts gnawing on my moccasins!"

He loved how their eyes widened the closer they got to the tall mud walls. Approaching from the southwest they reined for the circular bastion that stood more than twenty-some feet above the snowy plain. Extending to the right of that bastion stood two of the three corral walls, the top of all bristling with thorny cactus. Try as he might to squeeze his mind down on it right now, Titus could not remember this corral connected to the fort on his first trip here in the spring of '34, and he couldn't claim he'd paid all that much attention to its presence back in the autumn of '42 when he had traded off most of his Mexican horses for more than a thousandweight of jangly foofaraw and shiny girlews.

"Where is the door to this lodge?" Flea asked, a little perplexed as they continued to plod north along the west wall.

"Soon you will see, my son."

As they turned their horses at the far corner, he spotted a nesting of some three dozen lodges erected back among the riverbank cottonwood several hundred yards from the fort. More than two hundred ponies pawed at the frozen ground between the camp and the mud walls—

Suddenly an iron bell began to clang inside the fort, and a head appeared over the top above them. The man's face disappeared as quickly.

"The Mexicans are here too?" Waits asked him. "This bell rings for their holy meetings?"

He knew she was referring to how the Taosenos followed the dictates of the great iron bell rung in its tall church steeple. He said, "I don't figger we'll find many greasers here now."

"No holy meeting?" she repeated.

Wagging his head, Scratch said, "That bell rings only to announce the evening."

"Why, Popo?" Flea inquired. "I can look at the sun falling, and know for myself that it is evening!"

Halfway on down the mud wall three men suddenly belched from the wide gate and halted as soon as they spotted Bass's party. One of them waved an arm to the others, ordering the two on toward the small wheeled cannon while he stayed in place, shading his eyes as he inspected the new arrivals, calling out, "Howdy, stranger!"

"Ho, your own self!"

"What Injuns you brung with you, mister?"

"My family—wife and young'uns."

That man turned away and trudged over to the cannon the other two had begun tugging back toward the wall. As he helped pushing on one of the huge wheels, he inquired, "You folks fixing on staying inside for the night?"

Bass cleared his throat. "I reckon—if'n there's room."

"Just barely," he replied. "Got us more'n two dozen sick soldiers getting nursed."

Titus brought his horse to a halt as the man stopped pushing the cannon.

Together they watched the other two heave the weapon on through the open portal toward the inner plaza.

"Who's nursin' them soldiers?" Titus inquired as his family halted their horses around him. "Charlotte Green her own self?"

The man twisted suddenly and squinted up at Bass. "How you know Charlotte?"

"I been here years ago," he confessed, quickly glancing at his pair of dogs sniffing along the base of the mud walls for interesting scent. "Meeted her and husband Dick back then. Good folks. Bought these here two dogs off Charlotte—back when they was wee pups. That was just afore I got skinned by Savary. He here—Savary?"

"Naw," the man explained. "St. Vrain's been off to Santa Fe—gone last fall. I figger he's in the thick of things in Taos by now."

"Who's trader here?"

"Goddamn Murray. You hear of him?"

"Hell if I ain't!" Bass replied. "Did a piece of business with him that fall I come in here with some Mex horses from Californy. He's a square man."

"You was with the bunch what come in with Bill Williams back in forty-two?" the man asked, stepping right over to Scratch's knee to peer up at the white-bearded man, the old trapper's ruddy face all but hidden beneath the coyote fur cap.

"That was a time," Bass sighed. "Mex soldiers chased us down to the desert, then the Diggers up and spooked our whole herd."*

"Story was you fellas lost more'n half them horses on the way here."

Titus glanced at his wife, then grinned down at the stranger. "The things a man won't do when he's young and full of vinegar."

"My name's Haney Rankin," and he held his hand up. "I'm Murray's segundo while most of the fort hands are off with Bransford—gone to fight the greasers in Taos. You can head 'round to the east wall. You remember that corral over there?"

"I do recollect. There a gate on that side?"

Rankin nodded. "Bring your family on inside that small corral. Sun's down so we're bolting these here gates for the night. I'll meet you over to the corral."

"You don't s'pect trouble from them Injuns camped down in them trees?" he asked as Rankin followed the cannon through the darkened entryway.

"Naw. That's Gray Thunder's band," Rankin's voice echoed through the low, shadowy entryway. "They come in a week or so back—soon as they heard Charlie Bent was kill't by the Mexicans. Offered to go kill greasers if William wanted 'em to."

Bass waited till the three were swallowed by shadows, then reined his horse

---

* *Death Rattle*

away. "C'mon, woman," he said in English to his Crow wife. "We'll settle in for the night. Come morning, I'm fixin' to pay a call on that Cheyenne camp. Maybeso scratch up some news 'bout a old friend of ours."

"I will stay behind with the children when you go," Waits spoke emphatically. "Cheyenne are not so much friends with my people."

"Better I go down there by myself anyway," he agreed. "See what sort of mood them Cheyenne are in afore I go asking up about that ol' friend."

"Who is this?"

"You 'member the one about as tall a man as you ever seen?"

She thought a moment as they brought their ponies to a halt outside the narrow east gate. Then a grin crossed her face ruddied by the cold. "Shad-rach," she said slowly, deliberately, in her husband's tongue.

"Shadrach Sweete," he repeated as the gate was drawn back against the icy snow and Rankin was there with a candle lantern spilling its yellow patch on the snow around his feet.

"So where's this Titus Bass?" a loud, deep voice boomed in the dark behind Rankin.

"Who's asking?" Scratch demanded as he dropped from the saddle onto the snow and started his horse through the corral gate.

"Dick Green," the voice said as a shadow took shape and the huge, muscular man stepped up to the old trapper. He turned to hurl his voice over his shoulder, "As I live an' breathe—if it ain't him, Charlotte!" Then he was grinning at the old trapper, yanking on Bass's arm as he trudged backward into the corral. "C'mon in here, bring them folks all in here now!"

The blacksmith's big hand quickly seized hold of Bass's mitten and pumped heartily as Green pounded Scratch on the other shoulder.

"Oh, my! Oh, *my*!" a high voice squealed as a woman squirted out of the kitchen door, a low rectangle of light behind her. "It *is* the puppy man! An' he brung him his fambly, Dick! Lookee if he didn't bring his fambly—" Suddenly Charlotte Green lumbered to a halt on the ground trampled by moccasins and many a hoof, staring slack-jawed. "Why—is this them two tiny puppies you buyed from me?"

He watched her crumple to her knees in the snow, her ankle-length broomstick skirt fanning out around her as she began to pat the tops of her thighs and whistle as good as any St. Louis wharfside stevedore. "C'mere! C'mon over here, you li'l whelps!"

"This the woman who traded me for the dogs," Titus explained to Waits as the dogs bounded over to the black cook.

"That is easy to see." She turned and signaled through the open corral gate for the children to dismount, pointing them off to the right in this triangular-shaped corral strung along the full extent of the easternmost wall.

Watching the dogs lick the cook's face, Scratch grinned, saying, "They sure as hell remember you!"

"What brung you back here for such a hoo-doo season?" Dick Green asked him as Rankin took the reins from Bass's hand.

"We was down to Taos when the blood started running in the streets," he explained in a near whisper. "Got out by the skin of our teeth."

The big blacksmith wagged his head dolefully. "Figger to lay low here till it blows over, then head south again?"

Titus shook his head as Waits and the children came up beside him. "We're here for a night, maybeso two at the most, then we push on."

"Middle of winter the way it is?" Charlotte whimpered as she slowly brought her bulk off the ground and stood. "Surely you can find something to do here to keep these young'uns o' yours safe till spring when you can leave."

Titus smiled at her. "By first green we'll be long on our way to Crow country, Miss Charlotte."

He then went on to introduce everyone all around. While Dick went to fetch some short sections of rope to tie up the dogs there in the corral, Charlotte shuffled Waits-by-the-Water and the three children inside her warm, glowing kitchen.

"You manage the rest by yourself, Bass?" Rankin asked.

"Be just fine by myself, thankee."

The trader tugged on his blanket mittens. "We got a few more chores afore Charlotte sits us all down for supper. An' Goddamn don't like to be kept waiting on his supper 'cause I'm late getting my chores see'd to."

"Be off with you then," Scratch said with a grin as Rankin started away. "And tell Goddamn Murray that the blanket man has come to pay a call."

Rankin stopped in the snow. "Blanket man?"

"Time I was here last, I took near ever' blanket Murray had in this here fort—traded off a hull shitteree of horses to him."

A big smile crossed the clerk's face. "The blanket man, eh?"

"All them blankets I packed north on Cheyenne horses been keeping the Crows warm for the past few winters."

"Sounds to me I should ask Murray 'bout you sitting to dinner with us in the main room."

Titus shrugged. "No need to bother 'bout such foofaraw doin's." He gestured at Charlotte and said, "Looks like we'll be eatin' just fine with the cook her own self."

"Just the same—you still want me tell him the blanket man's come to call?"

"If I don't run onto him this evenin', just tell Murray I'll be round to call at the trade room in the morning."

It was just growing light when Titus Bass slowly rolled out of the buffalo robes and blankets so as not to disturb his family, pulled on his moccasins and heavy coat, then carefully dragged back the heavy cottonwood door and stepped outside beneath the low awning that ran along this southern side of the courtyard. The wheelwright's shop, where they had bedded down for the night, was located right beside Dick Green's forge, with the wagon alley running just behind those small rooms, arranged in a row with the gunsmith's and carpenter's shops too. No one was yet stirring in the plaza, where a light snow had dusted the massive fur press. He stepped into the cold air, turned, and dragged the door closed behind him, when off to his right he made out the soft notes of a woman's hum. Shuffling through the new snow he entered the kitchen, surprised to find it already warm, cozy, inviting.

"Well lookee here, Charlotte!" Dick Green's voice greeted Titus as the blacksmith stepped around a corner. "Mr. Bass is a early get-upper hisself too."

Charlotte poked her head around a corner, smears of flour dusting her nose, a cheek, and the side of her bandanna decorated with red Mexican roses. "You ready for some coffee?"

Scratch smiled. "Damn if I ain't allays ready for coffee!"

"C'mon back here where we got the pot on," Charlotte offered. "Mr. Green, I could use your help cuttin' the bacon for me."

"Be there straightaway," the blacksmith promised. "You get this man a cup of coffee, then I be right with you."

The Negro servants had spent a little time talking with the trapper and his family when their chores were done following dinner, at least until young Jackrabbit had fallen asleep in his father's arms in a toasty spot near Charlotte's fireplace where they all sat on stools and drank a rich, sweet mixture of Mexican chocolate seasoned with cinnamon. Their bellies filled with such delicious warmth, it wasn't long before Flea and Magpie began to get drowsy too—their eyelids growing heavy as lead and their heads starting to sag. Titus and Waits shuffled the sleepy children off to the wheelwright's room, right next to the residual warmth of the forge. Scratch and Dick Green had settled the family in that shop since the wheelwright himself had marched off to the south with Bill Bransford to exact revenge for the murder of Charles Bent.

"He ain't gonna be back no time soon," Green had prodded the trapper, who was reluctant to bed down inside the shop. "You an' yours stay right here long as you want. Likely he won't be back for to work again till winter's fair done."

"Thankee for the offer," Bass had replied as they shook out the robes and thick wool blankets across the narrow clay floor. "Maybeso only two nights, till we push on."

"Stay longer, why don'cha? Charlotte, she'd love the company—your woman and the chirrun too," Green pleaded. "There ain't much wimmins out to these parts, so my Charlotte sure do get the lonelies for a soft face to talk to."

Titus had straightened and stood beside the pile of blankets. "I know that feelin' . . . the lonelies. But, long as Charlotte's got you, Dick—and you got her, neither of you ever gonna be lonely, no matter where you go."

"But my Miss Charlotte—she likes to talk to other wimmins."

"We'll let 'em gab an' palaver much as they want for the next two days," Titus promised.

"That's right," Dick had agreed reluctantly. "They can allays talk some more next time you come by this here mud fort."

Laying his gnarled hand with its painful joints on Green's shoulder, Scratch had explained, "I lay this'll be my last trip here, Dick. Don't see a reason to wander this far south ever again, now that I saw to what I needed to down in Taos."

"Wh-where you gonna trade, you don't come south?"

"I s'pose there'll allays be a trader's post on the Yellowstone," he had confessed as they started back to Charlotte's kitchen last night. "Don't make much matter to me anyways. I think I've figgered out how to get by 'thout needing a hull passel of trade goods. The less I need a trader, the better off I'll be."

That morning over coffee as the few fort employees left behind began to stir with activity, and Jackson's dragoons came and went with steaming cups of Charlotte's hearty brew and plates of her fluffy, piping-hot corn muffins, Scratch told the Greens tales of that north country where his family belonged. Now, more than ever, as the army, and emigrants, and those religious pilgrims too were all crowding in on what had long been a quiet and ofttimes lonely land. When he could stuff no more in his belly, Scratch got up and moved his stool back against the wall.

"Keep a sharp eye out for them young'uns of mine," he warned the cook. "When they get around to rolling out, a hungry bunch gonna come runnin' in here to clean up all your bacon and corn dodgers."

Dusting her hands on her big white apron, she beamed. "That's why Charlotte be the cook, Mr. Bass. So's I can fill up bellies till they're bustin'!"

"You tell them young'uns of mine I'll be back after I've looked up an ol' friend down to the Cheyenne camp," he explained as he pulled on his coat and started toward the door. "I figger you'll keep 'em fed and warm right here till I come back."

"I can allays find something for your chirrun to do for me 'round here," Charlotte vowed. " 'Specially that girl of yours. My, oh, my—she's gonna be a sure-fire handful of ring-tail cats one of these days, you mind my word, Mr. Bass. She's got that light of trouble sparkin' in her eye!"

Didn't he know that already, Titus thought as he shouldered the corral gate closed, then strode off toward the far grove of cottonwood on foot, scuffing through the old snow in those thick, hair-on winter moccasins. He damn well realized how Magpie had her father wrapped around her little finger, what with the way she had learned to flash her pretty eyes at him all the time. Come a day when she'd be batting those eyes at some young buck of a suitor. Leastways, he had begun to hope it would be a young warrior . . . and not some half-baked, green-hided, soaked-behind-the-ears white youngster fresh out of the settlements.

Back when he had first taken a shine to Waits-by-the-Water, Titus Bass was notching his ninth winter in the mountains. With their daughter's mixed blood, Magpie deserved a man bred to these mountains, and not no snot-nosed young'un who didn't know prime from stinkum.

Three older Cheyenne men stood off to the side of the first lodges as Scratch came across the open ground. He was carrying no rifle or smoothbore—surely they could see that. All three wrapped in a buffalo robe, the Cheyenne watched him warily as he approached—he was sure they had a good suspicion that he wouldn't have come without some weapon on him somewhere. When he was less than twenty feet away, Titus stopped and held one arm up in greeting. Then he pulled off a mitten and quickly yanked at the long ties that held the flaps of his elkhide coat closed. There he patted the big pistol stuffed in the front of his belt.

The moment one of the trio nodded and started his way, the other two shuffled off in different directions. Bass stopped in front of the camp guard, realizing he didn't know a damned word of the man's language—wondering for a moment if any of these three had been among those Sioux raiders who had chased him and Shad Sweete down when they were on their way to Fort Davy Crockett in Brown's Hole. Too late for him to worry about them recognizing an old, gray-headed trapper from that many summers ago.

"Sweete?" he asked, using his friend's name.

The Cheyenne barely shrugged.

"Big man," and Titus held up a flattened hand half a foot over their heads. "Big, big man." As the warrior's eyes warily studied that hand, Bass brought both his arms up, fingers tapping his own shoulders, then moved his hands out all that much wider to show the wide span of Shadrach Sweete's muscular frame.

With no more than the slightest gesture, the warrior in the buffalo robe indicated he wanted the white man to follow him into camp. Follow him he did, scuffing through the length of the Cheyenne camp scattered among the old cottonwood growing back from the annual floodplain of the Arkansas. At the far edge of the treeline, the Cheyenne stopped and pointed out a young woman patiently trudging around the side of a squat, small-flapped hide lodge. She had a small, bowlegged infant slowly taking some first, tentative steps beside her.

"Sweete?" Bass asked. "She know about Sweete?"

"Sweete," the man repeated, speaking for the first time. Then he motioned for the white man to go on before the warrior pulled his hand beneath the buffalo robe's warmth once more and turned away.

"Sweete?" Titus asked as he approached the lodge, immediately drawing the young woman's attention.

She cocked her head to the side and repeated, "Sweete?"

"Yes—he here?"

"Shad-rach Sweete?" She repeated the three syllables with practiced certainty.

"You know Shadrach, do you?" he said with a grin, relieved. Then he started for the door of the lodge, figuring his old friend was inside.

"Sweete," she said, stepping between Bass and the open doorway as a young boy appeared from the firelit interior. Pointing off toward the far willows, she indicated a patch of open ground where some more of the band's ponies were grazing on grass blown clear of crusty snow.

"He's not here? That it? Sweete's gone off to the ponies?"

She bent her head this way, then that way, almost the way a dog would listen intently to its master's words. "Sweete go."

"Yeah, Sweete go to the ponies?"

"Goddamn!" the voice thundered behind him. "Can't a man go take a piss 'thout some mule-headed idjit come callin' after him?"

"As I live an' breathe!" Bass gushed as he wheeled around, spotting Shadrach threading his way through the bare-limbed cottonwood. "So you stand up and take a piss just like a real man now, do you?"

"Shit—what would you know about real men, you half-growed strip of spit-out mulehide!"

"Don't you ever say nothin' mean agin no mules!" Scratch roared back as the man who easily went half-a-foot again over six feet tall, just as Sweete enfolded the shorter man in his big arms.

The smell of Shadrach—a free man's mix of woodsmoke and gun oil, burnt powder and stale tobacco both—how it evoked so many bittersweet memories that Bass felt his eyes begin to sting. As his old friend loosened his grip, Scratch reached up with both hands and pulled Sweete's face down to his, promptly planting a wet kiss on both of Shadrach's cheeks.

"Damn, but it's good to see you too, Titus Bass," Sweete said in a husky whisper laden with deep emotion.

For a long moment there, Scratch could not speak. He hadn't expected to be choked up this way with the reunion. Finally he said, "Was told up to the fort you was down here with Gray Thunder's bunch. Knowed sometime back that you run off to the blanket with these here no-good Cheyennes."

Sweete looped a muscular arm over Bass's shoulder. "Pray tell, when you hear of that?"

"Can't recollect if it were someone right here at Fort William or not," he replied, a little aggravated that he couldn't scratch up the proper notion. "Or, maybe it were on up the Arkansas at Fisher's pueblo."

Sweete waved for the young woman to move in their direction. "What'd they tell you 'bout me?"

"Said you was lookin' to scare up some folks to take you in when Vaskiss and Sublette folded and closed down their fort on the South Platte. Said you was fixin' to head out for to find a band of Cheyenne where you ended up takin' a shine to a gal."

"This here's that gal," Sweete announced, strong affection in his voice. "Titus—want you to meet Shell Woman."

"Shell Woman." Scratch bobbed his head in recognition.

"She knows her name in American talk," Shad explained. "Ciphers more an' more American talk all the time. Most times I call her Toote."

"Toote?"

Shad smiled toothily. "Like them Frenchies say: *'Toote suite,'* I call her Toote."

Nodding his head to the pretty woman, Bass said, "Toote it is."

Dropping to one knee, Titus asked, "This li'l pup your'n?"

Quickly scooping the child off the ground and cradling her in his big arms, Shadrach said, "This here li'l doe-eyed gal is my daughter, Pipe Woman."

"She is a purty one, Shad," Bass agreed. "Good thing she takes after her mama, ol' coon. Ugly a nigger as you are, I don't figger you'd be a man to throw good-lookin' young'uns."

"Shit, look who's talkin' ugly!" Sweete growled, then turned to Shell Woman and spoke quickly in Cheyenne before she turned away. "My darlin' baby here was born year ago last winter. And I want you to see my boy—he's older'n my girl. I sent the woman to fetch him."

"Jehoshaphat! You got two young'uns?" Scratch cried. "Been keeping that poor woman heavy with child, ain'cha?"

The proud radiance on Shad's face drained to a look of pained sympathy. "When Shell Woman give birth to the girl here—she had her a long, hard fight of it. From that day on she said she knowed something tore inside her, knowed she'd never have 'nother child after the girl. I allays wanted more young'uns when it came my time to settle down . . ." A look of quiet resignation came over him. "These two—why, they be all any father could pray for—"

Bursting from the lodge door toddled a small boy, somewhat lighter skinned than his baby sister, but every bit as black-headed as their mother. He sprinted across the icy snow, his small capote slurring the snowy ground as his tiny legs pumped him toward his father. Reaching Shadrach, the child flung his arms around his father's leg and clamped on fiercely.

"He was still sleepin' when I left to take my piss in the brush," Sweete explained. With one of his big hands, he gently turned the boy's head so the boy was looking up at the stranger. After saying something in Cheyenne to the child, Shad told Bass, "This here's High-Backed Bull. He's allays been a cantankerous sort if'n he don't get his way."

"Some young'uns just like that."

"But, his mother an' me can usual' calm him when he gets real excitable," Sweete said. Then Sweete gazed directly at Bass. "You just come down from the north country?"

"Afore last fall."

"What you hear of Bridger up that way?"

Scratch smiled at the remembrance. "You an' him . . . allays was best of friends."

"You're the best friend a man could have too, Titus Bass," Shad admitted.

"Still, I reckon you an' Gabe allays will be best friends since't you come out west with Ashley together," Scratch explained. "Back then both of you 'bout as young and green as they come."

"Jim, he was seventeen in twenty-five," Sweete reminisced.

"An' you was a big lad for fifteen . . . seems how you told me that story a hunnert times if you told me once't!"

Shad tousled his boy's hair and inquired, "Didn't you reach the mountains in twenty-five?"

"Yep—come out on my own," Scratch reflected. "Prob'ly come close to starvin' half a dozen times afore three fellas run onto me and showed me the way the stick floats—"

"Why the hell didn't I think afore!" Shad exclaimed. "You come outta Crow country alone? Or, you bring your woman and young'uns?"

"They all come with me," Bass explained. "Never gonna go much of anywhere 'thout them now. Was too long out west to steal some Mexican horses in Californy—ain't gonna stay away from my kin nowhere near that long again."

"Stole Mex horses, did you?"

"Ol' Solitaire, Peg-Leg, passel of others—some good men, others awready turned snake-bellied thieves," Scratch declared.

"You tell me all about it tonight over some elk?"

"That mean you're inviting me for dinner?"

Sweete shook his head. "Naw. I figgered to invite Waits-by-the-Water for dinner, have your family meet mine . . . so I figger you'll be tagging along anyways."

Balling up a fist, he started to hurl his arm at his tall friend, but Shadrach caught the fist in his huge paw. "Best you save your energy, ol' man—'stead of throwing punches at me! Gray as you got in these last few winters, time sure has to be gnawin' at your heels."

"How long's it been, Shadrach—since we last see'd each other?"

"Was it them last sad ronnyvoo days back to forty?"

"Maybeso it's been that long," Bass admitted after a moment. "No matter how many year it was, allays too long to go 'thout seein' good friends."

"Companyeros from the shinin' times." Sweete laid his hand on Bass's shoulder.

"Them was glory days, Shadrach," he whispered with an anguished remembrance. "Them really was our glory days."

THREE

Shad Sweete passed the pipe to Titus Bass and asked, "How come you won't wait till green-up afore you push on north?"

"Wanna be in Crow country by summer," Scratch replied. "I lollygag around these parts with you till spring, why—summer gonna be over time I reach Yellowstone country."

As Titus brought the pipestem to his lips and sucked in that warm and heady smoke of Shad's tobacco smoldering in the redstone pipebowl, he glanced over at his wife as she gently rocked the sleeping Jackrabbit in her lap. Magpie and Flea were already lying back-to-back between their parents, curled up beneath a blanket, eyes closed to the crimson light flutting against the inside of the buffalo-hide lodge cover. Swaying shadows climbed with the converging poles toward the smoke hole and that black triangle of starry sky over their heads. Opposite the fire sat Shell Woman, her son's head propped against her leg and her infant daughter asleep at her bared breast.

Right from their arrival in Gray Thunder's camp late that afternoon, Scratch had sensed the courteous strain, a civil tension, that electrified the air as the two women were brought together in these most unusual circumstances. Their peoples, Crow and Cheyenne, had been at war all the way back to those generations of elders who remembered long-ago-told stories of conflicts and hatred between the tribes when they both had lived far, far to the east of the Missouri River. Migrating west had given the Crow only a temporary respite from war against the Cheyenne. Generations after they had fled the valley of the Upper Missouri for the

country of the Yellowstone and Bighorn Rivers, the Cheyenne had begun to
mosey west too.

"But Shadrach's wife isn't from one of those sneaky bunches who trouble
the Apsaluuke farther north," Titus had attempted to explain to his wife after
telling her they were invited to dinner that evening in Gray Thunder's camp.
"This bunch never has killed a white man. Always traded with whites. Made
friends with the Bents and others for their own good: guns and powder, beads
and brass."

"Maybe they are friends with your people, Ti-tuzz," she had responded
grimly. "But I see or hear nothing to show me Gray Thunder's people haven't
murdered my people when they had the chance."

"This village has never been north of the South Platte," he had explained in
American. "Other'ns do run with them Sioux. They're the Cheyenne making
trouble up north. But this bunch—"

"Stay south." She interrupted him in American too. Then continued in her
own tongue, "They are not my kind, Ti-tuzz. But because I feel safe with you, I
will go where you take me, as I always have gone to be at your side."

"What are your kind, Waits-by-the-Water?" he had made the mistake of asking, pricking her pride. "There any tribe what you Crow get along with good
enough to call your kind?"

"Flathead. Josiah's woman—Looks Far Woman—she probably is my kind,"
she declared in Crow.

"Dammit," he grumbled in exasperation. "It's clear as sun there ain't very
many of your kind, woman—because the Crow are at war with most ever'body
around 'em."

"Except the white man," she had reminded him with a soft smile. "I always
liked Shadrach fine."

"Then you come tonight to see ol' Shadrach again?"

With her lips momentarily pressed into a grim line of thoughtfulness, Waits
finally nodded once. "I will meet this Cheyenne wife of his, and see the children Shadrach has made with her too. Then I will judge if there is any chance
for two enemies to feel safe in the company of one another."

"And become friends," he urged.

Her eyes looked squarely into his. "Maybe to be friends is a lot harder thing,
so you must be patient for what may never happen. To feel safe . . . that is
enough for now."

All evening there had been that tense civility between the two women—both
aware their husbands had been the best of friends and trapping partners, men
who had protected and nourished their own friendship.

"Shell Woman may feel like she's the outsider here," Shad whispered as the
fire crackled in the pit near their feet.

"But, this be her home," Titus responded quietly.

"Can't you see—you an' me, an' Waits too, we all knowed each other years ago when the two of us trapped together, Scratch. Shell Woman an' our young'uns ain't been around the rest of you none, the way I was. I'm sartin she feels this here's a case where ever'body knows ever'body but her."

"Such things take time, Shadrach," Titus consoled as he handed the pipe back to its owner. "You'll recollect that no matter how many times you and me crossed trails in them early years, it weren't until the last of the beaver trade we finally come to be friends."

"Most all this afternoon while'st I was waiting for suppertime and you to be coming, I been thinking a lot on them times. How you said they was our glory days," Sweete sighed. "How you s'pose Gabe's doing over to his post?"

"What I heard, Jim's full o' pluck and doing fine."

"You ain't never been there yourself?"

"Not once," Titus admitted. "After we talked 'bout Gabe this mornin', more I cogitated on it, an' the more it made sense to take me a ride on west to the Green and have a look at what Bridger's been doing with hisself after all these years."

Shad leaned forward to whisper, "You s'pose he's still in business with Vaskiss over west of the mountains?"

"They're both likely lads; I figger they had the gumption to make a go of damned near anything they ever set their minds to."

Shadrach quivered a little with anticipation. "So you're goin' to see him, Scratch?"

He glanced for a moment at his woman, found her smiling at him as she sat listening to their man-talk, her legs folded to the side in that woman way of hers, rocking their youngest. Her smile always reassured him.

"Yeah, Shadrach," he replied. "Fixin' to drop in on Bridger, have a look at his new diggin's, sit and palaver 'bout the ol' days for a spell afore we tramp on down the Wind River for Crow country."

Sweete cleared his throat, that scratchy bullfrog of a voice dramatically softened now. "Sure would like to see ol' Gabe my own self."

"Why, child—you askin' yourself along?"

Shad's face brightened. "Figgered I'd have to work harder'n that to get you to come to the bait, pilgrim!"

"Who you callin' pilgrim, you lop-eared greenhorn?"

"Damn, if it wouldn't shine for our families to ride north together!" Shad gushed with enthusiasm. "So, how long afore you was planning on leaving, Scratch?"

He dug at an itch under his chin, then said, "When I first rode in here, I fixed my sights on laying over at the fort two nights at the most—so I was gonna pull out come morning."

It was like the air suddenly went out of Shad. With a grump of resignation he said, "Morning don't give Shell Woman much time."

"Hell, Shadrach—ain't a Injun woman what can't take down a lodge and pack it up in the time it takes you an' me to eat our lunch and have us a pipeful of that tobaccy o' your'n."

Wagging his head, Shadrach explained, "It ain't getting ever'thing tore down and packed up I was meanin'. It's just . . . Shell Woman's got family—folks, sisters, and a brother, ever'one she growed up with in this camp. I allays figgered I'd give her all the time she needed to say her good-byes afore I ever yanked her off with me—"

"Ask her if'n you give her a day, she'd be ready to go mornin' after next."

He watched the two of them talk back and forth, listening to the strange word-sounds in the Cheyenne tongue. But mostly he trained his attention on Shell Woman's face—watching how her eyes darted to the newcomer and his Crow wife. Finally Shell Woman rocked onto her knees and turned aside to lay her infant daughter on the robes, her back to the men as she went about putting her small children to bed. For those breathless moments, Bass had worked his expectations and hope into a lather.

Finally Sweete explained in a whisper, "She says no matter how long I'd give her, it'd never be long enough to say good-bye to her folks, her blood kin."

Disappointment flooded through Titus. "I'm real sad to hear that—"

"But Shell Woman said a day would be awright . . . long as I promised to get her back to her people one of these days soon."

His heart leaped again. "S-she says . . . you're all gonna go?"

Shad's head bobbed up and down eagerly. "Damn if we ain't!"

To Scratch's left, both Magpie and Flea were abruptly awakening to the noisy voices, blinking their eyes and squinting at the exuberant men who had bounded to their feet to begin pounding one another on the back and shoulders. Across the lodge little Bull Hump woke up, propping himself up on an elbow to watch the same strange scene as the two men jigged beside the low fire.

Finally turning back to Magpie and Flea, Scratch held down both hands. His children put their hands in his as he pulled them up and helped them into their heavy blanket coats, winter moccasins, hoods, and mittens, preparing to make that snowy tromp back to Fort William. At the doorway, he stopped Waits-by-the-Water and put his arm around her shoulder as she clutched the sleeping Jackrabbit against her shoulder.

"This gonna be good for us, Shad," he said, his heart filled with an exquisite happiness. "Not just you an' me. Good for all of us."

"Shell Woman—she and the young'uns—none of 'em ever knowed anything but this prerra country down here. They ain't stomped all around the mountains like your family, Scratch. Gonna be good for 'em to lay eyes on some new sights."

"You need help tomorry?"

Sweete shook his head. "The two of us get it done."

With a huge smile, Titus asked, "Be set mornin' after next, Shad? You'll have it all packed for Green River country?"

Bull Hump sleepily rubbed his knuckles into his eyes. The tall man knelt beside his weary son and tousled the boy's hair. "Damn if we won't be ready to prance north, Titus Bass. Back to beaver country come first light!"

Wind like this could make a horse downright fractious. The way it blew the old snow along the ground in gusts that swirled almost as high as a horse's nose—it frightened the poor, thick-headed animals.

"We best tie 'em off and leave 'em here," Scratch finally suggested after the horses had been fighting their riders. "Never get up close enough on them cows to get a shot, these dumb brutes making all this noise with the wind."

"We can slide off over there," Shad Sweete suggested, pointing his longrifle at a faint line of green that hinted at a brush-choked coulee.

As they came out of the saddle minutes later, Titus assured, "Shell Woman an' your pups, they're gonna be fine, outta the wind where we left 'em with my family. Them dogs of mine, they'll scare off most critters what try an' sneak close."

Sweete glanced up at the lowering sky. "We best make meat soon, afore this storm slams us but good."

"Gonna take us time to ride back to that notch in the ridge," he said as he poked his trigger finger out of the slot in his blanket mitten. Bass turned and looked over his shoulder, unable to see any of the distant landmarks for the roll and heave of the earth, not to mention the way the wind had kicked up, tormenting the old snow into what might soon become a ground blizzard.

Shad sighed, "Leastways, we got us a good chance to get back afore dark sets in."

They started down the barren, twisting bottom of the coulee, headed for the flat where they could hear the lowing of the shaggy beasts. Titus shouldered into the gale and whispered, "Pray our medicine's strong and the wind don't shift on us."

He swore he could smell those buff well before the two of them eased up to the end of the coulee and the first of the hump-shouldered creatures emerged out of the swirling snow. Strong, heady, an honest-to-goshen smell of the earth—a fragrance perhaps made all the stronger what with the sharp, metallic tang to the wind quickly quartering around to the north. It still made his senses tingle—after all these seasons, after all those years of waiting and wanting that had gone before he came west out of St. Louis . . . the nearness of these mystical beasts still made his blood run hot and throb in his temples like an Apsaluuke drum.

"You smell that?" Sweete asked, almost breathless.

"Buff."

"No—ain't buff what I smell."

Scratch closed his eyes and held his breath, drawing the freezing air into his nose. Finally he opened them and said, "How long it been since you hunted buffalo?"

"It ain't been that long," Shad growled defensively. "An' it ain't buffalo I'm smelling! Something else—"

"There!" Titus whispered sharply, the breathsmoke ripped from his lips as he spoke.

At least two dozen of them slowly inched out of the layers of gauzy ground snow swirled into tiny cyclones by the fickle wind. The dark animals were there, then they were gone. There again, and gone. Slowly plodding past the edge of the hill, their hooves kicking up tiny cascades of white, their long beards dragging over the top of the icy crust, frost steaming from their black, glistening nostrils like smoke belching from the double-barreled stacks of a Mississippi paddle wheeler. That hot breath encapsulated the huge, shaggy heads in wreaths of fog, tiny molecules of moisture quickly freezing into masks of matted ice.

The huge beasts snorted and blew, trumpeting their cold discomfort or their fright at the wind to those around them, some of the buffalo tossing their horns menacingly at those who crowded too close as they plodded past the unseen hunters.

"See what I told you, Shad?" he whispered. "That's buff you're smelling."

"Maybeso it was," Sweete answered in an unsure way. "I'll take a shot from here."

"Wait'll you see a cow."

"Bull's gonna be tough and rangy now," Shad agreed. "I can almost taste the boss right now."

"You miss, we're gonna have to chase this bunch, or find us some more—"

"You hear that?"

"Yeah," Titus responded as the bellowing grew louder.

"Bulls can't be fighting for the rut," Sweete said guardedly.

"Something's got 'em worked up."

"You figger I should shoot?"

"Way they're all on the move—you better shoot now or we ain't gonna have us 'nother chance."

Sweete immediately took three steps forward and went to one knee. After flipping back the frizzen to check the priming powder in the pan, he drew the hammer back to half cock, brought the butt plate against his shoulder, then dragged the hammer back to full cock before slipping his bare index finger inside the trigger guard.

She was no more than forty yards away when the gun roared. Staggering to the side, all but disappearing in the swirl of snow, the cow tumbled to the side, where she kicked her legs twice and lay still.

"You dropped 'er!" Bass roared, his words muffled by the bellows from the nearby beasts.

As Sweete quickly reloaded, Titus watched several of the other buffalo pause momentarily near the cow, stopping to sniff at her body, snort at the blood on the snow—suddenly they all bolted as if they were one.

"Can't stand the smell of blood."

Shad gazed over at Titus while he got to his feet. "Ain't blood what scared 'em off." Sweete sniffed the air again, nose held high.

"What you smelling now?"

"Same as it was before," the big man answered as the bellows grew louder. They were both drawn to turn by the unmistakable, snarling growls.

"See what you gone and done?" Bass grumbled.

"Me?" Shad replied. "What'd I do?"

"You gone and give them damn wolves some fresh blood on the wind."

As he and Titus started away from the mouth of the coulee, Sweete asked, "You think them critters comin' for our cow?"

"Only a matter of time afore they do."

"Let's butcher off what we can do real quick, then ride on back to the women," Sweete suggested.

"You start on the boss and some fleece," Scratch said as they inched toward the dark carcass sprawled upon the icy snow. "I'll get the tongue first off."

After propping their rifles against the ice-crusted flank of the cow, both men went to work as the wind picked up and the snow billowed around them all the more.

"Can't hardly see what I'm doing," Sweete grumbled from between the cow's legs.

"Just don't cut your goddamned fingers off, Shadrach."

By the time Titus had the savory tongue freed from the mouth, Sweete had carved off a yard square of the cow's hide and had it laid on the blood-streaked snow at his feet. Now they both put their knives to work with a growing urgency—listening to the snorts and bellows of the buffalo all around them in the blinding storm, hearing the growling, snarling, snapping wolves work their way closer and closer through the nervous herd.

"That be about all we'll need for now," Scratch said as he plopped some of the bloody, greasy strips of fat on that piece of hide stretched across the snowy ground.

What the mountain men called "fleece," this thin layer of fat lying just beneath the animal's skin could satisfy any man who had just about had his fill of the extra-lean meat trimmed from a buffalo.

"That packhorse can carry more." Shad raised his voice as the wind came up.

"Like you said, we ain't got the time," Bass argued. "Let's get while we can still find our way back to that notch."

The moment the last word was out of his mouth on a stream of breathsmoke, Scratch saw the first of them slip out of the dancing snow. Gray-black, their muzzles coated with hoarfrost. Their heads slung down and forward, brought this close to man by the luring fragrance of fresh blood.

"Scratch?"

"I see 'em, goddammit."

"Them bastards is what I was smelling," Sweete admitted with a loud snort as he dropped his skinning knife into its scabbard at the back of his belt.

"You got your pistol in reach?"

Shad nodded slowly. "Hooked on my belt."

Mentally measuring the distance from where he stood in the fold of the cow's neck to the rear flank, Titus shuddered when another five, no—six more wolves slinked up through the fog. "You get to the guns?"

"Think I can."

"Easy, coon. Easy at it."

Damn 'em, he thought as Sweete began inching sideways toward the two rifles.

Two of the biggest ones were slipping round to get behind Shad—just the way those creatures worked over any poor dumb brute that happened to land in their path. While most of the hunting pack held the victim's attention, one or more played the sly and got up behind their prey, where they could make a blinding dash, slashing at rear tendons, hamstringing the victim while others leaped up to sink their fangs in the back of the neck.

Shad was slowly reaching out for his rifle when Titus announced, "Watch them two—"

"Where—"

The first one streaked in low, its belly almost dragging the ground, jaws opened as it lunged for Shadrach's ankle. As Sweete attempted to spin away, the wolf instantly locking down on his foot, the second predator had already sprung high—its powerful momentum carrying it right on over the man and the cow's carcass too, landing in the bloodied, trampled snow. In a high-pitched, feral yelp of pain, Shad hammered away at the wolf clamped onto his leg. When that did not break its hold, Sweete seized the ruff at the back of the wolf's neck with his left hand while his right scrambled to lock around the butt of his belt pistol.

Having wrenched his own pistol off his wide leather belt, Titus dragged back the flintlock's hammer and quartered to confront the snarling wolf starting its lunge for him. The .54-caliber ball slammed into its furry chest just below the neck, the impact's force twirling the wolf's body in midair. As he attempted to twist out of the way, the furry body hammered against Bass's hip. Two more of them crouched menacingly less than ten feet away now, snarling yet wary of the man who instantly dropped the empty pistol and dragged out both of the butcher knives he carried in rawhide scabbards at his back. Clutching both of those long, much-used weapons in his bare, bloody hands, Scratch began to snarl at the wolves, feinting with this knife, then with that. Each time one of the wolves appeared ready to leap, he swung a knife in a wide arc. Inch by inch the lanky-legged predators steadily worked toward the two trappers, at the same time Titus inched his way backward in the direction of their rifles.

"Scratch!"

Just as he was twisting about to look for Shadrach, Titus watched the wolf free its hold on Sweete's ankle—and immediately whirl about to seize hold of the big man's forearm. Shad shrieked anew as he shook the arm violently, attempting to dislodge the predator's teeth from his flesh.

"Use your goddamned pistol!" Bass ordered over his shoulder.

Shadrach grumbled, "Shit—I'm trying to get to it!"

Finally freeing his pistol, Sweete hauled back on the hammer of the big weapon, jammed its muzzle under the beast's jaw, and blew a lead ball right on out of the top of the wolf's head. As the animal collapsed, its jaws still locked on the man's arm, it toppled Shadrach over with its weight.

A swirl of ground snow blinded Titus for a moment as the closest wolf growled, leaping for Sweete as the man hit the ground. Landing on the trapper's back, it sank its teeth in Shad's shoulder as Titus dove for his rifle. Wheeling it in an arc, Bass brought the hammer back from half cock and didn't wait to set the front trigger. Instead he pulled the back trigger with a powerful surge of adrenaline while bringing the muzzle down on the wolf snarling atop Sweete's back.

The bright muzzle flash flared against the murky snow scene as Shadrach sank to the ground beneath the dead animal's weight.

"Load me!" Scratch bellowed, dropping the rifle over the cow's carcass so that it landed right beside Sweete.

"Don't think I can move my arm," he groaned. "The shoulder, can't move it—"

"Your pistol?"

"Only one is empty," Shadrach admitted.

"Try your best to hold the rifle up 'cross't your arm, Shad," he begged. "The rest of this pack don't know your gun's gone empty."

"H-how many more?"

"I see'd four more of 'em out there in the snow," he replied, watching the dark shadows lope back and forth, no more than fuzzy blurs in the dancing snow.

"I—I'm bleeding bad, Scratch."

"Where?" he asked, not taking his eyes off those ghostly attackers.

"First'un got my leg," he answered weakly. "Likely I can wrap it tight. The last'un got my shoulder . . . it didn't have time to rip out a hunk of meat. But—when that first'un got his teeth in my arm . . . hell, I can't feel a thing from my shoulder on down."

"That's good, you don't feel the pain so bad," he soothed, worry already worming in his belly. "Wrap your other hand around your arm, Shadrach. Clamp down tight—see if that holds off the bleeding."

As Sweete did what Bass suggested, Titus went about quickly reloading. But after pouring in a measured antler tip of powder, he decided not to waste any more time fishing out a patch lubricated with bear grease from the pouch that hung at his right hip. Instead, he started the ball into the muzzle with his thumb, then rammed it home with the straight-grained hickory wiping stick.

"What's your caliber, Shad?"

"Six . . . sixty-two."

"Shit," he grumbled as he clambered over the cow's partially bared carcass. "Gonna have to dig a ball out for your gun. Pistol too?"

"It's the same. Sixty-two."

"Good man," he whispered as he knelt beside Sweete, quickly peering down at the arm his friend had clenched between the fingers of his big right hand. "Allays good to have the same caliber for rifle and belt gun too. H-how's that bleeding?"

"Dunno. Can't tell yet."

"Hold down on it tight for a little more," he sighed, fearing the worst would come through in his voice. "Lemme get all our guns loaded, then we'll have me a look at what you gone and done to yourself."

It took some doing, getting both rifles and those two big belt pistols reloaded as the wind drove icy snow against his bare hands. What with his trembling from the cold and the shaking from his fear in not knowing how bad off Shadrach might be, the process took longer than it should have.

"Don't see 'em no more," Sweete whispered as Titus laid Shad's rifle back against the man's bloodied leg.

He looked up quickly. "Them wolves?"

"Sounds like they took off."

"I ain't paid that much attention."

"You get the pelts for me," Sweete asked.

As he looked over at his friend's eyes, Bass said, "Forget the goddamned pelts—" then shut his mouth. "It's getting dark. Maybeso I can come back in the morning for 'em, Shad. Right now, I best take a look at these here holes them no-good prerra wolves chewed in your hide."

"Easy there, hoss," Sweete groaned as Titus grabbed hold and began to straighten the appendage. "That leg hurts fierce."

"Think it's froze for now."

"The bleeding?"

Titus nodded. "Likely I won't have to cut off your hoof, pilgrim."

Sweete screwed up half a smile and snorted, "That's good news to this child. Lookit my shoulder, too."

Scooting behind Shadrach, Bass rose on one knee to have himself a good look at that broad, muscular shoulder. "Lucky, coon. Damn lucky."

"Not bad, eh?"

"You got so much there for the critter to bite through—coat and shirt and all. Ain't any bleeding to it."

"Tore through my coat good down here," Sweete said, bringing his arm away from his belly.

"Lemme see."

As Shad brought his red, glistening hand away from the torn wound, it was easy to see the battered flesh wasn't going to stop bleeding from the intense cold, much less on its own.

Scratch sighed. "Put your hand back on it and hol' tight as you can."

"It bad?"

"We're gonna get that bleeding stopped." He turned aside, reaching for his oldest skinning knife at his back.

"Don't worry 'bout nothin' else—just get me to Shell Woman."

"Damn you," Titus snapped angrily, frustration threatening to overwhelm him. Despair lurked all around them, right out there in the snowy, dancing, swirling coming of darkness. "We ain't going nowhere till we get that bleeding stopped. I ain't gonna have you bleed out getting back to the women."

"You just don't want them wolves come follerin' my blood tracks, do you?"

He jerked up to find Shad grinning in the whitish light. "Good thing you can still laugh about spilling all your damn blood, Shadrach. Here, hold tight—right here, like that."

After he had Sweete's hand better positioned over the wound, Scratch scooted behind the carcass and butchered free a small rectangle of long, thick fur from the cow's front shoulder. Then he cut three narrow strips from the rear flank, each more than a foot long and no more than a half inch wide. Quickly wiping the knife off on the cow's frozen fur, he jabbed the weapon back into its scabbard and returned to Sweete's side.

"Here now, move your hand," and he positioned the rectangle of fur over the wounded forearm. "I ain't gonna take the time to cut the sleeve on your coat and shirt. Time enough for that once we get you to quit bleeding like a gutted hog."

In a rasp he said, "I love you too, Scratch."

As he finished wrapping the green, elastic hide around the wounded arm, fur side down, and looked up at his friend's face, Titus asked, "What you mean by that?"

"Just what I said," Shad admitted with a little difficulty. "Man does what you're doing for me—I figger that friend cares something deep for me."

"Don't know where you'd ever get that idee, Shadrach," he grumbled as his eyes smarted hotly in the bitter cold. "Hold down hard on this now," he snorted as he slowly moved his hands aside, allowing Sweete to grip onto the furry rectangle lapped over the wound.

One at a time, Titus looped the long, narrow strips over the green hide, pulling with all his might on the tough, thick, elastic hide until Sweete grunted in discomfort, if not in outright pain, then knotted each strip in turn over the buffalo fur bandage.

"If'n that don't stop the bleeding by the time I get back from fetching up the horses, I'm gonna have to tie off the arm, Shadrach."

For a long moment Sweete stared up at Bass's grim face while Titus stiffly got to his feet and stood over his friend. Shad finally asked, "You thinkin' I could lose the arm?"

"Better the arm than you dying right here."

Shad looked down at the arm. "Damn, I ain't ready to die . . . an' I ain't ready to lose my arm neither. If I'm goin' under, you gotta get me to Shell Woman. She'll know what to do. I swear—she'll know what to do for me, Scratch."

"Ain't much more she could do for you 'ceptin' what I awready done—"

"Get the horses back here," Sweete interrupted with a plea. "Leave me one of your guns case them other'ns figger to sneak back in on me 'cause I'm down."

"There's four of them bastards left."

"You leave me one of yours, that makes three guns," Sweete said, putting on a brave face of it. "For the last'un, I got my knife."

"Here," and Bass knelt, laying his pistol in Shad's lap. "I ain't gonna be long."

Sweete looked up into Scratch's moistening eyes. "I know."

Without another word, Titus laid a hand on his friend's shoulder, then turned and lunged into the wind, his bare face suddenly stung by the icy snowflakes hurtled this way and that by the capricious gales.

He knew he could get the horses back to Shad before the man bled out, maybe even get Shad back to where they left the women and children at a warm spot below the ridge, where they were going to build a fire and make camp after the men took off to hunt down some supper. But after that, Scratch didn't know what the hell to do.

Except for getting the man back to his woman. That was the least he could do for his friend. If Shad wanted to believe Shell Woman could heal her husband, then it was fine by him. Whatever a man wanted to believe in.

At those times when his hands had failed to make a difference in saving a friend's life, Bass had felt as if he had been brought to his knees—hammered down in frustration, in despair, in anger too. So he didn't rightly think what he was doing could be called praying, not real church praying, as he lumbered blindly through the stinging snow, making for the mouth of the coulee and their horses.

But if there were some spirits out there watching, or those missionaries' God hovering up in His heaven right now, then it stirred a fury in Titus Bass that such a powerful being as the First Maker could snatch his friend from him so quick and capriciously.

As much as he had wanted to believe before—just as he had been coming to accept the presence of a power much greater than himself . . . something always happened to make him doubt in the goodness of a creator or divine being. So if that holy and all-powerful spirit wanted to make itself known to Titus Bass . . . it damn well better do it now.

FOUR

"You figger I'll ever use this arm again?"

When Shad Sweete asked that of him, Titus Bass was stunned. He turned to gaze at his friend standing in the shadows of the tall adobe wall at old Fort Vasquez. "What makes you think you won't be back to wrasslin' bears and whoopin' Injuns real soon, Shadrach?"

"It's been a long time," he said with a heavy resignation. "Too long."

"Who're you to say it's been too long?"

Sweete shrugged.

So Bass took a step closer to the tall man and asked, "What's Shell Woman tell you? She ain't said it's time to take that sling off."

"No, she says I ain't ready for that . . . not yet."

"C'mere, Shadrach," he prodded, gesturing for the big man to walk with him to the center of the plaza at the middle of this small adobe trading post.

Near the western wall Waits-by-the-Water was giving Shell Woman a tour of this once-thriving fur post where Titus and his family had spent the better part of a winter years gone now.* Doing her best to explain this and that to Shell Woman by sign, pointing, and impromptu gestures, she was entertaining the five children to give the two men some time to themselves there in the deteriorating hulk of this fort, unoccupied almost five years now. Before it had been abandoned, Andrew Sublette and Louis Vasquez gave it their all in the Arapaho trade here on a wide, grassy flat

---

* *Ride the Moon Down*

along the east bank above the South Platte. It was here, Shad had explained to his wife as they approached the deteriorating mud walls, that he had worked a few seasons for the partners after the summer rendezvous were no more. Here stood a part of his past, a piece of his life before he first came among Gray Thunder's band and took a shine to a pretty, doe-eyed girl.

Even though the partners had raised their post more than two hundred miles north of Fort William down on the Arkansas River, the influence of the Bent brothers ranged far and wide along the Front Range of these southern Rocky Mountains. Within two trapping seasons, the Bents and Milton Sublette's own older brother, William, had consolidated the lion's share of the Indian trade, not to mention what few men still trapped on their own instead of slaving for the overbloated American Fur Company. While Andrew ended up throwing in with his older brother's economic fortunes, Vasquez had ridden north and eventually formed a partnership with Jim Bridger—the two of them constructing their first small post on Black's Fork of the Green River by early autumn in '43.

"Look 'round you, Shadrach," Titus suggested. "Look at ever'thing around you here."

"Ain't nothing left," Sweete grumped. "Nothing to look at—"

"That's where you're wrong, my friend."

Sweete looked down at him strangely, as one might regard a soft-brained town idiot. "Ain't nothing to see here but mud walls and them broke-down wood gates, a few corral posts, an' what's left of the fur press that ain't been burned to ash by the Injuns."

Wagging his head, Bass said, "You ain't lookin' close enough."

"At what?"

"Lookin' at all the shinin' times you had here," he whispered, a mystical enthusiasm rising in his voice. "Take a look over there," he said as he turned Sweete on his heel. "An' over there too. You was here for times that was some, Shadrach! Times got tough an' I won't argue with you that this place is drying up like a ol' buffler wallow . . . but it sure as blazes shined while you was here."

Titus stood looking up at his tall friend's face, watching something new come into Sweete's eyes as the big man studied the mud walls, the charred, half-burned gate barely suspended from its iron hardware at the entrance, at those empty, lifeless windows along the walls of the low-roofed huts appearing very much like the empty eye sockets of a buffalo skull . . . and realized Shadrach was finally seeing more than the abandoned facade. His eyes were finally looking back across the years to a day when this spot teemed with life. A long-ago day when he stood tall and bold against what the future might throw at him. Back to a day before their breed was abandoned and they were all left to wander evermore.

"You see what Shad Sweete was when he stood here many seasons ago?"

He nodded slowly. Then turned his head to look down at his older friend. "I can see more'n some empty post ever'body turned their backs on."

"Can you see what you was meant to do, meant to be, when they pulled the fur business out from under us?"

Shad went back to staring at the walls. "No, Scratch. I can't see that."

"Good." He slapped Sweete on the back. "None of us can see ahead into what days're still to come. We'll leave that up to them ol' rattle-shakers and Injun medeecin men. Now, lookee right over there."

"At them women?"

"Shell Woman. Hell yes, you idjit," he snorted. "Lookee there at that young pup o' your'n holding on to his mam's hand so tight, at that li'l girl Shell Woman's got in her arms."

"I see 'em."

"That's all the gonna-be you need to worry about, Shadrach. Don't go frettin' on what was—"

"But . . . my goddamned arm!"

"You're the only one worried 'bout it. Shell Woman sure as hell ain't."

"It's *my* arm," he groaned. "If'n I can't take care of that family over there—"

"You been doin' fine by 'em ever since that wolf chewed you up and spit you back out!"

Sweete's eyes narrowed menacingly. "I can't wait till I'm strong 'nough again to toss you in the river."

"The Platte over there?"

"Yeah—I'll throw your ol' ass in the Platte."

"Just be gentle with me, child," Titus pleaded, his hands clasped together prayerfully. "Promise me you won't do it till summer."

Looking down at that left arm bound close to his chest in a sling fashioned from a huge black bandanna of silk, Shadrach sounded wistful. "Hope by summer, I can toss us both in the river."

Overhead a ragged V of Canada geese curled low, making their noisy descent on the nearby river. In silence both men watched those final moments of flight as the birds ceased flapping, raised their wings into double arches all the better to catch the wind, and dropped their legs beneath them as they descended onto the South Platte, squawking with a flourish and a spray of water.

Sweete said, "First of them I've see'd this year."

"Honkers making their way north, Shadrach. Day at a time," Titus said. "Just like us: a day at a time."

That snowy, hoary night back south along the Front Range of the Rocky Mountains, Scratch had convinced himself that no one was going to stop Shad's relentless bleeding. But old as he was, despite all that he'd seen out here in these wild and mysterious places—Titus Bass was in for an experience he never could have imagined he would witness right before his eyes, especially back in those days when he was young and far too cynical to believe in anything beyond the reach of his own hands. Had that night happened to a younger

Titus, why—he likely would have refused to accept what he had seen, and passed it off as nothing more than his mind playing hoo-doo tricks on him with some strange and inexplicable occurrence. As it was, Scratch had witnessed something that rocked him down to the soles of his winter moccasins, then did his damnedest to wrap his mind around what marvel had overtaken all of them. By dawn he had come to accept that there was no other explanation but that they had all been in the presence of Shell Woman's protector spirits.

Bringing back their horses from the coulee, Titus had somehow managed to clumsily get Shadrach off the ground and into the saddle, weak and groggy as Sweete had become. With that small, lone pouch of buffalo tongue and boss meat lashed between the sawbucks on the packhorse, Bass had clambered aboard his mount and taken a moment longer to wrap a big bandanna over the coyote fur cap, knotting it beneath his bearded chin to hold the cap down against the growing strength of the icy gales. Then he had closed his eyes. Drawing in a deep breath, he dithered on whither direction they should go. With the disappearance of the sun behind the storm clouds, gone were the landmarks that had brought them here to the buffalo. Nowhere to be seen were the guiding stars he had always relied upon at times like these.

"You know where we're going?" Shadrach had asked him weakly sometime later after they had quartered into the storm's wintry fury.

Bass had stopped all three horses and pulled the big wool muffler down to his chin. "You got a feelin' I'm going wrong?"

Sweete shook his head. "I . . . I dunno. Just take me to Shell Woman, quickest way you can, Titus. Quickest you can."

"Ain't much quick about gettin' anywhere tonight, Shad," he said, then wished he hadn't spit out those words. He leaned over, helping his friend get a thick wool scarf adjusted over his face so that it protected everything below the eyes. "There now. Can't believe you don't trust a nigger like me after all our years partnered up. You just stay in the saddle an' you can count on me taking you right to Shell Woman. She'll have a big, warm fire going for us, and my woman gonna have some hot food waiting for your belly—"

"Shell Woman's gonna use her power to heal me, Scratch."

"You 'member that—how she'll go to work on your arm," he said as he tugged on the packhorse's lead rope. "Mend you up just fine."

"Just listen for her," Shad said in a raspy voice, muted somewhat by the wool muffler and the growing cry of the wind. "Shell Woman gonna lead us back to camp. All you gotta do is listen."

The sharp, icy snowflakes slashed at any bare flesh exposed as Titus led them on into the dark, plodding warily across the shifting, icy landscape. But for all that he strained, Bass couldn't hear anything but the faint keen of the wind as it slinked out of the coulees and whined along the tops of the ridges overhead. That, and the steady, insistent crackle as the icy snow slapped against the fur of his coat and cap. And the snorts of the horses. His had even started to fight the reins.

"Hol' up there."

Sweete said nothing, head slung between his shoulders, half conscious, likely half dead, as Bass stiffly lunged to the ground and felt his way up the horse's neck to its muzzle. Ice was building up, crusting around its nostrils. Poor beast couldn't breathe, what with the wind slinging that sleety snow at them nearly dead-on. Hammering his blanket mitten against his thigh, Scratch next used the mitten to rub over the animal's nostrils, then its eyes. Turning in the dark as the snow whipped around them, he did the same to Shad's mount, then the packhorse. Layers of warm, misty gauze haloed about him as the horses in turn bobbed their heads and whickered in gratitude.

Of a sudden the wind died—he turned on his heel. The hair rose at the back of his neck as the faint sound crept beneath the scarf and the fur cap, snaking its way into his senses. It was a voice. No, something *like* a voice. As he stood there, rooted to the spot, the wind came up again and he was instantly unsure if he had really heard what he thought he had heard. Maybe words . . . but he wouldn't swear to having heard what could be called words. At least not any language he knew of or had ever heard with his own ears.

Bass turned and peered up at Sweete. The way Shad had come awake, his face was raised, turned into the wind—Titus knew he had been listening too. But that wasn't Shell Woman, he told himself. What had made that sound wasn't someone who spoke Cheyenne. Scratch had been listening to enough of that tongue from the lips of both his old friend and Shell Woman too that he could recognize what that wind-borne sound *wasn't*. He might not know for certain what that noise was that made the hair stand on his arms . . . but he was for sure what it wasn't.

"You hear it too?" Shadrach asked.

"Thought it was the wind," he said guardedly.

"Foller it," Sweete declared weakly, his head sagging. "It'll get me to Shell Woman."

"It's coming from the wrong direction, Shad. We go off that way, we won't never—"

"Foller it, Titus Bass," he gasped in desperation. "If I never ask 'nother thing of you, just foller the voice tonight."

Stopping right beneath the big man and looking up at Sweete's shadowy form, Bass argued with himself a moment, unsure if Shad had gone soft-headed from loss of blood. Titus said, "A voice? Sound I heard wasn't no voice."

"I ain't got no strength to fight you," Shad admitted as his head sagged. "An' I wouldn't know the goddamned difference if you took me off somewheres else to die. But, I'm asking this one and only thing of you. Take me to Shell Woman. I know that's her calling to me in this storm."

Taking a step closer so that he stood right at Sweete's knee, Titus reassuringly patted the buffalo robe he had wrapped around the wounded man's legs to protect Shad from the driving force of the snowstorm. "I ain't gonna fight you neither, Shadrach. My best sense tells me that sound come from—"

"It was the voice."

"Awright, the *voice* . . . it come from the wrong direction," Scratch continued. "But, at the same time my good sense tells me to keep pointing our noses off in the direction I had us going, down in my bones something says to trust you on this."

"Shell Woman's calling me."

"Awright, Shad. I'm taking you to her."

When he settled into the saddle and wrapped that ice-coated half-robe around his legs once more, Bass took his bearings from that eerie call come on the wind, then reined the horses sharply to the left. The wind didn't feel right against them. The air itself didn't go down well when he sucked it through the warmth of that blanket muffler. And the horses? They fought him for a while, even though they were no longer nosing right into the storm. Eventually, his horse grew weary of fighting, dropped its head, and plodded on in the direction Scratch took them.

And every time the wind died, he strained to listen—making out the faintest drift of sound. Not no voice, like Shadrach claimed it was. Leastways, no sound he could call human, speaking a language he could put a name to. From time to time as the minutes, then hours, trickled past in an agonizingly slow procession, Scratch made a small adjustment in their direction. Each time the wind itself seemed to take a breath and that eerie sound came out of the dizzying black of that stormy night, he eased over a little more to the right or turned off a little more to the left. And every step of the way the deepening cold came to suck at what reserves he had always thought he possessed. But, that had been when he was a younger man.

So cold it had grown, Bass was sure his mind had started to numb. Having to remind himself to keep his eyes open in narrow slits—watching ahead for the edge of a coulee or an escarpment of boulders they might plunge over. Someone had to keep an eye open, and his ears alert. If they were being beckoned into hell by the devil hisself, at least it would be a damn sight warmer in those diggin's. Breath by breath, step by rocking, slippery step, they inched into the night, right into the growing fury of the storm . . . then right when Titus thought he had finally fallen asleep, all his senses so dulled by the cold and the chaotic frenzy of the wind—that wind up and died.

For some reason a small part of him had remained alert—expecting the unrepentant wind to keep on howling around them, whip at their robes and mufflers, bluster at the horses' manes, hurling icy snow at their eyes again after that momentary pause, but . . . the wind never rose above a whisper. A quiet, haunting whisper. It was as if Scratch came awake slowly, not with a start, but groggily, eventually becoming aware that all sound had died except for the crunch of each hoof as it plunged forward, the grunting heave of the played-out animals beneath them, the groaning creak of the ice-rimed saddle leather. Scratch had been in blizzards before. Times past when he had tucked his head down and gritted his teeth, riding on through the storm's battering to safety . . . but, he could never remember riding himself right on out of one.

This leaving the storm behind, this earth-shaking silence—it was damn sure enough to give a man the shakes, if he hadn't been shaking with the bone-numbing cold as it was already.

Scratch tucked his head to the side and turned about with slight, leaden movements to look behind them. Back there the snow swirled, the wind still whipping it into a froth. But here the howl was no more than a whimper, a mere shadow of its former bluster. He straightened in the saddle and glanced over at his half-conscious friend. Then he peered ahead once more, his eyes growing wide when he heard that faintest of whispers brought across the icy heave of the land.

Shuddering, he sensed the not knowing give way to those first slight twinges of fear. Ignorance did that to a man, he chided himself. But his scolding served no purpose. He didn't know what was happening to them, and the not knowing would do everything it could to make him afraid. As the whisper grew inexorably louder, Titus didn't know if it was really a sound from out there in the black of the storm . . . or if he was hearing something born of his own imagination, something bred to echo within his own mind. Between his ears, rather than coming to his ears from beyond—

Then it struck him brutally. With that thought of the Beyond, a molten, fluid fear slammed him hard, squarely against the middle of his breastbone with breath-robbing force. Suspicious, he twisted about again to look behind them at that dark bulk of the storm, the immense curtains of billowing ground blizzard—at that spot from which they had just emerged from the torment of its frenzy into this netherworld of near silence.

His eyes opened wide, transfixed on the horizon.

Was that a crack in the dark storm clouds, a crack in the heaving vapors of snow? Had they somehow blundered through that crack in the sky Ol' Bill Williams had instructed him about so many seasons before? Time was he had thought the superstitious Solitaire was just given to things a mite ghosty. But over time, especially in these years since the bottom fell out of the beaver trade, and those hardy few who had remained in the mountains had been retreating farther and farther from contact with civilized and genteel white society, Titus had encountered one small incident after another—no one of which was enough to make him a believer in Solitaire's mystical realm—but taken together now they were more than enough for even the most thorny skeptic to believe he was in the presence of the great unexplainable.

In the silence of that heart-stopping moment—overwhelmed with the crystal clarity of pinprick stars exploding against the utter black of the sky and the gaping endlessness of a snow-covered monotony of heaving land—something told him he had not only been lured up to the very precipice of, but sucked right on through, that invisible crack said to exist between the world of a man's everyday reality and the unseen realm of spirits and haunts, shades and hoo-doos.

Never a man who was incapacitated by the fear of what he could see, Scratch was beginning to think he had forgotten to stay awake, that he had drifted off to sleep in the mind-freezing bluster of the storm and was already in the process of dying . . . maybe even dead already—now that the roar of the wind had suddenly faded as if a door had been closed behind him. Probably dead, he thought. Maybe this is hell itself, looming right here on the other side of what had always been the sky—a hell of dark and cold, a void absent of all light and warmth. Why, even the stars had never seemed this far away. Was this his dying? Would this cold and ceaseless wandering be the endlessness of all time for him?

Of a sudden his horse jerked its head up and snorted, snapping Bass to attention. His senses responded, tingling, every fiber of him suddenly electrified. Just ahead the shadows shifted. The packhorse whinnied, then Sweete's animal sidestepped and pulled at the reins warily. Scratch could not remember his mouth ever being so dry.

Slowly a liquid shadow congealed at the horizon, as if a sliver from the black of night had itself oozed down upon the pale luminescence of the snowy, barren landscape. Closer and closer it advanced on Bass as he considered turning one way or another, to flee what he could not fully see. Then, the shadow's form sharpened on the bluish background hue of the icy snow and gradually became a rider. A huge horse, the figure seated upon it flapping as if with wings. It made him shudder to remember the tales from the Bible learned at his mother's knee, a terrifying mythology come to haunt a young boy's nightly dreams with frightful visions of winged horsemen racing o'er the land, bringing pestilence, destruction, doom, and death in their wake.

But . . . this was only one horseman. Bass looked woodenly left, and right. Only one rider come charging out of the maw of hell—

Its cry was almost human, even childlike. He might almost believe the oncoming creature's shrill cry called out solely for him.

Surely the maker of that disconcerting sound was attempting to deceive him, to make Titus Bass believe it was a human voice that had reached his ears. Something in that cry discomfited him . . . but he steeled himself, stiffening his backbone against their impending clash. No, he decided. He would not heed that mournful cry coming from the throat of that devil's whelp. Instead, he would prepare to fight its cold death with a fire of his own. Scratch clumsily wrapped his wooden hand around the big butt of the pistol stuffed in the front of his belt and pulled the weapon free. He doubted whether the lead ball could

harm this winged creature of no substance, merely passing through the horseman—

"Po . . . !"

That part of the eerie whisper reaching him now was even louder still, as the
figure continued to take on more shape, less fluid now.

Scratch's red horse stepped sideways, then he righted it with a savage tug on
the reins. Damned animal was fighting him more now than it had when they
were both being mangled in the teeth of the storm. Not a single reason for its
actions but pure contrariness, he supposed. No blowing snow clogging its nostrils or blinding its eyes. Only reason for it to fight him was that dumb beasts
could damn well act consarn and contrary in the presence of a formless demon.
As if the beasts of the earth had some sense that man did not possess which
warned them of what might not really be there—

"Popo!"

As the sound reached his muffled ears, Titus turned slightly to look off to his
right for Shadrach. The man had his eyes closed, matted with icy snow. Likely
sleeping. "You hear that?" he asked.

Sweete did not stir.

"Jehoshaphat," Bass grumbled, wondering for the first time if Shad was
dead and frozen. Losing all that blood. It was the blood, after all, that kept a
man warm, wasn't it?

As that dark figure loomed closer he pulled back the hammer on the pistol
by inching it along the wide, tack-studded belt he had buckled around his heavy
elkhide coat. From beneath the specter's hood came a high-pitched, shrill whistle—strange and wavering, not at all human . . . but a sound Titus felt he knew.
All the more uncomfortable again, and that discomfort made a haven for the
fear to grow. He realized he could reckon on hearing that sound in another
place, another time. But the high, shrill whistle did not fit here and now.

Raising the pistol at the end of his wooden arm, he brought the muzzle to
bear at the onrushing spirit that had just kicked its horse into a lope, gaining
speed across the dull glow of snow left between them.

The haunt whistled again—at which Bass's horse and the pack animal threw
back their heads and whinnied. That proved it to him. This evil spirit had the
power to command the dumb beasts of burden, to make them revolt against
man.

"G-go b-back to hell!"

As his words croaked from his throat, the specter's flowing arm came out,
and up, yanking back the hood from its evil face—

"Popo! It's me!"

He blinked. Then again. His mouth gone all the drier. By the everlasting!
This screaming hoo-doo had taken on the shape of his oldest boy!

"I'll send you straight to hell right here and now!" Titus roared angrily, pained to his marrow that this haunt would know exactly how to pierce his heart with fear and confusion—

"Popo! I come out to find you!"

"You go make your magic on some other poor child! I'm half froze an' I ain't in no mood for none of it—"

"My mother asked me to—"

"F-flea?" he stammered, baffled by the spirit's use of the Crow tongue.

"It's me, Popo!" the youngster pleaded as a gust of wind whipped his long, black hair across his face. The boy brought up a blanket mitten and tugged the wool muffler off his chin.

"D-d-damn!" Bass shrieked. "It is you, son! What in the name of tarnal truth?" And then he remembered not to shove so much American at his boy, not near so quickly. "What you doin' here?" he asked in Crow.

"For a long time after it became so cold, so dark, I begged my mother, told her I could find you, but she did not believe me," Flea explained as he halted his horse and Scratch's came to a stop alongside it.

"My heart overflows with joy to see you!" Titus bellowed as he leaned woodenly to the side and seized the boy in his arms, squeezing, pounding, hammering the youth exuberantly.

Once Scratch had leaned back and touched Flea's face with his left hand as if he were unable to believe the boy was really there, he asked, "Your mother did not want you to leave the place where you made our camp?"

"No."

Shadrach came to a halt beside them, all the horses raising wispy clouds of vapor in that small knot of man and beast. Sweete started to clumsily pull at the wool scarf that had protected his face.

Bass snorted, "So you waited until your mother was asleep, then you left on your own?"

Flea smiled. "I do not think she was really asleep. Only pretending to sleep. She knew how I wanted to come, and I believe she wanted me to find you. It had been so long for the dark, with no moonrise—"

"This means your mother will be angry with you," Titus said, patting the youngster's leg. "And she will be angry with me if I don't punish you for going against her wishes."

"But I found you."

"Perhaps that will soften her anger." Bass pointed off in the direction Flea's dim hoofprints led toward the horizon, eventually disappearing. "How far did you come to find us?"

"Not far," Flea declared. "I called to your horses all the way here. I whistled for them too."

"C-called for our horses?" Sweete asked.

Turning to the wounded man, Titus said, "The boy, my son—I didn't tell you—he can talk to horses. Has a special medeecin to understand what they say to him too."

Flea added, "I called out to them in the darkness, Popo. Every step of the way I came."

"And that's how you knew where to find us in the storm?"

Flea wagged his head, bewildered. "W-what storm?"

"You didn't come searching for us because of the storm that blew down on this ground where we went to hunt buffalo?"

"No," and the boy shook his head in confusion, "there was no storm this night."

"N-no storm?" Sweete echoed.

Titus turned slowly in the saddle to peer behind them, wondering anew if perhaps he hadn't really frozen to death in that ground blizzard, and had indeed ridden through that jagged opening between the world of mortal existence and the world of immortal and everlasting spirits the moment they put the storm behind them. Maybe this was only a part of the dream of death, the dream that came with a man's passage from all that was to what would always be. Flea and the trail his son would take to lead them back to the rimrock, back to the place where Shad and Scratch had deposited their families before riding off to hunt buffalo, could be part of the death dream too. A place meant to confuse him into thinking he was still alive—when it was nothing but what his heart most fervently hoped at the moment he had died.

What he was now experiencing was nothing more than what he had been praying for in those moments before he had lumbered on through that ragged crack in the sky. At least the haunts and spirits of this cold land of after-death granted a man his final wish. Now he would see and hold his loved ones just one more time.

"Take us back to the others, Flea," he said quietly, with no small degree of resignation that he had been swept up in something he could not understand. "Take us back."

It was still dark when the rimrock loomed out of the night. What a good place to camp, he prided himself now. The westward-facing rock would have held the last of the sun's warmth from the day, and once darkness fell the fire's heat would radiate from the face of the cliff, warming the narrow hollow where the women were just beginning to unpack the horses when the men set off on their hunt. There, to the right, he spotted the first flicker of light against the face of the rimrock—the dim dance of a fire. After the immense, bone-numbing darkness, after the absence of all light save for the subtle flicker of those frozen stars overhead, the reflection of that warm glow pulled him onward like the heat of her body as she always gave herself to him.

Shell Woman was apparently the first to hear their horses, even before Ghost and Digger did. She arose at the fire, turning, and moved in their direction.

Wrapped in her blanket, she was only a few strides away from the horsemen when she noticed the bloodstained coat and that crude bandage of frozen green buffalo hide—and lunged to a halt beside Shadrach's horse, her fingers in midair, hesitating to touch the thick wrapping.

"He said you'd know what to do," Bass started to explain, then stilled his tongue when he realized Shell Woman didn't understand much American, and he couldn't speak any Cheyenne.

As soon as she had freed the yapping, eager dogs from their rope restraints, Waits-by-the-Water was hurrying his way, her eyes flicking from his face to Shadrach and back again. "I'm whole," he said to her. "It's Shad. Got took by some wolves."

As he landed woodenly on the ground, she buried her face in his neck, wordlessly.

Having his arms around her again was like being home. But a thought scared him anew. Titus whispered against her hair, "Are you real?"

She pulled her face away from his chest, then tore off one of his mittens. Pitching it aside, she brought his hand to her cold cheek, where he could feel the tracks of hot moisture spilling from her eyes. "Can you feel how real I am?"

"I-I thought this all was . . . my death dream," he whispered as he crushed her against him anew. "Dreaming of being back with you, when I was really froze to death out there in the dark."

"You won't see your death dream for many, many seasons to come," she assured him with a sob.

Nearby, Sweete was clumsily attempting to twist himself around in the saddle.

"Wait, Shad," Bass ordered as he tore himself away from his wife. "I'll come help you an' Shell Woman."

As Titus pulled the big man out of his frozen saddle, he grunted, "Flea, get the meat off the packhorse. Give it to your sister. You build up the fire while Magpie cuts off some meat to roast for us. We ain't et . . . not in a long time."

Without a word of reply from either of them, Flea and Magpie went to work as Waits hurried away to fetch her parfleche filled with roots and leaves, spores and spiders' webs.

The moment she and Bass had Shadrach lowered to the ground at the side of the crackling fire, Shell Woman tenderly kissed her husband on the forehead. Her tears glistened on both cheeks, narrow, shimmering streams tracing the roundness of her cheeks as she turned away from the flickering light and went to search among her own baggage.

With a painful sigh, Shad began to talk to her in Cheyenne. Back and forth they spoke in low tones. Scratch figured Sweete was explaining to her what had happened with the wolves, how they fought off the beasts, and Bass's attempt to stem the flow of blood. On the far side of the fire little Jackrabbit sat up among the mounds of blankets and robes, rubbing at his eyes with the heels of his tiny hands. Though he made not a sound, his mother leaned over and whispered to him. The boy nodded, his eyes fixed on Sweete, as if realizing that something grave was occurring before his wide eyes, which were taking in everything. Patting the blankets where the small boy sat, Waits called to the two dogs. Digger and Ghost trotted over and lay down by Jackrabbit, protectively.

After she had set two small kettles of water over the fire, Waits carried her parfleche of medicinals to a bare spot beside the wounded man. Magpie quietly worked her knife down into the frozen meat, carving off thin hunks she hung from sharpened sticks at the edge of those flames young Flea was feeding with twigs he had broken off of the deadwood dragged into their campsite.

"You get me something lean back on, Scratch?" Shad asked.

He pulled over some prairie saddles and a canvas-wrapped bundle, shoving the bundle against Sweete's back. As the big man slowly eased backward, the saddles kept the bundle from sliding under his weight. Titus knelt beside Waits-by-the-Water at Shad's right side, opposite Shell Woman.

"Help her," Sweete asked. "G'won an' cut this damn hide off my arm."

One by one Scratch sliced through the stiff, narrow strips of frozen hide he had tied around the long section of skin he had bound around the gory wound. All around the edges of the crude bandage Shad's coat was ragged, torn, and blackened with frozen blood. Stiffened, bloody fragments of his cotton shirt-sleeve and the faded red-wool longhandles feathered up around the frozen edges of the buffalo hide.

When Shell Woman began to open a large, painted rawhide box she had placed on the ground beside her husband, Scratch asked Shad, "She gonna take it off?"

"Says she won't, not till it's soft."

"That water she's heating?"

Sweete nodded, his face drained of color. "I'm afeared this's gonna hurt something fierce."

"Only way to get her medicine on them cuts is to get that bandage off."

"You stopped the bleeding, you beautiful son of a bitch," Sweete whispered as he looked up with moist eyes. "You kept me from dying."

"Maybe, maybe not," he answered reluctantly. "I just done what you asked me—get you to Shell Woman. She's gotta mend you now."

Without a word, Sweete let his head rock back against the bundle and closed his eyes once more. Several minutes later Waits carried the first kettle over to the Cheyenne woman. Then she handed Sweete's wife a tin cup. From her rawhide box Shell Woman dug out some powders she sprinkled on the surface of the steamy kettle. Next she produced some dried roots, which she rubbed between her palms over the water, fragments and dust from the roots spilling into the kettle as she murmured over and over again a fervent prayer.

After dipping her bare finger into the hot water, Shell Woman nodded to her husband and scooped out a cupful. Positioning it over the frozen, rock-hard buffalo hide, she continued to whisper her prayers while she began to slowly dribble the hot water onto the stiffened skin. As the tiny, delicate stream of water steamed onto the arm and into Shad's lap, she closed her eyes.

At the far side of the fire Flea was making noise as he broke apart limbs and branches to feed the fire that was holding back both the frightening cold and the terrifying darkness. Titus signaled his son to stop, gesturing at the Cheyenne woman. The youngster understood the gravity of the ceremony.

For what seemed like the longest time as the cold stars swirled overhead and the Seven Sisters traveled at least a fourth of their journey across the sky, Shell Woman poured one hot cup of water after another on the buffalo hide. From time to time she would turn Shadrach's arm slightly, to moisten another part of the frozen skin. When she had scooped out the last of the water from the first kettle, she asked for the second container and prepared that kettle by crumbling dried roots and leaves into the steamy water, all without any interruption to her monotonous, repeated prayers.

Eventually Titus heard the scrape of the tin cup across the bottom of that second empty vessel. Shell Woman dropped the cup at her side, leaned back, and closed her eyes as she held her hands just above the soggy buffalo hide, her fingers spread wide. When she finally breathed the last of her prayers and opened her eyes, Shell Woman slipped her fingers under the edges of the moistened hide. Bass winced, knowing this was going to hurt Shadrach. No matter how moist Shell Woman could have gotten the thick, green hide, with all that blood drying, coagulating, and freezing too—it was going to cause some excruciating pain when she ripped the buffalo hair from that jagged spiderweb of deep lacerations.

Sliding up on his knees right beside his friend, Titus seized Shadrach's right hand so that Sweete wouldn't be able to fling the arm at Shell Woman, attempting to prevent his woman from ripping that bloodied, furry bandage from those wounds shrieking in agony. Inch by inch, she pulled back on the soggy hide; every new moment, with each new tug, Bass was prepared for Shad to try jerking away from the hold he had on him. But, surprisingly, the big man did not flinch, not one little twitch, as he and Titus watched in wonder while the last edge of the soggy hide came away in Shell Woman's hands—

Scratch felt the breath catch in his throat as he stared at what had been a series of messy, gaping, oozy wounds where the blood simply refused to cease flowing while he laid the green hide over them. Instead, what he now bent over to inspect was a series of thick, swollen welts, each long line appearing like a dark, oiled rope—the sort riverboatmen used on the Kentucky flatboats. And protruding from the tangle of dark welts was a gleaming white hair that shimmered in the fire's light. He glanced at Shadrach, finding as much amazement on Sweete's face as he knew was on his—then, unable to resist any longer, Titus reached out with a lone finger to brush along one of the welts. It really was fuzzy after all. He yanked the finger back, suddenly afraid. This was strange to the extreme.

"Where'd all the blood on my arm go?" Shadrach asked.

"Feel this here," Titus instructed.

"That can't be buffler hair, can it?" Sweete said as he pulled his finger away, leaning close.

Scratch himself bent over to inspect the welts again, rubbing a finger across the swollen wounds, sensing the stiffened fuzziness of the hairs sealed within the jagged lacerations. "Cain't be. The hairs ain't black, like the hair I tied 'round your arm."

"So is it, or isn't it the buffler hair?"

With a shake of his head, Bass leaned back and stared into Sweete's eyes. "Some hair, from somethin', got closed up in them wounds, slicker'n a nigger could do if'n he'd been trying to knit a wound in just that way."

"B-but, you didn't do that—"

"No, I didn't, Shadrach," he whispered. "I don't know for sure, but it seem to me the hide done it on its own."

Sweete followed Bass's eyes . . . down, down to gaze at the soggy buffalo hide spread across Shell Woman's lap.

"The damn thing ain't bloody at all," Shad gasped quietly with a shudder.

Titus swallowed with difficulty and croaked, "Lookit the color of that hide, Shadrach."

"W-we didn't shoot no white buffler . . . that cow we was cutting up when the wolves jumped us weren't white!"

Scratch leaned over, brushing his fingers across the wide strip of white fur lying across the Cheyenne woman's lap. He glanced up at Waits-by-the-Water and found she still held her hand over her mouth in astonishment. As Bass lifted the rectangular strip of soggy white buffalo hide off Shell Woman's lap, the Cheyenne woman leaned against her husband, silently beginning to sob, her shoulders quaking.

"You told me to bring you to her, Shad."

Sweete cradled his wife against him. "My gut told me that was the only way I'd hold off dying. Didn't wanna go under out there on my own."

"You wasn't figgering that her medeecin was gonna keep you from dyin'?"

With a shake of his head, Shad said, "I only knowed my heart'd be stronger if I died with her right there beside me. N-never really knowed for sure she had her mother's power."

"Her mother's power?" Titus repeated. "What power is that?"

"Been handed down, mother to daughter, for generations back in them Cheyennes."

"What medeecin?"

"White buffalo—an' it's a strong power."

"I figger Shell Woman knows she's just found out she's got that power handed down to her," Bass sighed, staring down at those white hairs bristling from the welts of torn tissue and coagulated blood. "I figger she knows her white buffalo medeecin saved your life."

FIVE

A cold, steady rain sluiced off the soggy, shapeless brims of their low-crowned hats as they came to a halt at the crest of the low hill and gazed down at the tall, weathered adobe stockade erected around the American Fur Company's Fort Laramie.

"Thar's Fort William, Shadrach," Titus said, flicking a droplet of moisture from the end of his cold, red nose.

"When they put up them mud walls?" Sweete asked as Bass's eldest son came to a stop on the hill with the packhorses.

"I dunno," Titus replied, failing to remember. "Last time I was here, I reckon on how there was timbered walls."

"How long's it been, you been here?"

"Years. Can't recollect how many gone by now. You?"

Sweete wagged his head. "Had to be afore beaver went to hell."

"Back near the end—when Bridger was a brigade cap'n for American Fur?"

"Naw," Sweete replied. "Bridger always stayed 'bout as far away from here an' them booshways as a man could keep himself."

Bass sniffled, "Likely was some time afore that last ronnyvoo we had us over on the Seedskeedee near Horse Crik."

"American Fur squeezed ever'thing outta the mountains," Shad grumped.

"Then they kept on squeezin' so hard they damn near choked ever'thing north from here, clear up to the Englishers' country."

"Only reason they ain't got a finger in the business south of the Platte is the Bent brothers—" but Sweete caught himself. "I mean, what them brothers did afore Charles was murdered down to Taos."

Titus smiled, flashing those crooked teeth the color of pin acorns. "You reckon they got some whiskey to trade, Shadrach?"

"What the blazes you got to trade for whiskey?"

"I figger it's you got some trade goods."

A quizzical look crossed Sweete's face. "I ain't got no foofaraw to trade. Ain't worked for Vaskiss or the Bents in many a season . . . an' I ain't laid bait or set a trap in longer'n that—"

"Can you still arm-wrestle like you done back in them ronnyvoo days?"

For a moment Sweete gazed down at his right arm, then patted it with his left hand. No longer did he wear the left one in that black bandanna of a sling. "Long as it's the right arm."

"Your other'n, it'll come, Shad," Bass reassured. "Don't you worry—I'll lay how you're getting stronger ever' day. You can still fotch ary a man with that right arm of your'n."

"That how you figger we're gonna get us some whiskey to drink?"

Titus shrugged. "Don't pay a man to trap beaver no more. Onliest thing the traders want nowadays is buffler robes. But neither of us got a camp o' squaws to dress out buffler robes. What's a ol' man like me s'posed to do but find a likely young'un with big arms like you to wager whiskey on?"

"What you got to wager against a cup of hooch?" Shad inquired.

He thoughtfully scratched at his chin whiskers. "That Cheyenne skinner hangin' off your belt sure to grab someone's attention at the trade counter."

"My skinner and this sheath Shell Woman worked for me?" he whined in disbelief. "An' my right arm to boot? You're just 'bout as slick as year-old snake oil, Titus Bass."

"Smooth talker, ain't I?" And he grinned as the rain splattered his face.

"Shit. You can't get away with nothin', ol' friend—you're so bad at lyin'."

"Then you'll buy me a cup of whiskey?" Scratch begged. "Ain't had none since Dick Green topped off my gourd back down to Bents' big lodge on the Arkansas."

"If'n you'll put up something of your own against two cups of whiskey, then I reckon I can throw in my arm for a match."

"Shell Woman don't mind you drinking?"

Turning to peer over at his wife, Sweete ruminated a moment, then said, "I can't callate as I've ever had a drop o' whiskey since I've knowed her."

"Nary a cup down to that mud fort on the Arkansas?"

He wagged his head. "Nope. Not a drop since I been around Shell Woman an' her people."

Titus chuckled softly and said, "Then she ain't see'd you drunk the way I see'd Shadrach Sweete get in the cups!"

"Nope. Them days belong to another man now, Scratch."

"You was a wild critter, Shadrach," Bass commented with fond remembrance. "Good damn thing you never got so drunk we'd had to rope you to a tree till your head dried out. Would've took a bunch of us to get you wrassled down and tied up."

"Can't say as I've ever see'd you get bad in the cups neither," Sweete admitted. "So you figger to tear off the top of your head and howl at the moon tonight?"

"Nope." And he shook his head dolefully. "Them times is over for me too, lad. I hurt too damn much for days after. Can't swaller likker like I used to and stay on my feet."

"We're just getting old."

"The hell you say! Speak for your own self!" And he shuddered with a chill that was penetrating him to the bone. "I'm getting damned cold sitting out in this rain, water dripping down my ass what's gone sore on this here soggy saddle—listening to you spoutin' off 'bout whiskey," Titus grumbled. "A few swallers'd sure 'nough warm my belly right about now."

The fifteen-foot-tall double gate was still much the same as it had been on his last visit to Fort William, but now the arch that extended overhead bore the figure of a horse galloping at full speed, painted red in a primitive design that reminded Scratch of how a horse might be rendered on the side of a Crow or Shoshone lodge. A little distance out, he whistled the dogs close and they all angled away from the mud walls, aiming instead for that flat just below the fort, where the La Ramee Fork dumped itself into the North Platte. Here they would camp close enough to the post to conduct some business, but far enough away that there was little chance of their families being disturbed. After Titus sent Magpie and Flea off through the brush to scratch up what they could of kindling dry enough to hold a flame, he turned to help Shell Woman and Waits-by-the-Water with that small Cheyenne lodge the two women erected only when the weather turned as inhospitable as it had this day.

"Here, I'll lend a hand," Shadrach offered as he grabbed an edge of the buffalo-hide lodge cover.

"Not with that arm of yours still mending," Bass scolded.

"A'most good as new awready."

Titus shook his head. "G'won and tend to the stock. Three of us raise the lodge while you get our goods off them horses."

The early spring rain finally let up late in the afternoon, not long after the women and Magpie got Shell Woman's lodge staked down and the smoke flaps directed against the breezy drizzle. Inside the women unfurled buffalo robes and blankets around the small fire pit, then got the little ones out of their wet clothing. To the left of the door Flea piled the driest wood he could find down in the brushy creek bottom, while the women stacked bundles of their belongings dragged inside, out of the weather. Again tonight the two families would gather beneath one roof, crowded hip to elbow, sharing their warmth and their laughter rather than erecting Waits-by-the-Water's lodge nearby.

"Go with you?" Flea's English caught his father as he and Shadrach ducked from the lodge right after a supper of some boiled venison.

"He asked that real good, didn't he?" Sweete remarked.

Bass nodded proudly, then told the boy, "Go tie up the dogs to a tree, close by, like we allays do, son."

Magpie's head poked from the lodge door as she asked, "Me too, Popo? Go with you to fort?"

"What's your mother say?"

The young girl stood just outside the doorway, speaking to her mother, then turned back to Titus and said, "We go, yes. Stay with Popo all the time."

"You both unnerstand what stay with me all the time means?"

Magpie moved up two steps and took Flea's hand in hers. They nodded their heads in unison as she said, "Where you go, we go."

"If'n your manners stay as good as your American talk, then there won't be no reason for me to scold you two," Titus replied. "Your mother's been here afore, you too, Magpie."

"Me?" she asked. "I don't remember."

With a grin he explained, "You was little. No more'n a year an' a half old back then."

She stepped over and squeezed his hand lovingly. "That was so long ago, this will be a brand-new visit for me."

"Like our visit to Bents' lodge on the Arkansas," Titus said, hugging her quickly, "this might just be your last an' only chance to see this here Fort William on the Platte."

"Platte?" Flea repeated.

"The river," Shad explained. "That's parley-voo for flat."

This time Magpie echoed, "Parley-voo?"

"Frenchie talk," Scratch said. "Lots of Frenchies out here. Not so many up to Crow country, but they're all over the Arkansas country."

"Frenchies—is this a tribe?" she inquired in her native tongue as the four of them climbed onto the flat and started crossing the soggy pasture toward the fort itself.

Both of the men laughed and Bass explained, "They're part of the white tribe. Like there are River Crow, and there are Mountain Crow. The Frenchies are part of the white tribe, but they come from a land far, far from here—and they talk with a whole different tongue of their own."

"But, the two bands of Crow speak the same tongue," Flea protested. "Why do these Frenchies talk a different tongue than the rest of the white tribe?"

Baffled, Titus shrugged as he came to a halt near the gates, the light growing dim.

Shadrach chuckled as he held up two fingertips barely spaced apart and exclaimed, "Because them Frenchies got a wee small brain—so they don't know no better than to squawk an' whine in that idjit talk of theirs!"

"They got the inner gate closed, Shad," Titus announced with a little worry. "C'mon."

Passing under the arch over the double gates, the four entered a passageway at the end of which stood the set of closed gates. Midway down the adobe wall to their left was a narrow window covered by wooden shutters that had been bolted shut on the inside of the wall.

Scratch pushed on them gently. "Throwed an' locked." Then he pounded on them with his fist. "Ho! The fort! Open up! Open up out here!"

Muted voices and the scrambling of feet on soggy ground drifted to them from inside the gates; then the scrape of iron was heard, and one side of the shutters was pulled back a few inches. A nose poked itself out. After the nose's owner made a cursory inspection of the newcomers, the shutter opened all the way and there stood a round-faced white man, his chin and cheeks clothed in a neatly trimmed beard, his upper lip naked of a mustache.

"What's your business?"

"We're thirsty," Bass declared.

"Them too?" the man asked, his eyes flicking to the children with their heads poked between the two trappers.

"Jehoshaphat!" Titus roared. "These here my young'uns! They ain't near old enough to drink."

"They're Indian?"

Scratch looked down at their faces as they peered up at him. "Yes, sir. These here pups o' mine be 'bout as Injun as you is white." He looked at the fort employee. "Now, let us in for to trade on some whiskey."

"Almost time for the store to close," he said, his eyes shifty. "Sunset, you see—"

Scratch wagged his head and clucked, "Never thought a trader would turn away a buyin' customer."

The man exhaled with that sort of sigh one used when they have been interrupted at what they regard as a most important task. "L-let me inquire of the factor."

His face was gone and the shutter closed and locked before either Scratch or Shad could ask just who currently ruled Fort William on the Platte.

"You bring something to trade, Shadrach?"

"I ain't wagering nothing Shell Woman made for me, if that's what you're asking," he grumbled. "You'll have to get your own self drunk tonight."

That prompted Flea to look up at his father and ask, "You drink the spirit water tonight?"

"I pray I can afford a little of the spirit water tonight, you damn bet, son."

"So what you bring to trade?" Sweete asked, looking Bass up and down.

He patted the front of his coat just above the spot where he had buckled the old belt decorated with what was left of its tarnished brass tacks. "Got me a little sack of some Mexican coins."

"You been holding on to that money since you was down to Taos a while back?"

"Got me some coins in Taos," he replied, "but most of 'em I got out to Californy."

"When you rode off with some Mex horses?"

"Some of them greasers come after us had a few coins in their pockets," Bass stated as the sound of iron sliding against iron echoed on the other side of the interior gate. "We took ever'thing we figgered we'd ever use off them dead bodies afore we kept on running for the desert."

"There's just the two of you?" asked a stout, broad-shouldered man in a thick French accent that reminded Titus of the back alleys and tippling houses of old St. Louis.

"An' my two young'uns here," Titus declared, then smiled as he said, "but, they don't drink much whiskey no more."

The Frenchman's eyes wrinkled and his lips curled up in a smile. At least this one, Scratch thought, he appeared to have some remnants of a sense of humor.

"So, tell me—if the four of you have come to drink my whiskey, just where are your furs?"

Scratch immediately wheeled on Sweete. "Furs? Didn't you remember to bring the damn furs?"

"Me?" Shad bellowed as if he had been insulted. "You was the one s'posed to remember to bring in them buffler robes with you to trade."

"Damn your hide anyway!" Bass said, then turned back to the Frenchman. "Looks like we didn't bring along any of our furs to trade tonight . . . so if you wouldn't mind figgering out how much some gold coin is worth, we'll know how much we can drink up afore moonset."

"G-gold?" The Frenchman's voice rose in pitch as he pushed the gate open a bit farther and stepped through the portal.

Titus nodded. "Mexican."

"Real gold?"

"Californy gold," Scratch replied. "I s'pose their gold is real out there. I only been to Californy once, but I don't care to go back to them parts for to fetch me any more of it."

The Frenchman started to hold out his hand, palm up as he asked, "You've got it with you?"

"I got enough for a li'l drinking, maybeso some geegaws and earbobs for our wives what stayed back to camp."

"My name's Bordeau," he announced with transparent eagerness. "And yours?"

"Sweete," the tall one answered. "An' my ugly friend here is named Bass."

Bordeau turned and started toward the tall, heavy gate being held open by another man. "Come in—and bring your children."

"You're booshway here?" Titus asked as they followed.

"No," Bordeau answered as the group stepped inside the inner courtyard. "Monsieur Papin is chief factor, but he is gone east. Gone downriver with a load of furs for St. Louis."

"Papin," Titus repeated the name. "That's a French name, just like yours."

"*Oui.*" He turned them slightly on the path for the trading room.

Scratch looked at Shad. "American Fur ain't very American no more, Shadrach. All these Frenchies leavin' St. Louie behind an' makin' for the High Stonies. From the sounds o' things, there likely ain't a Frenchie left on the Mississippi River by now."

Bordeau stopped at the wooden door and, with his hand on the iron latch, quickly appraised the two Americans again, then asked, "Did you, or you, trap the beaver for our company before the beaver was good no more?"

"I worked for Jim Bridger," Sweete explained. "When he hired on to run a brigade for American Fur."

"And you, *monsieur?*" Bordeau asked, his eyes falling on Bass.

"Never," he snorted. "It stuck in my craw when I was made to trade my plews* over to American Fur at ronnyvoo after Billy Sublette was bought out of the mountains. I dunno who done the worst to kill off my way of life—you niggers with American Fur or them John Bull niggers with Hudson's Bay."

Bordeau unlocked the bolt and shoved open the door, promptly stepping behind a nearby counter where he turned up the wick on a lamp. "But American Fur is the American company holding the English out."

"From the looks of you and that parley-voo booshway Papin, and all them other Frenchies working down at Bents' mud lodge down on the Arkansas—I don't know if there's much of what you'd call American in the fur trade no more. Them fat, rich Frenchmen back to St. Louie, they near bought up ever'thing. Their kind's been doin' business outta these posts where they don't need no American trappers like me an' him."

"This is my business, the furs that come to this place," Bordeau said as he stepped behind the counter and turned the wicks up on two more lamps that slowly pushed back the twilight's growing darkness. "The furs, are they your business still, *monsieur?*"

Sweete shook his head. "No, can't say as they are."

The trader asked Titus, "You do the fur business still, like me?"

"Not since fellas like you squeezed beaver to death and killed the way I made a life for myself and my own," Scratch replied sourly.

---

* The mountain trapper's term for a beaver pelt, borrowed from the French word *plus,* for a prime beaver skin.

Bordeau grinned. "So you see? I am the American in American Fur now. You two and all the rest of your kind—you are no longer around. But I am still here. I work hard, work my way up. Learn the business. You two, like the rest, you nevair want to learn to work for the company—so the company does not need men like you no more."

"A damn shame," Bass grumbled. "Badger-eyed li'l weasels like you come in and took over this business from men who stood tall and bold of a time not so long ago. None of you Frenchies ever gonna be half o' the men I knowed back in the glory days!"

Shad latched his hand around Scratch's arm and held him tight at the very instant Titus leaned toward the counter where Bordeau's face was darkening with crimson.

Bass glanced down at Sweete's hand, then at his friend's face. "Don't you worry, Shadrach. I ain't about to pop this parley-voo in the jaw."

Shad slowly released his grip. "It'd be hard as hell to trade with this booshway after you busted his nose an' made him bleed all over his purty shirt."

With a snort, Titus said, "Mon-sur Bordeau ain't gonna throw me out, Shadrach. No matter how low he thinks of me."

"Because I am a gentleman . . . and you are not."

Shaking his head, Scratch said, "Wrong, mon-sur."

Bordeau said, "Because you do not fight with blood in front of your half-breed children?"

"That's wrong too, pork-eater." Titus stuffed his hand inside the flaps of his coat. "No matter how bad you wanna throw me outta your fort, you won't do it because I got some Mexican gold you want pretty bad."

Between Bordeau's lips appeared the pink tip of his tongue. He licked the lips, then rolled them inward over his teeth with anticipation. Glee twinkled in his eyes as Titus brought out the small skin satchel and clanked it on the counter.

"Let me see these coins of yours." Bordeau rubbed his hands together.

"I'll show you one," he advised as he unknotted the leather string wrapped around the top of the pouch. From it he pulled a coin, which he loudly thumbed onto the counter and pushed toward the trader.

As Bordeau raised it into the light for an inspection, the gold shimmered.

"You held on to that Mex money a long time," Sweete commented.

"Most times, I got some furs, something to trade off. Not no more. So it seems like this is as good a place as any to dicker on some goods for these here coins," Titus said as he watched the factor slip the coin between his teeth and clamp down with zeal. "Appears to me Mon-sur Bordeau here knows good gold when he sees it."

"Is real," the trader attested.

" 'Course it is," Scratch replied.

He watched Bordeau turn away, still clutching the coin, moving aside some objects on a shelf behind him before he pulled out a small set of scales and weights. Placing the coin on one side of the scale, Bordeau selected one of the smallest weights. After he had it balanced, Bordeau looked up at the American again.

"How many of these you have, *Monsieur* American?"

"What's that'un worth to you?"

"How many you want to spend?"

"Only one," he said stiffly. "I figger it's more'n enough to buy some earbobs and hangy-downs for our womenfolk. A play-pretty or two for each o' the young'uns."

Removing the coin from the scale, Bordeau leaned back against the shelves and held the gold piece before his eyes, turning it this way and that in the lamplight. "Pick out what you want for your women and the children too."

How excited the youngsters became as Bordeau pulled wooden trays from the shelves behind him and laid them side by side on the counter, each one filled with hanks of sewing beads, or large multicolored glass beads from faraway Venice and the continent of Africa too, along with many styles of finger rings, an assortment of tin bracelets, and small rolls of brass wire. Magpie went right to work touching every single item to her satisfaction. Next, Bordeau set a small wooden pail on the counter; inside were nestled a bevy of tin whistles and string toys that snared the eyes of young Flea and Shadrach.

Scratch was bending over the trays with his daughter when the trader spoke.

"What do you think of this?"

Magpie and her father both looked up together, finding Bordeau holding a colorful shawl, delicately sewn with a tassel fringe at the hem around the bottom V of the broad triangle. Scratch noticed how his daughter clamped her hand over her mouth, eyes going wide as muleprints.

"She likes, eh?"

"Let 'er try it on, trader," he demanded.

Bordeau passed the shawl to her. With her father's help, Magpie laid it over her shoulders while Bass lifted her long black hair. She clutched the shawl closed at her breast and spun this way and that. As he watched her twirl to make the tassels flutter, Titus suddenly spotted six faces pressed against the thick window glass, six pairs of eyes watching Magpie preen, the young girl lost in her own little world.

Looping his arm over her shoulder, Bass quickly turned his daughter away from the prying eyes and faced her toward Bordeau. "You got 'nother of these here shawls?"

"Same as the one she's got on?"

"Lemme see all of 'em so we can pick out three of 'em."

"Three?"

"The other two for our wives."

"That's awful good of you, Scratch," Sweete said.

"You damn well can't go back to that lodge without presents for her, Shadrach."

"But I ain't got nothing to repay you for 'em—"

He whirled on Sweete. "Don't ever say that to me again. I do this 'cause I wanna. Don't take away the joy from me doing this for you."

"Aw . . . awright."

"Shell Woman don't ever need to know it weren't your money," he explained. "Ever' woman needs some geegaws an' girlews to make their eyes shine and their hearts go warm."

"Popo!"

He turned at Magpie's exclamation, finding her running her fingers over eight different patterns of shawls. Bass told her, "Pick out one for yourself, and Shell Woman, and a real pretty one for your mother too. Shad an' me gonna scratch through these here earbobs an' foofaraw for some pretty hangy-downs to go with them shawls."

In the end, after they had argued over the worth of Mexican gold this far north of the old Spanish possessions, Bass finally relented and let go of two of his coins for a treasure trove of trinkets and jewelry, along with the three shawls, four more blankets, and a burlap sack filled with at least three of every sort of toy Fort Laramie had on its shelves.

"An' you said I had some left over for a little whiskey," Bass reminded.

"Yes, yes," Bordeau answered in a gush as he scooped the two coins into a pocket of his drop-front britches.

Shadrach asked, "Where's your likker?"

"Bring it out, trader!" Scratch demanded.

"No drinking here in trade room," Bordeau stated. "Other room for whiskey."

"Awright, show us," Sweete said.

They stepped from the trading room just ahead of Bordeau as the trader snuffed the lamps, then pulled and locked the door behind him. As the group followed the Frenchman down the side of the square, Bass turned to study that group of six curious employees stepping away from the shadows near the trade-room window, slowly following the Americans.

"I dunno if there's trouble brewin', Shadrach," he said in a low voice. "Maybeso there's some nosy parley-voo niggers spotted my gold through the window."

Sweete glanced over his shoulder at the half dozen following them. "They're small, Scratch. Frenchies too. They can't cause us too much trouble. 'Sides, you allays had your back to that window. They couldn't see your pouch or your gold."

"Then why you reckon they follerin' us?"

With a shrug, Shad said, "Bet they know we're headed for the whiskey room. Pork-eaters like them figger to drink a horn or two on your money."

"Ain't enough Mexican gold in my pouch to make me pay for a round of whiskey for one of their kind," he growled as Bordeau stepped through a smudge of yellow light spilling upon the damp ground from a smoke-stained, dirty window and immediately flung open the cottonwood door beside it.

"*Alors!*" the trader called out to the fat man behind the counter as they came in. "Four whiskeys for my friends here!"

"For the *petite fille?*" the barman asked, his face drawn up in question.

"*Non!*" Bordeau exclaimed with a snort. "These mixed-blood children do not drink the whiskey. Two whiskeys for the one-eyed one, and two for his tall friend."

"This Injun gal looks old enough for a cup of whiskey."

Bass froze at the counter and slowly turned at the sound of the voice. On instinct, he quickly glanced around the room, counting enemy, hopeful of finding another female. But as he had feared most, he found but one woman in this smoky room, dank with the mingled odors of sweaty bodies, spilled whiskey and brandy, as well as the stench of clothing and anuses gone too long unwashed.

"Fill the cups, like the trader told you to," Titus ordered the barman, then cleared his throat as he turned back to the stocky man who had called out with the loud voice.

"I buy the woman a drink of my own, yes?" the badger-eyed one asked.

Shaking his head as he felt his breath come hard, Bass growled, "This here ain't no woman. My daughter she be, you gut-sucker of a parley-voo."

"What is this you say of me . . . gut-sucker?"

Sweete immediately replied. "It ain't good, what my friend called you."

Slowly the Frenchman's eyes tore from Shad's to look again at Bass. "So, she is your daughter. Still I think she looks old enough to drink the whiskey."

Bordeau slipped away from the counter, stepping behind the Americans and inching along the wall until he stood just behind the right elbow of his stocky employee.

"She's maybe a moon away from her thirteenth summer, you no-count dog." Titus reached out and gently snugged Magpie against his hip. With his other hand he dragged a cup of whiskey his way and brought it under his nose for a sniff.

"Me? A dog? That makes me laugh! You are the dog who sleeps with the Injeeans. Look at this half-blood girl. Now she is the best for a man like me, no? Half-blood women want a real man in the robes."

After smelling the strength of Bordeau's whiskey, Bass took a long drink, enough to make his throat burn and his eyes water. If it was going to be the only drink he'd have this night, then he wanted it to be a deep one. He set the cup back on the counter. So far, the Frenchman hadn't moved any closer. Made no threatening moves. Although the stocky man still leaned against the wall, Titus nonetheless knew it was but a matter of moments. Scratch turned, wiping his mustache with the back of his hand, and glared over at the antagonist. The man wore a pistol stuffed in his belt and one knife Bass could see over the right hip. Appeared to be a left-hander.

"We come to drink our whiskey, part of a trade," Shad began to explain as he set his first cup down on the counter behind Bass and tugged Magpie a step back from her father.

"Trade? You want to trade, *n'est-ce pas?*"

Bordeau leaned over to his employee, whispering something in the stocky man's ear. The Frenchman listened, nodded once, but never took his eyes off either the American or the half-blood girl.

"Awready done our trading for the night," Bass said as he squared himself and laid a hand on Flea's shoulder. "Son, move yonder toward the door now."

"Popo, I don't want to go," the boy said in Crow.

"We aren't going, not just yet," he answered his son in the same language.

Bordeau asked, "Does your daughter know the words that will drive a man wild in this same tongue you speak to the boy?"

"Let's not fight over her," the muscular employee said with a mocking kindness. "I will bring some goodness to your poor family, old man."

"How could a gut-eater like you do that?"

Sneering, he said, "Don't marry your girl off to no Injeean warrior who picks the lice off his head. *Non,* marry your girl off to a real man like me who can get her out of those dirty Injeean clothes and put her in a fancy dress and hair combs."

The thought of such a life for his daughter turned his stomach. "I'd sooner see her married to a half-starved Digger than to have a scum-lickin' parley-voo in my family!"

"Let her make her choice, old man," the Frenchman demanded. "A Injeean life with lice, the life you choose . . . or a life as my woman—"

"She's just a girl, you French pig."

"Old enough to me," the muscular man provoked. "Look at her ass. Is that not how you Americains say it—ass? And she has those little teats so small and hard now too."

"You're a coward," Titus growled, both hands flexing, wondering how much older he was than this bad-tongued bully, trying to calculate how many pounds of muscle the Frenchman had on him. "You stand here in front of a little girl and her father, talking bad with your pig tongue, only because you got all these other stupid gut-eaters around you. You're no man, mon-sur. You're just a soft-brained, scum-lickin' parley-voo what works for Chouteau's American Fur because you can't do a real man's job . . . an' the most you can ever hope for is to die in your sleep somewhere out of the rain."

"Me? The coward, Americain?"

"All you parley-voo bastards ain't got the spine of a yappin' prerra dog," Titus declared. "You ever hear what happened to one of your kind when he bumped up against a fighting cock named Carson? Kit Carson?"

The dark eyes narrowed. "Who is this?"

"Carson's the one killed the parley-voo called Shunar."

"Chouinard?"

Bordeau leaned over and whispered something more into the man's ear.

"Thees Shunar, he was not as good as me, eh?"

"You ain't half the man Shunar tried to be," Scratch said. "But . . . I figger you're gonna be just as dead as him afore I leave this room."

"You talk so beeg for such old man."

"I can pin your ears back, slice 'em off, an' feed 'em to you."

"No pistols!" Bordeau suddenly hollered as the employee reached for his belt weapon.

"Fine by me," Scratch replied, his heart thundering in his ears. He dragged the .54-caliber flintlock from his belt and clunked it on the counter.

His antagonist asked, "When I kill you, I have to kill the other one too?"

Before Bass could answer, Sweete announced, "I ain't leaving here with you on your feet, pork-eater."

"Ah! You sweet on the girl yourself, eh?"

"No," Shad said as he nudged Magpie behind him at the bar. "I got me my own baby daughter too."

"She half-blood, like his girl?"

"Yes," Sweete answered.

"Too bad now. She grow up with no papa."

Scratch slowly pulled his knife from its sheath, saying, "Is all you do is talk, mon-sur?"

The Frenchman laughed mirthlessly. "*Infant d'garce!* You hurt me with your leetle knife?"

"Big enough to open your gut."

"*Non,* thees is a real knife," and the employee pulled the large butcher knife from its crude rawhide scabbard.

"It's big, s'all," Titus said. "Big and stupid, like you, dung-head."

For a moment the Frenchman smiled, then said, "Thees will be fun. First I kill you. Then I kill your friend. And after some more whiskey . . . tonight I make a real woman of your leetle daughter. Tonight she will bleed from the hard rut I will give her—"

All words and other sounds were suddenly muffled by the roar of blood rushing to his ears as he raced for the Frenchman, whose eyes snapped as big as the trader's teacups. The man started to crouch as the American shot across the short distance that divided them. Without time to work his big knife into position, the Frenchman did his best to jab in toward his attacker, but Bass already had that figured out too.

As the stocky man's left arm stabbed forward with the wide blade, Scratch raked under the arm with his own thin-bladed skinner. At that same instant he felt the Frenchman's calf crashing against his ankles. The room turned around as Titus spun into some crude stools and an empty wooden crate where playing cards and bone dominoes went flying.

"Arrgggh!" the Frenchman cried in pain as he gripped his sundered left forearm in his right hand and slung about bright streamers of blood in anguish until he gritted his teeth and took the bloody knife into that empty right hand.

"Bordeau!" Sweete cried in warning. "I'll shoot any of your pork-eaters makes a move to help the bleeder! You understand I'll kill 'em if they make one move toward my friend!"

With a nod, Bordeau growled at the rest of the men in the room while Bass scrambled to his feet, his shins and right shoulder crying out in pain.

"Lookee there, pork-eater," he rasped. "You do bleed just like a fat pig."

With an ear-splitting cry, the enraged Frenchman lunged toward Titus, slinging blood and flashing the butcher knife in his weaving right hand. In a blur, Scratch sank to a crouch, leaning forward, then retreated in a half circle from beneath the attacker's arm, all in the space of a heartbeat. Bass inched backward until he was stopped by the counter, then stood motionless as the Frenchman slowly gazed down at his lower chest. His shirt hung open the entire width of his body, blood oozing from the long, gaping wound. Small, dark pools began to collect on the clay floor around the toes of his moccasins.

Shadrach stepped up right behind Bass's left elbow. "You say the word, we'll gut 'em all."

"You want me to finish you, pork-eater?" Titus asked his enemy. "Want me to kill you off so you won't have to live with the memory of this night your tongue ran away on the wrong man's daughter?"

His mouth curled up, "I keel you now—"

"Non!" bellowed Bordeau as he leaped in front of his bleeding employee. "You are losing too much blood already! You cannot win, and I do not want to lose you." The trader turned and took a step toward the Americans. "No more fighting. You go. Take your goods and go from this fort—nevair to return—"

"Popo!"

Scratch whirled on his heel at Flea's shrill call of distress. He found the boy sprawled on the floor right beside the door, holding a hand to his head. Then something suddenly awakened in him as the silence closed around the old trapper.

Magpie was gone.

SIX

"Magpie!"

As he shrieked his daughter's name in desperation, Titus Bass lunged across the clay floor to land on his knees beside his son.

"How bad you hurt, boy?"

Flea pulled his fingers away from the gash on his head, a trickle of blood oozing its way down to his left eyelid. "They steal my sister."

Spinning around in a crouch at the sound of footsteps and clatter of wooden stools, Bass growled, "Shadrach! You hold these bastards here."

As Titus began to stand at the doorway, Sweete protested, "I'm comin' with you."

"No you ain't," he growled. "Stay with the boy. They couldn't get far—"

"There, Popo! There they go!"

Flea pointed out the open door at the open compound, where the five men dragged the kicking, struggling girl across the muddy ground illuminated only by starshine and some random splotches of lamplight spilling from smoke-smudged windows.

Titus hurled himself into the doorway and screamed, "Magpie!"

One of the handful of kidnappers yelped and wrenched his hand away from the girl's snapping mouth as the other four continued to wrestle the child, who was proving to be a blur of flailing legs and whirling arms, very much like a snarling catamount.

"P-popo!" her thin voice called to him, the frantic pitch of it almost swallowed in the immensity of the mud walls the moment that hand was torn from her mouth—but another hand cuffed her, stifling her next cry.

For an instant he began to lunge on through the doorway, then suddenly wheeled about, dashing back to the counter to sweep up the belt pistol he had laid aside just before drawing knives with the stocky Frenchman. He quickly gazed down at the cluster of men doing what they could to stem the flow of blood from his wounded adversary.

Glaring into the man's eyes, Titus vowed, "I'll be back to finish you."

Dragging the hammer back on the pistol as Sweete stepped forward with his own pistol and knife drawn, Scratch leaped through the door, racing across the soggy, barren ground for those men who were just then pulling the girl toward a line of dark shadows at the back of the fort, where no lamplight reflected from the murky puddles of rainwater.

"Let 'er go!" he bellowed like a herd bull challenged by a ring of prairie wolves.

Three of the five turned as his voice reverberated off the mud walls. One man's face went white with fear. In an instant he turned to flee toward the shadows. In his wake fled a second.

"Popo!" she pleaded again.

One of the men immediately slammed his fist into the side of the girl's face to silence her.

Without consciously thinking about it, Scratch slid to a halt and had the pistol up at the end of his arm. A noisy explosion rocked the square. Then the big lead ball caught the man between the shoulders just as he was raising his fist to strike Magpie a second blow. His arms flung outward as he tripped over his own feet and Magpie's too, bringing the two of them down together. A fourth man took that moment to dart away, but the fifth knelt over his bleeding companion, glanced at the American, then brutally yanked the girl to her feet.

He cackled, "You only had one shot in your pistol!"

Titus was already sprinting across those last few yards as the French-talker shoved Magpie ahead of him. Her feet slipped in the mud of a shallow puddle and she went down in a sprawl. As the Frenchman stumbled up to crouch over, yelling at the girl in a shrill voice, Bass wrenched the narrow, curved head of the tomahawk from the back of his belt, gripped the end of its worn handle in his right palm like the feel of an old and trusted friend, then cocked his arm and flung it through the air.

With that small head of the tomahawk piercing his back, the last of the attackers arched violently with a scream of agony, wrenching one arm backward as he attempted to claw at the weapon buried deep in flesh and bone . . . his legs went out from under him and he pitched into a puddle glazed with the black reflection of that starless night, splashing Magpie with mud and water as she began to crawl away, whimpering.

"Scratch!"

Bass did not turn at the sound of Shad's voice until he had helped his daughter to her feet. Holding her quaking body against him, he turned to find the tall man backlit at the doorway.

"Flea there with you?" he demanded.

Shad reached out his arm and pulled the boy into the open doorway with him.

Pressing a moccasin down on the back of the man, Titus worked the tomahawk up and down several times to free it from the attacker's back. As he cupped her chin in his bloodied hand, raising her face, Titus asked her, "Can you walk, Magpie?"

She bobbed her head with nothing more than a whimper, clutching her father for fear she might otherwise fall.

One at a time he stuffed his empty pistol and the damp tomahawk into his belt, then bent over the dead man and pulled free the attacker's two pistols. With one in each hand, he started back for the grogshop, eye scanning the shadows for more of the cowardly kidnappers. "Stay right beside me, darlin'. C'mon."

"We're lucky more of 'em ain't wearin' guns," Sweete grumbled as Bass herded Magpie through the open door.

"If it was so, they'd made a rush and you'd blowed a hole through two of 'em with the same ball," Titus declared with great confidence. "If'n I know you an' that big sixty-two of your'n."

Sweete grinned. "Maybe I ought'n still blow a hole through two of 'em afore we leave."

"Yes, go! Get out!" Bordeau wailed. "You better run before more of my help comes for you."

"Help?" Flea repeated the word.

Scratch's eye quickly raked over the room, making a tally of those here with Bordeau and the wounded man, along with the four live ones who had fled into the shadows outside. "I don't callate how you got any more *engagés* working for you this time o' year, Bordeau. Way I see it, there's them four cowards somewhere out there, waiting in the dark to back-shoot us—an' there's the rest of you parley-voo pigs in here."

"How we gonna get the young'uns out of the fort an' back to the women?" Shad inquired in a harsh whisper.

"Oui?" Bordeau asked with a sneer as he knelt beside the wounded Frenchman again. "You kill two of my men, them both American Fur employees. Maybeso this third one too, eh?"

"I not die yet," grumbled the wounded man who sat in a splatter of black that stained the clay floor. "I live," and he coughed. "I live to keel this Americain!"

"Another day, mon-sur. Not this'un, you won't."

"We still gotta get outta here, Scratch," Sweete reminded.

His eye fell on Bordeau. "C'mere, you parley-voo cock-bag."

The trader stood slowly, but did not move.

"You c'mere now," he growled as he slowly aimed a pistol at the wounded man on the floor, "or I'll blow what li'l brains that weasel got in his head."

"Non," Bordeau protested.

He moved the muzzle of the pistol so that it pointed at the assistant factor. "Then I'll blow a ball right through—"

"You kill me, *monsieur,*" Bordeau interrupted as he stood his ground, "Papin will not rest until you are dead."

Titus grinned, his brain grinding on his extrication from the fort, making their escape from this North Platte country. "You're important to Mon-sur Papin and the company?"

Bordeau jutted his chin with too much self-confidence, *"Oui,* very important."

"Papin an' all Chouteau's money don't mean a goddamned thing to me," he declared as he stepped toward Bordeau and suddenly shoved the muzzle of his left-handed pistol under the trader's chin. "But if you don't come with me, I will splatter your brains all over the rest of your dog-sucking friends here."

His eyes grew huge. "C-come with you?"

"You're gonna get us outta the fort."

"How I do that?" Bordeau asked as he shuffled away from the others, almost on his toes, that muzzle still shoved up under his chin as Bass slowly backed them toward the door.

Titus did not answer until they stepped into the light spilling out from the doorway. "Tell them, those four cowards of yours out there—tell 'em I'll blow your shit-brains out the top of your head if they make any trouble for us getting outta the fort."

"You cannot get away—"

With a sharp upward jerk of the pistol, Bass forced Bordeau's chin toward the roof. "It's up to you, parley-voo. If'n I kill you, I can grab another an' another till I get my young'uns outta this mud hole. So you can come with me, or you can leave what you got left for brains in the mud at my feet. What's it gonna be?"

"He's cut up your li'l booshway," Shad explained, sarcasm dripping from his words. "An' there's two more dead out there in the dirt right now. You better listen to this'un. I ain't got no control over him when he gets like this. The man's lived through twenty year o' Blackfoot, Comanche raiders, and Mex soldiers too. Killing another fat, pissant Frenchman like you won't make no nevermind to my friend—"

"Oui! Oui!" Bordeau stammered.

"Now," Bass ordered and started them out the door, but suddenly stopped and wheeled about on his heel. "Flea, grab that sack with them geegaws and shawls in it. Bring Magpie two of them new blankets for her to carry too."

Sweete helped the youngsters quickly gather up the trade goods, then Titus said, "Awright—let's get outta this pigs' hole. You bring up the rear, Shadrach. Put them young'uns atween us. Stay close, stay real close to me."

His chin raised to the sky, Bordeau whimpered, "Wh-where you going with me?"

"To that gate. Shad, keep your eyes moving. You too, Flea. Watch the shadows—sing out if somethin' moves. Watch those shadows behind us."

Inside the tippling house arose a sudden clamor of voices, the scraping and clatter of wooden furniture. He glanced back over his shoulder, saw shadows flit the window, figures moving inside.

"Flea, wan'cha keep an eye on that door back there, son."

When they finally reached the interior gate Titus ordered, "Open it."

Bordeau slid back the iron bolt through its hasp with a grating rasp, dragged back one side of the gate, then took a step to the side. All through it Scratch never removed the pistol from under his chin.

His eyes grown hard once more, Bordeau hissed, "Now go."

"Oh, no. We ain't saying adieu, mon-sur. You're gonna get us back to our camp."

"You keeping him?" Shad said. "He's a li'l booshway—worth something to the company. We can't take him outta here, Scratch."

"Reason I'll take 'im is for what he is worth to 'em," Titus replied, shoving Bordeau through the open gate.

"*Non, non!* Please, *monsieur*—"

"Stay close to me, Magpie. Don't you see, Shad—we leave this bastard here, we couldn't make a run for it fast enough afore the rest'd be down at our camp, shooting up the women and young'uns."

Breathlessly frightened, Bordeau asked, "You let me go at your camp, *oui*?"

"Likely I ain't gonna let you go till I know they ain't follering us, mon-sur."

As they stopped for a moment just inside the outer set of gates and peered into the darkness, Bordeau pleaded, "Your friend said it true—you can't take me out of here! I am important to my employers—"

"You don't shut up, I'll shoot you in the foot and make it hard for you to hobble back to your goddamned fort when I'm done with you miles from here."

"W-walk? Miles?"

"I sure as hell ain't gonna let you ride back here on one of my horses!"

He started to struggle against the old trapper. "You can't!"

But Bass shoved the muzzle of the second pistol into the small of Bordeau's back.

"Maybe you're right, mon-sur," he growled as he shoved the trader toward the gentle slope that would take them down into the cottonwood bottoms. "Maybe I just ought'n gut you right here an' now, then go back in there an' finish off that mouthy one I started cuttin' on. No matter what happens to me—we just finish off all you sonsabitches right now for what you was gonna let them others do with my daughter."

"*Les filles* . . . the girls," and he paused a moment, "Injeean girls, they come with the tribes and maybe one of my mens, he takes a shine to one. He can buy her from her father—"

"No good, lazy bastards, sellin' off their own blood kin," he snarled. Jabbing the second pistol into Bordeau's kidney, Titus said, "I ain't the sort of nigger to trade my daughter to no stiff-necked parley-voo what ruin't the hull god-damned beaver trade, Bordeau."

"This night," the Frenchman whispered, "the men think maybe to have some fun with you, is all."

"Naw, this ain't no fun. Dead serious to me: takin' a man's family—you an' your weasel friends thinkin' they was gonna use up my daughter, tradin' her off from man to man like you fort loafers do down here."

"Please, we make a big mistake!" Bordeau pleaded as they reached the cottonwood and he spotted the beckoning glow of the firelight inside the small lodge. "Cannot we be friends and you go your way?"

"More I think about it, the more this whole shebang sours my milk, Shad."

"What's that, Scratch?"

"You heard it: these bastards figgerin' I'd sell off my own kin to 'em."

Thirty yards ahead, a figure emerged from the lodge, a shadow taking shape as the sky began to mist.

"Ain't that what the Injuns do?" Sweete suggested. "I s'pose I bought Shell Woman from her family—"

"She weren't no li'l girl!" he snapped.

Shad swallowed, suddenly contrite. "Awright. Ain't the same thing, not the same at all."

"No it ain't," he growled. "Flea—g'won ahead. Tell your mother start packin' in a hurry."

"We go from here?" Magpie asked.

"Far away from here as we can," Titus said. "Seems what trouble run us out of Taos been doggin' us north. You go on with your brother. Help your mother and Shell Woman pack for the trail."

"Scratch, I . . . I didn't mean nothin' by what I said just now," the tall man apologized. " 'Bout it bein' what a man does with Injuns."

"You got a daughter of your own gonna grow up one of these days, Shadrach."

Sweete nodded as he turned his head this way and that, peering into the darkness. "I thought of that too. Thought how I'd feel if'n she was Magpie."

"Maybeso it's that way with most Injuns: sell off their daughters to the nigger can put up the biggest cache of goods," Bass said as he jerked Bordeau to a halt near the lodge, where excited voices murmured and noises clattered.

"I s'pose white folk do it back east too, most times," Shadrach observed. "Folks fix up a marryin' for their daughters to the richest feller they can."

"I ain't back east, Shadrach. Left that all behind a hull lifetime ago," he said, his voice almost a hush now. "An' I ain't like no Injun neither. Never gonna sell Magpie off for a stack of trade goods."

"So where do fellas like us go, Scratch?" he asked. "Now that this country ain't the same as it was an' ever'thing's changed on us?"

"We keep running till we get to the next place, Shadrach," he admitted. "We can give up to their kind and give in to all the ruin they're bringin' to the mountains . . . or we keep runnin' till we drop in our tracks. Man does one or the other. Let the ruin eat 'im up alive, or he does his best to stay one jump ahead."

Much to Bass's surprise, none of the French *engagés* showed up in the cottonwood bottoms to spoil their escape.

Between the two women and Magpie, the bedding was tied up and the lodge torn down, all of it thrown on the travois and packhorses while Flea untied the dogs and helped Shadrach get Bordeau trussed up for his ride with a length of hemp rope. It wasn't until they were mounted and on their way out of the valley that Waits-by-the-Water finally began to sob, quietly.

"No bad come to her," Titus reassured in English.

Yet she said in Crow, "This time. What of the next? Will you be there? Will there be too many for you?"

"She's a pretty girl," he whispered, trying to explain it. "Bees will always flit around the honey."

With a long, stern glare at her husband, Waits said, "You don't understand. Other white men, they are not like you. Not like our friend Sweete. The other pale eyes, they will always buy what they can, and steal everything else."

Wagging his head, Titus argued in her tongue, "It isn't just white men. For generations and generations, your people raided for ponies and scalps, taking women and children too. It isn't only white men who steal what they want."

She sighed, her eyes getting even more sad. "Then where will we go to protect our daughter until she chooses a man of her own—the way I chose you, *Pote Ani?*"

He studied her face in the dark for a long time until he answered, "I haven't sorted that out just yet."

"I love you, husband. I always will," she promised. "But, more and more now, I am thinking that it was not a good day when the white man first came among my people."

"I am wounded by your words—"

"I did not speak their truth to hurt you," she said. "It is the other men of your white tribe who are evil and leave pain wherever they go. I know you are not like the rest of them. And, I know that this troubles you too."

"There was a time not so long ago when I understood this world," he told her as they rode into the dark. "I knew what to make of things. I could tell a friend from those who meant me no goodwill. But now my old life is gone like winter breathsmoke in a hard wind. I do not know people anymore, Indian or white. Perhaps you are right, woman: it is my people who have brought a great change to this land—but your red people have changed as well, changed over the summers since I left the land of the white man behind."

She nodded and stared ahead into the night. "I know your words. While it is true that your kind brought the first shift in our way of life, many of the red people made wrong choices and became bad like those whites who came among us. Those like you and me are few—people caught between two worlds. I feel a danger growing around us like a thick fog. Where can our kind go to be safe again?"

"I don't know where we ever will find us a place that will be safe from those who would crush in around this land—stealing what belongs to us, running off with those we love," he sighed. "Those who are ruining everything we ever knew to be true."

They had put trouble behind them before, but the trouble they were running from in Taos, or here along the North Platte, was unlike anything Bass had confronted before. This was not something that could be solved by simply escaping. Down to his toes, he was frightened that they would eventually discover they weren't able to run from what he feared was coming, that the evil of it was growing more vast as they relentlessly put the miles and days behind them.

From that very night, Shadrach and his family took the lead, setting a course up the north bank of the La Ramee River, striking south by west instead of following the well-beaten road along the Platte that made for the Sweetwater and the Southern Pass. They realized they stood a much better chance of escape if they stayed off that hoof-hammered trail used by trappers and trading caravans. Riding south around the Black Hills would prove much harder on the women and the animals, but it would likely deter any halfhearted pursuit.

As twilight put a close to each of those early days of flight, they would stop and build a fire, cook a little meat, and warm some coffee before moving on another handful of miles, where they would picket the horses and shake out their sleeping robes. Without the warmth of a fire, the only illumination shed on that high, barren land was cast down by the stars—if the sky hadn't clouded up and gone murky with the probability of rain. During their first stop each evening, Shadrach or Scratch would bring Bordeau the scraps after the rest had eaten their fill.

"You didn't give 'im much," Sweete commented after their first full night on the trail and the women had boiled some dried strips of elk shot the day before they had reached Fort William.

"Fat as he is, bastard won't starve afore we set him out on his own," Titus said without the slightest hint of mercy. "Stiff-necked parley-voo gonna have to use his wits to get back to the Platte. If'n he don't—well, now . . . I hope what takes him down makes it slow an' painful."

Their third night of flight, low along the fringes of thick timber at the southern end of those low mountains, where they had been following the climb of the La Ramee, they were suddenly caught by a late snowstorm and ended up spending three days and nights around a fire, until the winds died and the sky cleared. Through it all, Shad and Titus spelled each other, one of them awake at all times, watchful for pursuers. By the time the heavens blued again, Scratch had grown certain the *engagés* from the fort had given up their chase in the face of the storm. Slowly they plodded on out of the hills, following the river until it turned due south. Only then did the men leave the La Ramee and strike out overland, continuing south by west toward that high, broad saddle between the Black Hills and the Medicine Bows where an inviting patch of blueing sky beckoned them onward. Here was a country of sage and cedar, juniper and dwarf pine. Immense patches of snow still cluttered the hillsides and especially the coulees too as the weather moderated and the high sun temporarily turned the desert into a sea of mud that sucked at hoof and moccasin alike.

"Gonna send you back to the teat of your awmighty American Fur Company, Mon-sur Bordeau," Titus said one midday when they had stopped to water the horses at a small spring nearly hidden by a vast carpet of yellow-green juniper.

The Frenchman brought his dripping face out of the cold water. "Y-you set me free?"

"That's right," and Titus started working at the knots around the Frenchman's wrists.

"I have nothing," Bordeau whined. "You must give me a horse! A blanket and a gun too. Powder and shot. To stay alive—"

Yanking the rope from the trader's wrists, Scratch took a step back. "Told you when we left Fort William: You ain't wuth a red piss, much less one o' my horses. I need 'em all—so you're on your feet now."

"These boots!" he whimpered. "They won't last in this mud! Wh-what if it snows again!"

Sweete stepped up. "Give 'im a blanket, Scratch."

He nodded at Shadrach. "My friend says to give you a blanket, keep you from freezing. And, I'll let you have one of these here belt guns I took off the niggers was running off with my daughter."

"*Non*—I need a big gun. Smoothbore! Please!" he cried, lacing his fingers together as he implored the Americans.

"You'll get this pistol, some ball and powder," Titus said, remaining untouched by the Frenchman's plight. He tossed Bordeau a small horn of powder, then scraped out a dozen or so lead balls from his spare pouch. "Just don't waste 'em all afore you get back to your friends."

As Shad helped Shell Woman load up the children, Titus turned back to the trader. "You know where you are?"

His face was a gray mask of fear. "You can't do this—w-we did no harm to your daughter!"

"That's the only reason I left any of you alive, only reason I'm givin' you this chance to warn them others," he said flat and hard. "Now, do you want to know where you are?"

"*Oui*—yes."

He bent before the Frenchman's boot toes and pulled his skinning knife from its scabbard, using it to scratch out a crude map on the damp, flaky ground. "You foller our tracks back, you should make it fine in a week or so."

"A w-week? Seven days?"

" 'Pends how fast you walk in them boots o' your'n. But you best watch your step when you get to them foothills off yonder where we was hit by the storm. Likely to be a mite confusing for you—all them tracks goin' round and round the way we did till we finally found a place to make camp out of the storm. That's when you best use your savvy and figger out the right direction."

Bordeau was near to crying. "I can't do this! I never was for the wilderness."

Bass stood and stared a moment at the man. "The company brung you out to this country and they didn't teach you nothin' of how to last out here?"

Wagging his head, Bordeau started to reach out to touch Bass, imploring— but Titus took a step back and wiggled the skinning knife between them. "See this knife? It's the one I used to cut your friend."

"Gaston?"

"That's his name? Gaston. I'll remember it," Scratch vowed. "I figger he'll remember me too." Wiping the dirt and mud from the tip of the blade across his greasy legging, Titus said, "Should've cut his throat an' scalped him. Them other two grabbed my Magpie, just the same. But I wanted to get my girl and boy away from the sight of your kind quick as I could, Bordeau. 'Sides, what's Gaston's scalp to me anyways? I'd only spit on it afore I throwed it down at your feet."

"Don't leave me out here without a horse! I beg of you, *monsieur!*"

"Just stay on the high ground and you'll keep your boots purty dry." Scratch passed off the man's plea and took a step backward. He glanced up at the sky quickly. "Got a half dozen hours of daylight, so you can cover ground if you get after it."

Bordeau's face slowly changed from a look of fear to one of undisguised contempt. "From this day—your life is not worth the poor beaver pelt now, *monsieur*. There are plenty men to look for you too. I make sure they look for you."

"Only way you do that is keep yourself alive, Bordeau." He turned away to take up the reins of his horse. "None of your kind ever belonged out here . . . but I'll bet one day your kind will run all over this country, stinkin' it up—"

"The company will not forget this murder!"

"Your company be damned!" Titus snapped as he stuffed his muddy moccasin in the cottonwood stirrup and raised himself into the saddle.

Shaking his muddy fist at the old trapper, Bordeau shrieked, "You do not do this to the American Fur Company!"

Pulling his horse around, Titus took a moment to watch Shad start away with the others as Flea herded their pack animals at the rear of the march.

"Your company put its murderin' hands around the beaver trade—choking the breath an' blood out of my way of life, makes me wanna put my hands around your throat an' choke it outta you."

Bordeau laid a hand at his throat. "You nevair get away with what you do to me!"

Suddenly Bass kicked his horse in its ribs, galloping back across those few yards toward the trader. Bordeau shrank backward, putting both arms up and crossing them over his face protectively. Wrenching back on the reins, Scratch stopped just a yard short of the Frenchman. He leaned over in the saddle, looming over Bordeau.

"Maybe your kind has gone and kill't most ever'thing I hold dear, you parley-voo windbag," he growled as he straightened in the saddle once more and nudged his horse around in a half circle. "But I'll be damned if I let your kind kill me!"

Scratch didn't rein up and look back at Bordeau until he had reached the top of a low rise. The trader was still standing there, unmoved, as if he intended to watch the old mountain man ride away until he finally disappeared from sight. But the moment Bordeau saw the horseman stop and turn around, he scooted into the sage and crouched as if he could actually hide himself among that skimpy brush.

"I hope that scared fool won't come follering us," Titus sighed. "Maybeso he does, he'll find out soon enough there's no way he's gonna keep up on foot—not him wearin' them fancy St. Louie boots of his."

The sun was out for three more days before the next soaking storm forced them to huddle out of the wind in the lee of a ridge for a night and all of the following day. When it was plain that the sun would be rising into a cloudless sky the next morning, Bass and Shadrach got everyone up early and had Magpie cook them all a big breakfast while Waits and Shell Woman tore down the lodge and packed the travois. When he was given the word, Flea tugged on the lead rope tied around the neck of the friendly lead mare and started their extra horses toward the next wide gap, plodding ever westward.

"That the Winds?" Sweete asked late that afternoon, pointing at the jagged line of white-capped purple lying low along the horizon far to the northnorthwest of them.

"Southern Pass be a long, long ride from here, that's for sure," Scratch said. Then he asked, "How long it been since you was up there in that country?"

"Back when ronnyvooz died," Shad admitted. "How many winters is that?"

"I cipher it's goin' on seven, Shadrach."

Sweete chuckled, "So I can figger you know the way you're leadin' us west?"

"I only tromped over parts of this," he confessed. "See'd other parts of it from on high."

It was long before Sweete asked, "Maybe we should've took the old trail by the Platte to the Sweetwater, across the pass and down to the Sandy."

"Helluva long ways to get to Black's Fork. I'll lay we'll be at Bridger's back door afore Bordeau ever walks back into Fort William."

The grin disappeared from the tall man's face. "You know you cain't ever show your face on that side of the mountains again, Scratch."

Bass pursed his lips thoughtfully for a moment, then said, "I can't think of anything ever gonna pull me back to that side of the mountains anyway, Shadrach."

"I'll go back, eventual'," Sweete admitted.

"You will?"

"The woman—she's got family," Shad explained. "That means them young'uns got family down on the plains."

"But that's south of Fort William," Titus assured him. "You won't have to go nowhere near that post when you take Shell Woman back to see her kin down toward Bents' big lodge on the Arkansas."

Wagging his head slightly, Sweete said, "There I was—happy as a sow bug under a buffler chip, living the life of a Cheyenne warrior . . . and you have to come along an' pull me away for a long ride right into a mess o' trouble."

With a snort, Bass said, "Man like you only gonna waste away in the life of a Cheyenne warrior, Shadrach! Slowly go crazy bein' a layabout with nothin' to do an' nowhere to go."

"I go huntin'," Shad argued, bristling. "And I been on a few raids for Ute horses."

"You got lazy an' soft, way you been livin' the last few years, child."

They burst out laughing together, loud enough it made both women turn and gaze back at them a moment before the wives looked at one another in that way women do when men act in some new and bewildering way.

"Man needs to get out, breathe the air," Titus explained. "See some new country, a far land, just like the ol' days, Shadrach."

Sweete drew in a long, deep breath of the chill air as some sage grouse whirred away from their path. "How—how long you figger can a man hold on to the old days, Scratch?"

He thought for but a moment, then reflected, "Just as long as that man dares to hold on, my friend. Long as he dares to hold on."

SEVEN

A long and muddy spring greened the prairie, short and hardy shoots up-lifting beneath the aching blue of a sky that went on and on across those days while their tiny group plodded west through the stark and barren Red Desert so briefly aflower with a palette of heady color. The water in the streams and creeklets was poor for many days, laced with bitter salts, forcing them to search out hidden, bubbling springs or even fields of boulders where rain might be trapped in tiny pools. Most mornings the women found a thin crust of ice coating what water they had managed to collect in their brass kettles—the only sign they had begun their climb over the Continental Divide in crossing this austere and desolate stretch of country.

Eventually they reached the banks of the fabled Green River, lying by for two days while the horses ate their fill of the new short-grass and everyone soaked in those cold, legendary waters. After crossing the river, they struck west-northwest, following Black's Fork as it meandered through a country of red and yellow bluffs, and spent the next night where Ham's Fork poured in, camping in that verdant V of meadow formed by those two tributaries of the Green, here where the free men and fur brigades had gathered to celebrate the height of summer, eighteen and thirty-four.

While supper bubbled in the kettles that twilight at the fire, Titus called his long-legged daughter to come sit upon his knee.

"I grow so tall now, Popo," she protested in English, standing before him. "Magpie not fit so good now."

"You'll always fit on your father's knee," he scolded as he patted his thigh again. "Come sit, girl."

Waits-by-the-Water got to her feet at the far side of the fire, shifted her new shawl about her shoulders, and said, "Sit, because your father wants to tell you a story."

"I listen too?" Flea asked, scratching Digger's head. The dog had his muzzle laid on the boy's leg.

He nodded at the youngster. "I think it's good you listen to my story about Magpie."

She leaned back a little against her father's arm so she could gaze at her father's wrinkled face. "A story about me?"

"Yes, daughter. You got your name right here at this place."

Quickly peering down at the ground Magpie asked, "This spot?"

"Yonder, just across the river," he explained and pointed. "Your mother and me, we were camped on upstream some. This here is named Black's Fork."

"Color of war, Popo?" Flea inquired.

"Black is the color of war—but I figger it was given a man's name, son. Not for war."

As Ghost followed her, Waits stepped around the edge of the fire pit, one hand on a hip and the other clutching a brass ladle. "This place, long ago, your father promise he teach you and me speak his white man talk, teach us together."

For a moment, Titus gazed up at Shadrach, who stood nearby. "Near as I recollect, ronnyvoo of thirty-four was the last doin's where I got likkered on John Barleycorn something bad. Paid heavy for it too. But it were a time I drunk my fill with a old friend I wasn't ever to see again."

"He a free man, or skin trapper like me?" Sweete asked.

"Neither. English. Jarrell Thornbrugh—a real John Bull of a Englisher."

"Hudson's Bay man?"

"By damn if he wasn't," Titus replied, growing wistful. "Last time I laid eyes on him was right here in this valley. That's back to a time when them Britishers was dispatchin' a small brigade out to our ronnyvoo, for to keep a eye on us Americans. But, I never see'd Jarrell after thirty-four."

Flea asked, "He not come back? Not to mountains?"

His eyes landed on his son sitting nearby. "No. Jarrell died two years arter I last saw him. Others said he was took by some croup-sick or the ague. That's a wet and muggy country out there. I went, once. Long ago it was. This air, dry the way it is, keeps a man safe from the ague." He lowered his eyes and wagged his head. "Jarrell was a better man than to die in bed. Such is for cowards and sick ol' men—to die in bed. A good man like him, a brave warrior never lives forever. Only the rocks and sky live long, children. Only the rocks and sky."

"Tell story of Magpie's name," Flea asked as he sashayed up beside his father's vacant knee and plopped on the ground at Bass's feet.

"Well, now—that's where I was headin' in the first place." Scratch cleared his throat, remembering a precious and bygone heartbeat of time. "That summer night it seemed like the whole of the world held its breath, just for my baby girl."

He went on to tell Magpie how it was that ever since they had arrived at that long-ago rendezvous of the white traders and fur trappers, the infant had taken to chattering more with every day—a happy, cheerful babble. "And for your mother, it was not an easy day to wait."

"Wait?" Magpie asked.

"To learn your name." he answered, winking at his wife. "She's never been a patient sort, young'uns."

"I was patient to wait for you," she protested from across the fire.

"Damn glad you did." Then he looked back into his daughter's eyes, close as they were to his, and magnetically intent upon his every word now. "I sat by a fire, just like this'un, Magpie. Had you on my lap, just like I got you sitting right now. With the Apsaluuke, you know that menfolk are to name their young'uns, right?"

She nodded eagerly. "A name is a special gift, yes."

"Your mother'd been after me for some time to give our first child a name."

Magpie nodded. "Long time ago I was born in Mateo's lodge in Ta-house."

"So that evening I tol't your mother you'd allays had a name."

"Magpie was always mine?"

"Only took me a while to figure it out, daughter," he admitted with a shrug. "The Creator—the Grandfather Above your mother's people call First Maker—He was waiting for us to find out what name He'd already give you."

Confusion crossed her face. "So my Popo did not name me?"

"I s'pose I did, but I had some help from First Maker too, because I got it wrong three times."

"Three names you tried to give her?" Flea inquired as Shell Woman handed her young son to an enthralled Shadrach, who sat spellbound, listening to the story with the youngster.

"First I thought your name was Little Red Calf," Titus explained. "You was just like a li'l buffler calf when they're first born—all red and wrinkled up. But, wasn't long an' you changed—wasn't red no more. So my mind come up with Spring Calf Woman, since you was born in the spring."

Magpie's eyes squinted up a bit. "But in the spring, calves turn yellow."

"That's right—because your hair ain't rightly black like your mother's."

She lifted a handful of her own to inspect it.

"I have a sister got yellow hair," Titus continued. "Yellow as the bright sun. One of my brothers too. You won't never have yellow hair like them, but I did once't—an' I give you a little of that color afore you was born."

"But Magpie never had no yellow hair," Shad pressed, "so, what'd you name her for a third go at it?"

"Cricket," he said in English. "For all them happy sounds she made as a baby . . . but by the time we got here to ronnyvoo, I had me a strong feeling that wasn't the name either. I was starting to get worrisome: three tries an' I'd got it wrong all those times."

"Then Grandfather Above told you?" Magpie said, tugging gently on the front of his faded calico shirt.

"Said to name you Magpie. 'Cause you loved to talk, even before we could understand your talk. 'Nother thing He tol't me was your mother could smoke with me that night we called you Magpie for the first time."

"Women never smoke," Flea argued, his young face gray with seriousness.

"Your mother belonged to our lodge, son. I am leader of that lodge—the coyote band. I told her she could smoke to pray for our first young'un."

"You smoke and pray for me too?" the boy asked, turning to his mother.

"We have done the same for you and Jackrabbit," she answered in Crow. "Go get your little brother before he gets too close to the riverbank."

Scrambling up as he grumbled in complaint, Flea took after the fleet-footed Jackrabbit. That's when Scratch took an opportunity to whisper to his daughter.

"You wanted to smoke my pipe the night we named you."

She grinned at that. "So you let me smoke soon, like my mother?"

"No," he shook his head. "Not for women like it is for men. That smoke your mother had for each of her young'uns was real holy."

"I do not know this word, *holy*."

In Crow Bass explained, "Do you understand *sacred*?"

"Yes, now I see the meaning."

"You was all arms and legs that night, wriggling and squealing, when we took off all your clothes—so you was naked as the day you was born. Then I held you up to the sky, so First Maker could get Him a real good look at the beautiful creature He'd made through your mother an' me."

"Will this be my name for all time?"

He hugged her a little more tightly. "Your mother an' me have you with us for only a short time. One day, you'll belong to another—"

"But I don't wanna leave you!" she sobbed in Crow against his chest.

Rubbing the first spill of tears from a cheek, Scratch said, "One day soon you will be ready to leave us, and go with a man. The two of you gonna make a family of your own. You won't be with our family no more."

"No, Popo! I don't want to leave!"

"Daughter," he said, his throat clogged with emotion, "it is the way of the Creator. You're with us for just a short while, riding the trails we take. Then comes a season an' you'll go off on your own trail. A time when we both will cry for you're leavin'."

"I don't want that for a long, long time," the girl sobbed, pressing her face into the hollow of his neck.

"An' one day, a long, long time from now—the First Maker will call you back to be with Him again, Magpie. He'll lift your spirit back up there with all the rest of them stars so you can be with Him again—just like you was afore you come to live with us for a little while."

As Magpie turned her damp face upward to look at the sky, Titus glanced at his wife, finding her smiling at him, just as she had that night thirteen summers before, her cheeks glistening with moisture that spilled from her radiant black-cherry eyes. Just the way she had cried when they had given their daughter her name here beneath these same stars, beside these same waters. He was reminded how much had happened to him, happened to them all, in those intervening seasons. Then he was struck with how this place had remained unchanged—these bluffs and the rising half-moon, the rocks and the water. It all was timeless, perhaps infinite, while he himself was a mere mortal who came, and lived, then passed on in the mere blink of an eye compared to the everlasting earth and sky.

"Magpie." The girl whispered her own name, gazing again at her father's teary eyes.

He turned to his daughter, seeing how Magpie's cheeks were completely streaked with rivulets of tears, her eyes pooling like her mother's. "Yes, Magpie," he repeated. "The li'l talking one who came to stay with her mother an' me for a while."

She flung her arms tightly around his neck and whispered in his ear, "I will stay with you and Mother forever."

Titus felt his own eyes filling to overflowing as his tears began to spill atop his daughter's head. "Yes, you will stay in our hearts for all time, Magpie. Forever, and for all time."

The sun was nearing midsky two days later when Bass was surprised to spot a small log hut topped with a sod-and-timber roof. A thin spiral of smoke whispered from the top of a crude rock chimney. At the opposite corner of the cabin stood a small corral constructed of lodgepole pine.

He whistled up the dogs. Both Digger and Ghost came bounding up. He gave them a quick signal with his hand and they immediately heeled on his horse, tongues lolling, tails wagging . . . waiting.

Whoever it was raised this cabin, he thought as he emerged from the cottonwood, they had invested a lot of time and sweat to drag lodgepole all the way here from the Wind Rivers.

"Halloo, the house!" he sang.

A shadowy figure moved across the open doorway, just touched by the edge of sunlight. At the same moment a brown-skinned face appeared very briefly at the lone, tiny window, open and without benefit of glass. Poor doin's, Titus ruminated.

"Titus? Titus Bass?" a voice cried out in English as the horseman warily approached. "Is that your ol' gray head I'm seein' after all these years?"

Scratch reined up, curious as to who might possibly know him here in the middle of the overland trail. From the appearance of the hut and that tiny corral penning up but three bone-rack horses, this damn well couldn't be Bridger's post. This was no more than a poor man's shanty.

He squinted into the darkened doorway. "That's me, Titus Bass," he responded, leaning over his big pommel the size of a Mexican orange. "Say, friend, step on out here where I can see you too."

The figure took but a moment to prop his rifle inside the doorway before he ventured two steps into the spring light, shading his eyes as he gazed up at Bass, when he suddenly caught sight of the others some sixty yards back.

"Uncle Jack? That really you, coon?"

Jack Robinson* tore his eyes off the others and held his hand up to the horseman. "Damn, Titus Bass. I ain't see'd you since afore beaver went belly-up!" He gazed a moment at their joined hands. "It really you—not no ghost of your own self?"

Releasing his hand from the younger man's grip, Bass slipped to the ground. "Flesh an' blood, Uncle Jack. Damn, but I could say the same for you. Thort you'd gone belly-up yourself, or run off to Oregon country."

The skinny Robinson shook his head, the loose wattles of his fleshy neck shaking like a turkey gobbler's. "Here's as pretty a piece of country as I'd ever wanna lay tracks in, Titus Bass. Think I'll for sure stay in these parts till it's time for my bones to lay in the wind."

Scratch waved the others on. "I see'd a brown face in the window there. You got yourself a woman for company?"

Robinson glanced at the hut, putting his fingers between his teeth, and whistled. "My second. This'un's a Snake. One of Washakie's nieces. A real black-skinned bitch, but she's got her a good heart. Warm place to keep my pecker in the winter too."

"Can't beat a robe-warmer in this high country," Titus agreed.

Shading his face again, Robinson squinted at the pair of bounding dogs, then peered at those oncoming riders. "Looks like you got you a new squaw, Titus Bass."

"Naw, that's Shad Sweete's woman. Cheyenne, she be, from down near Bents' big lodge on the Arkansas."

"Sweete's his name?"

Titus nodded as the others got closer and started halting to dismount while Flea circled up their extra horses.

Robinson took a step closer to Bass. "That'un serve with Bridger any?"

"Him an' Gabe was real tight of a time," Bass explained as he led his horse over to the corral and tied off the reins to the top rail. "How far's Bridger's post from you?"

---

* John Robertson was better known throughout the fur trade period and beyond as "Uncle Jack" Robinson.

Uncle Jack pointed off to the southwest. "Should be there afore supper." He watched Sweete start toward them. "I was the nigger told Bridger he ought'n build his post here on the Black's Fork." He turned to face Shadrach, announcing, "C'mon over. Any friend of Bridger's is a friend o' mine."

"When you come to the mountains, Uncle Jack?" Sweete asked after they shook hands.

"Thirty-one. Rode west with Fitzpatrick. Mizzable trip: Jed Smith was kill't by Comanches on the Cimarron water scrape. After we took on supplies in Taos from Davey Jackson, I stayed on with Fitz and we come north. Next summer when we fought the Blackfoot in Pierre's Hole, I was wounded."

Titus asked, "Ronnyvoo of thirty-two?"

"Weren't nothing bad, really," Robinson explained. "I was off my feed for the fall hunt, but stayed on my feet through till winter." He turned and whistled again. "Madame Jack! Godblessit—get out here, now!"

He turned back to the two trappers and shrugged, saying, "She's a bit shy when there's other wimmens about. Just menfolk show up, why—she's there, lickety on the spot. But when squaws come about, she's a shy one."

From the doorway emerged a stocky woman with an amiable face, carrying a large gourd trussed up in a leather cradle complete with a wooden handle. From the fingers of her other hand were suspended four tin cups, two of which she passed out to the trappers, then poured each of them a splash of cool water from the gourd.

"You mind we noon with you, rest the horses?" Titus inquired.

Robinson smiled warmly. "I'd like that, like that a lot, boys. Gimme a chance to talk to new ears. Haven't yet had much travel on the road this year."

"Road?" Sweete echoed.

"Oregon Road," Robinson declared to the tall man. "Wasn't you coming over the Southern Pass from the east?"

"No, we come south, through that Red Desert country," Scratch explained. "That what they call that way over the pass now? The Oregon Road?"

"Ever since last summer," Robinson said. "Some say it's the Emigrant Road, for it's carried a few on to California."

"Some claim American soldiers took Californy. But I'll wager it's Mexican country, still," Bass said as he handed his cup to Waits-by-the-Water.

"Most of 'em we see'd come through last year are makin' for Oregon," Jack went on. "I managed to trade off some good stock for what animals they wored out getting this far west."

Quickly glancing about, Scratch said, "Not them skinny horses. What good stock you got, Uncle Jack?"

"Have 'em grazing over yonder, a mile or more, on some good grass aways up the Black's—trail you'll foller to get to Bridger's big post."

Sweete asked, "Injuns don't raid?"

"Hell," Jack snorted, "this here's Snake country. They take good care of us fellers. Both Gabe and me got hitched into the tribe, you see. Utes don't dare come north, and them Bannocks is afraid to make Washakie angry. Naw, we don't worry none 'bout Injuns runnin' off our stock. Maybeso you fellers ought'n think 'bout settlin' down on Black's Fork like me an' Gabe done."

"Just gonna visit for a spell is all," Sweete answered for them both. "My woman's country is back on the other side of the mountains."

"An' my family's home is in Crow country," Bass stated. "We only come to visit Gabe. Thankee for the offer but it ain't likely we'll be putting down no roots."

"Not in no country where there's settlers passing through on their way to Oregon country," Shad said as he took a cup of water to his young son.

Robinson explained, "Man does what he can, now that there ain't no furs the traders want—'ceptin' buffler hides."

"Much as I can," Titus offered, "I'll stay off this here road you said them corncrackers and sodbusters ride west."

"Same road Billy Sublette, Pilcher, an' Drips come west to ronnyvoo with their goods," Robinson explained after he shuffled his wife back into the hut to fetch some dried meat to offer their midday guests.

"That means these overlanders using the same trail?" Scratch inquired.

Robinson nodded. "From Fort Bridger, they'll break north to Fort Hall."

"An' where they go from Hallee?" Titus asked.

"Striking out through that Snake country."

Wagging his head, Sweete said, "That's 'bout the roughest piece of ground I ever put a horse through."

Scratch turned to Shad and asked, "You been west of Hallee?"

"More'n once. Was a time the booshways didn't want the English to have that country all to their own."

"Can't be fit for wagons," Scratch grumbled.

"Ain't," Robinson agreed. "Some'll try to get their wagons on from Fort Hall, take 'em clear to the Willamette. Other'ns gonna sell off their wagons to them English at Fort Hall—trade for mules and horses to get 'em on to the Columbia."

"Bet you ain't ever floated down that Columbia River, Shadrach!" Bass needled his tall friend.

"I s'pose you're claimin' you did?"

"How the hell other way a man gonna get to meet Doctor John at Fort Vancouver?" Titus sneered. "An' I sure as the devil didn't float around the horn in no sea ship to get there neither!"

"I forgot—you told me 'bout that trip," Sweete admitted.

In a quieter voice, Titus confided, "That float o' mine down the Columbia with Jarrell Thornbrugh was fearsome enough to make my ass stay puckered for a month of Sundays!"*

---

* *Borderlords*

Soon enough there was dried meat for them all to chew on while the horses cropped at the new grass growing taller and thicker in the meadows surrounding Robinson's poor hut.

"I enjoyed myself, Uncle Jack," Titus declared later, as he had stood and held his hand out to their host. "I truly did."

"You come on back an' visit any time. Both of you."

"We'll be close," Shad advised. "A fella can ride over for a visit 'most any time."

Robinson and Madame Jack, his Shoshone wife, stood outside their hut, arm in arm as they waved the others on their way.

The sun was warm on his face and the back of his hands as he gave his last salute and plodded on up Black's Fork. A spring breeze rustled through the sage, stirring a strong scent of turpentine through the air, just before a couple of dozen sage grouse whirred away from the path of their horses, the birds chucking as they settled back to earth and sorted themselves out again for their timeless dance on this patch of mating ground. It was a good day, here in a country where no emigrants plowed fields, no Frenchmen stole plews or a man's daughter, no Indians came to trouble a man and his hard-won peace. Maybe Bridger and Robinson did have things figured right . . . at least for themselves. Trouble was, Titus doubted he could stay planted in one spot for long enough to raise up log walls or sink down some roots. Yet walls and roots were what it took for a man to survive in this part of the world rapidly changing around him.

For men like him and Shad, they had to keep on searching out that shrinking corner of the world where it wouldn't matter if they refused to build walls and overlay them with roofs, refused to plant crops or tend a store. And if he was lucky, Scratch brooded, that shrinking sliver of the old life and the old world would last just long enough till Titus Bass could no longer load his gun, mount his horse, and ride away from what was closing in around him. Maybeso what he had come to call his used-to-be country would last long enough to see a used-to-be man clear through till the end of his days.

"See that smoke yonder?" Titus asked his son as the two of them reined up with Shad Sweete at the breast of a low ridge.

"Top of the trees?"

"Yep. What smoke you make it out to be?"

The youngster was thoughtful a moment. "Not grass, Popo. Fire smoke."

"Right again, boy. Bet we'll spot horses, maybe some lodges by the time we cover 'nother hour or so."

"How long you figger it from here?" Shad squinted into the late spring sunlight.

"I callate we'll be drinking from Bridger's jug afore the sun goes down."

From the mouth of Ham's Fork a day ago they had followed Black's Fork as it looped around and made for the southwest. Now they had entered a broad valley where this tributary of the Green River was splintered into numerous small creeks with springtime's mountain runoff, all of which relentlessly cut itself through the fertile, verdant meadows to form a series of narrow islands carpeted with tall grass. Tall, old cottonwoods stood stately on the banks of every rivulet, heads and shoulders above younger saplings. Willow, alder, and prairie ash cloaked the streams.

"Gabe picked him a sure 'nough good spot," Sweete marveled as they continued toward the smoke. "How you figger the winters in this country?"

"You forgot, Shadrach?" Titus snorted. "The whole blamed valley of the Green damned well gotta be about the coldest place in the mountains. Chills my bones just thinking 'bout it."

"Then why'd Gabe an' Vaskiss raise their post here?"

With a shrug, Scratch turned in the saddle and pointed to the northeast. "The Southern Pass—it's off that way, back to Fort John and the road from the settlements. An' Fort Hall, it's off yonder in that direction."

Sweete asked impatiently, "Which means?"

"Which means Bridger's post is right on this here road what takes folks on to Oregon."

"Lookit all the grass there is for stock, right close," Sweete added.

"Allays good to have plenty of grass—you never know who's gonna be droppin' in to pay their respects," Titus said with a grin and a wink. "Lookee there through the trees."

"More smoke. You figger that for Gabe's post?"

Bass nodded. "Hell if it don't look like peeled timbers to me!"

Quickly turning in their saddles, both men tore their hats from their heads and signaled back to their wives. Then Scratch said to Flea, "We set off an' your horses get to running, just let 'em go an' stay with them. Only thing to watch for: Don't let 'em find no prairie-dog town, or stumble getting down to a crik bottom, son."

The boy's face flushed with excitement. "Flea go with you?"

He considered it a brief moment, then grinned hugely. "Sure as shootin' you can come along, boy! Stay hard on my tail an' you'll see how free men like Shad an' your pa rode into ronnyvoo long summers ago—once upon a glory time! Whoooo-eee!"

Both Sweete and Flea were caught unawares with the sudden explosiveness of the old man's untamed yelp and his burst into motion. But those two rangy dogs were ready. In an instant they were lunging along beside the old trapper's horse. No more than a heartbeat behind him came his son and an old friend, hammering heels into their horses, a long and shrill cry freeing itself from their throats as they followed Titus through the last fringe of cottonwoods, clattered across another narrow rivulet of Black's Fork, then exploded up the last low riverbank that swept them in a gentle arc toward that corner of the stockade they could spy through the last intervening stand of trees.

Suddenly in full view were a half dozen small herds of horses, and even a few horned cattle too.

Damn! Titus hadn't seen beeves since trader Sublette brought a milk cow to ronnyvoo long summers gone now.

And far beyond the timbered walls stood more than thirty buffalo-hide lodges, where brown-skinned women worked over outdoor fires and naked children chased one another in their games. Bridger had him an outright settlement of his own!

In moments it became clear there were actually two stockades, one a bit larger than the other, but sharing a length of one timbered wall in common. The gates of both were visible to the riders as they came tearing in from the north, finally slowing their heaving horses to a lope on that broad flat . . . when a lone figure stepped into sight from one of the open gates, the lowering sun at his back. He tore the flat-brimmed, low-crowned hat from his head and O'ed up his mouth for a greeting.

"What's your lather for, boys? Can't be no redskins lickin' it after you—"

The instant his voice melted away in midsentence, the man slowly lowered his hat to his side and began to wag his head, a huge smile growing on his face. "As I live an' breathe . . . if'n you ain't a pair for these sore eyes!"

"Gabe!" Shad shrieked as he bounded off his horse and hit the ground at a trot to seize the shorter man in his big arms while Ghost and Digger bounded around the two like pups.

"Lordy!" Bridger gasped after several moments. "C-come peel this here b'ar off me, Scratch!"

Reluctantly Shad released the trader and lowered Bridger to the ground once more as Titus legged out of his saddle and strode over to the pair.

"Just look at you!" Bridger exclaimed to Sweete. Then he turned to Bass to ask, "He's growed some since I last saw him. Don'cha think he's growed some?"

"I'll allow I was still a pup when we first throwed in with the general,* Gabe," Sweete said as he threw an arm back over Bridger's shoulder, "but I ain't growed outta a pair o' mokersons in many a winter!"

When Bridger stepped toward him with his arms opened, Bass gave the trader a fond embrace. "Damn, but it shines to see you, Gabe!"

"How come you never rode down from Crow country to see me afore now?"

"Ain't been anywhere close to the Green in more summers than I care to count," Scratch explained. "Last time it was . . . I think I rode through here with Ol' Solitaire on our way south."

"South? Makin' to Robidoux's post?"

---

* General William H. Ashley, founder of the rendezvous system, wherein every summer a trader brought his trade goods out from St. Louis to a predetermined spot of "rendezvous" in the central Rocky Mountains, taking in the mountain man's beaver pelts in trade for powder and lead, blankets and beads, coffee and whiskey too.

"Gone farther, we did—all the way to Californy for some Mexican horses."

Bridger snorted, slapped his knee with his hat before he repositioned it on his head. "Was you in that bunch that throwed Peg-Leg out in the desert?"*

"Yep. I figger Solitaire gave him better'n a oily-tongued backstabber deserved," Scratch replied. "You ever hear what ever come of him?"

"Last I heard tell, he's still raising hell and putting a chunk under it too!" Bridger declared. "Someone said he aims to make California his own. From what folks has told me recent, American soldiers gone down an' took Santa Fe from the Mexicans afore they marched out to do the same in California. So, Peg-Leg figgers to make something outta himself out there."

"Just the place for his kind, out there," Bass grumbled sourly. "Keep Peg-Leg busy so's he won't come back to these here mountains to make trouble for the rest of us."

Bridger wheeled on Sweete. "How long you coons fixin' to stay?"

Shad looked at Titus with a shrug. "We ain't never thought 'bout it."

But Bass scratched at his chin reflectively and said, "Lemme see now. Ain't long afore it turns summer, when plews ain't worth the sweat off your ass. An' since there ain't gonna be no ronnyvoo to ride off to this year, so . . . I figger next best place for the season is Bridger's post."

"You mean that?" the trader asked. "The two of you stay through the summer?"

"Don't see a reason why we can't—do you, Shadrach?"

Sweete threw a big arm over Bridger's shoulder. "We're movin' in, Gabe!"

For a moment there, the trader's tongue was tied, until he blinked his eyes and finally confessed, "Gotta tell you both, that's some good news to this here child. Past winter was hard on me. I l-lost my Cora."

Bass took a step forward and laid his hand on Jim's shoulder. "Your wife?"

"She died givin' birth to our li'l Josephine last autumn," he explained. "Josie's our third."

"That mean you're raising all three of 'em by yourself?" Sweete asked with concern.

"Sometime back I sent Mary Ann off to Doc Whitman's mission up in Cayuse country!" Bridger declared proudly. "She's goin' to school with Joe Meek's girl. But my boy, Felix, he's been here with me, an' the baby too. So it'll be some punkins to have your women around to help out. Lately I've found there's a lot a man ain't really the best at."

Smiling with admiration for his old friend, Titus said, "I know a couple o' gals gonna be real happy to get their hands on that baby girl of yours, Gabe!"

Bridger looped an arm around both of them as his attention was held by the young boy leading his horse toward them. "Times'll shine, boys. Days gonna

---

* *Death Rattle*

get real busy, here on out. I can use a hand from you both when them emigrants show their faces on the horizon."

"Man just as soon stay busy as loaf in the shade, Jim," Titus said.

"Every train bound for Oregon gonna come by here," Bridger explained. "They'll need fixin's, trade off horses or a team of mules, maybeso dicker off some of their oxen too afore they push on for Hallee up on the Snake. Likely, most'll need some repair work on their wagons—"

"Blacksmithin'?" Titus asked, the first twinge of excitement squirting through him.

"Yepper. Size down tires with this dry air out here, repair yokes and tongues and even boxes too," Jim said. "You know anythin' 'bout smithing, Titus Bass?"

"Hell, I worked Hysham Troost's forge in St. Louie for a number o' years afore I come west in twenty-five," he announced proudly.

Bridger blinked in disbelief. "Hysham Troost teached you smithing?"

Bass nodded.

"Glorreee! That's good enough for any man!" Bridger exclaimed. "You'll sure as hell do, Scratch! My forge needs fixin' up—some corncracker burnt half of it down late last summer afore we could put out the fire . . . but we'll work out some pay for what you do to help around here an' what business you scare up, both of you niggers."

Fumble-footed, Sweete asked, "What you figger I can do, Gabe?"

"No shortage of work to be done 'round here, Shadrach. But"—and he paused reflectively—"what I need most is someone smart to oversee my ferry on the Green."

"Your ferry?"

"You didn't see my ferry up there on the Green River when you come over the pass an' down the Sandy?"

"Nope. We rode south of there."

"Where from?"

"Bad doin's at Fort John on the Platte," Titus declared. "Them Frenchies tried to make off with my daughter."

"Shit," Bridger grumbled sympathetically. "They can all go to hell, them parley-voos! Glad I'm shet of American Fur and all o' Chouteau's Frenchies for good! So, tell me how you two come over from Fort John."

Titus scratched the back of his neck and said, "We come south of the Black Hills, where the weather'd blowed the land clear."

"You come through the Red Desert?"

"Yep," Shad said. "It was tough doin's, but we finally hit the headwaters of Bitter Creek, and follered it down to the Green. Come across the Seedskeedee near the mouth of Black's."

"I'll be gone to hell," Bridger exclaimed. "I ain't been through that country since back to Ashley's day—when we come north through that country to strike the Green. Damn, but I'll bet that way'd cut a passel o' few days off a trip between here an' the North Platte."

"Some of it's rough," Titus said, "but the winds keep the snow blowed out most of the time, I'd reckon."

"Who's this boy you got along?" Bridger asked as the lean, copper-skinned youngster came up to a stop near the three men, leading his horse by a single rein. "He yours, Shadrach?"

"Nawww, he's Scratch's boy."

Bass said, "Flea, shake hands with the man. He's a ol't friend of your pa's. A good, ol't friend."

"Flea is my name," the youngster said a bit nervously, holding out his hand to the trader.

"Jim Bridger is mine, Flea."

"Bri-ger," he repeated thoughtfully.

"Call me Jim," Gabe replied. "How old's the lad?"

"He'll be eleven come winter."

Jim turned back to the boy. "Didn't I see you wrangling them horses your pa brung in?"

Flea nodded without speaking a word.

"He's got some strong medicine, Gabe," Titus declared, bursting with pride. "The boy's damn good with the four-leggeds."

Bridger laid a hand on Flea's shoulder. "If your pa don't mind, I'm sure we can find some work for you to do around here this summer too."

"Wor-work?" and his big eyes flicked back and forth between his father and Bridger.

Titus chuckled. "I don't think he knows what that word means, Jim."

"I figger you for a lad who'd like to tend to our horses," Bridger explained. "Ride 'em, brush 'em, see to the mares when they drop their foals?"

Flea glanced quickly at his father, then nodded to the trader. "I try do good for you, Jim."

Squinting into the bright sunlight, Bridger gazed over his friends' shoulders and asked, "So any of them women and young'uns comin' our way really yours, Shad? Or they all belong to that ol' bull named Titus Bass?"

EIGHT

They came that summer of '47 . . . those dream-hungry emigrants sure as sun came. But the first of them to show up on Bridger's doorstep weren't bound for Oregon at all. They would claim to be the chosen lambs of God desperately in search of their Zion.

In those weeks that followed the arrival of his old friends, Jim Bridger kept Scratch and Shadrach busy with this and that around his post. Waits-by-the-Water and Shell Woman pitched in to help in a big way, what with Gabe's Flathead wife, Cora, having died in childbirth. Both women started right up with baby Josephine, and gave a mother's affection to six-year-old Felix too. Besides helping the trader get his store ready for the emigrant season, Magpie was right there on the heels of the two women, mostly helping out by watching over Shell Woman's little ones when she didn't have her hands in something with the women. But Flea—now he was given the most grown-up job of all.

Their second night at Fort Bridger, the three families sat around a cheery fire built in a pit outside the post buildings, dug near the center of the open compound where they had taken their supper of antelope, served with some Jerusalem artichokes and wild onions Flea and Magpie dug up along the river. As the stars popped into view, one by one, and the winter-cured cottonwood crackled at their feet, Bridger called young Flea over to stand at his knee.

"Your pa an' me, we been talking," Gabe began, then looked at the boy squarely. "You unnerstand my American talk, son?"

Flea nodded, his eyes flicking once to his father's face.

"When I asked your pa if'n you was ready to be give a young man's work, he said he figgered the only way to find out was to see if you was up to it."

Flea gulped. "What work?"

"You unnerstand that word, work?"

"He does now, Jim," Titus replied. "Maybeso he didn't a couple days back when we rolled in here. But I think my boy's got a quick mind about him an' he's caught on."

Shadrach agreed, "He dove in like a snapper, didn't he, Scratch?"

So Bass prodded, "G'won and tell him, Gabe."

Bridger trained his attention on the boy, raising a hand to place it on the lad's shoulder as everyone quieted in that circle. "One of the most important jobs I got at this here post is my horses. Man don't have no horse in this country, he's likely to die."

"But Tom Fitzpatrick got hisself put afoot—back to thirty-two! An' he wasn't rubbed out!" Sweete admonished.

Jim flicked him an evil look and said, "That's another story for another time, Shadrach. Now, Flea—if'n a man ain't got a strong horse under him, he's likely good as dead too. Good animals always been important to your mama's people, and to us white folks too."

Flea nodded, his dark eyes growing all the bigger now.

"You figger you're up to havin' me put my horses in your care?"

The boy's eyes narrowed, and his brow knitted.

"Flea," Titus said in Crow, "our friend asks you if you would do a man's work to look after all his horses at this fort."

Without saying a word, Flea turned slowly from looking at his father to staring incredulously at Jim Bridger. Then he spoke, "Flea? You want *me* see to your horses?"

"That's what I'm asking, son."

"Ever' morning you'll bring 'em out of the corral over yonder." Titus pointed at the stockaded corral attached to the fort walls, its size a bit smaller than the post compound. "Take 'em down to water, then lead 'em up to a pasture to graze for the day. You understand ever'thing I've said in American talk?"

The boy's head bobbed. "I understand."

"You want the work?"

Suddenly Flea's smile lit up as if there were a blaze of stars behind his face. "I work with the horses, yes!"

"What about me, Gabe?" Sweete asked. "You still need me work up on the Green at your ferry?"

"You was my segundo years ago, Shad—so I know I can count on you being at my back."

Sweete leaned forward, his powerful forearms planted on top of his knees. "Just tell me what you need me to do."

"Where we need to be for the next few weeks is up to that ferry on the

Green. Got to haul a load of goods there, take us a small pack string: new rope to run across the river, saws to cut timbers for the raft big enough to hold a good-sized wagon, nails an' such we might need to build a cabin for the fellas gonna run the ferry for me."

Leaning back slightly, his shoulders sagging with disappointment, Shad admitted, "I gotta tell you I don't know a damned thing 'bout building a cabin, Jim. Ain't never built a raft to float nothing anywhere near the size of a wagon, an' I wouldn't know the first thing 'bout stringing rope so it works a ferry."

"By the time you an' me get done up there together, you'll know," Bridger replied. "I figger I can leave you at the Green to run that ferry as my segundo. Way I see it, we got us till late June, early July afore the first of them emigrants gonna show their faces on this side of the Southern Pass."

Bass nodded, saying, "Three of us can make short work of that."

But the trader turned to Titus and said, "Me an' Shad, we'll get it done, just the two of us."

Now Scratch's shoulders sank with disappointment. "You don't figger me to go along, what'm I gonna do around here?"

With a snort, Bridger waved his arm in a wide arc at the stockade walls. "Hell, coon—you're gonna take care of Fort Bridger till I get back!"

"T-take care—"

"Watch over things: the stock mostly. But, your boy's gonna help you do that. 'Sides taking over looking after li'l Josie, your women gonna help out with all that's gotta get done in the store afore them emigrants show up ready to buy up ever'thing we got for sale, then be on their way to Oregon. But the biggest job you gotta see to is to rebuild my forge so you got a place to work."

"Rebuild your forge?"

Jim shrugged. "You're handy—I figger you can get yourself set up soon enough, and start hammering out some hardware on my forge I got out under that awning next to our quarters."

"I-I ain't worked a hammer an' anvil since . . . spring o' twenty-five, Jim!"

"Hell, it'll come back to you slick as shootin'. You was trained by Hysham Troost, so I know it'll come back quick. Need you to start cutting and shaving down wheel spokes too, with one of them drawknives. Them emigrants gonna need new spokes, and we ought'n have a few spare ox-yokes on hand too. I got one you can measure against. We'll need clasps an' hasps an' joint brackets too—I figger by the time they get here, them eastern sodbusters discovered how their wagons been shrinking up an' nothing's fitting right no more."

He took his eyes from Jim's face and stared at the fire, wagging his head slightly. "I s'pose it may be just like breathin', Gabe. Fire an' sweat, iron an' muscle." Then Titus turned to look at his wife, admitting, "I ain't got near the muscle I had when I worked for Troost, but—for you I'll give it ever'thing I got."

Bridger immediately leaned over and slapped Bass on the thigh. "Damme if we don't have us a plan!" He leaped to his feet, reaching down to grab both of young Felix's hands, sweeping his young son to his feet and spinning him away from the circle of folks at the fire, taking the boy round and round in a clumsy, flatfooted imitation of a genteel dance.

Scratch glanced over at Waits, finding her eyes wide and sparkly as she giggled, watching Bridger and his son. Leaping to his feet, Titus surprised his wife when he yanked her to her feet and dragged her a few feet from the fire to begin spinning her about in the same fashion: leaning on the left foot, then his right, as they spun on the balls of their feet, her leather dress billowing out and back, out and back, while the fringes on his leggings flew and flapped, slapping his legs and hers too as they weaved around one another and back, again and again. In a matter of heartbeats Shad had Shell Woman up and clomping around too, the small woman staring intently at the ground, ever mindful of where her husband's big feet were landing as the pair hobbled in an ungainly circle. Laughing with the joy that only children could ever know, Magpie pulled Flea away from the fire and the two of them started spinning at full speed, their hands clasped, arms fully outstretched, heads flung back as they roared in glee.

Then suddenly it seemed everyone started to tumble onto the spring-green grass at once, spilling and tripping over one another, adults laughing and shrieking like children themselves—so much they all had tears in their eyes as they gazed at one another's happy faces, sharing this one delicious moment of such exquisite, undiluted joy before the real work would begin on the morrow.

With the arrival of both those self-anointed sojourners fleeing the States in search of their Promised Land, and with the appearance of a train of dewy-eyed dreamers come forth from their eastern woodlands—none of these laughing, carefree people sprawled on the grass of Fort Bridger had any way of knowing this would be a summer that was to change all of their lives . . . forever.

Bridger was back at the fort as promised, less than a month after he and Sweete had plodded off to the northeast with their pack train of supplies for the Green River. They hadn't been there a day before three old faces from the beaver days chanced by. Jim hired them on the spot to work for Shadrach at the ferry.

"Leastwise, they got him four walls an' a roof over his head," Jim explained. "Shad claimed it was for the first time in years. It'll keep the rain off ever' afternoon, an' the hot sun too."

"Summer's comin'," Bass agreed. "The heat be here soon."

"An' so will those emigrants, with their oxes and mules, every critter's tongue hanging out as they roll up to Fort Bridger, Rocky Mountain territory!"

"Hell if that don't have a good ring to it, Gabe!" Titus cheered. "Lookit all around you—this here's all your'n. I s'pose it's like them parley-voos over there at Fort John lay claim to ever'thing they put their eyes to. This side of the mountains is yours."

"Maybeso it is after all, Scratch," Bridger mused. "Once the emigrants cross over the pass, I'm all there is atween that American Fur Company post on the North Platte an' the Hudson's Bay post on the Snake."

"That's a helluva stretch of country, Gabe."

"That means we're in the right place to give them emigrants what they need as they go on their merry way to that Oregon country."

Titus grew thoughtful. "H-how you figger Joe an' Doc are doin' out there?"

"Meek and Newell? In all these years since that last ronnyvoo when they pointed their noses for Oregon, I only see'd Joe back one time, when he come to fetch up my Mary Ann, take her back to Whitman's school."

"They made farms outta that Willamette country, like they said they was?"

Bridger nodded. "Both of 'em likely young men, Titus. They didn't have near as many rings on 'em as you an' me. Young niggers like them can make a go of anything. There's nothing but time ahead for 'em. But—for fellers like us, most of our days are already on the back trail."

He nodded reluctantly but tried a valiant grin. "Man sure does do things a bit differently when most of his time is at his back. The choices he makes. What comes to be more important to him."

With a long sigh, Bridger said, "You done me real good here while I was away, Scratch."

"Didn't take longer'n a day afore the hammer felt good in my hand again."

Jim grinned, showing a lot of teeth. "So you like blacksmithing, do you?"

"Don't go getting the idee that I'm hiring out for no job at Bridger's fort!" he protested.

"It's a fine turn you done for us," Bridger said. "The young'uns an' me. I'll miss your woman's help, an' that boy of yours too, when you light out for Crow country."

For a moment, Bass toed his moccasin into the flaky ground near the corral gate where the two of them stood talking in the shade of the tall timbers. " 'Bout that, Gabe," he began. "Me an' the woman, we been talking while you was away to the ferry with Shad."

"You ain't thinking of taking off soon?" Bridger asked, then hurried right on. "Hell, I could've figgered that. I don't blame you none, Scratch: not wanting to be around when them emigrants come rolling through here with their wide-eyed young'uns screamin' and throwin' their Bibles at us an' their poke bonnets—"

"Thought we'd stay for 'while, Gabe." He interrupted Bridger just as the trader was getting to midstride.

"Maybeso till late summer. Till the last of them emigrants get on past here to Fort Hall. Me and the woman figger that'll still give us plenty of time to ride north to find a Crow village to put in a winter with."

"You'll stay? By jiggies, if that ain't the finest piece of news I've had in a long, long while!"

"I s'pose Shad an' his family gonna stay on till the end of the season too."

Bridger nodded. "Up at the ferry, he talked about laying through the winter here with us."

"Be good for all of you. Them young'uns of yours, they need women around," Bass admitted. "Hell, that Felix can make hisself understood to the gals, no matter he don't speak no Crow or Cheyenne!"

"Wimmens is just that way!" Bridger enthused, then held out his hand. "Thankee, Scratch. This summer's bound to be a season we look back on for many a year to come."

They shook as Titus asked, "What else you see needs doin' around here now afore them corncrackers show up on Jim Bridger's doorstep?"

"Why—I was gonna push on over Southern Pass to Fort William, buy me some trade goods afore the first wagons reach them. Don't figger any of those sodbusters gonna coax their wagons this far west till the second week of July."

He wagged his head. "Can't help you do nothing with Fort John. My face ain't welcome in them parts—"

"I don't need you to come with me. I can handle the pack string my own self," Bridger declared. "But, I'm taking Shell Woman and her pups with me when I light out, morning after next."

"I'm sartin Shad's got a case of the lonelies for her."

"An' he asked if'n you'd come back for a day or so," Bridger explained.

"To see Shadrach?"

"Yep. He figgered things was gonna get busy for 'im and the others, once the easters start showing up to pay their toll on the ferry, so he wanted to spend a li'l time with you while he could. Him an' me, we'll have the hull durn winter to catch up an' tell lies. But, the two of you ain't got much time to be knee to knee till you take off north come the end of the season."

Titus felt that smile grow not just on his face but all through him. "Damn, if you two ain't about the finest friends a feller could have, Gabe. Yeah, for sartin, let's us go see Shad. I'd like to lay eyes on this ferry you two strung across the Green River for them wagon folks!"

So Titus had scratched the dogs' ears and kissed his family in farewell, then helped deliver Shadrach's family to the banks of the Green River a few miles south of the mouth of the Big Sandy. It brought a sting to his eyes to see how happy it made all four of them to be reunited once more: man, woman, and young ones too. The way things were meant to be. Early that following morning the three men bridled the string of mules, then cinched on the pads and empty packsaddles Bridger would bring back laden with trade goods for the store at his post on Black's Fork.

"I figger I can ride on with you till we reach the Sweetwater," Scratch announced after they had muscled the mules across the Green by rope and pulleys, then had the animals strung out in line.

Sweete bobbed his head. "With the other fellas here to help, I ain't got nothing for him to do here, Gabe. Maybeso he can give you a hand with them cantankerous mules till you reach the other side of the pass."

"Sure you don't mind heading in that direction?"

"Ever'thing's near ready for them wagon folks back at your fort," Bass declared. "So my woman'll just shoo me outta the store when I stick my nose in there. Yep—I'll give you a hand with this here string till we hit the Sweetwater."

The grin shining on Bridger's face right then convinced Titus that a few extra days with an old friend were more than worth any struggle that might come with those contrary-minded mules. In fact, the following day as they were slowly making their way up the Little Sandy toward the Southern Pass, Titus had been reflecting on just how much more enjoyable it was to be in this high, dry country with a string of mules than it was to be back at Fort Bridger where he felt like he was underfoot and clearly not wanted around by his wife and Magpie, womenfolk who constantly fluttered from one task to the next—with the children and the trading post and preparing meals. With a mule a man realized what he was up against and could coax some occasional cooperation out of them . . . but, with women, it was nothing less than a tale of confusion, confabulation, and not a little woe sometimes—trying his best to sort out why a woman would sometimes utter the exact opposite of what she really meant to tell him.

"Man's just a simple critter," he declared to Bridger that afternoon. "We're the last of God's creations ever gonna figger out the heart of a woman."

Jim chuckled in the warm sun. "Soon as a man understands he ain't never gonna read the sign in a woman's breast, the sooner he'll make peace with life—"

"What's that yonder?" Scratch interrupted.

"Looks to be a string of riders."

Bass shaded his eyes with a hand. "The first emigrants come west 'thout wagons?"

Shaking his head, Bridger said, "Don't callate how they could. Have no idea who they be. Or what they're doing out here."

"Them riders is all dressed in civil clothes," Titus commented as he peered into the mid-distance with that one good eye, then turned in the saddle to dig in his bags for his spyglass. "Ain't any Fort John fellas, is it?"

"Not a reason they'd be comin' this way," Jim surmised. "Besides, them parley-voos wouldn't be dressed in settlement clothes, would they?"

"If it ain't Frenchies from the Platte, what bunch gonna march over the pass 'thout no wagons?"

Bridger waited as Bass brought the spyglass to his eye, then asked, "You see any women with that bunch?"

"Nary a one."

Jim said, "No womenfolk—squaws or corncracker—neither one. Such only makes me curiouser and curiouser who them riders are."

He squinted through the spyglass and surmised, "Maybe their wagons and women coming behind where we can't see."

Bridger nodded. "That's the story. Damn, if this first bunch ain't one helluva lot earlier'n I figgered they'd come. For the life of me—can't callate how they made it across the prerra so fast."

Titus watched the horsemen draw closer and closer, those in the vanguard suddenly spotting the small mule train already pulled up at the side of a low hill overlooking the Little Sandy. "Only way for 'em to be this far this early is they got 'em a jump on leavin' the settlements, or they hunkered down for winter right out on the prerra—ahead of ever'one else."

"Maybeso you're right," Jim declared. "This bunch had to spend the winter a long way out from the settlements for 'em to make it here now."

"S'pose we ought'n go on down there an' be civil, don't you, Gabe?"

"That's the hull thing 'bout being a trader in the heart of this big wilderness," Bridger confessed. "Man's gotta be a good neighbor to what all kinds come riding through his country."

The sun was suspended just past midsky as the first four riders broke away from the head of that gaggle of horsemen and loped toward the two old trappers.

"Elder Orson Pratt!" announced the long-faced one who was first to speak. He held out his hand. "What are your names?"

"Elder?" Titus echoed. "You don't look so damn old to me."

"That's a way our brethren have of addressing one another," Pratt declared with a self-assured grin. "The title doesn't refer to our age, just our wisdom in the word of God. What name do you go by, good sir?"

"Titus Bass," he answered, tapping the brim of his wide hat with two fingertips. "This here's Jim Bridger."

Pratt's face lit up, as did the countenances of the other three. "*The* Jim Bridger?"

"I'm the onliest one," Gabe replied.

Turning sideways in his saddle, Pratt said exuberantly, "Elder Woodruff, ride back and tell the President that God has surely blessed us this day. Explain that Jim Bridger himself has been delivered into our hands!"

As the round-faced man in the flat-brimmed black hat reined his horse around and loped back toward the main party, Pratt didn't get a word out before Bridger spoke up, "Me delivered into your hands?"

The stranger nodded enthusiastically. "We prayed we might run onto you, Mr. Bridger. Two days ago we met up with a small company of men come from Oregon."

"Oregon?" Jim repeated. "They was headed east?"

"On their way to the States on some business," Pratt explained. "Left Oregon on the fifth of May, horseback and making good time they claimed. Major Harris, their guide, was bringing them through to Laramie, where he would take his leave of their party and stay at that post until he could hire out to one of the emigrant companies if they wished to employ his services, leading them back to Oregon."

Titus asked, "That where your train is headed?"

Pratt shook his head. "My, no. We're on the way to a land of our own. Where the Lord Himself is guiding us."

"We are the Saints of the living God," declared the man beside Pratt, his face flushed with the heat. "We have come to find the paradise He has promised to our Prophet, President Young."

"Saints, you said?" Titus commented as his eyes moved across the three strangers. They did have the same look about them as those men camped near the Pueblo when he arrived to deliver word of the slaughter in Taos a few months back. "I met me a hull camp of fellers down on the Arkansas last winter what called themselves Saints too. There more'n one bunch o' Saints come west to find their promised land?"

The second man had turned to Pratt and was talking almost before Bass was finished. "That must be Captain Brown's party. Praise God for their deliverance!"

Then he turned back to address Bass and Bridger, "I am Elder James Little. This is good news you've brought us this day about our first pioneer party to push west from Winter Quarters on the Platte."

"Pioneers?" Bridger echoed as the rest of the main body came up.

"We are the vanguard of a mighty migration," stated a solid man as he brought his horse to a halt. The solid, big-boned man wore no mustache, only a full beard, and his eyes appeared to shine with the first sign of a fever. "Good day to you both. I am President Young. Brigham Young. Pray, which of you is Jim Bridger?"

"He is," Titus said, indicating his friend.

Young heeled his horse forward, stopping immediately on Bridger's off side, and held out his hand. "I am very, very pleased to meet you, Mr. Bridger."

They shook as Jim said, "Call me Jim."

"Then you must be sure to call me Brigham."

"You're chief to these here Saints?" Titus asked. "An' them Saints I met down on the Arkansas last winter?"

"Captain Brown's party is safe and well?"

"They was when I last saw them middle of winter."

Young smiled. "This is truly an auspicious day, brothers! We learn that our fellow Mormons are safe in the hand of God, and Jim Bridger has been brought to help us."

"Marmons?" Titus repeated.

"No . . . *Mor*-mons," Young corrected, his face hardening.

"That's what I said: *Mar*-mons," he replied. "Thought you said you were saints."

With a benevolent smile, Young explained, "We are known by both names. Ours is the Church of the Latter-Day Saints, but most folks call us Mormons, because of the Book of Mormon we read, revelations of the latter day."

"Two names for the same thing," Bass muttered to Bridger out of the side of his mouth. "Ain't that just like a confabulating religion?"

"Are you bound for your post?" Young asked Bridger, stoically ignoring Bass's comment.

Jim wagged his head. "Fort John for supplies."

"Could I prevail upon you to spend some time with us before we proceed on our way?" Young pleaded. "You see, we have these maps of Colonel Fremont's. It would be most helpful if you could—"

"Fremont?" Bridger snorted with a huge grin and a shake of his head. "Best you don't count on them Fremont maps none! Might end up marching right into the sea, you foller a map drawed by the Colonel Fremont I know!"

"They're not to be relied upon?" the Prophet asked, dumbfounded.

"Truth is," Jim said, "I'm ashamed of any map Fremont'd draw. He knows nothing of the country hereabouts."

Drawing in a long sigh, Young said, "Exactly, Mr. Bridger. That's why it was God's will that He delivered you to me here. Weeks ago I heard you alone were the man to know this interior country. And for weeks now I've prayed God would lead me to you."

Squinting his eyes, Jim asked, "What you want of me, Brigham?"

The man's face lit up. "Why, I want you to help me find the Promised Land for my people!"

That afternoon as Bridger and Bass joined the Mormon pioneers in making camp beside the ford of the Little Sandy, Scratch got to brooding that Brigham Young sounded more and more like the Moses of a bygone day, what with all the stories his mother had read him from her great family Bible back in Rabbit Hash, Boone County, Kentucky. This one, a new Moses, explaining how he was leading his people out of turmoil and despair back east, where they could not practice their chosen religion in Illinois or Missouri, guiding his flocks of faithful onto the prairie to escape to Zion, much as Moses led his people into the wilderness in search of their own Promised Land.

"The information you give us about the country west of here is considerably more favorable than the news given us by Major Harris," Orson Pratt declared at that great council of the Twelve held beside the ford of the Little Sandy, where Bridger and Bass agreed to tarry till breakfast, answering every last one of the Saints' questions concerning the unknown country ahead.

"If this here Harris is a feller of dark skin," Bridger explained, "I figger you run onto Moses Harris, but he goes by the name Black Harris. You read the same sign, Scratch?"

Bass nodded.

Brigham Young confessed, "Said he was a pilot—could guide for us. We shared a camp with him last night at Pacific Springs, but, I'll admit I never got the man's first name. Moses."

Bridger said, "I don't know how he come to call hisself a major, but I'd be curious to hear what he told you Mormons 'bout where you're headed."

"There's the lake where I feel I'm drawn," Brigham declared. "I asked him about that lake."

"Big'un, or small?" Bridger inquired. "Salt or sweet?"

Young grinned. "Salt. Yes! Salt."

"What'd Harris say 'bout it?"

"Not much good," Young admitted, his jowls working. "The whole region is sandy, destitute of timber of any size, and there's no vegetation but for the wild sage. Tell me, should I trust the word of Major Harris?"

Making a casual sign of the cross from brow to breast, Bridger explained, "Can't figger what he'd know of that part of the country. As for me, there's plenty of timber. Last twenty year, I made sugar from the trees. Right where Harris told you there ain't no timber."

"So you do know the valley?"

Titus snorted, "Know it? Hell, Bridger floated on the Salt Lake his own self."

The Prophet was taken aback. "You've *floated* the lake? Then it isn't all as big as Fremont shows it is on his map?"

"It's so durn big we figgered it for the ocean at first!" Jim explained.

"I 'member you telling me that story, Gabe," Bass said with fond remembrance. "Not long after I first met up with you. Same time I met Beckwith* too."

Bridger smiled. "I recollect that too, sitting by the crik an' scrubbin' the grease off our hides. Shit, weren't we the young bucks back then?"

The Prophet waved a hand in the manner of a man impatient to bring someone else's conversation back to his topic. "What do you know of Hastings's route?"

"It's a likely way to get where you're goin'," Bridger answered.

The Prophet drew a few lines in the dirt at their feet. "Through Weber's Fork?"

"Yep. Go right on by my fort, keep marching south by west instead of turning north for Fort Hall. That takes you on Hastings's road to California. He come out last summer—"

---

* James P. Beckwith (sometimes spelled Beckwourth).

"So that route will lead us to the valley of the Salt Lake?"

"Less'n you get lost off it. Been least a hunnert wagons go through there last year, by way of Hastings's road."

"What do you know of the country beyond the valley?"

Jim hastily scratched some lines on the ground with the tip of his belt knife. "After you get around these here mountains, it's purty flat for aways."

"From there?"

He jabbed his knife into the grassy soil. "A country covered with a hard, black rock. Ever' stone looks to be glazed, just like glass. An' ever' piece so hard and sharp it'll cut your horses' hooves to ribbons in a matter of a mile."

G. A. Smith leaned forward and asked, "South of the valley of the Salt Lake, what lies there?"

"You run onto the Green again," Jim answered. "The way runs through some level country, then winds into some hilly ground, but all of it bare as the face of hell, all the way to the salt sea."

Howard Egan interrupted now. "Hastings reports that from your fort to the Salt Lake it is no more than a hundred miles. How far say you?"

"I been that way more'n half-a-hunnert times," Bridger declared. "But I couldn't lay any number on how far it is from my post."

Wilford Woodruff asked, "Can we pass through the mountains farther south of here with wagons?"

"Sartin you can," Jim replied. "But there's places you'll be in heavy timber, where you'll have to cut your way through for wagons."

Now Young asked, "You said you'd floated the lake. Have you been to the other side?"

"I know a half dozen men or more been around that lake," Bridger said. "Had a brigade over there one autumn. Some of 'em got their horses stole by Diggers or Utes*—you best watch out for them Utes, they'll be troublesome for you—so we cut some canoes outta cottonwoods an' sent our men around the lake, looking for beaver."

"How long did it take for them to bring back the beaver pelts?"

He grinned at Young. "Never did find no beaver, and them boys was about three moons getting back to us. Said it was more'n five hunnert fifty miles to get around."

"What of these Indians stole your horses?"

"Utahs and Diggers both, bad Injuns. They catch you out, got you beat on the odds—they'll plunder your outfit an' whup you, if'n they don't just kill you outright. But, a bunch big as you got here, ain't got no worry. Them Injuns is yeller cowards less'n they got big odds in their favor."

"With my apologies, President Young?" James Little injected. "I'd like to

---

* Tribes of the central and southern basin and plateau region.

ask Mr. Bridger about the favorable conditions for growing our crops, like corn."

"Yes, how is the soil in the valley?" asked William Clayton.

"I know of a feller was a trapper too, he has him a small place up in the valley of Bear River," Bridger explained. "Soil's good up there for his growing season, so I figger it's good on south in the Salt Lake country. Only trouble is—"

"Trouble?" Young repeated the word with his stentorian voice.

"I figger the nights get too cold in the Salt Lake Valley for your people to grow Missouri field corn. Frosts of a night'll kill off most grain. Country south of Utah Lake better for your crops."

Three of the bystanders immediately leaned over Brigham Young's shoulders as the Prophet hunched in study of his Fremont maps.

"Ah, here it is," Young announced with pride. "Is this the valley?"

Jim squinted and asked, "A little'un? South of the Salt Lake?"

"Yes," the Prophet assured.

"That's the place I'm telling you of," Bridger continued. "There's a band of good Injuns down that way, got farms of their own, and they raise grains. I can buy the very best wheat from 'em. As I recollect that country, I 'member a valley down that way. If there was ever a promised land your God was leading you to, it's gotta be that valley aways on south of the Salt Lake Valley."

Surprised at that declaration, Young stammered, "W-why do you call it a promised land?"

"There's a cedar grows down there, bears a fruit, like juniper berries, but bigger an' yellow—'bout the size of a small plum. And the Injuns in the country ain't thieves. They feed themselves: pick them berries and grind 'em into a meal."

Little asked, "There's a lot of this fruit?"

"I figger I could gather more'n a hunnert bushels off one tree alone," Jim declared. "I've lived on that fruit afore, when I couldn't bring no game to bait."

"How's the water, Mr. Bridger?" asked Egan.

"Streams running outta the mountains all over, and many springs too."

Young sighed with impatience, "How far is it from the valley of the Salt Lake?"

Jim brooded a moment, then said, "Twenty days' ride from there."

The Prophet's face hardened. "That far?"

"Maybe not that far . . . just the country you gotta go through to get there is so bad. Nothin' much for your animals to eat. Not like it is here on the Little Sandy, where your horses got all the feed they want. But once you get there, you'll find a copper mine on one of the rivers running through the valley. Fact be, there's a whole mountain of copper. Gold an' silver down there too. I never had no use for such. You spot veins of coal in the hills. Yessir, that land is good.

That there's your promised land, Brigham Young. Soil is rich. Nights don't get cold in the growin' season. That country is thick with persimmons. Ever you ate a persimmon? That's a shame you ain't. There's wild grapes down there too, for a man to make the best wines."

"It takes a good climate to grow grapes, Prophet," commented Woodruff.

So Brigham asked, "How far north have you seen these grapes growing?"

"Never saw any around Utah Lake," he answered, "but I seen lots of cherries and berries. That's better country than the valley of the Salt Lake. But, it's far better south of there, where I told you. Plenty of timber, an' the fish in the streams ain't never been caught. Even found some wild flax growing down there."

Young asked, "How many years has it been since you were in that country?"

"A year ago, this coming July," Bridger declared. "There's good rain there, but not much wind. If your God brung you out here to a promised land, it's for sure it ain't in the Salt Lake Valley. By gonnies, you won't find no promised land till you get south of Utah Lake."

The Prophet brushed both hands down the front of his dusty vest and said, "Perhaps it would not be prudent of us to bring a great population to that basin until we have ascertained whether grain will grow there or not, to sustain our faithful."

At that moment three more men stepped up to the assembly, one of whom announced, "Supper is heated, President Young."

The Prophet stood and tugged on the points at the bottom of his vest. "I would like to take my supper in the shade of that tree over there, Brother Whipple. Would you throw down a blanket and set two places under the branches?"

"T-two, sir?"

Young turned to peer at Jim. "Would you do me the honor of eating with me tonight? I have so many more questions I want to ask you about the valley of the Salt Lake . . . and that valley you said was God's own Promised Land. Join me, please?"

"We be glad to," Bridger replied.

Young cleared his throat. "I don't want there to be any misunderstanding, Mr. Bridger. I invited only you to dine with me. Not your friend here."

"You don't wanna eat with him, then I ain't—"

"Gabe," Bass interrupted. "G'won ahead with this fella. S'all right. I ain't gonna go hungry."

Jim studied his eyes a minute. "Awright. I'll eat my supper an' then we'll make camp. Light out in the morning."

Titus nodded, then watched Brigham Young turn Bridger away, the two of them walking toward the tree where the three young men were spreading a blanket and preparing to serve supper.

A strange people, Bass thought to himself as he sighed and turned away. You'd think a man what calls hisself a prophet of God would know where God wants him to go already, Titus brooded. Wouldn't you think this Brigham Young would have no need to ask Jim Bridger for directions to the Promised Land?

NINE

"They call themselves Marmons," Titus explained to his wife as they stood at the open gates and watched the two dogs trotting toward the first of the Pioneer Party hoving into view more than a half mile from the stockade.

She did her best to mimic his English. "Mar-mo-o-o-o-ns."

He quickly glanced over his shoulder at the Cheyenne woman and all the children who had gathered with them to watch the arrival of Brigham Young's Saints at Fort Bridger. Then Scratch whispered in Crow.

"Gabe took to their chief right off; but I saw him as a hard-faced man," he declared as the sun shone hot upon them.

As Bass watched the riders approaching through the trees, crossing one small streamlet after another to reach the post, he ruminated on his confidential talk with Bridger some nine days back, late that night after Jim had finished his supper with Brigham Young.

"Not a bad sort," Gabe had observed as Titus put a few more limbs on the small fire as the summer night grew cold.

"I don't trust him," Titus snorted. "None of them others."

"But I don't read his sign same as you," Bridger said.

"Hell no, you wouldn't," Bass whispered as they unfurled their robes and blankets in a small copse of willow there beside the Little Sandy. "You just et supper with that preacher, an' now he's even got you seein' angels dancing on the top of a pin."

Bridger shrugged. "Simmer down, Scratch. He an' his brethren seem like they're honest, God-fearin' folk—just like Whitman."

"Like Doc Whitman?" Scratch repeated, incredulous. "Now, there was a good man, Gabe. He wasn't like most ever' other preacher I knowed: looking down their long noses at you from up on high, with them accusin' eyes full of fire an' the air around 'em filled with the smell of sulfur an' brimstone. No, I'll be glad to say our fare-thee-wells to this here Brigham Young an' his pack o' Marmons come mornin'."

For a moment, Jim had pursed his lips, then disclosed, "I was hopin' to talk you into turning around from here."

"You don't want me to see you on to the pass, e'en down to the Sweetwater?" he had asked. "I ain't see'd Devil's Gate, or that ol' Turtle Rock in a long time—"

"I was figgering you could take President Young and the rest on to the fort, Scratch," Bridger admitted. "Since I ain't got no choice but to keep on my way to Fort John to see about them goods we're needing for the store, you'll be the host for me."

"At your post?"

Jim leaned close to Bass. "I can trust you to show 'em your best manners."

He didn't have a good feeling from the start, and it wasn't getting any better. "I dunno—"

"Treat the Saints good an' they'll be on their way in a few days," Bridger said. "They need some smithin' done afore they move on. I told President Young you'd fire up the anvil for all they needed, an' he said they could do it themselves, or pay for your work in coin, or take it out in trade. They brung 'em plenty of supplies along, so maybe you can take a look over what they got to trade for. See what the women needs the most in the store, an' swap out your work for the goods."

"You're sure 'bout makin' these Marmons welcome like this, Gabe?"

"I get back from Fort John, I'll make it good by you."

"Not that," he whispered with a correcting shake of his head, "I mean, do you got your mind made up to help these here Marmons gonna set up their promised land right at your back door?"

"They ain't gonna be no trouble, not like Utes or Bannocks, raising hell an' running off with my stock if I give 'em the chance!" Bridger snorted. "The Saints only got a differ'nt God than you an' me, Scratch. Hell, this here Brigham Young really ain't no differ'nt from a Snake or 'Rapaho medicine man. Some shake a rattle or look at the dried blood in the belly of a badger for some sign of the One Above."

Bass scoffed, "An' this here Brigham Young listens to all that his angels tell him about what God wants him to tell all his flock."

Jim's brow knitted. "Where you get these notions 'bout angels an' his flock?"

"While you was havin' supper with your Prophet, them others had a hold on my ear, telling me all 'bout this here Brigham Young bein' the only one what knows the true word of God meant for the ears of man," Titus confided sourly. "Damn, but they was preachin' hard at Titus Bass. Harder'n any preaching I ever got whipped on these ol' ears. Made my head ache with all their Urim an' Thummin. Hell, they claimed they was the only folks bound to sit on a throne in glory. Angels named Moroni an' Nephi . . . Gabe, this bunch wuss'n all the hell an' brimstone preachers I knowed back in Kaintuck. These Marmons don't holler sayin's outta the Bible like McAfferty or Bill Williams neither! They got their own book they was thumpin' an' drummin' on—"

"Young showed it to me. Where they get called Mormons—from their own book on the word from God," Bridger said with an unmasked enthusiasm in his voice. "He said they still believe in the Bible, but it's older, an' their book is a newer word of God, meant for them what's chose for heaven here in the latter days."

For a moment, Titus had carefully studied his old friend. "Young change you into Marmon?"

Jim smiled and leaned forward to say in a hush, "Hell no, Scratch. But I give the man my manners an' listened to all he had to say. We talked some more about the country an' the Injuns an' crops they could grow down there south of Utah Lake, but in atween it all he was giving me a sharp lesson on all they believed an' why he's brought his people out of Missouri—"

"Missouri!" Scratch interrupted. "Why, them Marmons hate Missouri an' all the folks in that country! Afore I had my fill of supper for all they was poundin' in my ears, they told me the Garden of Eden—where Adam an' Eve was birthed by God—why, it was right outside where ol' Fort Osage stood, near the mouth of the Blue River, on the Missouri! No preacher I ever heard spout a sermon back in Kaintuck ever come anywhere close to saying God started the hull world back yonder on the banks of the Missouri River!"

"An' a Snake medicine man claims he can pull a evil spirit right out of a man's mouth so he ain't sick no more," Jim argued. "These here Mormons just got their own way of seeing God, an' Brigham Young says they only wanna be left alone by folks who don't understand 'em."

"You sure you ain't gone Marmon on me?"

With a shake of his head, Bridger stated flatly, "No. I been out here in the Rocky Mountains too long to swaller talk about angels coming down from the clouds an' Eden at our back door, an' one prophet gonna talk to God hisself so he can tell me which way my stick floats an' what don't smell o' horse apples."

"We're too damn old to change our ways now," Titus observed, feeling a bit reassured.

"Maybeso a old beaver trapper like me can make a life for hisself helping them emigrants bound for Oregon," Jim admitted. "But I ain't gonna change who I am or what I come to believe in after more'n twenty winters out here."

He plopped a gnarled hand on Bridger's knee and said fraternally, "Time was, I didn't figger I wanted nothing to do with no emigrants comin' through in their wagons, stirring up the buffler an' bringing their white women to the mountains. But, long as them sodbusters keep right on going west to Oregon an' don't dally long in our country, I can help some corncrackers on their way to their own promised land on the Columbia."

Jim grinned in the moonlight. "So we'll both hold our tongue an' help these here Saints find the promised land they chose for themselves. Them others, did they give you some bread with your supper?"

"It was mighty tasty, I do admit," Scratch said as he lay on his side in the starlight. "Been some time since I ate white folks' bread."

"When I sat down with Brigham Young, I told him I ain't see'd so much bread in years," Bridger confessed as he lay back on his blankets. "So he asked me, 'But, Mr. Bridger, how do you live without bread?' "

"What'd you tell 'im, Gabe?"

"Told him we live on meat. Dry our deer and buffler to eat in the lean times. And we also cook fresh when we can get it. Told him we have coffee to drink most of the time, for that we can have plenty of that brung out here."

They lay in silence for a long time, until Scratch asked once again, "You're sure 'bout bein' so friendly to these here strangers?"

"Yes," he answered in the dark. "Way out here on this side o' the mountains, we ought'n treat other folks the way we wanna be treated ourselves, Scratch."

Titus sighed, then said, "Long as it's gonna help my friend, Jim Bridger . . . an' don't ever hurt you to open your door to this here Brigham Young."

"Them Mormons gonna be putting down their roots and setting up shop so far south from here," Jim explained, "we'll never hear a sound from 'em."

Titus Bass went to sleep that night, wanting to believe that every bit as much as his friend did.

But for the last nine days that little wary voice of warning was about all Titus had brooded on as he stayed just far enough ahead of the column's vanguard that he would discourage any company as he dragged these saints of the latter days beyond that fateful meeting with Gabe and on toward Fort Bridger on Black's Fork. It was just past midafternoon when Scratch had recognized the faraway river bluffs. He immediately turned about and covered that quarter mile back to the head of the march where Brigham Young and a half dozen of his Apostles rode.

"You'll spy Jim's post when you round the bend in the river," Bass announced as he reined his horse around and brought it up near the group of riders. "I'm goin' on to see to my family. Let ever'body know you'll be comin' soon."

"Your family?" Young echoed. "You have an Indian wife like Major Bridger? Half-breed children too?"

His eyes narrowed at the judgmental tone the stocky man took. "Crow. My family's Crow."

"Are they a tribe from this part of the country?" asked Elder Woodruff.

He wagged his head. "North of here. Far . . . north of here."

William Clayton stated, "Another band of Lamanites we've read about, President Young."

"Band of what?" Titus asked.

"Lamanites," Clayton repeated.

"Indians, Mr. Bass," Young declared. "The red man, his women and children. They are a lost tribe of Israel—banished to this wilderness because they refused to turn their ears to the continued revelations of God."

He tried out the word, "Lay-man . . ."

"Lamanites," Clayton pronounced it correctly for the old trapper.

Titus asked, "All that what some Lamanite tol't your people back east?"

Young smiled that same hard smile he wore most of the time, the sort of smile a man would use when he was scolding a disobedient child. "No, Moroni appeared to our founder and told him the word of God was meant for His chosen here in these latter days. For hundreds of years the world has not heeded God, but now these faithful, holy people have been raised up by the Almighty to forge a trail west—following a pillar of cloud by day, and a pillar of fire by night, just as the thousands followed Moses out of bondage in Egypt to their Promised Land."

So Scratch had peered this way and that in the sky that afternoon, and saw no pillar of cloud. Nor had he seen any pillar of fire blazing in the sky after the Pioneer Party had made their camp each evening.

Yet, even while there had been no fire in the heavens for the past nine nights, there was no mistaking the flames in Brigham Young's eyes as he gazed into the distance and caught sight of something to make his case to the faithful.

"There, Mr. Bass," the Prophet declared as he pointed up the valley. "Behold—there is your pillar of cloud."

With murmurs of assent and wonder, Titus looked on up the valley of Black's Fork. A thin column of woodsmoke arose from the direction of Fort Bridger. A cold chill tumbled down his spine, so cold and shocking it reminded him of stepping into a beaver pond in spring, cracking a thin layer of ice with his moccasins as he waded in to his crotch, numbing everything from his waist down. He looked again at Brigham Young, at the Prophet's faithful, who were pointing and muttering in agreement that they were indeed seeing the pillar of cloud God had put before them, leading them onward to their Promised Land.

Chimney smoke.

Titus wagged his head and put heels to his horse. As the big red pony loped toward Fort Bridger, the old man did his best to pray that the Prophet and his chosen few would soon spot more woodsmoke to continue them on their way, to lead them far from the valley of Black's Fork, to take their kind on to a distant kingdom of their own . . . so they could not possibly lay waste to the simple, earthly dreams of his old friend, Jim Bridger.

"Think of the trade my flock can offer you and Major Bridger as we bring the Saints through this wilderness to Zion, marching those thousands right past your gates!" extolled the Prophet.

Bass's heavy hammer clanged against the short, glowing strip of band iron one last time, a splatter of crimson fireflies spewing from the anvil, a few of them snuffing themselves out on his grimy, cinder-stained moccasins. Bass laid the hammer on top of the stump where the anvil was perched and dragged the reddish strap of iron to the bucket with a pair of long, leather-wrapped tongs. As the crimson metal *sisssssed* into the bubbling water, Titus dragged the back of his right forearm over his eyes, smearing beads of moisture and blackened cinders across the top half of his face. Droplets of sweat had begun to sting his eyes already irritated by the thick smoke. No matter that he couldn't see with the left, both eyes still burned fiercely as he worked over fire and iron, flame and muscle.

"Jim's gonna be some pleased with that," he sighed, wishing the Saints would turn away and leave him to his work.

"Our migration to Zion should more than guarantee Major Bridger a handsome profit for a short season's work," Young continued, his thumbs hooked in the top pockets of his vest. "Those Gentiles going on to . . . the emigrants going on to Oregon or perhaps to California will only be the sauce for what income you can make from our faithful."

He dragged the iron from the bucket with those tongs, turning the wide hub band this way, then that, inspecting it closely before he stepped over to the fire hopper and began hauling down on the long bellows handle he had repaired just this morning, bringing his coals to full heat. As he yanked down again and again in rhythm with his heartbeat, Scratch let his eyes bounce from man to man to man, across all eight of those who had followed Brigham Young to this shady corner of the post, all of them standing there like a broad-shouldered, multiheaded shadow, having tagged along behind their leader, hanging on his every word, whim, and need, as if Young's every utterance was the very breath of God itself.

"What's this Gen-tile?" he asked as the coals began to glow anew with the infusion of air.

Young cleared his throat. "A Gentile is a non-Mormon. One who has not yet come to the faith that will save him everlasting."

"Me? I'm a Gentile?"

"What faith are you, Mr. Bass?"

"I don't figger there's a name I can rightly put on it."

"Were you raised up with any church teaching?"

"My ma, she tried hard," Titus explained. "With me an' her other young'uns. But I s'pose your kind would call her a Gentile—no matter that she was as good an' God-fearin' a woman as ever walked this earth."

"I would never mean to give offense—"

"Much as she tried to get the Bible into my head an' part o' my heart," Bass continued without waiting for Young to finish, "I fell into the life what snared most boys I knowed on the frontier, snared 'em same as me. Whiskey an' wimmens. Bad whiskey and even badder wimmens."

He liked watching how those temporal, carnal words landed on their ears: the averted eyes, the downturned faces, as each man did his best to stare at the ground; a few gazed upward as if asking for heaven to cast its gloried benevolence on this pagan sinner, perhaps even asking for a thunderbolt to be sent from above to strike down this blasphemer.

"Even Mary, the mother of Christ Jesus, was an apostate from the true church," Young instructed. "She herself was not redeemed by the blood of her son."

"He was the one they nailed on the cross, weren't he?"

With a smile, the Prophet nodded. "Yes. The Christ Jesus, who married the two Marys and Martha too before He was betrayed and crucified . . . married all three, whereby He could sow His seed before He ascended to the right hand of God."

"My mam didn't ever teach me Jesus was married afore," Bass admitted as he studied the iron band again. "Havin' three wives, hmmm—sounds to me like you're saying Jesus wasn't satisfied to be with just one woman."

"Do you doubt that Christ Jesus married the three?"

He shrugged and replied, "I don't know enough 'bout anything to answer your questions. I'm just a simple man who manages to sin a lot—"

"What sin was once in a man's heart is of no bearing to God," Brigham Young replied. "And therefore of no bearing to me. It's what a man decides to become that marks him for the Lord's work—"

"It ain't a case of what I'll become, you best unnerstand. It's what I *am* that I'll allays be."

The Prophet took a step closer, holding out his hands before him, palms up. "Look at these hands, Mr. Bass. Once these were the hands of a carpenter. I too was a simple man with the hands of a carpenter." He looked up from staring at his palms. "Did you know Jesus was a carpenter Himself?"

"Before you say He married them three women?"

"Christ Jesus—the Savior who came to the New World after He was crucified," Young extolled. "He appeared to God's chosen to tell them how all others in the land of Old Israel had forsaken Him and His promise. So Jesus left them with a new promise, and that word is told in our holy book. How Adam was God, conceived on the great star of Kolob, the site for the conception of all the gods. The most amazing story of all is told in our book, Mr. Bass."

He wagged his head and turned back to the coals, dragging the iron strip out of the fire again and looping its crescent over the end of the anvil. "I don't read much. Ain't since I come out here."

"One of the Apostles could read some of the holy book to you—"

"I got work to do."

But Young was not easily deterred. "While you continue with your work."

"I'm too old—"

"No man should deny himself a chance at eternal life, especially when he grows long in the tooth, Mr. Bass."

He picked up the hammer and gave the red-hot crescent a slam, sparks sputtering from the anvil. "I am what I am, Preacher. I see what I see, an' I hear what I hear. No man can see or hear for me."

"But you can see the truth, hear the truth of our word, and judge for yourself as the many who have already made a stand for the new nation of Israel."

Again and again his hammer rang against the crimson metal he inched around the anvil, slowly tightening the crescent into a solid circle the size he would need to work onto a wagon's wheel hub. "I been out here since twenty-five . . ." and the hammer rang. "I seen things with my own eyes . . ." that hammer rang again. "Things I'd never dreamed . . . back east . . . heard an' smelled an' felt . . . all manner of things out here . . . things what wasn't really there . . . they's called ghosts . . . or shades . . . or hoo-doos—"

"Spirits, Mr. Bass," Young interrupted. "Like the Holy Spirit that will enter your bosom and seize your heart with a fire of unquenchable flame."

"Hoo-doos or spirits . . . no matter what you call 'em . . . that sort of thing may give a man like you . . . the willies an' shakes . . . but such ghosty doin's don't make no nevermind . . . to the peoples out here . . . out to these here mountains . . . the red folks ain't the kind to preach an' push . . . what they have in their heart . . . push it on me the way you preachers push . . . a man's medeecin is his medeecin . . . so who the blazes am I . . . to make so little of what another man carries . . . in his heart . . . who the hell am I to say . . . what makes him a man? . . . or to say I'm a man . . . an' he ain't?"

"I've attempted to explain to you where the Lamanites have been judged wrong, where the Indians, the cursed ones of this continent, came from and how God turned His face from them because they turned their faces from His true word," Young said impatiently as he stepped around the side of the anvil to gaze directly into the trapper's face. "The Indian believes in the sanctity of his beliefs about his world because he is in a state of ignorance—he knows not the word of God, Mr. Bass. Be careful, very careful, you do not covet the ignorance of these savages, or you are a heathen yourself, destined for the pit of fire. The reason these heathens can't spread the healing power of their teaching is because they have no knowledge of the one true God."

Scratch slammed the hammer down on the red-hot iron with a vengeance. "Their God is the same as yours, Preacher."

Young's face brightened with that benevolent smile that made Bass realize the Prophet believed he was ministering unto a lesser man, one who was every bit as ignorant as a heathen Indian, totally unworthy of salvation for the color of his skin.

"No," the Prophet argued, "the spirits of these Indians are not the same as the one true Creator. These red savages live in a state of ignorance, for there will be no happy hunting ground for them when they die without the salvation of the word."

From the corner of Scratch's eye, the old trapper spotted his wife step from the open doorway of the store and stop against the building, then slowly settle to the half-log bench propped against the cabin wall. Waits-by-the-Water smiled at him, then closed her eyes and turned her face up to the warming sun. Apparently very much at peace.

Turning back to Brigham Young, he asked, "Your God an angry God, Preacher?"

For a moment, Young appeared to heft his thoughts around like a carpenter might take the measure of the grain in a piece of wood. "Yes, at times He can be an angry, vengeful God. When He alone determines He will smite the unrighteous—"

"What of all them sinners back to Missouri?" Titus asked as he continued to hammer on those last few inches of iron. "Other places too . . . where the folks riz up . . . an' throwed you Marmons out? Why didn't your God . . . smite them Gentiles . . . why did your God . . . make it so hard on your people?"

That question startled the Prophet. He quickly glanced at those followers around him with a look that Titus figured was Young's wondering if any of them had explained the story of their years of travail to this ignorant Gentile.

"It is not for a man to know the inner workings of the heart of God, Mr. Bass," he finally answered. "I suppose it will all be revealed to us in due time."

"Maybeso, not in your lifetime?"

Young finally nodded. "Perhaps not in my lifetime, yes. But just as Moses led his Israelites to the Promised Land but could not cross over, this might not be revealed to me before I close my eyes and take my final breath . . . then stand at the foot of the throne of God, when all things will finally be revealed to me."

Titus sighed, "Some things just meant to be a . . . a mystery, Preacher."

"Mystery, you say?"

In the tongs Bass held up the small hoop of iron that had lost all its crimson glow. Suspended between the two of them. The anointed Prophet and the dirt-ignorant old trapper. "Most ever' kind of folk I come to know out here—man, an' woman too—they figger what they can't wrap their minds around ain't for 'em to unnerstand."

"But God has clearly shown mankind that He wants us to understand."

"Where's this hoop start, Preacher?"

"Why—clearly at the end you curved in."

"Did your own hoop start when you was born?"

"My . . . hoop?" he asked with the sort of smile one would wear when answering the questions of a young child.

For a moment Scratch considered how best to explain that simple concept to this self-assured preacher. "The long journey your own spirit takes—ain't it like a hoop? You're born, live your life good as you can, then you die. So did your own hoop start when you was born?"

Young cleared his throat and reflected. "Certainly . . . no, it didn't. My spirit yearned for a place among God's faithful and chosen people at this very time in history."

"You're saying you was somewhere else on this hoop when you was born?"

"I don't understand your point, Mr. Bass—"

"An' where will you be on the hoop when you die and stand before the throne of your God?"

It was indeed a hot midsummer day—nonetheless the Prophet's brow was sweating a little too much for a man who was doing nothing to physically exert himself.

Titus asked again, holding the iron band slightly higher, "Where will you be?"

"When I die I will be in heaven with all God's faithful saints. Right where you can be if you accept His revealed word."

"So you do got a beginning and an end, Preacher?"

"As do all God's creatures."

"Me too? A ignernt Gentile like me?"

"Yes."

Bass lowered the hoop. "How 'bout my Injun wife and our young'uns?"

"Yes, they have a glorious end in paradise once they accept the teachings of God." Young smiled again, as if beginning to feel more at ease.

"You take this here circle," Titus began, gazing at that iron hoop, "why, this here's my life, preacher. Just like my coming out here to the mountains was a part of the journey. No beginning an' no end."

"But in death—"

"When I die, my body goes back to the earth, don't it?"

"That's the way of all mortal clay, yes."

"But my spirit goes on," he said quietly. "Like the earth and sky. That don't die, does it, Preacher?"

Young corrected, "Your soul goes to live with God in His heavenly paradise prepared for us."

"I don't want my soul—my spirit—to go nowhere," he said with grave intensity. "I want it to stay right here where I been the happiest I ever could be."

"There's far more happiness in heaven with the rest of the faithful souls—"

"Maybe for you an' your Saints, but for me I don't wanna be nowhere but here with these rocks and sky, here with the ones I hold in my heart. There ain't no other heaven, no other paradise for me to be in for all time."

"I . . . see," Young stated, then dragged a single fingertip along his upper lip beaded with tiny diamonds of sweat. "Elders—we see how the Holy Spirit can only speak to a man if his ears are not plugged."

"It ain't that my ears are plugged," Titus replied. "I s'pose I just hear a dif-fer'nt voice than you heard, Preacher."

Throwing his shoulders back self-confidently, Young said, "The devil him-self can whisper in your ear, Mr. Bass. What has that evil voice you hear been saying to you?"

"It said I don't need no other man to tell me what I need to hear, to see what I need to see."

"Then you will not trust to the word of God revealed through his chosen Prophet?"

"Who's telling me it's the word of God?"

He spread his hand upon his chest, "Why, those men God has anointed as His spokesmen here on earth—in the way of prophets, the way it has been since the earliest days of man on this earth."

"The earth was here first? An' the sky too?"

"Of course," Young agreed.

"Then that's the way it must be for me too," Bass admitted. "If the earth an' the sky was here first, they'll be here through the end of time. I want my spirit to last as long. The way I seen how Injuns look at all there is around 'em. Makes more sense to me than all your glory an' Thummin' an' your angel Moroni blowin' his horn."

"He announces the coming of the—"

"I hear my God speak to me good enough in a whisper, Preacher."

Young worked his lower jaw around several times as if chewing on the words he was considering giving voice, but finally said with great finality, "So be it, Mr. Bass. Many times in our troubled past we have been told by God that not all men will hear His call. Some have their ears plugged to God's glory." He sighed and started to shamble around the anvil, his bearded jaw jutting. "Here on the doorstep to Zion—I am once more reminded that we cannot save every-one, my brothers. Even these simplest lambs lost forever in the eternal wilder-ness."

Bass watched the Prophet and his Apostles turn aside and shuffle off toward the store. He plunged the iron hoop into the water. This time it barely raised a hiss or a bubble; it had cooled as he held it out before him in the tongs. Then he looked up to watch their backs as they stepped past Waits, each of them in turn touching the brim of their hats before they disappeared, one by one, absorbed by the shadows of that doorway. She turned and got to her feet, pushing a wisp of hair back from her damp brow, tucking it beneath that hair, which was pulled into one of her braids as she started his way.

"Ti-tuzz," Waits said as she ducked into the shade of the low awning of tree branches suspended above his blacksmith shop. "Your face is troubled."

It took him a moment to put his mind on the Crow she spoke at him, his head swollen with matters most heavenly . . . bringing his thoughts back to the temporal present. With a clatter he laid the hoop and tongs upon the anvil and let her step inside his damp, gritty arms.

"These men," she said with her cheek against his neck, "they are not like any of your kind ever come out here before."

"You are right," he replied softly in Crow. "This is a whole new breed of horse. Not trappers, not even stiff-necked traders with their whiny ways. No, this is a high-nosed breed, woman."

"They are not staying here at Blanket Chief's lodge?" she asked, using her tribe's appellation for Bridger. "They will be gone soon?"

"A few days at the most, then they will go on to a new country they are looking for."

"Will they turn north, or south? Or go on far to the west where Blanket Chief says the trail people always go—toward the sun's resting place?"

"No, these are not going on to the place the others go," he explained. "This new breed is turning south from here to find the land their god has picked out for them."

"It is good for them," she said with a soft smile. "The First Maker has picked out a place for every people to be. He gave the Crow the very best place."

He smiled too at his mind's image of an old friend. "I remember Rotten Belly telling me how Crow country was in just the right place: to the north the winters were too cold; to the south the summers were too long; to the west were enemies and the mountains were too tall; while to the east the water was not good."

"Was Arapooesh right?"

He combed his fingers along one of her braids wrapped in sleek otter skin and peered down into her eyes. "I have journeyed far, far to the north—up near the country of the Blackfoot where the English trade. And far, far to the south where the Apache roam the mountains and valleys. I have gone all the way to the end of the land where the deep, white-ruffled ocean touches the last place a man can stand with dry moccasins. And many times you have asked me to tell you about that country where I was born far to the east. Sometimes when I think of all the country I have traveled, all the mountains and rivers, valleys and deserts I have crossed in my seasons, my head starts to hurt with the remembering of so much . . . far more than one man can hold in his mind."

"Have you ever found a better place than Crow country for Ti-tuzz?"

Taking her face gently in both of his rough, weathered, cinder-blackened hands, Scratch said, "That's what I am trying to tell you, *ua*." He used the intimate word for *spouse*. "There is no better place, and all other country I have seen is dimmed by the beauty of that wild land we call our home."

"I miss my country," she admitted. "But I would miss you more if I were not with you."

"I promised to take you with me, everywhere I go—and our children too. Until our little ones grow and they are gone with lives of their own, we will be together."

"Magpie will be first," she said with a mother's resignation. "Although she professes that she never wants to go."

"Yes. One day soon she will admit that she is ready to leave us."

"Perhaps when she gives her heart away, as a woman will do for the man she loves."

Titus squeezed her, then said, "And Flea will be next—when he grows old enough to be with other young warriors and sleep in a shelter of his own."

"That will happen before he even picks a wife," she speculated.

"And little Jackrabbit," he said. "But, that time seems so distant now that it is hard to see even with far-seeing eyes."

Waits shifted her weight a little self-consciously and asked, "So what of Jackrabbit's little brother or sister?"

"It would be a long, long time before that child would be ready to leave its mother and father."

Then she pulled away from him slightly, within arm's length, so she could hold his wrists and gaze into his eyes. "So what child do you hope Jackrabbit will have? A little brother, or a little sister?"

"He is in his fifth summer, so what do you think Jackrabbit would like most?"

"I think he would like a little sister."

"And why would a boy want to have a little sister?"

"I only know that I want another baby girl," she confessed.

"Yes," he said in a whisper. "Magpie was so dear. Girls are very different from boys. A sister for Jackrabbit would be good."

"But," she said, the smile gone from her eyes, "you would not be disappointed if Jackrabbit has a little brother?"

He began to look at her strangely, something gradually coming into focus for him the way he would twist on that last section of his spyglass as he brought a distant object into the sharpest focus. He did not realize his mouth was hanging open until she placed a fingertip beneath his chin and pushed it closed for him. With other fingers she took hold of his hand, moved it down to her belly.

"I first came to know while you were gone with Blanket Chief, taking Shell Woman to Sweete," she explained as she pressed his palm flat against her soft, rounded belly with both of hers.

He stood there, still speechless.

"So this morning while you talked with these strange white men as you worked," Waits continued, "I sat in the sun, closed my eyes, and made a prayer of my own."

Bass swallowed hard. "Y-yes?"

"I prayed that you would find joy in this news."

"H-how could I not?" he exclaimed. "You are . . . we are? Another baby?"

She nodded, unable to speak at that moment, the tears starting to spill down her high-boned, copper-skinned cheeks.

Immediately he wrapped his arms around her in a fierce embrace, hoisting her off the ground in a half circle before he plopped her back down on the dirt of that open-air blacksmith shop at Fort Bridger.

"H-how soon will this child come?"

"Winter," she said, a little breathless. "Maybe as early as your day of birth, but probably later."

"Winter," he repeated, then suddenly kissed her, hard, on the mouth, and quickly dropped to his knees before her, pressing his cheek and ear against that slightly rounded belly.

"Do you want this child born in Crow country?"

She used both her hands to gently cup the top of that faded blue bandanna tied around his head. "This child will choose its own place to be born, Ti-tuzz. If we are back among my people, or if we are somewhere else of our choosing—this child will decide."

He pressed his mouth against her soft belly and kissed it.

"No matter where we are when the child's time comes, as long as we are all together there," she said as he got to his feet once more, "then it will be as the First Maker has intended."

"I will be there," he promised, tears stinging his eyes as he painfully remembered not being with her when she gave birth to Jackrabbit. "For you, I will always be there."

TEN

"Wagons coming!"

Titus Bass turned at the cry from his son's throat. Wiping sweat from his eyes with a scrap of scratchy burlap there beneath the shady awning, he squinted at the front gate, both sides flung open for the day. At that moment Flea burst into view, reined his racing pony to a dust-stirring halt, and leaped to the ground near the fire pit.

"Wagons coming, Popo!"

As the barefoot boy came racing up to him on foot, yanking the spotted pony behind him, Scratch smiled and said, "Your American talk is gettin' real good, Flea. Real good."

Then he raised that grimy hand clutching the scrap of burlap and shaded his brow, staring beyond the boy and through the gate at the thickening cloud of dust to the northeast in that valley of Black's Fork.

Bridger stepped from the store and glanced his way before he slapped his hat on his head, and he too regarded the distance. "That boy of your'n got the eyes of a hawk, Titus Bass!"

Looping his arm over his son's bare shoulder, he proudly said, "That he do, Gabe. You want he should go with you to greet 'em?"

"Hell, his American is good as can be. I'll tag along, but why don't we let Flea lead 'em over to that southwest meadow where the grass ain't awready been cropped down."

He gazed at his son and asked, "You understand Gabe?"

Flea stared up at his father and nodded. With a gulp he said, "I go ride. Tell wagon men follow me. Meadow camp, good grass."

"Can you tell 'em why we don't want 'em to camp near the fort?"

"Bridger's grass is Bridger's grass," Flea said, mimicking a stern tone. "Bridger's grass for all year round, grass for Bridger. Not for wagon men."

Patting the lad on the head, Titus said, "Get along with you now, son. You take them folks to the meadow on up the river two mile."

The boy's smile could not have covered more of his face as he wheeled away in a scurry of dust. Seizing a double handful of the pony's mane he heaved himself onto its back, settled, and brushed some of his unbound hair from his eyes as he yanked the reins to the side. With excited yelps, Digger and Ghost suddenly appeared from the side of the stockade, already racing at full gallop as they sprinted to catch up to Flea's racing claybank.

"I 'spect Shadrach bring his kin back here any day now," Bridger said as he stood there a moment longer.

Titus asked, "Figger they'll tag along with a train on their way down from Green River?"

"Could be," Jim replied. "Been two weeks since I sent up them four coons to take over at the ferry."

Fifteen days ago it had been. Barely a week before that four more former skin trappers from the old American Fur Company days showed up at Fort Bridger, men who had served in Jim's brigades during those last half dozen years of the beaver trade. Each of them had a woman along, two with children in tow, and a third squaw so swollen with child she waddled about like a melon ready to burst. Shoshone gals, they were. The old friends weren't looking for a handout, just a way they could manage to live something resembling the old life and still buy a few geegaws for their women. Jim offered them work at the ferry.

All four leaped at the opportunity handed them by their old booshway. One claimed he'd even worked a rope-and-pulley ferry across the Wabash back in the Illinois country. When Gabe dug in, he found out the former beaver man did know his stuff. Hiring the quartet to help out the three there already would allow Shadrach to bring his family back to the fort, turning over the operation at Green River to that party of old comrades. The four were to pass along Bridger's request for Sweete to return as soon as he could get packed up. The big man's help was sure to come in handy around the post while the emigrant season wound down, now that they were nearing the end of that summer of '47.

"Better get on that ol' horse of your'n, Gabe!" Bass cried as Jim shuffled away toward the gate, heading for the second, smaller stockade that served as a corral. "You figger to tag along with that lad o' mine, you best be quick about it!"

In that moment of watching his oldest son rein his pony around and around Bridger playfully, Bass felt an immense pride in the lad. What a figure he cut upon this three-year-old claybank Jim had given him as a gift to train several weeks back, right after the trader returned from Fort John with the first train of the season, piloted by Joseph Reddeford Walker himself. Seemed the former

Bonneville man had gone east to the mouth of the La Ramee earlier that summer to see if he could stir up any work guiding emigrants through to Oregon. By the peak of the summer season there had been seven parties already come by Fort Bridger, not including those Mormons with Brigham Young on their way to the valley of the Salt Lake.

Such pride he felt for the youngster as he watched him take off at a lope beside Bridger for the northeast. Flea wore his long, brown-tinted hair loose and unfettered in the hot breeze, floating gently as the pony bounded along to match its young rider's exuberance. Flea twisted around slightly and waved his arm one time before the two of them were gone beyond the edge of the gate, into the trees, following the much-scarred pattern of ruts where little of the dry, browning grasses grew any longer. In turn he waved to the boy, then clucked to himself and turned back toward the shady awning, where clung the heavy stench of cinders and fire smoke, white-hot iron and half-burnt coffee.

"He's a good lad," Titus said with a stirring in his breast for the child quickly becoming a young man. "No man could want for any better."

Come this winter, Waits-by-the-Water might well give him another son. Or, perhaps another daughter. Gawd, but it did not matter—long as Waits was delivered of the child with ease and the babe was whole in body and mind. He had seen a few of those infants born not quite whole: missing fingers, perhaps a clubbed foot, maybe their eyes sightless or they were unable to hear the sound of rattle or whistle when a grandparent gave them a naming ceremony. It was his only prayer—that this child and its mother would come through the birthing whole. He picked up the leather-wrapped handle of the hammer and looked at the shady doorway of the store. Thinking of her. Waits was not a young woman any longer. Her scarred, pockmarked face was much fuller than it had ever been. Three youngsters given birth, along with so much loss and sadness since she became his back in '33. Older than most Crow women when they customarily took a husband, she had preferred to wait for the husband she wanted— wait to have children and raise a family with him.

Twice he'd almost lost her.

Bass dropped the hammer on the anvil again and stepped to the fire hopper, stirring the glowing coals with the tongs, digging out the hottest of the short strips of repair metal he was fabricating. He plopped it down on the anvil and took up the hole punch in his left hand, the hammer in his right.

The first time, he had believed she was taken from him by Josiah Paddock, that winter after he and Josiah returned from lifting the scalp from an old white-headed friend. Finding the pair of them together beneath the robes, Waits as naked as she got when she lay with him, Titus tore off to the west, plunging into the dead of winter and danger, spitting in the eye of death as he undertook a mission so risky that only it could come close to easing the pain of losing her to his best friend. Losing them both at once was almost more than a mortal could bear. . . .

With the punch crafted from a solid spike of oil-tempered iron positioned a few inches from the end of the strip of band iron, Titus slammed the hammer down on top of it, jarring both of his forearms. If nothing else, he had mused nearly every day of this hot summer, his hands and arms, shoulders and back, were all the stronger for this smithy's toil.

Years later the Blackfoot had ripped her from him and the Crow. Warriors already grown sickly with the smallpox that ate up their flesh as it sucked away their life with an unquenchable fever. That deadly illness had consumed her brother, but Titus dared his damnedest to keep her alive. The scars it left on her face could never diminish the beauty she remained on the inside, although it took long seasons for her spirit to heal after that lonely walk she had taken with the ghosts along the edge of the sky.

It took more than two dozen strikes with that hammer against the flared top of the punch before he finally pierced a half-inch hole through the strap iron. He laid the punch aside and picked up the tongs, returning the strap to the fire for reheating before pulling another strap of iron from the glowing coals. With a series of holes punched in these short strips of iron, most every repair could be made to a cracked yoke, tree, or running gear, even hold together a wagon box itself. He could bind up what was broken with iron strap and coarse bolts, work everything down tight with the muscles in his back so the emigrant could move on to Fort Hall beside the Snake River. Follow the twists of the Snake all the way to the Columbia . . . and the sojourners found themselves in Oregon country.

With a repair to this or an exchange for that, Titus Bass would get those farmers a little farther on their epic journey. Fix up a busted axle, trade for a proper-sized wheel. Maybe even refit a tire to the wood shrinking in this high, desert climate . . . if the farmer relented and gave Titus enough time to do a proper repair during a brief layover at Fort Bridger, heart of the Rocky Mountains.

The sweat beaded down the bridge of his nose, hung there pendant for only an instant, then landed on the glowing iron with a faint hiss.

Twice before he thought he'd lost her. Old as he was now, Titus didn't figure he could live through losing her again.

"Titus Bass?"

He quickly turned at the unexpected sound of a woman's voice. She stood framed in a splash of bright sunshine, her fingers knitted together before her. A poke bonnet shaded her sunburned, weathered face as she peered at him standing in the shade of that brushy arbor, where he was plunging a new iron tire into a narrow trough of water with a resounding sizzle.

"That's me," he replied after a cursory glance—these settlement women all ended up looking pretty much the same—then turned back to his hoop of iron. With his empty left hand he scooped up a dribble of water and smeared it down his face grimy with cinders and smoke, streaked with rivulets of sweat. "You're from the train camped over west what come in yestiddy?"

"Yes. Just before noon yesterday."

"The store's off that way," and he pointed.

"I was just there," she confessed. "That's where I happed to overhear your name."

Squint-eyed, he turned his head to peer at her again. "Oh?"

"Major Bridger was speaking of you to some of our leaders," she explained, inching a step closer, but stopped again, her hands still clenched in front of her apron. "One of the men, he's needing some blacksmithing work done. That's when I heard your name."

"You said that awready, ma'am." Sensing some impatience with the woman, he dragged the heavy iron tire he had fitted for a front wheel out of the trough and carried it to the outside wall of the Bridger cabin, where he hung it from a wooden peg.

Quietly she explained, "I suppose there are far fewer chances of bumping into a Titus Bass out here in the Rocky Mountains than there are chances finding a Titus Bass along the Mississippi, or running onto him back in St. Louis."

He slowly turned toward her and snatched up that small scrap of burlap. He wiped it down his sweaty neck and across his bare chest, smearing more of the blackened cinders across his reddened skin. "St. Louie?"

"Where you and I first met," she said after another step that brought her right to the edge of the shade.

"W-where was that?"

"Emily Truesdale's sporting house."

A memory long submerged beneath the layers of seasons, miles, and a thousand other faces. But not near forgotten.

His heart misstepped as he searched for words his dry tongue could speak. "Did you . . . work for the woman?"

"Of a time, I did." She stepped beneath the awning, her hands kneading one another now, anxiously. "If you're the Titus Bass I later saw at Amos Tharp's livery back in the late winter of thirty-four, then I am . . . your daughter, Amanda."

Instantly he felt a twinge of shame—for his sweated body, smeared with dust and blacksmith grime, stinking no less than a horse would at the end of a long day's ride. "You're Amanda?" He quickly turned for the wall of the cabin, where his cotton shirt hung on a wooden peg. As he got it over his head and began to smooth it over his sticky frame, Titus asked, "Marissa's daughter?"

"Your daughter," she said, finally moving toward him without stopping. As he flung open his arms she pushed back her bonnet, letting it fall to hang suspended from her neck with her long, ash-hued curls. "Father—"

Scratch folded her into his arms, unable to utter a sound, feeling his legs going as weak as they had when she had declared her existence to him back in

Tharp's St. Louis barn. Every bit as quickly he brought her away from him to gaze down into her face. No longer did she possess the pudgy, childlike face of her mother the way she had when she confronted him so many winters ago.

"H-how long's that make it?"

Shaking her head slightly, she made a tally. "More than thirteen years, Father."

"F-Father," he repeated. "Sounds so . . . starchy an' high-backed to me." He rubbed the top of her shoulders. "How 'bout you callin' me Pa."

She grinned, and it lit her whole face. "Pa. Yes, yes, I can call you that, Pa." Then the light in her face was gone, replaced with one of concern as she stared at him intently. "Your eye. What's become of it?"

"Don't know," he admitted with a shrug. "Happened that same spring I rode back to St. Louie. After I come back west. At Bents' big lodge on the Arkansas River. Ain't see'd wuth a damn from the eye ever since."

"It's gone cloudy," she said, inspecting it closely. "I've known some folks that's happened to."

Hopeful, he asked her, "They ever get better of it?"

"No, Pa," and she shook her head. "Wish I could tell you different. But I never knew of a person, their eyes got better after they got cloudy such a way. Yours no better since?"

"Can't say it's got worse neither," he admitted. "Allays made do with the one."

Leaning close, she studied his one good eye. "I didn't remember till just now—but your eyes are green. Like mine. They're green like mine."

With a self-conscious swallow he realized his tongue was so dry it nearly clung to the roof of his mouth. "Talkin' is dusty work—lemme get a drink."

Releasing her, Scratch leaped over to his drinking bucket and pulled an iron dipper from it. A lot of it sloshed on his dusty moccasins as he brought it to his lips and slurped what he hadn't managed to spill. Then he suddenly thought of genteel manners. "You want some?"

"Yes, I would like that," she answered, coming over and taking the ladle from him after he had dipped her a drink. "I never knew there could be heat like this."

"You think it's hotter here'n it gets hot back to St. Louie?"

Wiping the back of her hand across her lips, Amanda said, "A different heat. Back there is so heavy, sticky with misery. But the farther west we've come, the drier it got. Like the sun's been sucking every drop right outta me . . . Pa."

He smiled at that, hearing her use that special word. "You come west with that wagon train?"

"Yes, all the way from Westport."

"That's a long way for a gal . . . for a woman on her own."

She laughed easily at that. "I ain't alone, Pa. I've had a family for some time."

"A-a family?"

Leaning toward him, she asked, "Lookit me, real close. I ain't the young gal you met back to St. Louie all them summers ago. Lookit these lines I see when I look in my mirror every night. Can't stand to look in it the mornings when I rise, what for all the aging I see. It's better to see my tired ol' wrinkles by candlelight when the children are put to bed and I have a few minutes—"

"Children? Y-you got young'uns?"

"Land sakes, Pa! I said I come west with my family—children and a husband too."

"You married and started your family," he said, on the verge of wanting to believe it. "Wh-where are they?"

"Back at the wagon camp," she confided. "After I heard your name early this morning in the store, and looked outside the door to find you pounding on that anvil—I bided my time."

"Didn't come right over an' make yourself knowed to me?"

With a wag of her head, Amanda confessed, "I wanted to be alone when I came to talk. So I walked back to the camp with Roman and the children. Told him I was coming back to wrangle a deal for some calicos at the store from Major Bridger's wife. He'd have to watch the children while I came back to the post."

"Gabe . . . Jim Bridger don't have a wife no more," he explained. "She got took givin' birth to their last child."

Her eyes filled with consternation. "But . . . it was an Indian woman."

"Which'un you talk with?" he asked. "Which Injun woman?"

"She was a taller one. Had a long face, not the round-faced woman—"

"You met my wife!"

"The . . . same one you were . . . with when you came back to St. Louis in thirty-four?"

"I got back to her down in Taos afore she birthed our first child, a daughter."

Amanda's eyes widened. "She's here too? Your daughter . . . your other daughter?"

"Magpie," he said. "My boy—he come with Bridger to lead your train down to the south meadow to camp. You see him yesterday, spy him with Bridger?"

"Our wagon was so far back in the train," she explained. "The dust and all— we never saw anything happened up front."

Bubbling with enthusiasm, he said, "He's a great boy, more'n ten years old now."

Amanda dabbed a fingertip at a bead of sweat that was collecting in the hollow under her lower lip. "So you have two children?"

"Actual', there's three. 'Nother boy. Four summers old now. An' there's one on its way this comin' winter."

"Your fourth?" Then she caught herself. "I mean, that would be your fifth, counting me—of course. I was your first!"

"That's some, for a ol' fella like me."

"Pa, I've got four of my own," she declared, glowing with pride. "My oldest, a boy, he isn't as old as your . . . Magpie."

He took a step back and regarded her with a big grin. "Your whole family's here? Goin' west?"

"Yes, Pa."

"Where away—California or Oregon?"

"Oregon." She said it with a special reverence. "Roman's been wanting to come west for almost three years now. They been hard years." The softness in her eyes melted away with what he took to be a sour-tinged remembrance. "Roman, he was gonna get to Oregon, or kill himself back there in Missouri."

"Kill hisself?"

She wagged her head dolefully. "First years of our life together, things went good for us. We lived on his daddy's farm, worked it together, one big family. Then his pa died, took by the lung sickness, coughing up blood till he got so weak he couldn't fight off the fever anymore. Next year Roman's ma was taken by cholera. They kept her in to town, in an old chicken coop an' away from folks so she wouldn't make no others sick. It near tore Roman apart. But, everyone said it was the best for our children. We had two who could walk by then, and one just born too."

"Losing your family ain't good on a body's heart," he said. "Your mother, Marissa, how's she now?"

"I haven't seen her in over five years," Amanda confessed. "Wanted to see her one last time before we started to Oregon, but by then she was married to a river man and moved east to Owensboro. On the Ohio. I pray she's been well— there's so much sickness back there. I hope we can keep on going to Oregon without losing any more folks."

"You ain't lost some of your own young'uns?"

"Mercy, no," and she shook her head. "Others. People we came to know as the train was forming up outside of Westport. Lost friends on the way here. All along the Platte, they took sick, one after another. A child here. A mother there. A father on down the trail a few more miles. Seemed like every Sunday morning we had another person already ailing so bad for us to pray over them. By the time the week was out, we'd have us a funeral. Wasn't till we got to Chimney Rock that we wasn't burying folks along the way."

"Air got drier," he explained quietly. "Maybe some of that ague an' tick-sicks got dried up."

"Yes, it does seem we're all healthier now," she agreed. "Thank God for His blessings."

"Yes, Amanda," he agreed as he pulled his daughter against him again. "Thank God for all His great an' many blessings."

She raised herself on the toes of her dusty, cracked boots and planted a kiss on his grimy cheek. The black soot she came away with around her mouth made him laugh. Dipping the cuff of a sleeve on his shirt into the water bucket, he dabbed it around her cracked lips.

"You ought'n keep some tallow on your mouth," he advised. "Won't get so sore like it is."

"I'll be fine," she claimed. "We'll all be fine once we get to Oregon. Everything Roman's read says it rains plenty there. Crops grow nearly by themselves, all the papers say."

"It's a good place for to raise crops, Amanda," he confirmed. "Raise up your family too."

"C'mon, Pa," she prodded him, pulling on an elbow toward the edge of the brush awning. "I want you to introduce me to your wife, to all your children."

He stopped in his tracks. "How'm I gonna meet your family?"

"I don't think the company's moving on for two, maybe three, more days," she declared. "I thought I'd see if you wanted to meet them tomorrow."

"Want to meet 'em?" he exclaimed. "Hell, I want you go fetch 'em right now and bring the hull clan back here a hour or so afore suppertime."

"T-today?"

"So we got some time to talk afore an' after supper both!"

That seemed to strike her speechless for a moment. "Is this an invite to supper with your family, Pa?"

"Damn right—er, 'scuse me, Amanda," he apologized. "Bring that husband of your'n, and those four young'uns over for supper. I'll tell Waits-by-the-Water to put another hindquarter to roast over the fire for supper—"

"Waits-by-the-Water," she repeated. "Ever since St. Louis, I've punished myself for not remembering her name. All these years, I wished I could have remembered your wife's name."

"S'all right now," he said. "I hope you two take to each other."

"When I was walking back here from camp alone to see you, I kept thinking that she must surely be used to white women, since you two live here at Major Bridger's fort where so many white folks come through all summer long. But I was afraid too that she'd look down her nose at me for being a silly young white woman."

"I don't think Waits-by-the-Water could look down her nose at anyone," he stated. "She's the kindest, most gentle an' loving person I met in my whole blamed life, Amanda."

"Wouldn't want her thinking any less of me because I'm younger than her, white and all."

"How old are you now?" he asked her, failing to recall.

"I turned thirty-two on the trail, Pa. Back in June, along the North Platte."

His face screwed up a minute as he did his best ciphering right there in his head. "Thirty-two? Why, you ain't much younger'n Waits is. She's in her thirty-second summer."

"Sh-she's the same age as me?"

He nodded. "Can't be more'n a few months older'n you, at the most. Why, that alone'll give you two so much to talk about."

"She speaks English?"

"Waits talks real good American. Magpie and Flea too. Jackrabbit, now he's getting the hang of it as he gets older."

She smiled. "Supper here sounds grand, Pa. If you don't think we'll be imposing on her, Waits-by-the-Water."

"I don't think there's a chance of that, Amanda," he explained. "Soon as I came back to Taos to fetch her north to her home country, I started telling her all about you, 'bout your mother and grandpa too. We even talked about me takin' her back to St. Louie some time, to look you up and spend some time. But . . . St. Louie and all them folks, all them farms an' houses an' crowded towns back there—just never seemed like a good enough idea for me to do."

Amanda nodded and reached out to take one of his gritty hands in both of hers. "So, I had to come west to find you, didn't I?"

"That what you was intendin' to do?"

"No, I really never thought I'd see you again, Pa," she confessed. "Figured you'd be dead, killed by Injuns or bears or froze in the mountains by now. Never figured I'd hear your name spoken again in the balance of my days."

"Then you heard tell of Titus Bass in the store at Fort Bridger."

She laughed. "Even heard your name cursed at Fort Laramie. The Frenchmen there swore they'd love to cut your throat, if they ever got hands on you!"

"So you figgered I'd gone under awready?"

"Chances weren't good for a man surviving this long out here, Pa—were they?"

"No, Amanda," he admitted. "But, I had the spirits smiling down on me ever' since I come west in twenty-five. Ain't no other reason I come through all the scrapes I put behind me."

"God's been good seeing me through this journey so far, Pa," she said, casting down her eyes. "Lately, we haven't had the best life, Roman and me."

His eyes narrowed. "He ain't been bad to you, has he?"

She looked at him again, saying, "No, no—Roman's been a good husband. Strong and full of love, Pa. For me and the children. God knows he isn't the brightest man I could have married, but he had the best heart."

"Why you say you ain't had the best life, you two?"

Shrugging her shoulders, Amanda turned slightly from her father. "Sometimes I think there's certain people just not meant to make a go of things in life. No matter how hard they try, no matter they throw their whole heart into something . . . time after time."

"There's some folks who wander this way and that afore they eventual' find the way of their life," he responded after a long moment of thought. "Your own pa was that sort, Amanda."

"There's been times when it was real hard on the children," she explained, looking up at him again. "Row . . . my Roman—sometimes he gets dark. Those were the times I could tell the failure was eating him up inside, Pa. He'd look around at other folks who had a store and they're making a little money for their family. Or, Roman would look around and see other folks making the ground work for them, feeding their family and putting a little money away for the lean times. But . . . seems like it's always been lean times for us. Never got any better. Last few years, we been going from bad times to worse times, no matter what Roman threw himself into with all his might."

From the look on her face and the sound of her words, he was almost afraid to ask her the question, "You still love him?"

Yet she nodded her head emphatically and smiled as she said, "Oh, yes, Pa. I love him. Enough to follow him to Oregon Territory where he wants to make a new dream happen for us. Roman's so sure that will be the place for us. You should see the way his face shines when he talks about the new life we'll have out there."

"Does my heart good to see that your man wants the best for his family," Titus replied, reassured.

"He does, Pa. I know it in my heart."

"So you're gonna stand by him?" he asked.

"Every step of the way," she declared with conviction. "We're doing this for the children, going to Oregon for our family. Make a new start we haven't been able to do anywhere else as we moved across Missouri, from one settlement to the next . . . hoping each new place was going to be the one where we'd really sink down roots and build up something good."

Holding out his arms, Bass stepped toward her. Amanda came into the shelter of her father's arms and laid her cheek against his shoulder. He said, "Ever'thing I hear about Oregon tells me it's the place for a farmer's family to put down those roots and make a life for themselves."

"We started out reading all the papers and books about Oregon we could find," she explained. "Right from the first, Row said it got much more rain than we got back home in Missouri. Some people wrote that it didn't take much for anything to grow out there: just scratch a hole in the ground, drop in the seed, and wait for it to sprout right up on its own!"

"Other folks what already come through this summer all said pretty much the same thing, Amanda," he emphasized. "On their faces is writ all the much trouble they been through getting this far west, but in their eyes is still the light of where they know they're going."

"I never knew the journey would be this hard on us, this tough on the children," she admitted. "Never gone through anything like this that sucks me dry of all my strength by the end of every day . . . laying my head down every night, knowing I gotta get back up in the morning and do it all over again."

"Sometimes your life can seem like it's taking you nowhere," he agreed thoughtfully. "But you just keep putting one foot out in front of the other, then one day—you an' Roman gonna be standing in Oregon where you was meant to be."

She backed up a step and gazed into his eyes. "There's been times when we made camp late in the afternoon, to give us time to cook and clean up after supper before it got dark—and we'd look back to the east. How it makes my heart sink when I can see where we got up that very morning, Pa! After miles and miles of dust and heat, rocks and creek crossings, flies and gnats, and the sun allays sucking every drop of water outta me . . . and I can still see where we got up that morning!"

"Them wagons, ox or mule, ain't made for covering ground fast, Amanda," he sympathized. "Hell, your family damn well could mount up on horses, take along some pack animals, and light out from here to Oregon. Make it in half the time, I'd wager."

"H-half?"

"But you'd be living off the land," he continued. "An' when you got to Oregon, you wouldn't have all them things you brung with you to make that new home for yourselves when you got there."

Staring at the ground, Amanda said, "I've got a set of my grandmother's dishes in our wagon. Packed down in the flour barrel. Brought her bed and quilt too."

"See? You couldn't leave none of that behind!"

Nodding, she agreed, "Others, they've left a little here, and a little there along the trail—lightening the load the farther we went. But me, I just gotta keep up my courage for the days to come, the way I kept up my courage ever since we put Westport behind us. I can only pray to the Lord that the road's gonna get easier from here on out."

He took a deep breath, let it out slowly. "Truth be, Amanda . . . the way from here gets tougher. What you've come through since leaving Fort John on the Platte, it's about the same clear on to Fort Hall. But from there to the Columbia by way of the Snake—that's some bad, bad country."

Her sunburned face went haggard, drawn. "We haven't seen the worst of the trail?"

Wagging his head, Titus told his daughter, "No. There's times out there a farmer or shopkeeper from back east gonna stop and wonder why he's in the middle of the wilderness. It's gonna seem like it goes on forever, with no way out, not back east or on west. That's where your Roman is either gonna have his dream go up in smoke, or he's gonna grip it even tighter'n he holds on to you, Amanda. Out there . . . where you're taking your family to find your dream— that's where you—*you,* Amanda—are gonna have to put your whole heart into the journey to see the rest of your family through."

"I kept hoping . . ."—her voice sounded small and weakened as she stared at the anvil—"that when we got halfway, the road would get better, easier on the animals and the wagons, easier on us, too. Ever since I couldn't see Westport behind us no more, I've been praying that the way would get better."

"But I'll bet you got harder, toughened up, as you come west, Amanda," he attempted to cheer her. "And what you come through awready is gonna make you able to last out the hard scrapes that lay ahead of you."

She reached down and took one of his hands in both of hers. "I've got a good husband, a loving man. In my heart I know he's gonna get us to Oregon. And the Lord is gonna watch over us—see us all the way through."

Smiling, Titus told his daughter, "Don't you feel your heart jump when you think about making this journey to a new home, Amanda?"

"It's about the only thing helps me get back up in the darkness before sunrise every morning, Pa. I look out there ahead of us, and think to myself: 'Just over that next hill I'm gonna see our new home.' Then we make it to the top of that rise, so—I pick out another hill to look at and dream on. Over and over I do the same thing through the day till we finally stop for the night, when I can shake the dust outta my hair and clothes, put some salve on the sunburn and them bites the flies gave me."

"That's the way I done for myself all these years," he declared. "Take a day at a time, take a hill at a time if I have to. Best part is seeing some new country, Amanda. Where I ain't never been before—"

"Why don't you come with us?" she blurted out, hope filling her eyes.

He could only stare at her dumbfounded.

"Bring your family," Amanda pleaded. "There's gotta be some new country for you to roam between here and there, Pa. Come see it for yourself."

"I don't think I wanna ever go to Oregon again, Amanda," he tried to explain. "It's become a place for settlers and sodbusters. Not the place for a wanderin' man like me."

Pressing her lips together, Amanda nodded. "You weren't the settling-down kind back when you knew my mother. Likely you never will be, Pa."

"But that don't make me no better or worse'n a farmer like your Roman," he explained. "Just differ'nt. I ain't never been the sort to want those things, Amanda. I run away from farming back in Kaintuck when I was sixteen. About the age you run away from your ma."

Taking a step toward him, Amanda looped an arm through one of his. "Won't do me any good to try talking you into bringing your family to Oregon with us?"

He gazed down into her green eyes and shook his head. "Can't. This here's where I wanna stay. Ain't never thought about leaving the mountains."

Disappointment clouded her eyes. "I won't say anything more about it, because I can remember how anxious you were to get healed up enough so you could get out of St. Louis and back to the mountains."

"Back to my wife, and where I was s'posed to be," he confided. "Now, you best be on your way to fetch up that family an' have 'em back here afore suppertime."

She took a few steps, then turned to him once more. "Pa, I need to ask you a favor. Please don't say nothing to Roman about what I said of me ever being afraid of us going to Oregon."

"I unnerstand," Titus agreed. "Just atween you an' me."

Interlocking her fingers again, Amanda appeared nervous. "I can't imagine what it'd do to Row if he was to find out I've been afraid of us finding a place to live out our lives. If he learned that I was able to tell you things I haven't said to no one in so long."

"That makes your pa proud to be the ears you told. We'll keep our talk atween ourselves. No one else need know. Now, you best get along back to camp so you're here before supper."

"I can't wait to meet my brothers and my new sister," she said, her eyes growing a little misty as she stood there at the border of shadow and sunlight. "I . . . I never had no brothers and sisters before, Pa."

"You do now, Amanda."

She asked, "And you know what you got in turn?"

"What?"

"You got four grandchildren."

That took his breath a moment, struck with the sudden sureness of the revelation.

"Damn, if I don't," he exclaimed quietly. "Here I am, 'bout to have my fifth child come this winter . . . an' I got four grandpups awready! If that don't shine!"

ELEVEN

"Ain't you glad to see me, Scratch?" Shadrach Sweete roared.

Bass felt troubled as he peered southwest across the valley of Black's Fork. "It ain't that I'm not happy to have you back," he explained with a little irritation, watching the big man rein up beside him and slide out of the saddle. "I spotted the dust from your travois and them animals—figgered it was my daughter comin'."

"Magpie?" Sweete snorted as he approached, leading his horse. "That li'l gal can't raise much dust by her own self."

They clasped forearms and shook, pounding one another on the shoulder there on the flat some forty yards outside the main gate at Fort Bridger. "Ain't Magpie I was meaning. I got another daughter."

Sweete inched back. "I never knowed."

He grinned with pride. "Name's Amanda. She come in yestiddy with the last train down from the ferry."

"How'd she know her pa was here?"

Titus shook his head. "Didn't. Bound away for Oregon with her husband. Got four li'l ones of her own too."

"Then she ain't a young'un herself," Shad commented as they started moseying toward the post walls. "When's last time you see'd her?"

"Late winter of thirty-four."

Sweete looked over at Bass with a moment of study, then asked, "You still recognize her after all that time?"

"She come found me," he declared. "Was in the store yonder when she heard Bridger give my name to some fella from the train what needed a li'l smithy work. Come over to see for herself if I was the one."

Sweete laid his big hand on the shorter man's shoulder. "You really her pa?"

"I am, Shad." It was then they stopped short of the gate and Titus turned to stare at the distance, his one good eye moving across the distant trees. "Thought she'd be back with 'em by now."

"Who?"

"Amanda an' her family. They was coming to dinner."

Sweete cleared his throat thoughtfully, then said with a sympathetic tone, "Maybe her husband ain't the sort to wanna sit down for no dinner with Amanda's pa."

He studied Shad a moment, a new worry intruding on his plans for a happy evening. "Why you say that: He won't wanna eat with me?"

"I dunno. Here this fella's been married to your daughter all these years— who knows if she ever told him her pa was still livin', or where you was in the first place, even when they started out for Oregon. Maybe your Amanda just let it out of the bag on him today real sudden, an' it took him by surprise. Some folks are a mite touchy like that, you see?"

Titus shrugged a shoulder, not wanting to believe it. He wagged his head, saying, "Not likely. What she told me, the fella seems like a good enough sort."

Shad peered at his friend's face. "Sounds like you don't got a thing to worry about."

"Nothing to worry 'bout," Bass repeated, unconvinced. "Just wanna know why they ain't showed up."

"What say we head on over to the camp, have ourselves a look? You an' me."

"I'll get a horse while you tell Shell Woman why you won't be helping her set up the lodge," Titus said in a gush as he started to turn aside. "Tell her she can fetch Waits-by-the-Water to give her a hand! Them two need a time to talk after all the weeks Shell Woman's been away at the ferry."

"I'll wait right here for you!" Sweete hollered back.

Bass suddenly dug in his heels and skidded to a halt. "By the by, tell Shell Woman you an' the young'uns are invited to a special feed tonight in the fort!"

Shad swiped at the sweat trapped at the back of his neck beneath the long, matted mane of hair. "What's so special 'bout tonight?"

"My family's sittin' down to dinner with my daughter an' my four grand-kids," he roared back at Sweete as he bolted away again, beaming anew. "That's what makes this evenin' shine for this here child!"

The two of them and that pair of rascal dogs were no more than a half mile from the emigrants' camp when they realized something out of the ordinary was afoot among these Oregon-bound travelers. Usually these camps were a bustling beehive of activity at this time of the day: young men and boys water-ing the hundreds and hundreds of animals, women and girls bent over fires as they prepared the evening meal, others of all ages moving about, going here and there on one mission or another now that the train was not rolling and they had these precious hours before darkness fell. Repairs to wagons, wheels, guns, or equipment. Medication administered and healing words spoken to those become sick or injured along the last few days of their journey. Older children assigned to watch over the youngest, noisiest, and quickest of foot in camp.

But even those few youngsters Titus spotted on the fringes of the gathered crowd seemed oddly quiet at this time of day; at long last they were allowed to run and play and burn off all that energy they had bottled up through the interminable hours of sitting still in those jostling wagons.

"Somethin' ain't . . . right 'bout this," he said to Shadrach.

"Looks to be a meeting to me," Sweete said, pointing out the large gathering near the bank of Black's Fork.

Most of the emigrants stood, some seated in the grass beneath the shade of a thick copse of overhanging cottonwoods. Men, women, and their children too.

As their horses carried them closer, Titus picked out one voice after another, some raised louder than others to drive home a point. Although he could not make out most of what was being bandied about, he could nonetheless tell from the tone that he had not come upon a lighthearted occasion. Drawing up to the outskirts of the crowd, the two old trappers momentarily caught the attention of the first emigrants to turn, then nudge their neighbors to have themselves a look. In heartbeats most of the hundred-plus people had given the horsemen a quick look of disapproving appraisal before they turned their attention back to what was clearly some grave business at hand.

As Bass peered quickly over the crowd he spotted Amanda peeling herself away from a nest of women and children standing behind an inner cordon of their menfolk. But it wasn't until she had reached the outer fringe of the crowd that he saw she wasn't alone. Her hand gripped that of a young boy, a barefoot child, who shuffled along through the dusty grass to keep pace with his mother's long strides. She turned and leaned down slightly to say something to the child as they circled around the gathering. In response the boy brought his tiny hand to his brow and peered into the distance at the two buckskin-clad horsemen. He still had his hand shading his eyes as Titus kicked out of the saddle and landed on the ground, only a moment before Amanda stopped before him.

"This is my daughter Amanda," Scratch announced as she held out her empty arm for her father. "Amanda, this here's my good friend, Shadrach Sweete. Him an' me, we've been through a lot together over the years—"

"Oh, Pa!" she interrupted him, pain in her voice. "Our train's breaking up!"

He took her shoulder in one strong hand and quickly glanced at the heated argument taking place nearby at the center of the crowd. "That why you was late comin' for supper?"

Amanda's eyes pleaded. "I'm sorry, for we got all caught up in this trouble—trying to sort out what we're gonna do."

"How's your train falling apart?" Sweete repeated.

"We got to Laramie with our company captain," she began to explain. "We elected him at Westport, mostly because he had a little experience on the plains. Last year he'd come out to Fort Laramie on his own to ride part of the trail for himself. Mostly, he got himself elected because he had more money than the rest of us . . . and that meant he had more wagons and guns for our protection, and some hired men along too. But, they weren't family men like the rest of us. Just single fellas, going out to start over in Oregon on the captain's pay."

The fear he read in her eyes made Titus bristle. "Now the rest of you got trouble with some of 'em?"

"Yes . . . well, no," she responded with a frustrated shake of her head. "The captain, his name is Hargrove—back at Laramie he ran onto a pilot who says he knows the country from here on out. Says he's been out to Oregon a half dozen times. Was a mountain trapper too, he claims."

"What's his name?" Sweete demanded suspiciously.

"I can't rightly remember," she answered, her face gray with concern. "Only that Hargrove said he was our Moses," she admitted.

"He here?" Titus asked.

She nodded.

"Point 'im out to me."

Amanda turned with the child still clutching her hand and stepped away to the right where the three of them would have a better view of the central actors in this dramatic dispute taking place beside Black's Fork.

"There he is," Amanda announced, bitterness in her voice pointing quickly. "That's him. Got a full beard like yours, and he's wearing those skin clothes— like yours, Pa."

Peering through the anxious crowd shifting from one foot to the other, Titus trained his good eye on the figure who was turned slightly away from him for the moment. Then the tall man addressing the group took a step forward, and Scratch easily made out the pilot.

"Harris," Sweete whispered it like a curse.

"That nigger gets drunk at the drop of a hat—an' when he does, he ain't leading no one nowhere," Bass grumbled in agreement of Shad's sentiment.

"No, he hasn't made any trouble with his drinking," Amanda argued. "Problem is, the pilot's going off with Hargrove and his wagons."

"Off where?"

"Taking them to California," she said with exasperation and a shake of her head.

Scratch turned from glaring at Harris to look down at his daughter. "Thought you said your train was bound for Oregon?"

Amanda pursed her lips, then said, "Back at Westport we was formed as a company for Oregon Territory. That's where most of us still want to go. But late this afternoon Hargrove sent around his men, calling a council meeting."

"Hargrove?" Shad echoed.

She explained, "When we got here a little while ago, he started off telling us he and his hired men would stay on with us till we reached Fort Hall. That's where Hargrove said he was turning off for California."

"An' your captain is taking your new pilot with him to Californy," Bass completed the dilemma.

"That's right," she answered, reaching out to gently squeeze his hand. "After that we won't have us our company captain and all his guns along. And we won't have our pilot to get us from Fort Hall to the Willamette."

Without turning to look at his tall friend, Scratch glared at the tall, well-dressed speaker named Hargrove and said quietly, "Let's go have us a listen, Shadrach."

Leading their horses, the pair inched forward on foot to the outer edges of the crowd. It was there that Titus whispered, "I didn't see him my own self earlier this summer, but them Marmons Gabe an' me run into on the Sandy said they come across Harris at Pacific Springs in the pass. Coming from Oregon hisself, he told 'em. When Brigham Young said he had no need to hire him to lead his bunch into the valley of the Salt Lake, Harris said he'd push on to Fort John—where he claimed there'd be plenty of trains what'd hire him to pilot them through."

"No-good bastard found him some work, he did," Sweete responded in a whisper so sharp that it made a few of the nearby emigrants turn their heads and flick a disquieting look at the pair in buckskins.

Bass leaned over and whispered to Amanda, "That's your Moses, all right. His name's Moses Harris. Sometimes, that nigger goes by the name o' Black Harris. His cheeks burned so dark the skin shines like burnt powder. How he come by that name."

With an involuntary shudder, she declared, "I'd just as soon he go off a different way, Pa. Never did like the way he looked at me or any other woman with the train. Them eyes of his all over me—makes my skin tremble like I was cold and had spiders crawling on me at the same time."

"From what I recollect, that'un's a coward . . . less'n he's got a bellyful of John Barleycorn," Shad observed.

"Shshshsh!" One of the emigrants turned and pressed a finger to her lips at the two old mountain men.

"—which means all of you are free to follow me to my new home in California," boomed the tall man who towered over the stockier Harris, "or, you can make your own way to Oregon without our help."

"I recall this company elected you our captain," protested a tall, wide-shouldered man as he stepped from the edge of the crowd, tugging at one of his frayed suspenders that threatened to slip off his shoulder. He was clearly growing agitated. "Back at Westport, before we ever headed out, we elected you, Hargrove—because you said you was gonna lead us to Oregon."

"A man has a right to change his mind," Phineas Hargrove argued now with a winning smile. "Between leaving Westport behind and the Green River crossing, I've come to believe California is where my fortunes lie."

Another, heavier man lunged from the inner edge of the gathering to growl, "But we was formed around you to take us to Oregon. That's where we all wanna go! We're a Oregon company!"

Hargrove turned to the shorter man with that look of disdain written upon his face. "And you're all free to follow your dreams from Fort Hall," he reminded them. "But any of you who want to see what California has to offer, I repeat that Mr. Harris here has agreed to lead us south and west from Fort Hall, to the Humboldt and on to northern California."

That's when the tall man with the thick neck that disappeared into the collar of his shirt took three more steps that brought him onto the open ground at the center of the great circle where Hargrove and Harris held court. Amanda raised herself on the toes of her boots and whispered into her father's ear, "That's Roman."

"Roman?" Titus repeated, appraising the man. "Your husband?"

She nodded.

As Roman Burwell came to a sudden halt before Hargrove, three of the captain's hired men stepped protectively closer to their employer, their flinty gazes full of intimidation for the farmer who said, "There was something about you, Hargrove—right from when I first laid eyes on you at Westport. Something slick and oily from the start."

"I got you this far, Burwell," the captain sneered down his long, patrician nose. "I can't nurse the rest of you all the way to Oregon. You'll have to get there on your own." With an amused grin, Hargrove stepped away from his hired men and walked around Burwell tauntingly. "Why, the rest of you could even elect Burwell here as your new captain!"

But that suggestion met with a strained, awkward silence while Hargrove waited for someone to speak up.

Instead, it was Burwell himself who shattered the silence, "Ain't no one gonna choose me for to be the captain, Hargrove. I ain't got the makings of a train captain. Just a simple man. I could never pretend to be nothing I ain't. But that's just what you done to the rest of us."

Hargrove ground to a halt and he leaned in at the side of the farmer's face. "What's that mean, Burwell?"

The big sodbuster struggled to keep his beefy hands at his sides, clenching and unclenching his fists. "One thing I can't abide by is a man saying he's one thing, when he's lying through his teeth at me. I brung my family all the way here—hell, we all got our families with us. We was bound for Oregon, following a man who said he was gonna lead us to the Willamette River . . . and now we find out that man's a damned liar!"

The short, black quirt suspended from the end of Hargrove's wrist flew out in a blur, the two ends of the horsewhip catching Burwell high across one cheekbone. It stunned the farmer as he stumbled back a step more in shock than pain, bringing his hand to his face. When he brought the fingertips away and looked down at the trickle of blood the whip had opened in his flesh, a gasp escaped from those emigrants close by. Amanda took one step into the crowd before Titus seized her arm and yanked her back, where he could lay an arm over her shoulder.

"Your husband don't need you making more trouble for him," he whispered sternly, then he and Shad shared a look that both men understood immediately. He leaned down, tousling his grandson's hair, then whispered to Amanda, "Daughter, you keep the boy here with you."

Then Scratch took a step away from her, stopped, and turned back to whisper, "Don't you move from this spot, Amanda. Chances are, you'll only make things a mite messier."

"No one . . . no one at all, calls me a liar, Burwell," Hargrove bellowed at the crowd. He held the short whip at the end of his arm menacingly, slowly dragging it around the crowd in an arc.

The farmer wiped his bloodied fingers on his worn canvas britches, then suddenly pointed at some children inching toward him. "Lem, you keep your sisters back."

The twelve-year-old boy obeyed instantly, putting his hand on the shoulders of his two younger sisters and nudging them back against the fringe of the crowd.

Burwell stood for a moment, as if he were a big, dumb brute working up a fighting lather, his eyes gone to slits as he flexed those fists open and closed, open and closed. "No man's ever gonna hit me 'thout me hittin' him back!"

But the farmer lunged no more than two steps in Hargrove's direction when he lurched to an ungainly halt, jerking back as he stared down at the pistols those three hired men had pulled out of their belts, their wide muzzles only a matter of feet from Burwell's belly.

Dramatically, Hargrove dragged the leather strands of his horsewhip through his open left palm. "The rest of you have got to understand, I am not doing this to hurt any one of you. I am not that sort of man. I simply have my own interests to see to. My own dreams to chase. And those dreams beckon me from California now. I will nonetheless bring you all the way to Fort Hall—"

"Where you're gonna take our pilot from us," Burwell grumbled, staring down at those three pistols. "And take your extra guns with you too."

"Why shouldn't I, Burwell?" Hargrove asked. "Have I been paid by this company to lead you to Oregon?"

"You asked us to elect you!" a voice cried from the crowd.

"We elected you to take us to Oregon!"

"But I'm not going to Oregon now," Hargrove argued. "And, this company of poor farmers never contracted to pay me any money to get you there—"

"Never was any talk of pay," the big farmer reminded. "You put your own name up for captain, said you wanted to lead us to Oregon . . . so you was chose as captain to take these people to Oregon."

"Mr. Harris here says the chances are better than good you'll find someone at Fort Hall who knows the road and can pilot the rest of you to Oregon," Hargrove suggested with a flippant gesture of that horsewhip.

A woman's voice cried out, "But we won't have us no captain neither!"

"You can elect a man to serve when you embark from Fort Hall. Till then, I will dutifully serve as your company captain. And as captain, my orders are that we move at dawn day after tomorrow." Drawing in a long breath, Hargrove quickly said, "Since I hear no other business, this meeting of the Hargrove Company is adjourned."

Some of the crowd stood rooted in their places, whispering among themselves. Others began to wander away from the shady banks of Black's Fork, slowly starting back toward their wagons laid out in an orderly pattern across the grassy meadow. Hargrove leaned close to Burwell and said something to the farmer that no one else could have heard, then turned away with his men and the pilot.

"Harris!" Scratch hollered as the crowd before him splintered into whispering knots. He gave Shad another nod, and they started toward their old compatriot.

"Shadrach Sweete! If this ain't a joy for these old eyes!" Harris bellowed after he had stopped and turned on his heel, recognizing the tall man coming his way through the dispersing crowd.

Curious, Hargrove and his hired men halted as well, forming a crescent behind the pilot.

"Finally talked yourself into leading a train I see!" Bass said as he came to a stop in front of the old trapper. "Don't know me, do you?"

Harris wagged his head. "I s'pose to?"

"Naw. I never run with Bridger an' Sweete," he grumbled as his eyes peered into Hargrove's face, taking a quick measure of the captain. "I was a free man, Harris."

Without a word of reply to Bass, Harris turned to Sweete. "Thought I see'd ye workin' for Jim Bridger at his Green River ferry when we come across the Seedskeedee."

"I was," Shad said.

"Ain't got no job? Maybe ye're hankerin' to find a li'l work with some emigrants, are ye?"

"I got work if I want it, right here at Bridger's post," Sweete declared.

That's when Bass interrupted, "Shadrach, you 'member how they had to tie this here nigger to a tree till Doc an' Joe got started off from ronnyvoo for Oregon a few years back?"

Harris's eyes glared like those of a diamondback rattler ready to strike as they instantly shifted to Titus Bass. "What kind of bullshit—"

"You was a no-good snake belly back then," Scratch continued as Amanda rejoined her husband, several yards away at the edge of the trees. "An' it looks like you've hooked up with your own no-good kind again, Harris."

"Are you referring to me?" Hargrove demanded as he strode up beside Harris, about half a head taller than either the pilot or the old trapper.

His eyes flashed to Hargrove's. "Way you side-talked these folks, you're a slick'un, you are."

"Who the hell is this, Harris?"

"Never met 'im. So I dunno—"

"Far as you need to know," Titus said, glaring at Hargrove, "I'm just a nigger what hates bald-faced liars even more'n that sodbuster you hit with your—"

Scratch's left arm shot up and out, his forearm cracking against Hargrove's wrist as the captain brought up his horsewhip. Bass immediately rolled his hand and seized the man's forearm, which compelled the three hired men to bring up their pistols, each muzzle pointed at Bass.

Hargrove snarled, "Best you let me go, mister."

"I ain't 'bout to let you go till these lizard-hearted bastards of yours put their pistols away in their pants."

Hargrove snorted a chuckle. "And if they don't? I figure they can put three balls in you before you even begin to reach for your pistol. Now—for the last time—take your hand off me."

"Maybeso these three cowards can shoot one man," Bass admitted after a moment of reflection. "But if I know my ol' partner, he's got his pistol pointed at *you* right now. So no matter what happens to me, *you're* the first'un to go down after them three cowards of your'n shoot me. No matter what, you die where you're standin'."

Titus didn't know for sure what Sweete had done behind him. Or if he had done anything at all. The only thing he could do was count on his old friend to be there at his back. And from that look in Hargrove's eyes when the captain glanced at Shadrach, Titus could plainly see there was reason enough to give Hargrove pause.

"No man calls me a liar and gets away with it," he hissed at the trapper.

"Seems to me there's more'n a hunnert folks here who believe that's just what you are, a low-down liar," Titus declared, sensing some of the building fury cause the captain's arm to tremble. "Best you cipher this too—I ain't one of your farmers, Hargrove. I don't cotton to no whippin's, an' I figger any man what's gotta sashay around with the likes o' these here hired snake bellies, why—that man's no more than a coward."

Hargrove attempted to yank his arm free. "Maybe I should shoot you myself," he growled as he rested his left hand on the butt of his pistol protruding from the front of his belt.

"Go right ahead," Scratch prodded. "You'll never get it out afore Shadrach kills you dead where you stand."

Harris's face was painted with worry as he took a step closer to Hargrove. "The big'un—he can do it, Cap'n."

"Damn right he can, Harris," Titus said, watching Hargrove's eyes fill with concern. "The man what got his pistol aimed at you ain't no peach-faced farm-boy bully like these three you got pointing guns at me. Tell 'im, Harris. Tell 'im how Shadrach's killed Injuns from the Musselshell clear down to the Arkansas, some of 'em with his bare hands too. These snot-nosed bully-boys of your'n ever done anything more'n jump on some poor farmer, three to one?"

"Lemme shoot him," one of the trio growled at Hargrove, his crimson face flushing with anger. "Benjamin can shoot the big one got a gun on you—"

"No!" Hargrove shouted, then repeated it softer, "No. There's no need for any shooting. If this man will release my arm, the four of us will be on our way. There's no sense in shedding any blood, boys. We'll be gone from here day after tomorrow. On our way to Fort Hall and California. Right, Mr. Harris?"

"That's right." Harris took a step closer to Bass.

"Maybe someone ought'n tie you up to 'nother tree, Harris," Scratch warned. "Leave you out there to die."

The pilot's face went hard as stone. "No one ever gonna tie me up to no tree again—"

"Hard to show these fellas all the way to Californy," Bass said, "if'n you're tied to a tree somewhere out there in the hills."

"I got lots o' friends now, so there ain't no chance of that," Harris snorted.

Scratch said, "Leastways, till you go an' get drunk."

"About time you let go of me," Hargrove repeated.

Slowly Titus began to open the fingers on his left hand, while he inched his hand toward the pistol stuffed in the front of his belt. The captain quickly yanked his arm free, slapping the calf of his leg with the wide leather strands of that horsewhip as he lunged a step backward. His eyes went back and forth between the two trappers.

Then Hargrove said, "You'll keep an eye out for these two, won't you, Harris? Let me know if you see them coming around again—between now and the time we'll pull out for Fort Hall."

"He's your lookout boy now?" Titus asked.

"I'll come let ye know," Harris growled.

"You allays was a good bootlicker," Sweete finally spoke, for the first time in minutes. "Didn't have much good sense of your own—but you was awright when your booshway told you where to shit an' how to wipe your ass."

"Damn you—" Harris started toward Sweete but stopped suddenly as he watched Shad shift the direction of his pistol.

"G'won now, train boss," Scratch suggested. "Better you an' your coward bully-boys go see what trouble you can cause other folks. I won't let you cause no trouble for this here family."

He watched Hargrove's head turn as the captain regarded the farmer with his family gathered nearby. "What concern are they of yours?"

Bass said nothing, but as Amanda was opening her mouth to speak, Titus shook his head.

"You related to her somehow?" Hargrove asked. "That it? That dumb farmer Burwell can't fight his own battles—he's got to bring in his missus and her relations to stand up for him."

"Thought you was goin'," Scratch said.

"I am."

Hargrove got four steps away before he stopped and turned around. "I don't know your name, or what any of this has to do with you . . . but, I want to suggest you stay out of our camp, and out of our way until we depart day after tomorrow."

"Why's that?"

The captain wore a half grin on his face. "Just a suggestion. You'd be wise not to let any of my men catch you around my camp."

Bass watched the man move off, trailed by Harris and those three hired toughs who reminded Scratch of the sort of thugs who peopled every riverport town along the Ohio and lower Mississippi. Amanda moved up with her husband and children at the same time.

"I didn't need none of your help," growled the big farmer who stomped up to stop before the trappers.

That caught Scratch by surprise. From the looks of Burwell's red face, the man was mad as a spit-on hen at most everyone in general right now. And he recalled how Amanda had spoken of her husband being proud to a fault. "I sure didn't mean to step into your business none—"

"It is my business," Burwell snapped. "And it'll please me if you stay out."

"Roman," Amanda said at his side, "I'm the one you ought to blame."

He twisted around and glared at her. "You?"

"I saw them come up to the meeting, went over to tell my pa why we hadn't come for supper. So if you're going to blame anyone for helping you stand up to Hargrove, blame me."

His jaw jutted, the ropy muscles below the temple flexing as the big farmer worked her confession over and over in his mind. "I . . . I got my pride," he said quietly.

Bass thought that as good an apology as the farmer could bring himself to utter. "If there's one thing I unnerstand, it's pride, son. You don't owe me no more words to explain. You don't want my help, I'll stay clear o' your troubles."

"I can accept that," Burwell replied, the harshness suddenly gone from his eyes. He watched his children, two boys and a pair of girls, happily rubbing the bony backs of those two lanky dogs for a moment, then turned to ask, "You really Amanda's pa?"

"Proud to say I am." He held out his hand. "She said your name was Roman. Awright I call you that?"

Burwell grinned as if all that bristling uneasiness of their first meeting was forgotten as he brought up his big paw that easily swallowed the old trapper's hand. "My friends back to home always called me Row. That'd be fine by me, for Amanda's father to call me Row."

Shad cleared his throat for attention.

"Shame on me," Scratch scolded himself. "Where's my manners? Get over here, Shad. This here's my good friend, Shadrach Sweete. An' that's my oldest child, Amanda."

"Should I shake your hand, ma'am?" Shad inquired as he stuffed his pistol back in his belt.

Amanda grinned a little, saying, "Of course it's all right."

"Sorry, ma'am," Sweete replied as he stuck out his big arm and quickly bent at the waist. "Been a while since I been in the company of a proper white lady."

She winked at her father. "I'm no proper lady, Mr. Sweete. But thank you for your manners anyway."

"Be pleased to have you to call me Shad—like all my friends do."

As Roman and Sweete shook hands, Amanda held out her left arm for her eldest son. "Pa, this here's Lemuel."

"You look old enough to shake hands, son."

Lemuel Burwell said, "I turned twelve this past spring, just before we set off from Westport."

"Likely you're a big help to your pa, ain'cha?" Titus asked.

Roman said, "He does ever'thing he can to help out on the road to Oregon."

"Who are these pretty girls?" Titus inquired.

The oldest nodded slightly, clearly self-conscious. "Leah," she said in a modest voice.

"Leah, that's such a purty name," he said. "How old are you?"

"Just turned ten."

"You really our grandpa?" asked the other girl as she sidled forward beside the oldest sister.

Bass said. "Would that disapp'int you—to find out a feller like me is your grandpa?"

"My, no!" she exclaimed. "Just wish I could take you to school back at home to show you off to the other'ns."

He laughed at that. "Good idee from such a li'l girl. What's your name?"

"I'm Annie," she replied. "Sometimes my mama calls me Spitfire Annie."

Quickly flashing a look up at his daughter, Titus asked the girl, "Why your mama call you that?"

"I dunno for sure. Maybe 'cause I get in trouble, Mama?"

With a grin, Amanda nodded. "That could be, Annie."

Annie never took her eyes off her grandfather. "What's your name?"

"I'm Titus, Titus Bass," he replied. "But my friends like Shadrach here, they all call me by a name what was give to me many winters ago when I first come to these here mountains. Like you're called Spitfire."

Lemuel asked, "What name is that?"

"Scratch."

"You want we should call you Scratch?" Annie inquired with a devilish grin.

"No, I want you to call me by a name no one else ever called me afore," he declared as he reached up and stroked the child's cheek with his callused fingertips. "Want each of you young'uns . . . to call me Grandpa."

Amanda bent over and whispered something into the smallest boy's ear. As she straightened, the youngster gazed at Bass with unerring and questioning eyes.

"Mama said to call you Gran'papa."

Dropping to one knee, which caused the dogs to bounce over to sit beside him, Titus held out his hand and said, "That's what I am—your grandpa."

For a long moment the boy stared down at that big, scarred hand, then brought his tiny fingers up and Titus gently enfolded the hand in his. Finally the youngster retracted his arm and took a step backward against his mother's skirt.

"He ain't afraid of me, is he, Amanda?"

She wagged her head and said, "I don't think he's afraid of anything, Pa. Sometimes he scares me so, what he'll do and where he'll go if he takes a notion. No, he ought not be afraid of you."

"You ain't afraid of these here ugly dogs, are you, son?"

The boy glanced up at his mother, then back to the old trapper, when he finally shook his head, but just barely.

Bringing his eyes to bear on the boy, Titus said, "That's good. Boys an' dogs just go together natural. What's your name, son?"

With the tiny tip of his pink tongue, the youngster licked his dry lips and said in a strong, unwavering voice, "Lucas, mister. But you can call me Luke, 'cause you're my gran'papa."

"That what your mama calls you?"

He glanced up at his mother, then touched eyes with his grandfather again. "No, she calls me Lucas."

With a chuckle, Titus declared, "Then, that's what I'll call you too—Lucas."

The boy caught them all by surprise when he suddenly asked, "Why you got them wires hanging from your ears?"

That question took him from his blind side, but after a moment's reflection Scratch answered, "I s'pose I wear my earbobs 'cause I like 'em, Lucas. I think these here shiny rocks an' beads are purty. What you think?"

Tilting his head one way, then the other, the child seriously studied both copper ear wires strung with tiny pieces of azure-blue turquoise and blood-red glass beads, then peered into the old trapper's eyes and announced, "I think they're pretty too."

"Thankee, Lucas," and he wanted to say more—

But the boy was already turning his head to look up at his mother and ask, "Mama, can I get some earbobs like Gran'papa's got?"

Even though she clamped her hand over her mouth, there was no disguising the merry laughter in her eyes at her son's innocent request. When she had finally gained her composure, Amanda quickly glanced at her father, then at her husband, and finally at the boy once more, saying, "I'm sure your grandpa didn't get those earbobs put in his ears till he was much, much older than you are now, Lucas. You can wait."

"That true, Gran'papa?"

With an impish grin, Titus replied, "Yes, Lucas—I was real ol't afore I got my ears poked with a sharp awl an' these here wires put in."

His little face scrunched up with concern. "Did it hurt?"

"Something fierce, it hurt."

Lucas deliberated on that for a moment, then said, "I'm not afraid of a fierce hurt, Gran'papa. But I'll wait like my mama says I gotta wait—till I'm older."

"That's a good lad," he said to his grandson.

"And maybe then I can even come help you out here in the mountains," the boy continued to everyone's surprise. "Mama told us you work making wagon tires and such. Maybe when I get older you can teach me an' I'll be your helper. I'm good at learning."

"There's plenty of time for l'arnin', Lucas. A lot of l'arnin' your hull life through. But I 'spect your pa here's got a passel of things to teach you his own self," he said, patting the child on the shoulder as he rose to his feet. Bringing his eyes to Amanda's face as he stood once more, Scratch explained, "Like I was saying—we was getting worried 'bout your family makin' it for dinner. Figgered I'd come see what was keeping you."

"Hargrove," Roman said with utter sourness. "Him and his trouble was keeping us."

"But we can come now," Amanda said. "I'm sure we're all real hungry, aren't we?"

Lucas craned back his head to stare up at his grandfather. "My mama got any brothers and sisters like I got brothers and sisters?"

Immediately Titus asked, "I'll bet you're a lad likes to ride on your pa's shoulders?"

"Oh, yes—I do!"

"Here," and Bass swept up the boy, swinging Lucas into the air and turning him just before he plopped the boy down on his shoulders. "There now. That's where you're gonna ride till we go fetch up our horses and you can ride mine back to the post."

"You didn't answer Luke's question," Leah stated as she hustled to walk alongside her grandfather.

"What question was that?"

"My mama got any brothers or sisters?"

"Yes, young lady. Your ma got two brothers an' a sister." Then he looked at Amanda and smiled. "An' 'nother one gonna be here sometime deep in the winter."

"How old are they?" Annie demanded to know.

"How old are you, girl?"

Annie said, "Gonna be eight in a few weeks, my pa tells me."

"Well, now—the oldest after your mother, she's thirteen winters now."

"W-winters?" young Lemuel repeated.

"That's how we count age out here, son," he replied. "So she's a li'l older'n you. An' then there's my oldest boy—he's ten winters. But my youngest boy—for now—he's only four summers old."

"They're really my mama's brothers and sister?" Annie asked, a furrow between her eyes.

"Your mama was born a long, long time afore I come out here an' . . . an' got married to 'nother woman."

From his shoulder-high perch, Lucas tapped his grandfather on the top of the head and asked, "Can your children play with me?"

"I figger they'll think it purely shines to play with you, Lucas."

Reaching the horses, Titus hoisted the boy onto his saddle, then bent to untie the reins from the foreleg where he had ground-hobbled the animal.

He straightened and the horses lunged to their feet. Together, he and Shad led their horses, with the Burwell family scattered around them. Bass turned to Roman and asked, "How many of them hired men that Hargrove fella got along?"

"Seven. Eight now, if you count that pilot, Harris," Burwell answered. "Why?"

After covering some distance on their walk back to the walls of Fort Bridger, Scratch finally admitted, "I was making my own tally of the sort of trouble there was in your camp now. The sort of trouble it sounds like most men don't dare to bite off."

Amanda looped her arm around her husband's waist as they moved along. "I don't want no more trouble in our lives, Roman. We've had enough already. So we're gonna stay far away from trouble as we can now."

"I think you're right, ma'am," Shad replied as he glanced over at Titus. "A smart man wouldn't be stirring up trouble for himself."

"Less'n trouble just drops right outta the sky an' into that man's lap," Scratch remarked.

"You don't figger it's smart just to stay outta that wagon camp and not to bite off trouble on your own?" Sweete wagged his head with a wry grin. "Like Hargrove told us?"

"I was just askin' how many guns Hargrove's got working for him, s'all," Titus replied. "It sours my milk, Shadrach—bullies like that wagon cap'n an' his sort. I had my craw filled up to here with their kind. American Fur bully-boys an' all the rest, strangled things for the li'l man."

"There's Hargrove, and eight others, like I said," Burwell repeated.

"Why you wanna know, Scratch?" Shadrach asked.

"Only need to see what trouble I'm bitin' into," Titus explained, "so I can figger how long it's gonna take for me to chew it up an' spit it back out again."

TWELVE

"Do you want us to go with you?" she asked him.

Titus looked at his wife. Last night, after they had returned to the post from having supper with Amanda's family in the wagon camp, he thought he had had that question all figured out. But as the two of them stirred now in the predawn darkness, in their lodge pitched just outside the post walls, he knew he already had changed his mind.

"It will be a long journey," he reminded.

"Not as far as it is from here to the land of my people," she declared. "You still did not answer my question."

For a moment he watched her as she laid more kindling on the feeble embers in the fire pit. "I thought you would stay here, for the children."

"They go everywhere we go, Ti-tuzz."

He heard the rustling of blankets. Looking over his shoulder, he found Magpie sitting up at the edge of the darkness. "You do your best not to make noise."

She whispered, "I wanted to tell you something before you decided you were going alone."

"I am not going alone," he explained again in Crow. "Shadrach and his family are going with me."

Magpie pushed some of her long hair out of one of her almond-shaped eyes. "We belong with you more than we belong here waiting for you at Bridger's post."

Scratch looked back at his wife again. "Much of that country will be new to me. Parts of it I've never been through."

"Many summers ago, that was the country where you met Big Throat for the first time." Waits-by-the-Water used the Crow's name for Bridger as she leaned back and put some larger wood on the fire that began to cast a warm glow on the inside of the small lodge. "But I would not worry even if it was a completely strange land to you."

"My popo will see us through it," Magpie chimed in.

He grinned, his heart feeling much lighter. "Then you want to go with me when the wagons leave this morning?"

Waits leaned over and laid her hand on his. "Magpie and I will take care of everything in the lodge—taking only what we need for the journey. Flea can see to the horses. So that means you will see to Jackrabbit."

"Do you want to take down the lodge and drag a travois with us?"

"We have enough of the heavy cloth we can tie up if we need shelter from the rain," she stated. "I will leave the lodge here. Big Throat can care for it while we are gone to this Snake River I have heard so little about."

So it was decided, not so much by him as by the two women in his family. They would be setting out together on this long journey this morning, all of them, as a family. Somewhere over the past day and a half he had first come to believe it would be far better for him to go alone, to leave her and the children behind at Bridger's post when he set off with Shadrach's family in following Hargrove's wagon train to Fort Hall. Sweete had eagerly volunteered to ride along during their big supper inside the fort walls two nights ago after Hargrove's meeting at the wagon camp.

After that brief and clearly unfinished confrontation with the wagon captain and his bully-boys, Amanda's family had come back to the post with the old trappers for what was to have been a supper to celebrate this reunion of father and daughter and families. But for a while there it had all the makings of a wake, what with Amanda and Roman quietly despairing on what they would do once the train reached the Snake River and Phineas Hargrove pointed his nose southwest on the California Trail.

But by the time Shadrach returned from fetching his family for supper, the tall trapper sashayed up to the fire as cocky as any prairie grouse, plainly ready to bust his buttons with what he just had to tell Titus before he would burst.

"We're gonna light out with the wagon train day after tomorrow." He unloaded his news the moment everyone fell quiet around that fire crackling in the pit at the center of the stockade.

Bridger's face grew worried. "You're leaving me, Shad?"

Sweete looked at his old friend. "Wanna see some new country, Gabe. I'll get to Fort Hall, then turn around. I'll be back afore you can miss me."

"What'm I gonna do 'thout you here?"

With a snort, he flung his thick arm around Bridger's shoulder and shook his friend. "Same as you done afore I showed up!"

Bridger looked a little jealous of that freedom Shad was taking to wander. "Tired of that ferry work you was doin'?"

"Them seven others gonna work out slick for you," Shad replied. " 'Sides, the season is winding down awready. If them emigrants ain't anywhere close to the crossing of the Green by now, they ain't gonna make it through the mountains afore winter sets in. I figger we've see'd all but the stragglers by now."

Jim chewed his upper lip a moment. "I'll lay you're right on that. Likely we've awready seen just about all of them what's gonna be passing through."

"Maybe some more of them Marmons," Titus growled.

Turning to Bass, Jim said, "Young told me there'd be a heap more Saints come through here next season—but wasn't no more coming through this summer."

"A good thing too," Bass declared with a slight shudder. "Didn't like the read I got off that man's sign. I seen my share of fellas glad-slap you on the back with one hand while'st the other hand's dippin' into your purse for all you're worth."

"That prophet didn't seem like such a bad sort to me," Bridger responded, "far as a preacher goes."

Bass declared, "Doc Whitman—now that was a good preacher!"

With a wave of his hand, Bridger said, "Young and his flock gone on to their promised land. Even if Brigham Young don't take 'em where I told him they should settle, I wish all good things for 'em. Sorry I couldn't do a li'l more trading with that preacher's folks. Likely them Saints won't have much to do with Jim Bridger from here on out."

"The farther they stay away from you, the better it is by me," Titus said, then turned to Shad and asked, "Shell Woman wanna go?"

"See some new country with me," he admitted. "Ever since I brung that gal out of Cheyenne country, her eyes has growed hungry to see more an' more!"

Titus looked down at Waits-by-the-Water, recognizing the interest that was apparent on her face as she managed to snag a few words here and there of the men's conversation. Roman Burwell stepped back to the fire, bringing young Lucas by the hand. Just before he had settled with the boy by his knee, Amanda rocked onto her toes to whisper something in her husband's ear.

The emigrant turned to Shad in a huff, asking, "You say you're riding along with Hargrove's train, Mr. Sweete?"

"Figgered I'd come along to Fort Hall with you, lend a hand in what I could," Shad said.

"I don't need no . . . we don't need no help," Roman grumped. "Got this far just fine. We'll make the rest of the way just fine too."

Ignoring the settler's peevishness, Sweete continued to explain, "Won't get in your way. Comin' only to see what I can do to help your bunch find a pilot what'd get you on to Oregon."

Gripping her husband's arm tightly, Amanda asked, "You really think we might find someone to guide us at Fort Hall?"

"Chances better up there at Hallee, than you waiting here," Titus explained. "That post sits at the edge of the country you need to be showed a way through, where the crossings of the Snake are, how to ford that river, some such. You'll do far better scratching up a pilot yonder at Fort Hall than you will anywhere along the road atween here an' there."

"What if we don't find us a pilot?" Burwell asked, his long brow deeply furrowed.

Scratch thought a moment before he said, "Worst you could do'd be light out from there 'thout a pilot."

Roman wagged his head unapologetically. "We can follow the wagon road where them who've gone before us come through that country. Ain't nothing to staying on the road all the way to Oregon."

But Scratch snorted, "What your family come through awready ain't but a piss in a barrel put up against what you got left to go."

"But we can't go back if we don't find a pilot," Amanda groaned. "There's nothing left for us back there but . . . lean times."

Titus stepped over and gently laid a hand on her shoulder. "I ain't sayin' you go back. Hell, I'd be the last man to ever tell 'nother he should give in, turn around, and go back."

That fuzzy patch between Roman's eyebrows wrinkled testily. "Then what the blazes we gonna do when Hargrove an' his pilot take off from Fort Hall for California . . . and we got no one to guide us to Oregon?"

Scratch gazed the settler in the eye. "You sit tight for the winter if'n you have to."

"The winter!" Burwell roared. "That means I'd lose a whole growin' season, time I finally got to Oregon next year."

Titus saw how Amanda hung her head with defeat. He rubbed his hand on the back of her shoulders and said. "Come the first train through next season, you an' the rest can throw in with them. But the worst thing you'd do is all you farmers set off down the Snake on your own, get stopped somewhere along the way with wagon trouble or early snows—have to fend for yourselves all winter long out in that God-forsook country."

"Rest of us, we can take care of ourselves," Roman snapped testily.

"This ain't sweet an' safe Missouri—" Titus bellowed, but immediately felt bad for it.

For a long moment he gazed down at his grandchildren, sensing a deep and nagging responsibility to see them safely through. He took a deep breath then said more calmly, "Roman, that ain't the sort of country where you wanna get caught out with your young'uns for the winter."

"There'll be someone there," Shad reassured as he inched over a little closer to Burwell around the fire. "Likely someone I know from the beaver days— someone I can vouch for. Ain't that right, Scratch?" Sweete's eyes pleaded a little.

Titus quickly glanced over his daughter's family, deciding there was no choice but to agree with his friend—if only for the sake of Amanda and the others. "Shad's right. There's a real good chance your train will hire a pilot soon as you reach Fort Hall."

"But if we don't?" Roman pressed.

"Then pick you a spot to spend out the winter there within sight of the fort," Titus reminded.

Just as Roman was about to open his mouth again, Amanda stepped up and slipped her arm through his, saying, "I know we'll find us a pilot to hire, Roman. I feel it in my bones. So there's no need to fret any longer over what isn't going to happen. We're going to Oregon, just like you said we'd do all along. No matter what Phineas Hargrove or that weasel-eyed Harris do to roll boulders in our path . . . we are going to Oregon, Roman!"

He turned sideways and gripped the tops of her arms a moment before he pulled his wife against him. "God bless you, Amanda. Bless you for your faith in this journey to our own promised land."

"It ain't the promised land I got faith in, Roman—it's you," she vowed. "No matter what the journey, I got faith in you."

"We was meant to go to Oregon," he said as he crushed her in his big arms. "It's there we'll have all the bad days behind us."

As the stars had blinked into view and the tree frogs began to chirp their friendly calls down in the slough, Titus watched how Waits fluttered close to Shell Woman, as if she were reluctant to let her new-made friend go. He had felt a stab of pain for her. She was a social creature, not a loner like him. From the dawning of their first days together, he had realized that it was much, much harder for her to be apart from her family and her friends than it was for him to be alone. Back as far as those Boone County growing-up days in Kentucky he had come to know he was not meant for needing much in the way of human company. Oh, for certain he knew he could not do without Waits and those children of theirs. It would be so hard when Magpie, or Flea, or even little Jackrabbit were older and went off to make a life of their own with another. But . . . he would always have her, and that gave him the greatest sense of belonging he had ever known. Hers was the only belonging he felt he had to have for the rest of his life.

From those days when his self-knowing was awakened in Rabbit Hash, time and again he had put his faith in the wrong people, more often in the wrong women. First there was Amy Whistler, who wanted him for reasons other than loving him. And then there was Abigail Thresher, the bone-skinny whore who had given him all the love his body could stand, but never came to love who he was. And then there was Amanda's mother, Marissa Guthrie—who had put so many restrictions and knots on him that he could do nothing else but flee while he still had the chance. By the time he reached St. Louis, Titus was not about to risk any deep affair of the heart. But try as he might, the high-born, coffee-skinned quadroon managed to get under his skin before she too went the way of all those saddest stories of unrequited love. Confused and despairing, he had learned too late what it would take to protect his heart. Titus vowed he would simply not let another woman in.

And so it was for more than ten years. While there were those who crawled in naked to join him beneath the buffalo robes, spreading legs and arms to ensnare him in their moist embrace, Bass kept hidden that most precious piece of himself. In its place, he had substituted the immutable bond of men . . . yet found that affection shattered by the betrayal of those who professed their protection of him. It took a long, long time for him to genuinely trust again in those who rode the same trails as he, trapped the same high-country streams, slept and snored, ate and laughed, hunted and fought, beneath the same starry skies. But he eventually found friends. Not many—for he had never, never, never been a garrulous sort who sought the reassuring company of the many. No, Titus Bass had been rewarded with a few true companions who asked no more of him than they were willing to give—that complete and utter trust as they stood at one another's backs and dared the fates, damned the gods, and stood mighty against the wind in those days of brief and unmitigated glory.

Good men, the best friends a man deserved—even those the likes of Asa McAfferty, who went bad for reasons he had never sorted out, a compañero who, in the end, asked one final act of faithfulness from an old friend. Better it would be, Titus had come to believe after years of mind-numbing consternation, for a man to be killed at the hand of a friend than by the hate of an enemy.

Good men, the best friends a man could ever have. So many of the best gone now. Gone to where those mortals still walking the earth could only suppose. Gone where no man alive knew for certain. These good men, gone to where Titus could only pray he would see them again at last on some far-off, faraway day. Like the bullet holes in his flesh, the arrow puckers and knife wounds too, the losing of each of those good friends carved its scar upon his heart. Perhaps even deeper, unto the marrow of his very soul. Such loss was all but unbearable, one by one wounding its own piece of his being.

So he did take friends unto his bosom, the few and the most trusted he had embraced, and made a home for these in his wounded, broken-in heart. Likely he could survive, live out the rest of his days with two or three of the old ones at his side, men like Sweete and Bridger. Save for his family, Titus Bass needed little more. But, his need of Waits-by-the-Water was a different animal altogether. She left behind everything she had ever known to come and be with him. In those first seasons they were together, Waits found a new friend in Josiah's wife. Later, Mathew Kinkead's too. But both were a far cry from the friends who had surrounded her before he took her away from Crow country. She needed friends much more than he.

Titus could do with the few who easily moved in and out of his life, as easily as he could do with being a loner. But it near destroyed him when he was apart from her. If he had to live with but one friend for the rest of his days, it could be no other but her. Yet, he had come to realize she was different. Waits thrived and bloomed with her woman friends. She needed that companionship far more than he ever would. Watching how she fluttered near Shell Woman, her bravest and most cheerful reaction to knowing Shadrach was taking his family far away for a time, if not forever, gave Scratch a sense of remorse for his wife.

Yesterday, before the others awoke, he sought out Bridger.

Jim listened, then asked in exasperation, "You too?"

"Time's come for me to stretch my legs a little," Titus had explained as Jim poured them coffee from that first brew of the morning.

"Your family goin'?"

"If I go, they'll likely wanna come too."

Bridger had wagged his head. "Won't be the same 'thout you, Scratch. Won't be the same not hearing that anvil ring from first light till suppertime."

"We'll be back long afore winter comes hard, Shad an' me."

"You ain't ever spent a winter in country cold as this here gets," Jim warned. "Best you get turned around from Hallee as soon as you niggers can."

"How far you make the journey?"

"I'd make it ten, twelve days on horse," Bridger estimated. "But these sod-busters with their wagons. Gonna be double, no . . . triple that. A month at the outside, you don't keep 'em moving hard."

"Hell, we'll be back well afore the first snowflake lands on that ugly nose o' your'n. Three weeks at the most getting there, an' we'll be less time coming back. All of us on horses then—won't nothing hold us up."

"That's *if* you two bring a pilot to bait for this bunch of corncrackers."

Dread of that had worried Titus into sleeplessness that first still night after his daughter's family trudged back to the wagon meadow and the others had carried sleepy children off to their beds. How, Scratch despaired, could he just drop this weighty matter into Shadrach's lap once they reached Fort Hall, and pay no mind to the looming potential for failure once the train was beyond the horizon and out of sight?

And if he finally decided he could do nothing less than go along to Fort Hall himself—what would he do, Titus brooded, if he and Shad failed to scratch up a pilot who could be trusted? In the final dusting he admitted to no one but himself that this whole dilemma might well come down to what Roman Burwell and the other hickory-headed settlers would decide to do when they were confronted with that impossible choice of staying out the winter near Fort Hall, or pushing on without a pilot because their feet had grown far too itchy with every mile they put behind them. Exactly what happened when these emigrants reached the Snake would likely turn not only on events Titus Bass could not foresee but also turn on folks Titus Bass had no control over.

And that powerlessness was just the sort of thing that had nettled him no end since eighteen and twenty-five when he fled to the Rocky Mountains, seeking to finally seize hold of his own life, wrenching it away from the control of others. This was another of those crucial, pivotal decisions in a man's life that offered no good choice versus the bad options. In the two paths he saw left for him, there was no solidly good choice. Only a matter of what choice appeared to come with less risk . . . what path came with an acceptable, manageable level of danger or the possibility of failure. Time and again in his life among these mountains, he had been confronted with less than ideal options. Only trouble now was that the safety of so many of those he cared for rested on what choices he made from here on out—beginning with the choice he had to make that very morning.

The sun was only hinting at just how hot the day would be when the three families gathered in the open square of Fort Bridger. Jim had thrown some wood on the embers and poked life back into those flames that cast their reflections as those who were departing embraced each and every one of those who were staying behind. Tears shared between the two women and Gabe's three children, hugs between all the youngsters who had been able to play and frolic despite the language barriers. Off to the side two men said farewell to an old friend in much the same way this breed once bid farewell to their comrades when the luster of summer rendezvous had faded and the brigades were stringing out in a half dozen different directions for the high-country hunt.

"Watch your topknot, Gabe!" Titus cried as he rose to the saddle, a sour ball caught in his throat, eyes stinging in the early light.

Blinking his own misty eyes, Bridger pounded Sweete on the back one last time, then let the big man go to his horse. Finally they were all mounted and turning from the timbered stockade, with Jim trudging along beside them, like a man who had one last thing to say before parting . . . but could not remember what he wanted to say for the life of him. In the end, he looked up at Titus with those imploring eyes.

And said, "Countin' on you. Bring 'em back, Titus Bass. Bring 'em all back soon as you can."

With Magpie and Flea riding the left flank among the packhorses, it was Jackrabbit, along with little Bull Hump and Pipe Woman, who giggled and shrieked with excitement as the party set off to the southwest for the meadow where the Hargrove train had put in more than two whole days of rest, recruitment, and repairs. The women chattered, their hands busy as they always were when people of different tongues wanted desperately to communicate. But there was really no need to understand Crow or Cheyenne to recognize the joy on their copper-skinned faces, the excitement in sharing this new adventure with friends. Out in the lead rode the two old comrades, as they had done countless mornings before.

One last time they both turned and gazed back at Jim's double stockade, then waved a final farewell to Bridger's shrinking figure before Bass held out his left hand to Sweete. Shad nudged his horse closer and took Scratch's wrist in his right hand. Gazing into one another's eyes with that long-buried smile of great anticipation, they squeezed hard before freeing their grip. Exactly as they had done many, many times before when setting out on a trail they knew not where it would carry them.

Even at this early hour the emigrant meadow was beginning to throb with noise and color. Oxen bellowed and mules bawled as men and boys brought back strings of the beasts from a long watering in Black's Fork. The wind out of the west brought Scratch a cornucopia of fragrances, from fresh dung to coffee on the boil, from the strong perfume of bacon crackling in cast iron to the heavenly scent of flour biscuits or ground-corn johnnies. Here and there rode men on horseback, their eyes taking in everything as they moved slowly from wagon camp to wagon camp, rarely uttering a word that wasn't some terse or scolding command.

"You figger 'em for Hargrove's bully-boys?" Shad inquired.

"That'un, see how he just spotted us," Titus replied. "Lookit him turn 'round an' lick it back to give Hargrove the word that trouble just showed up."

They watched that first rider off to their left give his horse a kick and lope away into the midst of the busiest place in camp, just before a second bull-necked horseman dared to ride a bit closer, standing in his stirrups for long moments while he satisfied his curiosity and got himself a good long look at the newcomers, then suddenly reined aside and tore off at a gallop.

"We ought'n find Roman's camp straightaway," Scratch declared sourly. "I figger company's gonna come callin' soon enough."

"Never thought about it," Shad admitted. "What if Hargrove an' his boys say we can't go along?"

Bass snorted. "You ever ask a by-your-please of ary a man to ride where you wanted to ride, Shadrach?"

"No. Onliest I ever give a thought of it was my first time in Blackfoot country up north."

"What if they tol't you, 'No, you can't ride across our country'?"

Sweete said, "We damn well rode across it anyways."

"Now ain't the time to change our ways, Shadrach."

"Titus!" Roman Burwell shouted as he stepped from the corner of the wagon. "Come to see Shadrach off with us?"

He waited a few moments longer until he had stopped near the wagon and dropped to the ground there as Burwell, Amanda, and their children came flocking toward the horses and those two happy, yipping dogs.

"My stick floats with Shadrach," he confessed. "Thort the young'uns an' Waits might like to see some new country!"

"Y-you're really coming along?" Amanda asked breathlessly, reaching out to take her father's hand in both of hers.

"Till we get you to Fort Hall," he confessed. "The two of us, we'll run down a pilot to lead your bunch the rest of the way."

Roman's eyes flicked away, then he turned back to the two old trappers. "Seems Hargrove is coming to welcome you to the train himself."

They all turned their heads, watching the three men approach. Train captain Hargrove, with two of his biggest men hard on his tail.

"Don't that appear to be a big ol' smile of welcome on that bastard's face?" Titus grumbled with mock cheer. "Amanda, why don't you take Waits and Shell Woman around the other side of the wagon with all the young'uns? Find 'em something to eat, maybe. Put 'em to helping you pack up your goods in that wagon."

She could read the seriousness in his eyes. "All right, Pa."

For a moment longer he watched Amanda gesture to the women, then start them around the back of the canvas-topped prairie schooner, where she would get them involved with more than the arrival of the wagon captain.

"Good morning, Burwell!" Hargrove sang out in that easygoing way of a man who always carried a smirk on his face and self-righteousness in his heart.

"Hargrove," Roman responded.

The hair at Digger's neck ruffed menacingly, and the dog growled, low at the back of his throat. Bass quieted him with a whisper. "Hush, boy!"

The captain's eyes raked over the trappers. "I trust you're here to bid farewell to these members of your family."

With a shake of his head, Titus said, "That ain't why we're here."

Straightening in the saddle and pressing his chin down against his puffed-up chest, Hargrove tried again. "Then it's probably for the best that you've come to try talking Burwell and his wife into staying behind with you here until another train comes through for Oregon. Admirable, my good man—that you should place their welfare so highly, rather than see them risk it all on an unwise gamble on their own."

"They won't be on their own," Titus declared. "My friend here, Mr. Shadrach Sweete, he was first to jump up an' offer to ride along to Fort Hall. Likely find some fella there what can lead the train on to Oregon country after you an' Harris gone off to Californy."

Hargrove's eyes appraised Sweete a moment. "You'll be part of the Burwell family since you'll be making the journey by yourself?"

Shadrach picked at an old scab on the back of one hand and said, "I ain't goin' alone. Got my family comin' too."

"Family?" the wagon captain repeated uneasily.

"Wife, two young'uns."

"Wife? She's come out from the East?"

Crossing his big forearms across the saddle where he stood on the ground beside his horse, Sweete peered over the animal at the man, saying, "She ain't been no farther east than the Little Dried River, or the Smoky Hill. She's Cheyenne."

"So you're a squaw-man?"

Bass slowly stepped aside and laid his rifle atop his saddle so that it pointed in Hargrove's direction. "That's a word you don't wanna use with neither of us, Cap'n Hargrove. Some things just get under a man's skin, an' make him see red."

He turned back to Sweete. "You're married to a squaw."

"Cheyenne, like I told you."

"An' my wife's Crow," Titus advised. "Her people come from far to the north. Likely you ain't heard of 'em."

Hargrove blinked a few times, then asked of Sweete, "Your . . . wife and children—you'll be part of Burwell's camp?"

"We will," Bass replied for them all.

The wagon master's head jerked in his direction. "We?"

"I figgered to go along, show my family some country, give a hand to Roman when he needed it—"

"I can't allow all of you to join our train!"

"That don't callate to me," Bass argued. "Two day ago you was tellin' ever'one how you an' Black Harris was taking off for Californy on your own. So what the hell say you got in who throws in with these other folks when you're dropping out soon as you reach Fort Hall?"

"It's my train," Hargrove growled. "I formed it, I—"

"You was elected captain," Burwell interrupted as he stepped up suddenly, causing a horse ridden by one of the hired men to shy and shuffle backward awkwardly. "You don't own none of us. Not our wagons. An' you sure as the devil don't own this trail."

"We'll see what the others have to say about that!"

Scratching the side of his cheek, Titus said, "No man's got a right to tell me where I can ride and where I can make camp for the night, Cap'n."

Hargrove glanced to his right, then to his left, in a way that unmistakably indicated his hired men. With a smile he said, "I think we understand one another. In this wild country, might always makes right."

"Most times," Sweete responded.

Hargrove wagged his head meaningfully and clucked, "It can make a man nervous, forced to watch over his shoulder for trouble creeping up on him all the time."

"These here friends o' your'n," Titus began, wagging the muzzle of his rifle at one, then the other, of those horsemen arrayed on either side of the wagon master. "You figger they very good at killing a man? Maybe good for killin' two of us?"

"I'm certain they—"

"I ain't," Bass interrupted. "This coon'd lay down good money none of your gun-toters ever kill't a man."

Sweete had his hat off and was wiping the sticky moisture off the sweatband as he said, "Hargrove, I want you to look at that rifle my friend is holding on you. See them brass tacks he pounded into the stock, up an' down the forearm too?"

"What business is it of—"

"Ever' one of 'em is a dead man he's kill't."

Titus watched how that caused all three of them to train their attention on his rifle, where it was propped atop the saddle.

"Near as I know, he ain't added the last two tacks he should," Shadrach continued. "Pair of Frenchie fellas who thought they was gonna run off with the man's half-blood daughter—figgered a half-wild white man wasn't gonna care 'bout his family an' all."

Hargrove's eyes grinned mirthlessly and he said, "Sometimes justice can indeed be swift out here on the frontier."

Shadrach added, "But I doubt any of your hired men done more'n rough up some poor folks they had outnumbered. They don't appear to have the stomach for killin'—just for making you look bigger'n you are to sodbusters and settlement folk."

From his right side, out of the corner of his good eye, Titus watched three of his grandchildren poke their heads beneath the wagon. Then a fourth shadow: little Lucas, plopping onto his belly and squeezing his way between Lemuel and Annie. All of them intently listened in on the conversation between the menfolk and that talk of the brass tacks on his rifle, talk of his life of killing. It wasn't the sort of thing he wanted his grandchildren to know about him.

Hargrove was already starting a sentence with something about the council he would call when they had reached that night's campground to decide the matter—

But Titus interrupted, "You best keep your boys away from our camp."

"They were hired by me to patrol the line of march every day," Hargrove huffed. "And they stand their rotation of watch every night, just like the rest of the men. As long as I'm captain, there can never be anywhere that is off-limits to my men."

"I warned you once, Hargrove. Won't waste my breath again," he declared, then turned a quick glance at those four grandchildren of his, wide eyes peering out from under the possum belly slung beneath the wagon, every one of them getting a real earful. "But, I'm sure men like you an' me don't want no trouble with the other. Do we now?"

"This is my train, Burwell," Hargrove fumed as he turned to gaze at the farmer. "You signed on with your family—but these . . . these others didn't."

"We ain't part of your train," Titus said. "We'll ride with this family. Keep to ourselves. Ain't gonna cause no trouble . . . but we ain't backin' off from trouble if it comes neither. Be sure to tell all your boys that. Don't want none of 'em crossing tracks with me or mine here on out."

The wagon master sputtered, "I can't have my train providing for you—"

"We take care of ourselves," Shad declared. "Don't we, Scratch?"

"We ain't taking nothing from another's mouth, Hargrove. We'll hunt for what we eat," Titus explained. "An' we'll camp off from the rest of your farmers."

Pulling himself up to full height again in the saddle, Phineas Hargrove took a moment to sneer down his long, patrician nose at the poorly dressed farmer and his two friends arrayed in greasy buckskins and faded calico. "Enjoy your day on the trail with these new companions of yours while you can, Burwell. After our council meeting tonight, the men and their families will have no choice but to turn back come morning."

Scratch watched the three ride off. First one, then the other hired man twisted round in the saddle or looked back over his shoulder. Only Hargrove refused to give the newcomers another glance.

"Better we gave 'em that warning right off," Shad explained as he stepped over.

Roman declared, "I don't believe we'll be troubled by them after that council meeting tonight."

Wagging his head, Titus felt weary, deep-down bone weary. As he turned to gaze down at those four young faces peering out at him from the early-morning shadows beneath the wagon box, he grumbled, "Way I read the sign—our trouble with that Hargrove an' his bunch o' bullies only gonna turn uglier from here on out."

THIRTEEN

Two hours after crossing the gentle loop of Muddy Creek some eight miles north of Fort Bridger, a pair of Hargrove's hired men came loping back along that path the scattered emigrant wagons were plying. As they huffed past on their dusty horses, the men bellowed their orders to one and all.

"Making camp ahead! Form up for camp! Form up!"

Titus Bass quickly regarded the rocky ground and reminded himself he would have to warn these woodland emigrants, especially his grandchildren, to be vigilant for the rattlers that grew numerous and bold in this high, arid country. The very thought of a white-skinned little one getting bit put a sour, queasy ball in Bass's stomach.

A little off to his left, Scratch saw Amanda stick her head around the front bow of the canvas top on their long wagon as her eyes searched for him and the family. The faded red gingham of that poke bonnet, which shaded her eyes and much of her face from most of the sun's cruel burn, was unmistakable even at this distance.

Right from the start, he and Shadrach had chosen to ride their families on the far right flank of the train rather than spend that hot morning, and even hotter afternoon, chewing on the tons of dust spun into the air by the four wheels of every one of those sixty-seven wagons. Where they could, most of the farmers gradually worked themselves into a wide formation rather than suffering the stifling dust in rigid single file. By this point in their journey, these sodbusters-turned-teamsters had learned that some duties on this overland journey, like guard rotation, required military precision. But this did not. When the land became wrinkled and the coulees sank deep, the procession slowed as one team after another slowly dragged their wagons into line behind the others, a process of crossing each gully one at a time that made for agonizing delays. But when the next mile or so ahead foretold easy going, the emigrants gradually loosened their tight formation and spread across a broad front.

Many were the times that first morning when Scratch and Sweete had stopped their group on a low rise to wait for the train to catch up, or even to allow most of the wagons to pass on by. No matter how fast they could travel on horseback, it made no sense to outstrip the plodding pace of the train. Excruciatingly slow, those teams of oxen preferred by most farmers managed to set one hoof in front of the other with a steadiness that saw that first day waste away by the time they had reached the south bank of Muddy Creek. Far in the advance, Titus watched Moses Harris ride to the east along the bank, then back to the west aways, before the pilot found the approach he most desired and led Hargrove's first wagon down to the ford of the shallow stream. This time of the year, Bass thought as he watched one after another begin the slow, but noisy, descent down the sharp slope and make the crossing, there wasn't water enough to worry a man in this narrow creekbed. Yet it was the bottom on these shallow western creeks that should give a man pause: sands shifting almost by the hour—what was solid footing beneath the first wagons could, by the time the last few teams entered the creek, have turned itself into no more than a bowl of mushy grits beneath the two-inch bands of iron welded around every wagon wheel.

It had taken him most all of yesterday, his last in Bridger's forge, but he and Roman had managed to swap off those much-worn two-inch-wide iron tires the Burwells had rolled away from Westport on, then hammered and shimmed wider, three-inch rims around their shrunken wooden wheels.

"Wished I'd had these back in May after we got ourselves out on the prairie," Roman had commented as they were muscling one of the hot tires onto a wheel there in the shade of the awning. "When all them rains come, day after day—a narrow tire sinks faster."

"Ain't nothing gonna keep your tires from sinking under a heavy wagon," Titus had told him, "but out here a wider tire do better crossing creek bottoms and rocky ground too."

The water in Muddy Creek was turgid and slow, brown as its name and tepid to boot. Only good thing about the stream, he thought as he watched his two oldest urge the pack animals across and up the north bank, was that the Muddy was running so shallow that it hadn't so much as lapped at the bottom of a wagon box or licked at the bellies of their ponies. Besides, these small western streams weren't all that wide. It wouldn't be until these farmers got to the Bear that they would face their first test, a crossing that would prepare them, or weed them out, for the crucial two crossings of the capricious Snake River before they ever reached the mighty Columbia.

There wasn't much water to speak of in the bottoms around that great grove

of cedars where Harris and Hargrove chose to stop the train an hour or so earlier than usual—but then, another hour wouldn't find them camping at any better a place. Here they would have to hack away at the wind-stunted cedar for
firewood, and scratch at the sandy bottoms in the nearby coulees to see if they
could pool up any murky water. Bass was sure they could find enough here to
satisfy their thirsty stock. But for the dust-choked humans, each wagon had
carried along at least one pair of hardwood kegs filled with clear, cool water
drawn from Black's Fork. Water enough to boil their supper and brew their coffee until they camped tomorrow night on the Little Muddy as they neared the
rugged north end of the Bear River Divide.

All three women pitched in to get a fire pit dug and a supper fire started,
while Flea and Magpie helped Lemuel and Leah lend their father a hand in
dropping the heavy cottonwood yoke from the thick necks of the docile oxen.
Four teams had managed to make it this far on the westward journey. With an
eager dreamer's foresight, Roman Burwell had started out from Westport with a
full six teams. Two of the oxen had fallen dead either of disease or exhaustion
back along the trail not far out of Laramie, and Roman had traded a third animal to Bridger for those four new three-inch iron tires Titus had fashioned for
him. That left the farmer with nine oxen to get them across the roughest stretch
of the road to Oregon. For the present, two of the beasts had the first signs of
cracked hooves, but the farmer was doing all he could with salves and plasters
to see those wounded creatures through each day's long, dusty journey. As it
was, Burwell carefully, thoughtfully, rotated his teams, so that after one day's
bone-jarring labor each two-ox hitch would have the next three days to rest up,
dawdling along under the watchful care of Lemuel and Leah, both of whom
herded them along on foot, using lean, seven-foot-long teamster's whips. And
when a long, steep slope was confronted, he could always bring up two or more
of the fresher oxen, temporarily chaining them in tandem to drag the heavy
wagon to the top of the rise.

Bass came back to camp with a small doe slumped across the front of his
saddle about the time the women had a bed of coals built up and their beds
spread out for the night beneath the shade of the wagon box, along with a large
square of waterproofed Russian sheeting they had strung from the side of the
wagon to the nearby clumps of cedar. The venison wouldn't make a meal fit for
kings, but they weren't about to starve either.

After shooing the too-curious dogs away with a pair of legbones Titus
hacked off the carcass with his tomahawk, the two Indian women showed
Amanda how to skin out the doe, then bone out the steaks they tossed in the
white woman's two large skillets. While the meat went to frying, they set about
showing Amanda how to chop up some of the liver and heart into fine pieces,
then sprinkle the cubes with a dusting of flour before they stuffed it inside short
sections of slippery intestine. Raking aside some of the gray ash and half-dead
embers at the outer extreme of the fire, Waits and Shell Woman laid more than

two dozen of their greasy treasures in the hot ashes, then promptly covered them with coals to slowly sizzle while they tended the steaks.

"This ain't the first you've et venison, is it, Lucas?" he asked his grandson.

The boy glanced over at his father. "My pa takes me hunting sometimes."

"You a good hunter?" Titus asked. "Like your pa?"

"We get some birds and rabbits, a few squirrels sometimes."

Roman cleared his throat self-consciously. "Don't always bring down big game. S'pose I ain't near as good with a gun as you've got to be all the years you been out here."

"Gran'papa gonna teach you how, Pa," Lucas declared.

A bit self-consciously, Roman reached down and pulled the boy against his leg, tousling his hair. "Yep, I s'pose your gran'pa can teach me 'bout hunting, son."

He instantly felt a stab of sadness for the man, having his own son point out his flaws and shortcomings to his face. But Lucas didn't know any better. He was just a sprout, a pup who didn't know any different, a child who would one day come to realize no man could be all things to his son.

Dropping to his knee, Titus said, "I can teach your pa to hunt in this country, I'm sure, 'cause he pretty damn good at ever'thing else, Lucas. Back where you come from, I know your pa was far better at ever'thing he done than I ever could be. An', when you get to your new home in Oregon country, your pa'll be the best at what he'll do out there too."

As he stood again, he glanced into Roman's face, finding deep appreciation written in Burwell's eyes.

The women had dragged the skillets off the flames to cool and Amanda had just put some water on to heat for cleaning when a trumpet sounded faintly at the far end of the long camp scattered and strung out through the cedar grove.

"What's that horn for?" Shadrach asked.

"They're calling the council meeting," Amanda said as she stood, kneading her hands into her apron, her eyes anxious as she stared into her husband's face.

Roman said, "That's the way they let everyone know Hargrove is getting ready to start."

"Fixin' to start in on Shad an' me," Titus replied.

"Maybeso we should leg on over there," Sweete suggested. "Since these doin's got to do with you an' me."

"Got everything to do with me too," Burwell said as he stepped around the edge of the fire pit. "Your families are with mine—so I think I got some say in this vote."

"Vote?" Titus repeated.

Amanda stepped up to loop her arm inside her husband's elbow. "Hargrove loves to take a vote on everything."

"Least he did when we was forming up our company back at Westport," Roman grumped. "But after he got hisself made captain of this train—"

"And after he got us to vote for all these rules he wanted for the journey," Amanda continued, "Hargrove hasn't had many meetings. And he hasn't called for any votes since we voted to give the lash to one of the men."

"The lash?" Shadrach asked.

She turned to him, her cheeks blushing slightly. "One of the married men, they caught him sneaking a look at the women while we was bathing in the Platte, back yonder by the Chimney Rock."

Titus asked, "So Hargrove give that poor fella some lashes?"

"Mr. Kinsey," Roman said. "From the look on Hargrove's face as he laid into Kinsey's back, I'd say our wagon captain would make a damn good hell-and-brimstone preacher!"

"He didn't stop till Mr. Kinsey passed right out," Amanda explained as she smoothed the front of her apron. "That's when they let Mrs. Kinsey and a couple of her husband's friends come and untie him from the wagon gate."

Titus ground his teeth in anger. "Tied the man to a wagon gate an' whupped him?"

Roman Burwell nodded. "Mrs. Kinsey, she knowed I had some salve along to put on the cuts our oxen or mules get. I give her some for them bad cuts on her husband's back."

"They out-an'-out whupped him like a dumb brute?" Scratch growled.

"I know he had some punishment comin'," Amanda confessed, "but Hargrove didn't need to cut the man to a bloody ribbon neither."

Burwell drew in a long sigh. "We all know how you gotta have rules, and how you gotta punish when the rules is broke. But, that was the first time Hargrove whipped anyone."

Shadrach asked, "He have the whole camp watch the whippin'?"

Roman nodded. "Women and children too."

With a wag of his head, Sweete commented, "After he cut that poor nigger's back up with his whip in front of every mother's child, growed or pup, he sure as hell didn't have to whip no one else from there on out, I'll wager."

"C'mon, Shadrach," Titus said as he stuffed a second pistol in his belt. "There's no telling what this Hargrove gonna do with us, if'n he'll whip a man half to death for sneaking a look at some gals takin' their bath in the river."

They took a few steps away from the fire before Scratch stopped and said, "Hol' on, Amanda. You ain't comin' along."

"You can't stop me," she argued. "Every other wife and mother gonna be there to see what goes on."

"But you can't vote," Titus said. "Maybe it's better you stay here . . . if'n there's a li'l trouble."

"If there's trouble, that just gives me an even better reason to come along."

"Titus," Roman used his father-in-law's name for the first time, "best you realize you aren't gonna talk her out of this."

"I ain't?"

Amanda wagged her head. "No, you aren't, Pa."

He snorted in disgust, but a grin crept onto his face as they started off again. "Lot of respect a father gets around here."

"Haven't you figgered it out yet, Pa?" she asked as Titus and Shad waved back at their wives, who were staying behind with all the children.

"Figgered what out?"

Roman jumped in to say, "That your daughter's just as mule-headed as you."

Bass smiled at Amanda. "Are you now?"

"Leastways," Shad said with a chuckle, "the woman's fortunate she got her mama's purty looks an' not your bird-dog face!"

"You best be careful who you call a dogface, Shadrach," Titus warned, squinting one eye at the tall man as they neared the assembly. "You damn well may need all your friends when you go up against a vote by preacher Hargrove."

A cool breeze stirred the air as Roman Burwell stepped through the women and children who parted for them. It was clear to Scratch how the lines had been drawn and solidified across the last day of travel. Those who had cast their lot with Phineas Hargrove now tended to cluster close by the wagon captain and his hired men at the right side of the circle, while the majority of the train comprised the other two thirds of that milling ring, with no clear leader to throw the weight of their votes behind. All they had to hold on to was that they knew far, far more about Oregon country than they knew about California. Most every pamphlet and news story published back east, most every backer of emigration, spoke only of Oregon. These settlers had cast their eyes on Oregon. They trusted the dream of *place* more than they could ever trust the persuasive charisma of that one powerful man and all his money.

As they entered the assembly, more than a dozen men made a point of crowding around Burwell to shake the man's hand, and that many more nodded or murmured with approval as Bass and Sweete followed Roman around the inner edge of the circle, stopping just short of that spot where Hargrove was holding court among his loyal supporters.

One of the faithful leaned in and whispered something to the captain.

Hargrove turned. "Ah, I see the principals have finally arrived," he gushed with enthusiasm and a metallic smile. "It's time we call this council of the Hargrove Oregon Company to order."

Titus leaned close to Amanda and whispered, "Ain't gonna be the Hargrove Oregon Company for much longer, is it?"

"Maybe call it the cowards-run-to-California company," she whispered back to Titus just before she stepped over to her husband's elbow and squeezed one of his big, rough hands. Just as quickly she inched back through that front row of men until she stood among the other women and children who would serve only as spectators for this rare practice of frontier democracy.

Only adult males possessed the right to vote. Their wives and children did not hold such a privilege. From that outer fringe of this assembly, Amanda could only watch what was guaranteed to have a bearing on her family's fortunes and its future from here on out, no matter how the vote came down.

Scratch watched his daughter take up her position with the other women, who all looked on in silence. Come what may this warm summer evening as the land finally cooled, he realized that the vote Hargrove would call for would affect his daughter's family, one way or the other. If Hargrove convinced enough of the emigrants to vote against Bass and Sweete tagging along to Fort Hall, then it was a certainty the two of them would have to push on ahead of the train so they could go through with their plans to help scratch up an old comrade from the beaver days to guide the farmers on down the Snake to the Columbia, on into Oregon country. But if enough of these emigrants turned aside the wishes of their wagon master, there might well be a chance that Hargrove would retaliate against the Burwells for what the wagon master would see as mutiny.

Titus Bass hadn't lived fifty-three years not to recognize an oily-tongued, snake-bellied, duplicitous bastard when he saw one. Dangerous thing was, Hargrove seemed just the sort of man mean enough to make anyone who turned against him pay for that transgression, and pay dearly. Throughout that day after the long procession had formed up and slowly rambled out of that meadow along Black's Fork, pushed for Muddy Creek, then dawdled through that easy crossing, Scratch had weighed out the heft of that dilemma.

Would it just be all the better for him and Shad to tell Hargrove that they would turn around and start back for Fort Bridger in the morning, then secretly slip around the far side of the Bear River Divide and march on to Fort Hall on their own—so there would be no more confrontations with the man and his bullies that might end up hurting his daughter and the ones she loved in the long run? Maybeso, the two of them didn't need to ride on to Fort Hall in any event. Wasn't it entirely possible that Roman and the others who would not be turned away from Oregon could find someone to pilot them to the Willamette on their own? Did these farmers and settlement folks really need two old hivernants throwing in to see them through to Fort Hall and their digging around for a pilot? Maybe this matter of his tagging along to the Snake River was causing more trouble than all the good he could ever do.

Phineas Hargrove stepped to the center of that open ground surrounded by the men who had selected him to serve as their captain all the way to Oregon, while his seven hired men dispersed among the others. Titus began to cipher how many men there were, how many votes there would be to count when it came down to a show of hands.

"I'm going to assume that most of you don't have any idea why I've heralded this meeting tonight with our trumpet," Hargrove began, his stentorian voice clear as a clarion bell over the crowd of hundreds.

"You don't want my father-in-law to ride along to Fort Hall," Burwell roared as the throng fell quiet. "Him and his friend, both men good on the trail—"

"They did not sign on at our Westport depot, the way the rest of you did," Hargrove interrupted. "If there is a rule, there must be a good reason for that rule. You all joined our company according to the rules, agreed to abide by the rules, and this wilderness is by far the last place we should be letting those rules slide—not here in the lawless wilderness."

"What harm does it do to bend a rule this one time?" asked a man at the edge of the crowd.

"I'll tell you what harm it does, Mr. Bingham. It begins the breakdown in civil order," Hargrove preached with that booming voice of his.

Another settler asked, "How will they break down civil order?"

Turning, the wagon master said, "Mr. Iverson, all a man has to do is look at these two . . . two ruffians Burwell wishes to bring along to see that there can be no good come of this to our wagon company."

"What are you claiming they're gonna do, Hargrove?"

He turned slightly again to address the new speaker, "Dahlmer, isn't it? Agreed, we have no idea what men such as these might do to disrupt the law-abiding orderliness of our company. These roughs have been freed of the constraints of civil society for more years than we could ever guess. They have lived without the fetters of responsible, God-fearing men, like the rest of you."

"How safe are our wives and daughters around these two strangers?" one of Hargrove's backers prompted.

"Yes, yes," Hargrove said. "Wouldn't you fear for your wives and daughters with such lawless, unscrupulous creatures as these ruffians and scoundrels along on the journey?"

"Hold on a minute!" cried a man standing near Burwell. "Why the devil we have to fear for our wives and daughters from these two? You know something about them you ain't told us?"

Hargrove took two steps toward the doubter. "Just look at them, dressed like Indians, their hair long and unkempt like a pagan savage keeps his hair. Do you want that specter residing in our camp?"

Off to Bass's left a man took a step into the ring before he spoke, "So what the blazes do you call that?"

Turning on his heel, the wagon master looked in the direction the farmer was pointing. "What, Ammons? Call what?"

"That pilot you hired back at Fort Laramie."

With a hearty laugh, Hargrove asked, "Harris? You mean Harris?"

"Yeah," Ammons responded with a tug on his soiled suspenders. "These two who came along with Burwell don't look no worse than your handpicked pilot."

"For God's sake, the man is our pilot!" Hargrove shrieked.

Roman Burwell snorted, "Sure as the devil looks like he's *your* pilot to California, Hargrove!"

"Listen, Burwell," Hargrove snarled as he whirled on the big farmer, "ever since Laramie, Harris has been our pilot. Each and every one of you trusted in me to engage a pilot when we reached Fort Laramie. This man is our guide. He's not like those other two who threw in with your family at Fort Bridger."

"The man's my father-in-law," Burwell growled. "An' the other'n is his good friend. That makes 'em both near kin to me."

"But we do not have room for any travelers to throw in with this company!" Hargrove said, frustration crimping his features.

A new voice called out, "What's it hurt?"

He turned on the man, "Why, Fenton—it hurts the rule of law and orderliness here in the wilderness. If we let things slip out here, even a little, then we truly are not bringing God's order and civilization to our new homes."

"These two won't ruin nothing!" another shouted.

Then a voice seconded that opinion, "And I haven't seen either of 'em coming round my wife and daughter like you claimed they would."

Hargrove countered, "This is but the first day! There hasn't been time for these beasts to show their true stripes."

"Maybeso we oughtta put it to a vote!" called a voice.

"No, Pruett!" cried the wagon master. "We haven't had our full debate."

Bingham took two steps away from Burwell and yelled, "We can call for a vote now!"

"No!" Hargrove bellowed his desperation, wheeling to gesture at his supporters. "We haven't heard anything from the other side!"

"I say let's vote!" Burwell called.

Titus felt the palpable surge of electricity that shot through the murmuring crowd like a jolt of lightning.

"No—you can't!"

But Burwell was not distracted. "Those who don't want my father-in-law and his friend along to Fort Hall—"

"Not yet, you can't vote yet!"

Yet Burwell continued, "—let's see a show of hands!"

Immediately those on the far side of the assembly raised their arms—perhaps as many as twenty men, along with Hargrove's eight hired men, while the train captain began to wave both of his arms frantically.

"No, no—there must be time for more debate!"

Roman Burwell continued, "So we should have a show of hands for those who see nothing wrong with these two men coming to Fort Hall with us."

Only a blind man without ears would have trouble sorting out which way that vote went. As soon as more than sixty men held their arms in the air, they began a spontaneous cheer of relief, of jubilation, of revolt against the tyranny of the man who had arrogantly turned his back on them and would be making for California, leaving them high and leaderless at Fort Hall.

Burwell turned to Hoyt Bingham and said in a voice just loud enough for those close to hear, "I think it's time we got this all settled here and now."

"The new captain?" Bingham whispered.

"Yep. Let's get this over with so we can toss Hargrove out on his ear."

Bingham quickly looked at the wagon master shuffling over to his supporters, listened to the noise of their arguing, then pursed his lips and nodded his head once in agreement.

"Friends! Friends! Fellow members of the Hargrove Oregon Company!" Roman bellowed, shaking both arms aloft for silence. "We have an important vote to make tonight. Even more important than the one we just made."

"Vote?" Hargrove squealed as he wheeled about on his bootheels. "What other vote? You can't do this without your captain's permission!"

Burwell took a step toward the center of the ring and told the crowd, "We oughtta vote on a new captain!"

For a long moment the entire assembly fell into a dead hush. Not a sniffle or cough, not one shuffle of a boot on the sandy soil or the murmur of a mother scolding a child—nothing for three long heartbeats. Then all hell broke loose. Hargrove's supporters and hired men began screaming their objections—which only prompted the man's detractors to cheer, clap their hands, and stomp their feet on the ground. Which drowned out most all of the naysayers.

Once more Roman was signaling for some quiet; then he yelled, "For our new captain, I throw in the name of Hoyt Bingham!"

"Hoyt B-bingham?" Hargrove yelled.

"I put a second on that vote!" Iverson shouted.

"How 'bout you, Roman?"

Burwell turned to the speaker, who stood at the side of the throng. "Mr. Ryder, I do appreciate your confidence in me an' all—"

"You stood up to that two-tongued no-good who lied about taking us all the way to Oregon," Ryder said as he scratched at his gray-flecked whiskers. "I say you showed you got the stuff to be our captain!"

A moment after some of the crowd began to roar its approval, Roman shushed them again and said, "No. I won't let my name be put in the vote."

"Why, Roman?"

Burwell turned to the man. "Mr. Truell, I won't let you vote on me 'cause I know I'm nothing more than a simple farmer. I know I haven't got the brains to lead this outfit to Oregon."

That's when Titus roared, "But you got the heart to do it, son!"

Roman turned and stared incredulously at his father-in-law with something in his eyes that told Scratch that the man was about to loose some tears.

Suddenly Bingham was beside Burwell, saying, "I don't believe what Roman Burwell says when he tells you he doesn't have the brains to lead this outfit. But I do believe that Roman has the heart to make a good captain of this

Oregon company. I will serve as your captain . . . but only if Roman Burwell will serve as my coleader!"

The deafening roar of more than two hundred throats drowned out the exasperated cries of the desperate knot of men and women which had tightened around Phineas Hargrove.

"All those in favor!" Bingham called for the vote.

But the noise was even louder still, frightening magpies and jays from their roosts in trees for a full half mile around the cedar breaks.

"Any opposed?" Bingham shouted. "Any 'cept Hargrove's California Company?"

"But we're going to the same place!" Hargrove growled as he parted his supporters and advanced on Bingham and Burwell, his hired men in tow. "I will serve out my term as the leader of this whole company—"

Suddenly Roman and Bingham stood shoulder to shoulder before him, more than two dozen friends closing in a phalanx behind their newly elected leaders. That stopped the wagon master and his young muscle in their tracks.

"Unless Hoyt Bingham has something against it," Burwell announced to the throng, "Phineas Hargrove and his people can travel with us till we get to Fort Hall—but only 'cause the rest of us gonna let them stay."

"Amen to that!" Bingham cheered. "Out here in this new country we're gonna build, a man can't stay leader if the people he leads decide they won't follow him!"

Burwell drew himself up and looked down at the smooth-faced Hargrove. "It's a new day, Cap'n. No more are you gonna walk on the rest of us just so you can get yourself and your guns to California."

The apologetic look that came over Hargrove's face appeared convincing enough to the crowd.

"I-I can see now where I've been a little harsh," he confessed with downcast eyes. "But, I had a job to do—a job you men of this train elected me to."

"Now you take your people to California," Roman reminded him.

"Yes," Hargrove agreed, appearing contrite and duly chastised. "I'd proudly serve as the leader of this train until we reach Fort Hall . . . but, it appears I must turn over command to your new leaders: Burwell and Bingham."

The crowd roared again as men pounded the new upstarts on the back. Hargrove reached out his hand, shaking with both of those new leaders as his hired men held back the gathering. That brief formality seen to, the wagon master turned abruptly and disappeared with his men forming a protective ring around him as they took their leave from the low knoll.

Maybeso, Titus thought, things just might be working out for these folks after all.

• • •

"You see'd Roman?"

Amanda turned to answer her father early the next morning, "He and Lemuel went down to the hollow to find one of the cows that wandered away last night."

"Together?" he asked, some small itch nagging him, small but buried deep enough he could not quite find it to scratch.

"Yes," she replied. "Something wrong, Pa?"

Titus shook his head and lamely tried out a gap-toothed smile on her. "Naw—I just 'spect they'll blow that trumpet anytime now an' the train be rolling out."

"We're about ready here," Amanda declared. "Team's hitched and the milkers are over there with Leah and Annie."

As she turned away to toss the last of the bedrolls over the rear gate of the wagon, Scratch slowly scanned the cedar breaks that surrounded them on three sides. There wasn't all that much tall cover, and it sure as hell wasn't a forest the likes of which you'd find against the foothills. Just some low scrub cedar that ran more than five miles in all directions across the rolling, rumpled landscape. But the thickets were nonetheless tall enough to hide a man on foot, and sure as hell thick enough to conceal a cow that had wandered off in search of a fresh mouthful of grass sometime during the night.

The trumpet blew, a shrill blare on the hot breeze that foretold a scorcher of a day.

And he turned, finding Amanda over by the wagon, wheeling suddenly, her eyes finding him.

The trumpet blew its warning again.

Scratch watched his daughter swallow as she blinked into the distance, smoothing her open hands down the rumpled pleats at the front of her dirty brown dress.

"Ma!"

They both whirled, finding Lemuel trudging out of the cedar breaks, the front of his shirt dark with sweat. This early in the cool of daybreak? As the youth lunged closer, Bass could see how his hair was plastered with dampness, his face glistening.

"Lem!" she cried, starting for him.

"I heard the trumpet!" he gushed breathlessly as he approached the wagon and his mother, who lunged forward to greet him. "Come fast as I could."

"Where's your pa?"

"He's not here?" the boy asked as his dusty boots slid to a halt on the flaky soil. "Didn't he come back with the cow yet?"

"N-no," she answered, her voice small, pinched off.

Titus was there immediately, his hands gripping Lemuel's shoulders, turning the lad toward him. "Where's your pa?"

"Dunno, Gran'pa," the boy said, fear starting to show in his eyes.

"Thought the two of you went out after the cow together?"

That third and final call of the trumpet blared brassily over the encampment. Titus turned quickly to the east. Saw how the sun would be rising soon.

Lemuel nodded and swallowed hard after his race to get back to camp. "We did, together. But, it was getting later and later. Pa thought we ought to split up so he could work the other side of the hill from me."

"You don't know where he went?"

Turning, the boy pointed. "I come from there. Pa was on the far side of the hill. I figured he or Hargrove's men'd find the cow afore I got to the end of the draw, then doubled back—like Pa told me to—"

"You say Hargrove's men?" Titus interrupted, his belly tightening.

With a nod and a gulp, Lemuel answered, "Three of 'em ran onto me. They was riding horses. Asked where Pa was, was he on foot like me. I told 'em we was looking for one of our cows wandered off. They said for me to start on back to the wagons—we was pulling out soon."

"Where'd they go?" he asked, a little desperation creeping into his voice, that tiny itch grown to a full-blown uncontrollable urge just screaming to be scratched.

"They said they'd find Pa, then headed off the way I told 'em he went," the boy admitted. "Said they could find the cow better on horseback than Pa could on f—"

"You say they was riding horses?"

"Yes—"

Titus had freed his desperate grip on the boy's shoulders and was turning away as Hoyt Bingham rode up with Hargrove and three of his hired men on horseback. Shadrach was coming over from the shady spot where his family had slept out the night.

"That's them, Gran'pa," Lemuel declared in a quiet voice just behind Bass's shoulder.

"Who?"

"The three who said they'd find Pa and the cow."

"Them three ridin' up behin't Hargrove?"

"Yessir."

"Great God, Amanda!" Hargrove bawled as Digger lowered his head and growled. "You haven't got your yoke of oxen hitched to that wagon yet?"

"We're . . . looking for Roman."

Hargrove acted as if taken aback by that pronouncement. "But, we're leaving right now. Already put the head of the march on the trail for the Little Muddy."

"Oh, no, no!" she whimpered. "Roman's not back—"

"The boy here says these three niggers o' your'n turned him back from helpin' his pa look for a missing cow," Titus interrupted his daughter, instantly snagging the attention of the five riders as he moved toward Amanda beside the wagon. Shad angled around so that he stood behind Bingham and the quartet of horsemen, his double-barreled flintlock smoothbore cradled across his left forearm.

"What about this, Hargrove?" Bingham demanded.

Turning to one of his hired men, Hargrove asked, "Yes, what about that, Corrett? You know where Burwell went?"

Corrett shrugged, pulling at an earlobe. "We run onto the boy out in the thicket, like the old man said."

Then a second rider explained, "But we never saw hide or hair of him. So we come on back afore we got left behind."

"No sign of him, Jenks?" asked the ousted wagon master.

That second rider shook his head convincingly. "No, Mr. Hargrove. No sign."

Turning back to Amanda and Bingham, clearly ignoring Bass, Hargrove crossed his wrists on his saddlehorn and said, "There you have it, Mrs. Burwell. My men weren't able to find your husband. Perhaps he's been bitten by a rattler."

"Oh, Pa—"

Titus looped his arm over her shoulder as she started to sag. He held her up against his side. "We'll find him, Shad an' me."

Worry creased Bingham's face. "Who's going to get your wagon moving?" He pointed off at the rest of the wagons, the last of which were rumbling into motion, oxen lowing, mules braying, men barking commands at the animals, and women hollering at their children to catch up. "The train's on its way."

"You've got to stop them, Hoyt!" Amanda shrieked, trembling fingers at her lips.

Calmly, deliberately, before Bingham could utter a word, Hargrove declared, "We can't do that. Wagon master Bingham was elected by all the people to get this company through to Oregon. We have these rules for the good of the entire group."

Scratch had to restrain his daughter as she attempted to lunge forward, sobbing, "But you can't go off and leave us!"

Bingham started to speak, then wagged his head. "Roman will show up soon enough."

"One man and one cow cannot stay this company from the miles we must put behind us today," Hargrove asserted as he leaned back and straightened his spine reflexively. "Your husband should have thought more about you than he did his cow, Mrs. Burwell," he said, putting a real emphasis on the word *Mrs.*

"Wh-where you going?" Titus asked as Bingham and Hargrove pulled their horses around in that jumble of hired men.

"Wagon master Bingham has got a train to move one day closer to Oregon," Hargrove announced with triumph brightening his face.

Then Scratch could only stare at the backs of those five men as they kicked their horses into a lope and shot away, intent on catching the head of the column just then winding its way toward the sagebrush bottoms, raising those first choking spirals of yellow dust for the day.

FOURTEEN

As he scanned the thick cedar breaks before him, Scratch wondered which of them he would find first: the cow, or his son-in-law.

There was no chance of uncertainty here. In his black-and-white world, there was enough evidence already in hand to assure himself that Hargrove and his cronies had something to do with Roman Burwell's not getting back to camp in time to depart with the rest of the train . . . with or without that missing cow. If one of the Burwells' cows had ever managed to wander off on its own through the night.

At the corner of his eye, he caught sight of Sweete again, coming out of a knot of horse-high cedar. They waved and gestured to tell one another the direction they were moving in their search; then each disappeared from the view of the other once more. It had been that way ever since the two old friends had mounted up and left their wives behind with several rifles and a pistol apiece for them and Amanda too. Titus Bass didn't trust Phineas Hargrove and them young bucks of his any farther than he could puke.

"I'm goin' with you," Sweete had announced as the backs of those five riders headed down the long slope toward the bottoms, where the grayed canvas of the wagontops looked like the back of a bull snake winding its way north by west for the Little Muddy and the north end of the Bear River Divide.

For a long moment Amanda had shoved herself against her father, clinging to him, sobbing into his chest. That's when Titus noticed his four grandchildren coming their way, their eyes filled with questions, even the beginnings of a little terror.

"Amanda, your young'uns," he whispered and pulled her away from him slightly so he could peer into her face. "They need you right now."

"B-but . . . Roman?"

His eyes narrowed meaningfully. "We'll find 'im. Shadrach an' me. You . . . you see to the young'uns while we're gone. Don't let 'em see you worry."

She nodded and swallowed deeply, quickly dragging a palm down both of her cheeks as she blinked her eyes clear. "Yes, you're right," she said bravely, then attempted a smile. "I'll wait here with the children while you and Shad go f-find Roman."

The children stopped right behind her, Annie and little Lucas both tucking themselves under their mother's arms as they pressed themselves against her legs. She clutched them desperately. "We'll wait here for Gran'pa to find your father . . . then we'll be on our way for the day."

"But them others has left without us," Lemuel said.

"It doesn't matter!" she snapped at her eldest.

Titus put a hand on the boy's shoulder. "That train ain't goin' nowhere we can't find it. All them tracks. We'll catch up afore end of the day, son. Tie up them dogs so they stay right here with the rest of you."

"Aw-awright, sir."

He patted the lad on the shoulder, then turned to his tall friend. "Let's see the women got 'em plenty of guns ready afore we light out."

Each of them had stuffed an extra pistol in their belts before leaving their two Indian wives with the spare rifles and smoothbores. Both of them could shoot center well enough. There was never any telling what sort of critter might wander out of these cedar breaks to pose a danger to the women and children they were leaving behind. Four-legged and clawed . . . or two-legged and snake-eyed to boot.

"Why can't I go with you?" Lemuel demanded as he sprinted up to them a few minutes later when the men swung into their saddles.

Titus had peered down at the boy's face. "Your ma, she needs you right now. An' I need to know I left a man behind to watch over the rest, Lemuel."

The boy took a step back from the horse, peering up at his grandfather from beneath the shapeless brim of his low-crowned hat, his eyes glinting with a newfound courage. "Yessir."

"That's a good man," Titus said quietly as he reined aside.

He made it a point to ride right past Amanda as she stepped toward them in their leave-taking. When she held out her hand he reached out with his. And seeing the tears streaking her dust-covered face, he gripped her thin fingers a brief instant as his horse carried him past. Then kicked the horse for all it was worth.

He was feeling his own eyes sting as the animal beneath him bolted into a gallop.

And he didn't slow the horse until he and Shad reached the bottom of the

This item needs to be routed to HOPE_MILLS:
Hope Mills Library

3411 Golfview Road

Hope Mills, NC 28348-2266

Request date: 2018-03-14
Slip Date: 2018-03-14 14:59
Sent by: South Granville Branch Library
GRANVILLE

next swale where he could no longer look back over his shoulder and see the wagon camp. Nothing more than that long smudge of dust rising yellow against the hot, pale blue of the summer sky as the sun finally broke the horizon—instantly creating shadows in the cedar thickets where before they had been only shades of gray outlines.

He found the body at the head of a draw.

Instantly sizing things up from the saddle, Titus did not find a single boot-mark until it was plain how the rider had dropped from his horse and approached the animal. Those weren't Roman Burwell's square-toed boot tracks either. Not deep enough, nowhere big enough for the tall sodbuster. Titus sighed, searched in three directions for Shad, took one last look around for sign of Roman or maybe a strange rider on the horizon, then came out of the saddle. Dropping the reins he stepped toward the carcass of the milk cow. A few flies were clustered on the udder, and by the hundreds they were already clotting the long, deep gash across the throat.

He followed the half dozen boot tracks to the carcass, saw how the man had walked right up to the docile animal, then slashed its neck then and there. There was a dribble of blood where the boot tracks ended, then cowprints as the animal stumbled sideways, flinging its head and blood in both directions until it fell several yards from where the boot tracks ended. Titus stepped beyond the last of those prints, right over to the cow, and knelt beside its head. He held out his left hand, fingertip tapping the wide puddle of dark brown molasses beneath the carcass.

Cold. A little gummy beneath the crusty surface. But soaked into the ground and hard for the most part.

Wiping his fingers across the gritty soil, he stood and turned back for the horse. Shoving his right foot into the wide cottonwood stirrup, Scratch heaved himself into the saddle and shifted the big .54 across his thighs. Things did not look good for Roman.

Whoever it was came out here did this sometime after dark last night. This killing wasn't done in the last few hours. The lone horseman had wrangled the cow away from the rest of the stock, then herded it over two hills and into the bottom of this draw. When he finally had the animal boxed at the head of the draw, he had dismounted and slit its neck.

Things did not look good for Roman Burwell at all.

Slamming his heels into his horse's ribs, Titus Bass tasted the sour burn of dread rising in his throat with the burn of gall.

"If You really do listen to folks," he whispered bitterly as he reined directly up the side of the coulee, "then I want You to listen to me. You can't do this to Amanda. Can't take Roman from her like this."

He suddenly saw Shad appear at the top of the next hill, farther south than he would have thought to look, but back in the direction that unknown rider would have herded the cow. Sweete yanked his reins to the side, hard, forcing his horse to make a circle, then a second tight circle as he held his rifle high in the air. When Shad stopped after that third circle, he pointed with his rifle and kicked his horse into motion down the side of the draw. Titus hammered his horse into a gallop a heartbeat later. They both reached the body about the same time.

That's when he raised his eyes to the sky and whispered again, but only one word this time, "P-please."

Finding it hard to breathe, Titus was the first to leap out of his saddle, sprinting those last few yards toward the gnarled, wind-sculpted cedar where Roman Burwell was tied—his arms outstretched, legs spread-eagled. His shirt had been ripped from his shoulders and hung in tatters from the high waist of his drop-front, button-fly britches. From the bruises up and down the washboard of muscles rippling over his chest and belly, it was plain to see they had done their best to break the man's ribs. And that gave him hope as he lunged to a stop a foot away from the body.

He grabbed a handful of thick hair on Roman's brow, pulled the head back so he could peer into the face. The eyes barely fluttered. By damn—he was still alive!

Sweete was trudging up behind him, swinging that big .62-caliber flintlock side to side as he covered Titus's back. For a heartfelt moment, Bass looked at the sky once more. "Thankee. Thankee more'n You'll ever know."

"He breathin' any?" Shad asked quietly.

"Some," he answered. "Barely. Roman?" Then he thought and told his friend, "Cut 'im down, Shadrach. I'll hold him up best I can while you cut—"

"He's a big lad, Titus," Sweete volunteered as he stepped right against Bass and propped his .62 against the foot of the cedar. "Lemme hold him and you cut the ropes."

Soon as he dropped his rifle against a clump of sage, Scratch slashed through the narrow rope that held the legs spread; then as he cut through the bonds around the wrists, the body sank from sheer exhaustion and the relentless tug of gravity.

Sweete supported Burwell in his arms as Titus dragged the farmer's legs out to the side. "Like they was crucifying him, Scratch. Tied him up this'a way— like they was crucifying this poor man."

"Cruci—" he repeated with a grunt as he helped Shad ease the big farmer's body down onto the rocky ground. "What's that?"

"Way they done to Jesus when they kill't Him."

Titus slipped the blade of his knife under the greasy strip of cloth the attackers had tied around Burwell's mouth. "Jesus, that fella in the Bible?"

Shad scooted back on his knees and laid a hand on Roman's chest. "That's Him. My mama always wanted me to know that story. How the man's enemies hung Him on a cross. Died. Later He come back to living for all time."

As he slowly patted Burwell's cheeks, Titus said, "I 'member how my ma told us young'uns that story over an' over too. Damn—wish I'd brung some water with us."

"I'll go fetch some," Sweete volunteered but hesitated to move.

Scratch laid his ear against Roman's bare, blood-crusted chest. Then lifted his eyes to Shad's. "We need to get him back."

"How?"

For a moment he cogitated on it, staring at the two horses. "He's a big chunk. You think you can hold 'im up?"

"Alone? On my horse?"

"Ain't gonna work," Titus agreed. "G'won back to the wagon. They got them ridgepoles lashed under the belly. Bring a pair of my woman's buffler robes too, an' two or three coils of rope."

"Rawhide all right?"

"Any rope—buffler, rawhide—just be quick about it."

Sweete clambered to his feet, swept up his .62, then paused a moment before he laid it back against the clump of sage beside Bass's. "You keep that. I got my belt guns along. I best leave that'un with you . . . 'case someone shows up."

Scratch shook his head. "Ain't no one gonna come back, Shadrach. They left him for dead after they beat him. Cowards like them, they're long gone now."

The big man's face hardened like stone. "You an' me both know who it was."

"Maybe not the three or four of 'em it took to drag the man down," Bass said, holding up one of Burwell's hands, studying the raw, bloodied knuckles. "From the looks of the scuffle, they didn't have a easy time of it. One of 'em's gotta have some bruises too. I figger that's why they beat him so bad—even after he couldn't fight back no more."

Sweete stood over them, casting a wide shadow on Titus. "How they get him down?"

"Back of his head's crusted with blood. They laid him out with a gun butt, maybe whacked 'im with a rifle barrel. Only way them bastards make a big corncracker like this to drop to his knees."

"I'll be back quick's I can," Shad promised.

Titus only nodded, watching his friend jump astride the big horse and saw the reins around in a tight circle, the animal lunging away with a grunt.

When he looked back down, he saw that the new sunlight was starting to reach Burwell's eyes. He shifted a little so he could keep the face in some shade. Swollen, cracked lips. Puffy eyes. Tiny cuts on the brow and cheeks, blood crusted in the six-day-old stubble on his chin. The wounds had hardened, their dribble almost completely dry. Hadn't been that long ago the attackers had approached the farmer, likely claiming they had come to help him find the cow that was already drawing flies and dung beetles farther up the draw.

As he held Roman Burwell across his thigh, out there a few yards away

Titus saw the scuffed ground where the struggle had taken place. Likely one had come up behind Roman as he struggled with one or more of them at his front, at least from the way the ground was trampled. And it was easy to see from the knees of his britches that the farmer had his legs knocked out from under him. But he was still alive.

That's when Titus looked back at the aching blue of that midsummer sky, cloudless, flawless, pristine, and pure. He had never asked anything of the First Maker, of his mother's Creator, from the God of Brigham Young's Saints, nothing for himself. Never had he asked, much less pleaded and begged the way he had this morning. When it came down to asking on behalf of someone else, Titus Bass would not hesitate to plead and beg. He was not ashamed as he cradled his son-in-law in his arms and shooed the annoying flies from the oozy wounds. He was not ashamed that he had asked for the help of a power far greater than he. Too many of those he had known did believe—be they the women of his Johnston clan back in Boone County. Or be they the shamans and rattle-shakers of the Ute, Shoshone, or Crow clans he had wintered among. They had a different One, but he figured it had to be the same One in the end.

More and more of late, he had felt the presence of something greater than himself.

In his coming to this country, Titus Bass had first sensed how his heart sang with the endlessness and exquisite beauty of the land, both plains and mountains. For a long time, he hadn't realized that the feeling making his heart swell had really been the One talking to him, those first simple words he could not recognize, much less understand. It was only the utter freedom, the timelessness of each new bend in a creek or the view from the crest of a hill just topped. For a long time, Scratch had only thought the music he felt in his heart was merely the fact that he was here and now in a place few would ever see.

But there was the God-talkers, old friends like Asa McAfferty and Bill Williams—circuit-riding preachers who, although they had strayed from the path, nonetheless laid claim to the impossible, so much of the impossible that Titus Bass could only have doubted all the more the presence of any spiritual force in all of this wildness . . . be it the nature of the wilderness itself before the coming of man, or the nature of man alone and unfettered in that wilderness. Those who claimed to believe, be they white or red, they were merely superstitious, and maybe to be pitied for their scary beliefs. He himself was not helpless in the face of what might confront him. He had stood tall and bold against the wind—and survived without clinging to a superstitious belief in something he could not see.

Then he had held his baby daughter in his hands. And over the next few weeks he listened to Waits-by-the-Water tell him more and more about the One Above, the First Maker, the Grandfather, each day as they plodded north from Taos, making for that next rendezvous on Ham's Fork of the Green in '34. By the time he had truly heard his daughter's name whispered in the softness of the breeze that caressed his face, Titus Bass had taken that first step in admitting to himself that there was something far more powerful than man himself, something far greater than this wilderness that challenged his courageous breed. Perhaps . . . just perhaps there was some force that had created him and this land, a power that had pulled him west into this uncompromising garden of beauty and sudden death where he could no longer deny its existence.

How, he thought, could he have ever gazed up at the tall and hoary peaks of these Rocky Mountains, still mantled with snow in the heat of summer here far below, and not admit that there was some great life force that had created all of this? How could he have ever lain on his back, elbow curled beneath his head, and stared up at the night sky with its countless, numberless, infinite tally of stars and not accept that some great hand was at work in this world, if not at work in the tiniest recesses of his own insignificant heart?

While a younger man, a man more prone to squinting out at the world around him through a cynical eye, might have determined that any belief in the spiritual was nothing more than a weak-minded person's attempt to explain away a magician's tricks or the vagaries of unexplainable happenstance . . . Scratch had simply had too damn much happen right before his eyes for him not to admit the presence of some all-powerful might at play here in this wilderness, where the trappings of civilized man and his society had not sullied this high and pristine world the way they had contaminated most everything back east. Leave it to others to refute the existence of a power outside themselves.

Titus Bass had seen how a white buffalo calf robe told the old sightless Porcupine Brush that Scratch and the rest of Mad Jack Hatcher's men were sorely in need of rescue from the Blackfoot days before the white men were attacked, telling Goat Horn's Shoshone warriors they must ride hard and fast to save their trapper friends.*

And Titus Bass had seen how some all-powerful spirit had worked its healing through Shell Woman to save Shadrach Sweete's life. Even to turning that bloodied black hump fur carved off a buffalo cow into a strip of creamy-white hide—the color of which was more sacred than anything else to Shell Woman's people.

How could Porcupine Brush, blind and nearly deaf as well, have known the white men needed help, if he hadn't been told by the First Maker through that sacred buffalo calf hide? And how was it that Shad's unstoppable bleeding was healed and that makeshift wrap turned white if not through a power that answered Shell Woman's fervent prayer, if not as an answer to Scratch's own prayer to spare the life of his old friend? The two of them hadn't talked about it much at all since that stormy night down on the South Platte. Some things a man found hard to describe, much less explain, even to himself, especially to

---

* *Buffalo Palace*

others . . . no matter that they had gone through the very same experience together.

So if not a man to pray for himself, eventually Titus Bass had begun to pray
for others. To ask that the power of that great hand be brought to bear on the
fortunes of those he loved and cared for. How he had asked to get Waits back
from the Blackfoot. Prayed that the pox would not take her from him. Asked to
be freed from the grip of the desert, and the Diggers, and the distance too. And
how he had begged that Roman Burwell be spared to his family.

In the end this simple man realized that what blessings were showered upon
his loved ones would be showered upon him too.

By the time they got Roman back to the wagon, even the train's dust had disappeared from the horizon. By then, the two old friends had put hours of work behind them.

Upon his return to the coulee, Shad explained he hadn't wasted a lot of time
when he rode up, yelling for their wives to fetch him the spare rope from the
pack animals while he himself untied six of the hardwood ridgepoles from beneath the wagon box where Burwell kept them secured. They, and eight shorter
poles, had been brought west with a large section of oiled Russian sheeting—
kept in the event they needed additional shelter and had to erect a wall tent, or
might use the extra canvas for repairs to the main wagon cover. With the two
long poles tied into a V and four shorter ones quickly strapped across them, he
laid the two buffalo robes over the back of the pack animal, then climbed into
the saddle once more. That's when he said Amanda had come running up,
pleading with him to take her back to Roman.

"I've got to see him!" she begged, gazing up at the tall man in the saddle.

"Can you ride?"

"I can ride."

As he began to turn, prepared to have his wife fetch up one of their saddle
horses, Amanda pulled herself up atop that packsaddle frame to which he had
lashed the improvised travois. "You ever ride 'thout a saddle?"

"No," she answered with determination. "But, I've never had my husband
near get himself killed neither. Let's go."

As soon as Shad and Amanda had neared the scene, Titus watched her pull
back on the reins of that packhorse and leap off, her skirts a'swirl as she
bounded to the ground and started leaping over the sage, dodging around the
wind-stunted cedar.

"Pa! Pa!" she cried, her cheeks streaked with moisture as she came sliding to
her knees beside him. "Oh . . . Roman."

Gently, Titus pulled himself out from under Burwell and held Roman's head
up while she fit herself beneath his bare, bloodied shoulders. Bass got to his
feet, feeling the cramped muscles protest in one leg where they had gone to

sleep while he did what he could to shade his son-in-law from the cruel mid-summer sun.

"Here," Shad called, then tossed Scratch an old oak canteen. "I brung that for Roman."

In turn Titus handed it over to Amanda and stepped back as he watched her drag up the end of her dress, then the bottom of her dirty petticoat. Onto a corner of this she carefully poured some water from the canteen, then dabbed it on the first of his cuts and puffy bruises.

"How far they ahead of us, by the time you got back?" Scratch asked.

"Can't see nothin' of 'em no more," Sweete admitted.

Titus wagged his head, all the more angry for it. "Hargrove gonna make sure he covers ground today."

"Make it so we can't catch 'em today, fast as he's driving 'em," Shad agreed.

With a nod of recognition, Bass took a step toward Amanda, but Sweete caught his elbow and dragged him back.

"Stay here with me awhile, Scratch. Ain't nothing you can do for 'im right now."

"You're right. But these hands what wanna choke those bastards need somethin' to do," Titus explained. "We need to be tying up a travois for Roman."

As they bent over their work repositioning the cross members, then started tying on the cradle of a double thickness of buffalo robes in which they would place the injured man, Sweete confessed, "I wanted to keep you over here, where your daughter couldn't hear."

"Hear what?"

"Hear us talk on what we're gonna do about Roman an' Hargrove, an' them badger-eyed bastards done this to your daughter's husband."

His hands stopped working at the series of knots and he stared at Sweete. "You're in for making 'em pay for what they done to Roman?"

"Even if I wasn't your friend, I'd throw in with you just to have a chance to see their faces when they realize they ain't getting away with treatin' folks like this."

Bass grinned hugely. "While you was gone, I was thinkin' my own self."

"Your notion gonna happen tonight?"

"Soon as we get these three families caught up to the train."

Shad wagged his head. "That'll take some doing."

"Then we'll do it tomorrow night."

It was all but dark when they had to admit that the oxen just weren't going to be goaded into any more speed, any more miles that day. Reluctantly, they made camp as the stars winked into view and the women scrambled around to build a fire there beside the Little Muddy. At least they had some water. And some scrub oak, cedar, and sage for their fire—enough to last out the night.

Amanda steadfastly remained inside the wagon with Roman, day and night. She and Lucas budged from the wounded man's side only to trudge into the brush and relieve themselves, once they crawled into the crowded box and set-tled in beside him. Mercifully, the farmer hadn't come to as the travois bounded and jostled over the sage on the way back to the wagon, or as the two trappers hoisted the big man onto the tailgate. Burwell had grunted a time or two, and groaned in some misery, but he never did awaken that first day, even though his eyelids fluttered from time to time as he was jostled about. Waits-by-the-Water brought Amanda a half-full bucket of water and a dipper. Toote brought them a kettle of her hot soup.

Not long after the moon came up and Titus had Lemuel put his little brother and two sisters to bed beneath a low awning strung from the side of the wagon, Waits came to find her husband talking with Shad as the two sat just outside that ring of light given off by the flames.

"Ti-tuzz," she said softly as she approached the two men.

He turned, seeing her, and smiled. "Your soup was good," he said in English.

"Toote make," she responded in his tongue. "Come now."

"Come?"

She pointed back at the wagon. "Call for you. Amanda."

"She needs me to come?"

Waits nodded. "Tell you come—Roman, he awake."

Bass scrambled to his feet quickly. "Stay here and keep a sharp ear to the night, Shadrach."

"I'll be right here."

Then Titus stopped and stood there a'swell with feelings and all fumble-footed. "Shad—I . . . I . . ."

Sweete bolted to his feet and held open his arms. They briefly pounded one another on the back. Shad said, "It's good news. Him awake an' all."

With a nod, Scratch pulled away from their embrace and said, "Tomorrow night, we'll cull a few outta Hargrove's herd for what they done to Roman."

Hurrying with Waits back to the wagon, he handed her his rifle and stepped to the rear pucker hole, pulling aside the curtain and peering over the tailgate. In a whisper Titus asked, "He awake?"

Amanda turned, smiling at her father. "Yes, Pa," she whispered, yet with some undisguised excitement in her voice. Then she leaned over her husband. "Roman, my pa's here."

Bass could hear the soft murmur of words but could not make any of them out as Amanda raised his head slightly from the pillow and propped his shoul-ders against her side.

"He says thank you, Pa."

That tugged at his heart something fierce. "You tell 'im that's what we do for family, Amanda."

"Before you got here, he said something about the sun," she continued, then put her ear down to Roman's mouth again. "Said you kept his face outta the sun for a long time this morning. That what you did till I got there?"

"Yeah."

Burwell murmured more, then she explained. "He said to thank you for that, but the sun really did feel good when it touched his face after he'd been so cold."

Titus took a deep breath, then asked her, "He tell you . . . anything how they come to leave him out there?"

"No," she answered. "He hasn't said anything about what happened. I decided I would have to ask you what state you found him in."

All the better to take some time afore that, was what he thought, but "Good" was what he said to her. "I'll tell you 'bout it soon. Tell Roman get his rest now. We don't want him lollygagging around much more'n he's done awready."

"Goodnight, Pa," she said quietly.

" 'Night, Amanda."

"Goodnight, Gran'papa," came a small voice.

"That sounded like you got a Lucas critter in there with you, Amanda."

"It *is* me, Gran'papa!" and the little youngster giggled.

"Shshsh!" he hissed with a finger at his lips. "You can't stay quiet in there so your pa can sleep, I'll come drag you out here with me."

This time the little boy's voice came out a delicate whisper, "I'll be quiet. Promise. Don't take me away—I wanna stay with my hurt pa."

" 'Night, son."

He had dropped the cover sheet and was turning away when Amanda's voice drifted softly one more time through the back pucker hole. "Thank you, Pa. Thank you for saving Roman for us."

"Thank you, Gran'papa," said that dear little voice.

He stood there, feeling the tears course down his wrinkled, scarred cheeks. It was almost enough to fill a man's heart to overflowing, listening to those quiet voices caress him in the still of that starlit night. That's what a man counted on his family for.

Late on the evening of that second day of goading the very most from Roman's docile oxen, they had managed to straggle into the wagon camp on the headwaters of a narrow stream draining the northwest end of the rocky Bear River Divide.* Three times that second day they had stopped just long enough to swap out the tired team for a fresh pair of the beasts. Midmorning. Noon. And again in midafternoon they made another rotation . . . desperately attempting to cover in faster time the same ground the train had crossed. Bass didn't know a damn thing about these dull-witted brutes, but he was sure they could make up more than the time they lost during the many changes with stronger, fresher

---

* Today's Bridger Creek.

animals setting the pace. His gamble paid off as they pushed each team to their lumbering limit through that second hot and waterless day.

When the first emigrants on the outskirts of camp spotted the Burwell wagon swaying down the long slope toward the grassy, lush camping ground, Bass watched them turn and hold up hands to their mouths—shouting for the others to look on their back trail. The sun had already set, but it was still light enough to recognize the faces of friends and allies as the families came streaming out of that orderly camp, racing for the lone wagon and that dusty menagerie walking or riding on both sides of the rumbling wagon. Behind them came the extra, weary oxen, a few head of Roman's mules, and those pack-horses—the whole herd of stock tended by young Lemuel and Flea.

Men whipped hats off their heads as they came rushing forward, waving them back and forth aloft, while women and girls came lurching up the long slope, their graceful movement hampered by the long, layered impediments of skirts and petticoats that easily tangled between their legs or snagged on the calf-high sage.

"Lookit that, will you?" Shad said, his cracked lips crusted with a coating of fine dust. "This here family's got some good friends."

"Lord's sake! Wh-where you been for two days?" hollered the one named Pruett, the first to reach the yoke.

Licking his bleeding lips, Titus jabbed his thumb back to the wagon. "Didn't that bastard Hargrove tell you folks nothing o' what happened to Roman?"

Fenton lunged up at Pruett's elbow and said, "We didn't know a thing till after we was in camp more than an hour or so last night."

"Any one of you ask after the Burwells?" Shadrach inquired.

Iverson peered at the wagon while he answered the horsemen, "Goodell was the first. I s'pose we all figured the wagon was way back in line till none of us could remember seeing any of you making camp."

Ryder spoke up, "That's when Carter an' me rode a circuit round the camping ground to have ourselves a look."

"Didn't find you," Dahlmer confessed. "We knowed something bad had come of it."

Titus squinted into the mid-distance, looking for some sign of the train captain or his hired horsemen. "Something bad did come of it—"

"Everyone alive?" Truell asked as he trudged past the trappers and was about to reach the front of the wagon box.

"Barely," Sweete replied.

"We'll have some company soon," Titus announced from his perch.

The emigrants hushed and turned to find Hargrove and four of his men emerging from the center of the encampment on horseback.

Hoyt Bingham turned back to look up at Bass. "Hargrove said it was likely you'd not find Roman alive."

"Did he now?"

Bingham nodded. "Figured a rattler got him when he was out looking for a milk cow what wandered off."

"That so." Nodding slightly, Scratch kept his eyes on the approach of those five horsemen as he said, "It were a snake that bit Roman. Fact be, least three of 'em."

"Three snakes?" shrieked Murray.

"Two-legged ones," Titus explained. "Near beat the man to death, then strung 'im up to a tree—fixin' to let the desert finish him off the rest of the way."

The crowd of women, children, and those men murmured a moment, then fell silent. It was quiet enough to hear the gentle breeze waft through the sage and dwarf yellow pine, to hear the clop of those horses' hooves as the riders plodded up the slope behind their leader. The emigrants parted for Hargrove and the quartet.

The wagon captain took off his hat, his face grave with worry as his eyes settled on Bass. "Burwell? Is he—"

"He's alive," Titus interrupted. "More today than he was yestiddy mornin' when you rode off with your train."

Hargrove slammed the hat back down on his head. "I had every faith in the world that you'd find him out looking for his cow and that you'd be right behind us."

"You an' these here spineless back-shooters knowed good an' well we wouldn't find Roman Burwell out looking for his cow, Hargrove."

For an instant the man's eyes glared into the old trapper's. "Perhaps you can explain your allegations to me later, in private . . . so that we don't ruin this group's celebration at your return to the fold!" He tore the big hat from his head again and whipped it around in the air, shouting, "This is glorious news! The Burwells have rejoined us!"

At that moment Amanda appeared at the front of the wagon, her hands gripping the backboard of the seat so tightly her knuckles were white.

"Hargrove!" she screamed accusingly. "You nearly killed my Roman!"

His mouth hung open a moment as the crowd watched in stunned silence. "I only did what any good wagon captain would have done, Mrs. Burwell," he explained in the most syrupy of tones. "How was I to know that your husband would not be collected within minutes of our departure and you would catch up to us by midday, by last night's camp at the latest?"

Scratch could see his daughter was near to tears as he urged his horse to the wagon.

She said, "Y-you didn't give a good goddamn for us, Hargrove! Didn't send no one back to see about us!"

Standing in the stirrups and reaching out, Scratch grabbed one of her rough, callused hands. "Hush now, daughter. We'll see to his bunch later."

"Thank you, sir," Hargrove exclaimed in his booming voice. "Yes,

Amanda—we'll all see to this matter later. For now, just knowing your husband and family are safe is cause to celebrate! I say we ask the musicians in this outfit to bring out their instruments straightaway!"

The crowd turned back to look at the gray-headed horseman who took off his big hat and wiped the back of a hand across his brow just below the faded, sweat-soaked bandanna. Bass quickly flicked his eyes to Shad, then turned back to the ousted wagon boss.

"Awright, Hargrove," he said as Amanda disappeared into the wagon, "I say let's do make us a lot of noise tonight!"

FIFTEEN

The music and laughter were good and noisy that night after dark, enough celebration to cover a wake for the dead.

Titus and Shad left their wives at the Burwell wagon with extra guns, instructing the women to keep a weapon trained on anyone who came near until Amanda could declare if they were friend or foe. Those dogs he wanted them to tie up would serve as guards too, announcing the approach of any danger. Part of Scratch wanted the women to go right ahead and blow a few holes through some of Hargrove's men for what they had done to Roman and his family. But, there was an even bigger piece of his heart that desired to take that revenge for himself.

Moonrise would be coming all too soon. With that milky orb only two or three days from filling itself out, the two of them had to be about this bloody business of retribution before the moon came up, shedding its light upon this barren high ground just west of the Bear River Divide.

They didn't know which three of Hargrove's seven had been in on the beating of Roman Burwell, which of them had left the farmer strung up for dead. And Titus didn't figure he could recognize the three who showed up at the wagon with Hargrove the morning Roman was missing . . . but then, it really didn't matter. All seven were the same. Just different faces, different names. But like most all scaly critters that slithered through a man's life, these seven were bad from the first jump.

" 'Least two of 'em gonna be out watchin' Hargrove's animals," Titus said as he and Shad moved like whispers on the periphery of the dancing, clapping, jubilant emigrants.

Bitter as he was, Scratch couldn't blame these simple folk for climbing right aboard when it came to a celebration, so starved were they for music and joy and happy abandon. Besides, with so much gleeful merrymaking, all he and Sweete had to do was show their faces here and there before they slipped into the dark to see about finding a couple of those bullies tending to their employer's herd of animals. As they walked around the edge of the celebrants, he managed to pick out three more of the hired men. In this group of homespun emigrants, the bully-boys stood out like whores stepping through the doorway of a country church. Most times they were off by themselves, since most of the farmer families did not much want to have anything to do with the single men who eyed their young daughters and never lent a hand with creek crossings, the roundup of strays, or a settler struggling with a troublesome animal when it came time to hitch up for the day.

"Three of 'em," Bass whispered as they eased back into the dark behind a wagon. "Means Hargrove's got more'n two men watching his herd tonight, or we ain't picked out all the weasels back at the hurraw by the fires."

"That leaves four of 'em out there," Sweete said. "Two for you, an' two for me."

Thirty yards out from the last wagon, they stopped and listened to the night sounds, letting their eyes grow accustomed to the starlit darkness here in the hour just before moonrise.

"Where's Hargrove camped?" Shadrach asked.

Titus pointed. "I figger his herd be down in that patch of grass by the crik."

"That's where we'll find us some critters to skin."

He looked up at the tall man in the dark. "Skin? You think we ought'n *skin* these niggers?"

"They half skinned Roman," Shad explained with disgust. "If we ain't gonna kill 'em, least we oughtta do is skin the yeller bastards."

"Awright," he whispered, sensing a little glee surging through him to accompany the hot fire of adrenaline squirting into his veins. "You set on what we're gonna do?"

Sweete nodded. "I know how your stick floats."

"Meet you back at the music when you're done," Titus said, holding out his right arm between them.

The big man clasped forearms with his old friend, wrist to wrist.

"Save a doe-see-doe for me, Shadrach."

Sweete turned away with a huge smile and he was gone in the dark. For several moments Scratch listened, straining in the night for the sounds of the tall one's big moccasins on the dry, flaky ground. Then he himself slipped off to the right, making for the far slope of the hill that would lead him down to the north side of that patch of grass, while Shadrach would make his approach from the south end. As he threaded his way through the dark clumps of sage, Titus remembered how he and Josiah, along with their two wives, had crept up on a war camp of Arapaho back in the Bayou Salade.* Those warriors had been out-and-out killers, come to take the lives of the white trappers and their Indian women. There had been little choice but for the four of them to plunge into that camp swiftly, brutally, and not leave a one of the war party alive.

The more he had thought about it across the last few days, what Hargrove's hired men had done wasn't just a beating. The way they left Roman lashed to that tree, half dead when they strung him up, was tantamount to leaving Amanda a widow. Even though only three had been in on the attack, all seven were every bit as guilty. The fact that they hadn't stabbed Roman with their knives because they didn't dare make noise with a gunshot didn't arouse any mercy in Titus Bass either. Far as he was concerned, any of them he got his hands on were as guilty of attempted murder as were those Fort John Frenchmen who had attempted to run off with Magpie guilty of robbery and rape. He'd just as soon gut 'em, every last one, and leave their bodies for the coyotes that sang from the nearby hills this night.

But, Amanda said she and Roman had talked about it—sure and certain were they both that a man like Titus would be eager to right the wrong done them by Hargrove and his help.

"Just like you did back in St. Louis with that fighting dog," she explained earlier that evening as darkness was coming. "But this don't have to end in killing, like that night in Troost's livery did."

He had studied her eyes a moment, seeing so much of her mother in them. "You never had the stomach for what you done in that barn."*

Amanda had wagged her head. "What I done was to save you, Pa. I'd do it again for my children. And I'd do it for Roman."

"We hadn't come on him when we did, Roman be dead."

"He feels the same way about this as I do," Amanda had explained after a long and heavy silence. "He doesn't want to spill any blood. Just stay out of their way till we get to Fort Hall and see 'em gone."

"Then you don't wanna know what I'm gonna do," Titus said.

"I don't," she admitted quickly. "All I know is that blood begets blood."

"Roman don't want a piece of these niggers?"

"No," and she had shaken her head. "Says he just wants to get us to the Willamette River, where we can put everything that happened behind us."

Titus had sighed. "And start a new life."

"Yes, Pa. Row and me don't think we could start a new life by shedding blood."

It hadn't been that way for Scratch. Not years ago, not out here in this same country. This harsh wilderness had required a squaring of accounts from those who believed they had what it took to stand tall and bold against the wind. And that payment was often made in blood—either their own, or in the blood they

---

* *One-Eyed Dream*

were forced to take in order to survive. How he wished his life had been different, somehow. But this wilderness had to be accepted on its own terms.
Maybeso things were far softer back east, the way these settlement and farmer
folks hoped things would be once they made it all the way to Oregon. Perhaps
the reason these sodbusters were on their way west was because they figured
that far country would be as easy a land as the East had been to them.
Otherwise, why would a man risk everything on staking a claim in a place that
would demand a payment in blood?

But to get from that soft country back east to that gentle country called
Oregon, these settlement folk had to pass through an unforgiving gauntlet—a
long, wide strip of harsh territory, a land that demanded a man must become
about as brutal and unforgiving as that wilderness itself.

"This here's my country, Amanda," he had quietly explained to her at the
rear of the wagon just as the music started and the joyful voices were raised to
the starry sky. "Out here folks like you an' Roman don't set the rules. That's
what sticks in my craw 'bout your sort on your way to a new life. You're gonna
come through here an' do what you can to make this place fit for all of you
what are running somewhere else. Don't you see the reason I lasted so long out
here is I took this land on its terms?"

She had stared down at her scuffed boots for a long time before she finally
looked into his face again and said, "I always thought that folks had a say in
how they lived, no matter where they were, east or west, Pa."

"Maybeso that goes for back there where we both come from, daughter," he
sighed. "But, out here in this country, the wilderness got the last say. What you
an' the rest of these folks think should be don't matter a red piss. An' that even
goes for oily men like Phineas Hargrove too."

"Because he struggles to make it all turn out for his good?"

"No, just because life in this country has a way of balancing things out in the
long run," he explained. "What he takes from others will one day be took from
him. And that day has come, Amanda."

She gripped his arm as he leaned forward to kiss her on the forehead, stopping him from immediately pulling away. "Pa, I'd like to tell you there's no
need to put yourself in danger—but I know I'd be wasting my breath."

He had squeezed her hand. "You take the risk and the danger out of my life,
that'd be like taking the breath outta my body."

Titus had heard her scrambling back up the rungs of the short ladder, over
the tailgate, and into the back of the wagon as he moved around the fire to that
spot where Shadrach stood waiting. Both of them bristled with weapons—not
firearms but the sort of sharp-edged weapons that called for close and dirty
work, knives and tomahawks. Along with the short sections of rope each man
carried inside his shirt where they would not swing loose, making noise or getting in the way of what was to come.

His nose picked up the smell of fresh dung before Scratch even made out the clot of shapes before him, as he neared the patch of dried, sun-cured grass where he knew Hargrove's men kept the moneyed man's stock grazing through the night. They worked in watches, he had been told, those hired men. Two of them spelling the last pair for a few hours, until the last three men would fire the four-o'clock gun to rouse the whole camp. This early in the night, he and Shad would be catching the first watch—meaning there would still be some time before the relief arrived to discover what had been done to their friends.

Into his nostrils the westerly breeze brought that strong perfume of sweaty animals and the clumps of green manure dropped when the horses had finished digesting the brittle plateau grasses. He stopped and smelled deeply, wondering if either of the guards were smokers. Looking into the dark, Titus figured he might see the glowing ember of a pipebowl even if he weren't downwind of their burning tobacco. But the only thing his nose could make out was pony droppings and the sharp tang of the breeze cutting through the sagebrush and bitter alkali flat. He'd hear the man soon enough, maybe see the guard move against the horizon, if the man wasn't squatting under some bush—

Bass heard that stream of water hitting the hard, dry, flaky ground with a hiss. But it wasn't the loud and powerful gush of a horse taking a piss. No, that was a man sprinkling the ground. At his most vulnerable, with his pecker in his hand and his mind on the relief he was experiencing. He moved forward, his nose alive and drawing him onward, his ears pricking as his senses led him toward the guard. There!

Titus saw him. The dark, the shadows, the hat—Scratch wasn't sure which one it was. But the guard stood there with his left hand propping up his short prairie rifle while his right hand was busy at his groin, shaking free those last few drops—

Surprised, the guard was barely able to start his turn when Scratch kicked the rifle out from under his left arm, then drove in another step, swinging his arm with all the power his old shoulder and hip could put behind the blow. His hard-boned fist connected under the taller man's jaw, staggering the guard back a step, then delivered a second crack as the guard's arms wheeled in an attempt to regain his balance.

The instant he started to cry out, his brief warning muffled with the suddenness of the attack, Bass was already on him like a calico sack full of mountain cats. Scratch struck with the left fist this time, causing the guard to go rigid for a heartbeat.

But somehow the man managed to growl, "Napps!"

The guard was shaking his head violently as he scrunched his neck down into his shoulders and hunched over, starting toward the old trapper—pulling out his belt pistol. Scratch desperately lunged to the side as he dragged free one of the knives at the back of his hip with his left hand, immediately passing the blade of the skinner into his right palm and flicking it forward as the guard cleared the pistol from his belt. The knife's impact froze everything for a moment in the black of that night. The guard stood in place, shock registering on his face as he slowly peered down at the bone handle sticking out of his lower chest.

"N-napps!" he gurgled, much weaker this time as he struggled to screw up the strength to raise the pistol.

As the weapon floated up, Titus was already lunging forward, quickly knocking the pistol hand aside before he seized the handle of the embedded knife with his right hand, clenching his left around the back of the young man's neck like talons. Grunting with pain and fear, the guard flailed away with his arms, pounding Bass with one while the other struggled to jam the pistol's muzzle against the old trapper's belly. Just as Titus was twisting away, his right hand dragging down on the knife's handle through flesh and sinew, he heard the click of the hammer spring, felt the hammer fall against his arm at the same moment his sleeve was trapped beneath the frizzen, preventing flint from striking steel and igniting power in the pan.

As Bass landed on his hip, the man went limp, crumpling atop dead legs. The guard hit his knees, staring down at the long, jagged gash high in his abdomen where a dark and shiny gush spilled over the front of his britches. Rocking for a heartbeat, the man tumbled backward.

As Scratch wrenched the tomahawk from the back of his belt and rolled onto his knees, he watched the guard arch his back in a brief leg-twitching spasm, yanking the knife free of his chest before he collapsed and moved no more. Bass got to his feet, took a single step, and laid one of his moccasins on the man's wrist, pinning the hand against the ground. Bending over, he pried open the guard's sticky fingers and reclaimed his knife. After wiping it on the man's gingham shirt, he stuffed it back into the empty scabbard.

For a few moments he crouched there among the stunted jack pine, listening, his good eye searching the darkness. Maybe no one had heard the man's call for help. Perhaps Sweete had already seen to the only aid the guard could have summoned. He waited a few heartbeats more while the animals stopped snorting at the scent of fresh blood on the breeze, then knelt over the guard.

"You stupid idjit," Bass whispered as he leaned over and seized the back of the man's collar, dragging the body around in a half circle, then starting for a nearby clump of trees.

It was there he propped the body against the narrow branches, then reached inside his shirt for a short coil of rope. Titus looped it around the dead man's chest and tree twice, then tied it off in a knot before he pulled his knife again to cut off what rope he hadn't used.

"Frakes!"

A voice cut the night behind him.

His senses on fire, Bass whirled in a crouch, finding the nearly full moon's brightness already raising some light behind the ridge they had spent three days trudging to get around. In a matter of minutes that moon would poke its head over the bluff and illuminate the valley.

"Where you, Frakes?"

Concentrating on the sound of that voice, Titus spotted the dark form punching a sliver out of the starry sky as the man stomped closer and closer. Then that shadow split in two and there were suddenly four legs coming his way.

A new voice growled, "I bet that bastard's catchin' a nap."

"You can whup his ass tomorrow, Jenks," the first one said. "But we got our watch to cover, you an' me."

"Shit, Corrett—you buckin' for a raise in pay from that rich man?"

"I oughtta get a good bonus from that high-toned bastard by the time we get to California," Corrett declared. "Hargrove promised us all some good money if we took good care of that farmer an' left him behind like he wanted."

"Lotta good we done whipping him an' stringing him to that tree," Jenks grumped. "Them old skinners saved that farmer's worthless life."

"Maybeso like Hargrove promised, he'll give us a chance to dance with them two skinners once we divide off at Fort Hall."

Jenks laughed with Corrett, then said, "That farmer was big and hard, but he sure was a stupid sort."

The other shifted the rifle across his arm and said, "The real fun's gonna be watching them skinners bleed when we hang them both upside down in a tree like a gutted hog—"

Suddenly Jenks halted in his tracks, throwing out his arm to stop Corrett. Their leather boot soles slid on the hard ground with a crunch.

"Where the hell's Frakes?" Jenks hissed.

"Likely he's crawled under a tree, sleeping—"

"Shuddup!" the first voice snapped, then began to call in a loud whisper there beneath the slinky drip of moonlight just starting to creep over the divide. "Frakes!"

"I don't like this none."

"Something's wrong. Bad wrong," Jenks growled. "You got your pistol loaded?"

"Both of 'em," Corrett responded.

Titus crouched in the dark, quickly sorting through the few options open to him. The darkness gave him an advantage in one respect, but it hampered him in another way too. Damn, if he only knew what Sweete was up to.

"Let's go look for 'im," Jenks's voice demanded. "You go off that way—see if you can find that sleepy son of a bitch."

Corrett grumbled a reply just before a whistle came drifting out of the gloom. The shrill mating call of a blue grouse. Both of the men froze and slowly turned. Titus knew, began to search the dark in the direction of that telltale sound.

"That you, Frakes?" Jenks questioned. "C'mon, dammit! You're getting me riled."

"Over here!"

Both of the men turned their backs on Bass, directing their attention at the direction of the distant voice.

Corrett whispered, "Coming from over there, that's gotta be Napps. But where's Frakes?"

"Show yourself!" Jenks ordered.

"Right here."

"Shit, Frakes," Corrett spewed with relief. "You didn't answer us there—I was thinking you was—"

Jenks growled his interruption, "Who the hell are you?"

Not far ahead of him in the dark, Titus saw the two men bring their guns up in the starlight.

Jenks demanded again, "Who are you?"

"And what you doing out here on Hargrove's ground?" Corrett joined in.

"Better clear out, sodbuster," Jenks boomed his order. "You know the rules. Hargrove don't like none of you around his stock."

The reply came that much closer to Titus now. "It's you niggers I come for."

Corrett suddenly sounded brave, "You asking for trouble?"

"Two of you," Sweete said, his big feet crunching on the hard ground, "only one of me. Sounds like fair odds to this here child."

"Maybe we should shoot 'im," Corrett boasted as Bass watched the big shadow take shape out of the gloom, congealing just beyond the two hired men.

"Yeah—maybe Hargrove gimme a nice bonus for taking care of this one." Jenks cheered himself as he brought his rifle up at his hip.

"I didn't bring my gun, fellas," Shad confessed. "Won't be a fair fight."

"Don't need to make it a fair fight," Jenks warned. "Only need you dead."

"Yeah," Corrett chimed in. "You come out here to steal some stock from Hargrove an' we shot you red-handed."

"I'll keep my gun on him, Corrett. You go bring him over here by the horses."

The stocky man stomped right over to the big shadow, cocky as a young bull in spring. But the instant he was within an arm's length, Shad swung out with his thick leg and knocked the rifle aside, stepping in quickly to whirl the hired man around and drag him backward by the scruff of his neck. Now Sweete had his hard arm crooked around Corrett's throat, lifting the man onto his toes as his legs flailed.

"Drop 'im!" Jenks demanded. "Drop 'im or I'll shoot."

"Shoot an' you'll hit *him*," Sweete said.

Jenks moved three more steps, a little to the right. "Hell if I won't shoot."

"You don't wanna do that," Shad warned. "Your gunshot'll bring folks down here, wanting to see what happened."

"That's right," Jenks agreed. "So let him go and we'll make this quick—"

The hired man heard Titus behind him at the last moment but didn't get fully turned in time as that shadow ripped itself out of the darkness and struck out with the short-barreled prairie rifle he'd taken off Frakes. The man's eyes were about as wide as his mouth at the instant the rifle butt slammed against the side of his jaw, catapulting him off his feet.

"Easy there," Sweete whispered to Corrett as the man suddenly stopped struggling. "You be good, I won't have to put you to sleep."

Bass stood over Jenks, straddling the body, ready to drive the iron butt plate down into the man's head again if he stirred. But the body remained limp, sprawled in the dust and sage.

"Damn if that weren't a purty head-bang, Scratch."

He whispered as he knelt beside Jenks, "Good of you to show up on time, Shadrach."

"Why you growlin' at me? Took me some doin' to get my fella dragged off and tied up," Sweete said. "Where you tie yours?"

"He's dead," Scratch admitted. "Wasn't as clean as you was with yours."

Corrett wheezed, "Y-you killed one of Hargrove's—"

Shad squeezed down on the man's throat even more. "I'll gut you if you make me."

"Bring him over here," Titus commanded. "We'll take 'em both across the crik, other side of the hill—"

"Why you gonna kill me?" Corrett whimpered.

"We ain't gonna kill you," Bass hissed. "Much as I wanna cut the heart outta ever' one of you. Shad, let's get something in his mouth to make sure he's real quiet."

"I won't make a sound," the man promised.

Scratch stepped right up to the man, sticking his nose an inch from Corrett's face. "First whack—you better tell me who it was rode off the other mornin' to give Burwell that beating."

Corrett's eyes immediately dropped to the body crumpled on the ground.

Titus asked, "Him? He was one of 'em?"

Inside the iron grip of Shadrach's arm, Corrett nodded slightly.

"Who was the others?" Sweete growled at the man's ear.

"F-frakes," he whispered.

"That's the one I killed over yonder," Bass said. "I know there was three of 'em, who was the—"

"Benjamin," he interrupted in a harsh whisper. "He come back bragging how his hands was so sore 'cause he was the one beat the farmer so bad while the other two held him up."

"Benjamin," Titus repeated the name in a whisper.

"You let me go 'cause I told you?"

"No," Scratch said, turning back to the body on the ground. "You an' this'un goin' across the crik aways."

"You don't tussle," Sweete advised, "you don't have to hurt. Understand?"

Corrett nodded as Bass stepped up to him. "Put your hands out front of you."

"Y-you tying me up?"

Shad leaned into the man's ear again. "Be glad we don't string you up on a tree just like your three friends crucified Roman Burwell."

"Th-they laughed about doin' that when they come back . . . but I-I didn't have nothing to do with it!"

"Gimme your hands."

Corrett begged, "You won't hang me in no tree like Benjamin done to that farmer—"

Wrenching the man's hands together, Titus snapped, "Ain't it just like settlement folks, Shadrach? They're all full of brag and windy big-talk when they got the bully odds on their side. Damn your kind, an' damn what your kind's already doin' to my mountains."

After the moon rose off the horizon later that night, Scratch had slapped Jenks into consciousness and dragged him to his feet. Then the two old trappers shoved their prisoners across the narrow creek and over the first hill, eventually finding a place with enough cover that the two would not be discovered right off.

"More shade than they deserve," Titus grumped as they pushed Corrett down at the base of the first tree. "Better that the sun grows so hot it peels their eyelids back."

"We'll tie 'em down so they're facing west."

"Them others, they'll come looking, they'll find us," Jenks vowed. "Hargrove an' Benjamin, they'll come lookin' for us."

"Then what?" Bass demanded, grabbing the hired one's lower jaw in his hand.

The younger man sneered at the trapper. "Then . . . all of us come an' find you."

"Smart-assed li'l greenhorn," Titus growled, bringing his thin-bladed skinning knife up, pressing its fine-honed edge up against the underside of the man's nose. "Maybeso I ought'n go ahead an' cut this'un's tongue in two, Shadrach."

He had to admit he liked the way the young bully's eyes got big at that.

It wasn't long before he and Shad were slipping back among the wagons well after the music and laughter were spent, but they did not have to wait until morning for Hargrove and the last three of his men to go stomping through camp in search of the four missing guards, yelling, kicking over cooking tripods and trivets, spilling contents of kettles and water buckets in anger and frustration. Eventually the wagon captain and his trio tore up to Burwell's wagon, to find the old mountain men armed for bear and not about to be blustered the way the settlement folk had been as Hargrove rudely awakened the entire camp and cowed them all.

"I know you two got something to do with this!" Hargrove roared with indignation as he stopped directly in front of Bass.

"Don't have no idee what you're so spittin' mad about," Titus remarked, his two pistols hanging in his hands at his sides, both Ghost and Digger barking loudly, barely restrained by Flea and Magpie.

Hargrove's eyes flicked aside at some movement. Shad stood a few yards away with his two pistols drawn and pointed at the three who had come to back up their employer.

"Which of you gonna be first?" the train captain asked.

"First for what?"

"First to die!" Hargrove said. "Tell me where my men are or I'll kill both of you. Perhaps when the first one is dead, the other will decide to talk."

Sweete asked, "How you figger you're gonna get away with killing us here?"

"Look at my guns. There's four of us against the two of you!"

"Damn, Shadrach," Titus groaned. "Appears we forgot to count. No—wait. What 'bout them two women of ours? They know how to handle guns, don't they . . . right over there, Hargrove." And he pointed at the end of the wagon where Shell Woman stood with Shad's double-barrel smoothbore pointed at the hired men. "An' over there too."

This time he directed their attention to Waits standing just at the edge of the firelight behind them, holding an old trade musket, both its barrel and its stock sawed off to make it a deadly close-range weapon.

Hargrove's eyes came back around to rest on Bass in that dim, gray light of the coming morn. With the blackest menace, he promised, "One day, old man."

"Yes," Titus answered quietly. "One day you an' me gonna dance for sure. If it ain't Roman chews on your gizzard first . . . someday it'll be me tears off a piece of you for myself."

SIXTEEN

As soon as that bloody night had begun to gray into false dawn, Hargrove and his trio were out on horseback. It hadn't taken them long to find Frakes tied to the tree not far from the grassy patch of ground. They brought the eviscerated body back into camp, slung over the bare back of a horse for all to see.

"Look at this—everyone!" Hargrove demanded with an indignant roar. "Look right here at the lawlessness I did everything I could to protect you people from! One man's dead for sure. Maybe three more!"

He came to a stop near the center of that largest cluster of wagons, shouting at the settlers as they interrupted their breakfast and early-morning chores. "We'll hold a funeral for this man in fifteen minutes. I want every one of you there to pay your respects, then I want you men, the able-bodied among you, to saddle up with me and my men. We're going in search of the others those old fur men must have killed too. And when the dead are buried, we're going to hold us a trial before we hang these guilty ruffians, then get on our way."

For a moment it seemed the whole train—man, woman, and child—were staring right at Titus and Shadrach.

Hargrove started away—but suddenly stopped and wheeled about. He glared hard at Hoyt Bingham. "You, Bingham. You'll bring your shovel to help dig this man's grave."

But before the emigrant could speak, another voice boomed behind Titus.

"He ain't digging no grave for any of your hired trouble."

Slowly, Hargrove turned and found Roman Burwell standing as straight as he could, on his own feet beside the tailgate of his wagon.

"I gave Bingham an order, Burwell," the captain snarled. "Since you're in no condition to help him dig this man's grave, Bingham will dig it for the both of you—"

"I ain't going," Hoyt said, taking a bold step away from his wife at their breakfast fire.

Hargrove's cold eyes narrowed menacingly as Benjamin shifted on his saddle, preparing for what violence loomed. "Trouble happens, Bingham. Folks get hurt, sometimes through no fault of their own. Then there's folks like you and Burwell—they get hurt because it's their own stupid undoing."

"You ain't gonna bully an' beat us, not from here on out." Burwell stood bravely, one arm braced against the bandage that was wrapped tightly around his broken ribs.

That sudden show of bravery appeared to buoy Bingham and some others with renewed courage. Turning back to Hargrove, Hoyt Bingham declared in a clear voice, "Don't you remember what happened a few days back?"

"You do remember that council meeting you called real clear, don't you, Hargrove?" Truell asked as he stepped up beside Roman Burwell.

"You was voted out," Bingham reminded with new backbone.

"Maybe you and what you got left of these toughs oughtta get outta our camp!" cried the smooth-jawed Fenton.

Iverson stepped up to the line slowly being formed against Hargrove and Benjamin. "You and the rest shouldn't travel with our company no more!"

"You can't do this to me!" Hargrove bellowed like a wounded bull surrounded by gaunt and hungry wolves. "You said we could accompany your train till we reach Fort Hall!"

Surprising them all, Roman Burwell unsteadily pushed himself away from the wagon's tailgate, wincing a bit with the movement. "Don't you hear what these men are saying?" he asked. "That's the voice of the people saying you been voted out. Now it's time you got out."

When Hargrove reined his horse aside so he could look squarely at Burwell, both of Scratch's dogs growled where they were restrained at a wagon wheel, their neck hair ruffing, as Amanda stepped under her husband's arm, attempting to support him on her shoulders. Roman gently pushed her away, wagged his head at her, and stood there alone.

The ousted wagon boss jutted his chin out and told the wounded emigrant, "Not one of you farmers here is man enough to go against me—"

"We aren't gonna force you an' your hired men out, less'n you make us," Burwell interrupted. "As for the rest of them who want to go to California with you, all of you can stay with us till we get to Fort Hall. We'll see your bunch is safe till you get to the Snake. But you ain't our captain no more."

At the edge of the gathering crowd a man named Rankin grumbled loudly, "I say the California folks go their own way from here on out!"

"No!" Burwell cried, wincing with a spasm of pain. "We aren't gonna become the sort of people Hargrove is."

Titus glanced at his daughter as she stood easily within reach of her weakened husband but gave Roman his stand. Amanda's cheeks glistened with tears, her eyes shiny with pride in her husband. A pride that had long lain dormant until Hargrove's unremitting cruelty had reawakened it.

"Why not, Roman?" asked a man named Winston. "He damn well tried to do the same to you!"

"Maybe that's the way things was for folks back there in the East," Roman said steadily. "Fact is, that's the way it was for most all of us. Them with money had the power to rule over the rest. If we was so happy with that way of things back there—why'd any of us decide to strike out for Oregon in the first place?"

"Better lives!"

"That's right!" Burwell responded to the anonymous cry from the crowd. "But, are any of us gonna have better lives if we all act like Hargrove and his kind when we get where we're going? What have we made better for our families if we still fight to grab money and power for ourselves?"

Bingham started for the wounded emigrant, saying, "How're you saying we're supposed to make things different?"

"This here journey to a new land is our chance to do something good for our women and our children," he explained to the hushed gathering. "We can make a new life for ourselves—not just new homes and new farms. But a new *life*! We're not going to Oregon to end up the same sort of folks that Hargrove and them others are! Let him and his kind go to California. We're going to start a new life in Oregon for our families. For our children's children."

Bingham stepped to Roman's side and laid a hand on the big man's shoulder. "My fellow captain is right! We must make new homes in a new land—not live things the way they were back east. We'll let those who are happy with the Hargroves of the world stay back there and live out their lives, or let them follow Hargrove to California. As for us, we're on to Oregon!"

Iverson leaped up and shouted, "The Bingham-Burwell Oregon Company!"

"Oregon or bust!" shouted Murray.

Pushing her way through the crowd that immediately surged toward Roman, Amanda threaded her way to his side, grabbed his face in both her hands, and pulled it down to her mouth as she raised herself on her toes. Watching them together at this pivotal moment, Titus felt his heart grow light, weighing far less than it had ever since that day at Bridger's forge, when she told him about her husband and the troubles they were running from back in Missouri. For days now Scratch had been consumed by the fear that they would never outrun their mistakes, never get beyond the failures of Roman Burwell. Fear that Amanda had married a man who would one day plunge his whole family into disaster, if not with Phineas Hargrove on the road to Oregon, then surely once they had reached the mouth of the Willamette.

But instead, his son-in-law had stood up for the right, as Titus saw it. He had stood up to power, greed, and bullies. Here with the coming of the dawn, Scratch had realized his son-in-law was not so simple a man as one might suspect at first blush. Roman Burwell was as loving a husband as any he could hope for Amanda, as good and kind a father as he himself could be to his own children. The farmer was, in the end, the sort of man Scratch believed he could call friend. And to the old trapper there was no finer distinction than that.

"Oregon or bust!" the crowd echoed again as they washed forward, forcing the two horsemen back from their rejoicing in a swell of noise and a surge of bodies.

Amanda and Roman were going to be all right. For the first time in days, Titus felt that clear to his marrow. They and their children were going to be all right. The family would get to Oregon, and that country would indeed prove to be their promised land.

He felt his eyes sting as he watched that crowd of jubilant men, women, and children tighten around Burwell and Bingham, clapping and singing trail songs of Oregon. How proud he was to witness this moment. Strong, simple, good people—the sort who could surely make that new land thrive the way nothing back east ever would again.

Titus Bass felt as if he was witnessing the birth of a whole new country.

Off in the distance there was no mistaking that narrow, winding tangle of emerald green, luring and seductive against the sere and sunburned sienna of the summer landscape.

"That's the Bear," Titus said to Waits in English, holding the first two of those fingers left on his right hand in front of his mouth, pointed down as if they were the mighty canines of the beast.

She repeated in his native tongue, "Bear."

"You said that good," he sighed with contentment. "Off in that country, south aways, I first met Jim Bridger."

"How long?"

"Hmmm," he considered. "That's some. Must be . . . goin' on twenty winters now."

"Too-wen-tee?" she mimed. Then asked again, "How long?"

So he balanced his longrifle across the tops of his thighs as the horse rocked beneath him, and held up both hands, fingers extended. Then he quickly closed his fists once and extended the fingers again. "Twenty."

"Old man, this Ti-tuzz now!"

"Yeah," he admitted. "Some days, I feel so goddamned old I wonder why I'm still livin'."

She looked at him with worry creasing the crow's-feet at her eyes. In her own tongue she asked the difficult question, "Your heart . . . it's ready to die?"

With a shake of his head, Titus answered, "No. Not ready to die."

He recalled that her people believed very strongly that every man would know when he was about to cross over. That same mighty power was what had prompted, provoked, and inspired Jack Hatcher to warble his favorite song as he lay mortally wounded in battle against the Blackfoot in Pierre's Hole.* And the very same spirit that compelled Asa McAfferty to pick his own time and his own place to make what Asa realized was coming down to his final stand. To these warrior peoples of the High Plains and the tall mountains, a man knew in his bones when his time had come to cross over that last, high, and lonely divide. Alone . . . for dying was at best a one-man job.

"You stay with me a long, long time still," she said, the worry gone from her face.

"Woman—ain't none of us know what's in store," he admitted. "Much as I'd love to die in my blankets with you and our children at my side, a passel of grandpups crawlin' on the floor of our lodge . . . in this here country nothin' lives long but the rocks and the sky."

Her eyes misted a little, gone cloudy as a stormy day when she turned away from him and nodded once in agreement. "Only the rocks and sky live long, husband."

"But—just look at you!" he exclaimed with good cheer, leaning over in the saddle and grabbing hold of her elbow. "Why, you ain't ever gonna grow old, are you, woman?" He gazed deeply into her eyes.

"Many winters have come and gone since you first looked at me," she said in Crow, gazing at him from beneath those black eyelashes with a profound gratitude for his compliment.

"But you don't look no differ'nt than the day you come to sit with me aside the Elk River."+

"But, what of the . . . sickness that ravaged my face?"

"I don't see that," he confessed. "When I look at you I never have seen the sickness scars."

"How long . . . you and me . . . was together?" She struggled some with his American tongue.

"Fourteen. This'll be fourteen winters since you come to talk with me on that rock beside the river."

She smiled at him. "You give me four good children."

"Four?" As suddenly as he spoke the question, Bass realized his mistake and

---

* *Carry the Wind*
+ Yellowstone River.

grinned at her, roaring, "Yes! Number four is comin' this winter near my own birthin' day!"

How he wanted to be back up in Absaroka long before then. Before the hard winds blew the yellow leaves off the cottonwood standing so stately along the Yellowstone, the Bighorn, on north to the winding valleys of the Judith and the fabled Musselshell. By the time the trembling aspen on the high slopes had begun to shed their leaves of gold and the snowline crept down, down, down toward the rolling prairie where the buffalo had begun to put on winter coats and take shelter in the lee of the mountains. How he hungered to be back among the places where the white man did not come with his women and wagons, with his ways meant to change everything that had been into what those stiff-backed folks demanded it must be.

To be back among a people living generations beyond count in a land that had always been. All a man could do was pray that the soft ones back east would never find a way to change that on him. For, if they did . . . then life would no longer be worth the living.

If a man could no longer hear the shrill whistle of a red-tailed hawk circling overhead but for the noisy clatter of mankind and his wagons, if he could no longer make out a wolf's howl drifting down from the nearby hills because the aching stillness of night had been ruined by the nearness of one dirty, stinking settlement after another . . . then life no longer was sweet. Life was no longer worth the living. Till then, he'd go higher, and higher still, farther and farther back—all to stay away from those who came to take what they could from each new place before they ruined it and moved on. Men like Phineas Hargrove and his kind.

But then, there had always been that kind.

Yet wasn't he much the same sort? Hadn't the beaver men come to take until there was little left to take? Perhaps it was so . . . and it made his heart ache with the weight of that realization.

Still, he brooded, there was a marked difference between the him he was in those early years and the him he had slowly become. When the bottom fell out of beaver and there was no earthly reason to wade ice-cold streams in search of the elusive flat-tails, most all the old trappers had given up and fled: east for what once was, and west in the hope of what might be. But only a handful stayed on, clinging to what could never be again. Maybeso, that proved he was not like the rest, not the sort who came, used, and moved on when they had taken all that could be dug up, cut down, or carried off.

Which got Scratch to wondering just how white a man he was anymore. Gradually, inexorably, more and more with every year, he had come to think of himself as a man in between, someone who could never become a part of his wife's Crow people, someone who would never again be considered completely white by his own kind. If most of the white trappers had fled back east to old jobs and old ways, and other white folks fled the East in their wagons, desperate to make a new start and new lives for themselves far to the west beyond these mountains . . . being neither white nor red anymore, just what the hell was he? Merely some mule-stubborn old man refusing to let go of a way of life that was in its death throes?

And all the more important: He worried about what the devil a man would do as he realized he would never fit into that world he saw coming down the trail.

Titus stood at the lower edge of a crusty patch of ground where the sulfur-laden waters had soaked into the earth over the eons, relentlessly leaving behind one thin layer of mineral sediment on top of another.

"That's boiling water?" asked young Leah.

"Hotter'n your mama has in her kettle," he explained to his granddaughter.

As Ghost and Digger traipsed away to sniff at new and intriguing smells off in the sagebrush, both young boys accompanied the old trapper on this excursion to witness a true wonder of nature. Jackrabbit gripped one of his gnarled hands, and Lucas clutched the other. On both sides of him stood the other children, all of them a little in awe at the sight. As soon as the first steamy gush of water spewed from the geyser,* more than a hundred excited, enthralled emigrants came racing out of the camp they were setting up that afternoon near Soda Springs.

Young Lucas asked "Can I touch it?"

"Don't you dare," his mother warned as she stopped behind the child and rested her hands on his narrow shoulders. "That'll burn you good."

"Like fire burn me?"

"Wuss'n that," Titus told his grandson. "Fire just burn you up and kill you quick. That there water burns so you die slow an' hurtful, Lucas. That ain't no way for a li'l man like you to go under."

Leaning forward, Lucas peered around the front of Bass's legs to get Jackrabbit's attention. "We can't go there to play."

Little Jackrabbit, about the same age as Lucas, shook his head with understanding and confirmed, "No go."

"No is right," Amanda said gravely. "You boys play close to the wagon while we're getting settled for the night. Over there, that side of camp, away from this here hot spring."

"Where, Popo?" Jackrabbit asked, gazing up at his father.

"You boys play yonder where Lucas's mama said," he explained and pointed. "In the sage there, but don't go far as them rocks."

---

* Today's Steamboat Springs.

The boys started to let go of the old man's hand as Amanda reminded them, "You two boys stay where I can see you! Hear?"

Lucas was darting off, Jackrabbit at his side in nothing more than a tiny breechclout and moccasins, as the white boy flung his tiny voice over his shoulder. "I heard you, Mama!"

Six and a half days after they had left behind Hargrove's California-bound party and the headwaters of what the emigrant maps were already calling Bridger Creek on the Bear River Divide, the Bingham-Burwell Oregon Company reached Soda Springs high on the gentle, looping, northward curve of Bear River. From here the train would strike out north-northwest, leaving the river behind, striking overland as they made the last stretch for Fort Hall on the Snake.

Most afternoons all Titus or Shadrach had to do was turn about and look back along the far horizon for a low column of dust rising lazily in the air more than a full day behind, telltale sign of the Hargrove California Company. The ousted wagon master and his faithful supporters had begun to fall farther and father behind every day across the last week, moving at a more leisurely pace now that the Bingham-Burwell party was pushing on ahead without them. As the sun began to slip into the last quadrant of the sky, off behind their left shoulders, the time had come for one of the old trappers to select a camping ground for the night. A spot near wood and water, with enough dry, brittle grass available that the stock would not become too restless because of the lack of forage by morning.

More than four and a half days had passed since Roman Burwell pulled himself out of that wagon bed and rose on his own two shaky legs, standing up to Hargrove long enough for the rest of them to get up their gumption too. Not that any of these farmers weren't man enough. Just, sometimes, most men need others to prod them, to give them permission to stand up for themselves. If Roman wasn't the sort who would ever make a charismatic leader, at least he was the kind of man who had inspired others to be what any new land needed.

For those first two painful days after the train broke apart, Burwell had remained in the back of his wagon as it bounced and rumbled through the valley of the Bear River. And for the last four and a half agonizing days, Roman had mustered the strength to walk beside the plodding oxen, grumbling that as much as it hurt to trudge through the rocky soil, it still was nowhere near as painful as the hammering he had taken in the back of that wagon box, no matter how many comforters Amanda piled around him. The wounded farmer ended up covering the last eighty miles to Soda Springs on foot.

"Pa!" Amanda cried. "Get outta that food box!" She and the Indian women were going about preparations for supper.

"I'm just lookin' for something," he admitted as he retreated a step back from the rear gate of the wagon, bumping against his accomplice, Shadrach Sweete. "One'a them sugar bags o' your'n."

She eyed him suspiciously as Roman hobbled up, asking her father, "You got a sweet tooth I didn't know about?"

"Not really. Just thought I'd make the young'uns a treat," he confessed.

"Sugar? For what?" Roman asked.

"Shad an' me gonna go fetch some of that soda water in our cups," Titus explained with a playful grin. "We come back, gonna stir some sugar in."

Sweete added, "Makes a tasty drink, it does."

The pair were back at the wagon within minutes, each of them holding two pint tin cups filled with the bubbly water. Scratch asked, "You got my sugar ready?"

Amanda set an enameled-tin bowl on the gate, filled with a mound of sugar. "Here you go, Pa. Something to soothe that sweet tooth of yours."

"I ain't got a sweet tooth," he snapped at her as he dipped a big pewter spoon into the bowl and dragged the scoop over to dump it into the first of the four cups.

Shad watched Scratch stir and stir before he took a sip of the effervescent liquid.

"Needs li'l more," Titus admitted.

After another heaping spoon of sugar was stirred in, he tried it again. "That's more like it!" And he handed Shadrach the spoon. "Waits! C'mere an' try this treat I made for you."

His wife took the cup from him, sniffed at it, then wrinkled up her nose with a giggle. In Crow she said, "It tickles me!"

"Taste it," he prodded in English. "Sweet."

"Like me!" Shadrach said as he finished tasting his and handed the cup to Shell Woman.

Bass took the spoon and began to mix some sugar into the other two cups. "Call them young'uns over here," he suggested. "All of 'em."

"You're gonna make some for every one?" Roman asked.

"Got all the water we'd ever need," Titus said with a wink. "How much sugar you got for me to drink up tonight?"

Amanda relented and said, "Go ahead on and use the rest of that bag for the children. I figure I've got enough left for coffee and baking till we get to Fort Hall."

"Sugar there gonna be high as a silk top hat!" Bass exclaimed.

"So if we can't afford the price and have to run out before we get to Oregon," Burwell commented, "then we'll drink our coffee straight and eat our biscuits sour!"

"Lemuel," Titus called the youngster over. "Go fetch us this kettle full of water at that spring yonder where we brung the cups from."

It wasn't long before they were all standing at the tailgate, dipping cups in the kettle of cold, bubbling water—mixing in sugar and stirring, taking a drink before passing the cups around—wriggling their noses and giggling with the burst of tiny bubbles.

Scratch looked over the jostling of the children all around them. "Magpie? You see'd your li'l brother and that Lucas?"

"They play out there, Popo," she said in a passable American, pointing out into the sage bottoms that extended toward the lava flats.

"Maybeso you better go fetch 'em both back here to have a treat with us afore all this sugar gets poured down our bellies an' it's gone!"

Titus watched Magpie get in one last long drink before she turned away for the open ground beyond the last wagon, out where the happy shouts of emigrant children rang out.

"How'd you ever find out to mix some sugar in with this water, Titus?" asked Burwell.

"Been so many years ago, I can't rightly recollect," he confessed. "You had it fixed like this afore, Shadrach?"

Smacking his lips, Sweete declared, "Many a time I come here, but never had no sugar mixed in. This is some!"

"Years and years ago, ever' mountain man knowed of Sody Springs," Titus explained as he cast his eyes around this beautiful, lush camping ground. "When a trapper an' his outfit was anywhere near, they come camp here and drink all this water they could. This here's some of the best medeecin a man could want going through him. Works its good right on down my gullet, into my paunch, an' all the way on out."

"You'd drink this without the sugar?" Roman inquired of Sweete.

Shad answered, "But this here sugar makes the sody a toothsome treat—"

"Popo!"

Scratch whirled at Magpie's shrill yell, the sound of it making the hair on his arms stand on end. Something about it that instantly spelled danger and trouble. Everyone around him fell silent too and turned with him to watch the girl dashing toward them, the dogs bounding around her legs. Every few steps she took she twisted the top of her body halfway around to point behind her at the open ground where a small knot of children had gathered, all of them bending at the waist, as if looking down at something on the ground. From all directions, more and more of the children were converging on that tiny group.

"Po-*po*!"

As she screamed for him a second time and lunged closer and closer, more and more adults at the nearby wagons stopped and watched the girl with grave curiosity.

"She hurt herself?" Amanda said as she stepped around the end of the tailgate, dusting her hands on her apron, then bringing both to her brow, shading her eyes from the late-afternoon sun.

Something in his belly immediately told him Magpie wasn't the one who was hurt. Not the way that girl was bounding over the sage like a doe antelope, all brown legs and fringed skirt flying. So he looked beyond her, to that wide-open patch of rocky sagebrush flat where the small boys had gone to play. No, he was relieved to see that they hadn't ventured anywhere close to the boulders as he had warned them not to do. So were the two boys in that handful of youngsters knotted around something on the ground? From this distance, Titus could not make out either one of them in that group as the sun slanted its light from the last quarter of the sky.

He started toward Magpie at a walk, leaving the others standing behind without a word of explanation—acting on a gut-hunch that something was terribly wrong. Everyone in this valley seemed frozen, motionless, just watching. Everyone still but for him and Magpie.

"Popo, Popo, Popo!" she was gasping as her knee-length buckskin dress flapped at her skinny copper legs each time she leaped over some brush instead of dodging around it.

With his next breath Titus broke into a trot for her, suddenly aware of the murmuring voices of those emigrants he was leaving behind at their wagons on both sides of the sagebrush bottom. He still could not make out either of the boys in that bunch of youngsters. Worry became dread and began to claw at him. Titus started running faster.

"Popo, oh, Popo!" she whimpered when she came slamming against him, as he captured her in his arms and clutched her tight.

They were both gasping as he brushed the hair out of her sweaty face, asking, "Where the boys?"

She pointed, gulping deeply for air.

"They hurt? Your brother get hurt?"

"Loo-kass . . . Popo," she rasped in a gush. "Loo-kass." Then she pointed impatiently at the group of youngsters again.

"Lucas?"

Her head bobbed and the tears spilled from her wide, frightened eyes as if a dam had been broken, so suddenly it scared him.

"What!" he yelled down at her, sorry for the harshness of it that same instant.

"S-sn-snake," she sobbed.

"Lucas? The boy got bit?"

She was just starting to nod even as he tore himself away from her. By the time he approached that mute group of children, Titus had no recollection of leaping over or scampering around the sagebrush on his way to them. Nor that the unkempt, dust-coated dogs had turned around and scampered back with him, as if this was some exuberant play. When he came heaving up the youngsters backed away in silence, their white faces gone pale as school paste, eyes so big and every one filled with unimaginable terror. As his moccasins skidded to a halt on the sandy soil, he finally saw the two of them. Jackrabbit was kneeling on the ground, his dusty cheeks streaked with tears as he looked up and saw his father staring down at him in utter shock. Strange, but Titus froze a moment, gazing at the way a few wild strands of his son's hair stuck to the boy's dirty, tear-tracked cheeks.

Jackrabbit had both of his tiny brown hands wrapped around Lucas's right leg, fingers interlaced and their knuckles pale with pressure, clamped just below the knee.

"P-popo," he croaked, runny phlegm oozing from his nose as he cried.

Slowly kneeling to keep from collapsing under his own weight, Scratch settled on the opposite side of Lucas and looked first into his son's eyes. "Sn-snake?"

His son nodded.

Then Bass looked into his grandson's face, afraid—so afraid—of what he might see in those eyes. And his heart broke as he recognized the sheer terror in those half-lidded eyes the moment he leaned over Lucas and caused a shadow to pass across the child's face. The eyes widened slightly, moved liquidly, eventually found him. That's when all the terror disappeared from his grandson's eyes, even though they continued to leak big teardrops from their corners, streams of them washing down the boy's temples through the dust matted on his face, in his ears and his dirty, corn-silk hair.

"Gr-gran'papa," he said weakly. "See, Jackrabbit? I told you it's gonna be all right now . . ." Then he brought up a sharp, hacking cough. "Be all right now—Gran'papa's here."

Laying his hand on Lucas's brow, Titus gently lowered the hand so that it closed those two lids and covered the eyes. He could no longer bear to gaze into them. Instead, he turned his attention to the leg.

"Your hands tired?" he asked Jackrabbit in Crow.

The boy nodded.

His heart surged with an immense pride for this small child, his youngest son. It brought tears to his eyes to think that the boy had done the only thing he could think to do for this friend, this playmate, this relation he was coming to know on this short journey and would likely never see again in his life.

"Y-you done real good, son," he whispered as he reached down with his left hand and yanked on the long whang that tied a moccasin around his ankle. "Keep a good hol't of your friend's leg just a li'l more. You unnerstand?"

Jackrabbit nodded again wearily, his lips trembling as he gritted his teeth with exertion.

Yanking a second time, Titus finally freed the long leather whang from the holes in his moccasin, then took his hand from Lucas's eyes, quickly dragging his skinning knife from the scabbard at the small of his back. With three short slashes, he managed to open a slice in the bottom of the boy's cuff. Dropping the knife, he grabbed the two sides of the cuff in his hand and gave it a brutal yank, ripping that leg of the britches clear up to mid thigh.

"Gran'papa?"

"Y-you be quiet now, Lucas," he whispered as he saw Roman and Amanda running their way with Magpie and Waits-by-the-Water right behind them. Farther back came Toote and Shad, Lemuel and Leah too. And from other directions came what seemed like a hundred other nameless, frightened folks.

"I be real quiet for you," Lucas whispered back from his dry, cracked lips. "Gran'papa make it better now."

"Yes, L-Lucas," he vowed as he stuffed one end of that narrow strip of leather under the bony leg, dragged up both ends together, then looped them in a knot. Now he pulled for all he was worth on those ends. "Jackrabbit—get me a stick."

"How big, Popo?"

"Big as a pin to close your mother's lodge cover."

Sweeping up his father's knife, Jackrabbit hacked off a short branch from a nearby sage, no more than the diameter of his stubby little thumb. As he knelt again beside Lucas's leg, Titus said, "Lay it on the knot. No, middle. That's good. Hol't it there, son. Keep hol'tin' it."

Quickly he flipped over the long ends of the leather strip and made a second knot atop the small stick. Then a third as Amanda came dashing up. She was about to spill toward Lucas when Roman caught her, held his wife back. Titus gazed up at his daughter, reading the fear on her face, not having seen her cheeks so bloodless since that moment she had plunged a pitchfork into a man intending to murder her father in Troost's St. Louis livery.

"Pa?" she questioned, weak and winded like a frail animal as Roman held her up, kept her from collapsing.

That's when Bass moved his gaze to his son-in-law's face—reading the stoic pain registered there. The iron set of a man's jaw when that man knows if he doesn't clamp his teeth tight his chin is going to quiver and he will betray himself . . . when a man realizes he must be strong for everyone else even though his own heart is already crying out in bitter anguish. In Roman Burwell's eyes showed the despair of a man who already knew.

"Snakebite, Amanda," Titus declared.

Burwell cleared his throat and asked in a whisper, "Rattler?"

When Scratch nodded, Amanda stifled a shrill sob and twisted about to bury her face in Roman's chest.

Titus looked down at the child as he stuffed his knife back into its scabbard with one hand, slowly continuing to twist the stick with the fingers of his left hand, tightening, tightening, tightening the tourniquet.

"Lucas," he said quietly, bending low so his face was just inches from the boy's, "we're gonna take you back to the wagon, son."

"Get me better there, Gran'papa?"

God, how he wanted to lie to the child, to tell Lucas everything the boy wanted to hear, deserved to hear . . . but instead he said only, "Jackrabbit, you help me help Lucas now."

"Yes."

"Take hold of the stick from me," and he waited while his son seized hold of the stick. "Don't let go of it. Keep hold of it—I'm gonna pick Lucas up."

"I-I can help you, Titus," Roman offered.

"No," and he shook his long hair. "You keep hol't of Amanda. Just keep hol'tin' her real tight too."

Once Jackrabbit had the ends of the stick steadied in his two tiny hands, Scratch quickly stuffed both his arms under the child. Raising first his narrow shoulders, Lucas's long, corn-silk hair spilling over Bass's forearm, Titus next raised the knees, then got his own legs under him and stood. Digger was the more inquisitive of the two dogs, rising on his back legs to momentarily sniff at the boy. He turned and slowly started through the sagebrush as the crowd peeled back from his path, he and everyone in that crowd on either side of him moving slow as a death march, both his loyal dogs easing along at his heels. Bending his face over the child's, Bass was constantly vigilant that he not let the sun's intense afternoon light touch the boy's face.

His left moccasin finally worked its way off and he began to walk through the sage across that rough, rocky ground with one bare foot. Waits immediately scooped up the moccasin and dashed in front of him, holding up the limp moccasin and quickly pointing at his foot. He shook his head and resolutely continued for the wagon. On both sides of him the crowd quietly murmured in wonder and fear, explaining to one another what they heard had happened; in that way a story was told in but a matter of a half dozen compelling words from one mouth to the other, to another, then to the next, on and on as they shuffled through the sagebrush on either side of him and the boy's gray-faced parents.

He could hear Amanda sobbing behind him, could make out Roman talking softly to her as he continued to clutch his big arm around her quivering shoulders, holding her up, helping her walk, getting her back to the wagon for the sake of their youngest. Eight-year-old Annie suddenly pushed through the crowd and stopped right in front of her grandfather, staring at her little brother Lucas, her eyes never so wide. She stood rooted to the spot as Titus approached. He realized she needed something to do.

"Annie, go lay some more wood on the fire for me."

In an instant the child had whirled about on her heels and darted back through the edge of the throng that made way for her. Titus took a deep gasp as his bare foot found some tiny cactus hidden among the dried bunchgrass. And kept walking with that boy cradled in his arms.

"Waits," he called out to his wife in Crow. "Gather your medicines."

She stared into his eyes a long moment, then understood. Her eyes fell to the ground.

"Everything you have," he choked in his wife's tongue as she turned aside. "We'll need it all . . . so we can do everything we can."

SEVENTEEN

"Is there anything we can do for the boy?" Titus whispered to his wife as he crouched at the fire beside her, their faces almost touching as they rummaged through Waits-by-the-Water's rawhide pouch filled with small skin sacks of leaves and roots, powders and mosses, bark and crushed insects too. All of it they spread out on a piece of old blanket between them, then waited for the water to come to a boil.

She looked into his eyes, and he already knew.

"There is nothing I know of that has enough power to kill the snake's spirit," she confessed in a barely audible whisper, even though she spoke in Crow.

"Except the First Maker," he whimpered as Shad came up to kneel beside him.

Sweete glanced at his wife and said, "Toote seen a lot of rattler bites."

"And?"

Shad's face was long and drawn as he answered, "But none of 'em ever made it, Scratch." Then Sweete laid his trunk of an arm across the thin man's shoulders. "You done all you could. You sucked him, you burned them bites too. There ain't nothing but the leaves and roots and a medicine man's prayin' left to do now."

How he wanted to let go so his own shoulders could quake with frustration, with utter fear, even some building anger too. But instead he turned and peered into the face of his old friend. "Ask Shell Woman to bring over anything she's got what'll help us make the boy feel a li'l easier. I knowed her medeecin saved your arm, likely it saved your life. I can only pray Shell Woman's power gonna save that li'l boy's life too."

Without a word, Shadrach stood and shuffled off. Behind him Titus could hear Amanda sobbing again as her feet dragged across the sandy soil. Other folks were murmuring around them too, everyone staying back aways, keeping a respectful distance from the wagon and the wide awning Roman had just finished stringing up between the top of the wagon bed and a pair of poles when Magpie came running with her terrible news.

Titus had Magpie and Leah pull out the canvas bedsacks and comforters from the back of the wagon as they approached, instructing the girls to make Lucas as soft a pallet as they could in the shade beneath that awning on the lee side of the wagon near the fire. It was where the children and the two dogs always chose to sleep each night on the trail. This is where Digger and Ghost now dropped to their bellies and scooted across the sandy ground to keep a watch on the humans. And here too Scratch slowly settled with the tiny body in his arms, Jackrabbit still clutching that tourniquet stick with both his tiny brown hands.

"Amanda," he had called to her in a quiet voice as Roman brought her up to the awning, the crowd stopping several yards behind mother and father. "You need to be strong, woman. This boy needs a strong mother right now."

She had nodded.

"Can you be strong for my Lucas boy?"

Her chin quivered so as she had nodded again, then slowly peeled herself away from Roman.

"C'mere an' sit beside me, daughter," he asked.

Once she had settled right beside her father, Amanda took a long, deep breath, then leaned over and wrapped her arms around Lucas, slowly taking him from Bass's embrace. Into Jackrabbit's ear he had whispered, "Your hands tired?"

The boy shook his head, and kept holding that stick with white-knuckled intensity, his big black eyes pooling, tears muddying his cheeks.

"Amanda," Titus said softly as he shifted onto his knees over her and Lucas, reaching back for his skinning knife, "I'm gonna have to cut 'im a li'l—"

"Cut him?"

"On them bites."

For a few long moments she had stared at those two punctures high on the side of Lucas's right calf. "Will it hurt him?"

He shook his head. "Don't think he's gonna feel nothin' much from here on out now."

After she had nodded reluctantly, he clutched the sharp blade down near the point and started work on those two swollen black holes, saying, "I gotta suck out what I can."

Gently, carefully, slowly he had sliced down with the tip of the blade through each of the holes, making the incisions long enough below each hole to account for the downward curve of the rattler's fangs as they struck the innocent boy at play. The skin bled freely, instantly, the flesh so taut, swollen, and already hot to the touch.

Lucas groaned.

"Stop, Pa!"

Softly Bass said to her, "I ain't hurtin' him. It's the p'isen, Amanda. That's what pains him so."

Gently he squeezed the two wounds between a thumb and finger, swiped off the blood with the side of his hand, then bent over the leg there below the narrow leather whang he had fashioned into a tourniquet. Continuing the pressure on the wounds with his thumb and finger, Titus formed a seal with his lips and sucked. When he sensed the salty taste on his tongue, the warmth against his lips, Scratch pulled back, turned his head, and spat onto the ground. Again and again he bent, sucked, and spat. Until he figured that he had done all the good he could.

"You get it all, Pa?" she asked as he leaned back after that last time and dragged the sleeve of his shirt across his mouth.

"Dunno."

Roman knelt before him. Looked down at the boy's leg. Then peered into Bass's eyes with a plea. "Can we burn him?"

"Burn him?"

Burwell swallowed and said, "I see'd 'em do it with bad wounds back in Missouri. Put a hot poker on it, burn it so it don't bleed no more."

"It ain't that he's bleedin', Roman," Scratch explained, watching the realization of it strike the man doubly hard. Then he thought. "But we can do something else to burn him. Flea, get me my powder horn."

When the boy had returned with his father's shooting pouch and horn, Titus pulled the stopper and poured a little powder into the two puncture wounds and the cuts. As he gently kneaded the powder down into the bloody, oozing tissues, he again instructed Flea, "Son, get me a small twig from the fire."

"Fire on it?" he asked his father in Crow.

"Yes, a good ember on the end of it."

Roman inched back when Flea brought the tiny branch, a small flame licking at the end. Holding his breath, Titus touched the ember to the first of the wounds. A sudden twist of gray smoke spurted from the swollen flesh as Lucas twisted violently in his mother's arms.

"Hold 'im still best you can, Amanda," he ordered as he pressed down on the boy's ankle with his empty hand, then gently laid the twig against the second wound.

Another spew of sparks and a curl of smoke erupted as Lucas flexed that swollen leg grown so filled with fluid that the narrow leather strip had nearly disappeared between folds of rock-hard flesh.

"We're ready, Gran'pa," Leah said behind him.

"Why don'cha move him onto the pallet the girls made for him, Amanda," he suggested quietly. "Cover 'im up too."

"You think he's cold?" she asked as she began to lay her son on the comforters.

"He's awready got the fever," Bass had said. "Gonna be burnin' up with it soon enough."

Once Amanda had the boy settled on the soft pallet, his head in her lap, Titus creaked to his feet and inched away. He had to find Shell Woman, to beg her to use her powerful Cheyenne buffalo medicine on this dying child.

"Pa?"

He turned there at the fire, his painful reverie interrupted by the desperation in Amanda's call. He went over and knelt beside her in the shade of the awning again. The sun was settling toward the far western hills. West . . . where they had been going as a happy family out to make themselves a new home in a new land with new hopes and new, new dreams.

"Something's terrible wrong," Amanda moaned. "He's been restless, real restless for the last little bit—"

Titus heard the boy's stomach lurch, that unmistakable gurgle as he instantly lunged over Amanda to grab for Lucas, getting the youngster turned on his side just before he spilled the contents of his stomach. The child whimpered when he was finished. Scared.

Bass grabbed up the wet towel they had been using to moisten the boy's lips and wiped Lucas's chin and mouth, then swiped it across Amanda's arm where it had been right under her son's mouth. "It's all right, Pa. This sort of thing don't ever bother a mother."

He looked deep into her eyes, finding himself filled with so much love for her, filled with so much sorrow for her too. "Don't bother a father neither, Amanda."

But he had to drag his gaze away from the pain in her face, looking now at that thin, frail leg still enclosed inside the dirty canvas britches—how vastly different that leg was in its skeletal boniness compared to the pale, red-mottled leg puffed up more than twice its normal size. On the outside of Lucas's bare calf were those two dark incisions he had made across the fang marks, powder-burnt now, both crude attempts at frontier healing made all the more stark against the youngster's white skin. For a moment he stared down at the slits he had cut into the muscle to suck the boy. Still a little oozy with blood and seep after the burning, those slits reminded Titus of a reptile's eyes. Eyes filled with the black of badness, glaring back at him, mocking his inability to save the boy. Sneering at his every effort to live up to Lucas's trust that his grandfather could make all things better once more.

While Amanda continued to gently rock the child against her, humming over and over again the same few notes of some barely remembered song as a mother is wont to do when she has to watch her very flesh and blood slipping from her grasp, Titus got down on his hands and knees to smell the drying puddle of what little had remained in Lucas's belly before the boy heaved it across himself, Amanda, and that baby quilt she had managed to get sewn just before the birth of her youngest. Leaning back, he scooped up a double handful of prairie sand and spilled it on the rancid puddle. Several more times he filled his hands with sand and poured it out until the whole spot was buried.

Buried, he thought. Just like this woman's gonna have to do to her baby. Sour and sickly, that vomit's stench clung in his nostrils—proof to the old trapper that the boy was already dying inside. Oh, how his heart ached for this mother now, knowing that all too soon she would be wrapping up her baby in that very same quilt and consigning his tiny body to a shallow hole in the ground. Burying him, the way he had attempted to bury that—

"Mama . . ." Lucas whimpered softly, the last syllable trailing off in a moan.

"Yes, Mama's here." She bent her head low across his face, brushing his cracked lips with her ear.

He croaked, "Water?"

Amanda looked up at her husband. "Row, get him some water."

Scratch studied the child's face as Roman fetched the canteen from the sideboard of the wagon. Lucas's face was bathed in sweat. No longer were tiny jewels beading his forehead. Now he was in the full grip of a last, excruciating fever. Amanda took the canteen, stuffed it between her knees, and started to worry the cork from the neck.

"Lemme," Titus offered.

"I gotta pour some water on his poor tongue," she said in desperation while she passed her father the canteen.

"No, not that way," he said as he pulled the cork and looked around them. "Here, I'll use the corner of your apron."

Picking up the corner, Bass pressed it against the canteen's mouth as he turned it upside down. Water soaked a bit of the apron. This he brought to the child's mouth, rubbed it across the dry, cracked lips.

"Here, Lucas—suck on it. Suck the water."

"For God's sake, Pa!" she whimpered. "Give him a drink of water!"

"He'll just throw it up," he wanted to explain. "This way his tongue won't be so dry—"

"It doesn't matter," Amanda snapped, her red eyes hardened with despair. "He's gonna . . . Lucas is going to . . . it damn well doesn't matter anymore if his stomach don't hold it."

He felt shamed, chastised by her words, more so by his lame attempt to do right by Lucas when the time to do anything for the child was past them all. No longer should any of them worry about the boy throwing the water back up.

"Y-you're right, Amanda," he said quietly, handing her the open canteen. "Give Lucas anything he wants what'll make him feel better. Anything."

Her eyes suddenly softened. "I'm sorry, Pa. So sorry." And she started to cry again, her upper body quaking with the force of her sobs.

Quickly Bass threw his arm around her shoulder, saying, "Don't do that now, Amanda. Time enough for that later. But right now . . . for what time you got left . . . you be Lucas's mother. You just be this boy's mama."

When he took his arm from her shoulder and rocked back, Amanda gently raised the child and delicately pressed the canteen's neck to Lucas's lips. She allowed only a dribble to pour across his tongue as he swallowed again, then again, greedily. Finally he opened his eyes into cracks and she took the canteen away.

"Mama," he groaned, barely audible. "I hurt so much."

"Your leg?"

"Ever'where," he sighed, lips glistening with the last drops of water.

Titus got to his knees, then patted the pallet next to Amanda. "Roman— c'mere. Be with your people."

For a long moment the big, burly farmer just stood there at the edge of the awning's shadow, staring down at his son, grief relentlessly chiseling away at his sharp, thick-boned features. His arms hung stiffly at his sides, those big callused farmer hands balling into fists with a white-knuckled intensity, then opening before they balled again with a fierce helplessness.

"Row?" Amanda whispered.

"We gonna just sit here and watch him die?" Burwell spewed suddenly, his face flushed red with fury.

Amanda glanced quickly at her father, then said, "Row, he needs you now."

Closing his eyes, Burwell wagged his head. "I-I don't think I can sit here with 'im, Amanda—"

"Pa—Pa."

Roman Burwell immediately collapsed to his knees there on the pallet with that pitiful groan from his son's lips. As tears started welling from the farmer's eyes, he scooped up Lucas's hand between both of his. How small and white it looked to Titus now, lying there, protected between the father's big, strong, hard-boned paws. How small and frail and helpless too.

Anyone close to that awning now, in the death-still quiet that held its grip on family and friends and fellow sojourners on this road to Oregon, could plainly make out how the boy's breathing came harder and harder over the next excruciating minutes. Almost as if he were struggling to breathe under water. Short, shallow breaths—each successive one seeming to come quicker and quicker, as if the child would never again catch his breath. And with these last few moments came that pale bluish hue of impending death, its once-seen-never-to-be-forgotten color smeared beneath the tiny youngster's eyes. How many times in all his living had Titus Bass witnessed that sheen paint its fateful crescent there against pale skin.

Grinding his teeth together the old trapper had gotten to his feet, feeling more weary than he could ever remember being. Without a word he turned away from the awning, his muscles tensed as he hurried on this vital errand to beg of Shadrach what he himself could not do.

At the front of the wagon he now spotted Sweete and Shell Woman. Lunging over the wagon tongue, Bass grabbed the Cheyenne by her shoulders and shook her, bringing her frightened face close to his when he snarled, "You gotta help that boy! Go put your hands on 'im, sing your prayers! Do what you gotta do to save him—"

"Scratch!" Sweete whispered as he jabbed an arm down between Toote and the old trapper, tugging them apart.

He looked up at his tall friend, desperation growing, a plea in his eyes, and in his voice, "You gotta tell 'er to come say her magic words, come help Lucas, Shadrach. For the love of all that's holy—she can heal 'im."

"I told you afore—the Cheyenne don't have no medicine strong enough."

The despair was growing, more than palpable in the pit of his belly. "How come she saved you . . . an' she won't save that boy?"

"Ain't that at all," Sweete said soothingly. Gradually he got Bass's hands pried from Shell Woman's arms and got his friend turned aside.

"You gotta make her save Lucas same way she saved you—"

Sweete suddenly shook the smaller man. "Goddammit! It's different, Scratch."

He stared at his friend's eyes and asked, "How?"

Taking a long sigh, Shad explained, "Because when she healed my arm with her white buffler medicine . . . there wasn't no spirit fighting her prayers."

Bass squinted his eyes, attempting to get his mind around what he had just been told. "N-no spirit fightin' her prayers?"

"All she had to do was stop that real bad bleedin', an' I was healed," Sweete declared.

"What's differ'nt here with that boy Lucas?"

Letting go of Titus, Shad said, "Toote told me the Cheyenne's white buffler medicine ain't no good fighting against a bad spirit."

For a long, long time he stared into the tall man's face. "The snake . . . it's a bad spirit she can't fight with her medeecin?"

"I . . . I'm real sorry, Scratch."

He looked at Shell Woman now, feeling so hollow and dry, like everything good had been sucked right out of him. "I'm sorry too. Tell 'er, Shad. Tell 'er I'm sorry I grabbed 'er, if'n I hurt her—"

"Ti-tuzz," Waits whispered behind him.

Turning, he found his wife standing at the corner of the wagon, holding a small brass kettle, steam rising from its surface in the full blast of summer's hottest fury. In her other hand she held what looked to be a wet towel.

"What you made—will it help?" he asked her in Crow.

Her eyes already spoke their grim answer for him. Then she said, "No, but I made it from a root that will make it easier . . . his last journey . . . for him."

Bass could see how hard it was for her to stand there without sobbing, without breaking down herself. After all she was a mother too, a woman carrying her baby in her belly right then . . . experiencing an unimaginable grief just in watching another mother hold her baby in her arms as that child lay dying. He took the kettle's bail from her and carried it around the front of the wagon to set it beside Amanda. Magpie followed with her mother, leaning in to hand the white woman a spoon, then stepped back into that fringe of stunned onlookers.

Amanda looked up at Bass and his wife, asking, "What is it?"

"Waits made it. Maybeso it's gonna help . . . help Lucas so he don't hurt so much."

Her eyes bounced back and forth between them for a moment, then she said, "If it will make his going easier, Pa."

While Amanda raised Lucas up again and held a spoonful of the steamy broth against his lips, Titus knelt on the other side of the child, by the lower leg that was already blackening with an impatient death rising inexorably from the wound. Unwrapping the wet towel Waits handed down to him, Titus found inside a mash of roots and leaves. This dripping pulp he scooped up with his fingers and laid against the wounds, knowing the boy's flesh was dying, if not already dead, the flesh darkening the way it was, those wound sites seeping a foul ooze. Lucas did not move the leg as Scratch wrapped the wet towel over the poultice.

After a half dozen sips of the steamy broth, Lucas barely managed to turn his head before his stomach revolted and emptied itself. As he watched his daughter, Scratch saw how Amanda positioned herself, refusing to look below her child's waist anymore, to look at the snakebite, at the bloated, blackening leg. Instead, she kept her eyes only on Lucas's face as she stroked his tiny arm and gently rocked the boy. Her tears spilled one by one onto the child's pale, dusty shirt, each drop making its own muddy circle on the much-faded cloth.

Titus turned at the rustle and murmur behind him, watching Hoyt Bingham come through the crowd with a green bottle in his hand. The train's other captain knelt just inside the late-afternoon shade of the awning and held out the bottle to Roman.

"May—maybe some whiskey help it," the man offered.

Roman nodded to Titus, and Bingham shifted his offering to Bass. For a long moment he stared at that bottle in the settler's hand, an old hunger raising its head in the pit of him—the sort of hunger that came when there was nothing else to do but numb a pain with the forgetfulness of liquor . . . then he looked at Bingham's face again and those eyes pleading that he could find some way to help. At last Scratch looked down at how Roman held his son's tiny hand, not thinking that offer of whiskey was such a fine idea after all.

"Maybeso later," Titus said softly. "Likely . . . we could sure use that whiskey . . . a little later. Thankee most kindly."

Again and again Waits and Toote brought steaming rags in a brass kettle, rags he held over the soupy poultice. Changing the rag that had cooled off for a hot one as the crowd around them breathed but did not mutter a word. Maybe they were all talked out for now. Nothing more to say. No words that could make any difference. Maybe not even prayer words. So he glanced up at those vacant eyes in those dusty faces here beside the Soda Springs where the small geyser spewed at that moment with a watery gush.

He was helpless as any of them were, these emigrant farmers who had no earthly reason to be out here in his wilderness when they should be back in their hardwood forests, or on in their promised land on the Willamette River of Oregon Territory. Anywhere but here, an unnamed, unmapped hell of the country more than halfway between where they'd come from and where they still dreamed of putting down new roots. Easy was it for Titus to read that despair on their faces. It could have been any child, their child, their youngest, the baby who would have grown up strong and bold in that far-off land of promise. But here they stood suspended in time and distance, much, much too far from their old homes to ever consider turning back for what was. Still too damn far from Oregon country to truly believe any of them could make it to that promised land without being forced to pay some terrible price for their wanting and hungering for it.

Everything came with a price, Titus brooded. The wanting of that paradise on the Willamette . . . it had come with a hard, hard price for this little family.

Was his wanting of a little paradise far, far to the north for his family going to come with some awful price as yet hidden beyond the horizon . . . somewhere out there where he could not see it coming, could not turn out of its way?

So he peered up at Bingham and Ryder, Murray and Truell, Fenton and Iverson, and all those nameless ones who had stood up against the way of eastern men like Hargrove. Good, simple, hardworking men who sweated into the ground, bled on the soil to coax something green from it. Men who had already spent months and much more than a thousand miles learning what it was going to take to reach Oregon. Not just the anvil one of them had abandoned way back on the Kaw, or a sideboard already some five generations old left behind on the lower Platte. Maybe that clumsy, bulky grinding stone thrown out by the time the great shallow river split in two and they began to follow the road's course as it northed to Laramie. Perhaps some heavy china that had belonged to a great-grandmother, now left carefully stacked and abandoned beneath a wind-stunted tree at the base of Chimney Rock. Treasures left behind for them that might appreciate what treasures they were, and what it had taken to leave them behind—forever.

All of these sojourners had left something behind . . . even loved ones. Blood of their blood, flesh of their flesh, bone of their bone. Each loss a supreme sacrifice paid on the altar of this wilderness crossing. A stillborn child laid to its rest in a tiny hole beside the Little Blue. Then the train's first cholera victim, who awoke one bright, clear morning with nothing more than a headache, was taken feverish by midday, and at death's door before the train stopped for the night. That woman wasn't the last to be taken, Amanda had told her father as tears had pooled in her eyes several nights ago at their fire, when she had attempted to explain what sacrifices these emigrants had been making all along. Seventeen more had died, gripped by the cholera that chased them right out of the settlements, she declared, chased by that scourge until they finally outran it somewhere close to Courthouse Rock on the North Platte. No more graves after that one they dug for the husband and father who had stumbled clambering out of his wagon, dropping his loaded rifle, and shot himself under the chin. He had been the last one of these Oregon-bound sojourners they had buried on the way. . . .

At least until this day. Why the babes and the youngest among them? He sat there in the coming twilight, asking this troubling question of that great, still being he was just beginning to trust. Why this little Lucas?

As dusk deepened about them, someone brought three lamps, and though a few left, going back to stir up fires and put supper on the boil, Titus was surprised that most of these people ended up staying on in silence. A watch, he thought. A wake they were making of the boy's slow, fitful death, but nothing noisy in the slightest. No, these were the sort of people who were standing out there in the gathering clot of night, wondering on this happenstance, thanking their capricious God that it hadn't been one of their happy, laughing, carefree children who had been sacrificed to this camping ground at Soda Springs. These simple folks with simple dreams and simple prayers, standing there on the edge of the fire's glow or lamplight four or five deep, watching without a murmur, trying to grasp onto some sense of how it must feel to be Roman or Amanda Burwell right now.

Every one of these sojourners sure to sense how the journey had just taken its heaviest toll, its tithe, its blood sacrifice from this little family. Perhaps praying—they were wondering if they would make it the next thousand miles or so to the Willamette without being required to make a flesh-and-bone sacrifice of their own to this life-altering journey. Secretly in their heart of hearts offering thanks to their God that it was someone else who had paid and not them.

So Titus brooded darkly on what kind of prayer-maker it would take to thank their God for taking some other person's child. How goddamned holy did that make them, even if they invoked the Almighty's name and His spirit? All these simple people inching west toward the setting sun, brazenly believing they were only moving from one old home to a new home . . . with only a matter of some miles and months in between. Stupid, simple people, he cursed them— thinking of this march across the prairie, onto the High Plains, and over the mountains, fording powerful rivers, fighting off the cold and dust and bugs and water scrapes too . . . who were these people to stand out there in the dark and pray to their God, a God who hadn't done a damned thing to help save the life of this small, happy, towheaded helpless boy who'd never done a thing to hurt anybody and was just coming to know his grandpapa? Who were these people to judge anyway?

"P-Pa?"

He turned at Amanda's weak, raspy call, found her leaning over Lucas. "Hol't that light up for me, Roman."

Burwell raised the lantern, its oil sloshing in the brass well as the farmer held it above them all, creating stabs of shadow and light in a half circle. Titus bent close, hoping—perhaps praying—to feel the soft brush of breath on his cheek as he stared at Lucas's face. A thick and greenish ooze seeped out from the corner of the boy's crusted nostril.

Titus stifled a sob, thinking, The p'isen has riz clear to the child's head now.

Which meant Lucas was near gone. Sweet mercy. Sweet, blessed mercy— the roots in that broth Waits prepared had given the child a little peace as he slipped into the hardest part of his passing. Mayhaps the soup had eased the boy's pain, because Lucas hadn't fussed after that one time telling his mama that he hurt so bad all over. Titus could only hope as Roman raised the lantern.

"Keep hol't of him, you two," he whispered, his voice cracking and the tears starting to stream there in the dark. "Here, put your hand there, Roman. An' you'll be sartin to feel . . . feel when he's . . . took his last air."

When he got the words said, the breath caught in Amanda's throat. But she let him lift her trembling hand and lay it on her boy's chest, right there beside Roman's. This little boy, so short on earthly days, now passing on, cradled here in the arms of his pap and mam.

Every now and then, he could hear Amanda's gut-wrenching wail.

It made the hair stand on the back of Scratch's neck.

But he gritted his teeth, swabbed the raw end of his nose, and kept on digging.

"Ain't it deep enough yet, Mr. Bass?" asked Hoyt Bingham as he stood on the rim of that grave they had begun gouging out of the hard, flintlike ground forty yards south of the Burwell wagon. Yonder aways on their back trail coming to Soda Springs.

"We're goin' down far as it takes to keep that boy from gettin' dug up."

He watched how the dozen or so men on the rim of the grave looked at one another, then stared into the dark, the light from four lanterns positioned on the ground at their feet radiating upward to illuminate only the lower half of their faces, that soft light causing everything from their cheekbones up to disappear in shadow.

"Dug up?" one of the sodbusters asked.

"Wolves." Titus plunged the shovel into the ground and scraped it forward in the dark. He was working by feel now. The light from those lanterns no longer reached the bottom of the short rectangle just big enough for one man to turn around in. Dark at the bottom where the old man sweated as he pried loose more and more of the dirt he wanted to lay on top of that little boy's body.

"Maybe you been in there long enough."

He recognized Sweete's voice and looked up. "I ain't tired, Shadrach."

Sweete went to one knee beside the grave and gazed down at him with his own red eyes. "I know you ain't, Titus. Just—I wanted to have a hand in digging some of this grave too."

For a moment he stared up at his friend's long, sad face. Then nodded. "I'll leave the shovel down in the hole for you."

Shad reached out with his long arm and seized Bass's wrist, boosting him up to the prairie just as the dozen others nervously stepped aside at the rustle of footsteps coming through the sagebrush. Into the gentle yellow glow of those lanterns stepped a big shadow, followed by those two Indian dogs that had kept a long vigil over the boy's last hours. Roman stopped within their silent circle, swallowed deep, and arched back his shoulders. An hour ago Titus wouldn't have put money on Burwell ever rising from that foul-smelling pallet again. He had looked as defeated as any man could be, his shoulders hunched over, quaking as he held Amanda, who was holding Lucas. Rocking them both: his dead, towheaded boy and that grieving, wailing mother. Moaning as he rocked them both in the cradle of his arms. Rocking and moaning with some wordless pain leaching out of his pores the way a clay pitcher sweats in the summer. Slow, so slow, drop by drop—that pain leaching out of him so slow.

The sight of the three had been more than Titus could take. He had to do something with his own private grief. So he had tramped off into the dark, where Waits eventually found him, held her husband as he cried in silence, not daring to allow the wounded animal that was shrieking inside him to have its voice just yet. And when he sensed that he had it all shaken out for the moment, she dried his tears with the wide sleeve of her calico dress and he had walked back into the light with her. Pulling out that shovel Roman kept in the possum belly slung beneath the wagon, he had grabbed up one of those lanterns brought to the death watch and stepped into the dark alone.

Come tomorrow morning when the rest of them were gone over the horizon and nothing was left of the train but a dusty smudge in the sky, he would remain here on the back trail and hide the grave. Build a big damn fire to kill the scent. Turn a few inches of topsoil after the limbs had gone to embers. And no wolf, no coyote, no poor Digger son of a bitch would ever know his grandson was buried there. Blood of his blood, bone of his bone, left there to rest in peace in this nameless, unmarked corner of the wilderness between what had been and what was to be.

"What's that?" Roman asked the moment he dropped into the hole and the racket of hammers arose out of the silence of that chill, desert night like a disembodied poltergeist. Rhythmic, hauntingly rhythmic.

"I give Rankin and Winston two of those wood boxes my ship's biscuits come in," Bingham explained to his friend, who stared up at the eerie lamplight on their faces from the bottom of the hole. "Goodell had him two more."

"Ship's biscuits?" Burwell repeated, not understanding.

Bingham bit his lower lip a minute, then continued. "We figured it was the best thing we could come up with for a box, Row."

"A box for my . . . my . . . for him?"

"Yes, we're makin' him a coffin," Iverson said. "Winston took one side outta each box and they was laying 'em together, nailing 'em into a real nice coffin, Row."

Ammons nodded his head, "It's gonna work out real nice, Row—ain't nothing gonna get in to your boy."

Then they all saw how that image slapped Roman across the jaw as hard as a hickory-boned fist. His eyes scrunched up and his chin started to quake. Then it wasn't but a heartbeat before that tremble started to work its way down through the rest of him until he was shaking as he stood in that dark hole. Slowly he sank down the long handle of that farmer's shovel, gripping it for support until he landed at the bottom of the small hole with a grunt . . . and began to moan once more.

"Row," Bingham pleaded as he leaned over the edge of the grave.

But Titus pulled the man back and knelt so he could look down on the grieving father. "Son, whyn't you come on out now an' lemme finish this up for the boy," he said quietly, his voice having a hint of an echo as the words fell into the hollow grave.

"That you, Titus?"

"It's me."

Roman's words drifted up from the dark, weak and plaintive, "How's a man, a man ever s'posed to bear up under this?"

At first he swallowed, then said, "I ain't for sure, Roman. Can't claim to ever goin' through what's eatin' a hole away at your heart right now. Fierce as my own heart screams in pain right now, I don't have no idee how yours must be."

"It's like my legs won't stand when I think of . . . of him."

"But, you're gonna have to stand, Roman," Titus explained. "Amanda gonna be countin' on you for that. Hold her up when it comes time we gotta put that li'l body down in this hole."

"I-I don't—"

"What about them other'ns? Three of the most likely young'uns a pa would ever want to light up his life. What about them three, Roman?"

"I didn't figure on—"

"You tell me, son—would your boy, Lucas, want you an' his mama to give up an' die right here when you're so close to where you was takin' him?"

"Don't have no way of knowing—"

"Lucas wants his folks to carry on," Titus advised. "Lucas wants you both to be strong for each other. Say your words over his buryin' spot. Then wipe your tears an' get on down the trail another day."

"L-leave him here?"

"Yes," he whispered it. "You gonna leave the boy's body behind, right here. Just like he left his body behind his own self a li'l while ago."

"Then what, Titus?"

"You go on to get up next mornin', an' the mornin' after that, and you take your family on to Oregon—"

"W-without him?" he shrieked in misery.

Scratch shuffled at the edge of the pit, stretching out on his belly so he could reach down with one hand, lay it on Roman's trembling shoulder. "No, you an' Amanda won't never be 'thout young Lucas again. He'll allays be with you, ever' mile of the way to that new land in Oregon. Lucas allays be young, just like you 'member him."

"It's gonna hurt like the devil to remember him."

"But you will . . . 'cause Lucas wants you to," Titus said softly. "You go carry Lucas's memory with you day by day now. 'Cause he'll be right there with you on ever' mile you put behin't you from sunup to sundown. Lucas goin' to finish this journey to Oregon with you an' Amanda."

It took a moment, but they heard the muted shuffling of the big farmer's boots on the flaky soil at the bottom of the hole. Then his head came into the light as he stood, his face upturned, long muddy streaks coursing down each of his cheeks. Red eyes he turned up now to Titus.

"You don't mind me doing the rest by myself, friends," he told all of them quietly as his eyes touched their lamplit faces. "I got a grave to finish for my son."

EIGHTEEN

He had helped Roman lay that little body in its coffin cobbled together from those wooden crates, just wide enough for the lad's narrow shoulders. Long enough for those two legs: one thin and gangly, the other black and bloated with a serpent's poison. A spare and bony body that so reminded Titus of the skinny tyke he himself had been at that age.

At the moment Lucas had breathed his last, Titus pulled a large flap of that old quilt over the boy's disfigured leg. No one would ever have to look at the awful wounds again. Amanda made sure of that. She kept the boy wrapped from his chin on down, holding him in her lap there beneath the awning as the thin sliver of new moon rose, rocked across the horizon, then set in preparation for the coming of a gray dawn. Not until then did she wash his face, and only his face, with a scrap of burlap, then held Lucas against her breast so steadfastly Titus doubted they would be able to pry the body loose from her arms when it came time to consign the boy to the ground.

But she had given him up to Roman. With her face screwed up into an ugly picture of pure agony, she had bottled up the wail behind clenched teeth and allowed Roman to take the quilt-wrapped bundle from her . . . only that deathly pale face poking from one end of the blanket a mother-to-be had stitched for her youngest. On the far side of the wagon the friends had laid the box, its cover propped against a wagon wheel in the charcoal-hued light of that cold morning before the summer sun came to rewarm this high desert. Once her arms were empty, that's when the women moved in—white women from the train, all of whom had stayed up through that long and sleepless night with Amanda—for this manner of grieving was something new to Waits and Toote. They stood back as the others swooped in to lay their hands on her, murmuring their prayers and wishes and condolences, brushing the matted hair back out of her face, bringing warm water in a china bowl to wash away the dust from her cheeks and the blood smeared on her hands, clean off that arm where her boy had spewed anything put into his belly.

From the bottom of a humpbacked sea chest, one of them brought out a black dress she had, not a formal mourning gown, but something that spoke a much simpler grief. It would do, most all of them assured her as they gathered round the grieving mother for cover and two of their number loosened every last tiny button from her bloodstained dress, slowly pulled it from her, then draped the black dress around her. They brushed and fixed her hair as they all listened to the dull, unanswered thud of that hammer driving one nail after another into the lid of that long, thin box they had cobbled together from the hard-biscuit crates.

Scratch looked around at the others, then handed the hammer to the one called Ryder with a nod of thanks. He found Roman still staring down at the box in that way of disbelief.

"You made him real comfortable, son," Titus reassured. He swallowed hard and fought the quiver of his chin. Knowing his voice was about to crack, nonetheless he said, "The look on his face . . . Lucas was at peace, son. His hurtin's over now."

"You ready, Roman?" Iverson said as he stepped up, his old, scuffed Bible held in both hands at the center of his belly, as if protecting the buckle of a belt that wasn't there.

Burwell nodded again, his eyes never rising from the lid of that long, narrow box.

Three of the others immediately stepped around Iverson and knelt beside the coffin, but before they barely had their arms around it, Titus and Shadrach tapped on those emigrants' shoulders and shooed them away. Together, without a word spoken, the two of them gently lifted the box and positioned it on their shoulders, on Scratch's right as he stepped away in the front, and on Sweete's left shoulder as he made his strides shorter, more deliberate—that much taller was he than Titus Bass.

"Bring them two coils of rope," Scratch whispered to Bingham as he shuffled past.

A long gauntlet of men, children, and now the women too was forming on either side of the path the two old trappers were taking through the gray of first light to that deep, deep hole Titus had wanted to be half again as deep as he was tall. In the end, so deep that Shadrach had been the only one who could pull Burwell from the grave after Roman had passed up the shovel to them, then that empty bucket on the end of a one-inch line they used to drag out the dirt the grieving father tore up from the bottom of what would forever be Lucas's resting place.

On his right just past the wagon tongue the crowd parted with a murmur, and through that gap stepped Roman, his right arm around Amanda's shoulders, his left hand gripping her arm across her body, holding her up, making her move with him, slowly, taking small steps as they fell in behind the coffin. Behind them came Lemuel, Leah, and young Annie—the baby of the family now that Lucas was gone. Up ahead in the graying light, Bass saw the faces of his children appear at the side of the gauntlet of white folks, saw how they poked their heads out to watch.

"Popo," Magpie whispered as he came near, one small step at a time, carrying the front of that coffin, "all right we come with you too?" Her words were respectful, filled with awe and a pain that hadn't subsided since yesterday when she discovered the boy not long after the snake struck. She had one arm laid over Flea's shoulder, her other arm holding up her smallest brother.

Jackrabbit looked frightened, confused, downright scared. Bass's eyes softened as he quickly peered at the boy. "You come with me."

They tore themselves away from the gauntlet as the coffin moved past, stepping into line at the end of the procession to join Annie, Leah, and Lemuel behind the sobbing parents.

And finally Iverson reached the hole where Titus had dug it, aways back from the trees and brush, in the open, where the trail from the east rolled through to this camping ground. In the open. Where a soul should be buried, he thought again. Not closed in by trees and rocks. And if it couldn't be at the top of a hill, then . . . in the open.

Bingham and Goodell shuffled ahead of the trappers, getting to the grave right behind Iverson to quickly lay out just enough length from the two ropes on one side of the hole so the coffin could rest on top of the ropes for these last few minutes before the box would disappear from sight. As Scratch and Shadrach knelt and worked the narrow crate from their shoulders, Iverson began motioning to the more than two hundred who were crowding up, silently forming them around the site more than ten to a dozen deep. From the quiet throng, Carter emerged carrying a large cast-iron oven, the sort the women used to bake their breads, cakes, and biscuits in, when shoved beneath the ashes of a fire. As soon as the emigrant set it down, Scratch saw it was without its lid, filled with what he took to be ashes.

Waits-by-the-Water stepped through a knot of women and came to him silently, reaching his side to grip his hand and put her arm around him as they stood across the narrow hole from the grieving parents. Titus sensed just how lucky he was to have a good woman at his side through everything life could throw at a man.

Iverson held up that Bible much stained with sweat and grime, asking for quiet as Titus and Scratch stepped aside, allowing the family to approach the box. When the parents stopped, looking down at the coffin, Amanda drew herself up there in Roman's arms. Then took a long, ragged sigh, and no longer sobbed or whimpered, but instead motioned with her free arm to the children, not just the three left her, but to her brothers and sister too: Magpie, Flea, and Jackrabbit.

"The rest of you children," she said quietly an instant before Iverson started to speak, which compelled the man to stand there with his mouth in an O as her small voice made its presence felt on them all, "all you children who played with Lucas every night on the trail . . . I want you to come up to stand around his grave with us now."

He must be the closest thing this band of sojourners had for a preacher, Titus thought as Iverson finally began a reading of this Scripture, then another, and still another. And when he finally closed that worn, brown-skinned Bible, Iverson held it against his chest and began speaking from his heart.

"Not one of us knows the why of the ways of the Lord," he reminded them. "On our journey we've lost babes, and we've lost old ones too. It is the work and wonder of the Lord, so we are left to doubt or to believe. I . . . choose to believe."

There was some quiet muttering from some of the women and a handful of the men as the heat of the coming day began to tell.

Iverson pitched in again. "Last night I heard the talk of people scared of what they had done in running from homes and family to find themselves in this wilderness where the innocent can be taken from us. So let me remind those of you who were gnashing your teeth—crying that this must be a curse because we chose to chance a journey to God's garden. What took young Lucas was not the devil, or his evil serpent. It was only one of many dangers man finds in this wilderness. Do not despair—we will get through to our Garden of Eden!"

With that last word pronounced in a louder volume, Iverson held everyone's rapt attention. Even the old trapper's.

"Yea, last night in the darkest of hours there were those doubters who professed to know that our Oregon company had been cursed—cursed by Hargrove and his men; cursed by young Lucas's terrible death. But, I tell you nay! Why—don't you remember that we have lost some of our number all along the way?"

There arose a quiet, begrudging agreement from the many.

"No," Iverson hammered on, "I will not go along with those of you who say that these deaths are because we left the Garden of Eden behind us. No, my friends—our garden lies before us, pulling us on."

Titus had to admit, the man did have a gift for preachifying, the way he used an alternate rhythm or different tone to hold this crowd's attention from one moment to the next.

"Oregon awaits us, my friends. This wilderness infested with serpents and bad water is only what we must endure to reach the land where the Lord is drawing us nigh. Do not let the devil convince your hearts that young Lucas paid a blood atonement . . . as some of you were saying in the dark. No. I want you to look now—yes . . . look and see how first light is coming!"

They turned almost as one and peered east along their back trail, from whence they had come, leaving most everything behind to go west.

"This is a new day for the Lord. We must complete God's work and bury young Lucas, for his family, for us all. Then we must be on to Oregon."

"Can we sing a song?" a woman asked from the crowd, plaintively.

"Yes," Iverson answered, then immediately closed his eyes and launched into a song Titus could not remember ever hearing.

Some of the crowd knew the song too, and they joined in self-consciously by the middle of the first verse. But because the entire group had not added their voices, Iverson ended after the second verse.

"Friends, it is time to consign young Lucas Burwell to the ground."

Roman caught Amanda as her knees turned to water. Steadying her against him, they watched four men step from the throng and pick up an end of the two ropes. Carefully they raised the coffin off the ground, then swung it over the hole and began to slowly lower it to the bottom. When it rested securely, two of the men pulled the ropes from the grave.

In the coming of day Iverson bent and scooped up a handful of the dry, dark earth piled next to that hole and tossed it down upon the top of that wooden box with a muffled clatter. "Dust to dust . . ."

Kneeling beside the cast-iron oven, Iverson seized a handful of the cold ashes he had asked be brought here. He opened his hand, allowing the flakes and dust to fall, most of them drifting into the hole.

"And ashes to ashes," he reminded them. "From dust we come. To dust we all will go."

Rubbing his palm against the leg of his pants, Iverson stepped back and made a quick gesture to Roman. Mr. and Mrs. Burwell knelt at the edge of the grave, where they each tossed in some dirt clods, landing hollow on the top of that crude coffin, then reached over to toss in some ashes. Roman got to his feet first, helping Amanda as they moved aside, and Lemuel brought his two sisters forward. At the side of the grave, Lemuel turned, signaling Magpie and her brothers to join them. All bent and made their offerings to the grave.

And as the children inched back, Iverson said, "Anyone who wants to come to the graveside, offer a prayer by throwing in some dirt or ashes—now is the time."

They shuffled around the small hole, long lines of silent folk coming from two directions. As they finished, then passed by, most every one of these emigrants reached out to touch Amanda's hand, or shake with Roman—offering in that quiet, unspoken way something of their own grief, and hope too. Titus stood there with his arm around Waits, watching this long procession, realizing just how many friends the Burwell family had made on this unfinished journey to Oregon. Friends these were. Friends who had stood watch, knowing nothing else to do. Friends who had offered to help dig, knowing nothing else to do. Friends who brought food and drink all through the night, not knowing what else they could do. But here they stood as the words and prayers and songs were said over this deep, deep hole dug for a tiny child . . . because it was what they could do.

It was what they would want others to do for them if tragedy had struck their family instead of the Burwells'.

But in the end, only the Burwells stood beside that hole with the two trapper families. The others had moved off, busy with breakfast, bringing in the stock, hitching up the oxen and mules, saddling the horses, rolling up the bedding, and dousing the fires once the trumpet sounded—high and brassy on the motionless air. It was still so cool, Titus thought. But soon the earth would begin to heat up and the breeze would stir. Restless wind. It would be restless all day long and into the evening as the earth cooled once more. Wind every bit as restless as was he.

"You take your family back to the wagon now," Titus said as he and Shad moved up after the last of the emigrants were gone. "Time to get your stock hitched up for moving out."

Roman gazed down at his wife, then nodded and turned without a word. The children started back with him, joined by Waits and Toote.

Scratch moved up and laid his arm across his daughter's shoulder. "Sure you wanna watch us finish this?"

She nodded once. And Sweete reached out to grab the handle.

"I can do this," Titus said.

"Let me," Shad offered quietly, his big sad eyes imploring. "You stay with your daughter."

They watched the big man scrape and scrape and scrape the soil back in on that tiny box at the bottom of such a deep hole, deep enough, Titus thought, that no wolf would do anything but give up, even if it was able to smell something on this tiny patch of ground. When he had the hole completely filled in, Shad began stamping around on the new soil, compressing it, before he tossed on some more of the dirt and compressed again with his big feet.

"I'll carry the rest away from here," Sweete explained as he took the first shovelful of the excess dirt and started toward a copse of trees fifteen yards away.

"Gonna stay behind awhile, Amanda," he said softly to her while Shad was coming and going. "Build me a fire over the spot. Make sure no critter can smell a thing and try digging it up. Too far down, made sure of that. But I don't even wanna think 'bout some wolf tryin'—"

He saw she was crying again.

"I can't go, Pa."

"Can't go?"

She wagged her head. "I gotta stay here. Not ready to go on. Not . . . just yet."

"Awright, Amanda. You want to, you can stay here with me. You can take your time for grievin', all you need."

Minutes later as Roman pulled the four-hitch team of oxen around in a circle nearby and halted, Titus announced to Burwell, "Come see her afore you go, son." Then he explained that she would be staying there with him to see to the grave.

"You gonna be all right, Amanda?" Roman asked, lines of concern deep in his brow. "You . . . you'll be coming, right?"

"Yes, Roman. I'll come along soon. I just need a little more time here," she confessed. "Not ready to let him go just yet."

The big farmer embraced her a long while, then kissed the top of her head and wiped the tears off her cheeks before he clambered back up the front wheel, squeaked onto the seat, and slapped the reins down on the backs of those oxen. Lemuel came up beside the lead ox and snapped it with a long whip, hollering at the animal to giddap as he turned to look back at his mother in farewell, wet streaks running down the young man's cheeks.

When the wagon came around, the two girls were at the rear gate, there above the swinging buckets, waving back at their mother from the rear pucker hole, sobbing once more.

Toote and Waits stood with the children, those two shaggy dogs, and the extra stock until the wagon caught up; then they all fell in on the road to Oregon, the last in line for the day's march. Shad swung into the saddle and waved his long .62 flintlock in the air before he wheeled around and heeled into the march, eventually disappearing with the rest.

"You wanna sit over there in the shade, Amanda?"

Scratch walked with her over to that copse of trees near some large boulders. "Stay here in the shade an' don't you go too near them rocks where the sn—"

He bit off the word too late.

So she looked up at him as she settled to the ground in the shade of that sunny new day. "Gonna always look out for snakes, here on out, Pa."

"You sit yourself, daughter, and you do your grieving. It's what a body's s'posed to do when a big chunk been tored outta their heart."

After a minute, while she sat staring at that patch of disturbed ground several yards away, he knelt before her and said, "I'm goin' off now—fetch some firewood from what's been left round the camp. Build me a fire on the grave."

He stood up in that silence, her sigh the only sound, along with the slight tremble among the leaves brought by a first breeze stirring through the branches overhead.

A good place for a body to rest in peace, he thought as he started away to scratch up a heap of firewood. This silence made for a mighty fine place for a mortal body to rest for all time to come.

It had taken the better part of the morning to drag in what wood was left behind by the others, logs and limbs scattered across the camping ground. Then he built his fire, fed it with new timbers, and let it burn down to embers before he began working at the fire's edges to turn the hot ashes and glowing embers over, mixing them with the dry, flaky soil, one shovelful at a time.

Hot work, what with the way the sun had come up mean and resentful in that cloudless sky, baking him from overhead while the rising heat from those embers scorched him from below. Both moccasins were permanently blackened now, along with the bottoms of his buckskin leggings and that fringe that trailed at his heels too. But fire was a good thing. Flames had a way of cleansing what they touched. Just the way he had rubbed that powder into Lucas's snakebites and set them afire, now this ground had been cleansed of the smell of man, the stench of death.

A harsh purging for this unmarked grave, cleansed with the ancient, renewing power of fire. Just like a lightning storm started a whisper of smoke, burnt down a whole mountainside of timber, then from the fallow and black ground rose new life the following spring.

As he slowed his digging, straightened, and wiped the huge drops of sweat from his face with a sleeve, for the first time since the others had gone Titus began to sense the unalterable numbness of that hole eaten away inside him again, a hole he had filled with all the nonstop work of digging and hammering and filling and burning. But now the fire was out and the embers lay scattered, turned over and over and over with the soil that had grown as hot as the sun's own scorchy breath. He stood there, leaning on the handle of that shovel, helpless to stop its pain from rising within him like the black, bubbling tar in those pits over on the Wind River, north from the mouth of the Popo Agie. Hot, thick, rising bubbles of pain that threatened to gag him with the bitter taste of clabbered gall.

Below him lay a child fresh and dewy at life, innocent of pain and evil, ignorant of betrayal . . . a child Titus was just coming to know. A grandson with a soul so beautiful—remembering how the boy held out his hand to shake with a grizzled stranger who wore beaded earbobs, or looked his grandfather squarely in the eye to ask a why to almost everything, or bounded upon the old man's knee for a story of grizzly bears and Indian warriors and rendezvous glories too . . . it nearly chewed away a hole inside the old man there beside the child's unmarked grave. A gaping void he didn't know how he'd fill . . . or where . . . or with who.

Amanda had her head buried in her forearms looped across her knees, where they were tucked against her breast as he returned to the shade. She looked up as he approached.

"Oh . . . Pa," she whimpered, her eyes still full as he dropped the shovel and collapsed in exhaustion beside her. "How am I ever going to remember where Lucas is buried?"

Enfolding her in his arms, he cradled her and said, "You will. You'll remember the Soda Springs, and remember how we done ever'thing we could to keep him safe."

Shaking her head, Amanda pushed back from him. "I shouldn't have let them bury him. Roman and me—we should take him on with us. And bury him there—"

"No," he interrupted her, again pulling his daughter against him gently, reassuringly. "Allays best to leave a body where he's been took from the living. It's the most fitting thing."

"I can't bear to leave without him," she confessed. "Don't know how Roman was able to go from this place."

"You can too," he vowed. "Because you're gonna take Lucas with you when you leave this place behind."

Her red eyes studied his a moment. "How?"

"You'll take the memory of him from this place, Amanda. Allays remember his smile. Remember the way that shock of his yellow hair fell in his eyes an' he had to keep pushin' at it? Take that with you to Oregon now. Keep the memory of your boy Lucas with you."

She pressed her face against his chest and murmured, "When I come back here I won't be able to remember where we laid him, Pa."

Gently raising her chin, he wanted to convince her she never would return to this place . . . but instead he wiped some of the tears from her dust-streaked face and said, "Yes, you will remember, daughter. Look there, at them hills. See that cone where the water bubbles up. Then lookit the cut in that ridge yonder." He turned her slightly. "See that saddle there, and the sharp rise of that butte. Look here now where the creek makes that horseshoe . . . an' you'll remember where we made camp here. You'll remember where we put 'im to rest."

She nodded confidently. "Yes, I will remember when I come back to see him again, real soon I'll come back—"

"No, Amanda," he finally admitted it as he held her tightly. "Once you get to that Oregon country with the memory of your li'l boy, there won't ever be no need of comin' back here again. Just keep the memory of Lucas in your heart . . . an' let his body, this place, an' this long, hard road to your new home be nothing but a distant memory. Once we turn our backs on this place, it's gonna be up to you to keep him alive in your heart, an' forget this place. There's nothin' here for you to ever come back for—"

The profane smack of a lead ball against the tree trunk reached him an instant before the low grumble of the gunshot from a distant rifle.

Immediately throwing himself across Amanda, Titus quickly searched to find where he had propped his rifles, laying both pistols across the shooting pouch he left at the base of the same bush before he had picked up the shovel and—

A second ball sliced through the branches right above them, and the weapon's roar floated overhead on the hot breeze.

Two shots, too close together for it to be one shooter. There were at least a pair of them.

"C'mon!" he cried as he rose to a crouch, counting off the seconds they had before that first attacker could reload, aim, and fire again.

Grabbing Amanda at the back of her collar, Titus dragged his daughter in a crouch toward the low boulders to their left, snatching up the pouch and one of the pistols on the way past the brush—

A third shot rang out . . . kicking up a spurt of dust near his hand—coming too quickly for that first shooter to have reloaded.

Shit. There's least three of 'em.

"Get in!" he ordered as he shoved her through a cut in the scattered rocks that stood about knee-high.

As Scratch was turning around he pushed Amanda down against the ground, slinging the pouch and powder horn against her shoulder. "You know how to load a rifle?"

She looked up at him dumbly, but nodded her head.

"Good," he said, and patted her on the shoulder. "All I gotta do now is go out there to them guns of mine and get back in here 'thout getting shot."

"I-I can help, Pa."

"I ain't lettin' you go out there—"

"Will you listen to me?" she said, scooting up on her hip. "Man like you, seems you're always attracting trouble like flies to syrup."

He snorted, flicked a glance at the open ground between them and the sound of those guns, then looked at her. "Awright, what you got in mind?"

"I can shoot, Pa."

"Pistol?"

"I can hold it."

He squinted a moment at her. "Maybeso you give me a break to get them guns, Amanda. Here," and he pressed the big horse pistol into her hand. "When I bust outta these rocks, they're gonna aim at me real quick. So when I start movin', I want you to count to three while you're aiming off there at them trees—"

"That where they are?"

"I think so, but I ain't for sure," he admitted. "You count to three, then you shoot that pistol at the trees. That oughtta make 'em flinch a wee bit. Mayhaps gimme time to grab them rifles an' get 'em back in here."

"If you don't get back here with them?"

"Then you reload that pistol from my pouch," he said, staring her hard in the eyes, "an' you keep it cocked till they come real . . . real close—so you can stop one of 'em."

"You think they're comin' for me?"

He shook his head. "I hope it's me they're comin' for. Now, cock that hammer an' tell me when you're ready to start countin'."

"I'm ready."

Quickly touching her cheek with his fingertips, Titus crouched in the gap between rocks, then rasped, "Start countin'!"

He was counting himself as he exploded from cover. While his mind roared with the number one, a gun thundered from that copse of trees off to the south. Too quick a shot, indicating he had caught them by surprise. The ball went wild as he reached the rifles on the count of two. And turned, scooping up the pistol and stuffing it in his belt as he kept moving in a half circle. Three—

Her pistol barked. Immediately answered by a rifleman she must have scared a shot out of, for that man's ball went wild too.

Scratch was thinking he was going to make it back to the rocks with his weapons, scuffing through the sage on that sandy ground when he slipped and spilled onto a knee. A ball cut a furrow across his hip, pitching him into the brush with a grunt.

"Reload, Amanda!" he cried as much in anger at himself as in pain.

"Pa—"

He started to gather the rifles against him again, painfully, when he interrupted her, "Reload!"

"Old man!"

Jerking his good leg under him, Titus froze at the call from the trees, trying his damnedest to place that voice.

"We come only for you!"

A second voice shouted, "Like to get my hands on that friend of yours too, but he can wait."

The lead ball plowed into the ground right near his cheek as he lay gasping with the pain of the hip wound, wondering how bad it was, if it had broken a bone, if he'd walk again, if it was the sort of deep injury that would eventually mean a slow and terrible death.

"You ready, Amanda?" he whispered with a grunt as he cocked the good leg under him.

"Ready."

"Shoot!"

Her pistol roared as he rocked forward, lunging a few yards before he landed again in the sage—almost to the rocks. "Take the guns from me!" he ordered.

Her hand came out, grabbing the muzzle of the first rifle, yanking it back inside her fortress. She was pulling at the second when another ball smacked the rock near her arm. She flinched, withdrew her arm, then quickly reached out again and snatched the rifle out of sight. Dirt exploded near his shoulder, and another ball slapped against the boulder—sending slivers of rock spraying over him, cutting his cheeks and eyelids as he tried to turn away too late.

"Pa!"

When he opened his eyes, he saw Amanda's arm sticking from the cleft again, farther this time. She was holding it out for him. As he brought his good leg under him again he stretched out for her hand, grabbed it. Together they pulled and got Titus between the rocks as another ball stabbed against the boulder overhead, showering them with tiny chips of lead and rock.

"How bad you hurt?"

Rolling onto his rump, Titus pulled up the bloodstained hem of his long calico shirt and saw how the ball had gone through the tie that knotted his legging to the belt, into the hip muscle, and must have come back out through his buttock.

"Damn," he muttered as he interlaced his fingers around that right knee and pulled the leg up. It hurt, but not the way it would have made him pass out with pain if the ball had hit bone. "I ain't gonna die," he told her, sweat dripping in his eyes. "Not just yet, I ain't."

"C'mon out, old man! Just get this over quick and we'll be on our way."

Titus dragged one of the rifles over and passed it to Amanda. "Here, you hold on to this while I shoot this'un. Then we'll swap an' you reload." He shoved the loaded pistol across the dirt toward her feet. "Keep that'un right by you. Don't use it less'n they get me an' you can take one last shot when they get close to the rocks. Keep it . . . keep it for yourself till the very end."

"Who are they?" she asked as she got to her knees and looked at him.

With a shrug, he said, "White fellers. Out here, shootin' at me—I got a purty good idee, Amanda."

"Who?"

That's when Scratch flung his voice toward the copse of trees. "Hargrove with you stupid niggers?"

"No!" the voice cried. "He's back with the train."

"Like I figgered," Titus yelled. "Just like afore, he sent you boys to do a man's work, again."

A ball smacked the rock, but this shot came from much closer. He was immediately worried, but didn't want her to know as he grinned and said, " 'Pears we made 'em mad."

"That was close, Pa." Amanda was shaking.

Likely she figured that out for herself from the sound. So he said, "Just gonna make it interesting—"

Bass heard the scrape of feet somewhere behind them. He dragged the hammer on the rifle back to full cock and prepared to rise on the good leg. Popping up with the rifle already into his shoulder, he spotted the man just darting away from a clump of brush, making for the rocks. The rifle slammed against him as it roared, the ball catching the attacker in the side of the chest. Spinning him back into the brush where his legs thrashed as Titus sank back into their fortress, two balls hissing overhead where he had been standing for but an instant.

Amanda was already reaching for his empty rifle, passing him the loaded gun. "That's one of 'em, Pa."

"You any good with one of these?"

She shook her head. "Roman, he taught me how to load, and shoot too. But, I didn't hit much when we went hunting. Everything was so far away I never did any good—"

"This time, things gonna be much closer, Amanda—"

A loud voice interrupted him, "Did he get Ohlman?"

Another voice, closer still, shouted in reply, "Dropped 'im. Ohlman's out of it."

"All right, Corrett, you an' Jenks work in on him."

"Remember you promised," a new voice was raised, "promised I could kill 'im."

"That's right, Jenks—you get to do the honors this time since you messed things up so bad for Hargrove before."

"Jenks?" Scratch hollered. "You the one I beat like a half-growed alley cat a few nights back?"

"Goddamn you, old man!" the voice shrieked in fury.

"I'm here for you, Jenks," he needled the young bully. "Just waiting for you, boy. You an' me here now. So you even the score with me . . . since these other niggers saw how bad I whupped you—"

A ball splattered against the rocks.

"Jenks!" the leader's voice shouted. "Don't be a damn fool like that!"

"Yeah, Jenks," Titus prodded as he watched Amanda pour priming powder into the pan. "Don't be doin' anything stupid like that again!"

"You hear that?" she asked in a rough whisper.

"Yeah."

Another one of them was coming. This time from the north side of their rocks, where they were more vulnerable. He waited, and waited, listening carefully each time the angry voices paused. Listening for the sounds of the man's approach. Then the voices fell silent. And he heard the sound of them coming from the south too. Three of them now. Two behind the rocks, one in front.

"Amanda, you just might have to show me you can hit something up close here real soon."

She swallowed hard, her mouth firm and determined though doubt showed in her reddened eyes, and nodded once.

"Gimme that pistol you loaded."

Passing him the second pistol, Amanda leaned back against the rock and clenched her eyes shut.

"Just like I told you when Lucas was passin', this here's come a time when you gotta be strong. Take a deep breath an' hold on the target. You're gonna be strong for me, ain'cha?"

Her eyes popped open. "Y-yes, Pa."

"Get ready for the third one behind us, that way. I'm takin' on the other two."

He popped up with that rifle, afraid he didn't give himself enough time to aim before he snapped off the shot. The ball went wild as the two men ducked aside, then immediately got their feet under them and started running at a full gallop for the rocks. Bass let the rifle slip out of his grip as he heard her gun roar behind him.

"You hit 'im?" he asked as he slapped the pistol into his right hand.

"I-I dunno," she whimpered. "I don't see him!"

Bass double-handed the pistol, held for a breath, and pulled the trigger as the man zigged through the brush. The ball caught him in the leg, spun him around a half turn as he flopped to the ground. But the second man kept coming at a crouch through the sage. With no time to reload, he'd have to use the only weapon they had loaded.

"Pa!" she shrieked as he was turning in a crouch to scoop up the pistol.

He saw him. The fourth attacker. Side of his belly was bloody, but he was back on his feet and still coming, that rifle held low in his hands, lunging toward them from the north side of the rocks. And the one who looked like Benjamin—advancing on horseback at a lope from the south.

"Reload me, Amanda!"

"Go on an' get 'em, Jenks!" the horseman yelled. "They ain't got a loaded gun between 'em now!"

Back and forth he looked, then decided on Jenks. Closer than Benjamin. Bass swallowed down the burning pain in his hip, setting the butt of the pistol on top of the rocks. Hunching up behind the weapon, he aimed it right as Jenks brought up the muzzle of his rifle and fired an instant before Bass's ball slammed into the bully's chest, just below the throat.

Titus was sinking to the ground and dragging the pouch toward him, sensing in the pit of him that one of the bastards would get him now. He didn't want her to see it—lose a son, then her father too.

"Now you're mine, old man!" promised that disembodied voice of the horseman.

Plug came out of the powder horn, and he spilled the black grains down the muzzle of the pistol.

The hoofbeats slowed, then stopped. Then there were footsteps as the voice came at him again. "Hargrove wants you real bad—had everything going his way till you came in the picture."

Desperation overtook him as his fingers scrambled for a ball from his pouch.

Pushing it into the muzzle with his thumb, he yanked out the ramrod and drove it home just as another voice yelled.

"Outta the way!"

Whirling with the pistol, he found the wounded man standing just outside the rocks, his rifle wavering as he growled at Amanda. Something in the bully's desperate eyes told Bass he was going to shoot anyway—

But Titus fired his pistol instead, sending ball and that short ramrod both toward the target.

"That means you're empty now, old man!"

He spun around with the empty weapon, realizing Benjamin was right. Dead right. Shifting the pistol to his left hand, Titus reached at the small of his back for a knife.

With a wicked and broadening smile, Benjamin stopped, as if enjoying this moment. When the bully brought the rifle to his shoulder and took aim at Titus down the long barrel, he laughed and said, "Looks like you just run outta chances—"

With the rest of his words swallowed by a sudden gunshot that made Titus flinch in surprise.

NINETEEN

The sun blazed down hot as a new blister now that it had ducked below the wide brim of his old felt hat.

Late afternoon and it was beginning to feel as if Shadrach had been dragging him for days already. Titus shifted his head slightly to get the sun out of his eyes and spotted Amanda bouncing on the horse she was riding off to the side of the travois. The whole bottom half of her would be sore by the time they reached the wagon camp, Bass thought with an anguished sigh. He'd never known a white woman who rode back east— the only ones were rich and fancy ladies perched atop their sidesaddle rigs as if they were the queens of all they chanced to survey. Every other gal he could lay a memory on had preferred a buggy, carriage, wagon, or cart to straddling a thousand-pound beast. *Poor girl—she got herself into this just so's she could spend a little more time at her boy's grave . . . ended up having her hash pulled out of the fire by Shadrach Sweete.*

Scratch gritted his teeth again as the travois poles chattered over the rough ground and bounced across the stumps of sagebrush Shad did his best to avoid as he led Scratch's horse northwest through the ancient lava fields, following the rutted tracks of this trail of dreamers and schemers, sojourners and sodbusters making for Oregon country. Near as he could recollect, the last time he was shot as bad as this was back in the early spring of '34, the doing of Silas Cooper. Bents' big adobe lodge down on the Arkansas River.

But over a multitude of seasons, round balls, knife steel, stone and iron arrowtips . . . they had all profaned his flesh. Yet, he had healed, his body becoming a veritable war map of his adventures, a litany of his hairbreadth escapes from the long reach of death.

Closing his eyes, he swallowed down the acid taste of gall that came from the continued hammering his hip was taking . . . and wondered how long he could manage to be so goddamned lucky. Just how much longer would it be before the last of his luck ran out? Scratch felt so damned old, more so now that he was unable to fork a saddle horse, deeply insulted that he need be carried on this bouncing travois. Luck? That was a laugh! Many were the times that another had stepped in to pull his ass from the fire. Likely there'd come a day when no one would be around to yank the hand of death from Titus Bass's throat.

He clenched his eyes shut against the throbbing pain and remembered the others who had saved his hash. At its best, dying would someday be a one-man job no one else could do for him.

"What the devil you doin' here, Shadrach?" he had sputtered when the big man clambered down from his perch atop the rocks, from where he had knocked Benjamin down with his big .62-caliber flintlock.

Sweete knelt to provide his friend a little shade. His eyes grinned. "Come back 'cause I was getting a mite lonely for you."

"Ain't you the honey-tongue sweet talker now," he had said, shifting position slightly, gritting his teeth.

"Hurt bad?"

"Pains me like hell," he admitted as Amanda settled next to him in a rustle of petticoats.

"You bleedin'?"

Titus shook his head and grinned. "Cain't tell, not rightly—ever'thing's behint me."

"Ball broke any bones?"

And he shook his head again. "Nothin' broke but my pride, Shadrach. Bastards shot me where I sit."

That got a big smile from Sweete. "Lemme take a look at you."

The two of them had rolled him over onto the good hip before Shad took to prodding.

"Maybeso Amanda could turn her head away," he grumbled, "while you got my bare white ass pointin' at the sky!"

"It's nothing I haven't seen a thousand times before," she had scolded.

Sweete chuckled at that, which had made Titus all the more grumpy.

"Don't appear you can fork a saddle, Scratch."

He squinted in the bright morning light. "What you got in mind?"

With a shrug, Sweete stood. "I'll fetch you some water, then I'll go see what I can find for to make you a drag."

When he again closed his eyes to the jarring pain of each bounce the travois took, Titus remembered how he had waited a heartbeat after that faraway shot, sensing it hadn't come from the attacker. Then cautiously inched his head up to find Benjamin stopped in his tracks, staring down at the blood starting to gush from the big exit wound in his chest while his knees turned to water. Pasty-faced with shock, he spilled forward, his nose in the sand, fingers twitching as he let out his last explosive breath.

Back among those rocks Scratch had warned the children to avoid, he had watched the shadow move, then a figure emerge: tall and shaggy, his shoulders almost wide enough to take the span of a hickory ax handle. Shadrach Sweete stepped through the sparse shadow provided by some low brush, emerging into the intense light of midmorning. Reloading as he moved toward his old friend.

Relief washing over him, Titus had sunk to the ground. "We're gonna be fine now, Amanda."

While he was out fetching some of that sulfurous water for Scratch to wet his tongue, Shad said he had looked over the attackers. "Your aim gettin' poor?" he asked as he knelt over Bass.

"What's that mean?"

"Had to finish one of 'em off," Sweete announced. "You didn't hit 'im clean."

But there were four bodies, and that meant four horses. So Shad and Amanda started in cutting up three of the saddles to make short strips of leather they used to lash together a narrow travois, just wide enough for one man—a contraption that bounced even rougher because its poles weren't wide. After stringing together a network of short crosspieces, they laid on the four saddle blankets, all they had to put under Bass when they were ready to set off. On his one good leg, he had hobbled next to Sweete, out of the cluster of low rocks, reaching the drag, where he stopped and turned, then slowly sank across the travois on that one good hip of his. His side was growing numb by the time the sun reached midsky, dead from the waist down by the time Shad boomed that they were approaching the wagon camp.

"You got a grand woman," Sweete declared. "That Waits-by-the-Water is a grand woman."

"H-how's that?" he grunted between teeth-jarring bounces.

"Here she comes, runnin' out from the rest."

Titus twisted, although he still could not see her—but in moments he heard her moccasins padding on the sandy ground—then she was there in a swirl of sunset light and calico and flapping fringe. Her eyes shiny with worry as she started babbling in Crow at him, the young ones rustling up on either side of the jostling travois, only a step or two behind their mother. Then he had heard Roman's voice loud over the others, calling for Amanda. The dogs yip-yipping, aware of the humans' elation. The three Burwell children cried out for their grandfather. And behind it all lay the sound of voices shouting the news of the attack by Hargrove's bully-boys, the excitement and commotion beginning its relay through camp. Soon the ground thundered with several hundred feet, all come to hear the story of how this man came to be dragged into camp when they had last seen him standing with his arm around his daughter's shoulder early that morning, both of them waving good-bye to their families with a promise to catch up before early afternoon.

And here it was almost nightfall. Supper was on the boil, bedsacks being shaken out, and stock picketed on the good grass before moonrise.

With help he hoisted himself off the travois and hobbled between the two taller men to the spot Waits-by-the-Water had chosen for their shelter. There Magpie had her mother's medicines out for the second time in less than a day. The two of them began ministering to that oozy wound that had crusted and bled, crusted and bled repeatedly across the aggravatingly slow hours of that arduous journey to catch up to the train. First Waits cleaned both wounds with hot water that stung like wasps as he gripped the edge of the blankets. She chattered constantly at him, or to Magpie, telling her how lucky Magpie's father was that he had not been crippled by the ball that had torn in, through, and out his body without striking a bone.

"Big bones, there—yes," he had muttered, wincing as she kneaded some softened roots into the holes.

But he didn't need convincing to realize just how fortunate he had been. Just from the touch of her hands on the spots where she was working, he knew how an inch this way or that, things could have turned out far different. As it was, the lead ball had entered just behind his hip, missing the femur and the hip cradle too, as it tore its way through the fatty part of his buttock, emerging near the crack of his ass. Which made him laugh again.

"What is funny?" she asked him in Crow as she pulled the flap of blanket back over his bare, bony rump.

He quickly glanced about, finding their children hovering near. "I just remembered," he explained in her tongue so the curious whites clustered nearby would not understand, "back down the trail, I told Shadrach the shooter almost gave me a new asshole."

She giggled with Magpie and the boys at the ribald joke, covering her mouth with her fingertips, her eyes twinkling in gratitude that he still possessed his unusual, off-kilter sense of humor. "One asshole is enough for my people," she said with a tinkle of laughter. "Why would you white men even want a second?"

For two of the next three days it took the train to reach Fort Hall Scratch was too sore to even consider climbing atop a saddle. Instead, Amanda and Roman insisted he ride inside their wagon, where Burwell had nested on comforters as he healed from his near-fatal beating. It proved a damn sight more comfortable than that travois Shadrach had dragged him back on. Still . . . there were times in those next half a hundred miles that the springless wagon nearly jarred his back teeth loose as it clattered over a rough patch of ground. But these sojourners kept their heads down and pushed through every tough stretch along the way.

They had been hardened by the trail, had to have been, Bass thought. Pressing wagons and stock hard now that the next important stop was almost within hailing distance. Farmers were that way, these folks who moved only of a purpose. People who had been born and raised, lived out their adult lives in the same small fifty-mile area . . . and now they were venturing to the end of the earth—leaving behind everyone and everything they had ever known. Sad thing was, that sort of person never could savor the journey for itself. No, for these emigrants the journey was merely something to be done, gotten through, conquered. Once in Oregon, they would get on with what came next: the making of a life in a new country, building homes, plowing fields, raising corrals and fences and hayricks. There was a stoic, even pragmatic order to these emigrants; going somewhere had to serve the almighty god of purpose—the gathering of communities, the organizing of schools, the forming of their new governments. Once the trail was behind these farmers, they were on to the next phase of their lives, and the journeying would no longer be a part of them.

Why, he even had begun to wonder if these ham-handed sodbusters laid their women down in the dark with this same sort of get-it-over-with-and-on-to-the-next-chore brand of single-mindedness. This was simply not the way it was for him, who enjoyed the flesh-to-flesh journey and was not at all concerned with the hurry-up-and-get-there.

Lying there, his arms bracing him between crates and chests as the wagon jostled and rocked, Scratch hoped he still had enough rough edges that could never be smoothed down by the sands of time. The sheer, sweet wildness of those early days after he had come to this land. Ho, for the Snake! The Wind and Bighorn! The Musselshell and Judith too! Ho, for adventure so wild and forbidden only the half crazed and certifiable came west a'seeking it! Adventure only those insane ones who could live nowhere else would truly savor and did their damnedest to suck dry!

Was it only that he and the others had been young back then? For the short-horned bulls were always hard to frighten with what they hadn't yet confronted . . . hard to frighten when danger and challenge stirred adrenaline into the blood, heady as any trader's whiskey! Despite the unknown dangers and the unheralded challenges, back in those days they'd all thought they would never grow old, that the beaver would last and last, that these high times would only shine on and on . . . and on.

Back in those days when they were young and strong, bold . . . and . . . and didn't know any better. In a time before they began to realize they had brought about their own undoing . . .

While for him the adventure still began anew with every sunrise, with these movers one day just seemed to bleed into the next. Good people as they were, Amanda's family among them, their kind seemed driven to be somewhere else rather than enjoying the journey of getting there. Sweat and suffering, fatigue and frustration—pushing on through the constant wind and the ever-present sun until it was night, then they closed their eyes for a short while before the sun was up again for another day while the train rolled a little farther, one more day with all the joy drained out of it but for the fact that they congratulated themselves that their train was one day closer to the Willamette.

He breathed deep, smelling the sharp, tangy fragrance of the sage crushed beneath the wheels. Whining hubs that, if a man didn't force his mind onto something else, was all he heard—their groaning against the axles. A constant squeak of wagon boxes shifting with the terrain, the rattle of everything strapped, roped, or hung from the sidewalls—this incessant symphony that carried these movers in a quest to find their dreams. So steadfast and single-minded were these emigrants that he knew they would make it to Oregon country. He had nary a doubt. If they had made it to the Southern Pass, Bridger's post, to the Bear and Soda Springs, and now to Fort Hall . . . they were no longer innocents, and toughened by adversity and loss—these sod-busters would indeed reach the Willamette.

They were of a kind, these farmers, settlers, family folk who brought their schools, churches, and a quiet tidiness to a new place. While not wild or smart, they bored on through life with dogged determination to do, to accomplish, to see things set right in their own image, town by town. Just as it had been for his grandpap, and his pap after him. Titus was so young when he fled those shackles others were about to rivet around his ankles and wrists, too young to realize that even though it would never be a life for him, it could be a life of honor and decency for the many. Older now, many more choices had he made and regrets piled up. Yet Scratch had spent enough time with these emigrants that he had come to understand something of them and why they were going, even if that going wasn't for him. The land out there in Oregon must surely be big enough for all their dreams, even if it wasn't big enough for his.

Only this country had ever been big enough to capture and contain his dreams. Only . . . this.

"Ti-tuzz!"

He heard Waits yell his name before he saw her appear at the rear pucker hole, reining her horse close to the rear of the wagon. She sat swaying in that woman's snare saddle, its high pommel and cantle both decorated with brass tacks and colorful quillwork and long, jiggling fringe.

Pushing himself up on an elbow, he asked, "What do you see?"

"White man's post!"

"Hallee?"

"Sweete go on," she said in his American tongue, still grinning as she made a gesture. "Ride to post first."

Shifting himself some off the healing buttock, he inquired, "How far now?"

Waits gazed up at the sun, then concentrated on the distance where they were headed, and finally back to look at him. "Not long, Ti-tuzz. Much light left after we make camp."

He wanted to see for himself as they crossed the broad, barren ridge and rumbled ever onward. Dragging his weight up by his arms, gripping those crates and boxes roped against both inside walls of the wagon's box, Bass rolled over with that good leg braced beneath him and found that it did not hurt all that much to put a little weight on the injured hip. Slowly, keeping himself braced with his arms, he inched his way forward to reach the front opening, hoisted himself up on the back of the bench behind the farmer, and peered out. These ox teams did not require the heavy lines and harness of a six-horse hitch. Instead, most of the emigrants did not have to ride at the front of the wagon, but chose to walk alongside their teams, nudging them with a judicious use of a whip or stick to make a change in direction.

"That's Hallee, Roman," he announced as those in the lead began to shout and cheer, laugh and whistle, rejoicing at their arrival.

Burwell turned with surprise at the trapper's sudden appearance, then smiled. "You're moving around a little more today, I see."

"Nothin' much keeps me tied down for long—"

"Is that my father you're talking to?" Amanda asked as her face came into view on the other side of the plodding team.

Titus asked her, "You know what that is off yonder?"

"Fort Hall?"

"Can't be nothin' else."

"Oh, Roman!" she gushed. "If only we'd . . ."

Bass watched her face gray with regret; then Amanda dragged a finger under one eye and appeared to give herself a new shot of resolve.

"Happy as I am to reach this place," she explained, looking up at him as the wagon jostled him from side to side, "it's a bittersweet arrival."

"Lucas made it here with you an' Roman," Titus reminded. "His spirit goin' all the way to Oregon with you."

"But you aren't," she complained as some of the rejoicing from other wagons around them died away. "Did you think any more about our offer, Pa?"

"Ever' damned bump along the way," he admitted.

Her face registered excitement. "That means you've decided to go on with us?"

"No," he said, watching the glee drain from her sunburned face beneath that bonnet. "Ever' mile we come closer to Fort Hall, I thought on reasons why I couldn't go with you two."

"Waits? And your children?" she prodded.

"Them, yeah. 'Specially them," he confessed.

She pushed a sprig of her oak-colored hair back under the ribbon of her poke bonnet and gazed up at him from beneath the bill that framed her face. "They'd have a fine place to grow up and live in Oregon, Pa. Safe, once we get to the Willamette."

"Safe." He repeated that dream word with a sigh, watching the figures appear at the top of the tall earthen walls of the fort there beneath the fluttering red banner, one small blue Union Jack tucked up in the corner above the three large letters: H B C. "I can't hardly recollect anymore how it was to live safe, Amanda—I been in this life o' mine for so long."

She asked, "You wouldn't come for your children?"

Then Roman added, "That's the reason we come to a new land."

"Much as you make it sound sweet to a man's ears," he replied, seeing the first wagon teams starting to curve gracefully away from the walls at Shad's direction, the big man standing in the stirrups and waving them toward a far pasture, "it's for my family that I can't go where the rest of you are headed."

"But mostly for you," Amanda said with resignation.

"Mostly for me," he confessed. "Maybeso, you are comin' to unnerstand your pa."

Three stone chimneys were visible over the twenty-foot-high walls, only one of them smoking at this time of day. A large square blockhouse stood at one corner, a smaller one at the opposite corner, both covered by shake roofs drawn up in a peak. Like the adobe stockade constructed by the Bent brothers on the Arkansas, the tops of these walls were rounded in places, crudely scalloped by wind and rain eroding the mud surface clearly in need of repair. Four low doorways penetrated the one wall he inspected as they inched past, causing little stir among the post's occupants.

"John Bull," Titus said.

"You know someone here?" Roman asked.

"No. John Bull's what we call . . . what we did call the Englishers, the Hudson's Bay Company."

Burwell wagged his head as he stared at the mud wall. "Gets my goat to find the English squatting down right here between the United States and Oregon."

"I knowed a good Englishman or two," Titus explained as they turned past another wall, where stood the main gate, a double just wide enough to permit entry to a wagon. "As for me, the rest of 'em you could throw into the sea an' never let 'em set foot this side of Red River of the North!"

"Does my heart good to hear you speak no ill of America, Titus," Roman said, goading the off-hand ox with his long stick.

"Speak ill of America?" he echoed, brow knitting.

"Wasn't sure, all this time, where you stood on making Oregon our territory," Burwell explained. "From what I heard you say to Amanda, sounded to me you were over and done with the country where you were born and raised."

"I am," he admitted. "But just because I turned my back on America don't mean I want John Bull in here!"

"Rally up for Oregon!" Roman cheered as they reached a campground with some untrammeled grass over on the east bank of a river that fed the Snake from the south. "Build it strong for America and toss the British out!"

"Ho, for Oregon!" another emigrant shouted as the wagons peeled off in two directions to pick their camps.

Came a new voice, "Oregon for Americans!"

"Throw the English out on their ass!" a man shouted lustily, their voices echoing from the timber.

Here they would lay over, rest the teams, trade for what they might need in a final push down the Snake to the Columbia before reaching the Willamette. Come so far, they now found themselves no more than eight hundred miles from their promised land. And it was here that Roman Burwell surprised the old trapper when he dragged the oxen to a halt and turned around to lay his arms across the back of the crude plank seat, gazing in at his father-in-law.

"I been wanting to tell you something for the last few days, back as far as the time we took our train away from Hargrove," he explained. "Wanted to somehow get across that I started out for Oregon with a reason firm in my mind. Was a time I figured I was going simply because it was best for Oregon to belong to America. Later on I thought I was going for the land—land they told us was so rich a man hardly needed to work it."

"Good land for a farmer, that," Titus said as Amanda and Lemuel came up to the front wheel.

Burwell's face went grave with the creases of a simple man not easily given to introspection. "But a strange thing come over me—not sudden, but slow, Titus. Slow, with every mile we come outta Missouri, making our way along the Platte. Farther we went, the more I wanted to see. Not just to get to Oregon—but to really see what new country each new day showed us."

Slipping her arm through her son's, Amanda said, "This is country that draws a body on and on and on, making you hungry to see what's coming next down the river, around the hill, over the ridge."

Roman dropped his hand on his son's shoulder. "Used to be, I had me a good reason to take my family to Oregon. Thought of putting every mistake and misstep behind us, thinking of the fresh start we'd make out there. But the farther we got into this land, the more I lost hold on the words I can use to tell you why I brung Amanda and the four of . . . these three children on this long road. This far from our old home, and this close to our new land—I don't have words no more I can use to make anyone understand. . . ."

As the farmer's words dropped off and he seemed at a loss, Titus said, "Maybeso you might just be doin' the right thing, for the right reason after all, son."

Sweete came loping up on his horse. "The women got a good spot picked out down by the bank. Cool and shady. Feel up to getting down on your legs an' walking over there with me?"

"If I never see the inside of one of these God-infernal wagon bellies again," he grumped as he hobbled around and started toward the back pucker hole at the rear gate, "it'll be too damn soon!"

"Thought you was comfortable, Pa," Amanda sent her voice in after him.

He stopped, looked back over his shoulder at her, saying, "You made me a plenty good bed, daughter. Soft as I ever laid myself on. Only trouble is—your pa's a man rather be sittin' on a horse when he goes through new country."

"Good," she sighed with relief. "Here I was thinking you weren't comfortable . . . when it was only a matter of you being grumpy!"

"Wouldn't want you to think anything else of me, Amanda dear."

Her face suddenly appeared at the rear gate. "I love you anyway, grumpy."

He stopped short in surprise, looking down at her dusty face and shiny eyes filled with the mist of sentiment. Bass felt his pooling too as she and Roman pulled the iron bolts from their hasps and lowered the gate for him.

"Amanda," he said softly. "N-no matter where your grumpy ol' pa goes here on out, or what he does with hisself . . . I'll always love you."

That evening Scratch asked his wife to accompany him on a walk to the fort walls and see who was about.

"Someone who remembers your friend, the man who is no longer here?" she asked in Crow, using that term of highest respect for the departed by not speaking their name.

"Yes, maybe someone here knew him, worked with the man back in better days."

They had reached the point where he would turn back with his family once the Bingham-Burwell Oregon Company started across the Snake River. Maybe Phineas Hargrove would arrive with his California bunch by then, and the two of them would have it out here in the shadow of this fort. Come what may in the next few days, Scratch felt at peace about Roman Burwell and where the farmer was taking his family. He was proud of the man Amanda had chosen to cling to. No matter that Roman could not dredge up the words to explain his feelings about why he was transplanting his family into that yonder territory. The look in his eyes was good enough for Titus Bass.

If Roman moved on to Oregon, if he never did return to these mountains with Amanda and their children, then the man had for a heartbeat in time been unable to put words to something that really had no words to describe it. After all, how could any man wrap his mind, his thoughts, his plain and simple vocabulary around this great and terrible wilderness Titus Bass himself had come to love so deeply? He had decided long ago that some things were indeed best left unexplained. Best not to attempt to put the artificial boundaries of gussied-up words around the now, around the being here. Once a man tried to express that sort of thing, why—a little of the utter freedom of this land couldn't help but leak out. So let the promoters, land speculators, and shysters put their snake-oil words on that yonder country, fancy words to sell the territory to the dreamers who had been waiting to find a dream. As sure as sun, attaching those foofaraw words to Oregon put a claim on the land, and somehow made it already tame.

But that frightened him to the quick. How long could he keep this used-to-be country wild before someone much smarter than he found the words to tame it? Titus Bass knew he wanted his bones to be bleaching in the wind and the sun long before any folk ever came north to lay claim to what he alone had known.

Even though he supported himself with a stout limb, the two of them moved slow, deliberate, as he put weight on injured muscle, stretching the leg for the first time in four days. Both of the dogs quickly grew tired of the snail's pace and darted off for the riverbank to investigate something far more interesting. Although she was curious about the fort, Waits was in no hurry to be anywhere, content to walk beneath his arm, one step at a time, as they ambled toward the fort walls while the sun bled from sight.

"Your traders still around?" he asked of a dark-skinned half-breed who was pushing a cart of firewood toward the main gate.

"Traders, *oui*," the worker replied with a thick voyageur's pull on the language. "Ovair there."

As they stepped inside the trade room, a man behind the long counter had his back to them, his fingers pulling through a bolt of cloth, measuring out one arm length at a time. "Be with you shortly. Make yourself comfortable and look about for what you might need."

"Would like to see some pretties for my woman and my daughter too," he explained to the man's back. " 'Sides a few earbobs and shinies, I was wonderin' if this here still a Hudson's Bay post."

"It is for certain, sir."

"How long you been workin' for 'em?"

The man turned and studied Titus a moment before he answered, "It will be twelve years come December."

Before he spoke again Scratch let the man pull out a large wooden tray divided off with various ornaments and jewelry in each small section. As his wife went to touching and studying every new eye-catcher, Titus asked, "Ever you know a man named Jarrell Thornbrugh?"

That caused the trader's hands to halt his work at a new bolt of cloth. "You are American?"

"Time was, yes."

"I knew Jarrell, well enough that I called him my friend. How is it you would know of him?"

"Met him on the Columbia of a time long ago," Bass declared wistfully. "We rode down that river to Fort Vancouver where I come to meet the doctor."

"McLoughlin?"

"That's the one. Tall man—wild white hair like a bald-headed eagle. Eyes like a pair of white stones too."

"You said you're American?"

"Was," Titus admitted. "Ain't no more."

It was clear the trader didn't understand. "I . . . don't see—"

"Me and mine, we live in the Rocky Mountains. They ain't American. Don't belong to your English either."

"When was the last time you saw Jarrell?"

Scratch dug at his chin whiskers, sorting through the rendezvous. "Don't rightly remember the year. Only was told the next summer he'd got took by the ague. Fell sick and died quick."

"It's been long enough now I haven't heard his name for many a year. Not till you walked in here and spoke it out loud." The trader held out his hand. "I'm Hanratty. Pleased to make your acquaintance . . . Mister . . .?"

"Bass, Titus Bass."

"Bass, is it?" Hanratty declared with a rising note of interest. "Odd that is, for there's a colored man, a Negro, who works about the fort, come from the States of America. Has the name of Bass too. Is it a common name where you come from?"

"Never met another soul out here this side of the Missouri River had my name," Titus declared. "A colored?"

"Yes, what your countrymen call Negroes."

"Neegras," he repeated. "Knowed a few good'uns in my time. You say this one's named Bass?"

The trader nodded. "He came up from the Mexican provinces some years back."

His chest tightened. "Could it been Taos he come from?"

Hanratty shrugged apologetically. "Never did pay much attention to his wild stories."

"Where'bouts can I run onto him?"

"This time of the day, hmmm—I might expect to find him still at the cooper's shop."

"He a cooper?"

Hanratty smiled. "A damned good one, Negro or not."

"Where's that—your cooper's shop?"

"Straight across the courtyard. Off to the left of that well-house there."

"Thankee. Awright by you, I'll leave my wife to look over your goods while I look up this cooper of yours."

He smiled as he went back to measuring out the bolt cloth. "She can look to her eyes' content."

Turning to Waits-by-the-Water, he explained in Crow, "I am going to see if I have found someone from long ago. You can wait here to look over the pretty things you and Magpie will like."

"You'll walk by yourself?"

"I have my stick," he explained in Crow, holding it up. "Not going far. I'll be fine. Just across a little open ground."

She studied his right leg a moment, then leaned forward to kiss him on the cheek and whispered in his American, "Come back soon. We go to camp before dark."

The air didn't stir near as much in this country as it did back where he called home. It lay heavy and hot, oppressive with the bothersome drone made by a few of the year's last mosquitoes. That shady overhang above the open door looked inviting, what with the way the setting sun felt as if it had chosen him alone to torture. Step by step he dragged the wounded leg with its babe-tender wound toward the row of small shops where this post's handymen sweated over iron, wood, and leather, besides some rifle repair thrown in on the side.

He noticed a shadow of movement pass the open door, a man-sized form. Scratch stepped under the eave to the jamb and stopped, peering inside at the figure for a long moment before the cooper felt him there and turned.

His dark eyes narrowed, squinting on the old trapper silhouetted by the last of the sun's glow. "Help you with something?"

"You sure 'nough got gray-headed over the years," Titus said softly. "Hell, I s'pose we all got old."

The black-skinned worker shaded his eyes with one flat hand and peered at the stranger backlit in that doorway. " 'Fraid I can't make you out in this light . . . we know each other?"

"Your name Bass?"

Laying the small hammer on his cluttered workbench, the cooper did not move across the smooth, swept-clay floor. "That's my name."

"Name you took in Taos many a summer ago."

The Negro inched to the side, where he might have a better look at the stranger without the sun's glare. "How you know that?"

"Your Christian name—name what was give you by your owner—it's Esau," Titus explained. "You still go by Esau Bass?"

His pink tongue came out and licked his lips. "Yes. That's my name. You say we knowed each other down to Taos years ago?"

"Might say," he sighed, bubbling with the wash of so many memories flooding over him of a sudden. "Been so long ago, ain't likely you remember me."

"Step on inside, here—where I can see you better." That's when Esau took three steps away from the bench, bringing him within an arm's length of the man who stopped just inside the door where the last bright flares of the setting sun no longer blinded the cooper.

Slowly, Esau's eyes widened as he looked the old trapper up and down, then up again. "T-titus Bass? By the holy of holies—that really you?"

"All what's left of me, Esau."

He reached out his strong, black, sinewy hand to touch Scratch's cheek with his callused fingertips, then withdrew the trembling hand. "By Jehoshaphat's breath . . . if it ain't Titus Bass walked right into my shop!"

TWENTY

"I been out to Fort Vancouver myself . . . twice't," Esau Bass told the three men at the fire later that evening, as the sky deepened and the stars came out.

Their tongues fell silent, all of them stealing looks at one another until Bass trained his eyes on the black tradesman and clarified. "You . . . been to the Columbia . . . twice't?"

He smiled and held up two fingers in a V. "Two times."

Already Esau had finished explaining to Titus, Shadrach, and Roman Burwell how he put Taos at his back in 1837, while the three families took their supper around a small fire in the wagon camp. He described how he had abandoned the Mexican country when life grew harsh and lonely for a black-skinned man living among the many shades of brown. There were lots of pale folks, Esau had explained. But he was the only one the color of night.

"At first, I must've been a pure curiosity to them Mexicans," he had told the group earlier, his English much improved through the last ten years among the British. "Later on, the hate was easy to see in their eyes."

Working at Josiah Paddock's side, they had struggled through three trading seasons in their store, slowly building their wealth and reputation while Esau listened to a litany of the tales about far-off places from daring adventurers. It wasn't long before he became enraptured with those stories told by traders from California, who ventured with their caravans into the desert wastes that lay far to the south on the Old Spanish Trail; along with tales told by those who marched out of the Northwest to buy goods, speaking with strange accents so foreign to his ear, men who had hard English money to spend, along with the lure of mighty rivers and forests to boast about.

"I was a curiosity again, at least to these Hudson's Bay men," Esau admitted, scratching his head well salted with plenty of gray hair. "When the factor asked if I'd go back with him to the Snake, the Boise, clear to the Willamette too—I took my leave of Josiah. Wasn't long after we'd moved from our little shop to a big store on the plaza."

Only weeks before Esau abandoned life in Taos, the daring American entrepreneur Nathaniel Wyeth had sold his Snake River post to the British. The Hudson's Bay employees had been making things as hard as they could on Wyeth's American upstarts from their Fort Boise less than three hundred miles downriver from the Portneuf. Now the powerful British presence had consolidated its grip on this side of the mountains just as affairs turned tense on the diplomatic front, both countries laying claim to the fertile and fur-rich Oregon country.

"You're English now, are you?" Shad asked. Near him lay the two dogs, both of them protectively gnawing on meaty bones Scratch had given them while the women had fussed over supper.

Esau shook his head. "Never thought of turning English. Was never asked neither. Come to ponder your question now, my coming from America didn't ever make no difference to me—so it made no difference to the company what I was. At Vancouver I stayed that first rainy winter through, where I learned my cooper's trade." He smiled with pride. "Fast to pick up too."

The following spring he was dispatched inland with the supply caravan being sent to outfit those two interior posts operating on the Snake, assigned to work the cooperage at Fort Boise. By the autumn of 1840 the company had moved Esau on upriver to Fort Hall, where he had remained as the fort's cooper until four years ago, when his post factor sent him downriver to Vancouver with the fall packet, instructed to return the next spring with the annual caravan and with a new trade: wheelwright. With so many company carts and wagons moving up and down the trade corridor, and with all the more Americans migrating out of the East, it would pay for Hudson's Bay to have a man handy at fashioning new wheels and repairing old, worn-out, or broken ones. By late in the spring of '44 Esau was back at Fort Hall from his second journey to the mammoth Fort Vancouver.

"That's just across the river from the mouth of the Willamette!" Roman Burwell exclaimed, barely containing his excitement as he leaned forward, his elbows propped on his knees.

"Quite a show of Americans already in the valley," Esau agreed.

"So you know the way there?" Sweete asked, a new and deep interest on his face.

Esau looked at the tall man. "I been there twice't, why?"

In that sudden, heavy silence, Shad set his tin plate aside, stood, and moved off, gesturing for Shell Woman to follow him away from the fire's light.

Drawing in a deep breath, Bass watched Sweete step away; then his eyes touched Roman's before he asked, "Esau, how'd you take to the idee o' leadin' this bunch of farmers to the Willamette?"

"Go with you?" Esau squeaked.

"I ain't goin' along," Titus confessed. "Not Shadrach neither."

Wagging his head, the black man asked, "Why'd I ever wanna lead these folks to Oregon City?"

"You know of Oregon City?" Burwell cried, nearly spilling his tin plate of boiled beans as he squirmed atop a small crate.

"Been there a time, once only," Esau admitted.

Titus leaned close to the black man at his left. "But you damn well know the way."

"I s'pose," he replied unsurely, "but that don't make for a good reason for me to pick up and leave behind everything I worked hard for just to go—"

"Here you only work as a hired man," Scratch reminded him. "When you put Taos at your back, didn't you ever wanna be your own man again?"

Esau swallowed thoughtfully. "I been fine," he responded firmly. "Been a good life for me in this place and with these men."

"You're a colored to 'em," Bass said.

"An' I'll always be a Neegra to them Americans I meet coming through to Oregon."

"How'd it be to stand on your own feet, be your own boss?" Titus tantalized him. "Maybeso to have your own shop in Oregon City?"

Scratch noticed how that sparked a light behind Roman Burwell's eyes as well.

"He could!" Roman asserted. "By God, he could at that!"

Titus felt his mouth going dry. "So what you think of strikin' out on your own?"

Esau's face was grayed with doubt. "That's a long, long way to go, just for a man to take such a chance. I-I ain't ever led . . . folks." He turned his head and gazed round at the wagon camp spread about the meadow. "To lead all these white folks—"

But Titus interrupted him, "The Esau I 'member knowin' years back was a man what had the sand to run off from the Pawnee, a man with enough grit to point his nose west 'stead of goin' back where things might be easy."

The black man hung his head in recollection, staring down at his unfinished plate of beans. "All things would've been hard, I'd gone back where I come from again."

"You the same fella I knowed years ago, with that same sand and fightin' tallow?"

Esau's eyes shone, as if he wanted to believe despite his deep misgivings. Still he resisted, "I got work steady. The pay isn't much, but it takes care of things, gives me everything I could want."

"Ever'thing . . . 'cept your own dream," Titus declared, almost in a whisper. "Like all the rest of these farmers, some shopkeepers too. They're all goin' west to snatch at a dream with both hands. An' you can grab your dream too."

"I-I gotta sleep on this," Esau admitted with a wag of his head. "This is a big . . . big thing and my head is hurtin' with it already."

"Yes, you sleep on it," Roman said reassuringly.

Scratch laid his hand on Esau's knee, saying, "Like we awready told you, Shadrach an' me come from Bridger's post to see if'n we could find these folks a pilot what could take 'em on to Oregon country. Hell, maybeso it's a bad idee askin' you if you'd lead 'em. Mayhaps better off would be you tell us if there's a old fur man still about, one what would make a better pilot for this company. Someone knows where the camping grounds are, where lie the best fords of the Snake—"

"I know where those are," Esau declared.

"I reckon on what you're saying: Not ever' man is ready to lead all these folks to their dreams," Scratch cautioned. "I feel bad we offered you something you don't want, Esau."

"Ain't . . . ain't that at all," the black man replied with his own reluctance. "Just . . . that it's a mighty thing to do all at once: leave my work, set off for a new home, start on my own—"

"Same as all these folks are doing," Roman reminded. "None of us any different from you. We just need someone who's been there before to help along the road."

As Sweete moved back into the light among them again, he remarked, "Did I hear you right, Esau—said you'd been there twice?"

When the tall man had settled on a stump and picked up his half-filled plate, Esau repeated, "Twice't."

"Scratch," Shadrach began, looking at his old friend, "I don't know but maybe it'd be better Esau had someone to ride 'long to Oregon country with him."

"So mayhaps he wouldn't feel like ever'thing's layin' on his shoulders?" Titus asked, studying Sweete's face for more clues to the mood of his old friend's mind. "You reckon we could find someone to go along, someone to help Esau?"

Shad's head bobbed eagerly. "Right. Someone to help pilot the train with Esau, someone what's handy at most ever'thing a pilot's got to do."

Titus licked his lips and asked, "So all Esau have to do is help that pilot by tellin' him where the next camping grounds is, or what ford to cross a river?"

"That's 'sactly what I was thinking," Sweete admitted.

Titus turned to the tradesman and inquired, "You know anyone like that, Esau?"

The Negro shrugged. "I dunno of any man hereabouts what could fill them shoes."

"Not a soul around?" Titus repeated. "Not a single man who could give you a hand with trail savvy?"

Esau wagged his head again. "I don't figger there's much call for such a man this far along the trail to the Willamette."

Turning then to look at his old trapping partner, Scratch grinned as he said, "Shadrach, you got any notion where we'll find someone what could help Esau pilot this bunch to Oregon?"

Combing his beard with his greasy fingers, Shadrach swallowed and declared, "Matter of fact, I-I went off an' asked Toote about just such a thing."

" 'Bout what?" Esau asked.

" 'Bout us goin' to Oregon, see some brand-new country for us both." He turned to find Titus's grin grown into a huge smile.

Scratch asked, "What'd Shell Woman say to your idee?"

"Said it was fine by her for us to get a gander at more new country. Maybe even have us a look at the big salt ocean too."

Rising to his feet, Bass stomped over to drag Sweete to his feet so he could throw his arms around the tall man. "I ain't got no itch to see the ocean my own self—so one of these days you'll have to come back to these here mountains so you can tell me if it's all folks say it is."

Shad pounded Bass on the back. "I figger to look up Meek an' Newell while I'm in that country."

"It's been some years since they run off to make new homes in Oregon," Titus said. "You gonna make yourself a home in that yonder land?"

"Naw," and he gazed straight into Bass's eyes. "This here's our country, Titus Bass. Your eyes'll see me coming back one day."

"If'n we both still wear our hair." Then Scratch turned to the tradesman. "So what say you, Esau Bass? Are you truly a free man? Would you care to make yourself one last journey to the Willamette with these here pilgrims?"

The black man swallowed hard, his brow furrowed in consternation. "Mr. Shadrach Sweete, you're going along, positively sure?"

"Same as Titus Bass when he tells you something, you can count your blood on what I tell you."

The Negro nodded and blinked. "You'll pilot these white folks if'n I go along?"

"We're both pilots, Esau."

With a long sigh, the tradesman scratched at his graying head, then asked, "What if I figger to stay put right here?"

Shad glanced at Titus a moment, then returned his gaze to Esau. "I reckon

I'll have to lead this company to Oregon by my own self. Won't be as easy as it'd be with you helpin' me . . . but we'll just have to make do."

"This is a hard thing to think on," Esau admitted. "I ain't never had nothin' near this hard to work on."

"You sleep on it," Bass said, "then tell us come morning."

The wheelwright nodded tentatively. "Hard thing to turn my back on is you, Titus Bass—I never had much of anything till I was give a chance by you. That give me the courage to try another brave thing later on, when I come north to work for Hudson's Bay. I got a good life now . . . so I don't know if I can be so brave to leave everything behind again."

Sweete agreed, "A man's got him the right to give such important doin's a night to think on—"

"When you fixin' to put away?" Esau asked.

The two trappers both looked at Roman. He stood and said, "Two days. Give everyone a chance to lay over and visit the fort, stock to graze and get their strength for the crossing."

"Two days," Esau repeated quietly.

That's when Burwell stepped up to the black man to say, "Esau, I ain't ever had much to do with . . . with your kind back to home in Missouri. Hell, till this evening when you come to supper with Titus, I'd never shook hands with a black man before. But . . . I just want you to know you ain't alone when it comes to putting everything you know behind you and having to stare down something that gives even a brave man some doubts."

Bass took a step closer to the two, gazing intently at his son-in-law's face, feeling such a wave of deep admiration, and newfound affection too.

Roman took a step closer to stand right before the shorter wheelwright. "Back east, I tried my hand at what I figured was one brave thing after another . . . but nothing gave me the scares the way setting off on this journey did. What I want you to know while you're thinking this over: There's as many chances out there for a man as he dares take them chances. Hell, none of us can guarantee what waits for us on what's left of that road to Oregon. The folks on this train watched stillborns and babes die, seen men shoot themselves with their own guns and a passel of good people die of the fever before we finally outrun the cholera too."

Then he paused of a sudden, struck speechless as he looked at his father-in-law, his eyes glistening, before he said, "Esau . . . I even lost my youngest child a few days back, bit by a rattler. Better than most anyone, I know life doesn't hold any guarantees for us but what chances men like you and me make for ourselves."

As Amanda came up to stand at her husband's left side, Burwell held out his big paw to the Negro. "I offer you my hand, Esau Bass. For what miles we got left to go, you can take your meals out of the same pot my family eats from, and throw your blankets down beside my young'uns, outta the rain and cold . . . from here on clear to the Willamette. Any man Titus Bass would ride with is a man Roman Burwell be proud to ride with too."

Esau Bass's eyes moistened as he gazed at Roman and Amanda with gratitude, reaching out to seize the big farmer's hand. "I-I don't know quite what to say," he confessed in a quiet voice. "Ain't been but three other white men ever give me a chance to make something of myself."

Roman laid his left hand over Esau's in a firm grip, saying, "If you're brave enough to leave behind everything you got here at Fort Hall, the way all the rest of us left behind what we had, I'd be proud to call you my friend from here on out."

Esau stared down at the big, hard-boned hands that encapsulated his, white enfolding black there in the soft flicker of firelight. His eyes slowly crawled back up to Burwell's before he said, "Y-you sure you want ol' Esau come along with you?"

"You have my hand on it."

Smiling, the Negro blinked his pooling eyes. "I s'pose I better see to what needs lookin' after back at the fort come morning . . . seeing how there's only two days left before I'm bound away for Oregon with you brave folks."

Times were in a man's life, days passed so lazily. But on those occasions when he wished to hold the moments and hours prisoner in his hand—to stay time's relentless march—Titus Bass stood helpless in the face of what lay just ahead.

Two days . . . all that was left for Titus Bass to romp with his grandchildren in the shade of the trees, or fish the waters of a nearby creek, and with the help of young Flea they made a little time to give Lemuel, Leah, and Annie their first bareback ride on a horse.

Not very long at all for Waits-by-the-Water and Shell Woman to spend some final hours before parting. A happy, expectant air of excitement hung over those last two days as both women struggled not to grow melancholy as the sad hour inexorably approached. While they had not been friends for all that long, they nonetheless shared the same life: married to men who had come west in search of beaver, men who now were groping to find their way in a changing world, men who had fathered their children, fully intending to bring up those half-blood youngsters in some world not quite white. Now it seemed that these two men and their families would be parting for a time. No one knew how long the journey and their stay in Oregon might last, least of all Shadrach.

"If'n there's a place where ol' beaver men are layin' by," Sweete had explained outside those dirt walls of Fort Hall, "that be Oregon."

"Fair 'nough to see how it sets by you," Titus had agreed reluctantly.

"An' how it sets by Toote."

Bass had nodded. "Maybeso there's a new life waiting for you an' your'n out there with Meek an' Newell an' the others too."

"You tell Gabe I'll be back," Shadrach said dolefully. "I'll be back one day."

"Two of us keep our eyes on the skyline for you," Titus assured.

"You goin' on back to stay at Bridger's post?"

Shaking his head, Scratch said, "We'll go back there first, spend a li'l time. Tell Jim 'bout your plans an' all, afore we start north for Crow country."

"Winter up, or for good?" Sweete asked. "Where you figger on me findin' you—"

"If'n you ever come back to the high Stonies?" he interrupted with his question. "Can't say as where I'll be come the fall, least off next summer. Just feel the pull to get back north to that country."

"Country where Waits will birth another scrappy Bass child this winter!"

Titus smiled at that, sensing the warmth spread through his breast in great anticipation for the coming child. "We'll get Magpie north where I don't gotta worry 'bout no man stealin' her away from her mama."

"Purty as she is, there'll be a passel of bucks steppin' up to give you a herd of ponies and a kettle full o' geegaws for her hand to marry."

"An' Flea's comin' to the age when both his head an' heart will start turnin' from the matters of a boy to the matters of a man," Scratch remarked.

"You still got Jackrabbit, an' that baby comin'—both of 'em keep you young for years, Titus!" Sweete cheered.

He looked at his old friend, remembering how sad it must be for Shad, knowing Toote could bear him no more children. Titus laid his hand on Sweete's wrist, gripping it firmly as he said, "Make the most of these days ahead, Shadrach. These days to come with them two young'uns of your'n, with Shell Woman . . . and with your ride to Oregon to see what life has to offer you out there."

Dragging the back of his hand beneath his nose, Sweete said, "Wish't you was comin', now that you're mended up."

With a grin, Scratch admitted, "If I was to give my wounded arse a long poundin' on a saddle, it best be on a ride back to that north country, Shadrach. I ain't got no business goin' farther west. Amanda's family an' the rest of these good folks got 'em a fine pair of pilots gonna lead 'em all the way to the Willamette. No need for me to go on with you."

"You fixin' on waiting here till that California bunch comes in?"

Shrugging, he let go of Sweete's wrist. "I reckon if I was meant to meet up with Hargrove again, we'll do it somewhere on the road. I don't need to wait around for it to happen here."

"How you figger Harris will throw down his float-stick when you run onto 'em?" Shad asked about Hargrove's pilot.

" 'Less that nigger is drunk, I don't figger Harris is gonna get hisself in the way o' what's mine alone to do."

"You sure you don't want us wait 'nother day or so till they roll in here," Shad offered. "It'd give you someone at your back with the two of 'em."

Peering up at his friend's crow-footed eyes, Titus said, "You're the sort of friend the best of men deserve, Shadrach. Don't know why you ended up my companyero—but I'll just take it that you're my friend for a damn good reason."

"Ever' man sticks up for his friends the way you do," Sweete declared, "he deserves to have his back covered by them he's helped."

"Don't fret 'bout lollygagging 'round here with Roman's train till Hargrove an' his bullies get here. I've faced worse'n them. 'Sides, Waits and Magpie both purty damn good with a gun—so my women can cover my back if them bastards wanna raise some hell an' put a chunk under it."

No more was ever said about it between the two friends.

Then came the gray of that last morning together with family and old friends, before the parting, before some got on with the going on, and the rest got on with the turning back.

"Will you write to us, care of Oregon City?" Amanda asked when the oxen were hitched and the last of the coffee was poured on the breakfast fire. "Tell us what becomes of you and Waits when that child is born?"

"I-I can't say I will," he admitted. "Not just 'cause I can't write—"

Taking his two hands in hers, she pleaded, "Find someone who can do it for you."

That's when he confessed, "Never been one to write—not back to my folks in Rabbit Hash."

Nearby, Roman Burwell stabbed at the soggy, blackened embers at his feet with a thin branch. Wispy puffs of gray smoke rose into the chill, gray air here before the sun thought of appearing. Nearby, Hoyt Bingham was pulling the loud brass trumpet from the back of his wagon.

Amanda quickly glanced at her husband, then told her father, "Both of us, we've decided we'll write to you. To that post on the Yellowstone you told the children stories of. We'll tell you all 'bout how we make out in our new home. How Esau's doing with his shop. And Shadrach's family too. Just tell us who to post it to . . . where you'll pick it up in the years to come—"

"No, Amanda," he said quietly to shush her, squeezing his daughter's wrists in his roughened hands. "Th-this 'pears to be good-bye for us."

Her face screwed up in some momentary pain. Eyes pooling, she stared up at him, then said, "Y-you never know about that, Pa. We both thought we'd said our good-byes back in St. Louis when you left Amos Tharp's place."

He felt his heart stabbed with regret, a profound remorse for not giving her some hope to hold on to. So he hedged the truth and said, "You're right, Amanda. Never know when we might run onto one 'nother come the years ahead."

"So I can write you?"

Titus nodded, smiling behind his tears. "Yes, daughter. You write me much as you an' them young'uns of yours can. I'll find me someone can read your letters to me."

"Where?" she asked breathlessly, using the fingers of one hand to smear the tears from both cheeks.

"Where else, girl? Fort Bridger. Black's Fork of the Green. Rocky Mountains. Them letters'll keep with Gabe till I get back round to see him."

Roman Burwell took three steps and stopped there, towering over his father-in-law. "I can remember that. Black's Fork. Rocky Mountains."

"Lemme hear from them children too," he requested. "As fine a bunch of young folk as there ever was, Amanda. You two made a gran'pa right proud . . . right proud."

He turned to Roman, holding out his hand to the man. "I ain't a prayin' man—not like no Bible-talker is, Roman Burwell. But, you an' your family gonna be in my prayers for a long, long time to come."

Instead of seizing the old trapper's paw, Roman shoved the arm aside and stepped against Scratch, surprising him as he wrapped up his father-in-law in his big arms. The fierceness of that embrace nearly robbed him of breath and made the hot moisture leak from his tired, red-rimmed eyes.

"I ain't ever gonna forget you, Titus Bass," Roman Burwell whispered in the old trapper's ear. "Don't know how I ever deserved to marry into such a fine family as yours."

Then the big farmer inched back a step, and finally held out his hand. "Someday, I'll figure out a way to properly say thank you for all you done for us—what with Hargrove an' them men of his—comin' out to find me and bring me back . . . doing your best to s-save our little Lucas . . ."

Titus could see how tough that was for the man to get out. "We all done our best—"

But Roman interrupted him, saying, "For all you done, down to seeing we had these two pilots what'll get us to Oregon afore the snow flies. I laid in my blankets last night, tossing and rolling—fretting on how I ever could thank you proper."

This time Titus embraced the farmer, then stepped back and said, "You don't owe me a thing, Roman Burwell. Knowing how you care for my daughter, how you love her—knowin' you're gonna take care of her an' your young'uns . . . that's all the thanks I'll ever need, son. You're 'bout the best a father could hope his daughter'd marry to."

"I-I hope I can live up to that—"

Scratch felt the tears come. "You awready have, son. You awready have."

Amanda's children were moving close when Hoyt Bingham trotted up on his horse with that brass trumpet propped against his hip.

"Sun's coming, Roman!" he announced, pointing at the far ridge.

"You 'bout ready to have a blow on that trumpet?" Burwell asked as he dragged the back of his hard-boned hand under his nose.

Bingham's eyes quickly surveyed the melancholy group; then he relented and said, "When you're ready to lead this train to Oregon, Roman." Then Bingham nudged his horse forward, leaned off to the side, and held down his hand. "Mr. Bass—"

"Name's Titus," he interrupted the train's other captain as they shook.

"Titus, I just want to thank you for all you done for these people, since you've been with us. There was a time when I thought the only way we were going to find our way to Oregon City was on pure gumption."

"You'd done it," Titus said, his eyes landing on Roman for a moment before he looked back again at the man in the saddle.

"Now we're sure to do it—sure to get these folks to a new country," Bingham continued. "And it's your help going to get us there, same as Mr. Sweete's and Esau's too."

"I had family what needed my help," he tried to explain as Waits-by-the-Water came up to slip her arm through his.

"Gonies, but I almost forgot! Want you to know just how much the whole train is beholden to you," Bingham explained. "We ain't got much extra to our names, but we took up a collection." He reached under his belt and took out a faded bandanna, its four corners knotted together.

Scratch immediately put up his hand to signal and took a step back, shaking his head. "I ain't gonna take that, Hoyt. You folks save it till you get to where you're goin' . . . then you give it to Shadrach and Esau."

Bingham stared at the bandanna, where a few coins were tied. "You're sure you don't want this?"

"I ain't got a need for your money," he explained as Esau walked up with Sweete and their horses. "Keep it for your pilots. They're the ones you should pay for leadin' you to Oregon."

"A fine idea." Bingham nodded and stuffed the bandanna knot under his wide belt, then peered down at Esau. "How far downriver till we reach the first ford of the Snake?"

"Less than three miles, by my reckoning," the tradesman replied.

"Then we'll likely spend a good piece of the day getting across to the north bank," Bingham said, shifting in the saddle. His eyes touched Shadrach Sweete. "When you two are done here with your farewells, I'll blow the trumpet and have Iverson help me line out the wagons for the march downriver to the crossing."

They watched him turn his horse and move away, leaving behind that group of family and friends, all of them still in that nervous way of folks who don't know quite how to say what needs saying.

To everyone's surprise, Esau Bass was the first to make the attempt. He stepped up and held out his strong hand. "Titus, I said my fare-thee-well to you many a year ago . . . then you went and raised your head back into my life again. So, I've got a feeling this can't be the last I lay eyes on you. If it ain't out to Oregon, maybe sometime back here in your mountains."

As he shook with Esau, Scratch pulled the tradesman against him. In that tight hug he whispered against the Negro's ear, "You won't ever know how much it means to me for you to lead these people west."

They parted, still gripping hands. Esau's eyes crinkled. He looked like a man searching for words to say, till suddenly he asked, "You like my new hat, Titus? Bought it special for the journey."

He smiled. "A good'un. Gonna keep the sun outta your eyes."

Nervous as he dropped his hand and took the reins Shad passed to him, Esau cleared his throat and said with difficulty, "Till the next time I see you, Titus Bass."

"Make the most of your life out to Oregon, Esau," he declared. "You done a heap for yourself awready."

Swiping at an eye, the black man turned aside, leading his horse a few paces away as Shadrach edged up. Around the two of them Titus's children were jabbering and patting the two small Sweete youngsters on the head. Talking in low tones, their Indian mothers held hands, sobbing and wiping tears, touching one another's faces with wet fingertips in that way of Indian women taking their leave of one another.

"Watch your back trail, Titus Bass," Shadrach choked.

"You watch your'n, Shadrach Sweete."

He dropped the reins to his horse and seized Scratch in a last desperate bear hug. "I'll see you in the mountains again one day," he whispered in Bass's ear.

"That'd shine, Shadrach. I'll lay stock on that, 'cause that'd purely shine."

When Sweete stepped back, Shell Woman inched away from Waits-by-the-Water, who came to stand beneath Scratch's arm.

"You fellas take good care of these farmers," he said, his voice thick and all but clogged. "There's new homes waitin' for 'em out yonder."

Esau swung into the saddle and turned his horse away to follow Shadrach and his family as they mounted up.

Lemuel, Leah, and little Annie suddenly rushed against Titus and Waits, standing by that dead fire pit in a big knot as the five of them embraced.

"Gran'pa—we'll see you again," Lemuel said, his eyes glistening.

"I know you will, son."

Pushing their poke bonnets off their heads so they hung at their backs around their necks, Leah and Annie both surrounded him with their arms at the same time. Little Annie was blubbering and could get nothing said, but Leah's voice cracked when she spoke, "You made everything a lot better for Mama when Lucas was took from us. I won't ever forget that about you, Gran'pa."

He leaned down and kissed his granddaughter on the forehead, brushing some of the sandy-blond hair out of her eyes. "I won't ever forget 'bout you girls neither. Both of you make your gran'pa real proud. I'm gonna count on you to help your folks ever' step of the way, and 'specially when you get to Oregon. The same goes for you, Lemuel."

"Yes, sir."

"Make your pap an' mam proud of you, ever' day." He patted the girls on the head, then shook hands quickly with Lemuel before the children stepped away with their parents.

Roman waved at the five nearby riders. Bingham raised that tarnished brass horn in the growing light of this new day and blew his martial call. As the two Indian dogs suddenly lunged to their feet, expectant and prepared to move out as they had done many times before, on three sides of Scratch folks began to yell—at their oxen and mules, at their children, or just in an explosion of emotion as they rejoiced to be on their way once more, ready to confront the unmitigated might and power of the great and untamed Snake River. Step by step, mile by mile, day by day, these sojourners would always begin the next eight, twelve, or twenty miles this way. Voices raised as the dust began to stir and animals strained into their harness, lunged against the heavy yokes, whips snapping and milk cows lowing as they were nudged into motion.

"Ho, for Oregon!"

Burwell turned back one last time as he and Lemuel put their stock on the move. He touched the shapeless brim of his hat. Scratch held his arm up, steady and still in that coming light of day. Then the man and boy turned back to their duties, this getting on to Oregon.

Shell Woman was sobbing bitterly now, clutching her youngest against her as their horses moved off. And he felt Waits-by-the-Water quaking against him too as he held her tightly, so tightly against his side. Frozen there on the empty ground between the groups stood the two shaggy dogs, confused why their master was not joining the caravan on its way out of sight, eager to go, prancing nervously, as if seeking to goad him into motion, into catching up with the others.

Knee to knee with Esau, Shadrach reached Bingham and the four other riders, then wheeled his horse around one last time, ripped the big hat from his head, and waved it high at the end of his arm.

Titus felt the big, hot tears spill down his leathery cheeks anew as he yanked the hat from his head too and held it aloft.

"Yes," he whispered. "I'll lay eyes on you again, my friend."

He started to tremble then too, doing his best to contain the grief as he watched till the last wagon disappeared through the curtain of tall green cottonwood. Gone down the Snake. Making for Oregon.

With those two loyal dogs whimpering and whining in confusion, his three children stepped close, silent, while the creaking and groaning, all the noise of animals and those shouting voices, faded from their ears. Eventually swallowed by the distance stretching out between the here and the yet-to-be-seen there.

He waited, listening until all sound had been sucked from that dawn-kissed air. Then Titus Bass felt himself shuddering with a terrible sense of loss and held fast to his woman, all things made endurable with her at his side.

TWENTY-ONE

"Magpie, you take your brothers to those rocks," he ordered, conscious of keeping the timbre of his voice as steady as possible. "Take them two dogs with you too an' tie 'em up to the horses."

He could feel their eyes riveted to him as he continued to stare into the distance with that long leather-wrapped spyglass. The shimmering, faraway objects danced in the rising waves of heat. Already close enough that he could make out the snaking line of fewer than two dozen canvas-topped wagons, figures on foot plodding on either side of the train, and at least four horsemen riding purposefully out front. Even without the spyglass, a man could see it was Hargrove's bunch.

"Now, Magpie."

"Popo—"

"Do as I tell you!" he snapped at her in Crow.

Despite the uncertainty on her face, she held her ground and demanded, "Popo—you give me a gun to use."

He turned to look at her in disbelief, taking the spyglass from his eye.

"Me too," Flea supported his sister. "I can shoot a gun good as anyone my size."

Blinking, his eyes smarting with pride of them, Titus turned back to the wagons and swiped a droplet of sweat from the lid of his good eye, then fixed his gaze on the riders again. He was able to pick out Moses Harris from his slouch in the saddle. The tall one who sat ramrod straight next to Harris had to be Phineas Hargrove himself. The other two horsemen had to be emigrants . . . because those who were left of Hargrove's seven were likely busy at the helm of the first two wagons. That's where he figured Hargrove would continue to keep his teams and his men: right at the front of the column as they worked their way closer and closer to Fort Hall.

Did the man actually believe he would ever catch up to Titus Bass and Shadrach Sweete on this road before the trails split? After the train had broken apart and the California-bound emigrants remained behind with Hargrove, the wagon boss had tarried long enough to give the Bingham-Burwell company some berth before they themselves continued on their way to the British post. Somewhere in those next two days Hargrove had dispatched the four riders to catch up to the Oregon party and settle with the two old trappers. With all the confidence in the world, he would have expected Benjamin and the others back with evidence of success in the murders.

Jehoshaphat! How Titus would have loved to see the look on Hargrove's face when he came upon those four bodies at Soda Springs!

Shadrach had wanted to drag them all into the middle of that road cut with hundreds of iron-tired wheels . . . but from his travois, the wounded Scratch didn't want any part of it.

"Just think how that's gonna make his insides salt up when he sees them four all laid out neat and purty on the road, side by side by side," Sweete had proposed.

"No," he had whispered in pain. "I don't want Amanda seein' us do nothin' of the kind."

So they had left the four where each of the hired men had fallen in making his attack. A day or two under the late-summer sun, those bodies would have swollen up quite nicely, beginning to blacken with decomposition. And the stench? Why, if the wind had been from the right direction, that big nose in the middle of Harris's face would have picked up the scent long before they reached the springs. What a happy night that would have made for Phineas Hargrove and the two remaining guns he had brought west to protect all that he held dear in those wagons of his.

Come to think of it, without his drivers, what had Hargrove done with that extra cargo he would have had to leave behind? Would he have thrown what he could in the wagons he could bring along? Had he bullied and cajoled others into packing some of his cargo in their wagons? Or would he have offered good money to a few of the unattached men along in return for driving his wagons on to California? From the looks of things, Hargrove hadn't been forced to stoop to driving a team himself—still riding out front with the pilot, setting himself apart from the rest.

And just what would the other emigrants have thought when they came upon those bloated corpses? Bass had wondered as he started his family south from Fort Hall, riding for Bridger's post. Would those who had elected to stay with Hargrove and turn south for California instead of Oregon look at the carnage and finally say among themselves that the murderous feud had come far enough? Had any of them secretly decided that when they reached Fort Hall they would push on in the hopes of catching the Bingham-Burwell party instead of remaining behind with Hargrove's Californians? Hadn't any of those farmers and shopkeepers the eggs to stand up to those three bullies and tell Hargrove they wanted no part of him any longer?

Or would they keep their mouths shut as they had up to that point and figure such bloodshed was nothing more than the way of the wilderness, the price one had to pay for passage through a wild and brutal land? The toll taken in having anything at all to do with such mountain ruffians as those two old trappers?

"Ti-tuzz," his wife said at his side.

Bass pulled the spyglass from his eye and gently nudged its three brass sections together before he tucked it away in his shooting pouch.

Waits-by-the-Water waited patiently for him before she asked, "Do you want my gun with the children's weapons?"

Quickly appraising the ground, he decided where to put the horses, where to position what firepower he had against the many.

"Magpie and Flea, they will stay in those rocks." He pointed. The rest turned their heads and looked. "But you, Waits—take Jackrabbit with you into those rocks over there." Again they all looked in the direction he indicated.

"That will mean our three guns will be pointed at them," Flea declared.

"Four guns. I'll be right here," Titus said, gazing into the distance at the approaching column of dust shimmering with the intense, late-morning sun.

She stepped around in front of him, her sad eyes appealing. "We can get out of their way. Let them pass. There is enough time—"

"Hargrove an' me," he said in English, then thought that he better speak in Crow so there was no question of her understanding. "The wagon chief and me, we both have known we were going to reach this moment of our dance together. He never wanted Shadrach or me along with his group, because he knew that one day the two of us would be the whole reason the others finally showed the courage to stand up to him, the courage to break away from his hold over them. So Hargrove blames Shadrach and me. Now our friend and his family have gone to Oregon, so that leaves me to dance with Hargrove . . . alone."

"But he will not be alone," she pleaded. "The fur-catcher, he will be another gun—"

"I don't think Harris will pull down on me," Scratch interrupted her with a wag of his head. "That leaves Hargrove and the two who take orders from him."

"Three of them," Magpie counted.

Flea added, "And we have three guns already pointed at those three men, Popo."

"But we don't have to shoot them!" Waits snapped at her son.

Taking his wife by the shoulders, Titus said, "This is between me and

Hargrove. I pray that the rest of you won't have to shoot. Keep your guns on the others so they do not make trouble for me."

Her eyes smiled first, then she said, "We are getting too old for this, *chilee*."

He held her cheeks and kissed her forehead. "Now help your husband get the horses out of sight."

By the time they had the animals hidden in a nearby coulee and the extra guns distributed, they could hear the plodding hooves and the squeaking wheels, the yelling drivers and the lowing of the teams. Titus stepped toward the clearing between the rocky walls where his family crouched in hiding. He stopped at the edge of the well-trampled road and waited as the first horsemen came up over a low rise a little more than a hundred yards ahead of him. Scratch knew they had spotted him when he saw the squatters turn to one another and gesture—pointing on up the trail at the solitary figure. The tall rider turned around in the saddle and appeared to shout some warning to the first wagon as a couple of the horsemen abandoned the others, which left Hargrove and Harris alone at the front of the column.

That done, the two riders urged their horses ahead, cautiously studying the ground on either side of the spot where Titus Bass stood alone, bringing his smoothbore down from his elbow—clearly leveling it at the approaching horsemen. He watched Harris's eyes for several moments as the old mountain man and one-time confederate of William Sublette peered about suspiciously.

Suddenly Harris threw out his arm and snagged hold of Hargrove's elbow. They reined up together.

"Where's Shadrach Sweete?" Harris demanded sourly as he rolled his long-rifle over the head of his hammer-headed cayuse.

"He ain't here."

"He ain't?"

"I ain't gonna lie to you, Harris."

The two of them whispered where they sat atop their saddles, just out of earshot.

Then Hargrove spoke, "Why should we trust what you tell us, old man? I figure sneaky back-shooters like you two would lay an ambush for us like this."

"I ain't never been a back-shooter," Titus declared evenly. "Not like your kind."

"We found the bodies of my men," Hargrove explained. "Benjamin was shot in the back."

"Had to be," Scratch said.

"Then you admit you're back-shooting murderers?"

"No. Shadrach killed that'un to pull my hash out'n the fire."

"I stayed outta this all the way down the line!" Harris suddenly shouted to the rocks. "You hear me, Shadrach Sweete? I never had nothin' to do with any of this killin'!"

"Tol't'cha, Harris," he called out to the old trapper. "Shadrach ain't here."

"Where is he?" Hargrove demanded.

"Long on his way to Oregon with the rest of that bunch you an' Hargrove were going to leave 'thout a pilot."

"Sweete's guiding them his own self?" Harris asked in disbelief.

"Him . . . and a feller what's been out there twice't awready."

Hargrove rocked back in the saddle a bit as the first of the wagons came up behind the two riders and noisily pulled up just within earshot. "That makes things neat and tidy for Burwell's folks, doesn't it, Mr. Bass?"

"I s'pose. You take your outfit off to Californy, an' them others stay on the road all the way to Oregon."

The train captain grinned. "Sounds like everything is turning out rosy in the end, doesn't it?"

" 'Cept for one thing, Hargrove."

"Ah . . . yes," he sighed as the third wagon clattered to a stop and its driver turned to holler back at the others to halt.

Already the drivers of those first two wagons had clambered down from their seats, dragging their prairie rifles after them, those short-barreled, percussion-capped weapons being manufactured on the borderlands for the new breed of frontiersman coming west. Titus hoped the three family members he had secreted in the rocks would each remember to choose a different target, on their side of the open ground—and keep their rifle trained on their particular target . . . no matter what happened to him and Hargrove when the shooting started.

"Listen, Hargrove," Harris said, his eyes narrowing as they bounced over the rocks once more, "I've managed to keep my hair for all these winters already . . . I ain't gonna lose it to this son of a bitch what wants a piece of your tail."

The moment Harris attempted to turn his horse away, Hargrove reached out and snagged the reins. "You're staying. In for a penny, in for a pound, I always say. If I don't come out of this—you don't get paid, Harris. Simple as that."

"This ain't got nothin' to do with me," Harris complained. "Between you an' him."

"Let me explain it to you again," Hargrove growled, dragging the pilot's horse closer. "The other men that old bastard has killed, they were expendable. Practically speaking, I could count on a certain number of my employees not reaching our final destination with us. That always meant there would be more of the pie to share, don't you see?"

Hargrove waved one of the riflemen left, the other to the right, both of them stopping just ahead of the two horsemen so that it would be hard for the trapper to swing his weapon far enough from right to left before someone dropped him.

Hargrove cleared his throat dramatically and continued, "Do you get the import of what I'm telling you, Mr. Harris?"

"You figger me to sit here and shoot that man with the three of you?"

"If you want to get paid when we get to California."

"Th-that ain't part of being a pilot," Harris protested. "I kill't my share of Injuns, an' I've done a helluva lot I ain't real proud of in my life . . . but I ain't ever out-an'-out shot no man for money."

Hargrove's jaw set with a jut as he ruminated on that. "Very well. You've cast your lot with spineless cowards, Harris—"

"I ain't no coward!"

But the captain was already waving his pilot off with a disdainful gesture. "Be gone with you. Get out of the line of fire, you coward."

"Tol't you—I ain't no coward!" Harris was starting to fume.

"Move aside and let the real men finish this once and for all—"

Titus interrupted, "You better listen to him, Hargrove. Moses Harris may be a lot of things, but he ain't ever been no coward. Dead of winter, he's walked back to St. Louie from the mountains. Not once't . . . but twice't."

With a sneer, Hargrove shifted his rifle so that it lay along his right thigh, pointed in the target's general direction. "More myths of your brave breed? So Harris has performed mighty deeds. That still doesn't alter the fact that he's grown spineless in his old age."

"I ain't spineless—"

Yet Hargrove paid Harris no mind as he continued, "Which is something it appears you still have, old man."

"A spine?"

"Some backbone, yes."

Harris leaned forward, reaching down to tear his reins from Hargrove's grip. "Take your damn hand off my horse!"

The captain did just that, but brought that very fist up so fast and hard beneath Harris's chin that the pilot's head snapped backward, his wide-brimmed hat flying off before he slid from the saddle, dazed, spilling onto the sand.

Hargrove tapped heels into his horse, urging it forward at a walk as he brought up the rifle in his right hand. "Which ball will get you, Mr. Bass?"

"Won't be yours, Hargrove."

The man gentled back on the reins and halted, still clutching that short-barreled carriage gun on Scratch. "What makes you so sure it won't be mine?"

"Have to be one'a these other hired niggers," Titus said as he pulled the hammers back on the big pistol he gripped in the right hand, on the sawed-off trade gun he kept loaded with drop-shot that was in his left.

"My aim is excellent," he replied to the trapper.

"Not when you can't even get off a shot," Scratch declared. "You're the first'un I'm gonna shoot."

"You'll take your chances on these other two?"

Titus quickly appraised them. "Neither one of 'em look like killers to me, Hargrove. I figger you sent the ones what could kill on ahead to get me. If'n either these two had the stomach to cut a man down, you would've sent 'em along with Benjamin. But this'un an' that'un too . . . I think they like breathin' a li'l more than you give 'em credit for."

That appraisal clearly unsettled Hargrove. As the hired men turned their heads to look at their employer, he ordered, "Don't listen to his rantings. If he makes a move to use either of those guns, drop him where he stands."

"Come down to just you an' me, Hargrove," Titus said as he flicked a look at Harris starting to stir among the sagebrush.

The pilot wagged his head, groggily rolling onto his hip behind Hargrove, rocking onto his hands and knees shakily.

When he fixed his eyes again on the train captain, Titus found Hargrove had cleared a pistol from his belt, yanking it into sight with his left hand.

Without considering those orders Hargrove had given his two henchmen, Titus brought up his two weapons on instinct, instantly deciding he would take the horseman with the pistol, then use the trade gun loaded with shot to deliver a scattered pattern at the man to his left because he stood a better chance of hitting him with a wide pattern than with a single ball.

He pitched forward onto his knees after firing his first shot with the pistol, with barely enough time to watch the ball slam into Hargrove's shoulder before he pulled the trigger on the scattergun in his left hand. He felt the hired man's ball snarl past his ear at the very moment that double load of coarse drop-shot chewed through the gunman's belly like a nest of angry wasps, flinging him backward, his feet pinwheeling in the loose sand.

But a gunshot rumbled from the rocks behind the bloodied man, knocking his body forward. He landed with the side of his face down in the dirt.

Immediately afterward a second weapon roared from the boulders, off to Bass's right this time, the ball furrowing into the ground beside the second gunman's boot.

"No! No! Don't shoot me!" the henchman screeched in utter panic as he hurled his rifle loose and raised his arms.

Fury clouded Hargrove's face as he gazed down at his bleeding wound, angrily nudging his horse forward. "Isn't this a predicament, old man?" he crowed. "You've emptied both of your weapons . . . but I still have both of mine."

Scratch hoped Waits could place her shot close enough to Hargrove that it would give her husband at least a heartbeat to dive out of the way, perhaps even make it to that loaded rifle the hired man had just pitched aside before the bully shuffled back in terror, his arms still high.

"I'll still make it to California, old man," Hargrove growled, "but your bones'll rot here in the middle of nowhere."

The instant Hargrove whipped both of his weapons into play, Bass dove for that loaded rifle in the sand. One of the captain's bullets kicked up dirt at his heel the moment he smacked onto the ground and his hands scooped up the weapon. He was just beginning to wheel with it, not anywhere near ready to fire, when he winced the instant Hargrove's second gun boomed—

But the horseman's shot went completely wild.

Titus watched the man's back arch suddenly, a reflex that forced his pistol to fire at the sky. A long moment, then Hargrove peered down at his chest, beginning to gurgle, finding that patch of blood beginning to seep around the bubbling black hole at the middle of his brocade vest. Then, as Hargrove slowly turned around in the saddle and Bass rolled onto an elbow so he too could look behind the man's horse—they both found smoke curling from the yawning muzzle of that big-bore flintlock held by Moses Harris.

"D-don't shoot me!" the hired man blubbered repeatedly as he crumpled to his knees, sobbing.

After swallowing his heart back down from his throat, Bass hollered in Crow at the rocks, "No more shooting—hold your fire!"

Mules and oxen were braying and bawling from the echoes of that noisy gunfire behind Hargrove as the train captain brought his red hand away from his chest, stared down at the blood on it, then inch by inch keeled out of the saddle and fell onto the sand. Shrieks erupted from the first women to reach the scene with their men. Children surged forward between grown-ups' legs, held back by their parents as the crowd swelled up behind Harris, pressing in on one another for a view of the carnage.

As Titus got to his hip, then pushed himself to his feet with that rifle in hand, still uncertain if this had been played completely out or not, Harris lowered the weapon he held in his hands and trudged those few steps that brought him to Hargrove's body with a sad weariness.

When he stopped to peer down at the wagon master, Harris grumbled, "Idjit son of a bitch."

Scratch came to a halt on the other side of Hargrove as the captain spewed blood, trying to speak as his half-glazed eyes stared up at Harris; then his head rolled slightly so he could peer at Bass. Dropping to his knee, Titus held his ear close to the blood-covered lips.

Harris asked, "What's he say?"

Titus looked up. "Said he'd see both of us again . . . in hell."

The instant Harris raised his rifle in the air as if he intended to smash it down into Hargrove's face, Bass knocked it aside with his loaded weapon. Harris took a step back, his dark face hard as slate, glaring at Titus with fury-tinged eyes.

"Leave 'im be to die," Scratch said quietly. Then watched some of the anger disappear from the old trapper's face. "Likely he's right."

"Right about what?" Harris demanded.

"Chances are, we'll both see 'im again in hell."

"Damn this son of a bitch," Harris growled, his tone one more of disappointment than fury now. "Owes me money, an' a spree in California too. Señoritas an' some pass brandy. Damn this dead son of a bitch anyway."

"I'll lay you can scratch up some money back there in his wagons," Titus suggested.

A bright light dispelled the last remnants of darkness in the old trapper's eyes. "By doggies, you're right!"

The crowd was inching forward as Scratch said, "Why'n't you go an' take these here folks right on to Californy like you was set on doin' anyway. I figger you'll be set for quite a spree out with all them Mexican señoreetas."

With a growing grin, Harris looked down at Hargrove's wide, unmoving eyes. "S'pose I still could take 'em on to California at that—"

"What're we going to do without Hargrove?"

Looking up at the new voice, Titus found the face, one of those who had been Hargrove's biggest backers when it came time for the mutiny by the Oregon company.

"You wanna go to Californy, this pilot gonna take you folks there," he snapped at the man. "Elsewise, you all can rot right here waiting for Hargrove to raise hisself from the dead."

"What'm I gonna do now?" the last hired man asked, still frozen in place, his arms raised.

Harris eyed him menacingly.

But it was Titus who spoke, "You ever fire a shot at me or my kin?"

"N-no, I didn't," he admitted with a frightened wag of his head.

"Ever you do harm to any of these other folks?"

Again he shook his head. "No."

Scratch turned on those men and women, and the children clutching their mothers' skirts, wide-eyed. "This man ever raise a hand to any of you?"

Some hung their heads, others continued to stare at the dead bodies, and a few mumbled their answer.

Turning back to the hired man, he said, "Then I s'pose they might let you stay on with 'em all the way to the end of the trail."

He could hear the weight of that breath escaping the man's lungs. Jabbing his head toward Harris, Bass told the young man, "Seems like you can throw in with your pilot now, an' the two of you have yourselves a grand time. Makes no nevermind to me."

"Wha'chu gonna do yourself now?" Harris asked as Bass handed him the hired man's rifle.

"Me? We was headin' back to Bridger's post," he declared, spotting the forms stepping out of the rocks. A woman and a young boy. "Eventual', we need to be back in Crow country by the first deep snow."

"Who's *we?*"

"Them," and he pointed to Waits-by-the-Water bringing Jackrabbit toward him, the child's hand in hers, the long flintlock at the end of the other arm.

Harris turned back to him and said, "You wasn't takin' no chances, was you?"

"Onliest way ol' coons like us got to be so old, Moses. We don't take scary chances."

"Them too?" Harris asked.

Titus turned and found Magpie and her brother emerging from the boulders.

"They don't have to be the best shots in the mountains," Titus explained. "Just good enough to keep ever'body else busy."

Harris grinned and wagged his head. "I'll be damned if you don't take the circle, Titus Bass!"

Gesturing to Flea, Scratch said, "Get the horses. We're leaving this place."

Having turned and started away with his wife and youngest son while the two older children headed off to fetch the animals, Titus was surprised when Harris called out to him. "Don't you want anything off this son of a bitch?"

He stopped, thought a moment, then shook his head.

"Not his scalp?"

"Only hair I ever raised I took off a proper warrior, Harris."

"Then you don't want none of his money?" Harris asked in a loud voice.

"Money?" and he snorted a laugh. "Why, coon—that's the sort of addle-headed stuff you need out to Californy. What in blazes would I do with money in these here mountains?"

"Suit yourself!" Harris cackled with glee.

"For all I care," Scratch flung his voice back over his shoulder as he moved toward the horses, "you can keep ever' damn dollar of it. Man like me won't ever need money again."

"You don't s'pose Shadrach gonna stay out there in Oregon for good, do you?" Jim Bridger asked not long after Titus Bass had hit the ground outside the tall stockade timbers and informed Gabe why Sweete wasn't along for this return to Black's Fork of the Green.

"You just never know about that boy," Titus said as he wiped a droplet of sweat from the end of his nose. "But I don't figger he's the sort to put down roots in that country. Lad big as a stalk of corn the way he is needs his sun to grow!"

"Gonna fix us up something special for supper," Jim proposed. "An' after we fill your paunch with venison, I'll lather up your tongue with some barleycorn so you can tell me all 'bout your li'l sashay up to Fort Hall."

It was a merry return. If not a crowded homecoming, then the best they all could make it. This post wasn't home, but Gabe and his two children were nonetheless the very best of folks. And the way that Waits-by-the-Water and Magpie dove right in, making themselves comfortable around the place, chattering and giggling too, it did a lot to put the trials of the last few weeks behind him. It had been just like holding a gaunt and hungry wolf at bay . . . until the strong liquor loosened his tongue and the floodgate of memories came washing back over him in a way he hadn't allowed since that fateful day at Soda Springs.

"D-dead?" Bridger whispered. "That towhead young'un . . . your grandson?"

His eyes teared up uncontrollably as he peered at Gabe. "You know what it does to a man when he can't do a thing to help someone he loves?"

Laying his hard-boned hand on Bass's shoulder there beside the fire as his wife and Magpie talked, Flea chasing Jackrabbit and Felix about in the cool of the late-summer evening, Jim said, "You 'member how I lost my Cora last year, just after Josie was borned . . . but, still, I don't have no way of knowin' how that's gotta cut you clear to the backbone, what with losin' a little'un like that."

From the beginning Titus had promised himself that he would not get down in the cups with the grief he felt crushing in on him like an inescapable weight. He had resisted the urge to prevail upon Esau for a little of Fort Hall's hooch, either for some wallowing in misery or for a parting celebration. He had resisted this long—but now the fire of that whiskey pouring down his gullet matched the burn he suffered in that hollow spot that had been growing a bit bigger inside him with each new day. Maybeso he needed to roar and wail, to weep and moan, to release the grief after it had been bottled up for so long. At the very least to get it flushed out of his belly before it ate away at him from the inside like a terrible hydrophobia . . . like the snake's own poison had eaten away at Lucas Burwell's will to fight until there was no more strength left holding on to life.

The flames of that merry fire wavered in a blurry dance the longer he talked. And the longer he talked the more he drank. Magpie sat with her arm around Waits-by-the-Water, the two of them listening intently while Titus spilled his grief like a drunk would puke his belly on the ground—stinking and noxious and loathsome . . . but this was something that made both the drunk and the griever feel all the better for it.

"Shit, I warned 'em, Gabe," he had long ago started slurring his words, what words he managed to choke out around the huge lump wedged down in his throat. Something that just wouldn't budge no matter how he kept washing it down with Bridger's whiskey. "Told them young'uns stay back from them rocks."

"But, Ti-tuzz," Waits reminded in her language, "the snake did not get the boy who died near the rocks."

He squinted at the fire, trying hard to make the swimming images hold still for just a heartbeat. Struggling too as he attempted to get his grasp around what her words meant.

"Sounds to me there ain't no reason for you to think you could have done a thing different," Bridger consoled. "The boy didn't go to the rocks. He just crossed paths with one of them rattlers out huntin'."

For a long time he watched the flames with his half-lidded, pooling eyes, sensing so much of the poison leaching out of him, the way on a hot summer day back in Boone County moisture would sweat beads on the outside of his mam's clay pitcher. Like it was being pulled out of him a drop at a time, one heartbeat at a time. Gradually healing himself from the inside out as he wallowed in this despair so long rising to the surface.

"I tried my best to understand it, Gabe," he admitted. "All the time me an' Waits sat by that fire, makin' a poultice for them bites, or boilin' down some roots for Lucas to drink so's his dyin' wouldn't hurt so goddamn much."

"Tried to understand what?" Bridger asked.

He raised his eyes, struggling to focus on his friend's face as the tears spilled down his cheeks. "Understand why it is that these here Injuns we white fellers got for wives know so much more'n we men do."

"How you figger?"

"I see it's because we're white, Gabe," he confessed, staring at the dogs working over old bones nearby. "Ever' time I work so hard to get my mind around something I can't figger out, my wife tells me I can't unnerstand because I ain't meant to unnerstand. She says I ain't s'posed to work so hard to find a answer. She says I'll find out soon enough why ever'thing works out the way it does, an' why any of the rest of it don't matter none at all."

Bridger glanced at Waits-by-the-Water, then concentrated again on his friend. "Don't matter none at all?"

"You been around Injuns near as much as I have, Jim," he whimpered. "You sure as hell gotta awready know!"

"Know what?"

Licking a drop of whiskey that clung to his mustache, Titus spoke low, "Injuns say this here life of ours—what I'm doin' sittin' an' jawin' with you by this fire—this here life ain't real at all."

"Ain't real?" Bridger scoffed with a wide grin. "Quit your yankin' on my leg!"

Titus leaned forward, his elbow clumsily sliding off his knee, then quickly regained his composure. "Just what I said. You an' me here now . . . this ain't real."

Bridger's eyes narrowed as he turned to Waits-by-the-Water. "You understand what this here drunk is sayin'?"

Her head bobbed.

"Awright—spill it all for me," Bridger prodded. "Can't say I've ever heard nothing about any of this dreams an' such."

"This here's hard work," Scratch declared, then licked his lips. "Workin' my brain like this makes a man even more thirsty than that trail comin' down from Fort Hall . . . so maybe I should loosen my head-hobbles with a li'l more of your whiskey."

"Just as long as you don't pickle yourself and pass on out afore you tell me what these here Injuns of ours know that we don't."

Promptly Titus pressed one greasy finger up to his lips. "Shshshsh!" he hissed in a coarse whisper. "I ain't figgered out if we're really s'posed to know or not, Gabe." Slowly, with his oversized head swimming unevenly, he turned to gaze at his wife. "Gonna tell my friend here 'bout it."

"Bridger good man," she said in understandable American. "He knows dreams good too."

"What the hell is she talking about?" Gabe inquired. "Me knowing dreams good too?"

Scratch took another big swallow, then dragged the back of his hand across his damp mustache. "Your dreams, Gabe. That's the answer. Injuns I know believe your dreams are your real life . . . and this here, where we're talking by this fire? It ain't real at all."

With a loud snort, Bridger growled, "Shit, if you ain't way down in the cups, Scratch. Here you had me believing—"

"Injuns figger their dreams—'specially their medeecin visions—those are their journeys they take back to the real life," Titus interrupted with an impatient wave of his empty cup. "Them places we see in our dreams . . . that's where our spirits come from, where our spirits really belong."

Wagging his head, Jim confessed, "I don't think I understand any of this—"

"We ain't s'posed to!" Titus said with glee. "Don't you see? That's the way it is with these here Injuns. They get their minds around what they can understand an' they don't let the rest of it fret 'em at all. It's the way of things out here in these mountains."

"How's that?"

Leaning forward, his elbows on his knees, Bass whispered, "Injuns say I just gotta quit worryin' 'bout ever'thing I don't understand."

"Why?"

"Because it's what I ain't meant to understand . . . till ever'thing is showed me an' the answers is given."

"When's that gonna happen?"

Titus explained, "Waits told me it's when a warrior's spirit takes off from his body."

"When he dies?"

Nodding, Scratch said, "I s'pose that's it, dead center, Gabe. When a warrior's spirit is free of his body . . . we'll get all the answers."

"Answers for things like what happened to heal Shadrach's arm?" Jim asked. "Answers for why Lucas was took by a rattler?"

He swallowed hard on that lump in his throat. "Makes this here child feel a lot better just knowin' he'll unnerstand all the questions one of these days, Gabe. One of these days . . . eventual'."

TWENTY-TWO

This part of the day always smelled the very best. Here when it grew light enough for him to stir and muck about, but still well before sunup. The air had a special quality to it as the night was just beginning to relent and give itself to the day. These breathless moments were undeniably the best, no matter what season it was.

In spring, you could drink it in deep and smell the fresh, full-bodied, fertile readiness of the earth about to renew itself. And in summer this was the last of those cool moments before the sun began to radiate down from the sky, heat baking back up from the earth in waves of oppressive torture. Now in late autumn the air captured a tang, that aroma of things dying lifting from the ground where leaves and plants lay moldering, where little creatures dug themselves in for a long nap. Come winter, those creatures meant to sleep would not stir, while those meant to suffer and die would indeed endure and withstand, or die. Come winter in this far north land, a time when life could be decided quickly, brutally—when survival hung by a slender thread—each new terrible morning could taste as sweet as winesap on his tongue, at the back of his throat. The long, black night of winter would eventually leave, like a man reluctant to abandon his lover's bed, unwilling to give itself over to the light of day, to the warmth of those brief hours when about all a man could do was to prepare for the coming of the next long winter's night.

Autumn mornings in this far country north of the Yellowstone smelled the best. This was the time of year when matters of life and death were held in the balance, when it was decided what would live on and what would not see the coming of another spring. Mornings cold, hoarfrost coating most everything with a layer of icy death, breathsmoke wreathed around his head as he was always the first to stir. But by afternoon the sun had melted away the frost, steam drifted up from the thawing ground, and a man actually began to believe that the finality of winter had been put off for one more day.

Autumn in the north was what he had longed for so when they set off on their hot march north from Fort Bridger, back when Gabe's calendar had confirmed September was drawing to a close.

"Won't be no more trains coming through," Bridger said to Bass one afternoon some two weeks following their return to his post on Black's Fork.

Scratch had wiped the sweat from his eyes and stared west a moment before he said, "Any pilgrims show up now, like to be caught by snow in the mountains."

"You got a itch to tramp, this here's the time to scratch it good."

Turning to gaze at Bridger, Titus had explained, "I'll lay as I been here in one place long enough, Gabe."

"Reckon that's so." Jim sighed. "Time was, I kept movin' too. Been here four years now. Don't figger I got any reason to move on now, the way I did when I was younger."

"Likely I ain't growed out of it like you done," Bass responded. "Not ready to call one place my home. For while longer, my home gonna stay where my woman an' me set up camp for the night, or for the winter."

"Where you fixin' to stay out the robe season?"

"Gotta be back in Crow country afore the land goes hard, Jim," he had admitted. "We got us that young'un on the way."

Bridger had stood and held out his hand. "I can put some store credit on the books for you . . . or you can take out your wages afore you go."

"I'll do some of both," he had declared. "The young'uns deserve some new pretties, an' we ought'n have some presents to give out when I take this here family north back to their relations."

He knew the way well enough that with a three-quarter moon Bass decided they would leave the following day at dusk instead of with the coming of dawn. Travel out those short hours of the late-summer night, pressing on into midmorning while the heat began to rise again from the earth. Only then finding shade in those leafy trees bordering Ham's Fork, later the Sandy, then the Sweetwater, and on to the Popo Agie. Climb north to the Wind River as they watched for any sign at the curve of the earth ahead: dust rising from a village on the move, or smoke from those who had planted their camp in some oxbow of a pleasant stream. Come every sunrise as he studied the distance for a place to spend out the heat of the day, Titus Bass also surveyed the land for some sign that they had located Yellow Belly's Crow. But chances were better than good that the bands were north of the Yellowstone for now. This was the time of the year the camp was moving, when the Crow went in search of the herds in earnest, making the kills and drying the meat against the deep snows and ever-lasting cold so hard the trees would boom like those cannons the American Fur Company kept atop the walls of its fur posts. Here in the last days of Indian summer the Crow would be hunting with a missionary zeal before the beasts began turning south with that biological imperative buried in their marrow eons before the first man ever raised his first stone-tipped arrow, flung his first stone-tipped spear at the shaggy creatures. Ages ago when winter and the wolf were the only killers.

Hot as it had been, winter was no more than a fond hope now.

As if summer would never release its grip on the central mountains, the springs and creeks had shrunk like alum thrown on a green hide—little more than sparse, cool trickles—while the grass for the animals had withered and was harder to find day by day, the talc-fine dust rising from each hoof and travois pole, coating the inside of mouth and nose, burning the eyes with the sting of al-kali, making him yearn all the more for the high places where a man found com-fort and took sanctuary, no matter how steamy it became down below.

When they stopped on a nearby hill for a look into the narrow valley, he found no one camped near the colorful cones and terraces of the hot springs. The Shoshone must be ranging far to the east on the other side of the Bighorn Mountains in search of the herds of buffalo and antelope. For days now he had not spotted any sign of them, much less stumbling across a Snake village in one of their usual haunts in that Wind River country.

"This will be a good place to stay for two nights while I go hunting with Flea," he told Waits-by-the-Water late that morning.

As she slipped to the ground, Waits arched her spine a little, a flat hand pressed at the small of her back. "Two nights to rest here. That will do my bones good."

"Your back hurts from the long rides we've made?"

"This new child of yours," Waits groaned as she slowly slid out of the sad-dle, "he is not a good rider like the rest of your children were."

Legging off his horse, Titus hurried to her, putting his arm around her shoul-der and bringing up her chin so he could gaze into her eyes. "We'll stay here till you're rested and ready to go on."

"Should we pitch the lodge?" she asked. "What of a storm?"

"Magpie and Flea can help me," he offered. He studied her belly, how she had really begun to show. "You rest over there in the shade for now."

Gazing at him with a grin, she said, "I am not a helpless baby, Ti-tuzz. I can still do everything I have always done when I carried a child in my belly."

"Enough, woman," he chided her. "Jackrabbit, take your mother with you over there to the shade." Then he turned back to his wife, saying, "I'll let you put everything away when we have the lodge staked down for you. Now go sit with the boy."

By the time they had the cover pinned against the poles, the air had grown warm—especially when the breeze gasped and died. So they could avoid the strong sulfurous odors of the gurgling springs, he had made camp upwind of the steamy pools, where shallow pools of hot water collected on a series of terraces. On downwind from them stood a tall cone composed entirely of minerals deposited over the eons by a single spewing spring, one microscopic layer after another. As he began to drag the baggage off the packhorses, Scratch had Magpie and Flea roll up the bottom of the lodge cover so the light breeze could move through the shady lodge.

"Now it's time to take the horses to the crik," he instructed his eldest son. "Water them good, much as they wanna drink. We don't need to worry 'bout them gettin' too much because we'll be stayin' put for two nights."

"Do you want me to picket the horses when I am done watering them?" he asked. "Or, do you want me to let them wander?"

"They should be awright on their own," Titus replied. "Let 'em find the grass they want to eat by themselves."

What plants grew in this narrow valley not only tasted good but were highly nutritious, fed by the mineral-rich waters beneath the soil. It was clear to see from the many tracks and well-used trails crisscrossing their camping ground that the nourishing and flavorful vegetation attracted both deer and antelope to this valley too. As Flea moved off, herding the horses before him, Scratch considered taking the boy hunting at first light the next morning, when the game was moving out of their beds and down toward water. Yes, this would be a good place to lay over for a few days, he thought as he dropped to the grass in a patch of shade near the lodge, watching Waits and Magpie dragging their few belongings through the lodge door.

"Jackrabbit! Come over here to your father!" he called out in Crow.

The boy clambered into his lap and sat.

"You stay here with me," he told his son. "Where you won't be in the way of those women. Always best for a man to stand back and stay completely out of the way when a woman is at work. This is a good lesson for a boy to learn."

As Jackrabbit slid off his father's lap and laid his head down on Titus's thigh, Scratch leaned back against a tree and closed his eyes.

Here at the springs they were more than halfway to the Yellowstone from Bridger's post. They could afford to rest here before they marched on to find Yellow Belly's Crow, who wouldn't cross the Yellowstone and start south until the weather began to cool. Until then, the hunting bands would stay north, perhaps as far away as the Judith or the Musselshell, on the prowl for buffalo and wary of the Blackfoot. Time enough to be pushing on before the cold arrived. For now the second summer was hanging on—

"Popo!" Flea called excitedly as he rode up on the bare back of his claybank.

Titus immediately came out of his sleep, raising Jackrabbit's head as he started to slip out from under the small boy. Magpie and Waits sat in the shade of the lodge cover, watching. "Trouble?" he asked.

Flea watched his father reach around for the rifle he had propped against the tree. "No trouble . . . I think."

"What did you wake me up for?" He blinked as he stepped into the intense sunlight.

"Someone is staying near the creek."

Alarm troubled his belly. "Indian?"

His head bobbed. "But they have no lodge. Only a small shelter made of branches and blankets."

"How many?" he asked as he came to his son's knee. A branch-and-blanket shelter sounded like a war lodge, a horse-stealing party on its way into enemy country.

"I don't think there are many of them. I only saw three horses grazing nearby."

"Did anyone see you?"

"I don't know," he admitted. "I don't think so, but I'm not sure."

"How did you find this shelter?"

He patted the claybank beneath him. "I heard a horse whistle. My pony heard it too and asked me if we should go see. I thought we should go because we didn't know anyone else was camped close to us."

"You were careful?" he asked, then whistled low for the dogs. "Did you see if you were followed?"

Flea nodded. "I watched my back trail carefully."

"Where is this shelter and the three horses?"

Turning to point as the two dogs bounded out of the brush, the boy said, "Over that low ridge, where the stream makes a slow circle at the base of the hill."

"Our horses are safe?"

"Yes, Popo. I brought them back from the water and put them out to graze on the other side of that willow."

He looked downstream at the bottom of the hill where the sun glared brightly on the rustling leaves. "I see them now. Good. Magpie?"

She poked her head from the lodge. "You need me?"

"Come help me tie up the dogs so they will stay here with you and your mother."

When Ghost and Digger were secured at the ends of their tethers, and he had knotted a bandanna around each muzzle to keep them quiet, Scratch turned to his son and asked, "Flea, can you take me to look at this shelter you found?"

"Come up with me and I will take you." The boy patted the back of his horse.

Titus retrieved two pistols and stuffed them in his belt before he handed his son the rifle, then bounded onto the rear flanks of the claybank pony. Once he had scooted forward against the boy, Scratch took back his rifle. He looped his left arm around Flea's waist and said, "Let's go see who these strangers are."

They left the claybank tied in a clump of alder, then scrambled up the side of the hill at an angle. Scratch followed his boy to just below the top, then they both dropped to their bellies and crawled on up to the crest. At the top he peered down at the narrow creek, unable to find the shelter at first. Eventually he spotted a patch of what looked to be greasy, smoke-darkened canvas in the midst of a large stand of eight-foot-tall willow.

"Where are the three horses?" he whispered.

"On the other side," Flea said. "You come around the hill, that way, and you see them."

"Tied up?"

He nodded. "Long ropes."

"Saddles?"

This time Flea shook his head. "I saw no saddles. White man or Indian."

"But you saw the horses, son. What tribe are these strangers?"

"Don't know, Popo."

"Any weapons hanging outside?" he asked. "Shield or medicine bundle?"

"No. I saw nothing." He grew thoughtful a moment, then told his father, "It is a poor camp, no signs of wealth. Maybe we leave them alone, and they won't bother us too."

"Can't take that chance, Flea. With us camped just over the hill at the springs, these strangers are too close. Best to know who your neighbors are."

Titus slid backward, then rolled onto his hip and sat up, pulling the first pistol from his belt. Handing it to the boy, he said, "Here. You know how to use this if you need to?"

"I remember."

"Good. I want you at my back when we walk in there."

When they reached the bank of the narrow creek opposite the shelter, Bass saw how much thought had gone into placing the structure where it was all but concealed, except from straight on. It had all the signs of an old camp: footpaths tracking upstream and down, all the grass around the stand of willow trampled by moccasins if not hooves, and a small portion of the sharp cutbank worn down by the strangers as they knelt while dipping water from the stream. He was certain this wasn't a war lodge—a shelter hastily constructed for one night's sleep as a war party walked or rode deep into enemy country. No, from the signs of things, this trio of strangers had been here for some time and didn't appear to be in a rush to leave.

"We'll wait here and see how many are inside," he whispered to the boy. "If all three strangers are here, I will need to send you back for your bow. But if only one of them sleeps inside, we are in no danger with our three guns."

"We just wait?"

He looked at his son. "Patience is something good for all young men to learn."

Minutes later Flea whispered close to his father's ear, "Were you very different from me when you were my age?"

Grinning, he tousled his son's long, black hair and said, "Boys are the same, no matter where they grow up, no matter if they Crow like you, or a white boy like I was."

"Sometimes I think that I will never grow up to be as good a man as you," Flea confessed.

"That's where you are wrong," he said in a hush, deeply touched by the honor in his son's words.

In exasperation, the boy said, "But you know all these things that I don't think I ever will know."

"I suppose I make you feel that way because I try to teach you all that I have learned—to help you understand all those things I did not understand. I want to give you my hand in growing into a man, the help that I did not have. So, I am sorry if I have not been a good and gentle father to you. Sorry if I tell you that you should learn patience . . . then I am not patient with you myself."

"You have been a very good father," Flea responded, his eyes filled with respect. "Maybe there are times when it is hard to be my father."

Laying his hand on the boy's shoulder, Titus whispered, "I will try better to remember that there are times it is difficult to be my son—"

"Look!" Flea whispered harshly.

A shadowy form appeared at the shelter's low doorway, bent at the waist and knees, as the stranger stepped into a patch of shade and stood. A woman!

She straightened and shook her clothes around her—a long leather skirt that fell just below her knees and an ill-fitting cloth shirt once of a bright calico pattern, but now so crusted with grime and fire soot that it was hard for Titus to make out what color it had ever been. She wore no moccasins, her feet coated with a thick layer of ground-in dirt. She pushed back her unkempt hair and began to brush at it with a porcupine tail that had its quills clipped short, slowly and painfully yanking at the ratty knots, beginning to shake loose the bits of grass and ash that had collected there. She was not a young thing, he could see. Her hair hung well flecked with the snows of something more than forty winters, and her breasts sagged with not only the pull of age but the mouths of babes who had suckled at them what had to be a lifetime ago.

Perhaps there was a child inside that shelter; if not a child, then a youngster not quite become an adult—

A second figure stepped from the dark interior and emerged clumsily, one hand clutching onto the left side of the shelter to steady himself. Barechested, his legs naked as well, and not wearing any moccasins, the man tugged at his long breechclout, straightening it on the narrow strap of leather tied around his waist, then adjusting his manhood beneath the front fold of what had once been a bright red piece of trader's wool. The bright colors of selvage at the edges of the breechclout were faded, frayed, and almost indistinguishable with soot and filth. He rubbed the heels of both palms into his eyes, then spread his fingers apart to push back what unruly sprigs of his graying hair had refused to stay bound within his long braids also dusted with flecks of dried grass.

"Where is the third one?" Flea asked. "Inside?"

"Wait, and we will see."

The woman walked to the edge of the bushes, past the ground where the three horses raised their heads and followed her toward the hillside. There she yanked up the bottom of her short skirt, one side after another, raising it to her hips, then squatted and moistened the ground, unaware of the father and son across that narrow ribbon of water. When she stood, shifting the skirt back around her legs, and started back to the shelter, the three horses remained near the bottom of the hill to crop at the grass.

Quietly lifting the flap to his shooting pouch, Bass pulled out the spyglass and snapped out its three sections. He quickly looked over those three animals, inspecting their muzzles, manes, backs, and tails. These were not the proud possessions of a warrior: groomed, painted, a tail bound up for battle. All three showed their age, and two of them clearly had healing sores on their backs from an ill-fitting saddle. Slowly he dragged the spyglass across to his left, hoping to get himself a better look at these two aging and disheveled strangers.

He stopped first on the woman as she took down from a tree branch two small carcasses he had not noticed hanging there before. Rabbits; gutted, but unskinned. Plopping them beside a lifeless fire pit, she bent over the game and picked up a small knife, using it to slowly work the hide off the meat. As she squatted over those rabbits, Scratch studied her—unable to make out what tribe she was from her manner of dress or decorations. But he could only assume these two had to be Shoshone. This was, after all, near the northern border of Snake country, but close to the southern extent of Crow land as well. Still, in the absence of lodge symbols, pony paintings, or distinguishable hairstyles, Titus could only guess the couple had to be Shoshone.

When he inched the spyglass on to the left and found the man settling onto the trampled grass, Bass twisted the sections of the tube together until he brought the stranger's face into sharper focus. The man leaned back on his elbows in the shade and closed his eyes as if relishing that particular moment. He spoke to the woman without looking at her or opening his eyes. The sound of his voice drifted across the creek to the rocks and willow where Bass and Flea lay in hiding, pricking a remembrance, perhaps even a warning, at the top of Scratch's spine, there at the base of his skull. He held the spyglass as steady as he could, concentrating on that aging face. It had been so long, so very long, that he could not be certain . . . because the last time he had laid eyes on the man was more than—how many now? More than fourteen winters ago. How the years had taken a toll on the old warrior.

"I know him," Titus whispered, not taking the spyglass from his right eye.

"The man?" Flea asked.

As Scratch watched him through the spyglass, the man's eyes suddenly popped open and he gazed intently across the narrow creek, slowly turning his head as he studied the base of the hill where Bass and his son lay in hiding. It was clear the warrior had heard something of the unseen spies. He spoke to the woman, and she looked up, peering across the creek too as she wearily got to her feet. The man slid his legs under him and stood, backing toward the shelter as the woman hurried behind him, quickly ducking through the low opening. In a moment her arm appeared again, handing out an old trade gun to the man. Just before Bass took the spyglass from his eye, he saw how poor a weapon the firearm was—repaired with rawhide wraps at both the wrist right behind the lock, and again along the forestock, just in front of the rear sight. Both crude repairs clearly showing signs of age.

Titus put his lips to Flea's ear and whispered, "Stay down until I tell you to show yourself."

"Where is the third one?" asked the boy. "Should I watch for him?"

Sliding his knees under him, Bass said, "I don't think there is a third stranger. Just that old woman and a man who was once an old friend. One who became an old enemy long ago."

As he stood, Scratch raised his rifle in the air, held high at the end of his arm. He wasn't certain when he shouted across the narrow creek if he had remembered the smattering of the Snake tongue he had learned that winter he was healing, after the Arapaho had ambushed him and taken part of his scalp. Maybe enough of what he said would make sense to the old man who readied that ancient trade gun to shoot and to the woman who crawled out of the shelter with a brace of horse pistols.

"I mean no harm!" he hurled his voice, waiting for the low echo to end. "We are old friends."

"Who is this claiming we are old friends?"

Cautiously, he inched into the open, still holding the rifle in the air. "See this? I cannot shoot this weapon at you."

"Answer my question: Who are you?"

"Look at me and tell me you don't remember," he urged the warrior. "I know you are called Slays in the Night."

That seemed to stun the Indian a moment. Eventually he said, "Who knows my old name from so many winters ago?"

"Titus Bass!"

The man appeared to work that over in his mind the way a wolf bitch would work round and round making a bed for herself when it came time to birth her pups. Finally he demanded, "Let me see more of you!"

Scratch slowly lowered his rifle and moved more to his left, coming into the open, knowing he was putting faith in this old friend made into an old enemy from so long ago. It was faith and nothing more, because he had no solid reason to trust Slays in the Night. Nothing more than the sense of it in his gut that he could give the warrior this benefit of the doubt.

Even though the Shoshone did not lower his weapon, the tone of his voice was no longer strident. The way it had sounded when he cursed Titus Bass that morning in Brown's Park.* And now he spoke in a stuttered English, "You not dead, Titus Bass?"

"You learned to talk some American, Slays in the Night?" he asked as he lowered the butt of his rifle to the ground and crossed his wrists over the muzzle, staring across the stream.

"Some little, yes."

"Last time I see'd you—said you was gonna kill me next time you laid eyes on me," Titus declared. "You still fixed on killin' me?"

He mulled on those foreign words a few moments, then looked down at his old trade gun a heartbeat before he lowered it, suspending it in his hand at the end of his arm. "No. I am too tired, too old, kill you now. Maybe long winters ago. Too tired now kill Titus Bass."

As he finished speaking English, the old woman said something to him in low tones and he turned slightly toward her to mumble.

Seeing how she lowered her pistols and turned for the doorway, Titus asked, "Is that your wife? The woman who makes the good-tastin' pemeecan?"

Shaking his head sadly, Slays in the Night explained, "No. Not this woman. Old wife now . . . gone. Other wife, she . . ." and then he grew frustrated that he could not explain in English. Speaking Shoshone instead, he said, "That wife so many summers ago, she left Slays in the Night. That's not really right. It is better to say that my old wife stayed with our people when Slays in the Night left the village for the war trail."

"In all those years," Bass inquired in Shoshone, "you never gone back to your people?"

"I couldn't," he confessed. "The headmen drove me away and did not allow me to return . . . so my old wife stayed with her relations. She no longer wanted to be with me. She did not come with her husband."

Bass gradually put the words together, at least enough of them to understand what the warrior had spoken to him in Shoshone.

"Do you still ride the war trail?" Titus inquired.

Slays in the Night snorted sadly. "Look around at what I have, Titus Bass," he said in his native tongue again, gesturing toward the poor shelter. "I am not a fighting man no more. No herd of ponies. Three old horses only. Sick, old horses now."

"And your wife?"

For a moment the warrior glanced at the woman before he said, "She is a

---

* Sometimes referred to as Brown's Hole; *One-Eyed Dream*.

good woman for a sick old warrior now. She . . . spreads her legs when I want her. She cook the rabbits and deer I can shoot for us. She keeps me warm at night . . . and—she never runs away, afraid of me."

"Is she from your old band of Shoshone?"

"No," he admitted. "She is a Digger. I don't have very much to give a woman now, but what poor things I can give is far better than any Digger can give a woman . . . so we are both content—for more than ten winters now."

"Children?"

"They stayed with their father when I stole her."

That surprised Scratch. "This woman, she is your wife?"

"Now she is. For the first winter, she was just my woman. I tied her up and made her stay after I stole her from her camp. But the following summer when I untied the ropes from her wrists and ankles, she did not run off from me. She stayed. Maybe she stayed because she had learned to feel sorry for this man who had very little left in his life."

Taking the seven steps that brought him down to the edge of the stream, Titus signaled for Flea to come out of hiding. "Maybe, Slays in the Night—she stayed because she had a strong heart for you."

When the warrior turned to glance at the woman, he caught sight of the second figure from the corner of his eye. Slays instinctively raised his rifle again as Bass shoved the boy behind him.

"No, no danger—this here's my son," Titus explained in English, his mind working back and forth between the two languages. Then he tucked the muzzle of his longrifle under his armpit and, for better understanding, he began to sign with both his hands as he spoke. "His name is . . . I can't remember what the Shoshone word is. A tiny crawl-on-their-belly."

Slays in the Night made the prairie sign for his tribe. "Snake?"

"No. Smaller. Bites animals."

"A deerfly?"

"No. More . . . smaller."

"Buffalo gnat?"

"Not that either."

"Tick?"

"No, smaller still . . ."

"A flea," the warrior said in Shoshone, making a sign with his thumb and forefinger as if pinching himself.

Titus brought the boy out from behind his back. "Yes, that is the word for him. His name."

Slays in the Night stepped down to the bank and motioned them across. "Come over here and let me see this boy who has grown far too tall for his father to call him a little flea! Come over now . . . so I can look into the face of the man who used to haunt so many of my dreams."

He wanted to trust this old friend who had taken to stealing horses from white men even though he had had a long history of loyalty to trappers. None of the man's reasons for that startling turnaround had ever been explained by the nightlong chase he and Josiah made going after the horse thieves back in '33, nothing but a nagging hole left by not knowing why some men turned bad the way they did, why some men became something different, were not the friends he had once known them to be. But Slays in the Night hadn't been the first. No, likely that had been Silas Cooper, along with Bud and Billy, his two obedient compañeros. Then Asa McAfferty came along to twist things around and tangle things up the way no one else ever had before. No, Slays in the Night was not the first to ride off on a trail Titus could not understand. And he sure was not the last to yank the ground right out from under Bass's feet.

"Hold the pistol careful," he reminded Flea. "By the barrel. Point it down when you jump across the crik."

Titus stayed on the bank while the boy took two steps, then vaulted across the narrow stream to grab the Shoshone's outstretched hand. When Flea was steadied up the bank, Scratch shuffled down to the edge of the water and jumped across with his rifle in hand, planting the butt in the dry grass on the bank as he reached the opposite side. Slays in the Night put out his hand to the trapper.

For a moment he looked into this old friend's eyes, pushed his rifle into his left hand, then clasped the Snake's wrist. They shook once in a firm up-and-down motion, then freed one another.

"That night so long ago—we could have killed you in your camp," he told Titus in his language and with his hands, the expression on his tired, wrinkled face unchanged.

"You didn't because we were in Snake country," Scratch replied. "And white men have always been safe in Snake country."

"When you killed the first Shoshone warrior riding with me, I should have killed you then," he retorted, his expression grim. "It would have been right for me to kill you."

Titus wasn't sure if he should feel uneasy that their meeting had taken this turn. "It would have been right for me to kill you for stealing our horses."

Slays in the Night sighed, then said, "But you didn't kill me."

"What was worse, old friend?" he asked. "For me to shoot you, that would've made ever'thing easy on you."

Nodding, the warrior admitted, "To go on living with my shame after you had killed all the others but let me live . . . that was worse than a quick and merciful death."

Titus noticed the woman's face as she watched them from where she sat, just inside the low shelter. He asked the old warrior, "So life is better now than it was so many winters ago?"

Digging at an itch behind an ear, Slays in the Night came away with a louse that he cracked between the nails on his thumb and forefinger. "Once I was a rich man—many horses, a fine wife and children, owned many nice things. Then everything disappeared, even my friends and finally my wife. I took the wrong road trying to get back what I had lost. When I finally had nothing more to lose . . . when you left me standing there in the valley without a weapon, without a horse, without a single one of my friends . . . then I had nothing left in the world."

Slays in the Night motioned them over to the side of the fire pit, where the three settled on the grass in the shade.

Titus laid his rifle across his lap and asked, "What did you do that morning after I left you, cursing me?"

Before he answered, the warrior turned and looked over his shoulder, signaling to the woman to return to her work skinning the rabbits. When she had knelt nearby, her nervous eyes darting over the white man and the young boy, he explained, "I started to walk south. I struck the big river and found berries to live on. Tried to throw rocks at rabbits and lizards too. You can see I am not a very good hunter!"

She whispered something.

"My wife wants me to tell you her name," he declared. "Red Paint Rock. She is named for some country where she was born far, far to the south of where I found her."

"You said you stole her?"

"Yes," he admitted quietly, his eyes falling to the ground. "By that time I had stolen an old gun from a trapper's camp and a horse too. It died many summers ago—but by then I had another horse, and a woman."

"You were able to steal her because you had a horse and a gun."

"Yes. I had a horse and a gun," he agreed, "but . . . I was very lonely. It took a long time for her to want to touch me when I forced her legs apart. But I think she finally understood how alone I was in the world."

"She'd never leave you now," Titus said.

"And I won't leave her till the day she dies." Suddenly his face grew animated. "We don't have much—just these two poor rabbits. But you are welcome to eat with us when they are cooked."

"I have a better idea," Titus signed with his hands as he was struck with the thought. "Both of you come eat with us. We have some antelope that I shot two days ago."

"Go get it, bring it here, and you two can camp with us," said Slays in the Night.

He wagged his head. "We already have our camp set up. My wife and two other children."

"There are more of you?"

"Save your rabbits for another day," Titus suggested. "Come have supper with us tonight instead."

"How far away are you camped?"

"Not far—down the creek by the tall cone."

"I know the place like I know my own hand!"

"I thought you would," Scratch remarked. "It isn't far, even for those tired old horses of yours."

Slays in the Night stood as the white man and the boy got to their feet. "Do you think we can go with you now? I don't want to wait until evening. It has been so long since I have had new ears to talk to."

Bass looked at the woman's expectant face, then studied the old warrior's wrinkled eyes, the deep clefts, and his sagging jawline. "Yes. It will be good that you two come join us now."

TWENTY-THREE

That Indian was a proud man, one who had made plenty of mistakes, owned up to his faults, yet was still paying for what lay in the long-ago past. It didn't seem fair to Titus Bass, since he'd made a heap of mistakes in his own life.

Still, he damn well understood just how few things in his own life had turned out anywhere near fair. Scratch could admire the warrior's dogged persistence, as well as his survival savvy. And he got to thinking that perhaps there was a reason why he had run onto Slays in the Night after all these years, now that they were both no longer young and frisky as bull calves in spring . . . now that they had rubbed their old horns down to a polish and they no longer frolicked, the sap of youth no longer coursing through their veins. Considering the odds that once stood against the Shoshone warrior, it was nothing less than a wonder that Slays in the Night was still alive at all. *The Injun had the ha'r of the b'ar in 'im, for sartin.*

Even in her youth, that Digger woman could never have been a comely gal, Titus thought the more he looked her over that evening at supper. She didn't talk much either, mostly keeping her eyes lowered except when she stole furtive glances at Waits-by-the-Water or one of the children. Red Paint Rock had to be half again as old as Waits. She was built sturdy and close to the ground, but it was the pear shape to her body that made the woman seem all the more squat—especially when she stood next to the tall Shoshone.

"This is really the old friend who stole our horses long ago?" Waits whispered at his ear when he called her to the lodge after everyone had eaten supper and wiped their greasy hands on their hair.

"Yes," he responded in a hush. "The man's medicine has seen better days."

"Our horses, our things are safe from him now?"

Laying his hands on her shoulders, Titus reassured, "That was a long time ago, far away, a wrong committed by another man."

"You can be sure of him?"

"I want you to believe in me when I say I can."

She looked into his eyes. "Then I will trust you, even though I do not know if I can trust him."

"You can trust me." He turned to kneel at the stack of blankets.

She stepped up behind his shoulder. "What are you doing?"

"I am making gifts to them," he explained, feeling her eyes on his back as he pulled out a red blanket, and a multistriped one too. Sensing her waiting there behind him made him a little edgy, feeling as if he had to explain this act of charity when she herself was the most giving person he himself had ever known.

He turned slightly on his knees and asked, "Them extra guns—where'd you lay 'em?"

"You're going to make a gift of a gun?" she asked, surprised enough that her voice rose an octave.

"Yes. He has nothing but a poor gun that is only good to shoot a few poor rabbits."

"There, back where you sleep. I laid them under that green blanket."

"The extra lead and powder we got for my work at Bridger's fort?"

She pointed. "In the basket—there."

Scratch crabbed toward the back of the lodge on all fours, pulled back the blanket, and started appraising all the extra firearms he owned, most of them taken from the bodies of dead enemies over the years. He picked out a rifled flintlock, then selected a pistol that could use the same size ball.

"What does she have to cook in?" Waits asked.

Her sudden question startled him. Scratch turned and peered over his shoulder at her with a shrug. "How'd I know what she's got to cook in? Didn't pay no attention. Only saw her skinnin' a pair of poor-lookin' rabbits—"

"Isn't that just like a man." She let her words whip him even while she grinned. "This woman needs something too, but all you can think about is your gifts to the man."

He smiled back at her. "What you got in mind for Red Paint Rock?"

"I have a kettle she can have," Waits began as she crouched on the robes and went to digging through her belongings. "And a new knife too."

He stood, scooping up the rifle and pistol, then started for the door—stopping to lean over and plant a kiss on the top of her head as she dug out a few yards of some cloth and several feet of red ribbon. When he had ducked out of the lodge, Scratch called for his children.

"Flea, take your sister and little brother into the lodge to help your mother," he directed. "I want you to bring me the two blankets your mother will show you. And help your mother bring out all that she is gathering up too."

It wasn't long before Flea and Magpie carried the heavy wool blankets out and laid them on a shady patch of grass so Titus could prop the rifle against the stack and lay the pistol on top of it all. He went back to the lodge to pick out some powder and lead while the children helped their mother bring out the rest of her gifts. Through it all, Slays in the Night and Red Paint Rock watched with growing interest and curiosity as the white man's family bustled back and forth to the lodge and the dogs whimpered to be let off their ropes.

At last, Scratch settled again at the fire, where the antelope haunch roasted. He pointed at the spit, then signed, "How long has it been since you ate antelope?"

Self-consciously, the warrior said, "A long time. They move too fast for my . . . for my old gun."

"You and the woman are lucky that old gun of yours can keep you both fed."

"We get a little to eat. Enough for her and me," the Shoshone replied. Then, pointing at the rifle leaning against that stack of blankets, Slays said, "I like the looks of your gun. Such a gun shoots straight, kills a lot of game."

"That ain't my gun over there," Titus corrected. "Used to be."

The Shoshone looked at him quizzically until Scratch explained, "It's your gun now."

"M-my gun?" he signed, tapping his breast with a trembling hand.

He stood up again, reaching down to pull the warrior's arm. "C'mon. Let's go see how your new rifle feels in your hands."

As he stepped away from the fire with the white man, Slays said something to the Digger woman. Her eyes grew wide, bouncing back and forth between the rifle, the old trapper, and Bass's family, who stood nearby, watching their guests. After a moment of stunned silence, Red Paint Rock quietly said something to her husband.

The Shoshone stopped just feet short of the blankets and rifle. "Friend," he said in his language, beginning to sign again, "we do not have anything of value to repay you for this kindness."

That poverty tugged at his heart. "There's no need to give anything back to us for the gifts we make to you and your wife."

"G-gifts?" he asked. "M-more than the rifle?"

"Lookee there," and he pointed at the stack, "first whack, you both likely could use a couple new blankets. Them come right out of Jim Bridger's storehouse a few days back. Brand spankin' new they are. An' you're gonna need some powder an' lead to shoot your new rifle—so I give you some of that."

Slays's lips moved slightly, but no words slipped out.

"Here, lookee," Bass said as he picked up the small skin pouch from the top of the blankets. "Inside is a worm"—which he brought forth and held up for the

Shoshone to see—"so you can pull a patch from your barrel. An' . . . this here's a screw—good to yank a dry ball from your breech." He saw the mortified look on the man's face. "Don't you worry none. I'll teach you how to use 'em afore we push on north in a couple of days. Show you how to give your barrel a good cleanin' with some boil't water too."

"Clean, this gun?" signed the Shoshone.

"You don't clean that barrel?"

He shook his head.

Laying a hand on the Indian's shoulder, he said, "Got some presents for your woman too. We'll give 'em to her while you go back an' fetch that gun of your'n."

"Get gun?"

"Yepper—go get your old gun for me to look at."

By the time he came trudging back with that well-worn smoothbore trade gun, Slays in the Night found his wife crying uncontrollably as she sat on the grass, surrounded by those two new blankets, the gift of a new brass kettle, along with a small iron skillet and ladle too. In addition, Magpie, Flea, and even Jackrabbit were handed small gifts by their mother to present to Red Paint Rock. A few yards of coarse cloth, some blanket strouding and shiny ribbon, along with a little brass wire, a handful of brass tacks, and a few nails too. But what made her lose control was the earbobs Waits put through the holes in her earlobes: wires from which were suspended small pewter turtles. Slays found the woman rocking back and forth on the ground, blubbering like a baby from her joy.

The Shoshone halted a few yards away, struck dumb himself for a moment before he could sign: "She never had someone give her anything pretty. Now so many pretty things."

"Maybeso, we all know what it's like not to have somethin' what makes us truly happy," Titus said gently. "I'm truly proud we made you both happy with our gifts."

Tearing his eyes away from his wife, Slays looked at Titus. "W-why do you give us all of this?"

"When I look around at my family, an' where I'm livin' out my days, I see how much I have—the good things I been given." He tried to explain that intangible warmth residing in his heart. "I got a lot more'n I ever deserved, friend. More'n I can ever use, so there ain't no use in keepin' it to my own self. I figger I should share with other folks all the good what's been give to me."

For years now Scratch had struggled to sort out why he had ever deserved a woman anywhere as special as Waits-by-the-Water, or the children who brought him such joy and made his heart swell with pride. After the oft-misspent life he had led to reach this day, after the mistakes he had made and the people he had hurt along the way . . . exactly why he was so richly blessed remained an unsolvable mystery to him.

Swallowing hard, Slays began to sign, his hands trembling. "This is so difficult to ask, the words to find . . . but why do you and your family do this for a man who stole horses from you many years ago?"

"That was a long, long time in the past," he explained. "Ain't ever been one to carry a grudge. I just figger you was a differ'nt fella back then. The two of you need help now. Me an' my family can help you 'cause we got more'n we can ever use. Ain't no sense in holdin' on to any of it when we could pass it on to some folks who'll get a real good use out of it."

"I can't remember when I ever felt this rich!" he signed as he spoke Shoshone. Then he asked, "How do I ever repay you, friend?"

Titus smiled at that. "You called me friend."

"Yes, because that's what we are?" Slays asked. "Even when I stole your horses, you did not kill me because you were still my friend. So you need to tell me, how can I repay you?"

He thought for a moment, his eyes looking at the pleasure it gave his wife and children to see such joy on the face of the Digger woman, a happiness that came from helping those who had little of their own but their lives, the poor clothes on their backs, and a few old weapons. Scratch sensed that this moment beside the hot springs with these two people might just mark the start of some healing for his injured soul, battered and wounded by deep loss. He knew his healing had begun this day.

So it was he looked at the tall Shoshone, the man grown as old and wrinkled as he, then said, "The way you repay is you help the next person you can, same as you been helped along your own self."

"My horse smells his own kind," Flea announced days later when his father brought his animal to a halt beside the boy.

Scratch looked at the claybank's eye, finding that it seemed to be studying him. Then he peered at his son. "You know this from the way he is acting?"

"He told me, Popo."

Bass took a moment to peer back over his shoulder, into the broad valley where he signaled Waits-by-the-Water to hold up with the other children and their pack animals. "Where are these other horses he smells?"

"Beyond the ridge."

Drawing in a deep breath, he said, "That's a long way for your pony to smell his own kind, Flea. Especially when the air is so heavy with the coming storm."

"I believe him and what he told me," Flea asserted. "But do you believe me?"

After a moment's pause, Titus responded, "I believe you, son." He took the big-brimmed hat from his head and waved the signal to Waits. She raised her rifle high, a black silk bandanna fluttering where it was knotted around the muzzle, to show she understood she was to remain where she was near the trees. "Let's go find these horses you've found."

From the morning they had put the hot springs at their back and continued north into the land of the Crow, they had not come upon any recent sign of the Mountain or River bands. A week ago they had put the Yellowstone River behind them and pressed on for the valley of the Judith, finally encountering fresher horse trails and even the remains of a recent campsite. But still no dust on the horizon or columns of smoke curling wispily into the chill autumn sky. The farther they rode in search of buffalo, the closer they drew to Blackfoot country, and the greater the odds the Crow village would invite an attack from those inveterate enemies. For days he had been as wary as a bull elk during the high-country rut, sleeping little at night, thinking how good it would have been to have another man and his guns along—Josiah Paddock, Shadrach Sweete, even Slays in the Night.

But one of them had become a storekeeper in old Taos; by now another had likely reached the new territory of Oregon leading a train of emigrant dreamers; and the Shoshone protested that he was as close to Blackfoot country as he ever wanted to be. Slays said he and his woman might start south toward Bridger's post; then again, he might just remain right there near the hot springs for the winter. Cold as the rest of that country could become, the narrow valley stayed a bit warmer, most hospitable to man and beast alike.

Each time he brooded how having another gun along would have made him ride a mite easier in the saddle, Titus remembered how unflinchingly Waits, Magpie, and Flea all took up weapons at that final eye-to-eye with Phineas Hargrove. So he had decided they would push north another two days in search of the hunting bands. If they hadn't found Yellow Belly's bunch, then he'd turn south by east, striking off toward Fort Alexander. Chances were trader Robert Meldrum would know where both the River and the Mountain bands were using up the last of these precious autumn days in making meat for the winter. After all, Meldrum's American Fur Company had a vested interest in every one of those shaggy hides the warriors managed to get, after the women had skinned the beasts and dressed the hides into soft sleeping robes suitable for the market downriver in St. Louis and beyond.

Winters upon winters ago, when King Beaver ruled these mountains, who would have ever conceived that buffalo would one day be the only hide worth trading? Or that there'd be only one outfit a man could sell to when he had furs for barter? Or that the traders would no longer pack their goods overland to a midsummer rendezvous in some central valley . . . hell, he groused—nothing ever would be the same again, nothing like those glory days when he and a few others walked this land as giants. As bold and brassy as young bulls in the spring of their lives! Why, back in those heady days how could any of them even begin to believe those shining times would come to an end?

So full of life were those seasons that not one of them gave a thought to what might lie on the horizon . . . until it was too late, until the first emigrants were moving through with their white women and their preachers too, until the big fur companies had choked the life right out of the beaver business and only buffalo were left, until every man jack of them had shuffled on to Oregon country or limped back east with his tail between his legs . . . except for a hardy few who held on and on and on. Become half Indian, half white . . . but not near enough of one race or the other to make a home or find some peace in either world.

And the saddest thing was these princes of the wilderness had brought about their own ruin. The big fur brigades had trapped many of the richest streams entirely clean of beaver, taking even the kits before they moved on to strip another section of the river, keeping the harvest out of the hands of the English and other American outfits. Over time in those final years a man could ride into a valley and not find a dam or a pond, nary a beaver lodge—much less hear the warning slap of a tail striking water, or the industrious chawing through the tender saplings, the branches of each young tree rustling as it fell and was dragged through the meadow. Greed—and the belief that if a man did not take everything he could for himself then others would come along to take it all for themselves—had turned this brief ride through glory into an endless, wandering search to recapture some shred of that magnificent era—

He heard the whistle, jerking awake suddenly, aware that he had been dozing in the saddle, the sun splendidly warm on his face, lulled asleep.

Titus found Flea pointing at the line of trees ahead of them. Shadows tucked back in the cottonwood. Beyond that fringe of trees the valley stretched north into an irregular bare meadow that meandered along the east bank of a stream that eventually poured its bounty into the Musselshell. Some three miles away at the end of that open ground grazed some horses, a sizable herd content and unalarmed in the midday autumn sun. Narrow spirals of dusky smoke lifted into the sky from lodges beyond the timber, hidden from view. That was not a war camp; instead, a large gathering made before the first hard snow arrived and the bands eventually broke up into smaller clan units, dividing off to last out the winter in the lee of the mountains.

Three riders appeared from the trees ahead, one of them raising a shield as signal. For the first time Bass turned to look to his left, the bad side, and spotted the horseman who seemed to appear out of nowhere on the ridgetop across the stream. The rider waved back with what appeared to be a piece of faded blue blanket. Off to the right he heard the snort of a horse. Four more horsemen brought their animals out of the trees nearby and came to a halt.

"Hold up, son."

Flea drew back on his reins and turned around in a half circle, gentling the lead mare who controlled their packhorses. Keeping an eye on Waits, Magpie, and young Jackrabbit, Titus waited several moments until he was assured they were close enough, then turned back to peer at the horsemen. The three riders in their front had already put their horses into motion, while the four off to the right approached more slowly, cautiously, at an angle.

"*Pote Ani*? Is that really you?" one of the voices called out.

"It is me!" Titus cried in Crow with growing excitement, squinting in the bright autumn sun at the trio, unable to discern which one had called out his name.

"The old shaman—Real Bird—he said he had seen you in a dream a few days ago . . . that you were going to return twice more," the young man explained as he approached. "But after that second return, you would never leave the Crow again . . . without a terrible end coming to you and all those around you."

A cold fingernail scraped its way slowly down his backbone with that prediction from the old soothsayer. He trained his eyes on the youngster and asked, "Who are you?"

"Stiff Arm!" the young man cried.

"No! You are grown so much in this past year!" Titus marveled, immediately forgetting the ominous prediction with the joy of returning home to his wife's people. "When we left last summer you were but a youngster, growing quickly . . . but a youngster still the same . . . and look at you now! A young man! Is this what happens when you put away the things of a boy?"

"Do you remember me too?" one of the four asked as they came up and halted on his right.

Turning, Bass studied the youth's face. "Is that you, Three Iron?"

"Has it truly been a year, *Pote Ani*?"

Titus nodded. "Long enough for boys like you to grow into such fine young men."

He watched how that made both of them beam there before their peers.

"Could this be little Flea?" Stiff Arm asked with a grin, pointing out the young horseman sitting next to Titus. "The boy who was so small when you left us last summer?"

"Like my father said, a year is a long time in the life of a young warrior," the boy replied, his face glowing.

Three Iron agreed, "Well said, Flea! Well said!"

Then a young man Bass did not know asked, "So that must be Magpie?"

Seeing how they all had trained their eyes beyond him, Titus turned in his saddle to find his wife and the other two children approaching with the lone travois horse.

"No, Turns Back," Stiff Arm said, "that cannot be little Magpie!"

"But who else could it be, *Pote Ani*?" asked another youngster Scratch did not know.

"*Pote Ani,* please forgive our brash manners," Three Iron apologized. "These boys—Turns Back and Don't Mix—they are as amazed as I am just how beautiful Magpie has become in the year since she has been away."

With a guarded sigh, he took a moment and studied his daughter as the last three members of his family came to a halt around him. The girl was every bit as beautiful as her mother must have been at that young age—which made Scratch wonder if Magpie herself would choose to wait for just the right man . . . or if she would allow herself to be swept off her feet by the first suitor who turned her head with sweet talk and a bevy of pretty presents.

"Magpie?" breathed the youngster named Don't Mix. "You are now the prettiest girl in our camp!"

She dropped her eyes as Waits asked, "Husband, who are these young men?"

"We are some of the camp guards. My name is Stiff Arm," the horseman introduced himself.

"Who is this one who talks to my young daughter without waiting for her mother's permission?" Waits asked, her eyes boring into the guard next to Three Iron.

"I-I am Don't Mix," he answered, grown a bit anxious in the face of a mother's sternness.

"Who is your mother, Don't Mix?" she asked him abruptly. "Do I know her?"

"I d-don't know—"

"Maybe I should know her first before you take the liberty of talking to my daughter, Don't Mix."

"I apologize for him," Turns Back volunteered, off to the side. "Maybe we forget ourselves and our manners when we see how pretty a girl has come back to live in our camp."

She turned to look at the one who had spoken up. "Do I know your mother?"

"Yes, I think you do," the boy declared. "She has told me you and she were friends when you were children yourselves."

"What is her name?"

Turns Back said, "Bends. Her name is—"

"Yes, Bends," Waits repeated. "She is your mother?" When the youngster nodded, she looked him up and down. "Are you sure? You are not the skinny little boy I knew as the son of my friend. Where is that little boy who had such big feet and skinny legs that I was always afraid he would trip over his moccasins and break a bone?"

All around Turns Back the other youngsters were sniggering behind their hands, just the way young men would do when one of them had fun poked at him.

Turns Back swallowed hard to keep down his anger at them and said, "That little boy . . . he is no longer a little boy, Waits-by-the-Water. He has grown up . . . and wears even bigger moccasins now!"

"I can see," she told him, gazing down at his sizable feet. "This name of yours, Turns Back, is it a new name?"

"Yes," the boy answered. "I was given the name last spring."

Stiff Arm explained, "Turns Back got his name when he turned back into a buffalo herd on foot to kill one more cow for his family. All the older men, they said it was a brave thing to do for his family, that no one else had ever done such a thing—and on foot! Later that day, the old shaman, Real Bird, said it was just as he had seen it in a dream."

"So you were very brave that day?" Titus asked the youngster.

"My uncles gave me the new name for my bravery, yes."

Waits took a deep breath and rocked back in her saddle, wriggling there between the tall cantle and saddlehorn, both of them ornamented with long fringes and colorful porcupine quills. "I am glad to see you again, Turns Back, who is no longer a little boy with big feet. I am very much looking forward to seeing your mother again. I want to tell her how proud she should be that you remember your manners so well . . . when there are other young men who do not remember what their mothers tried to teach them."

As she said these last few words, her eyes fell on the youngster called Don't Mix. His eyes were promptly downcast, and a crestfallen look crossed his face. By all appearances, he was duly chastised by an older woman, the mother of a young and beautiful girl—right in front of that girl, no less!

"Tell me," Bass inquired, "where is Yellow Belly's village headed now? Are you still hunting for buffalo?"

Many of the others turned their eyes to look at Stiff Arm, but it was Three Iron who spoke up first.

"The One Who Used to Lead Us . . . he died night before last."

"Y-Yellow Belly," Titus stammered, forgetting the custom of not speaking the name of one who had passed on. "He's dead?"

"Yes," answered Stiff Arm. "The old ones met for a long time last night, but they did not decide on a new chief. So they went off to their beds and will meet again tonight."

"He wasn't killed?" Titus asked, astonished at the news.

"No, he fell sick many days ago while we were far to the north," Three Iron stated. "He immediately ordered the camp to start south again for the Elk River."*

"The One Who Used to Lead Us firmly believed that if he got back to the Elk River and could cross it to the south, touching once more the land where he was born," Stiff Arm continued the story, "he would be healed."

"But . . ." —and Three Iron paused—"he did not live to make it back to the river."

Titus gazed at Waits a long moment, watching how the gravity of this news

---

* Yellowstone River.

struck her too. When he finally looked back at these youngsters, all of them less than a third of his age, Scratch said quietly, "He was . . . your chief was younger than me. Healthy, and strong as a warhorse. I cannot believe that he would be brought down by anything but the hand of his enemies in battle."

"Everyone thought the same thing," Turns Back suddenly commented. "That is why the news caught every man in camp by surprise. Our chief was so strong and vigorous."

"How did this happen?"

Three Iron explained, "He grew sick one day while we were out hunting buffalo—most of the men in our camp were on the hunt."

"Who was with him?" Titus asked. "Any of you?"

They turned to look at Don't Mix.

The brash youngster now said, "I was near him, watched him rein up his horse. By the time I got my head turned around to find out why he was stopping in the middle of the buffalo chase, he had both hands clawing at his chest . . . and he was slowly falling off his horse."

"Did you go back for him?"

Don't Mix nodded. "I called for help, from anyone in the sound of my voice. Those who were close enough to hear came running to help, but I don't think there was anything any of us could do."

Now Stiff Arm took up the story, "The older men called up one of the travois the women had brought out to the hill overlooking the buffalo herd. We loaded him on it and hurried him back to camp."

"Real Bird was called to make ready his medicine," Three Iron said. "Even before we got our chief back to camp."

Titus asked, "Was he still alive when he reached the village?"

"Yes," Stiff Arm replied. "He was breathing hard, like a man running uphill on foot. And sweating too, even though it was a very cool day."

"Did he say anything to you?"

It was quiet a moment, then Three Iron said, "He did not speak until Real Bird was standing over the travois when it arrived in camp, when the healer started to pray. That was three nights ago."

"What did he say to the old shaman?"

Three Iron looked at Titus, explaining, "Our chief wanted the healer to hurry him back to the Yellowstone as fast as the men could drag him on that travois. To start immediately and not stop until he was on the south bank."

Stiff Arm continued. "He swore he did not want to die north of the Elk River."

For a moment he studied their young faces, their averted eyes. These young men had something more to say than they were telling him. Finally Bass prodded them, "Why was your chief so afraid to die north of the river?"

When the rest would not speak, Turns Back admitted, "When our chief finally stopped breathing, Real Bird made his announcement to the camp . . . and said that he had always been afraid of dying so close to Blackfoot country."

"Why was he afraid of that?" Titus asked. "Many a good Crow warrior has died *in* Blackfoot country."

"It was the old seer, Real Bird, who made him afraid—many, many summers ago, when he was a young man like us," Stiff Arm declared. "Back before he became a war chief, Real Bird told him that he had a vision that as long as He Who Is No Longer Here stayed close to the Elk River, he would live long as a leader of the people. But if he ever stayed too long north of the river, venturing too far into the land where the Blackfoot roamed . . . that the spirits would not be strong in him and he would be weakened, grow sick, and die."

"Then your chief had every reason to be afraid," Titus said. "The old healer had seen his end in a dream . . . and it came to pass."

"And the same for you?" Three Iron asked. "Will it come to pass too? What Real Bird saw in a dream about your final day?"

Bass strove to wave off the old seer's prophecy, saying, "Not every dream comes true." He looked at Waits a moment, saw her eyes cloud with doubt.

"That old man has rarely been wrong," Stiff Arm declared.

"For more winters than any of you have been alive, I have come and gone from Absaroka," Titus explained to them. Just the saying of those words, made him suddenly feel all the older here before these youngsters. In those days among the hardwood forests of Boone County, he had been like them: their blood running hot like a potent sap through their veins—undeniable and unstoppable, with their whole lives ahead of them.

Sore from the long rides they had been making every day on this journey north, he flexed his sore back. Then Scratch responded, "Then—if old man Real Bird's dreams are true it means I am destined to leave and return to the land of the Crow one more time. From that day on I must make sure I never leave my wife's people again, so no trouble comes to all who are around me."

Three Iron smiled, glancing quickly at Magpie when he said, "I think some of our young men truly would like it if your family never left the Crow at all!"

Gazing at his daughter, whose high cheekbones were blushed with the rose of embarrassment, her eyes fixed on the withers of her horse, Scratch said, "You be sure to tell all those who have ears that it will be a long time before Magpie's father entertains a suitor for her. This is only her fourteenth winter, so they are wasting their time if they come scratching at our lodge door."

Some of the older guards quickly turned their eyes on the younger members of their group. But instead of looking away, Don't Mix said, "Your daughter is a fine prize, no matter how long a man has to wait."

"But you stay away from her," Bass reminded. "Don't come around our lodge at all."

Looking squarely at the father, Turns Back asked, "Will you let the camp

know when you decide Magpie is old enough for us to court her? In the old tradition of telling the camp that your daughter is ready to take a husband?"

For a moment he caught his wife's eyes. Waits-by-the-Water barely lowered
her lids and dropped her chin slightly, just enough to signal him. Scratch turned
back to the handsome young warrior and said, "Yes. We will tell all the people
when Magpie is ready to leave our lodge and start a life of her own, with a husband of her choosing."

Don't Mix tapped himself on the chest and asked, "You will give your
daughter away to one of us?"

"Perhaps," Scratch replied. "Maybe only Real Bird knows what the future
holds for any of us. As for you and me . . . the seasons to come will have to remain a deep mystery."

Which is the way he had always preferred it.

TWENTY-FOUR

"T-T-Ti-tuzz!" Waits whispered softly.

As he awoke Waits-by-the-Water was already huffing—gritting her teeth while her breath came quick and labored. Scratch rolled toward her, onto his right hip, and propped himself up on an elbow, about ready to ask her what troubled her so . . . then felt the dampness. Slipping a hand between them, his fingers brushed over the blanket she had been sleeping on every night for the past two weeks. Initially he had thought she folded the blanket up in four layers beneath her to provide a little more insulation from the frozen ground.

But that first night she stretched out upon that old red blanket, Waits had explained, "I think this child's time is soon."

Now he discovered the blanket below her buttocks was damp, quickly growing chill. Worried, he immediately brought his fingers to his nose and sniffed at them. Not the smell of blood, more so her fragrance.

"How long ago?" he asked as he sat upright.

Her head plopped down onto the horsehair pillow, weary from the effort. "Not long now," she said, exhaustion apparent in her voice.

"Why didn't you wake me before?"

She turned to gaze at him in the dim light, a grin written on her face. "What are you going to do to make this any easier for me, husband?"

Turning, he pitched some small pieces of broken limb onto the embers. "I could make more light, warm the lodge for you too."

He leaned forward, grabbed his long hair in one hand to keep it out of the ash and coals, then blew several times on the fire to excite the flickering flames. "And," he continued, considering whether he could call upon the services of a midwife, "I could go get Bear Below to help us—to help you give birth to this child."

Before she had a chance to answer, Waits-by-the-Water looped her hands beneath her thighs and scrunched up with another strong contraction, her eyes clenched shut as she huffed noisily. So noisily he thought she was going to awaken the children. Titus turned and looked at Magpie's side of the lodge. The girl was already awake, her eyes wide as capote buttons as she watched in silence. He turned to the boys' side of the lodge, finding Flea's eyes open. But Jackrabbit hadn't moved.

"Is your brother awake, Flea?"

The boy looked closely, then said, "No."

"Let him sleep," Scratch whispered. "Do you want to stay while your little brother or sister is born?"

For a moment Flea looked across the fire at Magpie, then answered. "I'll stay here with our mother while she delivers this child."

"Magpie?" he asked his daughter.

"S-stay," she confessed. "Last time—when Jackrabbit was born—I was too little to understand. Now I can see, and I want to know how a woman suffers when she gives life to a child."

"This is a good thing," he said, but thought better of it and turned back to Waits. "The children, they can stay to watch this event with their own eyes?"

She nodded clumsily, huffing her way through the end of that long contraction. "Y-yes, they can stay with us."

"Flea," Scratch directed, "put on your coat and go to Bear Below's lodge. Tell her your mother's time has come and we need her here now."

Carefully crawling over his little brother, Flea sat down next to the rekindled fire and pulled on his heavy, thickly furred winter moccasins. Then he dragged his blanket coat over his arms, stood and lashed it around his waist with a sash before ducking from the lodge door. A cold gust snaked its way through the portal before Flea got the stiffened door flap closed, along with a dusting of powdery flakes.

"It's snowing again, Magpie," Bass prodded her. "Get up and come help me."

She immediately kicked her way out of the blankets and robes, sliding on her knees closer to the fire where she rubbed her hands together over the rekindled warmth. "What can I do, Popo?"

"Bring more of that wood beside the door over here by the fire. You're going to start heating up some water as I hold your mother while this baby comes."

After she had begun to drag some of the broken limbs toward the fire pit, Magpie asked, "Did you hold my mother like that while I was being born?"

"I did at first," he declared. "Then I was shooed out of the room."

"In Mateo's house." She repeated the lesson she had learned in Taos last winter. "And when Flea was born?"

"I always promised her I would be with her when a child's time came to be born," he explained. "Except I was a long, long way off when Jackrabbit came along."

"B-but you did not even know"—Waits huffed—"that I was carrying—your new child when you—left to go trapping that spring."

"I would have been there for Jackrabbit, Magpie," he apologized, "if I had known not to go to the land of the Mexican horses. Bring your mother some water to drink."

He had Waits propped up against him by the time Magpie brought over a half-filled tin cup. After her mother had finished the next long contraction, Waits took a sip of the cold water, then a long drink, letting it wash down her dry throat deliciously. He heard the crunch of footsteps outside, the low murmur of voices just before the heavy, frozen deerhide was dragged aside and in came that spindly leg wrapped in a wool blanket legging, a buffalo moccasin so big that it made her feet look three or four times as big as they really were. Bear Below stood hunched over, one of the old woman's arms supported by Flea. This was the boy's eleventh winter, and he had begun to shoot up in the same weedy way his father had when he had been the same age back in faraway Rabbit Hash on the Ohio River.

"Did the boy wake you?" Titus asked.

"I have been waiting for this baby too, so I heard him coming to get me," the old woman responded, tearing off her coat. "Look at those feet of his!" and she pointed at Flea's moccasins. "This one could never creep up on anyone!"

She passed her blanket coat to Flea, then started shuffling around the fire pit to the rear of the small lodge. "You have had three births already?"

When Waits could only nod, Titus said, "Yes, this is her fourth birthing."

"So, child—tell me how it is for you."

"Not hard. I think this child will come easy."

"I will see for myself," Bear Below stated.

She slowly collapsed to her knees on the bedding, squatting at the feet of Waits-by-the-Water, and dragged back the top blanket so she could reach under it with both hands. Closing her wrinkled eyelids, Bear Below turned her head as if staring at the fire with those closed eyes while she felt about. Just about the time Waits began to pant through her nose again, Bear Below said, "That's good. Let it come over you and carry you with it. Do not tense . . . do not— that's it. You must remember not to tense your body, girl. Stay loose and the child will slide on out into this world."

Bear Below rocked back onto a bony hip and settled there between the up-folded legs of the mother.

"Did you see or feel the child's head?" Waits inquired.

"Not yet," the old woman reassured her. "But very soon I think." Then Bear Below turned to the white man. "Tell me, do you make good coffee?"

"I do—but I want to stay here beside my wife."

Bear Below shifted her bottom so she could look over her shoulder at Magpie. "What is your name?"

"Magpie."

"Do you make good coffee?"

She looked at her father, and he nodded. "Y-yes, I . . . well, my father tells me I do."

"Make us a pot of your coffee, Magpie."

As his daughter busied herself with the pot and some coffee grounds they brought north from Fort Bridger, Titus instructed his son, "Bring some more of that wood over here by the fire."

The pot hadn't been on the flames very long when Waits-by-the-Water announced, "It-it's time now."

Bear Below was already there between the mother's knees, pushing the blanket off her legs, folding up the bottom of the long hide dress onto the swollen belly so that she had an unobstructed view of the birth opening. "Yes, girl—I think I see the head coming now."

"I feel him coming!"

"A boy?" Titus asked his wife. "You think this is another boy?"

She nodded as she gulped air, huffing between her gritted teeth.

The old woman cooed, "There you go, easy now. That's the head. Let's turn a little and let those shoulders out too."

Doing his best to keep his wife propped up as he leaned to the side, Titus attempted to get a look at this babe being born.

"You are doing good, mother," Bear Below cheered as Magpie crabbed up close behind the old woman, looking over her hunched shoulders. "Just a little more. This next time you can push hard for me."

Staring transfixed on the child emerging into the world, Magpie's mouth hung open. "Little brother—do you want to see this?"

Flea asked, "Are you talking to me or to Jackrabbit?"

Magpie finally turned, finding Jackrabbit awake on the far side of the lodge, curiously watching the adults. "I was asking you, Flea."

"N-no. I am fine right here where I am. I can see plenty well right here."

"It's a good thing too, Flea," Titus told his eldest son. "You don't want to get in the way right now—"

"It is done!" Bear Below cried out, moving that small child out of the shadows and into the fire's illumination.

"Wh-what do we have for a child?" Waits inquired expectantly when the babe let out a gush of air, then began to howl.

Holding the newborn aloft, the long, purplish umbilical cord descending from its belly to disappear between the mother's legs, Bear Below announced, "You have another girl!"

Waits began to cry, her tears tumbling off the edge of her face onto his arm. Bass wrapped up his wife in his arms, clutching her against him tightly. Then he slowly lowered her back onto the horsehair pillows and wiped the beads of sweat from her forehead. "We have another girl!"

"Here, white father of this new daughter," Bear Below grumbled at him. "Hold your baby while I cut this cord and finish delivering this mother."

Starting to tremble as he held out his hands to the old midwife, Titus felt his tears spill down his hot cheeks, his vision blurring with a salty sting. "L-look, Magpie!" he whispered as the child was laid in his arms. "You have a sister."

Waits attempted to raise herself onto her elbows. But Bear Below scolded her, "Lay down while I finish the birthing, girl."

So the new mother asked her husband, "Which of us does she favor?"

Bear Below looked up, her eyes briefly assaying Magpie. "Your oldest daughter—she clearly favors her mother, and a pretty creature at that."

"Let me see her," Waits begged.

"I think she will be a pretty one too," Titus observed.

Stopping the work of her hands, the midwife said, "Even if she does look more like her father."

"Oh, she does!" Waits gushed, clapping her hands together. She then reached out with both arms, imploring. "Here, I want to hold her too, husband."

"Yes, see if she is ready to suckle," he suggested as he positioned his infant daughter in the cradle of her mother's arms and rolled her cheek against a swollen breast. The babe blinked its eyes in the flickering firelight and latched onto the nipple Waits rubbed against the girl's lower lip.

"I-I wish my mother were here to see this granddaughter," Waits sobbed, her shoulders trembling as she brushed a dark lock of her newborn's damp hair back from the brow. She looked up at her oldest daughter. "How proud my mother was of you, Magpie."

She was crying too when she told her mother, "I think she would be very proud of this new granddaughter."

Waits looked at her husband a moment, then again at Magpie. "Tell me, daughter—you watched your sister come into this world. Are you ready to be a mother yourself?"

She shook her head emphatically. "No. Not yet, anyway. Someday. But not soon. I don't have a husband yet. Not even a suitor to court me."

"And that won't be for a long time to come," Scratch admonished, patting the robe beside him so his daughter would come sit with them.

"Here," Bear Below said, holding up a six-inch section of the whitish umbilical cord to the new father. "You will want this for your daughter's amulet."

"Put it in this empty cup," he suggested.

"You will help me make your sister's lizard," Waits declared to Magpie. "It will be good training for you—when your time comes to start having children of your own."

"I am not ready to be married yet, I already told you that," Magpie protested, then softened her tone, saying, "but I will do all I can to help you with my baby sister."

"I am relieved to hear you say you are not ready to marry, Magpie," he told his daughter. "Because your father isn't at all ready to give you away to a young suitor!"

Three winters had come and gone. That new daughter born in the deep of an awful winter night was walking and getting her nose into everything, if not her busy little hands. And what a talker she was, almost from the start. Noisy as a little bird.

In fact, Waits had named this little girl Crane, after her own mother who had taken sick not long after Bass brought his family back to Absaroka late that autumn of '47. Whatever it was that sucked away at Crane's strength and made her weaker by the day had been merciful in taking the old woman quickly. In that year they had been south to Taos and away to Bridger's post, this woman had wasted away to little more than skin and bones, so light when Titus picked up her body and carried her to their lodge there beside the Yellowstone as the first snowfall whipped around their camp opposite the mouth of the Bighorn River. She almost felt dried up, desiccated, as if she had been lying out in that hot, endless desert the Ammuchabas* called their home.

The family cared for the old woman at that camp, and at two more campsites in the weeks that followed, until Crane finally gave up breathing one morning, no more tears seeping from the edges of her tired eyes. While she had been ailing, slowly dying, Titus hadn't thought he would end up crying when she was gone . . . but there he was, tying the pieces of broken, discarded lodgepoles across tree branches for her scaffold, the hot tears spilling down his cold cheeks and disappearing into his whitening beard. After Waits and Magpie had cleaned the old woman's body and dressed it in her finest, they sewed the body up in a brand-new blue blanket—her mother's favorite color—a blanket brought north from Fort Bridger as a gift to the old one. Now it would weather in the rains and snows, in the ceaseless winds that haunted this high, hard land. The bright blue blanket slowly rotting like the body sewn inside it, returning to the winds that moaned through the bones that would bleach beneath the sun, winter and summer, and winter again in that endless circle that was life, and death, and life anew.

On the village moved, under the new chief—Pretty On Top—Titus's old

---

* The mountain man's word for the Mojave Indians.

friend.* Over the years the once-impetuous horse thief who had been but a brash and daring youngster when Titus met him twenty winters ago had become a warrior of great note, offering wise counsel, bravely holding off his people's enemies, kind and thoughtful in the tradition of the great Arapooesh. Often were the times when Bass had hoped a young leader much like Pretty On Top would court his daughter when her time came. But in the past few weeks those hopes had been hung out to dry. During this warming time of the year, when thunderstorms rumbled out of the west and Magpie celebrated her eighteenth spring, the first suitor to come scratching at the doorpole was Don't Mix.

"Stay away from my lodge," Scratch grumbled at the handsome suitor. "Don't come around me or my daughter and there won't be trouble between us."

The brash young warrior took a step back and spread out his arms indignantly. "There doesn't have to be any trouble for us, Uncle," he said, using that familiar term of respect for an older man. Don't Mix glanced left, and he looked right. "I don't see any other young man come to call on your daughter. I think I am the only one who will marry her."

"Go away," Titus snapped. He did not like the man's cockiness, wondering too if he had ever come off sounding so sure of himself when he was a youngster full of rutting juice. "Even if you are the last one she could marry in all of Absaroka, I would still not accept your presents!"

"One day soon I will bring you a lot of presents, Uncle." The young man again used that term of familial closeness that served only to grate down Scratch's backbone. "But for now—I must first make Magpie fall in love with me. So I will return tonight with my flute and play love songs for her."

"I'm warning you—don't come back," Bass hissed menacingly, his eyes narrowed at the warrior who started to turn away with a wide grin on his handsome face. "You will make a lot of trouble for yourself if you bother my family."

"Tell your daughter I will play my music for only her," Don't Mix promised, as if he hadn't paid any attention to the white man's warning, "tonight, when the moon rises off the hills."

"No one will be listening!" he bellowed at the young man's back, angrier still as the warrior walked away.

"Don't treat him so badly," his wife said behind him.

Surprised, Titus turned there in front of the lodge and found Waits-by-the-Water stepping from the open doorway. Right behind her came Magpie.

"Why shouldn't I treat him that way if I don't like him, don't want him around Magpie?"

Glancing quickly at her daughter, Waits said, "We don't have to like our daughter's suitor, Ti-tuzz."

"W-we don't?" he asked, bewildered by his wife's assertion as his youngest

---

* *Crack in the Sky*

daughter followed them into the sunlight. "Wait, I get it. I suppose this is again one of those matters of the heart that a man is simply too stupid to figure out."

His wife took one of his old, bony hands in both of hers and said, "No, we don't have to like our daughter's suitor. Only she has to."

It slowly dawned on him, the way the sun came up at the edge of the earth. He looked from his wife's face to Magpie's. "Is this true, daughter?"

Magpie bent to pick up her younger sister and positioned the child across her left hip. "I think he is handsome, Popo."

"You've told your mother this, and you did not tell me?"

Magpie dropped her eyes. "We've talked about him, the two of us, yes."

"Your daughter told me of her feelings, Ti-tuzz," Waits explained to her angry husband. "Don't Mix is a very handsome young man. Any girl would be proud if he came to court her with his flute songs under the stars."

"Even though I never played a flute for you—"

"You didn't have to, husband," she declared. "I already knew my heart belonged to you. Your flute songs didn't have to capture it from me."

After a moment of fuming that he was the last to be let in on this secret, he asked, "Are you trying to talk me into accepting this Don't Mix with your sweet words, woman?"

"No, think for yourself, husband. Don't Mix is a good warrior—since we met him those winters ago, you have seen how many successful raids he has led. Not only his good friends like Stiff Arm and Three Irons and Turns Back, but many others are always ready to go on Don't Mix's raids into the land of the Blackfoot or the Lakota."

He did his best to calm the squirm of apprehension wriggling inside him, feeling as if these two women had already made up their minds and now they were going to twist him around to their way of thinking about this young suitor.

"So Don't Mix is a handsome man—"

"Very handsome, Popo," Magpie interrupted with an enthusiasm that made her eyes sparkle. "The most handsome man in the camp!"

Titus continued, "And he is a good war leader too."

"Yes," Waits replied. "As a man, that is something you can easily agree on. You want a strong war leader for your daughter's husband."

"Wait!" he growled, holding up his hand as he whirled on Magpie. "Your mother is telling me you not only are ready to have suitors call on our lodge, ready to let them play their flute songs for you and talk to you beneath the blanket . . . but you are ready to marry?"

Her head nodded tentatively. "Are you angry because I want to marry?"

That made him stop and consider a moment. "I . . . I don't know, Magpie. Perhaps I am not ready to think of my little girl moving away from her mother and father, marrying a man and leaving us to start her own family."

"But I am not moving away," Magpie protested. "I will always be close. We will live in the same village."

"W-we?" he stammered. "Already you and Don't Mix are a *we*?"

Waits quickly hoisted little Crane from Magpie's arms and set the child on her own hip, laying an arm over Magpie's shoulders as she said, "Your oldest daughter has had her eye on that handsome young warrior ever since that first day we came back from the Blanket Chief's post on Black's Fork, when Don't Mix proclaimed just how beautiful he thought Magpie was."

Titus looked at his daughter closely. "You have made up your mind on him?"

"Yes." Then she tried out her winning smile on him.

"There is nothing I can say to convince you to leave your mind open and entertain other suitors until you can decide among them?"

Waits answered quickly, "This is not a matter of her mind, Ti-tuzz. This is a matter for her heart."

"I want Don't Mix to play his flute songs for me," Magpie said, holding up her folded hands before her as if pleading with her father. "I want all the other girls in camp to see him courting me—all those other girls who swoon when they watch him walk past them, when they talk about him among themselves at the creekbank. I want them to be so jealous of me."

He wagged his head slowly now, eventually admitting, "I have never been afraid of taking on two enemies at one time in battle. Most often, they get in one another's way. But against the two of you . . . I am beaten even before I can start!"

"You will let Don't Mix come to our lodge and play his love songs for our daughter?" asked Waits-by-the-Water.

Titus nodded once, very grudgingly.

Magpie lunged against him, wrapping her arms around him tightly. "Oh, Popo! You will never be sorry for letting me have who I want for a husband."

Laying his cheek down on the top of her head, he breathed in the sweet smell of her hair and remembered how Waits-by-the-Water had scented her own braids with crushed sage and dried wildflowers in the days of her youth. Then he reluctantly said, "I never want to regret letting Don't Mix court you, Magpie. But even more important—I don't ever want you to be sorry for that either."

The camp was on the move early that summer of '51, travois swaying under the weight of extra winter hides the men were hauling to the white trader's post standing west of the mouth of the Rose Hip River* on the Elk River. After bartering for some supplies, Pretty On Top's headmen had decided the village would move southwest toward the low mountains, where they could stay in those cool elevations through the hottest days of the summer, capturing wild

---

* Rosebud Creek.

horses for breeding and even making a visit to the small cave where monumental slabs of ice kept a water seep cold all summer long. Twice each year the band made this particular pilgrimage to Fort Alexander: once in the early summer, and again late in the fall—trading those furs fleshed, grained, and softened by the women, bartering for days at a time for all that the Apsaluuke people needed as they moved through the seasons, in the footsteps of the same circle they had followed since ancient times on the Missouri River far to the east.

Every evening last spring, when the skies cleared off and the sun had set behind the fiery clouds, Don't Mix had shown up to play his love songs for Magpie. That first night he had stood right in front of the door, blowing the sweet notes from his flute. But Scratch would not let his daughter go outside the first time he showed up, nor the next two. Not until the fourth night. And then, only with her mother standing nearby, watching the two as Don't Mix finished his love songs, then stepped close to Magpie to talk in tones so low even Waits-by-the-Water could not hear what the two young lovers were saying to one another. It wasn't too many more days, she had explained to her husband, before the two young people stood with their foreheads touching, holding one another's hands, gazing into each other's eyes as they whispered their sweet entreaties beneath the spring starlight.

Sometimes, Titus found an excuse to slip outside the lodge after dinner as the night sky grew dark, carrying his clay pipe and tobacco pouch with him, finding a patch of nearby shadow beneath an overhanging tree or sometimes nestled back against a neighbor's lodge—where he could watch and listen as this young man courted his daughter. It still rankled him that both women had convinced him that Don't Mix was a superb catch for Magpie . . . because something still troubled him inside about the union. He did not know why he suffered those misgivings, but he believed that if he watched from hiding, he might learn enough either to refuse the young man as a suitor to Magpie or to grudgingly accept the young warrior.

"Can Flea come with me, down to the horses?"

Scratch looked up in surprise at Turns Back. The young man hadn't made a sound as he came out of the trees behind the spot where the white man sat at the edge of the clearing—a father watching those two young lovers standing near the lodge, both of them wrapped in a single blanket, their foreheads touching as they whispered in low tones.

"Yes," he said.

Scratch patted the ground beside him. The youngster settled close before his own eyes went to staring directly at the couple. For a long time Titus was aware that Turns Back kept his attention trained on his good friend and Magpie without saying a word to explain why he had come to ask about Flea.

Clearing his throat, Bass said, "Many nights you come to spend time with Flea."

"Yes," Turns Back agreed, his eyes landing briefly on the white man before he concentrated again on the couple some distance away, young lovers totally unaware they were watched by a friend and a father. "Flea may be much younger than me, but he is nonetheless a good companion."

"You like spending time with my son?"

"Yes, he has taught me a lot about horses in the time we have been together."

He reflected on that, watching how the young man kept looking at the couple. Then Titus asked, "You come no other time to see Flea. Only in the evening."

"After supper, yes."

"Now that I think about it, you come to see Flea whenever your friend Don't Mix is here courting Flea's sister."

His eyes slowly came to the white man's face. "Is that true? I did not realize I came to see my friend when Magpie was talking with Don't Mix."

Again he did not immediately speak, but instead watched as the young man's gaze went back to the couple. Eventually Bass dared to flush out the inner ways of this youngster's heart, asking, "Are you ever jealous of your friend Don't Mix?"

"Jealous? Why?"

"Because he has won the heart of Magpie."

To that point Turns Back had been wearing a mask stoically devoid of emotion. But now his face showed a visible hint of regret. "Has h-he won Magpie's heart? Is this true?"

"I think so," Bass said with his own regret. "After all, no other has come to court her."

"Don't Mix, he is a handsome man."

"Is he?" Titus asked. "That's what the girls think, but is he handsome to his friends as well?"

"Yes, I can see why any girl, and especially someone as pretty as Magpie, would give her heart to such a handsome warrior," Turns Back explained. "For years now I have seen how the girls look at Don't Mix."

"And you've wished the girls looked at you the same way?"

"Yes . . . I mean, I used to wish that," the youngster said. "But, after some time, I realized that they never would, especially Magpie, because I am not a handsome man the way Don't Mix is so . . . so—"

"Pretty?"

Turns Back looked at him. "Yes, he is so handsome he is pretty. I can see why Magpie gave him her heart."

"But does he have a good heart to give her in return?"

"Yes. You will be his father-in-law. Don't worry about your daughter. Don't Mix will take good care of her, and treat her well."

"But is he the best man for her?" Titus prodded. "Isn't there another who would treat her far better, love her far more deeply than Don't Mix ever could?"

"How could that be?" he asked, looking at the white man.

"Because a big part of Don't Mix's heart is in love with himself," Titus explained. "Couldn't there be someone else who has a very strong heart for my daughter, someone who has never spoken up to her about his feelings . . . some young man who will love her better than any man ever could . . . because his love is truly hers alone, and not mixed up with his love for himself?"

"I-I don't know what you are getting at."

Titus reached out and laid his old hand on the youngster's bare knee, saying, "I have always thought that the most important reason why Don't Mix began courting my daughter is that she is pretty enough for such a handsome warrior to have as his wife. She will look good with him. Everyone will say that they are a handsome couple. He did not ever think that Magpie's beauty could lie beneath her skin as well. He was never interested in what lay inside my daughter."

"Perhaps he has not thought to look inside to see how beautiful she is—"

"Tell me what you think about my daughter, Turns Back." He nudged the warrior, squeezing the youth's knee paternally. "Better yet, tell me why you never came to court her yourself."

He turned, stared at the old trapper, and swallowed hard. "I don't know what you want me to say—"

"Say what is in your heart. What you feel about Magpie."

The young man looked again at the couple, staring a long time before he finally spoke. "I think she is the finest woman any man could marry."

"Because she is beautiful?"

Turns Back shook his head. "No. Because she is gentle. I have seen her with Jackrabbit, and little Crane. She will make a fine mother to her children."

"What else do you think about her?"

"I think Don't Mix is the luckiest man alive."

That made his heart feel so heavy and sad. Titus felt the hot sting of tears there in the dark as a tall, thin, and weedy youngster emerged from his parents' lodge and noticed the couple. Flea shook his head in adolescent disgust, then turned and hollered into the darkness.

"Popo!"

"Over here, son!"

Flea started toward them. Turns Back clambered to his feet, dusting off his breechclout. Titus got up much slower than the young man. He grabbed the warrior's wrist.

"Don't you think Magpie deserves to hear what you think of her?"

"I-I never could—"

"My daughter deserves to know," he whispered insistently.

"Don't Mix is my friend. I don't want to embarrass him or Magpie."

"Maybe Flea deserves a good brother-in-law too," Titus reflected.

"I like Flea," he said as the fourteen-year-old youth stepped up to them in the shadows.

"I hope you like me," Flea said, with a fraternal grin. "I've taught you almost everything you'll ever know about horses."

Turns Back laughed at that, in an easy way that made Titus feel all the more affection for this shy and selfless warrior.

"So," Turns Back said as he laid a hand on Flea's shoulder, "I know as much as you about horses, my friend!"

Flea snorted with that same easy laughter that had always had a special place in his father's ear. He said to his older friend, "That's where you are wrong, Turns Back. I've taught you everything you'll ever know about horses, right?"

"Right."

"But," said Flea, "I haven't taught you everything *I* know about horses!"

All three of them laughed together as Turns Back pounded the young man on the back. Already Flea stood an inch taller than his father, almost as tall as Turns Back. Then the young warrior sighed and turned, gazing again at the couple.

"I will speak to her for you," Scratch said quietly. "If you won't speak for yourself."

"No, no. I could not have you do that," Turns Back protested. "There's no reason to cause trouble for the two of them."

Flea studied the two older men suspiciously and asked, "Are you talking about Magpie? Are you?"

"Yes," Titus answered, laying a hand on his son's shoulder. "I think the wrong man is courting your sister, Flea."

The youngster whirled on the warrior, saying with exasperation, "All this time I thought you were *my* friend! Why couldn't you be honest with me and tell me you were only acting like you were my friend because you wanted to be around my sister—"

"I do want to be your friend." And he put out a hand to grip the young man's arm.

Flea shrugged it off, taking a step back, saying angrily, "How can I believe you anymore?"

"He's telling you the truth, Flea," Titus soothed. "Turns Back has never said anything to Magpie because he did not want to wreck his friendship with Don't Mix."

"But he doesn't mind wrecking his friendship with me!"

"I don't want that to happen, Flea," Turns Back pleaded.

"This is an honorable man," Scratch told his son. "If he could never bring himself to confess his feelings for Magpie, how was that being dishonest with you?"

Flea stood there, staring at the ground for a long time. "I don't know—"

"Listen, Flea," Turns Back said. "To prove to you just how much I want to be your friend, I want you to know that I will never tell your sister what I feel for her."

"Y-you'd do that for me?" Flea asked.

"Yes, because I want to stay your friend. I would rather know that you trusted me than to have your sister fall in love with me. I could never marry your sister knowing that you thought I had betrayed you."

"Do you see how honorable a man he is?"

Turning to glance at his father a moment, Flea looked at Turns Back and asked, "You . . . really do feel this strong in your heart for my sister?"

"Yes," he admitted.

"But—you never told her?"

"No."

Flea looked at his father and said with a grin, "I think Magpie is going to marry the wrong man."

Titus himself smiled, his heart swelling with pride and happiness. "I am glad you see things the same as I do, son."

Turning back to the warrior, Flea said, "If you do not want to tell her yourself, I will tell my sister how you feel about her. Tonight, after Don't Mix has gone—"

"N-n-no, Flea," he pleaded. "I cannot make things hard on Magpie, or for my friend Don't Mix."

"But," Titus said, "didn't you tell me Magpie deserves the very best husband? The man who can love her the way she deserves to be loved?"

The young warrior eventually nodded with great reluctance.

"So," Scratch asked him, "which of us will it be who tells Magpie that she is making a mistake to marry Don't Mix? Will it be me, her father? Or Flea, her brother . . . or—"

"It will be me," Turns Back interrupted, drawing back his shoulders there in the dark. "It is my heart the words must come from."

TWENTY-FIVE

By the middle of that summer's moons, the two young lovers were no longer standing with the blanket wrapped around them and their foreheads touching. Instead, Waits-by-the-Water told them they could put the blanket over their heads to give them just about all the privacy young lovers could enjoy before they exchanged commitment vows in front of their families and friends.

But, it hadn't been an easy journey seeing Magpie to her wedding day. For some time Titus Bass had known women were a headstrong bunch. He'd not encountered anything to change his opinion on that until he found out there was indeed a creature more headstrong than any woman he had ever known . . . and that was an adolescent female with her juices all stirred up for a handsome young warrior. How the family had ever gotten to this warm summer day without killing one another would be a story worth telling his grandchildren over and over again. A tale of pain and tears, a tale of just how the heart could shatter into innumerable pieces. A story of how Magpie eventually won a victory, how she had triumphed in what her heart wanted most.

Above the grassy meadow in sight of the log walls of Meldrum's Fort Alexander the sun was reaching its zenith and the crowd had gathered, murmuring quietly, as Titus led Waits-by-the-Water through their midst, slowly making a circle of the great camp crescent, moving at the head of the throng, gathering more and more onlookers, who followed them back toward their lodge. Eventually they stood before their own door as the crowd parted and the pony carrying the young warrior came through the whispering people. Yes, he had never looked more handsome—this proud, young war leader. On a pony beside the youngster rode the old seer, Real Bird, his eyes grown even more milky of late. The pair of horsemen stopped before the lodge of the white man and his Crow wife, dismounting and handing their reins to young herder boys who led the animals away.

The crowd fell to a hush as the young man took the old prophet's arm and led Real Bird those last few steps, so that they both stood before the trapper who had made his home among the Apsaluuke people.

"Who is this comes to my lodge this day?" Titus asked as the crowd hushed.

"I am Don't Mix," the young warrior replied with a strong voice. "And I bring the holy man, Real Bird, with me."

Already Scratch had a hard lump in his throat. The words came with difficulty as he croaked, "Why do you bring this holy man, this physician, this great healer with you today, Don't Mix?"

"I bring the holy man here this day so that he can perform a wedding."

"A wedding for who, Don't Mix?"

He stood tall, a few inches above the old white man, as he proclaimed, "A wedding of your daughter—Magpie . . . and the man who loves her more than any other man ever could."

"Who . . . who is this man who dares say he loves my daughter more than any other man ever could?" Scratch demanded. "Who dares to say that he loves my Magpie more than her father?"

"I would tell you his name," Don't Mix declared in a clear voice as he took a step aside, leaving Real Bird there before Waits-by-the-Water and Titus Bass, "but he will proudly tell you himself."

"Who is this man?" the trapper demanded again, hurling his voice over the silent crowd. "I want him to show his face and tell me how much he loves my daughter before he hopes to take her hand in life's hazardous journey."

"It is me!" Turns Back announced at that dramatic moment, standing far to the side of the throng.

Expectantly, the crowd parted for his spotted pony. Behind him, Turns Back led a dozen of the finest horses in all of Absaroka. On two of them he had packed everything he owned, what few clothes and weapons were his alone, along with his shield and totems and the small shelter he and his new bride would erect at the edge of camp for their wedding night.

"Who speaks up, brave enough to say he is prepared to take my daughter from her father?" Titus roared, the lump hard in his throat, his eyes smarting as he looked upon this young man who came to a halt before the lodge.

"Turns Back is my name," he said as the crowd fell breathless and he slid from the back of that spotted pony. Then he handed Titus Bass the reins to his warhorse. "I have come here to ask that you let me marry your daughter."

Scratch turned to glance at his wife, finding that she too was crying, tears streaming down her bright copper cheeks, her eyes glistening in the midday light. He turned back to the young man, stared down at the reins in his hand, then held out those reins to the suitor. "I could never take a man's war pony, Turns Back."

An anxious murmur shot through the crowd.

"I will give away everything I own," the warrior vowed, turning slightly to indicate his poor possessions and those twelve horses. "Give you all that I have if you will only say I can marry your daughter, *Pote Ani.*"

"Take back your war pony," he declared, lifting the warrior's hand and placing the reins into his palm. "I can't accept such a gift from a courageous warrior of the people."

Turns Back stared at his hand and those reins, fear and surprise in his eyes—for this was not the way things were supposed to happen at this very moment in the ceremony.

So Titus did his very best to reassure the young man who had despair written across his face. "You are a warrior of our people," Scratch told him as his voice slowly grew stronger. "And a warrior must have a war pony to fight our enemies."

"Then take the rest of these horses," Turns Back pleaded before that hushed crowd of onlookers, murmuring about the father's refusal of gifts. "Take everything that I own—"

"You do not own very much, so it seems," Scratch chided him, looking over what little was loaded on those two ponies.

Turns Back hung his head. "I know it is not enough to pay you for the hand of someone so wonderful as your daughter, Magpie. In fact, I realize I will never own anything near enough to pay in return for a woman like Magpie."

"Look at me, Turns Back," he commanded. The warrior raised his eyes, unflinchingly steady at the white man. "I think a good man is one who gives away much of what he owns. He returns from a raid—and he gives away the horses he has stolen. He brings back blankets and weapons—he gives them away as well. Is this what you have done, Turns Back? After every raid against the Blackfoot, the Assiniboine, the Lakota, and others?"

"Yes," he answered in a clear voice. "I would have kept it all in trade for Magpie if I had known that you would want it in return for your daughter."

"No, Turns Back," he said with a stone face. "I don't want your horses. I don't want all that you own. None of it is worth anything to me."

The crowd gasped. This had never been done before. No father had ever turned down the offer of gifts for his daughter when a marriage ceremony was announced and the whole village brought together in this way. People all around them were whispering, many of them leaning in to get themselves a look at the face of Turns Back as he stood there in abject shock. This white man had just broken the long-standing tradition of the Apsaluuke.

Turns Back started to stammer, "I-I have n-nothing more to offer—"

"I want only one thing from you, Turns Back," Titus said as he reached out and took hold of his wife's hand with his left. Then he raised his right hand and held it out between himself and the young warrior, palm up. "These ponies, these weapons and totems—they are not worth anywhere near as much as what it is that I want my daughter to have from you."

"Wh-what can I give you to make you let me marry her?"

"It's not what I want from you, Turns Back," he said, seizing the warrior's wrist firmly. "It's what I want to know that you will give my daughter."

"Anything!"

"Your heart," he said to the youngster in a whisper. "Tell me she will forever have all of your heart."

Relief washed over the young man's face, and his eyes began to pool with emotion. "Yes! Yes, this I promise you!"

"Promise her . . . promise her this now," Titus said as he released his hold on the warrior's wrist and took a step back to the lodge, pulling aside the door flap.

Out of the darkness stepped a radiant white light as Turns Back gasped in surprise. Magpie had never looked more beautiful.

Her hair gleamed, shiny with bear grease, both braids intertwined with red silk ribbon, each wrapped with white ermine skins, the black tips of their tails spilling across the tops of her breasts. The fringes on the sleeves were so long on that snowy white dress they nearly brushed the ground, where she stood in a pair of matching white moccasins tied around her ankles. The entire yoke of the dress, both front and back, was covered with the milk teeth of the elk, the umber crowns which tarnished those teeth stark against the blinding whiteness of the gown. Down both shoulders ran a four-inch-wide strip of porcupine quills of brilliant colors: oxblood red, greasy yellow, robin's-egg blue, and a hint of moss green. It was truly the most beautiful dress Waits-by-the-Water and her eldest daughter could have created for this most special day.

Down the center part of her hair, Magpie had rubbed a dark strip of purple vermilion dye, and a smear of it to highlight each cheek, in addition to one wide strip of the reddish paint extending down the center of her chin. This would be the last day she could ever wear paint as a woman of the Crow. From this day on, she would no longer be a virgin. Now she would be a wife—

"Tell my daughter, Turns Back," Titus spoke in the hush of that crowd admiring the beauty of this bride who stood in their midst. "Tell Magpie what you wish to give her."

Turns Back took a step forward so that he stood right before the young woman. At last she raised her eyes to his. They never once left his face as he took the wide eagle-feather fan from her hands and passed it on to Magpie's mother.

"Magpie," he said, his voice cracking with nervousness, this time in the way of a young lover declaring himself, "I give you everything I own."

"Turns Back, I was standing inside my parents' lodge when you spoke of this to my father."

"I don't have much to give you . . . but I give it all to you." He wrapped his hands around both of hers and held them midway between their breasts.

"Do I have your heart?" she asked. "This day, and for all days?"

"Yes, oh, yes," he answered fervently.

"That is all I could ever ask of you, Turns Back," she said in the stillness of that moment. "There are others who can offer me many fine things . . . but you are the one who has won my heart. You are the one who can give me what no other man can ever give me."

"Then you will be my wife?"

"Yes, Turns Back," she said, starting to cry, smiling in spite of the tears. "I will be your wife . . . and bear your children . . . and I will wait for you when you ride off to make war on the enemies of our people . . . and—I will grow old with you, Turns Back. Like the seasons of the year, we will know our spring and summer, our autumn, and we will know our winter too. I will grow old with you . . . and I promise my heart will love you more each day of our life together."

Tears spilled from Turns Back's eyes as he looked over at the old prophet. He asked, "Real Bird, will you step over here and give us your blessing? Will you say a prayer for our union?"

Titus helped the old man shuffle closer, then pulled Waits-by-the-Water close, so that the three of them stood around the young couple, joining their arms to form a circle of love around Turns Back and Magpie as Real Bird began to sing, his high, reedy voice sailing on the breeze of that hot summer day.

The four of them were crying for joy, tears streaming from their eyes as the old prophet gave wing to his prayers for these young newlyweds, his own blind eyes closed as he raised his face and shouted at the sky.

"Creator Above! Hear me! Grant this man and his woman your every blessing. May he be strong in protecting your people . . . and may she be fruitful in bearing the generations to come!"

Opening his eyes he held out his thin, bony hands to the young couple. Slowly he raised their arms in the air with his and gave a wild, shrill cry. All around their small circle the many hundreds lifted their voices, drunk with triumph and celebration. Men yipped exuberantly, women trilled their tongues in victory calls, and children screamed and laughed, suddenly freed to dart in and out of the crowd, shrieking joyously in play.

Turns Back seized his new bride, clutching her against him tightly as they both gushed with laughter on this happy, happy day. Scratch leaned in to kiss his daughter on the cheek as Waits-by-the-Water kissed Magpie's other cheek. Then the old trapper pounded his new son-in-law on the back of his war shirt, which was draped with black-tipped winter-white ermine tails and enemy scalp locks. Suddenly among them were Jackrabbit and Flea, the tall youth lifting up little Crane so the girl could give her big sister a congratulatory embrace.

"The feasting and songs will begin as soon as we walk down to the grove by the river!" Titus roared above the tumult as the throngs surged in to shout their wishes at the newlyweds.

Led by Don't Mix, all of Turns Back's loyal friends had been helping the white man over the last few days, hunting buffalo, digging long trenches, and dragging in a great store of firewood before they started roasting huge slabs of lean, red meat over the immense beds of coal they had begun firing day before last.

"I could not have done this without you, Don't Mix," Titus said to the young warrior as they reached the crowded grove, where Magpie's girlfriends were helping to carve off chunks of buffalo for everyone pressing forward in a great wave.

"Everything is as it should be, *Pote Ani,*" he said to the trapper. "Your daughter is in love with my best friend. If she could not marry me, then she deserves to have Turns Back as her husband."

"Thank you for not standing in their way and making things hard on them when he finally went to her and spoke of the feelings in his heart," Scratch confided. "And when Magpie came to you and told you she wanted to marry another."

He smiled in that handsome face of his. "It is for the best! Now I have lots of time to look over the other girls in the village and pick one of them for my bride!"

"Titus Bass!"

He turned at the loud call, recognizing the voice of the old friend before his eye found Robert Meldrum threading his way through the milling crowd, a small brown jug suspended at the end of one arm, two tin cups looped in the fingers of the other hand.

"Round Iron!" he cried, using the Crows' name for the American Fur Company trader, which referred to Meldrum's blacksmithing abilities practiced here at Fort Alexander.

The trader had himself married into the Crow tribe, making him an invaluable asset to his employers. He had a long history in the fur trade, all the way back to '27, when he first came west with William H. Ashley's brigades, tramping across the Rocky Mountain West with the likes of Bridger, Carson, Meek, and Fitzpatrick.

"I brung some of the company's special brandy for this very special day," Meldrum announced as he stomped up in front of the old trapper and held out the cups to Bass. He winked at Waits-by-the-Water, who stood at her husband's side, clutching Scratch's arm. "This here's for a very special father of the bride!"

"Brandy, eh?" Scratch growled. "You ain't got no more hard likker buried in that hole under your bed?"

Meldrum brought the neck of the jug to his lips and bit down on the browned cork, quickly worrying it out of the top. Around the cork he said, "This here's the finest I got. Never knowed you to pass up any alcohol, Titus Bass!"

"Shuddup an' pour!"

When Meldrum had both of their cups halfway filled, he turned to Waits-by-the-Water and hoisted his tin, saying in Crow, "Here's to the mother of the bride, who always has been one of the most beautiful women in all of Absaroka!"

"You still got a eye for the ladies, do ye?" Scratch roared, and then took a long drink of the thick and potent brandy, feeling its fiery burn coursing down the back of his throat.

Meldrum swallowed and bobbed his head from side to side, peering over the crowd. "My wife is here, somewhere. Over yonder—helping cut slices off that buffler. What I wanna know is—where that pretty daughter of your'n went. This child's got a hankerin' to kiss the bride!"

"She pretends she don't mind getting a kiss from her dogfaced ol' man, Meldrum!" Titus roared as he held his cup out for more brandy. "But I don't think Magpie's gonna want a thing to do with your hairy mug! Jehoshaphat, if you ain't 'bout the ugliest man I ever knowed!"

"That puts me right next to you, Titus Bass!" he said as he hoisted his cup in toast again. "For you surely be the ugliest man I ever did see!"

Smacking his lips, Titus licked the tip of his tongue through the shaggy ends of his unkempt mustache, savoring every drop of the sweet fruit brandy the American Fur Company sneaked upriver only for the use of its post factors, but not in the robe trade itself. "Meldrum, you ol' Scotsman," Scratch grumbled, "you're doin' your damnedest to get me hooked on the company's goddamned stuffed-shirt brandy!"

"What—you're acquirin' a taste for brandy, Titus Bass? Why, you ol'—"

"Mr. Meldrum!"

They both turned at the call, spotting one of the trader's three employees riding toward them from the direction of their log-walled post. As the crowd stepped out of the way of the man's horse, Titus spotted the five buckskinned riders close on the employee's tail.

"Mr. Meldrum!"

The trader wiped his lips with the back of the same hand that held the cup, and his eyes narrowed on the newcomers as they approached. "What is it, James?"

"Visitors, sir! You got visitors from far away!"

By the time the six riders halted their horses several yards away, Scratch could see the five strangers weren't Indians at all. Instead, they appeared to be French-blood half-breeds.

"Far away?" Meldrum asked as he took two steps closer to James.

Bass gently lowered his wife's arm, then inched away from her so he could stay at the trader's elbow.

"Fort LaRamee," one of the strangers announced.

It suddenly struck him that Meldrum was an employee of the same company that Bordeau worked for down at Fort John on the North Platte—the site that was only now becoming better known as Fort Laramie. Quickly he peered at the faces of those five strangers, looking for a hint of someone familiar . . . perhaps one or more of them had been a part of that bunch who had tried to harm Magpie, who had made trouble for him and Shad Sweete back in the spring of '47, bad blood more than four years gone now. If Bordeau had made it back to the post on his own hook, would he have carried a burning grudge this long? Finally tracking down Titus Bass and sending a handful of half-breed gunmen to kill the old trapper?

Meldrum demanded, "There's trouble?"

With a shake of his head, the half-blood who had spoken waved his hand at the young white clerk. "Give him now."

The employee reached inside his belt and pulled out a folded piece of foolscap about as big as a man's palm. As he held it down to Meldrum, Titus saw it had been sealed with a huge dollop of dark blue wax, at the center of which was imprinted a seal. "Here, sir. This is what they brung for you."

"When they get here?" Meldrum asked as he reached up to take the folded packet.

"Just now," the young man explained. "Give me the note—but I didn't want to open it. Brung it to you right away."

"Good man," he said, gazing down at the symbol hardened in the wax. "Who's this from?"

Clearing his throat, the clerk said, "These here couriers said it's very important, Mr. Meldrum. They've come all the way north from Fort Laramie, carrying this here letter from a man they called Fitzpatrick."

Scratch took a step closer now, studying the dark, swarthy faces of those five strangers. That name of an old companion from their beaver days just did not fit into the scenario he was constructing with Bordeau tracking him all the way to Fort Alexander—

"Thomas? Thomas Fitzpatrick?" Meldrum asked.

The half-blood who had spoken before now nodded, echoing the name. "*Oui,* Thomas Fitzpatrick. He is . . . my booshway."

The trader held his finger beneath the dollop of wax as he inquired, "Your booshway?"

"Hay-gent. In-gee-an hay-gent for all the mountains," he said in a thick, barely understandable accent.

"If that don't beat all," Titus said with apparent relief that this special day would not be marred by the eruption of violence. "You hear that, Meldrum? Ol' Broken Hand's a'come the Injun agent out in these parts!"

"I heard tell of that last year, as I recollect," the trader explained as he turned to the trapper. Then he looked back at the half-breed. "That ol' white-headed boss of your'n sent this note to me?"

The half-breed nodded. "Is your name Meel-drum?"

"Close enough, it is."

"Thomas Fitzpatrick write it for you," the horseman declared. "You name on dis let-tair."

Meldrum immediately turned over the folded paper. There it was, written in a strong hand.

Robert Meldrum, Trader to the Crow
Fort Alexander on the Yellowstone

He immediately flipped the folded paper over and dragged his index finger beneath the folds held down by that thick dollop of cracked and faded blue wax. Quickly he spread the paper with his hands, and his eyes danced over the neat swirls of ink made upon the foolscap. When he was done reading it in silence a third time, his lips moving soundlessly, Meldrum raised his eyes from the paper, gazing up at the older trapper.

"How you feel about making a journey with me, Titus Bass?"

He glanced at his wife, then asked, "What sort of journey?"

"South to Fort Laramie."

"That's where Fitzpatrick wrote you from?"

"Yes. You'll come?"

"I . . . I dunno," Scratch said. "Like I told you couple years back . . . last time I was there, I left 'thout good terms. Bordeau an' some of his Frenchies—"

"That was long, long ago." Meldrum interrupted. "I don't even think Bordeau's around anymore. 'Sides, you'll be with me—I'm part of the company too."

"Be with you?"

The trader nodded. "I want you to make this important journey with me."

Despite Meldrum's enthusiasm, it still didn't sound all that good: the two of them riding off with these five half-breeds who might have been put up to some murder by an old antagonism. "Just you an' me goin'?"

"Hell, no!" Meldrum exclaimed with his engaging smile, shaking that stiff sheet of wrinkled foolscap.

"I ain't never trusted the Frenchies—"

"Them?" asked the trader. "They'll be outnumbered all the way south."

"Outnumbered?"

He stuffed the paper inside his shirt and poured a little more brandy in their cups. "I'm s'posed to bring along the chiefs and headmen of the Crow nation: Pretty On Top, Flat Mouth, Falls Down, and young Stiff Arm, all of them comin' with us. And more too."

He wagged his head in deliberation, holding out his arm for his wife to come stand by his side. If the chiefs and headmen were coming along, then it made sense that his family could ride along with the delegation as well. Titus asked, "What in tarnation for?"

"Sounds of it, Fitzpatrick is callin' in all the tribes to join him for talks at Laramie," Meldrum said dramatically, patting the paper he had placed between the folds of his shirt. "Broken Hand says he's gonna sit down with all them chiefs, and he's gonna make 'em all smoke a pipe with their enemies."

"Fitzpatrick figgers he'll get all them war bands to make peace, one to the other?"

Meldrum nodded. "So I want you to come with the leaders of the Crow."

Turning to Waits-by-the-Water, Scratch asked her, "You understand what Round Iron's sayin'?"

"Yes."

"We'll go together?"

She nodded. "Yes."

Turning back to the trader, grinning, he said, "Looks like we'll go see for ourselves if ol' Broken Hand gonna make a good peace with all them bad cases. Now, pour me some more of that there booshway's brandy—I got me a wedding to celebrate!"

He didn't awaken until the early afternoon of the following day, his head pounding like a hammer on an anvil as the sun finally slipped in beneath the bottom of the upturned lodge cover, making his flesh hot and causing his head to swim. When he eventually sat up and opened his eyes, Titus realized there wasn't much left in the lodge. Someone had come and stolen most everything that belonged to his wife. His wife—

"Waits?"

She bent to her knees and stuck her head under the rolled-up lodge cover. "You are awake? How is your head?"

"Pounding like a drum," he moaned, cradling his temples in both hands.

"Little wonder," she scolded him in Crow. "You stayed up most of the night dancing and singing and pounding on any drum someone would loan you."

"Don't talk so loud," he growled. "I can hear you just fine if you'd talk softer."

"Go back to sleep until you feel better," she said with a giggle. "I have too much work to get done before we leave for me to sit and argue with a drinker man—"

"Leave?"

"With Round Iron and the chiefs," Waits reminded.

"Oh . . . right," and he remembered foggily. "When?"

"Tomorrow at sunrise. Before then, I have to finish packing what we will take along for the children, and leave the rest with Magpie."

"M-Magpie, yes." He remembered her wedding too. And for some reason, that really saddened him. "She . . . doesn't live with us anymore."

"She has a husband, and they have their own lodge now."

"Are they going with us?"

"No," she answered. "Turns Back and those war chiefs staying behind are leading the people into the mountains—the Baby Place, *Baah-puuo I-sa-wa-xaa-wuua*, where there are the children's footprints. They will find it cooler there, until autumn."

"Right . . . the mountains," he said as his head sank back onto the horsehair pillow. "The children's footprint mountains, where the Little People live?"

"Yes. They might run into some of our holy friends, the Little People."

Closing his eyes, Titus heard her shuffle off and felt himself drifting back into a blessed sleep. The idea of cool, shady mountains sounded damned good to him; at that moment he wasn't so sure the air was moving at all. Heavy and hot. Maybe if he prayed right now the sacred Little People would answer by blowing with their breath, causing a breeze to drift down from their mountains that lay off to the southwest. He'd never seen one for himself, but the Crow steadfastly believed in these beings who were half human, half furry creature. Ever since the Apsaluuke people had come to this land from the Missouri River, they had been visited by the Little People. The beings came to heal the sick and wounded when the Crow healers could not. They came to protect the faithful who believed in them. And, they sometimes portrayed their sense of humor too—often making off with some small object or another that they took a liking to. From time to time a Crow man or woman might realize they were missing something shiny and explain that the Little People had taken it. Then, years later, they would find the missing object lying on a prominent rock, or hanging from a tree branch beside a well-used trail somewhere in those mystical "children's footprint mountains,"* always in plain sight where a shiny trinket would sparkle, catching the rays of the sun.

He tried to imagine what shape the creatures took, how they looked—because while every one of the Crow believed in the Little People, few, if any, had ever had themselves a good look at one of the mysterious and sacred creatures. Most times, the elders and prophets, seers and healers caught no more than a glimpse of the Little People out of the corner of their eyes. The hint of a shadow, the mere suggestion of fleeting movement . . . because the legends always told of the Little People doing their good in secret, away from the eyes of man.

---

* The Pryor Mountains, in present-day south-central Montana.

Titus felt himself dreaming at last. Floating up the mountainside toward the cool and inviting darkness lit by a bright full moon and innumerable stars that seemed so close he felt he could reach out and tap each one, even set his big-brimmed hat right down on top of that gauzy, gibbous moon. He heard a rustling on either side of him and stopped, looking down to realize the horse that had been between his legs was somehow gone . . . and he was standing barefoot in the cool grass, the breeze nuzzling his long, graying hair. He turned to the side at the sounds of tiny feet scampering, but glimpsed only a half dozen shadows as they disappeared behind the trees.

From his right he heard more faint rustling and turned that way to look. All he saw was the tail end of some flickering movement as the creatures vanished before he ever saw them.

When he held his breath and concentrated, Titus heard the whispers. Straining into the black of that night, he listened intently, straining to make out the sounds. Voices, but not quite human. And the language they spoke . . . not anything he had ever heard spoken before in his fifty-seven winters on earth. For sure not American, but not Ute or Snake, Comanche or Crow either, not even what little Blackfoot or Mojave had fallen about his ears, and not a thing like Mexican talk.

Scratch took a deep breath and let half of it out, the same way he held a breath in his lungs when he was aiming his rifle . . . then listened some more, doing his best to recognize a word, some fragment of the foreign sounds.

These had to be Little People, he decided. For some reason, he knew he was the only human around these parts. Titus wasn't sure why he felt so certain about that . . . but, after all, this was his dream. While the Crow could accept that they would never really see one of the creatures, Titus Bass wasn't a Crow. He wanted to see one of them, talk to it—have the being talk with him, perhaps even show him some of their magic that so amazed generation after generation of the Apsaluuke people. Waits-by-the-Water and their children could believe in these holy beings out of hand, but Titus wanted to see for himself some of their notorious tricks and sleight of hand. The Crow had many long-held legends about Old Man Coyote—the well-known spiritual trickster . . . so maybe these sacred Little People had some tricks they could teach him.

"Come out here an' lemme take a look at you."

He heard a rustling to his left, then felt a brushing against the back of his leg. But as soon as he looked, it was gone.

"Stand still, so I can have me a good look afore you run away again."

Scratch suddenly turned at more rustling, trying his best to catch a glimpse, for he was sure they were all around him at that very moment—and as soon as he had turned his head he felt as if something had trundled across his toes, the way a badger or porcupine might, had they not been such slow and lumbering creatures.

"Titus Bass."

He understood that.

He grinned and said to the night, "You do speak American after all."

"We talk so you understand us, yes," the voice answered. "In the tongue of the listener."

"Why won't you show yourself to me?"

There was a pause while more leaves and branches rustled on all sides of him. Then the voice said, "We never show ourselves to you until you need us."

Scratch smiled at that. "I need to see you, know you're real an' not just some dream of mine."

"Dream? Why, you're dreaming right now, aren't you, Titus Bass?"

"Yep, s'pose I am."

"Then—if this is your dream, you should realize this is very real," the voice said as the rustling quieted.

He struggled to wrap his mind around that. Not since that night at Fort Bridger so many years ago had he given any thought to the two opposing worlds of unreality and dream, any thought to that unknown country where the two worlds converged, where they could ensnare a man into belief.

So he begged, "Why can't you lemme see you?"

"Not till you need us," the voice sounded soft, and only in his head, as if his ears weren't hearing it. Instead, as if it were just inside his head all along. "Not till you really . . . need us badly."

"When? When's a man really need you badly?"

"Are you wounded?"

"No, I ain't wounded."

"Then you aren't dying?"

"No," he said testily. "I told you, I ain't wounded an' I ain't dying."

"Then why did you call us here to help you?" the voice sounded, edgy with anger. "We can't understand why you've come here to this place and why you brought us here to help you."

"Don't you 'member: I'm dreaming this," he reminded them. "I'm dreaming I was ridin' up this mountain, into these here trees—when I thought I heard noise. I wasn't thinking of you Little People, not thinkin' 'bout your kind at all till I heard you movin' around out there in the brush."

He heard the immediate scampering of feet, untold numbers of feet, fading into the night.

"Wait!" he pleaded. "Don't go!"

From farther away, this time certainly not within his head at all, the voice replied, "We have others to see to, Titus Bass. Ones who are in need of healing, people who are very ill—those who are dying—and the First Maker has sent us to find them because we are the only ones who can save them."

"I ain't sick . . . an' I ain't dyin' neither," he groaned. "I just wanted to get my own self a look at you."

Now the voice whispered, so far away it was just barely audible. "You will see us one day, Titus Bass. But not until that day when there is nothing anyone can do to save you."

"S-save me?"

"You will see us at last . . . on that day when you are prepared to die."

TWENTY-SIX

"Jumpin' Jehoshaphat, Meldrum!" Scratch shouted above the noisy hubbub of those war chiefs and headmen pressing up behind them. "I'll be et for the devil's tater if'n that don't look ever' bit like ronnyvoo camps down there!"

"Can't claim as I ever saw that many Injuns in one place myself!" Robert Meldrum hollered. "Look at all them lodges and pony herds too."

Both of those white men could understand the Crow tongue being growled back and forth among the thirty-eight warriors, chiefs, and old headmen who had accepted Tom Fitzpatrick's invitation to join the other tribes of the High Plains and Rocky Mountains at this momentous gathering near Fort Laramie. These men of the north had every right to be more than a little anxious as they started down the long, low slope into the broad, yawning valley of the North Platte, where more than ten thousand of their most inveterate enemies awaited their arrival. Because they had the shortest distance to travel, the Cheyenne, along with bands of the Oglalla and Brulé Sioux, had been camping here for close to a month, since the end of August. In addition, a large camp of Titus Bass's most implacable foes—the Arapaho—had come in to join the talks.

Two days back, when the Crow delegation had been nearing Fort Laramie, Meldrum sent Fitzpatrick's couriers on ahead to learn where they were to camp. No chance for a big council to be taking place anywhere near the post—they found the entire countryside deserted. As the small party from the northern mountains drew closer, two of the half-bloods came galloping out from the adobe walls.

"They move the camp," one of the men shouted as he reined up in front of Meldrum and Bass. He pointed to the east. "Over to Horse Creek."*

"How far are they?" Meldrum growled testily. He was fighting some raw saddle galls on his rump, a trader unused to spending so many weeks nonstop in the saddle.

The half-breed squinted his eyes as he calculated it. "Less than two days."

"Maybeso we ought'n stay the night right here," Bass had suggested. "Close to the walls."

Rising slightly in the stirrups, Meldrum agreed, "Let's get down out of these saddles soon as we can, Scratch. Let the others make camp while we go have us a look around the fort."

Throwing up a hand in protest, Titus said, "Naw, I left enough bad blood here years ago. I'll just hang back with the family and these chiefs. You go have yourself a look an' tell me 'bout it when you get back to camp."

"Where you suggest we throw down our bedrolls?" Meldrum had asked.

Titus tugged down on the wide brim of his hat to make a little more shade for his eyes and peered across the 180 degrees of the compass. "If we're headed east at sunrise tomorry—I'd say we might as well camp yonder in them trees, far side of the stockade. We'll have water and a little grass for the animals."

"Good idee," Meldrum said as he started to rein aside. "You tell the chiefs that we still got a two-day ride."

"Just you 'member you don't tell any of them bastards Titus Bass is in shootin' distance," Scratch said with a grin.

Meldrum tipped his hat, saying, "I'll meet you in camp soon as I get my how-do's said to them booshways over at the fort."

Later that evening after supper, when the trader arrived back at the Crow camp, Meldrum brought with him some of the company's headmen and a young soldier. Since that spring of 1825, when he had run into three dragoons at the oft-abandoned Fort Osage, Scratch had seen only one other bunch of soldiers in all his travels—some of General Kearney's men spotted along the road outside Taos back in the early winter of 1846. First to come had been preachers with their Bibles and whiny cant, then their white wives reminding a man of all the thou-shalt-nots he had tried to escape . . . and eventually came those wagons loaded with plows and milkers.

"With so many of our citizens emigrating to Oregon along this central road," explained the fresh-faced officer, "the government determined it was best to bring all the warrior groups to a peace council. That way we could not only assure safe passage along the Oregon Trail, but do our level best to see the tribes made peace with one another too."

"You figger the Sioux and Cheyennes gonna treat these Crow or the Snake any better just because you had your peace meetin' with 'em?" Titus asked at

---

* Thirty-six miles down the North Platte.

the fire, where most of the delegation from the Yellowstone country stood with grave interest, waiting for translation of the white men's words.

"Yes," said the officer. "Like Superintendent Mitchell and the others who came west to make this conference a success, I believe the lion can lay down with the lamb."

Titus asked, "How many dragoons come out here to watch over things at this peace parley?"

"Just under two hundred, sir," the soldier replied. "Officers and enlisted both."

Meldrum gave Bass a knowing look before Scratch said, "Your army thinks that's enough guns to keep all them Injuns off the Crow an' Shoshone when them Sioux an' Cheyenne take a notion to cut through their old enemies?"

"Mitchell has already made it clear that there will be no bloodshed between the tribes," declared the officer with certainty.

"If you soldiers aren't right, an' you can't keep a lid on the Cheyenne an' Sioux," Scratch responded, "there'll be more blood shed at this here peace parley than you ever thought to see in your life."

Even though Meldrum told Titus that the hated Bordeau had been relieved of control at Fort Laramie when the army bought the post back in '49, Scratch never had been one to take unnecessary chances. Might well be some old friends of those employees Bass and Sweete had killed were still hangers-on, living a half-blood, squaw-man existence. Someone might just recognize that old gray-headed trapper who wore a distinctive bandanna, not to mention that long scar that traced itself down from the outside corner of his left eye.* That night, and the next as they made their way east for the broad valley said to lie at the mouth of Horse Creek, Titus slept loose, restless, half aware of every noise in the night—whether the snort of a pony, the howl of a prairie wolf, or the booming rattle of Meldrum's snore. That second morning east of the fort, the Crow had acted more nervous than they had since the day they put Fort Alexander and the Yellowstone country at their backs.

"They know there is great danger waiting for them in that camp of their enemies," Waits-by-the-Water quietly explained as she rolled up the last of their bedding after breakfast.

"The Crow been outnumbered before," he responded. "But never nothing like this."

"Maybe you should tell them the thoughts in your heart, Ti-tuzz," she suggested.

For a long time he had regarded the thirty-eight warriors and chiefs, who went about their special toilet, painting their faces and brushing their hair, tying on feathers, stuffed birds, and spiritual amulets, dressing in their very finest— then removed the covers from their shields and weapons with great ceremony.

---

* *Carry the Wind*

Although they had been riding through the heart of their enemy's land for many, many days, by this afternoon these delegates would be entering what they believed might well prove to be the valley of their death. Surrounded by enemies many times stronger than their few numbers, the Crow began to sing their brave-heart songs as they tied up their ponies' tails, rubbed their animals with dust, and made ready for one last fight.

"My friends and fellow fighting men," Scratch had addressed them in their native tongue, then waited as they fell silent and stepped close to hear his words.

"No man here can doubt that I have fought the enemies of Apsaluuke. I have been a brother warrior to the great chief with the sore belly, and my father-in-law too. I held my wife's brother in my arms as he died after we had pursued those Blackfoot into the mountains. So measure my words carefully, friends. They come from a fellow warrior."

Flea came up to stand beside his father. Scratch put his arm around the taller fourteen-year-old's shoulder and continued. "Pull the old loads from the barrels of your weapons and charge them with fresh powder. While there are not many of us, nowhere near as many as there will be of our enemies as we ride down into their gaping jaws, remember that we have far, far more medicine irons than do the Sioux, the Cheyenne, or the Arapaho. Your trade with the white man, with trusted men like Round Iron, who has married into your tribe like me, has assured that your men have always had more firearms, powder, and lead to protect your people and the land of Absaroka too."

The first of the younger chiefs growled with agreement, a few of them yipping in excitement as his words worked up their martial feelings.

"We have more guns, my friends," he reminded them again. "So do not be afraid. But—even more than the guns we can use to fight these enemies, who we will soon see face-to-face—know that the Apsaluuke have stronger hearts than these enemies, who will tremble when they finally see, for the first time, you warriors and fighting men who carry the scars of many battles against the mighty Blackfoot!"

Beside him Flea shouted with the older men, all of whom raised their muskets and flintlock rifles, shook their powerful war totems, and pounded on their shields, invoking their magic and the mystery of the spirits who watched over those who rode into battle, those men who put their bodies between those of their people and the weapons of their enemies. Gooseflesh rose along Bass's arms, and the hair stood at the back of his neck as the three dozen surged forward as one, sharing this brotherhood one last moment before they rode on down this trail into the unknown.

Below them now at the bottom of that wide, verdant valley where Horse Creek flowed from the south into the North Platte, camp sentinels—both red and white—spotted the newcomers drawing up at the top of the low rise and looking down upon the treaty grounds, where tens of thousands of horses and more than two thousand lodges dotted the grassy bottomland. The horns of every camp crescent pointed east, one lodge circle after another of those browned buffalo-hide cones teeming with horsemen, women, and children at play in the summer sun of that late afternoon.* From the very tips of the lodgepoles fluttered long cloth streamers of varied colors, along with a few black scalp locks. As the Crow delegation watched from the knoll, activity began in the soldier camp—easy to spot by its orderly corral of wagons, fancy Dearborn carriages, and dirty canvas A tents, each with its single upright pole arranged in company row after company row, squared to their sense of worldly order while the world of the Indians was lived inside a hoop.

Titus thought on that as their horses blew atop the hill and Waits-by-the-Water brought her horse to a halt beside his. Brooding how the Indian lived his life in a circle, while most everything in the white man's world was made with straight lines, angles, corners, and squares—whether it was the long rows a farmer like Roman Burwell was likely scratching out of the earth of Oregon Territory, or the angularity of the log house Row and Amanda would have raised for their children that first autumn in the valley of the Willamette, south of the Columbia River. There were no corners in a lodge. Besides those hours spent working at Bridger's forge, or standing inside a trade room at Bents' big lodge on the Arkansas, or back at Fort John on the North Platte, even down south to Taos at Josiah's store, or in the Paddock home, Scratch could not remember feeling all that comfortable inside a squared-off building with its walls, corners, and no-nonsense roof too. To his way of thinking, the best home had neither walls to support a roof, nor a roof to rest upon its walls.

"See how they're sending out a proper escort for us!" Meldrum announced in English above the hubbub of chatter, then turned and told the chiefs that they were about to be welcomed by that small squad of a dozen soldiers splashing across the knee-high Platte and lurching onto the north bank, where they set off at a lope toward the newcomers.

"What are these men?" Pretty On Top asked as he reined his horse around the front of the group so he could stop and await the escort detail between the two white men.

"They are fighters like your men, warriors for the white man's people back east," Scratch explained.

The chief measured him with his eyes, then asked, "These white warriors, they do not fight for you and Round Iron?"

"Not for me," Titus said. "Maybe they help out the fur traders, but I don't think they're here to fight against the Crow."

"How is it they all wear the same coats?" asked Stiff Arm.

"Maybe it's easier to see one another when they are in a battle," Scratch advised.

"Our fighting men dress the way their medicine tells them," Three Irons said

* September 10, 1851.

with disdain for the approaching soldiers. "They do not wear another man's medicine."

"These fighting men do not have their own medicine," Bass explained. "They take their orders from their leader, and they do what he tells them."

Stiff Arm wagged his head and said, "How can a man fight like that, following the will of another man?"

"Maybe that is why the soldiers will always have a hard time if they ever have to fight a band of warriors!" Titus cheered. "These soldiers will stand around waiting for their leader to tell them what to do while warriors ride right through them!"

"Are you white men?" called out one of the soldiers as they slowed, drawing near.

Meldrum looked Bass up and down, then regarded himself, dressed in canvas drop-front britches, a calico drop-shoulder shirt, and some moccasins beaded by his Crow wife. The trader sang out, "I'm a white man, for certain . . . but, I don't rightly know that this nigger with me is a white man anymore!"

The soldiers came near enough that the leader with a lot of gold braid looped on his upper arms signaled the rest to stop. Then the leader glared at Bass and stated, "You look to be a white man to me."

"Shit, son—I been working a lot of seasons so I don't look like a white man no more."

Rather than responding to the old trapper, the soldier quickly looked over the group and asked Meldrum, "Are you more Shoshone come in for the peace talks?"

"These here ain't Shoshone," the trader snapped. "You got Snakes down there in that camp too?"

"Yes." The soldier wiped some sweat off his bare chin. "A band of them came in a few days back, under an old fur trapper, Colonel Bridger."

"Jim Bridger?" Bass squealed in delight.

"If I remember correctly, that's his name, yes. If you aren't more Shoshone, who are you two and what tribe are these men representing?"

"These here the finest fighters in the northern mountains, my good man," Scratch announced. "They're Crow."

"C-Crow?"

"That's what he said," Meldrum reiterated.

Turning to the trader, the soldier said, "We didn't think any Crow were coming. No representatives had shown up when we opened the councils—"

Meldrum grumped, "Any of you folks know just how far it is from Fort Laramie up to Crow country on the goddamned Yellowstone?"

Blinking in embarrassment as he absorbed the strident words, the soldier said, "Mr. Fitzpatrick had all but given up hope that a Crow delegation would make the journey."

"Where's Broken Hand?" Scratch asked. "I wanna see that ol' whitehead for myself."

"Y-you know Mr. Fitzpatrick?"

He looked at the soldier. "We both do. Fitz was a friend of ours from the beaver days. A glory time. Now we hear Tom's the Injun agent for these here western tribes. That really be the certain of it, son?"

"It is, sir. He sent out the invitations to the bands to join us at Laramie," the soldier said, "but the feeding grounds near Fort Laramie were soon depleted and the whole council was moved here to Horse Creek five days ago."

Bass inquired, "That when you start palaverin' with the tribes?"

"No—not until two days ago," he explained, his bare upper lip glistening with sweat. "This is the third day of the ceremonial talks."

Rocking back in his saddle with a sigh, Titus said, "Good thing we ain't too late, Robert."

"No," the soldier answered, "not too late at all."

"Maybeso we ought'n ride on down there to find ol' Fitz hisself an' ask him where's a spot we can camp these here Crow," Bass suggested.

Clearing his throat, the soldier asked with a nervous rise to his voice, "These Crow you're with—they friendly with the Sioux or Cheyenne?"

"Hell no, they ain't!" Meldrum roared.

"There's plenty of bad blood atween the Crow and them tribes down there," Titus added.

Wiping the sweat from his upper lip, the soldier said, "Then I suggest you wait here until I can ride down to find out from Mr. Fitzpatrick where he and Superintendent Mitchell want to camp your delegation—"

"I'm comin' with you, son."

The soldier was opening his mouth in protest when Bass turned aside and spoke in Crow to his wife. "I won't be long. Going with these riders to see an old friend from the trapper days—he's the one called this meeting . . . and he's the one who will tell us where he thinks we should camp, here in the lap of such a strong enemy."

The instant Bass finished talking to his wife, the soldier said, "I'd prefer you wait here with the rest of your delegation while I—"

He harrumphed, "I ain't a Crow, which means none of them Sioux or Cheyenne gonna try to take what I got left of my hair."

"But, mister," the young officer said, then cleared his throat before continuing, "you don't understand everything going—"

"Unnerstand what?"

"Understand that the situation here is a bit tense," the soldier explained. "On their way to Fort Laramie, Colonel Bridger's Shoshone delegation was attacked by the Cheyenne and two of the Shoshone delegates were killed."

"Thankee for spellin' that out for me—but I ain't an Injun gonna be run off by no Sioux or Cheyenne," he said with a firm set to his jaw. "Besides, I got friends down there in that camp: Agent Fitzpatrick and Colonel Bridger both. I'm fixin' to go see where these fellers lay that my Crow friends should set up our camp."

Tapping his heels into his pony's flanks, Titus set off on down the long, grassy slope, moving past the soldier detail. In a handful of seconds he heard the soldier growl the order for his men to about-face and follow him after the old man. It wasn't long before he heard the officer set his horse into a lope. He caught up to the old trapper, coming alongside as Scratch approached the outskirts of the largest and most extensive village.

"I suggest that you cross the Platte here, mister. This is the Sioux village, here on the north side of the river. Just past the end of the Sioux camp stands the Cheyenne, then the Arapaho villages, on this north bank too."

"Whose tents are those?" he asked, pointing across to the south side of the Platte, where more than a dozen wall tents stood in the V formed by the river and its junction with Horse Creek flowing in from the south.

"They are for Superintendent Mitchell and his peace commissioners."

Titus reined his pony to the right and entered the shallow river. "Then what's all them tents over there?"

"Across Horse Creek?" the soldier asked, pointing ahead. "That's the army's camp."

"An' them lodges near 'em?"

"The Shoshone—Colonel Bridger was asked to camp them near us for their protection."

As his pony carried him onto the south bank of the Platte, Scratch reined to the left. "That be where I wanna go. I figger I'll find Bridger with his Snakes."

The soldier didn't utter another word until their horses were crossing Horse Creek. "But you do realize the treaty grounds are across the stream too? The Sioux and Cheyenne, they're holding talks with Fitzpatrick and the commissioners at this moment."

"Then Fitzpatrick's campin' here with the soldiers too?"

"No, he and his interpreters have their shelters pitched farther upstream," the soldier explained, pointing off to their right, up Horse Creek.

"I'll g'won over to these here talks with you an' see if I can spot Fitzpatrick or Bridger."

Leaving the escort detail behind at the edge of the wagon corral with Meldrum and the Crow delegates, the old trapper and the young soldier ended up being momentarily stopped by the first row of pickets, dragoons who were posted at an outer ring around the treaty grounds, then halted a second time by an inner ring of guards too, as the horsemen neared the huge canvas awnings erected for shade. Despite the glaring intensity of the late-summer sun, the Indian delegates sat outside in the heat during the long speeches and wrangling.

Only the white men sat beneath the awnings, stewing in their heavy wool uniforms, continually fanning themselves with their hats or folded papers.

Bass and the soldier dismounted several yards back from the massive crowd of Indians, then handed their horses' reins to a hairy-faced guard before they walked around the throng, finally spotting Fitzpatrick's long white mane. The agent sat in the midst of a mass of pale-skinned easterners. At his knee two dark-skinned interpreters squatted on a buffalo robe, speaking from time to time, their hands flying in the broad gestures of sign language.

"He looks a mite busy right now, don't he?" Titus remarked. "Can you tell me where them Shoshone are in this bunch?"

"I can't say I recognize one Indian from another, mister," the soldier apologized.

"There he is! I see 'im!" Titus yipped with excitement, stepping away to his right around the throng toward the large band of warriors and chiefs who sat off by themselves, nearest the commissioners' awning.

Once he got up behind the Snake delegates, Scratch whispered, "Gabe!"

Bridger turned, bringing a flat hand under his hat brim to shade his eyes while he studied the caller. His face immediately lit up and he scrambled to his feet, waving Titus to come his way. The instant Bass had threaded his way through the Shoshone, the trader looped his arms around him and exclaimed, "Scratch, you ol' buzzard! It's been three winters already! Damn me if I didn't think you'd gone under for sure up in Crow country!"

"But here I walk, Gabe!"

"Sit," Bridger said as they both settled on the robe and leaned their faces close to whisper. "Hell, if it ain't four years this very month since you took off north."

"You see'd any sign o' Shadrach?" Titus asked. "He ever come back from Oregon?"

Wagging his head, sadly Bridger said, "No. He ain't."

"You hear anything from him?" he asked with disappointment. "Figger he made it there with that emigrant train?"

Bridger snorted, "Oh, that tall boy made it, all right. I heard it from Joe Meek's tongue hisself."

"When you see Joe?"

"He an' Squire Ebbert come through, late that winter," Bridger confided. "They was on snowshoes they'd made themselves: willow an' rawhide. Had to put down their horses and eat 'em back up the trail. Starvin' times."

"What the hell they show up at Fort Bridger in the winter for?"

Jim explained, "Joe was hurtin' something bad. He an' Squire was the last of a bunch headin' east for the States. Figgered to rally up some soldiers to come help out in Oregon."

"The Britishers makin' trouble?" Titus asked, bristling.

Shaking his head, Bridger said, "Injuns. Cayuse. They murdered Doc and Mrs. Whitman."

"The sawbones what dug that arrowhead out'n your hump meat back at ron-nyvoo?"

"Yep."

"An' that purty yellow-haired wife of his too?"

"Cayuse killed some young'uns what was at their mission school," Bridger said gravely. "Joe lost him his daughter to them red buggers. Found her body dug up by wolves."

"Murderin' sonsabitches!" Titus grumbled, grinding a fist into his left palm. "Killin' women an' young'uns. Damn 'em to hell anyway. So w-what become of it? Them Oregoners make war on them Cayuse what started killin' white folks?"

"Wasn't a war on white people. Joe told me them red-bellies had it in for the Whitmans—so they killed 'em all at the school. Medicine men got 'em stirred up, to Joe's way of thinking. Medicine men what didn't like the Whitmans teachin' their people 'bout the white God."

"Joe go back to Oregon?"

"He's back there, much as I know," Jim replied. "But I ain't see'd Shadrach."

"Heard you come over here with the Snakes."

Bridger nodded. "Where away was you bound, when you happed on Fitzpatrick's big peace council?"

"We was invited," Titus announced.

"In-invited?"

"Not a lonely ol' badger like me! But Meldrum, trader up to Fort Alexander on the Yellowstone. Fitz asked him an' the Crow to come."

Bridger's face lit up. "So you rode down with the Crow chiefs?"

"I did. Meldrum asked me. Brung the wife an' young'uns too."

"Let's see now," and Bridger scratched at his cheek with a widening grin, "I'll bet you're havin' to use a big stick to knock them young Crow bucks away from that oldest girl of your'n. She was a purty thing."

"Magpie? Why, we got the girl married off just afore we set off for these here peace talks."

"Married! I'll be dogged—I wouldn't thought you were a coon old enough to marry off a daughter—"

"Mr. Bridger!"

They both turned to peer into the shade of the council tent, finding all the faces looking their way.

Scratch whispered from the side of his mouth, "Who's that?"

"Mitchell—big white Injun father from back east," Bridger hissed.

The big-bellied man gestured toward the open ground in front of the council awning and proclaimed, "Mr. Bridger, time has come for the Shoshone to give their speeches—"

"Who the hell's that sittin' with you, Gabe?" Fitzpatrick roared in interruption, lunging to his feet and starting their way.

"Been a long time since I laid eyes on yer white-haired carcass, Fitz," Titus said as he got to his feet too and started toward the agent.

"Wasn't sure that was really you, Titus Bass!" the agent's voice boomed as they met near the Shoshone delegation and pounded one another on the back. "Heard stories every now and then. Lots of stories 'bout you. Most of 'em got to do with some new way they said you gone under!" When they backed apart, Fitzpatrick said, "Wasn't all that sure when you come through the crowd an' sat down with Bridger there. Neither of us look much the same as we did years back when beaver was high an' we was young."

Reaching out to stroke the side of Fitzpatrick's long hair, Scratch said, "You ain't changed much, you ol' whitehead. Shit, I 'member when them Injun trappers brung you into Pierre's Hole back to thirty-two. Lookin' at you was like we'd all see'd a ghost our own selves. Your ha'r used to be sleek an' black as a otter's . . . an' after what you come through, gettin' chased down by them Blackfoot, it'd turn't white as snow."

"Can you figger it's been almost twenty year now?" Fitzpatrick asked.

"Agent Fitzpatrick?" Mitchell intruded with a scolding tone. "Can you and your old crony wait until tonight after we've concluded the day's negotiations to reminisce?"

Fitzpatrick grinned and shrugged as he whispered, "Back to business, Scratch. We'll talk later. I'll come look up you an' Jim at the Snake camp after supper—"

"I didn't ride in with Gabe's Shoshone."

"Just come to see these here doin's on your own?"

"Hell, Fitz," he said with a growing smile, "we got your invite clear up to the Yallerstone country. Meldrum talked me into coming down with—"

"Meldrum?" he wheezed. "The trader up there in Crow country?"

By this moment Mitchell had come right to the edge of the shade, growing irritated at this rude delay. "Agent Fitzpatrick, will you and Colonel Bridger bring the Shoshone over for their speech—"

But Fitzpatrick wasn't paying the slightest attention to the stuffy official from the East. "Robert Meldrum? From Fort Alexander?"

"That's him!"

"You mean you two brung the Crow down?"

"A old friend like you asks us," Titus said, "how you figger we're gonna let you down?"

Fitzpatrick wheeled on the official, bubbling with joy, "The Crow are here!" Then he suddenly whirled on Bass again. "Wh-where are they?"

Turning Fitzpatrick away from the side of the awning, Scratch led the agent a half dozen steps so they had a clear eye-shot at the long, low slope. "There they be, Fitz—waiting for you an' this impatient hotheaded son of a bitch to tell us where to camp—"

The superintendent's cheeks were flushed with anger. "Agent Fitzpatrick—there's important business at hand to conduct!"

Wheeling about, Fitzpatrick flapped his arms at the superintendent. "And we'll get to that business, Mr. Mitchell . . . but for now I've got to tell my friend here where he can camp with the delegation he and Robert Meldrum just brought in from the north country."

"D-delegation?" Mitchell echoed, his crimson face marked with lines of irritation as he took three steps forward to stand bathed in the bright afternoon light.

"The Crow!" Fitzpatrick bellowed. "By jigs, if the Crow ain't here for your peace talks!"

Mitchell demanded, "Where?"

Scratch pointed, saying, "On the hill, waitin' for me to tell 'em where to camp."

"You brought their delegation down from the Yellowstone country?" Mitchell inquired as he quickly started toward the three former trappers.

"Robert Meldrum did," Scratch admitted to the superintendent. "I just come along 'cause he asked me to."

"Who are you?"

But the white-haired Indian agent answered before Scratch could. "This here's Titus Bass. There ain't nowhere you go in these here mountains what you won't hear ghosty stories told about this nigger, Mr. Mitchell. Titus Bass been about as far north as you can get afore a man gets chewed up by Blackfoot war parties, and as far south as Taos and the Apache country too. Hell, I even heard a tale you went out to California with Bill Williams sometime back!"

That's when Bridger joined in, "This man an' the fellers he was with stole more Mexican horses than ever come outta California!"

"So what do you have to do with the Crow?" Mitchell asked.

"My wife's people," he replied. "Live with 'em, hunt an' fight with 'em too."

"Mr. Bass," and Mitchell suddenly held out his hand. "May I say I truly appreciate your efforts in bringing the Crow chiefs down to make a most momentous peace."

As they were shaking, Titus said, "They got the wrong man. Wasn't me. Robert Meldrum's the man you an' Fitz here invited to come with the Apsaluukes."

"Still the same, I personally appreciate your efforts," and Mitchell tipped his hat.

"I was in the mood for a trip," Titus replied. "Brung my family down this way for to visit some ol' friends, Mr. Mitchell."

After sundown that evening Bridger and Fitzpatrick came to eat supper in the Crow camp with those two companions from the beaver days. The Indian agent explained that he had come by himself rather than bringing his Arapaho wife and infant son from his camp, worrying over the reception that might be given her by the Crow. But Scratch sent him right back for the woman and the boy.

"Way I see it, we've had us a long ride down from the Yellowstone, so my woman's got a hankerin' for woman talk, Fitz," Titus said. "Much as there's real bad blood atween me an' the 'Rapaho, I figger that's atween me an' their menfolk. Not atween my wife an' yours."

Soon as the agent returned with his family, the women eventually got to communicating about children and the never-ending work of a woman, using their hands in sign language at the cooking fire, where they roasted the haunch of a tender young pony Fitzpatrick and his interpreters had butchered earlier that morning. After Jim related the grim story of how the Cheyenne had ambushed the Shoshone delegation far west of Laramie, he and Fitzpatrick went to work explaining all that had gone on since the first of the warrior bands began gathering at the fort.

"We stopped at the post," Titus explained, "an' Meldrum found out the place been sold to the army couple years back."

Fitzpatrick wagged his head. "Everything would've been run better if the fur company still saw to things 'stead of the army."

"You picked a good time of the year for this peace council," Bridger said. "No emigrants on the trail. So there's no problems with the Sioux and them Cheyenne for white wagon folks."

" 'Cept that we started runnin' outta grass a mite soon," the agent declared. "That's when we moseyed on downriver, here to this valley."

"You had to see this confabulation, Scratch!" Bridger said, his face animated. "How that bunch of soft-brained pork-eaters got all them supplies loaded up in wagons and hauled over here, I'll never know!"

"Beads an' blankets, knives an' coffee for the chiefs, eh?" Titus asked.

That's when Fitzpatrick wagged his head dolefully. "No. We still don't have any presents for these Injuns."

"N-no presents?" Meldrum squawked with indignation. Then he lowered his voice, saying, "What the hell you think I promised these here Crow you'd give 'em—"

"Hold on," Fitzpatrick argued. "The presents is comin'. Just ain't got here yet."

"Better be any day now," Bridger groaned. "That's all I gotta say."

"You mean you convinced all these Injuns to come talk peace with you an' each other," Titus said, "but you didn't bring no goddamned presents for 'em?"

"I said the wagons are comin'," the agent snapped. "Ah hell, Scratch—it ain't you I'm angry at. It's these damned officials from back east, and their soldiers. This summer they used my good name to invite all these warrior bands here. My name! And now I'm the one gonna be huggin' two handfuls of bare ass if those trade goods don't get here by the time these talks are all over and the chiefs put their marks on Mitchell's treaty."

Bass clucked in sympathy, "You're in a bad way if them goods don't reach us soon. What with old enemies camped closer'n you an' me could spit tobaccy at each other. They don't get their blankets and kettles, beads and paint for their women . . . what do you think this many warriors gonna start doin'?"

"Hell if I don't already know what they'll start doin'," Fitzpatrick complained. "And, to tell the truth, I hope they start with Mitchell and his bunch!"

"I'll drink to that!" Bridger cheered. "Where's some whiskey, Tom?"

"We ain't got any of that either," the agent groaned. "Mitchell didn't want any likker in camp—seein' how it's contraband out here in Injun country."

Bass made a sour face and looked over at Bridger. "You got any whiskey wuth drinkin' over to your post on Black's Fork, Gabe?"

"That's a mighty long way to ride for a drink, Scratch."

For a moment he thought about his loneliness for Magpie, then realized how safe she was up there in Crow country. She now belonged to another man. Reassured, Titus burst out laughing. "I wasn't talkin' 'bout tonight, you idjit! I just figgered I could foller you back to your post when these important folk got their peace talks all wrapped up here."

"C-come to visit?"

With a shrug, Scratch said, "You an' me got four years of catchin' up to do, Gabe. An' we can do a lot o' palaver with some whiskey to wet our gullets."

Bridger slapped Titus on the knee exuberantly. "My new wife gonna be tickled as a hen what's just laid her first egg!"

"You got a new wife?" he asked.

"She's my third," Bridger confessed to his old friends.

Titus grinned. "I didn't even know 'bout what happed to your second wife."

"Ute gal," he said, staring into the fire. "Married back in forty-eight. But she died givin' birth to my li'l Virginia Rosalie, that next summer of forty-nine."

"A Flathead gal, an' a Utah gal too," Titus recounted. "If you ain't the marryin' fool! So who's your third wife?"

"Li'l Fawn. She's a Snake, daughter of Washakie his own self. But I call her Mary," Bridger boasted a little behind a big smile. "Still, there's time she gets hungry for woman talk so she takes off to see her kin over at some camp. But if your wife comes over for a visit to the fort, she's gonna be just the poultice to put on Mary's case of the lonelies! Tell me true now, you'll really come visit for the fall when we turn back for the Green?"

"I damn well couldn't think of a better place to be than visitin' with ol' friends till our tongues get tired!"

TWENTY-SEVEN

Those nights during the great peace council in the valley of the North Platte were given over to feasting and dancing. One hell of a feast and a lot of nonstop dancing.

Because no buffalo roamed anywhere close to that great overland road by the end of a busy, bustling emigrant season, the tribal bands had depleted their supplies of fresh meat days ago. In fact, to Titus Bass's way of thinking, it stood to reason that this sad business with the great buffalo herd having been split in two by the white tide sweeping west to the shining sea had to be the sorest spot for these nomadic Indians of the plains. Not only did the shaggy beasts refuse to wander close to the Oregon and Mormon trails, but most of the abundant game in the region had either been killed off or driven away, miles and miles to the north or the south of this great migration highway. Too, there wasn't much for the ponies of those wandering bands of brown-skinned hunters to graze on either—not after the oxen, mules, and horses of the white sojourners had cropped every edible shoot right down to the ground, starting with the first train through in early spring and running right on through until the last wagons had rattled through late in the summer.

For white and red alike, a glorious era had come and gone by that autumn of 1851. There were now, and forever would be, two great buffalo herds. But even put together their numbers came nowhere near the infinite black multitude that had once blanketed this endless and incomprehensible buffalo palace.

It wasn't long before the bands ran out of their supply of dried meat and they took to making a dent in the dog population. Sioux, Cheyenne, and Arapaho all had long favored the canine—the younger the pup, the better. So too was dog a delicacy with the Crow delegates. But not among the Shoshone. They did not eat dog. Instead, Washakie's Snake representatives sacrificed one of their fine young ponies each day. With tens of thousands of horses grazing the bottomland and hillsides, no one was about to go hungry as the Laramie peace council crawled toward a final agreement.

Just as each day's parley had begun, that final morning Superintendent D. D. Mitchell had the cannon fired promptly at 9:00 A.M., his signal for the delegates to assemble at the treaty grounds. Again the Sioux made a grand and showy entrance when they crossed the river. In the lead rode an ancient warrior. Tied to a long staff carried above his head fluttered a faded and worn American flag.

"That ol' fella claims he got that flag from the redheaded chief, Clark," Thomas Fitzpatrick explained to Scratch.

"St. Louie's William Clark?" Titus asked.

"Him and Lewis took the Corps of Discovery all the way to the Pacific Ocean back in 1804, thereabouts."

That had shaken loose a little memory for him. "I 'member him from St. Louie. Injun agent for some time after his outfit come back from the far salt ocean—agent while I lived there."

While each delegation approached the site in a grand procession, the proud horsemen—who had tied up the manes and tails of their ponies, coloring the animals with earth paints and dyes—all pounded on handheld drums and sang their noisiest national songs, doing their best to outsing every other throat. Every delegate wore his finest, draping himself with all the colorful trappings he owned. But none of the delegates who entered the treaty grounds could bring a weapon. Superintendent Mitchell held fast to his edict that no man would be allowed a role in the peace talks if he carried a means of making war. Following the horsemen came the great throngs of women and children on foot, streaming across the river and up the banks, all of them painted fiercely and wearing their showiest ceremonial clothing for these auspicious talks of peace on the High Plains. At the end of each day, many of the government officials and reporters, who had come west for this treaty council, remarked on their surprise at the courteous and peaceful conduct of the children throughout the lengthy speeches and formal ceremonies in the late-summer heat.

Since Mitchell himself was an old beaver man, he knew how important was the giving of presents to these red delegates. So every evening he hosted a dinner at his camp, during which the superintendent handed out little packets of vermilion and twists of tobacco, until he had no more to give. In every village the young men paraded about, expecting to be noticed by the young women. But those girls did their very best to attract the warriors: greasing their hair, coloring the part with vermilion, draping themselves with the gaudiest bead- or quillwork, wrapping their arms and wrists with coils of brass wire, looping every finger with a bright ring, all to catch the eye of a particular young man.

But when Mitchell had called the council to order each morning, the clamoring hubbub fell silent and an air of solemn dignity descended upon the valley of Horse Creek that September of 1851. Only the chiefs and their important counselors moved forward to sit in the council arena itself. Since the Sioux were the most numerous tribe present for the talks, their headmen filled both the north and west sides of the treaty ground. The Cheyenne were assigned to sit next to them on the south side of the circle, while the Arapaho were situated beside them. The enemy peoples, both Shoshone and Crow, completed the eastern side of the great open circle.

The morning after Robert Meldrum arrived with his Crow, September 11, the ceremonies were largely consumed with welcoming these thirty-eight delegates from the north. As Chief Pretty On Top and Takes Horse rode up, the last to arrive so they could make a showy entrance, an eastern reporter named B. Gratz Brown found himself so impressed with their grand entrance that he came over to kneel beside Agent Fitzpatrick, who was seated on a robe.

"That is the finest delegation of Indians we have seen!" Brown gushed his praise to the other white men as the Crow approached and dismounted. "Look at them! They make a most splendid appearance with their beautiful mounts and trappings. From everything I can see, these Crow ride better, hold their seats more gracefully, and are dressed much more lavishly—but with finer taste—than any of these others who are here!"

That evening of the eleventh, Alexander Culbertson, trader for the American Fur Company and agent at Fort Union on the high Missouri, had arrived with Father Pierre DeSmet and a mixed delegation of thirty-two Assiniboine, Crow, Minnetaree, and Arikara chiefs. The appearance of the much respected black robe caused quite a stir among the camps, and was warmly welcomed by longtime friends Fitzpatrick, Bridger, and Robert Campbell—now a wealthy St. Louis merchant—three old fur men who had met DeSmet years ago in the heyday of the beaver trade. Starting out from St. Louis immediately after plans for the treaty council had been laid, DeSmet took a steamboat up the Missouri to Fort Union, where he joined Culbertson, who had been given the honorary title of "colonel" on the northern prairies, along with those Indians the trader had chosen to make the journey south with them. Taking a circuitous route on horseback, the party made its way overland almost to Independence Rock before striking the Oregon Trail, then marched east to Fort Laramie.

With other details of the treaty finally put to rest, September 12 was devoted to intense discussions of tribal boundaries the white man wanted demarcated on those large maps Mitchell unfurled across his tables. Trouble was, as Scratch saw right from the first speeches that Friday morning, every one of these tribes boldly and unashamedly claimed more land than their neighbors

wanted to allow. Even worse for the commissioners' plans, none of these warrior bands cared a whit for fixed boundaries. From ancient times their tradi-
tional and nomadic way of life was itself completely antithetical to what the
white men were now asking of them. A warrior culture had always wandered in
the hunt of buffalo or the taking of horses, captives, and spoils, wherever they
dared to go, no matter what tribe might claim that country.

That same evening of the twelfth, Agent Fitzpatrick and his wife,
Margaret, presented their half-breed infant son, Andrew Jackson Fitzpatrick,
to Father DeSmet for baptism by firelight. And the rest of that night proved to
be no different from any other during the great council: Scratch found it hard
to fall asleep, and if he did, to stay asleep, what with the drums and singing,
yelps and shrieks coming from every camp. On the thirteenth followed another day of heated debate on the matter of tribal boundaries, but all matters
of business were suspended for September 14—a "powerful medicine day,"
as the white men explained to the Indians. DeSmet made use of the vacated
council arbor that Sunday, calling to him all those who wished to attend a
special religious service he conducted at midday. At the end of the mass,
eight more half-breed children were brought forward for baptism, along with
five adults who also wished to receive this holiest of blessings from the
renowned black-robe.

For another two days those territorial debates raged on, until three of the old
fur men stepped in to prove their worth in this weighty process. In their youth
they had crossed most every river and stream, mountain range and pass, in
those trackless regions claimed by one tribe or another. Fitzpatrick, Bridger,
and Robert Campbell too talked and wheedled and argued their position nonstop, until by the evening of the sixteenth the tribes had relented and
Superintendent Mitchell could finally ink the lines across his great maps, tribal
divisions and territories that the mighty warrior bands had agreed to. The following morning, the seventeenth, the delegates gathered to watch Mitchell,
then Fitzpatrick, sign the historic document. That done, they began the most
solemn process of all, as the chiefs and headmen of each band came forward in
small groups to affix their marks, each one a crude cross, inscribed beside their
names printed on the white man's treaty. When all the Indians had completed
the ceremony, the remaining government officials gathered to add their signa-
tures as witnesses to the compact.

"I reckon you ought'n sign too," Fitzpatrick whispered to Bass as Robert
Meldrum got to his feet and joined the other white dignitaries at the table.

Shaking his head, Titus declared, "Been so long, I don't know if I'd 'member how to write my name, Tom. 'Sides that, this here's a day for others to
shine. I ain't done nothin' to make this treaty, not the way you an' Bridger
worked. It's your day to stand in the sun, Tom Fitzpatrick!"

"We still got one matter to attend to," the white-haired agent announced as
the last of the witnesses stepped back from the table.

Mitchell inquired, "What's that, Major Fitzpatrick?"

"This business between the Cheyennes and the Snakes."

Staring down at his treaty for a long moment, the superintendent asked, "Do those killings really matter now that both tribes have signed this document?"

Fitzpatrick leaned on the table with both hands, glaring at Mitchell, and said with firmness, "That there paper ain't worth spit . . . if these tribes don't make things right in their hearts for one another."

After a long sigh, Mitchell asked, "How do you suggest we call for a reconciliation between them after the Cheyennes wantonly killed two of Washakie's delegates?"

"It's all up to the Cheyennes," the agent explained. "So I figger John Smith has to be the one to convince them Cheyennes they've got to cover the bodies."

"C-cover the bodies?" Mitchell repeated. "What do you mean by that?"

"That's Injun term for the killers making gifts to the relations of the ones they killed," Fitzpatrick explained as he waved the Cheyenne squaw-man over to his side. "John, you think you can get them chiefs to understand what they got to do to make things right with the Snakes?"

Smith gnawed on the inside of his cheek a moment, then nodded. "I'll give it my best try, Fitz."

By late that afternoon, Smith had convinced the Cheyenne delegates that their best interests lay in settling this grave matter of taking those two Shoshone scalps. Four riders accompanied the white squaw-man to visit Bridger and Washakie in the Snake camp, bringing their invitation to attend a feast. Knowing that the Shoshone did not eat dog, the Cheyenne roasted a pair of young ponies that evening, along with some boiled and crushed corn. On into the night the speeches were made by both tribes, then the pipe was lit and passed around the fire as more than a hundred of the headmen of both bands smoked to their reconciliation. Only then could the presents be brought forth. Cheyenne women were called forward, carrying blankets for the relatives of the two dead Shoshone in way of apology. By accepting the blankets, the Shoshone acknowledged that they accepted this personal expression of regret. And the matter was buried.

All that remained for the more than ten thousand visitors to do on the morning of the eighteenth was to await the long-overdue wagon train that was bringing what Mitchell had promised was a mountain of gifts.

For as far as the eye could see, the grassy hillsides had been cropped all the way down to the prairie. Every step of a hoof or moccasin, every little gust of wind, stirred up clouds of dust. After two weeks in this same location, the human refuse, pony droppings, and offal from all those butchered dogs and ponies made for an unimaginable stench. The first to go were Major Chilton and his soldiers, who struck their tents and moved their camp two miles on down the North Platte to a sweeter-smelling locale. Yet Mitchell and his commissioners held fast.

"We will stay with these Indians," Mitchell vowed. "We have asked them to believe our word that the presents are coming. The least we can do is to stay here with them till the annuities arrive."

So the warrior bands waited out the eighteenth, then the long, hot nineteenth, feasting both nights, since the camps still boasted plenty of dogs. Then on September 20 the long wait was over! With Chilton's dragoons posted on either side of the long train, the freight wagons finally rumbled into the valley, down to Mitchell's arbor, and squared themselves into a large corral as some ten thousand Indians cheered, sang, and shouted, all of them eagerly pressing forward, expecting the flow of presents to begin. But the superintendent had his interpreters explain to their wards that he would not be presenting the gifts until the following morning because he had to go through the annuities and separate the goods.

At long last the great day arrived. Again Mitchell had the cannon fired, and the chiefs advanced on the brushy arbor. The crowd waited breathlessly while the most important men in each band were presented with army uniforms. Dealing with rank among the plains and mountain tribes was always an extremely sensitive and touchy affair, something that would have been horribly botched if it weren't for men like Fitzpatrick and Bridger firmly establishing the order in which the chiefs and their subalterns were called forward for their individual ceremony. To each Mitchell presented a wool coat dripping with braid and ribbon, along with a pair of wool army britches. To the most important of the delegates, Mitchell also presented a sword and a peace medal suspended on a bright blue ribbon.

One after another the chiefs put on their coats, patting the shiny brass epaulettes on their shoulders, running their tawny hands over the gold braid and glittering buttons, strutting before their people with unabashed self-importance. When Pretty On Top and the other headmen returned to the circle with their gifts, britches draped over their arms, Scratch leaned over and whispered to his wife.

"What you figger our chiefs gonna do with them pants?"

"Pants?" she echoed the English word.

He patted his leggings, then pulled up the hem of his cloth shirt and tugged at his belt. "Pants."

With a grin she said, "They cut off."

"Cut off?" he asked.

"See how Flat Mouth does now," she said, pointing at the war chief.

The war leader had dropped to his knees, pulled out his belt knife, and begun cutting both the crotch and the seat out of the light blue army britches until he had a pair of wool leggings. Quickly untying his buckskin leggings from his belt, he cut some pieces of fringe from them and threaded it through the belt loop that remained at the top of each wool tube. Then he stuffed one of his bare appendages down the pants leg and tied it to the outside of his belt. In a few easy steps Flat Mouth had made himself a new pair of fancy leggings, warm for the coming winter.

"I'll be gusseted for a hog!" Titus exclaimed in a whisper. "If that don't beat all. I figgered for sure them fellers was gonna throw those white-man pants in the first fire they come to!"

Now the murmurs of the crowd grew to become bedlam as Mitchell called the chiefs forward again, this time to assist in passing out more than $50,000 worth of blankets and beads, kettles and bolts of cloth, along with all the rest of the shiny new trade goods to their respective peoples. Each band impatiently waited their turn through the rest of the morning, into the afternoon, and on till sunset, when Mitchell suspended the presentation of the annuities. But at 9:00 A.M. the following morning, the ceremonies continued. It wasn't until early afternoon of the twenty-second that everything had been distributed. Rather than waiting until the next morning, some of the bands began tearing down their lodges, gathering their herds, and starting away for the fall hunt.

At sunrise the following day, Robert Meldrum waited with the Crow while Scratch went to fetch Fitzpatrick for some final words before the trader started Pretty On Top's delegation back for the north country.

"When do you reckon I'll see your face up near my post again?" Meldrum asked as they watched the white-headed agent shaking hands with each of the three dozen Crow delegates.

Titus shrugged. "Don't rightly know. Late in the season as it is now, we're likely to lay over the winter with Bridger. Maybeso see what comes next summer when them emigrants start rolling through."

"It's for sure Jim can use your help about his place, busy as I hear he is with them folks bound for Oregon."

Titus gazed at Meldrum, held out his arm to the trader. "Don't know when I'll find myself on your doorstep again."

"Been a long, long time since you ever had to be anywhere." And Meldrum grabbed Scratch's arm, shaking it vigorously.

"Onliest place I ever had to be was ronnyvoo!" he said. "I'll see you again one of these seasons," Titus promised. "Leastways, that's what Real Bird promised me."

"Real Bird? The old seer?"

"That ol' rattle-shaker said I was gonna leave the Crow two more times, but no more after that," he explained. By then the Crow were mounting up all around them. "So I figger I still got some travelin' to get outta my mokersons afore my bones go white and groan in the wind."

"Stop by the fort when you come back to the Yellowstone, Titus Bass," Meldrum said with melancholy as he started for his horse. "We'll share us a drink of that special brandy you don't like at all, the stuff you still guzzle down like a thirsty man stumblin' in off the desert!"

He smiled at the trader and tugged down the wide brim of his floppy hat. "Watch your back trail, friend."

"You watch what you got left of your topknot, Titus." Meldrum reined his horse around, then suddenly brought it around in a half circle again to stop beside Scratch for one last word as the Crow delegates set off. "I like your company, Titus Bass. I like your company a lot. I sure hope the First Maker sees to it we have more time to share together."

That sentiment brought the hot sting of tears to his eyes. "Me too, Robert Meldrum. I pray you an' me got a lot more time to share together too."

While the Crow slogged their ponies through the shallow, muddy waters of the North Platte, Bridger rode up and dismounted. Together with Fitzpatrick, the two old mountain men came over to stand with Bass and his family.

When Titus turned at last to look at the Indian agent, he got tickled looking at the wide grin carved on Fitzpatrick's face. "Shit, Tom—you look like the barn cat what just ate a nest of swallows!"

"I s'pose it's bound to show."

Bridger held out his hand and shook with Fitzpatrick. "You done good here, Tom. You done real good."

"If this peace holds—I will feel like I done some good," the agent responded. "All of us tried to make a go of the fur trade, but the big money ripped the beaver out from under little fellas like us. I've tried my hand at this and that for the last ten years . . . so everything I've set my mind to now is resting on this treaty."

"By Jehoshaphat, you done it, Tom!" Bass cheered.

"I sure as hell hope so," Fitzpatrick replied. "Maybeso, we can count that treaty paper as the promise of a lasting peace here on the High Plains."

"What's your plans now, Fitz?" Bridger asked. "Can you come over to the post with us for a visit, maybe do some huntin' like the old days?"

"You 'member when we cut our way right into Blackfoot country, that brigade you an' me was leadin'?" Tom replied. "I'd like to do that sometime, come over to your place and have us a good talk about the old days."

"Ain't no better time'n now," Scratch advised.

Fitzpatrick shook his head. "Official duties, fellas. We're lighting out this morning for Washington."

"W-Washington?" Scratch echoed. "You an' who?"

"We're going east with Mitchell," Fitzpatrick explained. "Now he's gotta sell Congress on the treaty terms we wheedled outta these chiefs."

"Just you an' him?" Bridger asked.

"No—we convinced eleven chiefs to go with us."

"All the way east to Washington," Titus enthused. "That's a piece of travelin', Tom."

"Sioux, Cheyenne, an' some Arapaho too," he said, then looked at the ground a moment. "I sure hope them government fellas can hold the promise of what we guaranteed these Injuns over the last few days."

Bridger laid his hand on Fitzpatrick's shoulder. "Soon as you get back to the mountains, come on over to Black's Fork."

"That's right," Bass said, holding out his arm to clasp the agent's wrist. "No matter what them gussied-up, stuffed-shirt folks do to you an' your treaty back in Washington . . . count on me an' Jim bein' there to share a jug with you—either to celebrate your treaty, or to cry in mis'ry with you, that too."

The two of them threw their arms around one another, then Fitzpatrick embraced Bridger. Without another word, the whitehead turned and trudged away for the council grounds.

"Damn," Titus grumbled in a whisper after the Indian agent was out of earshot.

Quietly Bridger said, "You thinkin' what I'm thinkin'?"

"What's that, Gabe?"

"Fitzpatrick's treaty don't stand a ghost of a chance, does it?"

"Nothin's gonna change, Jim." He turned to look at his old friend. "Those white men back east ain't gonna keep givin' a few presents to these tribes out here . . . but these warriors ain't gonna give up their fightin' for a few beads and blankets. The tribes been makin' war on each other for longer'n there's been white men out here to the mountains."

"No piece of paper ever gonna change that," Bridger agreed.

Scratch looked at his family gathered nearby, busily rolling up their bedding, as he said, "Only thing what might change one day is them tribes gonna stop makin' war on each other . . . an' they'll start makin' bloody war on them white, gussied-up folks made all them tomfool promises to 'em way back when."

Bigger than life, Shadrach Sweete himself was standing with Bridger's long-time partner, Louis Vasquez, outside the stockade walls of Fort Bridger, both of them watching the return of the Shoshone delegation. On up the valley from the post stood more than five dozen lodges, pony herds dotting the meadows. Down in the creek bottoms the cottonwood blazed with a golden fire, touched by the late-autumn sun. For the old man known as Titus Bass, this place and this moment had the feel of homecoming.

"Jim Bridger!"

Gabe shouted in glee, "Shadrach Sweete, his own self!"

As Vasquez waved his hat and the tall man started toward the riders, Sweete suddenly stopped, his huge moccasins kicking up dust. "Could that really be Titus Bass?"

"Hell if it ain't!" he roared back as he reined up, kicked his right leg over and plopped to the ground. "Damn, but you're back from Oregon!"

All three of them met at once there in front of the open double gates while curious Shoshone men and women came out from camp to shout their greetings to Washakie's returning delegates.

"You give up on farmin'?" Titus asked as he and Jim gazed up at the face of their old friend.

"Never was much for scratchin' at the ground," Sweete admitted.

"Been four year now," Bridger stated as he pounded a hand on Shad's shoulder. "What you done with yourself, young'un?"

"Pray tell how's that daughter of mine—Roman an' their li'l'uns?" Scratch inquired before Shad could utter a word.

"I spent some time with them, raising a cabin an' a barn with Roman," he explained. "At the same time I was helping Esau get a roof over his head for the comin' winter too."

Bridger asked, "You have Hudson's Bay folks lookin' over your shoulder?"

He nodded and stepped between the two of them, looping an arm over Jim's shoulder, another thick arm around the bony Titus Bass, as they started moving slowly toward the open gates where Vasquez had disappeared, headed for the trading room. "We never went hungry, my family didn't. Plenty of folks needed help, an' they paid us in vittles. Me an' Esau even lent a hand to Meek a'times."

"He ever come back to Oregon after them Cayuse troubles?"

"Sure did," Shad remarked. "Don't know why he took a southern trail after he got word of the Injun murders back to Washington. But he traipsed on down through Santa Fe."

"I was wondering where he went," Jim said. "After him and Squire Ebbert come through late that winter of forty-eight, I 'spected to see 'em come back through again inside of a year."

Coming to a halt just inside the double gates, Sweete turned to Bridger and said, "That had to be hard on you too, Gabe—losin' your li'l Mary Ann—"

Grabbing the front of Jim's cloth shirt, Titus interrupted, "I didn't know you'd lost your daughter too, Jim."

"Like Joe lost his li'l Helen, my Mary Ann was carried off by them Cayuse," he confessed as he stared at the toes of his moccasins. "She was less'n thirteen summers by then. No tellin' if them bastards killed the girl . . . or a buck took a shine to her an' made her his squaw."

"Vaskiss's missus told me you took a new wife," Shad announced as women and children dismounted and kept their horses at a distance from the walls.

"Hell—sounds to be you've been here long enough to catch up on all my news!"

"Little more'n a week now, I callate," Sweete said. "Snakes was already camped yonder when I got in. I s'pose they been markin' time for Washakie and his chiefs to get back from the big talks over to Laramie."

"Truth be," Titus whispered, "Gabe's been married twice't since you left, Shadrach."

He stared at Bridger incredulously. "Two wives?"

"Married a Ute gal that next spring after you rode off for Oregon," he explained. "But she died the followin' summer givin' birth to our girl. Forty-nine. Named the baby Virginia Rosalie."

"That's a good name," Shad remarked. "You give 'er that 'cause you was born in Virginia?"

"Takes a friend to remember somethin' like that!" Bridger replied.

Sweete said, "Mrs. Vaskiss says you married a Shoshone this time."

"Washakie's daughter," he announced with a grin. "Last year. So we ain't had no young'uns of our own yet."

While Sweete and Bridger continued catching up on years of news, Bass called Waits over and suggested she pick out a nearby spot to raise their lodge. When his family had started toward the gold-hued cottonwoods, he turned back to his old friends.

Shad was saying, "With Mary Ann disappeared, you only got Cora's two younger ones around the fort now."

"Felix, he's turned ten years now, and li'l Josie, she's almost six."

Titus said, "I 'member how you lost your first wife, Cora—not long after she give birth to Josephine."

"An' then three years later you lost your Ute wife givin' birth too," Sweete said, wagging his head in sympathy.

"That was a patch of rough country there for a while," he confessed, his eyes gone sad with the remembrance. "After Virginia Rosalie's mama died, I had my hands full of a newborned baby an' no way to feed the poor thing . . . till this child come up with a idee."

Bass inquired, "You had a emigrant's cow, a milker?"

"Had two, an' both of 'em was dry," Bridger admitted. "So ever' mornin' I rode out to find me a small herd of buffler. Looked 'em over and picked out a likely cow. Dropped her quick with a ball in the lights. After a time, I got real good at cuttin' out her udder 'thout spillin' too much of the milk."

Scratch beamed with admiration. "That's how you fed your daughter ever' day—on buffler milk?"

"You see'd her yourself over to the treaty doin's at Horse Creek, Titus Bass. An' on our ride back here—ain't she a pistol? An' I owe it all to buffler milk!"

Shadrach looked about. "Which one is she?"

"That'un," and Bridger pointed to the scampering toddler set down upon the ground by her stepmother. "Blazes, but she's fat an' sassy! Just like her mama was. So I still got three young'uns around, but me an' Mary plan on havin' a fortful more of 'em on our own!"

Turning to Bass, Sweete asked, "How's Waits-by-the-Water took to Jim's Shoshone wife?"

"Hell, they get along slick. Seems that's the way it is with Injun women. They can make their way with gals from 'nother tribe easy enough," Scratch mused. "It's the bucks can't get along with bucks from 'nother tribe at all."

Bridger asked, "Why you s'pose that is?"

Titus thought on that puzzlement a moment, then answered, "Maybe the

reason they can is their bucks is allays off stealin' squaws from some other
tribe, bringing them squaws back to have more children for the band. I figure
because of that the women get used to takin' to squaws from other tribes like
it's no great shakes."

"Likely you're right," Bridger agreed. "Leastways, the three of us bound to
see for ourselves on that 'count. What with us three coons havin' a Snake, a
Cheyenne, an' a Crow gal too—three unfriendly tribes all mixed up together
here at this post."

Shad snorted a laugh and said, "Why, if the three of 'em didn't get along,
these here ol' stockade timbers couldn't hold all the hell those gals'd make!"

Titus jabbed an elbow into Sweete's ribs and said, "From the looks of
Gabe's new wife, I figger her for the kind what can raise hell way up an' stuff a
chuck under it so hell'll never come back down!"

Bridger slapped them both on the back, and they started toward the post
store. "I see'd that Louie come up from the Promised Land. You talked with
him much since you been here, Shad?"

"He come in couple days after I did," Sweete said, then held his two hands
out in front of his belly. "That's a man ain't ever missed a meal!"

"Louie has put on some meat since he's livin' so high on the hog," Jim declared. "He have any news 'bout Brigham Young's Saints?"

"Vaskiss only said he rode up here to sleep with his wife, since it'd been a
long time he'd poked a woman. Down there with all them Mormons, he says he
ain't got a chance of finding a part-time night woman to keep his pecker
warm."

"Why's Vaskiss makin' hisself cozy with the Marmons?" Scratch asked, a
little concerned about such a relationship.

"Them Saints been comin' through here ever' summer since forty-seven,
when you an' me met their high president," Bridger explained. "Brigham Young
sure has been workin' hard to change folks over to his religion. Hundreds and
hundreds of 'em roll through here ever' summer since you was here last."

"So Vaskiss went down there to the Salt Lake to become one of Brigham
Young's Marmons his own self?"

Jim chuckled. "No, he ain't no part of their religion. But as much business as
we was doin' with Brigham Young's Saints up here, we figgered we could open
up a tradin' store down in Salt Lake City itself."

"That where Brigham Young ended up planting his promised land?"

"Yep," Bridger answered. "He didn't take 'em on south of there, down
where I suggested they should go."

Shad inquired, "So most of the time Vaskiss is mindin' the store down there
with them Mormons, while you're tendin' to things up here at the post?"

"That's the fix of it," Jim responded. "Vaskiss hired him a couple Mormons
to help out down there. Shows we done ever'thing we could to make things
good atween them folks an' us. Hell, two year back—right about the time Louie

was settin' up the store in Salt Lake City, some bad blood got started atween the Bannocks an' the Mormons."

"What sort of bad blood?" Titus asked.

Bridger's eyes flicked around, then he said in a low voice, " 'Cause of what's happened with things down there—sometimes I don't know if I can trust Louie's wife no more."

"So Vaskiss is wrapped up in this bad blood atween the Bannocks and Mormons?" Sweete asked.

With a shrug of his shoulders, Bridger said, "Most times, I don't know which way Louie's stick is floatin' anymore. But when a whisper of troubles started two years back, we heard some Mormon settlers killed a Bannock who was making a brave show of things, trying to order the Mormons off Bannock land."

"Them Marmons just up an' killed that Injun?" Titus asked.

Jim nodded. "So that got the fire started in their red bellies. Them Bannocks was makin' plans for war on them Mormons homesteadin' outside the Salt Lake Valley. So when we heard 'bout the rumbles of trouble, me an' Vaskiss thought we ought'n let Brigham Young's folks know the Bannocks was fixin' to make raids on 'em. Louie wrote Brigham Young a letter, warnin' him them Injuns was buyin' up lead an' powder an' talkin' mean about killin' off ever' Mormon they caught."

"What ever come of it?" Shad asked.

Shrugging again, Jim said, "Never heard nothing more of any troubles. Bannocks never did start them raids . . . but over the last two years, Vaskiss got closer'n closer to Brigham Young. Real cozy when he's down there in that City of the Saints."

"You still trust 'im as your partner?" Scratch asked.

It took a few moments before Bridger would answer. When he finally did, Jim said, "I don't ever wanna think any man I did ever'thing I could to help would ever jab a knife in my back."

Titus studied his old friend's face a long time, then asked, "Who was you talkin' about, Gabe? Louie Vaskiss . . . or, was you meanin' Brigham Young?"

As his eyes narrowed and he peered around to be sure the three of them were alone, Jim Bridger confessed, "Sad thing is, Scratch—my belly tells me I better watch my back for the both of 'em."

TWENTY-EIGHT

"Father!"

Titus Bass had already turned at the rapid hammer of the pony's hoof-beats, Jim Bridger at his elbow, both of them tying off their horses to branches before setting off into the thick brush of the river bottom in search of mule deer . . . when he heard the boy's warning call.

"Father!" Flea cried out again.

This was the youngster's seventeenth summer, eighteen and fifty-three. For the briefest flicker of a moment, Scratch felt an immense pride in his son, how the young man sat a horse at a full gallop, the pony's tail held high, mane fluttering in the hot August breeze, and Flea's long, un-bound hair trailing freely behind him. But that pride swelled in his breast but an instant until the rider got close enough for Titus to recognize the pinch of fear on his son's face.

He stepped away from the horses, more toward the opening formed by the willow and cottonwood that rustled with the hot, late-summer breezes.

Bridger started to say, "Damn, but that boy's gonna scare off all the—"

He broke off his friend's complaint. "Somethin' ain't right, Gabe." And as his son approached, he called out in American, "Is there trouble at the fort?"

Yanking back on the single rein that was knotted around the pony's lower jaw, Flea shuddered to a halt atop the animal, then flew off its back and landed barefoot in the dry, brown grass, his breechclout flapping.

"Visitors," he growled in his father's American tongue. Then shook his head as he thought of better, perhaps more descriptive, words. "Riders. Many . . . riders!"

All the boy's life, his American talk had been getting better, but especially in these seasons just shy of two years, while they had remained at Fort Bridger following the Fort Laramie treaty, a time when his children experienced more and more contact with a new outfit of white emigrants every few days.

Winter had come early to the valley of the Green in '51, so Scratch ended up keeping his family right there at the post till spring. By that time many things stood in need of repair, both at the fort and up at Bridger's Green River ferry too, keeping him and Shadrach more than busy. About the same time those wet and muddy days of 1852, the first of Brigham Young's Mormon migration for the season had shown up at the fort. But these resolute Saints weren't making an arduous journey *to* the valley of the Salt Lake . . . instead, they were bound from Salt Lake City for the valley of the Green River itself, where the Prophet had commanded them to establish themselves and profit in the emigrant trade under the spoken will of God.

"Will of God?" Titus Bass asked that spring day as he, Shadrach Sweete, and a half dozen other old mountain men interrupted their repairs to Bridger's ferry when the column of Mormons rode up to the crossing.

They claimed they came with charters from Brigham Young himself, stating that they, and only they, had legal right to operate in trade with the emigrants inside the territory of Utah.

That's when Bass snorted and wiped some sweat off the end of his nose. "Territory of Utah, you say? You fellers be a long way off from the territory of Utah. This here ain't the United States. Why, this here's the free Rocky Mountains. Free! Far as you can see off in all directions—we're standin' in the free Rocky Mountains."

Shad Sweete joined in, "You'll have to ride a long way to the south afore you get to your territory of Utah—"

"You do understand that our Promised Land of Zion has become the territory of Utah, under a mandate by the federal government in Washington City—back in 1850—don't you?" one of the horsemen declared as he inched his horse forward. He was a hard-jawed, fiery-eyed zealot if there ever was one.

"No," Bridger himself replied, "ain't heard nothin' 'bout the government makin' no new territory for your people."

The zealot continued, "Then you haven't heard that this country all around the Green River, including that back down at your trading post too—it's all part of the territory of Utah now."

For the first time, Bass stared from under the wide brim of his hat and really studied the man. Then he took a few steps closer to have himself a better look at just who this tarnal fool was, and asked, "You there, the feller tellin' us all this news we ain't got no use for—what's your name?"

"Hickman," he replied. "My name is William Hickman. Being an attorney I can attest to the legality of the rights transferred to these people by the new governor of the territory, Brigham Young. You men are clearly operating your business without the necessary charter granting you the legal right to operate in trade with the emigrants. I am here to inform you men that you must stop your work, pack up your belongings, and move away from this crossing."

"You're full of horse apples," Bass roared with laughter as Shadrach pounded him on the back.

The hard-eyed zealot inched his horse closer until it made Titus nervous enough to lay his hand on the butt of the big pistol sticking from his belt. At the sight of that, the Mormon immediately reined back, glaring at Scratch, then eventually turned his granitelike gaze on Bridger again.

"Jim Bridger, I hereby notify you that you are illegally operating a trading establishment inside the boundaries of the legitimate territory of Utah, County of Green River, without the necessary compact signed by the duly appointed governor—"

"Illegal?" Titus squeaked, taking one step closer to the rider before Bridger flung out his arm, grabbing Bass by his collar, and stopped his old friend in his tracks.

"What you mean I'm illegal?" Bridger echoed.

Hickman said, "You'll have to quit operation at your post—"

"Quit?" Jim squawked. "I been in business more'n ten years right there on Black's Fork, son. Afore Brigham Young ever knowed about me an' my post . . . afore there ever was your god-blamed territory o' Utah! You don't have no right to tell me I gotta move . . . an' Brigham Young sure as hell ain't got no business sayin' he can throw me outta business—"

"He's the governor," Hickman said, patting a hand against a pocket of his wool coat, "and I am carrying his compacts here, documents that state you are operating illegally within the boundaries of the territory of Utah."

In frustration Bridger glanced at Shadrach, then at Titus, and finally back to Hickman. His eyes narrowed, "Was you in that bunch of Pioneer Saints what Brigham Young brought through here back in forty-seven?"

"No," and the man's eyes fluttered in embarrassment, "I did not have the honor to accompany the Prophet—"

"Then you best understand I'm goin' to say this one time, so mark my words afore you fellers clear out of my sight," Bridger interrupted him with a stony firmness. "It was near here, over yonder on the Sandy, where I took my supper with your Prophet, this Governor Brigham Young, when he was first comin' to these parts . . . an' I sure as blazes was already doin' business outta my tradin' post up on Black's Fork long afore your Prophet, or your governor, or whatever the hell he calls hisself now—long, long afore any of you Mormons come trompin' through this here free country, stumblin' around like blind barn rats asking folks to help you find your Promised Land."

"Under designation by the federal government, our Zion is now the territory of Utah," Hickman repeated, "which includes the County of Green River, where you are standing, and back on Black's Fork where you operate your trading post—"

"You've wore out your welcome, Mr. Hickman," Bass interrupted, his voice harsh but even. "It's high time you moved along." While flat, his tone nonetheless carried a level of threat as his eyes touched a few of those horsemen on either side of Hickman, then came to rest once more on their spokesman.

"You're . . . not going to leave this place, Mr. Bridger? Or close down operations at your post?"

Bridger sighed, "No."

"It's time you folks left," Sweete said. "We got work to do."

Bass tightened his grip on the pistol, having decided that if guns were brought into play, the first one to fall would be thick-tongued, big-talking William Hickman. "You been told get out. So while you Marmons can—git!"

"This is the territory of Utah, ruled by Governor Brig—"

"Git!" Bass roared this time. "Go on back to your Salt Lake Valley an' tell your Marmon prophet that he don't rule rabbit squat up here in these free mountains. Never will!"

Mumbling something to the other riders near him, Hickman savagely reined about in a half circle and retreated up the long slope of the cutbank. Two by two the others turned their horses about and followed that band of leaders angrily talking with one another, some of them peering back over their shoulders at the trio of old mountain men and those six others who had stood back from the confrontation, their long guns at the ready.

"This here's the free mountains!" Shadrach echoed Bass's sentiment to their retreating backs.

"You an' your Prophet ain't the rulers here!" Titus shouted, his fury unabated. "This is the free Rocky Mountains, an' by God we're free men!"

Before they realized how many days and weeks had slipped by, while they busied themselves performing repairs and making ready, it was time for the first train of emigrants to breast the horizon and rumble into the meadows—eager for trading at the store, looking forward to a day or two of layover to rest the animals, perhaps picking up a bit of news from Bridger on the condition of the trail ahead as he used a piece of charcoal from the fire to sketch out his map of the region on the rough-hewn planks of the trading room's door. That year of '52 had certainly been a busy season, one filled with sojourners—far more Saints pressing southwest for the Promised Land than folks headed to either California or Oregon.

And by the time the crush of travelers trickled off late in the summer, Bass and Waits-by-the-Water found one excuse after another to hang on for another day, then one more week, and eventually the first icy flakes began to fly. Winter set in. Truly a blessing to have good friends to wait out the season with, the incessant winds moaning through the timbers, winds working incessantly at the clay chinking stuffed between the log walls of their low-roofed shelters, winds that scooped up most of the snow and hurled it along in an icy blast that deposited great white drifts of it against both the northern and western walls of the corral stockade and the fort itself. Inside and out, the bitter winds sculpted beautifully hoary patterns on the snow it packed and hardened into something resembling the consistency of prairie sandstone.

And when the spring of '53 arrived for certain—no, not the false spring that came every year, when the weather warmed and a man's blood coursed a little stronger in his veins, but was quickly interrupted by another bout of bitter cold and a snowy, icy sleet that descended on this valley of the Green for one last onslaught of winter—but a genuine and warming spring, it was finally time to put things aright and make a hundred different repairs for his friend Bridger once more.

By then Waits was beginning to show, no mistaking that. Their fifth child this would be. Most every night after they had pulled the blankets over them and lay in the dark, she talked about how she was likely a grandmother by now, that Magpie probably had delivered her first child sometime around the beginning of last summer or so. And here she was, a grandmother, carrying another child of her own!

But she wasn't old at all, Bass told her again and again. Hell, if she wanted to look at old, all she had to do was look at him! Why, he'd be celebrating his sixtieth birthday this coming winter. The coming of the child was an unexpected joy to them both, but it was even more so a special blessing from First Maker for him. Right from the moment he first noticed Waits's belly beginning to swell, Titus had considered naming the child Lucas. Perhaps the way the Crow often named their young after a revered and respected elder who had passed away. Maybe, he asked the First Maker in the dark after the cabins went silent and only the tree frogs peeped softly down in the slough, maybe the Creator could tell him if it would be all right to name this child after that grandson who had been torn from him at Soda Springs so many, many summers ago.

So what with all the work that needed doing around the post that spring of '53 and performing the extra repairs for the emigrants who dragged their wagons through the valley of Black's Fork, the summer got later and later, and Waits got bigger and bigger . . . until they decided they'd just wait until this fifth child of theirs would come into the world at Jim's post. This was, after all, the very place where they had first met Amanda's youngest boy. Truth was, in the past few weeks Titus had begun to like the sound of Lucas Bridger Bass. If the boy was going to have a white first name, he might as well have the whole caboodle—down to carrying his pa's last name too.

Rare were the times he and Jim had stolen off to hunt together, both of them so busy at the post or up at the ferry, what with that fat and lazy Vasquez and his wife living their high life with Brigham Young's Saints down in Salt Lake City, and hardly ever showing their faces at the fort anymore. What a high-nosed hypocrite Vasquez had turned out to be, to his way of thinking. Why, word was Vasquez and his wife even rolled around in a splendid coach and four matched horses bought off the Mormons! A goddamned coach-and-four! If that wasn't taking on airs, Scratch didn't know what was. Seemed to be that Louis Vasquez had forgotten the old days and the old friends from those hard, lean times, and with every year seemed all the more eager to throw in with his new friends and business associates down in the valley of the Salt Lake.

So rarely did Titus and Gabe have any time to themselves, time like the old days when men rode off to hunt together, never really having to say much at all because they just enjoyed the moments and didn't need to spoil it with a lot of talk—just like the old days when they were young and strength flowed through them like the rush of an icy spring runoff breaking through a high-country beaver dam. The old days when it seemed as if their way of life could never end . . . that all of them would live on forever and this glory life of theirs would never, ever ebb.

So he and Gabe had promised themselves a hunt that morning,* down in the bottoms a couple miles above the post, where the mule deer loved to make their beds. A hunt for the spirit of the old days, a hunt in the old way . . . a hunt they would never get to make now that Flea had come galloping up with that look of fear on his face.

"Riders?" Bridger echoed the way the youngster had growled the word in American. "Not wagon people?"

"No wagons. Hicker-man come, with riders."

"Hickman? Bill Hickman?" Titus said, bristling at the mere mention of the Mormon's name. "You hear that, Gabe. Son of a bitch is back to try bullyin' you outta these here free mountains again!"

It had been more than a year since they had glared at one another up at the Green River crossing. Hickman's bunch of Mormons had retreated from the valley and hadn't been seen again until this past May when William A. Hickman had moved his wagons filled with Salt Lake City trade goods past Fort Bridger without so much as stopping or so much as a by-your-leave, first attempting to erect a store not far from Jim's ferry on the Green River, hoping to capture some of the emigrant trade. But, Jim's employees—old mountain men all—at that well-established ferry hadn't let Hickman and his bunch of Mormons bully them away. No, not since those ferrymen were all old veterans of the fur trade, men not about to knuckle under to the bluster and bravado of Brigham Young's chosen people. Hickman's outfit hadn't stayed long on the Green before pushing east to Pacific Springs, which lay right on the western side of the great saddle that was the Southern Pass. There his operation finally began to capture a little of the emigrant trade, siphoning off some of what

---

* August 26, 1853.

would have otherwise come on down to Black's Fork to trade at the far better-known Fort Bridger.

Hearing the name of William A. Hickman was clearly not a good omen.

Seething, Scratch cursed the day the Saints had ever come into this wilderness in search of their Promised Land. Day by day, season by season, Brigham Young and his zealous faithful had gone and changed things far, far more out here than all those Oregon- and California-bound emigrants ever did. The others had gone on through to faraway lands, but the Saints had plopped down right in these mountains, where it eventually had become clear as sun that Brigham Young did not at all look favorably upon the notion that the influential old trapper-turned-trader was sharing this Rocky Mountain wilderness with the Prophet of the Lord. Especially now that the Saints' Promised Land had become a United States territory, one that encompassed this wild and beautiful valley of the Green River, now that Governor Brigham Young was prepared to waste no effort to see that only his faithful would thrive in this new territory of Utah. No Gentile, especially the renowned Jim Bridger—who had been the real visionary to reveal the Promised Land to the Prophet himself—was bound to last long if he went up against the might of Brigham Young and his personal army of Avenging Angels.

"What's he come to see me for?" Jim asked Flea.

"Take over your post."

With a snort, Bridger scoffed at that with a grin. "You must've got that wrong, son. Hickman is a oily sort, that's for certain, an' I wouldn't trust the bastard no farther'n I could spit—but I don't think he's got *huevos* big enough to try takin' over my post—"

"Hickerman and many, many riders," Flea interrupted.

"Where, son?" Titus asked, growing concerned as he studied his son's face—heard how the youngster emphasized that word: *many.*

Flea pointed back in the direction of the post, less than two miles off to the east.

"At the fort awready?"

"Yes."

"How many?"

Flea dropped his pony's rein and held up both hands, closed his fingers quickly, again and again, until he had tallied more than 150 horsemen.

"Jumpin' Jehoshaphat!" Scratch exclaimed as his son's hands finally dropped to his sides. He turned to look at Bridger. "All men?"

"Yes," Flea answered again.

"He brung a goddamned army!" Jim growled.

Clamping a hand on his son's bare shoulder, Titus asked, "They know you come to tell us?"

Flea shook his head. For a moment he sought the American for it, then broke into Crow. "I was in the trees with Jackrabbit. We heard horses coming. Everyone heard that many horses coming. Men with many guns. Guns here," and he pantomimed stuffing his hand in his belt like a pistol. "And here," he gestured for another pistol stuffed in the belt. "Lots of long weapons too." Flea quickly raised an imaginary rifle to his shoulder.

Bridger's eyes were wide and lit with flame as he lunged closer to Flea. "The women, the young'uns—they all right?"

Glancing quickly at his father, Flea looked at the trader and said, "Hickerman no hurt womens and youngs."

"What'd he do with 'em?" Jim demanded as he gripped both of Flea's broad shoulders.

"Put all in your lodge."

"All of 'em?" Titus asked.

Flea nodded.

"How'd you get away?" Bridger inquired.

"I send Jackrabbit back to fort," he explained. "Said to him: tell mama—tell her I go for you men folk. Be sure to tell her in Apsaluuke, brother. No word in American talk, I told him. Jackrabbit went slow from the trees to fort gate. Hickerman's riders come out and jump around Jackrabbit, pulled him off horse, throwed him through gate . . . last thing I see—they pushed him on ground again."

Titus felt his gorge rising. Those goddamned bastards abusing and muscling around a ten-year-old boy! Damn, but he'd hated bullies all his life—be it men like Silas Cooper or Phineas Hargrove, Bill Hickman or even Brigham Young his own saintly self.

Licking his lips in anger at the taste of bile drenching the back of his throat, Titus asked, "How you come from the fort?"

"Down the creek," he answered in Crow. "These gun riders don't see me for the trees and the brush. When they pulled Jackrabbit off his pony and into the fort, they didn't see me in trees."

"Did you watch Jackrabbit get to the cabin with the women and young'uns?"

"No," Flea admitted. "Hickerman pulled Jackrabbit off ground by his hair at the gate, then I saw them no more. I led my pony to the water, got on and stayed in the creek till no eyes could see me from the fort."

"Good," Bass said. He turned to Bridger, his tone grave. "You an' me go in there—don't think we can count on doin' any good agin' more'n a hunnert fifty of Hickman's gunners."

"I don't know what he's fixin' on doin'—come to take my post," Jim groaned, desperation thick in his voice. "Or why he's done it." Then his eyes lit with hope and he said, "Maybeso you an' me ought'n head to the ferry and get the rest o' the fellas up at the Green."

"Seven of 'em is all we could scrape together, Gabe," Scratch declared. "That don't make for good odds, even if we're goin' up agin' bad-shot Marmons."

Bridger snatched hold of the front of Bass's shirt. "What the hell we gonna do? They got our women! Our young'uns too!"

Gently taking hold of Bridger's shoulders, Titus said, "I dunno, Gabe. I ain't never stared somethin' like this in the eye, somethin' where I had . . . no way out of it."

Slowly, the trader released Scratch's shirt. "Awright. How we gonna find out what Hickman wants and get our families out of there . . . 'thout gettin' ourselves killed?"

"Only thing we can do is wait him out for a day or so—"

"Wait? They got our families in there!" Jim protested. "What'd you do if'n it were Injuns took hold of your woman an' young'uns?"

"The Blackfoot done that to me once't," Titus reminded.

"You went after 'em too. Back when Waits got the pox and her brother was kill't freein' her from Bug's boys with you."

"Then you know there's nothin' gonna stop me from goin' after Hickman once them Marmons light out for the Salt Lake with our families," Titus vowed.

"We just sit?"

"No," and he was struck with an idea. "We got Flea here. He looks 'bout as much a Injun as them Marmons ever see'd."

"Flea?" Bridger echoed.

Scratch turned to his eldest boy. "Son, I want you to ride in there like you come to do some tradin'—"

"He ain't got nothin' to trade!" Bridger interrupted.

"Shit," Titus grumped. "Awright. You just come ridin' in there to have yourself a gander at all the shiny geegaws the trader got for sale. You unnerstand?"

Flea nodded. "No American talk?"

"Not one word, 'cept to say *Bridger,* an' maybe the word *trade,*" Titus explained. "That way them Marmons won't know you unnerstand much American."

Jim stepped up the youngster. "Can you do this?"

Unflinchingly, he answered in his harshest American, "I can damn well do."

"This gonna be just 'bout the most important thing you ever done for your mother," Scratch declared. "For your friends too."

Flea looked his father in the eye steadily as he said in Crow, "I am a man now, Father. There are many ways for a warrior to fight to protect the ones he loves. Sometimes a man doesn't have to raise a weapon to defend his family. Now is the time to show you I am a man."

That declaration brought tears to the old man's eyes. He blinked and swiped at his cheeks, then laid his arm around his tall son's shoulders and brought the young man against him in a tight embrace.

When he took a step back and looked at Flea, Scratch said, "I-I didn't realize how much you'd growed, son. Jupiter's fire, if you ain't shot up taller'n me in the last year or so. Yes, you're a man by anyone's 'count—an' that makes your pa real proud."

Bridger held out his arm and clasped wrists with the youngster. Then Flea snatched up the long buffalo-hair rein, a handful of mane, and leaped onto the pony's bare back.

Titus stepped up, laying his hand on the lad's bare knee, and asked, "You know them rocks way upstream what look like a mountain lion's head?"

Flea nodded.

"That's where you'll find us when you got some news," Scratch concluded.

In Crow, the youngster said, "I hope to rejoin you by sunset." Then he spun his pony around and kicked it in the flanks to set off at a lope.

"What'd he say there at the last?" Bridger asked.

Bass watched the young man's back until rider and pony disappeared around a brushy bend in the stream. "Said he'd come to us by sundown."

Gazing at the sun blazing high at midsky for a moment, Jim growled, "Sundown. Damn, hot as it is right now, I'll lay it's gonna get cold for our old bones afore sunup tomorrow."

"C'mon, Gabe. No sense thinkin' 'bout what's gonna be hard of it," he cheered. "That Hickman's got blood in his eye so he's bound to put out searchers now that he ain't found Jim Bridger sittin' round home."

"I s'pose you're right," and Jim yanked at the knot tying his horse to a willow limb.

Scratch swung into the saddle and stuffed his moccasins inside the big cottonwood stirrups. "We better scat into the hills afore Brigham Young's bully-boys come beatin' these bushes so they can get their hands on you."

Which is exactly what the Danite posse did.

But those noisy Mormons didn't search upstream far enough to get anywhere close to where Bridger and Bass lay in hiding, waiting for Flea to bring them some news as to who these interlopers were and what they wanted. Instead, two different groups of riders were spotted heading down one side of Black's Fork, busting the brush for their wanted man, then crossing the creek to turn about for the fort by riding down the other side of the stream. The sun had just set behind them, but the sky was still radiant with an orange-hued summer light when Titus spotted the lone horseman moving down from the hills through a narrow coulee, hugging the willow.

Damn if that didn't make him proud of the boy. From the looks of things, Flea had come around the long way, climbing north toward the ridge before he made a long and circuitous loop back to the west. Now that he had reached Black's Fork, every fifty yards or so Flea reined up his pony, turned around, and waited. Likely listening for the sounds of anyone dogging his back trail. Then he advanced a little farther before he stopped again and waited.

From their perch up on the rocks, the two old trappers could clearly see the Danites hadn't followed the youth, or—better yet—that Flea had shaken any who had attempted to tail him by leaving the fort in the opposite direction before circling back around behind the low hills. The young man's face was a stony mask of determination mixed with utter hatred when the two men stepped out of the brush and made themselves known.

"What you find out, son?" Titus asked in American as Flea slid from the back of his pony and pulled off the thick saddle blanket he had been sitting on.

The youngster stuffed his head through a slit previously cut through the middle of it so that it hung from his bare shoulders like a greaser's poncho. "I hear these men talk to my mother. They ask, she Bridger woman? She say other woman, point to The Fawn." Then he looked at Jim to say, "Sheriff, he come for you."

"One of 'em's a sheriff?" Bridger asked.

But Titus interrupted to ask, "What's a sheriff come to take Jim for?"

"Sheriff shake paper in hand. Say come take you away—you sell powder and guns to bad Injuns . . . Injuns gonna kill their people."

"Injuns gonna kill Mormons?" Bridger asked.

"I s'pose that's what they come to arrest you for, Gabe." Then Scratch spat a brown stream at the dry grass near his moccasin toe. "We both know that's horseshit."

"Here I was the one what even warned 'em two year ago that the Bannocks was gettin' a mite fractious an' was comin' to raid their settlements!" Jim grumped.

"None of this has to make sense to no one but that goddamned Brigham Young," Titus said. "He's the one wanted you out of here right from the start. Can't you see that now?"

"Why the hell he'd want to get rid of me for?"

"Man like him—all his high-an'-mighty kind—these here mountains ain't near big enough for him an' the rest of us too," Bass growled. "Way they're showin' their colors, Brigham Young an' his Marmons ain't no better'n a pack o' plunderin' Blackfoots. Come to steal away ever'thing they can . . . an' what they can't steal—they'll kill."

"You don't think they'll harm them women an' young'uns in there?"

"I dunno," Titus admitted. "Don't know what to think anymore now. The hull durn mountains is turned topsy on us, Gabe. The used-to-be's don't count for nothin' anymore."

Bridger's hands flexed into fists as he asked, "What's a man to do when that Lion of the Lord sends out a murderin' bunch that outnumbers us the way they do?"

Scratch said, "Only thing I figger on us to do is get word over to Laramie."

"Fort Laramie?"

He nodded. "Yep. Them soldiers is the only law you got to go to for help."

Bridger shuddered. "Used to be, we settled things here ourselves. Took care to right a wrong on our own."

"Don't bet your last pair of wool drawers on it," Scratch said, "but I'll bet Brigham Young knowed you was the sort to take care of yourself. That's why he sent more'n a hunnert an' a half up here to steal your post away from you. With that many of them niggers swoopin' down on your fort, that Marmon president knew damn well there was nothin' you could do to fight back."

He watched Bridger grind his teeth on the dilemma for a few moments, until Flea laid his hand on his father's forearm.

"Popo, these raiders," he spoke quietly in Crow, "they found Bridger's whiskey."

"They bust open the kegs, them gut-bait, high-talkin' preachers?"

Flea shook his head. "No, they took down cups, poured the whiskey, passed it around. Drank up one barrel. Then opened a second barrel too."

"They're drinkin' my goddamned whiskey?" Jim squealed after Titus translated. "That ain't good for them women and our young'uns—"

"Maybe it might just be," Scratch said, clutching at hope. "Could be, them Marmons gonna have themselves a hurraw on your free whiskey. I'll lay a wager that Brigham Young is the sort of preacher what figgers whiskey is the devil's own squeezin's, so he told 'em to destroy all your whiskey they found."

Bridger's eyes gleamed. "So they're destroyin' it drop by drop in their cups?"

Titus nodded. "Right. An' if I can put my faith in them gals of ours, they'll slip off with the young'uns when them Marmons is drunk an' our families got the chance to get away."

"My mama, she told these sheriff men they don't touch her or any child," Flea explained. "Bridger woman, she told sheriff that he hurt her or any child, her father was the great chief Washakie. This great chief of Shoshone people hear they hurt her—then Washakie put ten-times-hundred warriors into battle to wipe out sheriff men . . . then go wipe out all the villages where sheriff men come from."

Bridger grinned, "Damn if Mary didn't tell 'em off!"

Still, Bass asked of his son, "W-what'd these Marmons say to The Fawn's speech?"

Flea smiled. "Sheriff men good now. Said they want no trouble with Washakie people. Said they don't hurt no woman, hurt no child either. Leave them alone in Bridger lodge—go drink on Bridger whiskey barrels, drink lots on whiskey barrels."

"They put out guards?" Titus asked. "You see any guards when you rode off?"

He thought a moment, then held up some fingers.

To which Scratch said, "So Hickman an' Brigham Young's sheriff got less'n a dozen guards out for the night, while the rest of 'em are bathin' their gullets with your whiskey, Gabe. I don't think them women gonna sit over there in that fort of your'n for long tonight."

"Likely Waits-by-the-Water can help Mary an' all the young'uns slip off afore first light?"

Bass nodded with a grin. "I figger them preachy Marmons gonna be dead drunk by then, my friend."

There was nothing better in the world than the feel of Waits in his arms, her head nestled in the crook of his neck—just the smell and sense of her as Waits-by-the-Water shuddered against him in utter relief. For the first time in these past few months, Titus suddenly realized how big she had become, her belly swollen with their child she was carrying.

It was at that moment he noticed how his two youngest stood off to the side in the dim light of false dawn. Titus waved them close. Jackrabbit and little four-year-old Crane both came up to their parents, one arm hugging their father's leg, the other arm hugging their mother's leg.

"What kind of god do these white man worship?" she sobbed against him in Crow. "A god that is no better than the Blackfoot spirit that allows them to attack a woman's home, to capture her children—the same god who commands all his evil followers to commit misdeeds in the name of the First Maker?"

"I haven't figured that out," he whispered quietly in the first hints of a coming sun. "But from what I've seen, the leader of these people is every bit as evil as any Blackfoot war chief I ever ran up against. Maybe even more evil, because he parades around in all the trappings of the one man God has picked to lead His chosen people."

Within minutes of their emotional reunion with their wives and children, Mary Bridger began to tell her husband about the conversations she had with Hickman, as well as the Mormon sheriff and a few of the 150-man posse sent from Salt Lake City with Brigham Young's orders to arrest the trader for providing powder and lead and firearms to Indians who were reportedly hostile to the Mormon settlement of the Great Basin. Mary went on to confirm Flea's story of how she had cowed the posse leaders and protected the fort's occupants by immediately telling them in her best English that she was the daughter of the great chief Washakie—so that if these raiders dared hurt anyone her father would see to it that a thousand Shoshone warriors swept the land clear of all Mormon outposts.

"One of them Saints told her they had nothin' but the deepest friendship for Washakie's Shoshone," Bridger declared. "But they said they still had orders to take me down to Salt Lake City with 'em so I could stand trial for my crimes against the territory of Utah."

"What'd she tell 'em then?"

"Mary lied an' told 'em she hadn't see'd me for a few days—I was out huntin'," Jim replied. "So that's when they sent out them four search parties to look for me in the hills." Then he grew pensive, staring at the thin red line across the far horizon, where a new day was coming. A new day.

"What is it, Gabe?"

"Mary said there was a bunch—forty men she counted—ordered north to the Green River," Bridger stated grimly. "From the house where she an' Waits locked themselves in, she heard the orders give to them forty Mormons to ride straight for the ferry on the Green an' take it by force."

"Shadrach's up th-there," Bass stammered. "An' more'n another ten ol' hivernants we know—friends of ours workin' that ferry till the river freezes up for the winter. Them Marmons go to shootin', I don't know how long them boys can hold out."

"That's where we oughtta go first," Bridger declared firmly.

"Awright. I figger them Marmons down in your post won't be risin' real early this mornin'—seein' how Mary let 'em all get a real snootful of her husband's whiskey," Titus said. "We'll light out for Green River to see if we can help Shad an' the rest hold off them snake-belly, back-stabbin' thieves."

TWENTY-NINE

"Who the hell's out there?" a harsh voice called from the night.

"That you, Jack?" Titus hollered, having shushed Bridger. He did not want Gabe announcing his presence to anyone now that Jim was a wanted man. "Uncle Jack?"

"Yep—who's askin'?"

He located Robinson's shadow blackened against the backdrop of starshine. "Titus Bass."

"Why the hell you didn't come on in, Titus?" Robinson said with some irritation.

But Scratch did not move. Instead, he stayed in hiding beside Bridger and asked, "Who else here with you, 'cept for your woman, Jack?"

"Wasn't you down to Bridger's post, Titus?" Jack hollered.

"I was, sometime back," he answered, wanting to trust the old mountain man, who had squatted on Ham's Fork even before Bridger and Vasquez built their post on Black's Fork.

"Jim with you?"

"Why you askin' that, Jack?" Bass demanded, suspicion squirming in his belly. "You see'd a bunch o' Marmons come through day or two back?"

Robinson did not answer immediately. Rather, there arose the rustle of unseen movement, the crunch of sandy ground beneath rawhide moccasin soles.

"Scratch—it's Shadrach. C'mon in—"

"Shad, you're awright?"

"Big as life," Sweete answered. "Bring your mangy face over."

Before he did, Bass wanted to assure himself that Sweete didn't have a Danite gun to his back. Maybe he should ask first to see just how Shad answered. "We heard trouble was headed your way at the ferry."

"Mormons?" Sweete asked. "Damn if they didn't hit us yesterday. The bastards got—"

That was enough proof for him. Titus scrambled to his feet, whistled into the night, then started for Robinson's earthen dugout, hearing Flea whistle back to Bridger, who had stayed in hiding with the women and their children.

"Who's that with you, Scratch?"

"I brung Gabe," he answered as he started toward the two figures. "Our families got out of the post after Mary set them Saints to swillin' down Jim's whiskey like they'd never heer'd of Brigham Young's temperance sermons at all."

Shad embraced him quickly, and Robinson grabbed his wrist to shake. Then Titus started to ask, "Any more of the fellers get away from the crossin'—"

That's when the figures came out of the brush, or bent low as they made their way through the low doorway of Robinson's hut. He quickly counted six of them.

"This all?" Titus asked as he heard the hoofbeats and footsteps coming up behind him. Suddenly, he remembered, a panic rising in him as he asked, "Where's Shell Woman? Your two young'uns, Shad?"

"They're inside with Jack's woman," Sweete replied. "Good thing was, they was over here visitin' when the Mormons come down on us. No tellin' who'd got hurt, the way the bastards was shootin' us up—"

"How many was up there with you, Shad?" Titus asked now. "How many workin' when the sonsabitches come down on you boys?"

"Twelve, countin' me," Sweete admitted. "Them Mormons had us surrounded afore any of us got up in the mornin'. Kill't the first one of us got out to take a piss. Shot down two more through that day. Night come an' the rest of us we slipped off one at a time—every one of us makin' tracks for Uncle Jack's diggin's."

Bridger came up and embraced both Sweete and Robinson. Then he asked, "Them Saints shot three of my men?"

"Maybe more," Shad replied. "Don't know for sure. Only seven of us made it here—on foot."

Titus had been working it on his fingers. He said, "That leaves two more what ain't made it yet."

"Likely dead," Robinson advised sourly. "We been waiting for them shooters to show back up here to ambush the rest of us, way they did on the Seedskeedee."

"Goddamned murderers!" Bass growled menacingly. "Five men murdered, Gabe! I tell you—we should let Washakie's Snakes tear right on through them Marmon settlements, right on through their God-blessed Utah Territory, an' be done with the lot of 'em. We can hang back, waitin' for Brigham Young hisself to try sneakin' out from the safety of his city . . . then we can be done with that evil son of a bitch—"

"We can't do that," Jim interrupted. "Not just yet."

"How come they didn't get their hands on you two?" Shad suddenly asked.

Titus snorted without a lick of humor, "Me an' Gabe been hunted down by Diggers an' Blackfoot, Sioux an' Cheyenne. You wanna stand here an' tell me you think some flat-footed Marmons gonna find Titus Bass or Jim Bridger in these hills?"

"Wouldn't give 'em a snowflake's chance in hell!" Robinson roared, setting the other old mountain men to laughing.

Sweete suggested, "With them Mormons come up to take the ferry outta our hands, maybe all the rest of us can move on down to your post an' take it back. You got plenty of powder an' lead for us to hold off—"

"There's more'n a hunnert of the bastards still down there at Gabe's fort," Titus snarled. "Not countin' the bunch ambushed you pilgrims, that's still some ten-to-one odds agin us goin' up agin them oily Marmons."

After a moment of reflection, Shadrach wagged his head and laid a hand on Bridger's shoulder. "What to do now, Gabe?"

"I ain't for certain sure," Bridger admitted, his face long and sad. "But somethin' tells me I got to have a look at things down there on Black's Fork."

Titus could not believe his ears. "You mean—head back to your post where all them Marmons is waitin' for you to show back up in that country?"

Resolutely, Jim nodded once. "I reckon I better see what's become of them Saints, what they're doin' to what's mine."

"No tellin' what'll happen, they catch us out in the open, Gabe," warned Shad.

"You can stay here, any of you," Bridger suggested. "I ain't askin' you to come back with me to my post."

"Your mind's made up?" Titus inquired.

"This here's my country," Jim answered. "I was here long afore Brigham Young. So as long as the mountains is free, I'll be here long after Brigham Young an' his Saints is gone. Just as long as these here Rocky Mountains stay free—"

"I'll ride with you, Jim," Titus vowed as he stepped up to his old friend. "I'll even ride with you to Salt Lake City so you can lay your hands on Brigham Young hisself. Don't you ever doubt me, Jim Bridger. You can count on Titus Bass to ride into hell with you."

Ghostly tendrils of gray smoke still rose from the half-burned timbers.

The valley of Black's Fork stank, the late-summer air heavy with the stench of those smoldering piles of hides the Mormons had set ablaze.

But nowhere they looked as they slowly advanced on the blackened gates of Fort Bridger did they see a sign of life. Not one of Brigham Young's Saints. Not a single horse or mule. Not even so much as a wagon or a milk cow left in the paddock of the corral.

"They cleared out, Jim," Shadrach Sweete said as they all came to a halt at the edge of the cottonwood in the chill of that early morning.

"Appears to me them Marmons put great stock in what your Mary told 'em 'bout her papa bein' Washakie, chief of the Snakes," Titus observed. "I figger they woke up with their achin' heads, an' got to thinkin' they didn't have the stomach for fightin' the Shoshone. Their kind allays gonna skeedaddle when they gotta fight men even up."

Sweete said, "I bet they scared themselves, Jim. Once they found Mary gone, figgered she went off to fetch her pa an' his warriors."

Bridger said nothing but continued to wag his head as he started slowly toward the smoldering walls of what had been his peaceful bastion in the wilderness. An uneasy silence hung over the valley . . . not at all the sort of silence the man had settled here to enjoy. This was the utter lack of sound after a piece of ground had been gutted of all life. Not the twitter of a sparrow, the caw of a magpie, or the shriek of a robber jay. Only the occasional whisper of the breeze that kept the last of the embers glowing, their smoke rising, an oily-black stench filling their nostrils as they stopped at the open maw where the double gates had once hung. The charred ends of those timbers lay in a heap on which a small fortune in buffalo, bear, and other skins had been sacrificed to the flames of a bonfire.

A sudden creak made them all spin about, their hearts leaping to their throats . . . but it was only the dawn breeze nudging what was left of one half of the broken corral gate as it swung on a huge iron hinge. A lonely, forlorn sound. Where once this place had reverberated with life unleashed, now it felt like it was the empty pit of a man's belly, gone hungry three days or more.

"You cache anything, Gabe?" Titus asked quietly as he stopped at Bridger's elbow.

"No. Did you?"

Bass shook his head. "S'pose we ought'n look to see if the sonsabitches left anythin' behind when they set fire to the place."

Jim sighed, his face long and gray with despair. At least half of every low hut was burned, the logs tumbled to the ground, charred and smoking. About a third of the outer stockade still stood, but the rest had burned nearly to the scorched earth, both the walls around the fort itself and the adjacent corral.

"The wagons're gone," Bridger said. "No sign they burned 'em."

"They took them too," Sweete declared.

"After they loaded 'em with ever'thing they wasn't gonna burn," Jim growled, a fury finally beginning to glow behind his eyes. "After they stole ever'thing right out from under me for Brigham Young."

"This ain't right," Jack Robinson said in a weak voice. "This just ain't right. Even if they said they come to arrest you for sellin' weapons to the Injuns . . . it ain't right they just up an' steal ever'thing from you an' your family."

"From me an' my family too," Titus reminded him.

Robinson muttered, "Stealin' an' murder ain't right—"

"These folks ain't like you an' me, Uncle Jack," Titus interrupted. "Ever'thing these Marmons do agin us an' our kind . . . why, they figger it's the work of their god and his awmighty prophet, Brigham Young."

"Damn Brigham Young!" Bridger shrieked. "I give him my hand. I offered to guide his people down to a valley where they could settle in peace an' grow their crops an' no one'd ever bother 'em again! The night I took supper with that bastard Prophet, he told me he an' his people was runnin' from folks what wanted to hang him, folks what wanted to kill all his faithful believers."

Jim turned to his friends, tears of frustration and rage pooling in his eyes. "Can you believe I was took in by the son of a bitch? Here I was gonna do all I could to help him an' his folks who he said just wanted a place of their own to live out their lives an' believe the way they wanted to believe . . . an' Brigham Young puts a butcher knife atween my shoulders!"

"You just say it," Titus offered. "I'll ride with you to the valley of the Salt Lake so you can strangle that evil son of a bitch with your own bare hands, Gabe."

"Th-there ain't near 'nough of us no more," Bridger said quietly. "Time was, we could ride out in the four directions an' be back inside of two weeks with more'n a hunnert . . . likely two hunnert trappers. Time was we could've rid right down on Salt Lake City an' dragged Brigham Young out of his house— quakin' an' shudderin' an' blubberin' for me to spare 'im before we dropped a rawhide rope round his fat preacher's neck . . . but not no more."

"There ain't a hunnert of our kind in these mountains anymore," Titus declared. "Ain't nowhere near half that many, not all the way from the Marias on the north to Taos an' Santy Fee on the south. Them what ain't gone west to Oregon like Meek an' Newell, or run back east to what they used to be . . . the rest is standin' right here with us." He swept his arms around the group. "Lookit us, fellas. Just lookit us. We're all that's left of a glory breed . . . an' ever' last one of us is barely hangin' on to what was by our fingernails."

Slowly the handful of men drifted off in different directions, not one of them uttering another word, each of them wallowing in his own thoughts, recollections, memories of a brighter day, shining times when they were still kings of this mountain empire, before the big fur companies choked the very life out of the beaver trade . . . long, long before the settlers' wheels cut through the heart of these mountains. Long, long before these self-anointed Saints came to murder, plunder, and steal everything worth living for.

Funny, Titus thought as he and Waits-by-the-Water walked arm in arm toward the smoldering log hut near the southeastern corner of the stockade, the one that Bridger had turned over to them, but that night back in '47 when Gabe had supper alone with Brigham Young by the crossing of the Sandy, the Prophet had swayed Jim with tales of how the Saints had been persecuted by the majority of folks wherever they had attempted to build their temples and live out their lives according to the dictates of their holy leader. Funnier still it was, now that Brigham Young's Saints had come to this land and through the sheer strength of their numbers had become the majority for the first time in the history of their church.

But what did these Saints do when they finally found themselves totally powerful over others already living in these free mountains? Did they let those other folks be, let others live their lives according to their own beliefs? No— Brigham Young's holy, self-righteous people turned out to be murderers and thieves even worse than those who had hounded the Mormons out of every city back east . . . for the Saints committed their evil, stole from Gentiles, staining their hands with the blood of innocents—all in the name of their gods!

There wasn't much of anything the Mormons had left behind. They had plundered everything of any value: blankets, clothing, weapons, cooking vessels stolen from every hut. And what they hadn't loaded up on Bridger's wagons before heading south for Salt Lake City, they had destroyed. Waits bent to pick up the remains of a brass kettle, smashed in half by the butt of a rifle or the heel of a boot, then stabbed with a bayonet until it could never be used again.

All that he and his woman had managed to acquire over twenty years together was gone in one fit of murderous thievery. Even when the Blackfoot, Sioux, or Cheyenne had raided, none of those tribes had ever completely stripped Titus Bass of everything. He gazed around, his heart aching and his eyes stinging with bitter tears. All it seemed they had left were their children—

Waits-by-the-Water suddenly hunched over in a spasm of pain, huffing loudly.

"Mary!" he cried from the ruins of what had been their little cabin as he threw his arms around his trembling wife. Sensing the volcanic quake shudder through Waits-by-the-Water, he hollered again, with even more urgency. "Shell Woman! Mary! Someone, come help us!"

Titus heard the footsteps pounding up behind them. Still holding her tightly against him as she caught her breath, her knees gone watery, Scratch peered back over his shoulder from the charred ruins, finding their children frozen in place, their wide eyes locked on their mother. Jim and his wife ran up and ground to a halt with Toote and Shad, the smoking timbers staining the air.

Seeing that frightened look in Mary's eyes, Scratch realized the woman knew what they were up against.

Quietly, calmly supporting his trembling wife, Titus Bass said, "Mary— we're gonna need your help. This baby's comin' too early."

•　•　•

He had asked Waits-by-the-Water if she wanted to come with him, but he knew that no matter how strong she was, she still was in no condition to straddle a horse.

He could have cut some saplings and tied together some sort of travois to carry her in . . . if she had wanted to go along with him into the hills.

But she had shaken her head, bit down on her lower lip almost hard enough to draw blood to keep from crying out loud, and buried her face against him until it was time for him to go. Alone.

They didn't have much they could do for a proper burial shroud, what with the Mormons stealing most everything and burning what they didn't take with them when they cleared out of the valley. But Jim Bridger did manage to find some scraps of flour sacks his wife, Mary, and Shell Woman quickly stitched together with some delicate and narrow leather whangs until they had a piece of coarse burlap big enough to wrap twice round the tiny corpse. Into this mourning sack they sewed the infant, this one and only garment the child would wear on this earthly veil. Soon enough, he thought as Gabe helped his wife with those stitches, soon enough the burlap would fall to tatters beneath the howling winds of this coming winter . . . then the tiny body would begin to go the way of all flesh. Back to dust, set upon the winds for all time to come.

When the little bundle was ready, Jim came over and nodded, then turned away. Neither he nor Shad had been able to say anything, their grief was so palpable.

"I will go now," he said to her as the fire's light flickered on the sheen across her wet cheeks.

"Say the prayers," she begged him in Crow.

She didn't have to. "I know the prayers to say. Through the seasons, I have said the words over so many. Over your father, and your brother too. These same prayers we both said over the grave of my grandson. And finally . . . the words spoken over the body of your mother too."

"Wh-why?" she whimpered again, grinding her face into his shirt. "Did we do something wrong to bring all this pain? Is there something we could have done to change this—"

Pressing two fingertips against her lips, Titus reassured her with words he did not yet believe, "This is not about us—not about what we did or what we didn't do."

"How can this be about that little man who died coming too early?" she asked in a husky whisper, her throat sore from the hours of hard breathing and the difficult labor.

"It isn't about our son either," he said. "It's about whoever makes these choices. Who decides what's to live . . . and what's to die."

"Will we ever know?"

He squeezed her shoulders against him for a long time, then finally said, "If we're lucky, we might figure it out one day. But . . . I don't think we ever will know why it was us, why it was here and now . . . why it was that little boy of ours."

She sobbed for several more minutes; then her trembling slowed until she finally pushed herself back from him enough to gaze up at her husband's eyes. Waits said, "Make it a safe place for him who has no name. Make it a very, very safe place."

He leaned down and kissed her on the forehead, right where her hair began, and drank in the fragrance of her, then slowly peeled himself out from under his wife and stood. Without a word he passed by his children and went to untie the reins to his horse.

As Scratch put his left moccasin into the big hole of the cottonwood stirrup, he stopped, stood still, feeling so damned weary. Then without turning to look back over his shoulder, he said, "Flea, I want you to bring me the body of your little brother."

With great effort, Titus dragged himself into the saddle, settled himself down, and toed his right foot into the stirrup as the tall, muscular Flea took the tiny bundle from Shell Woman's arms and brought it over to where his father sat on the horse.

"I can come with you, Popo."

His eyes were wet, tears falling down his leathery cheeks as Flea laid the burlap shroud across the crook of his left arm. "You stay with your mother. Sit with her. Do anything she needs of you. I . . . I must do this alone."

Not able to choke out anything more, Titus Bass dragged the reins to the right and heeled the horse in a quarter turn. The animal slowly carried him away from the smoking rubble that remained of Fort Bridger on Black's Fork in the valley of the Seedskeedee. The stars were still in bloom early that morning as the sky began to gray in the east. Just the faintest hint of rose at one spot on the horizon. A reddening, deepening, bloody rose that so reminded him of the smears running up and down the newborn's body, of that blackening pool of blood there beneath his wife's buttocks as her legs quivered in pain and exhaustion while she delivered the tiny lifeless body.

The boy had never breathed.

Scratch let out a long sigh, watching the thin, gauzy wisp of breathsmoke trail from his mouth as he began to sob again. This tiny son of his had never taken a breath, never known the simple joy of tasting life in his lungs.

First Maker breathed His spirit into each of us, he thought as he started the horse upstream toward the lion's head rocks where he and Gabe had waited out the Mormons' sacking of the fort. So it was the Indians of these mountains believed. The Creator of all blew His breath into the mouth and nostrils of every newborn at the moment of emerging into the world so that the child gasped with the powerful spirit that infused the tiny lungs and made the babe cry out with life.

But where had the First Maker been for this child he clutched, here in the crook of his left arm, just beneath his broken heart? Where was this all-powerful Creator, this Grandfather Above, whose place it was to watch over the tiniest and most helpless of creatures? Where had the First Maker been when Mary and Toote sat staring down at the child's lifeless, blue-tinged body, lying limp across Shell Woman's arms until Bass desperately shouldered Mary aside and took the child into his own hands, pressed his open mouth over its tiny nose and lips . . . where had the Creator been as he desperately fed his tiny son the breath from his own body?

With that one hand gently laid on the babe's chest, Titus had felt each of his breaths make the tiny chest rise. After each attempt, Scratch had stared down into the wrinkled face, looking for some flicker of the eyelids, some cough and sputter, some bawling response as the legs and arms would start to flail . . . but instead his child lay still and lifeless, no matter how he breathed into its lungs or rubbed its cold, blue body. So helpless, so goddamned helpless as he had started to sob, his tears spilling to mingle with the thick, milky, blood-streaked substance smeared all over the limp newborn.

Titus had pressed the tiny body against him as his head fell back and he let out a primal wail that shook him to his very roots. As he rocked and rocked and rocked there by his wife's knees, Waits-by-the-Water cried, clutching Mary and Shell Woman, clawing at their arms in grief, finally burying her face in the Shoshone woman's lap. Finally Bridger came up and knelt beside him, put his arm around Bass's shoulder.

"Let me take 'im, Scratch. I'll hol't 'im for a while."

"No," he had growled, like a wounded animal with its paw caught in the jaws of a trap—hurting, angry, and preparing to chew off his own foot to free himself.

But this was not the sort of pain he could swallow down and be shet of it. No bloody chewing through the gristle and bone, fur and sinew, would make this loss any better.

"G-get me something to bury the boy in, Gabe. Just you do that."

Bridger had risen there beside him and moved with Shadrach off to locate the charred pieces of those once-used flour sacks. He had brought them back and showed them to Mary and Toote. When Titus nodded that they would do, the two women had slowly inched away from Waits while Scratch went to sit at his wife's shoulder. Propping her against him, Bass laid their stillborn son in her arms and rocked them both in his.

"Day's comin'," Bridger said before he turned away with Shad and the women to see to the burial shroud and to give them privacy. "Couple hours, maybe three at the most."

"I'll go when you're done wrappin' the boy up," Titus whispered.

"What if it's still dark out there?"

"Even if it's dark, Gabe. I'm gonna do this right by the child."

Holding her, embracing both of them, from time to time he asked Flea to bring in some more firewood. Waits-by-the-Water felt as cold to him as the tiny stillborn. He knew she had to be freezing, shaking the way she was. Just keep the fire going so she did not die on him too. He didn't know what he would do if that happened . . . couldn't possibly go on without her. Wouldn't even want to go on without her, even if he could.

Strange now that the light of a new day was coming, brightening out of the east at his back, even though he felt his own spirit withering, shriveling, darkening like a strip of rawhide left out in the elements to dry and twist and blacken. Should have been that he went to bury this little body after dark, with the coming of night instead of the start of a whole new day. The way life had of giving a man a new chance all over again every dawn.

Miles upstream on the far side of the rocky outcrop, he found the tree that had several high, thick branches. Titus dismounted below its rustling leaves touched with a gentle breath of breeze every now and then. He shuddered once at a chill gust, pulling the flaps of the old, stained blanket capote together. This was always the time of day when it was coldest, just as the sun was deciding to raise its head into this gray world of little color and contrast. Sitting there, still and silent except for the occasional snort of the pony, or the creak of cold saddle leather beneath him, Bass listened to the wind sough through the leaves of that tree—wondering why the wind blew now, this holy breath of the First Maker . . . wondering why that life-giving breath of the All Spirit had not entered his son's mouth.

Damn, but he didn't want to grow bitter. Not here and now holding this boy's tiny body. Not when it came time for a father to do the only thing a father could for his stillborn son. He did not want to get hard and crossways with the First Maker, not now because in the last handful of years he had been sensing more and more that spirit breath move through him as it never had before. Maybe only because he was getting older. Maybe most everything he'd cared about before just didn't matter anymore, while some things meant more than they ever had in his life.

No, he did not want to become embittered, even though he so convinced himself that he possessed the power of that spirit in his own lungs that he could breathe its wind from his body into the lungs of his infant son, giving the stillborn babe a breath of his own spirit wind. But he had found himself helpless in the face of death. Every bit as helpless as he was in understanding why the First Maker had refused to save the baby. And Lucas too. Why had young life been snuffed out in its innocence . . . when men like Brigham Young and their evil flourished?

But, that wasn't for him to know, was it? Not . . . just yet.

Titus kicked his right foot free, gripped the round saddlehorn, and slid down from the horse's back. A gust of wind tugged at his long, gray hair, nudging that single, narrow braid he always wore—and carried a moan to his ear. An eerie, melancholy sound strangely like the final sigh a man makes as the last air

in his lungs comes whispering out in a death rattle. Drawn by that moan's direction, he turned slightly, made to look at the high slope of loose talus that had
torn itself away from the foot of the rocky cliff. Jagged seams and fissures
streaked down from the top of that ridge.

One of them would be the most fitting place for the tiny bundle.

Turning back to his pony, he untied the short length of buffalo-hair rope
looped at the front of his saddle, laid the shroud on the ground, and quickly
knotted together a sling so that he could carry his son on his back. He stood and
studied the slope covered with sage and juniper, scattered with loose rock and
talus shale, knowing he would have to use both hands to make the climb if he
was ever going to reach the crack he had selected, that fissure where the wind
would enter at the top of the ridge, moan down the entire length of the crack,
then whisper out at the bottom, making the sound of some language he did not
understand. But a sound that continued to call to him nonetheless.

Planting his foot for that first step, he immediately slid back down. Clawing
with his hands, he managed to hold on for the most part, but as he made a little
ground, he always seemed to slide back, losing more than half of what he had
gained. Eventually he found that if he kept himself low, digging in with his toes
and crabbing up on his knees, he didn't lose so much. The sun was beginning to
warm the air, and he had begun to sweat inside the blanket coat by the time he
reached the bottom of the narrow fissure. There on a ledge less than six inches
wide he set a knee, dug in the heel of the other moccasin, and balanced himself
as he turned slightly, slowly slipping his arms free of the rope loops.

For a long, long time he cradled the body against him and let the tears flow
as the sobs wracked his body with spasms. As the sun emerged from hiding, he
eventually blinked to clear his eyes and turned to peer over his shoulder at the
coming sun. The very top of that bright, glowing orb was spraying the horizon
with a luminous, orange iridescence. Scratch turned back, pivoting on that one
knee, and raised the bundle toward the crack in the rocks.

Turning the tiny body sideways, he managed to get the infant back more
than a foot, as deep as his elbow. When it would go no farther, he quit nudging
and pulled the arm out of the fissure. As his left hand clutched a fingerhold in a
nearby seam, Titus leaned over and grabbed hold of the first of the loose rocks
around him, one no bigger than his own hand. He stuffed it into the fissure.
Then another. Again and again he shoved loose rocks in after the burlap shroud,
pounding each one in with the succeeding rock so they wouldn't easily come
loose with freezing and thawing, freezing and thawing across untold seasons.
Finally he had all the rocks the fissure could hold.

He had buried his son within the folds of the earth, here in these free mountains.

Sweating with the heat of the rising sun, Bass pulled one arm, then the other,
free of the coat, and flung it down the slope. It made him too damn hot and, be-

sides, he might trip himself on its long tails as he slowly inched his way back down the treacherous slope of loose talus.

Sighing, he turned and closed his eyes, letting himself feel the warmth of the sun as it pressed its light against his face. A feeling came over him as the wind moved through his hair. But he regretted that he didn't have a whistle. Not a whistle carved from the wingbone of an eagle and wrapped with colorful porcupine quillwork the likes of the one he had taken off that dead Blackfoot warrior, then hung around the neck of the dead man's younger brother. No matter, he thought.

Wetting his parched lips with his tongue, Scratch began to whistle—doing his best to imitate the shrill cry of a diving hawk on the wing. Then making his best rendition of a sound he had heard ten thousand times in these mountains: the harsh call of the golden eagle. A war cry. A high, sliding screech that he laid upon the wind as his offering for this stillborn child. Nothing more than his lips, and his prayers.

That's all he could offer the boy now. Prayers for a child who would never learn to crawl or toddle, for a boy who would never learn to run and ride, for the man who would never hunt or fight enemies alongside his old man. This child who would never become a warrior, protecting his woman and their children . . .

And that made him sob all the harder, making it nearly impossible for him to raise that whistle as an offering to the wind.

Then he swallowed down the pain, shoving it as far into his belly as he could so he could whistle loudly as the sun baked him and the insects began to whir in the brush below at the base of the slope. Each time he raised the shrill cry, he felt a little better . . . until he fell silent and dried his eyes.

Titus turned and faced the fissure once more, kissed his fingertips, then laid his hand on those rocks he had hammered in upon the tiny body. That last good-bye said, the father began to slide down the slope, yard by yard, reaching the blanket capote and dragging it with him as he descended to the brush and dry grass. Rolling up the coat as he stepped over to the pony, Scratch tied it behind his saddle, stuffed a foot in the stirrup, and swung up for the ride back to the gutted, half-burned ruins of Fort Bridger and his wife.

She would likely be about as empty as Gabe's plundered post. Waits needed him. He needed her. Together they would have to sort through the why of this.

What to do now, and where to go . . . and how would he convince Waits to go on?

She was waiting for him when he came out of the trees at the edge of the far meadow. His wife was sitting against a section of the corral wall the Mormons hadn't burned down. He knew it was her, the way Jackrabbit sat on one side of his mother, little Crane in her mother's lap. And standing guard over them all was his eldest son, Flea. The tall, sinewy young man waited with his shoulders back, his pony's reins in one hand, Scratch's long flintlock in the other—watching his father approach from the southwest across the open ground.

The summer wind moved through Flea's unbound hair, whipping it across his face, as the youth turned to the side and his mouth moved. Titus could not hear the words at this distance, but in a moment Bridger appeared at the sundered gate. Behind him came Shadrach and their families. With them the last of Bridger's ferry workers came to stand. They all waited in silence as Flea and Gabe helped Waits-by-the-Water to her feet. No one moved as Scratch drew near, reined back, and let his eyes touch each face.

Gazing down at his wife, he said, "It's done."

Bridger said, "I'm goin' to Laramie, Scratch."

His eyes moved to Gabe's face. "What you decided on doin'?"

"Maybeso them soldiers will help," Jim sighed.

"Help you do what?"

"Go after them Saints in the Salt Lake Valley."

Titus wagged his head. "I told you I'd ride with you, Gabe. But them soldiers ain't gonna be wuth a red piss to us."

"What you think I ought'n do?"

"Do what folks in these mountains allays done," Titus said as he slid from the saddle. "You gather round you them what you can count on—then go to right the wrong what's been done to you."

For a moment, it appeared Bridger didn't understand, but he eventually said, "You figger I ought'n find Washakie?"

"Yep. He can put his warriors on the trail behind us, fightin' men what them Marmons can't never stop."

But Bridger stared at the ground for some time before he looked up at Bass again and said, "That means I'd be startin' a Injun war, Scratch."

"No, the way I see it, them Marmons started the war on you," he snarled. "You'd just be finishin' what they was goddamned fools enough to start by takin' ever'thing from you but your life an' your family."

Gray-faced, Bridger finally said, "I'll go on over to Laramie. Give them soldiers a chance to help me, or turn me down."

"An' when they turn you down," Titus asked, "what then?"

"We come down to playin' our hand," Jim said, then paused. "You an' me gonna see about makin' Brigham Young pay for what his Saints done to us an' our families."

THIRTY

It was a damned shame, he brooded as an icy snow swirled round them like tiny lance points.

Time was a man knew what he could count on, who to count on. But from those final days at the end of the fur trade when white man first turned on white, things got real murky. Tragedy of it was, the more white men out here, the muddier the water, and the muddier the water, the harder it was for a man to see his way through his troubles. Used to be a man knew the straight way on through to making right of any trouble that came his way. Used to be . . . hell, Titus thought, everything about his own self was used to be, so it seemed.

A used-to-be man who only belonged in a used-to-be country. But—even that was shrinking smaller and smaller with every season. Folks what didn't give a damn about things like honor and decency, folks what trampled on the rights of others, folks what claimed they was the chosen ones had come to kill and steal all in the name of their prophet and his god. Titus Bass wondered how folks like Brigham Young and his Mormons could act so self-righteous when they sure as hell hadn't acted as if they possessed a single shred of honor. How was it that the First Maker could let these false prophets and their followers get away with hurting good folk?

How was it that the Creator could stand idly by while not lifting a hand to help decent men who were willing to right a terrible wrong?

But that's just the way things turned out when their bunch hurried over to Fort Laramie that fall of '53, eager to talk with Major Chilton about using his army to retrieve the stock and goods stolen from Bridger's post.

"I'm sorry, but there's not anything I can do," Chilton sighed after Bridger presented his case before the major and some of his officers.

"N-nothin' you can do?" Titus roared, lunging forward a step before Jim snagged his arm and held him in place.

Gabe said, "What're you tellin' us?"

The major ran fingers through his graying goatee. "I haven't got the authority to take any action against the duly constituted government of Utah Territory."

So Bass said, "Maybeso we ought'n go ahead on an' do what Mary Bridger suggested we do in the first place, Major."

Chilton turned to him with a stony, disapproving gaze. "And start an Indian war?"

Setting his jaw, Scratch snarled, "No Injun war. Just takin' a li'l revenge on some Marmons—"

"You can't do that!" Chilton snapped.

Glaring at the officer, Titus said, "It's Jim's right. His family's been hurt. An' his wife is Washakie's daughter. Best you soldiers l'arn it's the way of Injuns to hurt back them what hurt you. Likely them Snakes are north of here right now, huntin' buffler, makin' meat for the winter. Jim's father-in-law could put ten times the warriors on the war trail than you got soldiers here."

Chilton turned from Bass to Bridger and pleaded, "I haven't got enough men to stop that sort of bloodshed if you get it started. Nonetheless, my superiors will order me into the field to put down the Indian troubles, which means I will be forced to fight Washakie and you too."

Bridger appeared to chew on that a long moment. Finally he said, "You'd have brung your soldiers to fight us?"

"Brigham Young is governor of Utah Territory," Chilton explained. "If he screamed and hollered that Washakie's warriors were killing and plundering Mormon settlements, the Department of the Army would send me into the fight . . . against the Shoshone, and against you."

Then the major leaned forward on his crude desk littered with sheets of foolscap and maps, saying, "Besides, Mr. Bridger, you ought to think about who you would be leading Washakie and his warriors against."

Jim glowered at the officer, saying, "Mormons: the folks what stole ever'thing from me an' burned down the rest."

"No," Chilton argued. "Those Indians would be murdering and plundering the settlements of innocent farmers and their families. You wouldn't be taking revenge on the men who robbed you and murdered your employees. You and Washakie would be taking your revenge on innocent folks . . . folks just as blameless as you claim you are, Mr. Bridger."

Gabe twitched in anger, "I ain't to blame for gettin' robbed of everything—"

"Damn you!" Bass snarled.

Chilton jerked aside to stare at Titus, saying, "Mr. Bridger, maybe I should go ahead to arrest you and your two friends here and now before you incite more trouble than we could ever put a stop to."

"Trouble with you, Major," Titus growled, "your preachin' words about hurtin' innocent folk only works on the hearts of good men like Jim Bridger here. That's why I damn you—because one way or 'nother, you know the sort of men you have standin' afore you right now. We're men what got a code of honor . . . honor what wouldn't ever let us hurt no innocent women an' children—not even a man innocent of what his leader's done to Jim."

"Like havin' his gunmen murder some of our friends," Shadrach said as he finally stepped out of the shadows at the corner of the room. "Bastards cut us down without givin' ary a one of 'em a fighting chance. That's cold-blooded murder!"

"To my way of thinking, that business at the ferry is an entirely different matter than the one involving how they seized Jim's fort," Chilton argued. "But bringing in the actual murderers would be a hopeless task. Who is to say which of those Mormons killed your friends, which of them are to stand trial for murder?"

"You can't even make a try to bring 'em back here for a trial?" Bridger demanded.

"No," Chilton said. "Not when those men were acting with what is called duly constituted authority. I would be undertaking a fool's errand."

"We're the damned fools," Bass growled, "fools for thinkin' this here army ever gonna help us do what's right."

Chilton arose from his chair. "Mr. Bridger, it's far better you worry about what crimes you've been accused of."

Gabe stared at the major in disbelief. "My crimes?"

"From the sound of things," the major expounded as he inched around the side of his desk, "that posse was operating with a writ to arrest you and bring you back to Salt Lake City for a trial on charges of inciting the Indians against the outlying Mormon settlements."

"Like hell I did!"

Chilton glared at Bridger, saying, "I'm not so sure of you anymore, Mr. Bridger. You might well have incited those Indians against the Mormons . . . because you've stood right here in front of me and talked about leading Washakie's warriors against Brigham Young's Mormons!"

"He claims I armed the Bannocks," Jim protested. "They was the ones been causing trouble with no help from me—"

"The army can't help you," Chilton cut off the debate. "And if you give me any reason to believe you'll cause problems in the future—any of you—I'll have you sleeping in the guardhouse until you can whistle a different tune."

Titus leaned in. "You threatenin' to arrest us, army boy?"

Chilton wheeled on him. "You'll be the first, you arrogant, disrespectful scalawag."

Bridger seized Bass's arm, but Scratch didn't move. Instead, he looked at Jim for a moment and said, "That ain't necessary, Gabe. I ain't gonna do nothin' to get throwed in their jail. I may be a scalawag—just like the soldier says—but this here scalawag is smart enough to know this here's a empty stretch of stream, boys. No beaver comin' to bait here. I say we go."

"Go where?" Chilton demanded, his voice surly.

"I say we go back to Fort Bridger," Scratch suggested.

"Why would you want to do that?" the major asked.

Turning to Gabe, Titus said, "Because that's where them Marmons gonna go first when they come back lookin' for Jim Bridger."

The major asked, "Why are you so sure the Mormons will send another posse to arrest Bridger when they've failed once already?"

"Because I know Brigham Young ain't gonna sit still till he's got Bridger locked up down in his City of the Saints," Titus explained. "He'll send 'nother war party to find Gabe awright."

"And?" Shadrach asked, a smile growing huge on his face as he stepped forward to join his two friends.

Bridger laid a hand on Bass's shoulder, another on Sweete's, then said, "That's when they'll find us waitin' for 'em."

"I think you're a damned fool, Mr. Bridger," Chilton said, wagging his head.

"A fool what's had nearly his whole life stole from him by some God-spoutin' bastards," Jim growled. "Now, I'd sure appreciate it if'n you'd tell me where I could find this Mr. Hockaday you told me about when I first got here to see you."

"The surveyor?"

"Yeah, him. Where can I find this surveyor?"

"We've put him up in the barracks," Chilton answered without enthusiasm, starting back to his chair. "I don't really think he can help you, since that would involve him going back with you into Utah Territory to survey your claim."

"I think Mr. Hockaday deserves the chance to turn me down hisself," Bridger said firmly.

"It's up to him, although he is a government employee," Chilton declared. "If he wants to put himself at risk, I can't stop him."

"Why'd this surveyor be puttin' hisself at risk?" Titus asked.

The major explained, "Because he would be caught with Mr. Bridger here."

"Ain't no Mormons gonna catch me," Jim said. "They tried once, a hunnert fifty of 'em. I got away from Blackfoot an' Sioux, Cheyenne an' Pawnee too. Ain't no soft-headed Mormons gonna catch me."

"Mr. Bridger," Chilton warned, "for the last time I'm suggesting in the strongest of terms that you stay well clear of your fort."

"Why?"

"Fort Bridger lies inside the boundaries of Utah Territory, where you—like it or not"—Chilton sighed—"are a wanted man."

"Mr. Hockaday?" Titus Bass addressed the surveyor as the man emerged from his simple A tent pitched just outside what was left of the charred stockade of Fort Bridger. "You any good with a gun?"

John M. Hockaday shifted the shooting pouch on his shoulder and tapped the hunting rifle he held across his body. "I've been known to hit my share of game."

Bridger stepped up to him. "You ever shoot at a man before?"

The surveyor swallowed hard, but there was no fear in his eyes. "No. Never had to shoot at a man, white or red."

"You're a good sort, Hockaday," Bass replied as he flicked his gaze at the distant rider laying low against his horse's withers. "Chances are, if'n you was born earlier, you'd been out here years ago. I figger you'd do to ride the river with."

"That some sort of compliment?"

"Damn right it is," Sweete said as he walked up with the six other old mountain men, who had returned to the ruins with Bridger the latter part of October, camping their families in a protected valley miles away.

Grim-faced, they were all bristling with weapons as they turned, the sound of galloping hoofbeats becoming distinct, peering at the lone horseman racing toward them. The gray-bearded man dressed in buckskin leggings and a heavy blanket capote pushed back the hood at the same time he yanked back on the reins and skidded to a halt by Jim Bridger.

"They comin' on down the valley?" the trader asked the horseman.

He swung out of the saddle and said, "More'n three dozen of 'em, Gabe."

"Doesn't sound like good odds," Hockaday said grimly, looking over the old trappers.

Bass patted the surveyor on the shoulder. "I figger you can find yourself a place to lay into, place where you can stay outta the way, somewhere back inside the walls. Keep your head down an' you won't catch a stray ball—"

"I'm not going to hide from this fight," Hockaday interrupted with firm conviction.

With a smile of admiration, Scratch replied, "Like I said, you're a good man. Stay close to me an' we'll show these Marmons how to shoot center."

Knowing full well that he might be venturing into what could well turn out to be a deadly confrontation, government surveyor John M. Hockaday nonetheless had accompanied Bridger, Bass, Sweete, and the other ferrymen on their return trip from Fort Laramie following their unproductive talks with the dragoons about righting the wrongs committed by Brigham Young's "Avenging Angels." In a matter of a few autumn days, Hockaday had completed his survey of Bridger's claim on Black's Fork—a site both Jim and Louis Vasquez had long ago claimed the Mexican government had given them title to back in the days prior to that brief war with Mexico. Rod by rod, Hockaday had carefully measured the ground Bridger had heretofore marked with piles of stream-washed stone. By the afternoon of November 6, the surveyor had completed his duties and been paid what Bridger could afford. As it turned out, Hockaday had reveled in the company of the old trappers and preferred staying around the gutted ruins of Fort Bridger for a few more days rather than immediately returning to Fort Laramie. Those few days turned into nine by that midafternoon of the fifteenth, when the sentry came racing up with his news.

Bass and Bridger turned the sentry back around with orders to keep a watch at the far end of the valley, more than four miles off—not returning to the burnt-out hulk of the post until he was certain of the riders' destination.

"They got wagons too," the sentry declared as his winded horse tugged at the reins he looped around one hand.

That news worried Titus. He turned to Bridger. "They're comin' to settle in, Gabe. First they burn you out, take ever'thing the two of us own. Them wagons mean they come back to stay—just like folks with a eye to settle down in Oregon."

His brow wrinkling beneath the brim of his hat, Jim looked at the sentry. "Was there any women along?"

"Didn't spot a one, but . . . couldn't rightly tell."

Shad stepped up to ask, "Possible they got their women inside the wagons?"

With a shake of his head, the sentry said, "Ain't nowhere to hide anyone in them wagons. They ain't covered with bows—just got oiled sheeting tied over their plunder an' sech."

"Three dozen of 'em—all men," Titus reflected. "An' they're gonna come sashayin' on in here—figgerin' there won't be a soul around, Gabe."

"Let's fix us a li'l surprise for 'em," Bridger declared.

On the face of it, most men wouldn't have dared face more than three dozen armed Mormons with only ten men. But, nine of these weren't your ordinary settlement folk. No, not these double-riveted, iron-mounted, battle-scarred mountain men. Their sunburned, wrinkled, lined, and weary faces were nothing less than the war maps of their lives—and the light aglow behind their eyes now as they prepared to go into battle once more was like a lamp turned on all the victories they had won and the coups they had earned. As things stood, they knew they were outgunned . . . but this bunch sure as hell wasn't outmanned. Scratch looked around the small group of friends for a moment, his heart growing stronger. One of these old hivernants was clearly the equal of five, six, or more of those Mormon thieves riding back in to occupy what was left of Bridger's post.

Jim sent Shad with three of the men off to the timber on the north side of the meadow and another three just south of the half-standing walls. Then he and

Bass took Hockaday and secreted themselves just inside the charred ruins of the corral, where they hunkered down out of sight and watched to the west, up the fork, for the first sign of the invaders. It was here in the cold they waited and shuddered as the shadows inexorably crawled with the low tracking of the late-autumn sun, and when the sentry returned with word that the Mormons were near, they waited some more.

"There!" Bridger whispered harshly, the breathsmoke spewing from his lips in the freezing air.

"It's yours to open the dance, Jim," Titus reminded. "This here's your show."

Gabe turned to look at him. "You lost almost as much as me when they drove us out, Scratch. This is gonna feel good to us both."

He patted the scratched, nicked, octagonal barrel of "Ol' Make-'Em-Come," his .54-caliber flintlock rifle. "Ever since last August, I been waitin' to get them thievin' murderers in the buckhorns of my sights, Gabe. That's a mite long for a man to wait for justice—don't you think?"

"But we ain't really like them, are we?" Jim asked.

"Not in no world I'd ever be part of," Titus replied.

"You 'member how Shad told us them Mormons shot our friends down in cold blood up there at the ferry?"

Titus took his eyes from Bridger's face and stared through the gap in the timbers where his barrel lay . . . peering out at the oncoming riders and wagons, the muted sound of voices, the jangle of bit chains and clopping of hooves just beginning to reach their ears. Brigham Young's Avenging Angels came on slow, riding easy and not at all on the alert. Gabbing as men do when they don't have a concern in the world that they are being watched and are riding into an ambush. He sensed a cry for justice welling up within his empty belly, burning at the back of his throat—or, was it a scream for revenge? To shoot four or more of these Mormons out of their saddles the way they had cut down five of his unarmed, defenseless friends at the Green River crossing might go a long way to quieting its angry voice.

His mouth had gone dry by the time he struggled to ask Bridger, "What's your thinkin' on how to play this, Jim?"

"We both seen our share of killin' . . . an' killin's easy for men like us, Scratch. Hell, all them red niggers the two of us put under in more'n twenty-five winters—why, we could wait for them Saints to ride right up to us afore we let fly an' there'd be more dead Mormons on the ground than I care to bury."

"Spill what you got to say, Jim," Titus said, angry with the way Bridger's words had pricked his own conscience as the enemy got all the closer.

"You was once a fair shot with that ol' table leg you call a rifle," Gabe said. "You think you can knock that big gray hat off the one riding that roan out in front?"

Before he answered, Titus laid his cheek along the comb of the buttstock and peered down the worn, browned barrel, lining up the sharp rise of the front blade in that notch of the curved buckhorns of his rear sight. He held it on the hat, let out half a breath . . . then he said, "I think I can do that for you, Gabe."

"Awright," Bridger replied. "When that roan of his comes even with that pile of stone off there by the willows—you knock the bastard's hat off."

"You better signal the others, so them boys don't think we're openin' up the fight."

Jim turned, put two fingers between his lips, and whistled with the call of a meadowlark. Of the three signals they had agreed upon, that was the signal telling them to hold their fire. The other signals ordered them to fight for their lives, or to turn and slip away into the hills. Only three choices facing the ten of them now.

From those men waiting on the south, and from Shad's bunch on the north, came the answering calls. Scratch peered over the barrel of the flintlock, waiting, amused that not one of those oncoming riders had paid any attention to the bird calls. Flatlander settlement types didn't know a jay from a whippoorwill no how.

"He looks about there, Scratch!" Jim whispered low.

"Hush," he said quietly. "I'm trying to concentrate over here, Gabe."

Bringing the hammer back to full cock, Titus slipped his finger inside the trigger guard and set the back trigger. Then lightly touched the front trigger and slowly let his breath out as he blinked, blinked again, and held high on the Mormon's big gray hat. Just a twitch here and he could put a lead ball through the man's forehead, maybe right on up the bastard's big nose, or right on into his grinning, gaping, stupid mouth. . . .

The gun went off a bit by surprise—and everything exploded into action at once. The hat went sailing, tumbling through the air as the roan's rider threw himself onto the ground and started crawling backward toward the first wagon on his hands and knees. At the same instant other horses bucked and shied, men bellowing orders or screaming in surprise as they peeled this way and that—

"You there!" Bridger hollered as his eyes crept over the top of the low, burned timbers. "You Brigham Young boys! There's only two ways outta this valley now!"

Scratch had turned and already had the barrel blown out and a load of powder poured down the muzzle.

"Who the blazes are you?" a voice demanded as the wagons rattled to a halt.

"I'm Jim Bridger! Right now, you an' all your wagons are on my land!"

"It's Bridger!" another voice hollered. "We got the reward! We got the damned reward!"

"Shuddup!" the first voice snapped. "Bridger, this isn't your place no more. The lawfully appointed authority of Utah Territory has seized your land and all your worldly goods, in partial payment for your crimes against the citizens of Green River County—"

"This here ain't no court of law!" Scratch hollered as he finished ramming home a ball and shoved the wiping stick into the thimbles beneath the barrel. "Quit your spoutin' an' start fightin', you murderin' sonsabitches!"

"Who-who's with you, Bridger?"

"Enough to empty half your saddles afore you get turned around an' off my land," Jim attested.

"You're a wanted man in this territory!"

Rolling back onto his belly to stuff his barrel out between the timbers, Scratch bellowed, "An' you'll be a dead man afore the sun goes down!"

"We don't want any violence," the voice shouted. "Only came to occupy what's left of the post where you were selling weapons and powder to the Indians—"

"You an' your bunch will come in here over my dead body!" Jim protested.

A third voice called out from the milling horsemen, "If that's the way you want it!"

Another of the Mormons cackled, "The reward on your head is good no matter if you're dead!"

Titus spit behind him, the warm tobacco juice steaming in the subfreezing air. "You give them Marmons 'nough of a chance awready, Gabe. They showed they ain't the kind to appreciate what you're doin' to let 'em ride on outta here with their hair."

"S'pose you're right," Bridger replied as the Mormons started forming in a broad front. "Best get your head down, John."

The surveyor looked at Bridger, then at Bass, his eyes wide. "I'm here to defend myself, Jim."

With a grin, Titus said, "Go find yourself a shootin' hole, Mr. Hockaday. We're 'bout to send these here Marmons straight on to heaven!"

"Give the boys a whistle, Scratch!" Gabe growled.

He and Titus signaled the other groups with a quick, short blast of the Stellar's jay, then Scratch leveled his gun again at the riders just as the Mormons kicked their horses into a lope and started a ragged charge toward the charred walls.

Scratch's gun was the first to speak. The bullet slammed into a horse's chest, the animal skidding to a halt and collapsing on its haunches, tossing its rider clear. All around the Mormons, guns began to explode. Riders screamed in pain and terror as lead sailed through their midst. Other men bellowed orders. Horses reared and neighed. Wagons lurched onto two wheels as their drivers careened them about in a half circle as tight as they could, beating a retreat.

As he was digging at the bottom of his pouch for a lead ball, Bass watched how two of the Mormons were screaming at the others—ordering them off their horses and into the brush. Must be leaders of the bunch.

"I-I got one of them!" Hockaday announced.

"Kill 'im?" he asked.

"No, don't think so," the surveyor said. "Hit him in the leg."

"Good enough," Bridger growled. "Ain't likely he can do any good with a gun no how, not now."

The Mormons made it to the timber with their wounded as the wagons rattled up the valley and out of sight. Six horses lay on the crisp, brown grass of the meadow just now getting dusted with an icy snow—some of them lay dead in a heap, the others wounded and neighing pitifully. Two more hobbled around with broken legs, crying out. Bass wanted to drop them both and put them right out of their pain, but for the time being he'd save his shots for those Mormons hiding in the brush.

"Shad!" Bridger shouted. "Work your way in on 'em to the west!"

"You want any of 'em left alive?" Sweete called out.

"Only kill the ones what won't run off, boys!" Gabe instructed. "Put them others afoot an' let 'em walk outta here!"

"You don't stand a chance, Bridger!" that voice cried again, the one with the mean edge to it. "Give up now and we won't have to kill you to get you back to Salt Lake City as our prisoner."

Scratch roared, "I'm afeared you Marmons don't know what you bit off comin' back here!"

"Only a matter of time, Bridger!"

The two of them both fired shots into the brush, then looked at one another. Gabe was the first to speak.

"He might be right, Scratch," Jim whispered sadly. "Looks to be only a matter of time afore them an' their kind run all over these mountains."

"Naw, don't go thinkin' like that, Gabe," he pleaded. "There's still places for men like us. Get back far enough, up high enough . . . there's still places left for our kind."

"How far away, Scratch?" Jim asked as he began reloading. "How far's a man gotta go to find such a place?"

"North," he said as he poked his barrel back through the slot between the timbers. "Far enough from this here road to Oregon. Go far enough I can't see trouble no more."

"That's where you're fixin' to take your family?"

He was sprinkling some priming powder in the pan when he looked up at his old friend. "This gotta be my last trip back to Crow country, Jim."

"Why, ain't you ever gonna come visitin' again? Gonna let these here Saints run you off?"

Scratch wagged his head. "I'm talkin' 'bout the dream one of them ol' Crow rattle-shakers had for me. Said I was gonna go under if I ever left again."

"So, when you go back now—you ain't leavin' no more?" Bridger asked, a grave look on his face.

Glancing quickly at the wide, questioning eyes of Hockaday, Titus said, "I got tired somewhere down the trail aways, Gabe. Don't know where . . . can't rightly say when neither. But, I wanna get my woman an' our young'uns back north where there ain't no white niggers stirrin' up trouble for us."

Bridger grinned and snorted, "Just Blackfoot!"

He laughed too. "That's right. Man allays knows what to expect outta Blackfoot, don't he?"

Turning to Hockaday, Jim explained, "With them Blackfeets, there's more killin' and stealin' too, than there be with any other red niggers."

Bass nodded. "Up north, near them Bug's boys, a fella puts his nose up like this . . . an' he can tell what's in the wind, Mr. Hockaday. Down here in this country a man's gotta work to figger our which white men are good, which white men ain't. Up there, life ain't near so confusin'. You hunt an' you live. Life goes on easy, 'cept for one worry. Only one worry, Mr. Hockaday. When the Blackfoot come 'round . . . there's allays the worst kind of trouble. It's a good an' simple life."

The surveyor asked, "Y-you'd rather live with that sort of worry than down here where Bridger has made his claim?"

He stared along the barrel of his rifle at that patch of brush where some muzzle smoke appeared a second time. The Mormon hadn't moved so was doing his damnedest to make himself an inviting target.

"Think I would rather live where folks don't make out to be something they ain't, Mr. Hockaday," he said, turning slightly to look at the surveyor again. "Some folks, like these here Marmons—they gussy up their talk with all the Bible words, but they ain't no God-fearin' folk. Hell, Jim, even Ol' Solitaire— Bill Williams his own self—was more a holy man than Brigham Young an' a hull territory of his Marmons, all of 'em throwed together in a tater sack!"

Titus looked back down along the barrel at his sight picture and set the back trigger. "No, Mr. Hockaday—these here Marmons are the sort to parade around in the clothes of some holy folk . . . when all along they really set out to steal ever'thing they want an' murder ever' man what stands in their way."

Scratch waited a few moments after firing at the leafless brush, staring at that spot where he had been aiming. But he never spotted another puff of muzzle smoke. Fact was, during those heartbeats he waited, the Mormons started yelling a lot at one another, and their return fire was quickly withering.

Then through the trees upstream, Titus saw what blur of movement the other old free men could see from their positions. Their enemy was mounting up, helping those bleeding, wounded men onto what they had left of horses, every one of them retreating without much grace or ceremony.

"Ain't that downright ill mannered of 'em, Gabe," Titus growled as he pulled the barrel back through the opening, blew down the muzzle, then stuck the plug to his powder horn between his teeth.

"Ill m-mannered?" Hockaday asked.

"That's right," Bass replied, pouring a measure of powder from his horn into a brass charger. "I 'spected them holy folks to have better manners than they showed, Mr. Hockaday. You see, Brigham Young's murderers just run off with their tails atween their legs . . . but 'thout givin' any of us the slightest by-your-leave or fare-thee-well!"

Gabe was laughing as he clambered to his feet and peered over the top of the timbers, shaking his fist at the sky. "You tell Brigham Young he's gonna have to send more'n you milk-teat pilgrims if'n he wants to drive me outta my home!"

By that time Scratch was scrambling to his feet, having rammed home a lead ball. He cradled the flintlock across his left elbow and began to prime the pan on the gun's ignition. "Only way them murderin' thieves ever gonna take this here place from you, Jim—they're gonna have to come agin us with a army."

When Titus turned to look at him, Bridger's smile of victory had faded. His face was like a fruit gone sour and pithy.

"That's just what Brigham Young's gonna do now that we throwed this bunch back, Scratch," he said, barely above a whisper. "You an' me both know it. Lookit us, just lookit us—there be less'n a dozen ol' hivernants left in these here mountains now. We won't ever hold back that bastard's army when he sends it next time."

Bridger turned away slowly, his shoulders sagging with regret and more while he started trudging away from the charred wall. Titus turned, his eye finding the rest of their friends emerging from the brush and cottonwoods, stepping into the open and starting for the ruins of Bridger's post, their breath become long streamers in the icy air.

"Jim!" he cried as the snow began to turn serious. Bridger stopped in his tracks and turned around to look at Bass. "Come north with me, Gabe. Come north."

The trader deliberated on it for a long moment as he stared at the toes of his moccasins, then raised his eyes. "No. I'm gonna take Mary an' the young'uns to the Green River. That's where Brigham Young's territory of Utah ends. Where his Saints don't rule."

"What's there?"

"Nothin' right now," Jim admitted as Shad and the others slowly moved up and stopped in silence. "But come spring, I'll scout for a better crossing, build me a better ferry too."

"You gonna run it your own self?" Titus asked.

For a moment Gabe looked at the others as if he were a man who regretted dragging his friends through any more of his tribulations, and finally said, "If'n I have to, I will run it myself."

"I'll help," Shad offered. "I ain't got nowhere to be in a hurry."

Then one by one the other old mountain men offered their services too, even though Jim was quick to remind them that Brigham Young's Saints had already murdered five of their friends in a vicious and surprise attack.

"Don't know for the rest of these fellas," one of them replied to Bridger's warning. "But for me, I ain't got nowhere else to be neither. Like for Shadrach here, I figger the Seedskeedee is good a place as any for a man to stay out the rest of his days."

Then Bridger took a step toward Bass as icy pricks of snow danced and swirled about them. Standing beside Titus, Hockaday tugged up the collar of his coat and shivered as a gust of wind slapped some of the sharp, cold lancets against their exposed skin.

Jim asked, "How 'bout you, Scratch? You got any place better to be than Green River come next spring?"

"Crow country."

Sweete inquired, "Why you fix your sights so far away up there?"

"Yeah," Bridger added, "this here's a good country too."

"For some folks, I'll lay as that's so," he sighed. And finally said, "One time a ol' friend of mine named Rotten Belly told me Crow country was right where First Maker intended it to be. A man goes south, he must wander and worry over a desert, where the water's too warm an' folks grow sick. If a man goes north, the summers are short and the snow lays deep a long, long time. To the west the people eat fish and they grow old too soon, their teeth rotten too, since't they don't have proper meat. And in the east, a man finds the water muddy, the land closed in so he can't see far at all, and too many folks creepin' out from the settlements. No, Gabe—I'll head for that Yallerstone country. Seems to this child he's been showed the right place."

"You gonna winter your family on the Green with us, or you figger to head north now?"

He squinted his eyes and drew in a long breath of the cold, shocking air. Then he answered, "Now's the time my bones tell me go north, afore winter sets in too hard."

"What you say to ridin' with us to the Green?" Bridger asked.

With a sad smile, Titus said, "I'd like to ride with you fellas that far. One last journey together, till it's time for me to cross the Seedskeedee. Cross the Green . . . one last time."

THIRTY-ONE

A week later as they were nearing the Green River, they ran onto Washakie's village marching south. Word of the troubles had reached Bridger's father-in-law, and he was leading more than twelve hundred warriors south to spend the winter in the Black's Fork country, if need be to drive off any more of the Mormon attacks.

But Gabe and the others had sat in that council circle with the headmen of the Shoshone nation while he tried to explain to them that he did not want them to take up his cause. Eventually the Indians came to understand in their own way that if they sought to protect this friend and relation from those white men who stole and murdered, then the white man's dragoons would be called upon to come after Washakie's people. And even if the Shoshone won the first few contests with the white soldiers, more and more would keep coming . . . just as the Snakes had watched more and more white men flooding through their country, heading for Oregon, California, and—the valley of Brigham Young's Saints.

"I do not profess to understand the heart of the white man," Washakie admitted sadly. "I do know the heart of other red men. I know if those hearts mean to do me good, or if they seek to do me evil. Their hearts are there for me to read."

"Like the hearts of the Blackfoot who struck your people a few days ago?" Jim asked.

"Yes—a large war party of them," Washakie said, nodding with pride. "They came far to the south to attack my people—because they did not expect us to be so strong. They have not been as powerful as they were since the spotted sickness wasted so many of them away like breathsmoke. So our fighting men ran them off, like yipping dogs with their tails curled between their legs. The mighty Blackfoot!"

"This is good!" Bridger exclaimed, and quickly translated again for the rest of the old trappers who did not understand the Shoshone tongue.

"But," Washakie warned, "a hurt animal is a dangerous animal. And the war party may try to hurt others—the Flathead, Assiniboine, or even the Crow. But," and now he smiled as he said, "I am assured they have learned never to come south again to raid Washakie's people!"

He and Bridger were the same age, and between them had been a strong bond that dated back to when Jim's trapping brigade was fighting off an overwhelming number of Blackfoot, slowly being bested, until Washakie and his warriors showed up and drove off the attackers.

"Sometimes I do not understand the things the white man does," the chief continued. "The Grandfather far to the east, who told us to make peace with the white man and with the other tribes at Horse Creek, he tells us we must no longer steal ponies from our enemies."

"That's right," Bridger said.

Washakie continued, "The Great Father tells us we must no longer raid and plunder and kill our enemies. Is this so?"

"When you put your mark on that paper, that is what you agreed to," Jim declared.

Drawing himself up Washakie asked, accusingly, "Then where were these other white men when we put our marks on that paper and promised not to steal or kill? Where were they?"

"Who?" Bridger asked.

"The white men who came to your lodge, stole your horses and stock, drove my daughter and your children off into the cold, then carried everything else away before they burned your lodge? Where were those white men when we made our promises?"

Gabe wagged his head. "They did not sign the paper."

"Why does the Grandfather and his soldiers allow this?" Washakie demanded, slamming a fist into an open palm. "How can this be right, for white men to steal from those who have been their friends? How can those white men come kill their friends?"

Bridger shrugged. Without an answer.

"You white men have a strange justice, my old friend," Washakie replied sourly. "You are my son, you are my brother. So I will do what you ask of me, instead of driving these bad white people from our land forever. For your sake only, I will not draw my knife against them."

Bass leaned over and whispered into Bridger's ear, "You unnerstand what you just done?"

"What?"

"You just saved the life of the one man who's set out to steal ever'thing he can from you," Titus explained. "The man who's set out to murder friends of your'n if they stood against him. You unnerstand you just saved the wuthless, flea-bit hide of Brigham Young hisself."

Turning to his old friend, Jim's eyes reflected the pain and frustration that Titus was himself feeling. Gabe said, "If'n it turns out that I saved Brigham Young's life by savin' these Shoshone from even more trouble, then that's the way it's gotta be, Scratch. One day, Brigham Young an' me gonna square accounts. That's as certain as sun."

"I ain't so sure of that," Bass grumbled. "Brigham Young's the wust cut of coward. He's not man enough to stand an' fight you square, Jim. He's a yeller-backed, throat-cuttin', weasel-gutted coward who's gone high an' mighty, hidin' behin't all his believers, lettin' his army of Avengin' Angels do his dirty blood work for him. No man I ever had respect for gone an' hid behin't a murderin' mob the way Brigham Young does."

Near the end of their council, Gabe explained to Washakie that he was going to spend the winter on the Green, and when spring arrived he and his friends would build a new ferry for the white-topped wagons heading west along the Great Medicine Road. Once the ferry was in operation, Bridger declared that he intended to take Mary and the children back east, as far as the settlement of Westport perhaps. There they should be out of harm's way, either white or red.

"Will you keep my daughter far from her father for all time?" Washakie asked solemnly.

"Long as I see it's safe out here, old friend," he sighed, "I'll bring her back one day. But I want my father-in-law to understand I've lost two wives already. I could not go on if I lost Little Fawn too."

Nodding, Washakie said, "A woman goes the way of her husband. If he rides into trouble, she rides too. But if he takes his family far, far away from harm, then she must go with her husband. My heart will grieve for our separation, but I know you will take her where she will be safe."

That was all any man ever wanted for his family, Titus thought that night through and on into the graying of the morning. Somewhere safe where a man could live out the last of his days in peace. Maybe in Absaroka.

Washakie's camp was slow to awaken that cold morning as a few errant snowflakes bobbed and danced on a cold wind, scudding along an icy rime that coated the ground. But somehow Shadrach and Bridger sensed what was afoot. They awoke the other old friends early and kicked life into their fire, then set coffee on to boil before they pitched in to help bundle up what few possessions Waits-by-the-Water owned after the Mormons had burned or stolen everything from Jim's post. Old friends joked and kidded one another, like they had in the old days, squatting around the fire, drinking the steamy coffee, and chewing on strips of lean, dried buffalo. But by the time the sun was rising low upon the southern horizon, Scratch knew he could no longer put off this one last crossing of the Green.

"We'll be here all summer long," Bridger reminded, "somewhere along this stretch of the river."

Sweete stepped up with them, his eyes sad. "C'mon down for a visit."

"You're welcome at my lodge anytime, Titus Bass," Jim said. "I figger we'll make our home here till the army goes in down on Black's Fork an' throws Brigham Young off my land."

Shad shrugged. "But it don't sound like the dragoons gonna do that anytime soon, so I figger you'll find us here when you mosey down for a visit."

For a moment he looked over at the three women, always saying their good-byes while their menfolk stood off and stumbled through their own. It damn well had to be easier tearing yourself away when everyone believed you'd be seeing one another on down the trail, somewhere else, another time. Then again, maybe it was easier like this after all—just making the break clean and quick, not laying out any hope of the impossible.

Because Titus Bass was never coming back.

Scratch knew that now. It wasn't so much a matter of his not wanting to see old friends ever again—hell, there was a passel of 'em he'd never lay an eye on now, dead they were. No, Titus realized he'd soon have a hankering to see old faces, hear familiar voices on his ear, feel their arms around him and their mighty hands lustily pounding him on the back. It wasn't that he didn't want to return to Green River, or go wherever the old free men might hunt in the seasons to come.

It was simply that he knew down in the marrow of him that it was never to be. Titus Bass was never coming back again. This was the last time he would look at these wrinkled, wind-scoured, sunburned faces. The last time he would gaze across this piece of country. He was going home for the last time. Every bit as well as he knew the aches in his bones and the scars on his body, Titus Bass accepted that he would never be back.

So he swallowed deep, working up the courage to explain it, and finally said, "Very ol't man, name of Real Bird, some years ago, he said if'n I go back to Crow country this time, I can't never leave again."

"C-can't leave?" Sweete echoed, worry graying his expression.

He patted his tall friend on the shoulder and said, "My heart's telling me that's awright, Shadrach. Because my spirit wants to get back north to the Yallerstone."

As the others moved in close, forming a tight semicircle about the old man, Sweete cleared his throat and asked, "Th-that mean none of us ever see you again?"

Sensing the sting of tears, Scratch explained quietly, "Maybeso you niggers won't ever see Titus Bass like this again, not like you see me standin' here now.

Gray, an' ol't, an' awful tired. But . . . ever' night when you boys close your eyes to sleep, close your eyes to dream—you'll see them days that used to be." He looked directly at Bridger then, smiling. "Gabe, you 'member back to that night at your post, round a fire, when I come back after takin' them emigrants to Fort Hall?"

"I 'member the night."

"You recollect I was in the cups, an' how we talked of what was dream . . . an' what was real?"

Bridger swallowed. "I 'member that too."

"Them dreams you fellas will have of the used-to-be days are gonna be real . . . an' all the rest of these seasons without beaver, these seasons when the unhonorable men come crushin' in on us—why, that won't be real a't'all," he told his friends. "Way I see it, the dreams is just about all we got to hang our hands on to now. So them dreams of what was our glory time are gonna be all the sweeter for it."

Few of them could hold their eyes on him now, most of the old friends dragging hands beneath their cold, dribbling noses or smearing an eye here or there.

"I ain't got no doubt you're gonna see me again an' again, over an' over, in your dreams," he explained with difficulty at putting the feelings into words. "But I don't figger you'll ever see me like this again. In your dreams I won't be feelin' all my war wounds an' all these here battle scars."

Quietly, Sweete said, "We lived through a high time when other'ns went under, Scratch."

"That's right," he responded. "An' in them dreams each of us gonna have in the seasons to come, we'll all be fresh an' brand-new again, boys. Can't you see them dreams now? Why, we'll be settin' foot out here again for the first time— just like this land was brand-new. The day after God made this country for our kind, when we was the onliest white niggers to put down a mokerson track out here."

Scratch could tell by the way tears were trickling from their eyes that most of these old friends were remembering those glory days already. Veterans of more than two decades of survival, countless seasons and battles, victories and losses. Friends moved on and friends gone under. These last holdouts were remembering those bright and shining times when this country was brand-spanking-new . . . and they had been the first.

The goddamned very first to walk this high and mighty land.

"I'm going back north to live out what I got left of days, fellas," he confessed in a voice cracking with emotion. "Spend it with my family, up there with my wife's relations. Now that it's come my time to cross the river an' go, I don't want none of you to stare at this here ol' nigger too good. Don't want you to 'member his gray head or the tired way he moves in his ol' bones."

"Don't look at you?" Sweete asked.

"I want you ol' friends to do me honor," he started to explain, "to remember me when we was all like young bulls come spring green-up: strong, an' wild, an' with the sap runnin' through us so heady that no man dared stand agin' any of us, red or white."

Dragging his coat sleeve beneath his nose, Scratch quietly said, "That's the Titus Bass I want you to 'member. When you boys close your eyes, I want you to dream on them glory days we had. An' I'll be there. No matter what happens to me from here on out, I swear to you under this great sky that them dreams are gonna be more real than us standin' here right now."

Shadrach impulsively threw his arms around the shorter man, hugging him fiercely. As Sweete took a step back, the others came up and embraced their old friend in turn. Until it was time for Bridger.

With a deepening melancholy, Scratch looked into Jim's face and said, "Nothing lives long but the earth an' sky, Gabe. Only the earth an' sky."

They hugged and pounded each other on the back, then stepped apart.

Smearing the back of his powder-grimed hand beneath both eyes, Scratch cleared his throat and told them with a strong voice, "That dream I tol't you about . . . that's where Titus Bass is gonna live for all time to come. That's how Titus Bass is gonna stay with you."

Quickly he turned on his heel and went to his gray pony before any of them could say or do something that would stay him any longer. Settling in the saddle, he gestured for his son to start the others down to the crossing. When his family were on their way toward the bank, Scratch turned for one last look at these old faces he would only see in dream from here on out.

"I'll see you again—soon enough, my friends!" he cried out, his voice cracking with painful emotion. "Just dream of them glory days, by damn, you dream it in your hearts . . . for that's where I'll allays stay!"

They didn't have all that much when they put Fort Bridger behind them and started for the Green River, not after the Mormons had stolen all the extra weapons, blankets, buffalo robes, even unto what extra clothing an old mountain man, his wife, and their children possessed.

But by the time Mary Bridger finished explaining to her people what had happened to all of them at the hands of Brigham Young's Avenging Angels, Washakie's Shoshone opened up their hearts and their hands to the family of Titus Bass. A blanket from this person, a buffalo robe from another, an old saddle someone wasn't using, a worn kettle or dented coffeepot—nearly everyone gave something to the old mountain man, this good friend of Jim Bridger who had married the chief's daughter.

Once again Titus was stunned by the generosity of these people who lived with far less than any Mormon family ever would own, yet were a people more than willing to share what little extra they had with this stranger and his Crow wife. On top of that, it had struck Scratch, the Shoshone and Crow held no undying love for one another. So it was with deep gratitude that he had watched as Little Fawn brought the first gift to place upon the ground in front of the brush shelter where Titus and his family were preparing to spend that cold night after running onto Washakie's people near the banks of the Green River.

"While we menfolk was in council with Washakie's headmen," Jim had explained in a whisper as one person after another came forward with a gift for the Bass family, "that wife of mine went round the camp, tellin' ever'one just what you an' your'n been through to help us, Scratch. What you give up, what you lost just to be there to help a old friend like me."

Scratch's eyes brimmed as he looked over the goods given by people who did not have great wealth but were rich in spirit.

He said, "Don't know how I'll ever come to thank 'em all—"

"You awready have, Titus Bass," Jim interrupted in a whisper. "These folks know you chose to stand by a friend against a whole damn army of thieves and murderers—an' your family lost near ever'thing for it. These folks is honoring me by honoring my friend, Titus Bass."

For a long time he could not speak, the lump so tight and raw in his throat. Instead, the old trapper stood on his tired legs, one arm wrapped around his wife's shoulders, as they watched the procession of Washakie's people bringing gifts to the family of that man they honored as a faithful friend.

Many times in the following days he squinted his eyes against the low winter light glinting off the icy skim of snow . . . and remembered back to that afternoon as the sun sank and the weather turned bitter. His wife and children had been doubly warmed with those gifts of clothing, blankets, and robes. From there on out, they had no fear of freezing before seeing Crow country. Enough robes to throw over a small shelter made of willow limbs he and Flea could tie together, forming a low dome. Two old kettles to boil the meat he and his son had somehow managed to scare up in the coulees and at the foot of the ridges as they plodded north for the Yellowstone. When at last they would reach the land of the Apsaluuke and found Pretty On Top's people, they could crowd in with daughter Magpie, her husband, Turns Back, and what was sure to be their first child of their own. As soon as Titus, Turns Back, and Flea could, they would hunt for enough robes the women would flesh free of hair, grain to a smooth finish, then sew together to construct a small lodge for Waits-by-the-Water, replacing the one burned by the Mormon raiders.

By midwinter, life would return to normal. Something as close to normal as it could be for a man and his family who had lost a stillborn child, had everything else he had accumulated over the years either carted away to Salt Lake City or burned to uselessness in the cinder-choked ash heap that was Jim Bridger's fort. What bright hope it had taken to raise those walls back in '43, more than ten winters ago. The same hope that now carried Scratch and his family north through the short days, traveling between sunup and sundown, huddling through the long, bitter, winter nights as they chattered of the joy to come with seeing the faces of family and friends, gazing at familiar landmarks and that place a man called his home.

That used-to-be country where things might just stay the way they always had been for . . . just a little longer. A hope that it would be for all of them as it always had been for just . . . a little longer.

If that could be called a prayer, then it was the prayer of Titus Bass. The plea of a man who found himself caught in a world he did not recognize, a world where he felt lost and adrift. Better for him to flee that world the white man was changing into his own image. Far, far better for Titus Bass to strike out for what he knew, for what he remembered was tangible, for what he could embrace as the way things had always been, and might always be. That didn't make him a coward, did it? he asked the First Maker. To escape all that he knew was wrong, to flee where he knew men still valued honor above all? As he considered it, Scratch tallied up every ill and evil wind that had befallen his family—from the attack by the Arapaho in Bayou Salade to the troubles for Magpie at Fort John, hired St. Louis killers to the devastation of the smallpox, Comanche kidnappers to a Taos uprising . . . against one travail after another they had prevailed, until Brigham Young's Mormons came riding into their lives to kill their friends and steal everything Titus Bass had ever owned. And all of their troubles seemed to happen south of Crow country.

So this was the best a man could do—taking his family north away from all the trials they had ever encountered. Up there along the Yellowstone, back into the country of the River and Mountain Crow bands, life had remained virtually unchanged over these last twenty-some years. Few white men had ever come, fewer still had stayed on. The Blackfoot had their post up at the mouth of the Marias. The Assiniboine, their Fort Union at the mouth of the Yellowstone. And the Crow had "Round Iron" Robert Meldrum at Fort Alexander near the mouth of the Rosebud. Despite those far-flung outposts, few white men had come to stay . . . sure as hell not the way it was to the south, from the Sweetwater and Devil's Gate country all the way down to troubled and bloody Taos. Once a man got on the north side of Shoshone land and was headed into Absaroka, he would find life was quieter, more predictable, this far north—

"Friend!"

Scratch jerked back on the reins and brought the old rifle up, realizing he had been dozing, daydreaming, not paying a goddamned bit of attention. Behind him he heard Flea's hoofbeats as the youngster's pony hurried him from the far right flank.

He blinked in the waning light of that windy winter afternoon. Blinked again, clearing the water from his one good eye, and found the figure emerging from the brush. He wasn't sure what to think, what the devil to expect as Flea galloped closer, protectively vigilant in the face of any danger to his father. But, that was not the sort of term an enemy would use, was it?

"Who calls me friend?" he demanded of the figure bundled in a long capote and fur cap, heavy hide mittens.

"I am Slays in the Night!" the man cried. "You 'member me, Ti-tuzz friend?"

"Damn, if it ain't you now!" he exclaimed as he reined up near the old warrior. He looked about quickly while the lone Indian scuffled over, his moccasins crunching through the ankle-deep snow, dodging clumps of sage and juniper. He gazed at the face of this old friend with wonder now as the Shoshone's features took sharper focus. "What the hell you doin' out this far from your stompin' grounds, down south at the hot springs? A mite close to Crow country for your likin', ain't it?"

"I come looking . . ." he started to explain, then stared at the ground, as would a man searching for the words.

"Lookin' for what? Where's that woman of your'n? What's her name? Painted Rock? Something such—"

"Red Paint Rock." He looked up, his eyes filled with great pain when he interrupted. "She is gone."

"That's a damn shame, friend," he said quietly, glancing at Flea as he struggled to find some words. "I know how that can cut a man to the marrow to have your wife die on you—"

"No die. She is gone."

He squinted at the Indian for a moment, then dropped from the saddle. Waving his wife and family to close up and join him, Scratch asked, "Gone? She run off from you?"

"Blackfeet!" Slays snarled the word.

Of a sudden he remembered how Washakie had informed the party of old trappers that the Blackfoot were raiding, far south of their usual haunts. "You see 'em come through?"

His head bobbed. "North," and he started to sign as well as speak his birth tongue to tell the story. "Big war party of Blackfeet. Sweeping north. Striking down the Bighorn River . . . riding strong. Very big war party, go for Crow country."

"They hit Washakie's camp," Titus said. "But his warriors were too strong for them Blackfoot."

"Washakie," he repeated the chief's name. "We were friends . . . long time ago."

Stepping closer to the old Shoshone, Scratch noticed again just how gray the man's hair had become in the last few years—the black streaked with the snows of many, many winters and more than his share of trials too. He laid a hand on the Indian's shoulder. "They kill Red Paint Rock, or they run off with her?"

He swallowed. "Take her," he signed, one hand suddenly sailing off the other. "She is not a pretty woman. She's no good to them. Why take my Red Paint Rock from me?"

"They took her," Scratch explained to his wife as Waits-by-the-Water and the children came to a halt behind him on foot, leading their horses. "That means she's still bound to be alive."

Suddenly the old Indian dipped his face into both of his hands and wailed, his shoulders trembling. Bass understood loss. Goda'mighty, did he ever understand loss. Quickly he folded his old friend into his arms and let the warrior quake against his shoulder.

"You been hidin' since they took her?"

Stepping back, the Shoshone snorted and said with his hands, "Eight days now. This eighth day. They take her. I follow on foot. Blackfeet take my woman, my horses. They take everything else."

And Scratch understood how it felt to have the Blackfoot swoop down and ride off with a man's wife. How it felt to have the Mormons sashay off with everything he had accumulated in his life of wading crotch-deep into streams or punching all the way into California to steal some Mexican horses. Bass understood how a man could feel everything being jerked out from under him by forces he could not comprehend, much less control.

"The gun I give you?" Titus asked, hopeful.

Pointing back at the brush where he had been hiding, the Shoshone said, "I have the gun still. Balls and powder too. I go hunting."

"Man's gotta eat."

But Slays shook his head. "I go hunting for Blackfeet. Eight days, I follow their horses down the river."

"Was you gone when them Blackfoot come through?"

"Hunting antelope with my friend's gun," he replied with his hands. "I come back, see them riding away. Big, big war party. Dressed like Blackfeet. My lodge is empty. Horses gone. But I still have my gun, and my legs, and a small piece of buffalo robe—so I start following their trail down the Bighorn for the Elk River into Crow country."

Scratch looked into the eyes of his wife. She nodded slightly to tell him she had understood the import of the Shoshone's sign language. Then he glanced at Flea.

"Son, take the packs off that red horse there," Titus instructed in Crow. "Spread those packs among the other three horses. Our friend can ride the red horse."

He turned and explained to Slays in the Night, "Crow country is dangerous for one lone Shoshone man."

Slays snorted. "I am old and the rest of my days are on my fingernails. Crow kill me if the Blackfeet don't. This is all dangerous country now, when a man is ready to die for one he loves. It makes no matter. I am not running away from this one last fight."

Bringing his hand down on the warrior's shoulder, Scratch said, "Ride the red horse for now. Until we get your wife and your horses back from these Blackfoot. Maybe they don't realize they're headin' right into the heart of where the Crow are probably killin' buffalo for winter meat."

"You want me to ride with you?" Slays asked. "With your family?"

"My friend will be safe with me," Scratch reassured as Flea led the red horse over. "Now, let's get movin' again. My feet get cold standin' here in this hard wind. We gotta scratch us up a place to stay for the night, somewhere the wind won't find our old bones!"

"And in the morning?"

"With tomorrow's sun," Titus answered in sign, "we'll follow those tracks to get your woman and horses back."

But the cold wind that was picking up near sunset had brought with it new snow. Big, fat flakes the size of ash curls had started to fall not long after dark and continued past sunrise. Falling slow, except when the wind gusted like a frantic child, then rested before its next spasm of blustery fury.

Try as they did, neither of them could make out the trail, so snowed over and windblown it had become during that long winter night. But they forged on that following day, and the next two, continuing on down the Bighorn toward the Yellowstone. And by the middle of the fourth day they stopped on the high ground and gazed north into the narrow valley that lay off to the west, discovering a smudge of smoke laying low against the winter sky, hanging in among the leafless cottonwoods.

"That many fires would not be the war party," Scratch observed. "Not this time of day."

"No," Slays in the Night remarked. "War party was riding off there." He pointed to the northeast.

"The Rosebud, maybe the Tongue, maybe as far east as the Powder too," Titus said. Then he looked back to the northwest at that smoke and the first dark hints of a pony herd slowly inching about on the white background. "That's gotta be a Crow camp."

"This where you go?" Slays inquired.

"Yes. And where you'll go with us."

"No," and the Indian shook his head and pointed north-northeast. "The Blackfeet go that way. I follow them to the end."

"Come with us to the Crow village, friend," Bass pleaded, feeling hopeful that he could talk Turns Back and others into helping. "My son-in-law, he will gather friends—many warriors—we will go in search of the Blackfoot who came raiding this year."

For a long time the Shoshone sat there on the red horse, clutching that old smoothbore Bass had given him seasons before. His breath streamed from his mouth and nose into the subfreezing air as the setting sun struck their backs, riding low in the winter sky. Finally he took his eyes off the north-northeast and they came to rest on Titus Bass.

"All right. We go to this Crow camp where you get help for us to find my wife. You, me—we ride together against the Blackfeet." Then the Shoshone's eyes brightened with moisture, glowed with fond remembrance. "You remember old time we fight Blackfeet together?"

He shook his head, failing to recall any time he and Slays in the Night had battled those implacable foes. "I don't recall—"

Slays licked his lips and interrupted with a stammer as he gave voice to the white man's words, "Pee . . . Pierre's Hole."

The long-forgotten scenes exploded into view there in his mind. Back in '32. One of the biggest and finest of summer rendezvous ever held, company brigades and free men joined by many bands of mountain Indians, drawn by the trade goods and the nonstop gambling. A big band of Blackfoot had stumbled onto the white man's trading fair, forted up, and been surrounded. Mountain men and their allied warriors dashed south down the valley to do their damnedest to wipe out every enemy they could.

"Yes," he said with something close to reverence as he squinted his eyes and focused on the long-ago scenes. "I remember that now, old friend. A very long time ago—more'n twenty winters now."

"Long time," he repeated the white man's words, then signed, "We were young."

With a smile, Scratch asked, "How about you an' me do this for the ol't days, my friend? We go kill us some goddamned Blackfoot for the ol't days?"

"Goddamn these Blackfeet!" Slays agreed in American. "We kill. You and me, we kill goddamn sonofabitch Blackfeet!"

With a whoop, Titus shoved heels into his pony and they all started off the high ground, down the first of the long slopes that would carry them toward the cottonwood-wrapped meadows where that Crow village stood. With enough help from Turns Back, Don't Mix, and the rest of Pretty On Top's warriors, they could confront any threat from a large Blackfoot war party, inflict a lot of damage, drive their old enemies out of Absaroka, and reclaim Red Paint Rock from her captors. Which would be right and square with the world as he saw it.

If them dragoons at Fort Laramie didn't know how to exact a little justice from them murdering Mormons who did wrong by Jim Bridger and so many others, or the dragoons simply didn't have the stomach for it, at least life was still sane and real up here in the north country . . . up here where a man could still right what wrongs had been done him and his friends.

Being able to right an injustice committed against him by either Brigham Young and his thieving mobs or by a plundering Blackfoot war party was something a man had to count on when there were few things in life that really mattered. Maybe the Trickster, Old Man Coyote, would be capricious enough to punish a man by not allowing him to right a terribly unfair iniquity . . . but Titus knew the First Maker would never turn His face from His people in a time of need.

"Who is this stranger you bring?" asked Don't Mix as he led a small party of guards loping up to the newcomers.

"He is an old friend," Titus explained in Crow. "He was treating me and mine with kindness even before you were born."

With that characteristic smirk of his, the young warrior studied the old Shoshone. "Who are his people?"

"I am Snake," Slays in the Night responded in sign without hesitation.

That he understood enough of the Apsaluuke tongue to understand what had been said around him surprised Scratch. Bass touched the rider at his knee and announced to the others, "This is my friend, Slays in the Night. Side by side, he and I fought Blackfeet more than two-times-ten summers ago."

"He is still a fighter, this one?" Stiff Arm asked.

Just as Slays was opening his mouth to speak, Titus spoke up, "Many days ago my friend's camp was raided by Blackfeet, not far to the south. His horses and his woman were stolen. I told him I would ride with him to reclaim what has been taken from him by our old enemies."

Don't Mix inquired, "Just the two of you are going after these raiders?"

Shaking his head, Titus replied, "No—I want you to come with me, war chief. And strong-hearted others. There are many, many raiders we must chase from Absaroka!"

Most of the other camp guards whooped at that call to action, causing some of their ponies to jostle and shimmy in nervousness. From the corner of his eye, Scratch saw how Waits signaled him with that particular look in her eye.

"Where is my son-in-law, Turns Back?" Titus asked.

"The last I saw of him," Don't Mix answered, "he had just returned from the hills with a deer and was dressing it out over beside his lodge."

"And my daughter?"

Don't Mix smiled as he looked first at Waits-by-the-Water, then back to the white man. "She is as beautiful as ever. More so now that she is a mother."

Waits barely got her hand over her mouth to squelch a squeal of delight.

"This is good news!" Bass roared. "Tell me, have you taken a wife yet?"

With that sly look in his eyes, Don't Mix said, "My heart was so wounded, and my soul hurt so bad after your daughter married Turns Back . . . I knew it would take me a long time to heal, a long time before I could ever give my heart to another. But, it wasn't long after we returned from the big council at the white man's warrior fort in the south country that I found a pretty girl to help me heal my heart!"

"Has there been the cry of a newborn heard in your lodge?"

"No—but it will be any day now," Don't Mix said with a proud smile. "Big as my wife has grown, she must be carrying two—"

"Ti-tuzz," Waits impatiently interrupted their man-talk.

"Ah, yes," Scratch said, realizing his mistake. He urged his pony into motion. "We must hurry on to the village to see our daughter . . . and my wife's first grandchild!"

THIRTY-TWO

"Enemies!"

Titus Bass did not need to be told.

He had heard those faint, out-of-the-ordinary sounds drifting to him through the cold of that winter's dawn. Then the first distant cry of alarm. Followed by the muffled hammer of hooves reaching that ear he had lying against the ground in Magpie and Turns Back's lodge. Had to be a lot of them from the thunder of their coming. That, or the thieves were running off with every horse Pretty On Top's band owned.

Across the lodge, Flea was hurrying on with his winter clothing, tying one blanket legging to his belt, and then the other. Turns Back hugged Magpie, then touched the cheek of the infant between them, before he threw back the robes and began to dress in the cold stillness of that breathless lodge.

Yanking on the heavy, furred buffalo moccasins over his others, Scratch quickly dragged on the capote, buckled a wide belt around his waist, then pulled the coyote fur hat over his ears. Into his belt with the two knives went his only pair of pistols. Then he turned to the side of the lodge over the bed where he and Waits had slept for the first time last night. Two leather thongs were knotted in loose loops from the narrow rope that held the liner to the lodgepoles. He freed his old flintlock from the loops, bent to scoop up his shooting pouch, then touched her face with his bare fingertips before stuffing his hands in his blanket mittens—

The first gunshot roared from somewhere on the far side of camp.

He bent to kiss her mouth, recognizing the unspoken fear in her eyes.

As Slays in the Night shoved aside the frozen door flap and hurled himself outside, Scratch rolled up onto one knee and started for the door.

"I am right behind you, Popo!" Flea cried as he lunged onto his feet and followed his father into the gray before dawn's arrival.

All around them in that instant, men were bursting from their lodges to join those few who were already scuffling across the snow, gathering at the middle of the lodge crescent. Loud voices were raised: a few of the clan chiefs shouting orders to their men, others demanding answers for the unanswerable, fragments of songs and sacred chants just beginning as a few took up the reins to their favored war ponies staked securely at a lodge door . . . and through it all came the high-pitched wailing of the women and the screams of children from the far side of camp.

In that direction, gunfire became steady, hot. Hoofbeats, male voices louder still, and coming their way.

"The enemy has entered the camp!" Pretty On Top called out from behind the lodges.

Suddenly the young chief appeared in view through the frozen, misty air, gauzy and stinging to the skin with sharp and invisible ice crystals. The old friend caught Bass's eye, waved him on.

Grabbing the white man's elbow, Slays in the Night said, "That one, he is a brave man. He wants us to go with him into the fight."

"These are the men who took your wife, your horses," Scratch explained hurriedly with a rasp. "They have been brought here to your hand, my friend."

"*Yi-eeee!*" Slays called out in a shrill voice as he bolted into a run beside the white man.

"Nothing lives long but the rocks and sky!" Titus reminded him as they lumbered across the snow behind others on their way to stem this challenge to their camp. "If this is our day to look at last upon the face of the First Maker . . . then let it be known that we died protecting everything dear to us!"

By the time they had covered not more than thirty yards, Bass and Slays in the Night rushed up to a line of warriors, most of whom were kneeling against some lodges, firing their weapons against a crescent of unseen, shadowy gunmen. All a man could tell of his enemy was the flicker of some movement, the orange and yellow muzzle flashes of their firearms. Balls whined overhead, slammed through the stiffened, frozen lodge hides, splintered poles. Inside a few of the lodges, tiny voices cried out in terror.

"Some of our people are trapped!" one of the Crow bellowed.

"Cut them out!" Titus roared as he started forward off his cold, stiff knees. "Cut them out of their traps!"

Flat Mouth was there ahead of him, just as a ball whined past his cheek. Wrenching his long and well-worn skinning knife from its scabbard, Titus plunged it into the back of the rock-hard, frost-stiffened buffalo hide of the lodge and attempted to drag the blade in a downward motion. The knife would not budge. Quickly propping his rifle against the lodge, he gripped the knife in both hands and put his weight behind it, managing to slice a five-foot-long laceration in the back of the lodge cover. Even before he could get his knife yanked away from the bottom of the opening, the first child appeared, all legs and arms, terror-filled eyes and screeching throat. Six of them squirted through the opening before he realized Slays was calling to him in the noisy tumult.

Whirling on his heel as a warrior raked a slice open in a neighboring lodge, Scratch found Slays in the Night with Turns Back and Flea—all three of them pointing behind them . . . back to the side of camp where their lodge stood.

"The enemy!" Turns Back cried in frustration, shaking his smoothbore.

Flea's breath streamed out of his mouth like a white streamer, "Father! The enemy has made us fools! They have circled around the camp and are attacking our rear!"

"Come, you fighters!" Slays shouted, standing in the open and making a grand target of himself. "Come, my Crow friends! Kill them all!"

A long, long time their peoples had themselves been enemies—but in this dim light, on this ground, Turns Back and Slays in the Night stood fighting a common foe, side by side.

"Go!" Bass shouted at the trio and started toward them across the trampled snow. "Go to the lodge! I am coming!"

The Blackfoot had arranged a fine diversion for their attack on the Crow village: staging their feint on the north side of camp where part of the herd was grazing in a windswept meadow, while most of their attackers plunged in among the lodges on the south part of the village—where Magpie and Waits waited with the children.

When they were no more than ten long strides from the small, smoke-blackened lodge, horsemen swirled out of the mist ahead of them. Evil faces, eyes glaring with hatred. Faces smeared with dabs and streaks of color. Feathers fluttering from fur caps and the hoods to their blanket coats. Bass heard the *thung-thung-thung* of bows as he raced on, his cold, aching knees protesting. First two, then more than a dozen riderless horses suddenly careened into view, forcing the four men to leap aside in both directions. Right behind the horses came the first of the Blackfoot raiders—some of them leaning off to swing a stone club or taking quick aim with their short, elkhorn bows, others attempting to aim and pull off a shot with their firearms—

That's when Titus recognized their cries.

His eyes went directly to the lodge, finding that opening like a black oval in the frost-coated buffalo hides where Waits and Magpie had their faces, watching the battle, waiting for a chance to leap into the open.

"Don't!" Bass cried as he ducked out of the way of a warrior's wild swinging of a war club.

The round, stream-washed rock grazed the top of his right shoulder, pitching the white man onto his side in the snow, knocking over a warrior's medicine tripod erected in front of the man's lodge. As he rolled onto his hip, he saw Waits already stepping out of the lodge door with Crane positioned under her arm. Magpie was right behind, clutching her babe in her arms.

"Don't come out!" he screamed at them, his voice high and shrill. "Don't—"

Waits was already running across the icy rime, hand in hand with little Crane. Her pockmarked face was gray with terror as her moccasins repeatedly slipped on the trampled ground. But still she heaved and stumbled toward her husband. Slowly, slowly lumbering into the open.

"Go back!" he cried, standing to wave at her with that arm. How the shoulder hurt! "Please! Go back inside!"

Behind Waits and Magpie more horsemen appeared out of the frozen mist. Grayish-black forms suddenly squirting between the lodges, weapons leveled, mouths O'ed up in some war cry as their eyes narrowed on a selected target.

Once more he hollered, "Get back inside—"

—as the muzzle of a short smoothbore spit a dirty yellow flame just behind Waits-by-the-Water.

"No-o-o-o-o-o!" he shrieked at the instant Magpie tripped and spilled to the side, almost under a horse's slashing hooves.

But it was not his daughter, or the grandson he had held for the first time last night, that was the enemy's target.

Instead, the ball's impact slammed his wife's body forward, her back arching reflexively as her fingers flew free of Crane's tiny hand and the little girl stumbled, tangled up in her mother's flailing legs as Waits-by-the-Water desperately attempted to maintain her footing.

But there was no ground beneath her moccasins. She was already in the air, sailing awkwardly until she spilled onto the dirty, hoof-hammered snow. The side of her head skidded across the trampled crust as he brought up the rifle at his hip instinctively. There had to be more than ten of them. No matter. He wanted only the one in the red capote, the one who jumped his horse over the woman's body and bore down on the white man with a frightening cry.

Jerking back on the trigger, Bass felt the weapon jolt in his hands, watched the ball strike the warrior in the side, twisting him slightly on the bare back of his war pony. Clutching his wound and crumpling over on the animal's withers to keep from falling, the Blackfoot managed to stay atop his horse as he and the rest thundered on past, shrieking their war cries and shouting in triumph. His ball had struck the warrior, but not near good enough to unhorse the man.

Then Titus was spinning round, not intent on reloading—no matter the danger now.

He skidded to his knees beside his wife's body as Magpie scrambled onto her knees and crawled over with her baby in one arm.

"Mother?"

Scooping Waits into his lap, Titus stared down at her scarred face, wiping some of the crusty snow from her cheek and mussed, unbound hair. Her eyes fluttered half open, found his face, and then widened as she held her gaze on him.

"Ti-tuzz—"

"Sh-sh," he whispered as the roar of battle ground around them, slowly rumbling into the rest of the village. "L-look at me. Yes, keep looking at me." He knew that if she did not, her spirit might well fly away—

"I don't feel my legs," she groaned. A ribbon of bright blood leaked from the corner of her mouth.

Tears already burning his cold cheeks, Titus crushed her against him and rocked slightly back and forth—pressing one hand harder and harder against that warm, wet gush of blood from the gaping hole in the middle of her chest. Harder and harder still he pushed against the blood and frothy bubbles, moaning himself . . . not words, just wild and feral sounds as he blinked and blinked to try clearing his eye of tears. His spilled on her cheeks, smeared with the ooze of blood on her chin as more and more gushed from her mouth.

"Don't go!" he commanded her, feeling her rigid, quaking body begin to loosen.

"Ti-tuzz . . . ," she whispered with difficulty, heaving with a shudder, her eyes glazing as she continued to stare into his. "Always with you, Ti-tuzz."

"You can't go!" he yelled at her as the gunfire withered, fading to the far side of the village. *"No-o-o-o!"*

"See me soon . . . on the mountaintop," she whispered with another gush of blood, her eyes fluttering. "In your dreams . . . see me real—always see me . . . in your dreams . . . real for all time to come—"

He knew it when her body went limp and her head slowly sank against his arm, a last gush of blood spewing from her mouth onto his wrist. Bass pressed harder and harder on the wound, but the more he tried to plug up that hole, the more limp she became. Finally he stopped pushing so hard and slowly brought her against him again, folding her limp, lifeless body into his as he crumpled over her with a wracking sob that shook him to his core. His loose, gray hair spilled across her face and neck. Never had he felt such a cold hollowness like this—

"Mother!"

He heard Magpie's cry.

Suddenly his head jerked up and his eyes narrowed on his daughter's face. "Get Crane and your baby into a lodge!"

"Mother? Is she—"

"Hide them in a lodge with you, Magpie!"

Her eyes widening, she was once more his daughter, his little girl again. Magpie's eyes registered the same mixture of grief and terror as was in little

Crane's as she scrambled to her feet. Crane instinctively lunged toward her mother's body, clawing at Waits's limp arm.

"Take her now, Magpie!"

As he pulled the little girl's hands off her mother's arm Crane began shrieking.

"Go with Magpie!" he ordered, his words harsh, mechanical. "You must get out of danger. I will bring your mother with me. Now, go with your sister!"

Reluctantly Crane let him pull her hand free from her mother's blood-soaked sleeve as Magpie dragged her younger sister away toward the closest lodge—

Five riderless horses suddenly hammered through the lodge circle, lunging this way and that to avoid the small child and woman clutching her baby. Magpie shoved her little sister into the neighbor's lodge, both of them gone from sight through the gaping black oval. He was alone with the body of his dead wife.

And an emptiness he had never before felt swallowed him whole. Nothing he had experienced with the death of friends or that young towheaded grandson. Not even with the unexpected death of their stillborn infant. No, none of the pain he had ever suffered in life had prepared him for the cold, gaping emptiness that had instantly taken a ravenous bite out of his insides and left nothing but a hollow, oozing pit.

It was only slowly that Scratch became aware again of what existed outside his own flesh as the sounds swelled around him once more, the roar of blood that had surged in his ears gradually lessening now as the hole within him yawned all the deeper—threatening to suck him in after it.

Gunfire and the hammer of hoofbeats thundering on the iron-hard winter ground. Men's angry shouts and the shrill wails of frightened, mourning women. The snarl of camp dogs and the high-pitched, frightened cries and chatter of terrified children.

Of a sudden he felt the warmth touch the back of his shoulder, almost like a fingertip brushing the back of his neck where his tousled gray hair had bared the skin. Slowly he looked up, over his shoulder, saw how the light was just then tinting the frosty branches of the skeletal cottonwood with a pale rose, the color of her blood smeared on his hands. The sun was coming up. A first, pink light had entered the river valley.

"*Arrrghghghghgh!*" he cried in utter anguish, hot tears spilling from his eyes onto his cold cheeks, spittle spewing from his lips as he cradled her lifeless body against his hollow breast.

"D-don't take her from me!" he roared as he tore his face away from her hair, from that most familiar scent of her, and stared at the newly awakening sky.

"Damn you!"

How he cursed the spirits, the First Maker, this God who could chip away at him life by life. Leaving him hollow, empty of everything but for a smoldering hate that he immediately knew would drive him on until he had brought these killers to a reckoning. How long that would take, he did not know . . . but this craving for revenge was like a force of its own and would carry him on for as long as it took.

Bass's face hardened as he started to sob once more, slowly rocking his wife in his arms, groaning in a feral way like some wild thing caught and with but one way out of a trap. Except—this time he knew it was different. This time he would be required to sacrifice more than a paw imprisoned in the jaws. Gazing down at her face, he sensed those glazed eyes still somehow looked into his . . . then Titus reached up with his bloody fingertips and gently closed her eyelids.

The coming of the sun set the cold ground mist to steaming.

This first day of the rest of his life without her had begun.

They weren't hard to track, not these brazen Blackfoot, these remnants of a once-unstoppable force in this northern world. Decimated by pox many, many winters ago, the tribe was now but a shell of its former greatness.

Perhaps that was why they had raided into Shoshone country, then swept back through the land of the Crow—attempting to recapture some semblance of their days of glory.

Titus had to laugh at that. There was no goddamned way any of them could recapture their glory days. Red or white. Nothing was left for the old warriors but to die. Either die quiet in their robes, sucking desperately at a last breath as they lay inside a lodge . . . or to die as a warrior. Out in the open, among the rocks, out under the sky.

We who are warriors—

Remembering how Whistler, Waits's father, had died, how Whistler's son, Strikes In Camp, had died too. Brave men who had unflinchingly stared death in the face at that final moment and not been found wanting. Surely there must be some sort of reward for such men, surely there must be something more for each of us—he found himself brooding again and again over the three days following the attack on the village. Three days of chasing, riding, stopping only to water the horses, then chasing some more until a short halt was called because it was too damned black to dare moving on till dawn.

Slays in the Night and the others slept in fits and starts on the cold ground, wrapped in a blanket or a piece of buffalo robe. But not him. There was nothing more he needed—not sleep, and surely not food. No hungers now . . . only to get his fingers around the windpipe of the one who had killed her. Titus knew he would remember that face, remember the pattern of the man's war paint, for as long as this chase took. Something like that was burned into the back of his head like a red-hot iron brand would scour its imprint into a piece of smoldering wood. He saw the face, the paint, the warrior's clothing every time he merely closed his eyes in weariness. The image was emblazoned behind his eyelids, refusing to release him.

So much the better, Bass thought. It would draw him on until he found the man.

The raiders had at least half a day on their pursuers, time that the camp of Pretty On Top gave over to caring for the wounded and the dead, reaching some count of the stolen horses, calling together the chiefs and headmen of the warrior societies.

"It does not matter how much you argue on who is to go and who is to stay," Scratch had snapped at these younger men. "It matters little what plans you feel you must make to pursue these enemies. Every word you waste is one more step they take away from Absaroka. Every heartbeat we stand here is one more it will take until we taste the blood of these murderers."

Quietly, Pretty On Top said, "You are not the only man here to suffer a loss—"

"Then the rest of you who have lost someone you love can do what you want," he interrupted and shrugged off those war leaders with a wave of his arm. "There is talk . . . and there is action. I am putting my feet on this last warpath now."

Titus had turned away and started back toward Magpie's lodge, his son and his Shoshone friend caught by surprise but quickly catching up to him, one at each elbow. Of a sudden, Turns Back had lunged ahead of him, stopping right in front of the old white man.

"Uncle," he said to his father-in-law with respect. "I will go with you. With the three of you. She was my wife's mother. I will go with you—"

"No," Titus growled as he shoved his flat palm against the young man's chest. "You stay here with Flea. I don't want—"

"Stay here?" Flea echoed as he circled around to stand in front of his father, towering over the white man.

Titus looked up at the angry eyes of his son. "You have a brother and a sister to watch over."

Shaking his head furiously, Flea protested, "My sister, she can care for them while we are gone."

"Magpie has a family of her own," Titus scolded his son. "Jackrabbit and Crane, they are your family now, Flea. Your only family."

"My wife, she can watch her brother and sister," Turns Back said. "Flea will go with us—"

"No—you two must stay and protect them," Titus refused with a resolute wag of his head. "Someone brave must stay behind and watch over these lives that mean so much to me."

Flea drew himself up and looked down at his father. "Turns Back can stay and watch over them all until we come back to bury my mother—"

"No, son—you will do that today. Yourself. The last act of love for your mother," Titus explained.

"Then I will do it before we go," Flea said desperately. "So that my mother will be buried before—"

"Don't you understand, my son?" he snapped at the young man. "My feet have already begun a journey from which there is no return."

Titus started to step between them, but Flea caught him, held his father tightly by both of the old man's arms.

"Y-you are not coming back, Father?"

He first looked into the eyes of Turns Back, then at his son's face, seeing how the eyes started to pool. "When you watch my back disappear through the trees, you will then be the leader of this family—the protector of your brother and sister."

"I'm coming with you."

"No . . . because you are now the one called Holds the Fight," Titus said, watching the new name register on his son's face.

"H-holds the Fight?"

"You need a new name, son," he said, the hard lines of his face softening. "Flea was a good name for a boy . . . but now you truly are a man. A man who has a family to hunt and provide for, a family he must protect. A father is the one to name his children . . . when the First Maker finally tells that father what to name the child. Just now I have heard our Creator tell me that you are Holds the Fight—because you will stay behind to protect your family."

With deep respect Turns Back quietly repeated the name, "Holds the Fight," then put his arm across his young brother-in-law's shoulders, struggling to speak as he held back the tears. "Yes, old warrior—the two of us will do as you have asked. Even though it will be painful to watch you ride off after these enemies without us at your side, we will honor She Who Is No Longer Here by obeying your last wishes."

"And we will honor you, Father," Holds the Fight added, his chin quivering even as he stood taller than the older men. Quickly he unbuckled the narrow belt he had around his waist, that belt he had worn from the day Jim Bridger had given it to him when he was a gangly youngster that first summer at the post on Black's Fork. From the long strap he dragged the beaded rawhide sheath and knife. "Take this knife with you, Father. Use it to cut the scalp from the one who killed my mother."

For a moment he stared down at the weapon held out between them, wanting to refuse his son's request. Then he took the scabbard into his hand and peered into the young man's eyes.

"If I return with the scalp, I will bring back your knife," he said in a whisper, his throat clogging with emotion. "But if I do not return . . . remember me always to my youngest children. Raise them to honor the memory of their father."

Holds the Fight lunged against him, encircling his father with his long arms, and they sobbed together for a moment before they tore themselves apart. Titus touched his heart with his empty right hand, then placed those fingertips against his son's breast.

"Let the memory of me always rise in your heart like the coming of the sun," he croaked painfully. "It is here—in your heart—that I will always remain."

Holds the Fight clamped a hand over his father's fingers, squeezing it against his chest. "I am h-honored to be your son, old warrior."

With his eyes tearing up again, Titus said, "Come now—I must say goodbye to Magpie, to Jackrabbit and to Crane too, before I go."

A large Crow war party had caught up to the two old men late that first night, not long after Scratch and the Shoshone had stopped in the dark to rest the six horses they were pushing so hard. The two of them had ridden out with three horses each, the strongest the old trapper owned. When one animal tired, they had changed to another throughout that first afternoon and on into the starry, moonless eventide as they loped, loped, loped north up the serpentine trail, across the wide patches of snow and long straights of hard, flat, flinty ground where the sun had burnt off most traces of the last storm. Theirs was a joyless reunion of determined men.

"These enemies haven't come into our country like this in many seasons," one of the older men had explained.

"Why now?" Bass had growled with bitterness.

Pretty On Top said, "Perhaps we will know when we catch up to them."

"No," Titus shook his head in resignation. "Chances are we will never know why they came."

They had pushed on as soon as it was light enough to see six horse lengths ahead. And by the time the sun was rising they spotted the Blackfoot raiders and their stolen horses far off in the distance. No longer was it merely a trail of hoofprints they were following. Now they saw their quarry. He even imagined he could smell these enemies in his nostrils. Maybe it was the strong turpentine scent of the sagebrush crushed under each hoof as the enemy pushed toward the Judith Basin. Strong and wild, the wind in his face, this pursuit infused him with youth once more. Just seeing those warriors and their stolen herd out yonder in the distance felt as if years had been shaved off his old hide. This was meant to be, he thought.

This is the way it was meant to be.

It wasn't long before he admitted to the pang he was feeling somewhere behind his breastbone—the pain of regret and remembrance, the faces of his children swimming before his eyes as he yanked on the long lead rope to the next horse, a strong, long-legged pinto. At first the wild-eyed pony protested and jerked back its head, but Titus eventually had it loping alongside the tiring claybank he had been riding ever since first light.

"Here, friend," he called to Slays in the Night. "Hold my rifle for me."

"A new horse?" asked the Shoshone as he urged his pony close, on the white man's off side, and took Bass's old flintlock.

It took a few moments, heartbeats really, to match the strides of the two horses as their hooves thundered across the iron-plated ground, heading up a long, long slope—the last before they reached the winding valley of the Judith. He knew this place well. Lo, the many times he had trapped these grounds, walked the thready paths of these feeder streams, fought grizzly here. If the Blackfoot were thinking to lose their Crow pursuers in this maze of hills and stands of cottonwood, to confuse those who followed in the tapestry of alder and chokecherry, willow and sawgrass, then they hadn't reckoned on Titus Bass riding up on their tailroots.

He leaned over with his right hand, intertwined his fingers with a handful of the pinto's mane—then held his breath and rose up to one knee on the clay-bank. Up and down, up and down he moved with both horses, then suddenly leaped across to that painted pony that ran with its rib cage brushing against the tired, lathered claybank. The pinto grunted at the man's sudden weight landing on its back. He shifted slightly, his crotch sliding into that natural groove behind the withers. Then he played out the claybank's long rein, letting the tired horse seek its own pace some yards behind them as Slays in the Night eased over to his side again.

"Here, you will need this soon," the old Indian said, his eyes glistening with an inner peace.

Bass took his rifle. "Your turn for a new horse." And he took the Shoshone's smoothbore, clutching both weapons across the crook of his left arm.

When he looked ahead into the distance at the figures once more, Bass felt his heart leap in anticipation. He thought he saw that red blanket capote at the far right edge of the herd now. In the first dim, gray light of this cold morning the figures had all been black as sow beetles scurrying out from beneath an overturned cowchip. But now, with the coming of the sun, colors came alive. And in the fiery hue the sun gave this high, hard land, Titus finally saw the only one he had been chasing all along. The tails of the Blackfoot's bright red coat fluttering out behind him in the cold wind that had quartered around to the northwest, smelling strong with the tang of coming snow.

The horizon far ahead looked heavy with it too. All the way north to the Missouri itself, where it was surely snowing already. That mighty, mythical river a man had to cross before he could make these legendary mountains his own. A fabled and fated crossing that few men would survive. Some who had reached this land had already gone back, recrossing the Missouri to what had been before. Still more had gone on until they reached the end of the land and the great salt ocean washed up at their feet. But Titus Bass had stayed here in this high land that few would believe ever existed. Surely the stuff of a schoolboy's myth, legend, and tall tales. Not possible for a man to have lived out the life Titus Bass claimed he had, those stiff-backed settlement types would say.

It made no difference now. None of their nay-saying made a damn bit of difference. He was here, on the bare, narrow back of a young painted pony, and he had the cold, icy wind in his face . . . his enemy in view.

With the coming of the sun at their backs, he realized it had turned even colder. So cold it felt like it would never get warm again. The ground beneath him hard as hammered iron. The sky above so blue it hurt his one good eye. The bitter wind made it tear, making colors run and swim.

Turning to his old friend, Titus said, "Soon we will be close enough to see which one of those riders is your Red Paint Rock."

For a long time, the Shoshone studied the figures, staring into the distance, but not as if he were trying to choose among the distant horsemen. When he finally turned to speak to the white man, his cheeks were wet with frozen tears. "No . . . our women are dead, Ti-tuzz. Both us have nothing left but the killing now. Our women—they both dead."

"And soon our enemies will be too," Titus spoke into the growing strength of the northern wind as the black belly of the horizon darkened, "unless they kill us before we can raise their scalps."

The Shoshone smiled at that, his eyes brimming, then pounded a fist twice against his left breast and pointed that hand into the distance at the narrowing gap between the Blackfoot and their pursuers.

"Yes, two hearts," Titus replied with a roar as he pounded his fist twice against his own breast and smiled at this old friend. "Two women. Two old warriors. And two scalps we must take."

Just as they both shrieked with a feral cry at those icy-blue lowering clouds, the Blackfoot raiders suddenly boiled into action. The enemy horsemen reined this way and that into the captured herd, splitting the Crow ponies in half, then even more pieces, as the raiders divided and divided, and divided again—a few warriors taking a small bunch of the horses and slowly peeling off from the direction they had all been taking together.

"I must follow the Red Coat!" Titus shouted.

The Shoshone nodded. "It is good! You see the one riding beside your red coat?"

"The one wearing the headdress with one buffalo horn?"

Slays grinned, his eyes hard. "That one, I remember from the taking of my woman."

"They go together," Scratch cried happily.

"So will we!"

Five of them. That Red Coat. And the Buffalo Horn Headdress. In addition there was an elkskin painted an earth yellow. Then a faded, green-striped blanket. And finally a buffalo robe decorated with wide bands of earth-paint color running its full width. Five would not be so many that he and his old friend could not whittle them down once they caught these Blackfoot. Five had never been too many for a man who put his head down and kept on coming. Nothing else a man could do when he found he had nothing left to lose.

Magpie. His sweet little Magpie all growed up and married, a mother too. And that oldest boy of his. How he had already made his mother proud. One day soon he would cast his eye on a girl and take a bride—perhaps even this coming spring, when the days lengthened and the weather warmed and a young man's blood pounded hot and strong in his limbs. Holds the Fight would father his own children. And so the blood of one tired old warrior would be reborn again and again and again, and again. If Titus had not made his son stay behind, chances were Holds the Fight would never have known the pleasure a woman could bring a man, never experienced the joy of holding his own new-born child naked in his arms, all arms and legs and screwed-up red face staring into his.

The same mighty blood coursed through young Jackrabbit, already coming of age. And in little Crane too. The one who looked more like her mother than any of the others. They both had this chance, both stood on the cusp of a changing world their father could not begin to fathom, dared not even attempt to imagine. His youngest two now belonged to their brother, and to each other. They were family—even without their mother and father. They were family.

"Children," Scratch had said as he dropped to one knee on the snow in front of Magpie's lodge and wrapped the youngest two into his arms, "you will go with your brother soon, and pray at the foot of the tree where he will lay your mother."

"You will not be there to pray with us, Popo?" Jackrabbit asked.

"No, your brother is a man now. He will watch over you for me, instead of me, from this morning on," he whispered, then hid his tears in their hair as he crushed both of the youngsters against him and kissed the tops of their heads.

Little Crane squirmed her way loose so she could peer up into her father's lined and war-tracked face. Her tiny hand came to the long scar that coursed its way down from the outside corner of his left eye. She stroked it with such intense seriousness, and finally asked, "When will you come back to us?"

He smiled through the tears. "One day, I'll see you both again, Crane. Just like you will see your mother again one day too. When what I have to do is finished . . . I will see you both again."

The flesh between her eyes knitted up in confusion. "Where are you going?"

"I'm going to a place where I hope to put your mother's spirit and mine to rest, little daughter."

This time a suspicious Jackrabbit inquired, "How far away is that?"

Tousling the boy's hair as he got to his feet and pulled those young ones against him, waving Hold the Fight and Magpie against him too, wrapping all four in his arms, Bass said, "I hope it is not too long a journey, children. When you go to the tree and pray at the foot of your mother's body . . . ask the First Maker to be sure it is not too long a journey for your old father."

One by one, he kissed them each, on the eyes, on the mouth too, touched their faces one last time, remembering the golden, shining moments of their squirming infancy and how they had brought such exquisite joy to their mother . . . then before the agony of this separation would delay him any longer, or he would decide against leaving them without both of their parents, Titus Bass suddenly spun and walked away from his four children—

Ahead of him now those five Blackfoot raiders yipped and cried at one another, repeatedly glancing back over their shoulders at the pair of horsemen who followed, closing the gap.

"You are not alone, old warrior!"

Titus turned and looked over his shoulder, surprised to find the face of the one who had called out to him from behind. Bear Who Sleeps urged his heaving pony up to the white man's side. He smiled at the Crow. "Is your heart strong today?"

The warrior grinned and shook his old smoothbore. "It is a good day to die!"

That made him yip like a young warrior, the cold wind and lowering sky whipping tears from the corners of his eyes. Titus slapped his chest and cried out, "Nothing lives long but the rocks and the sky! All the rest of us must die!"

"A good day for this!" Slays bellowed on his other side. "A good day!"

"Goddamn right!" Titus roared to the heavens rumbling toward them, boiling with a storm right over their heads, blue sky turned black and heavy with winter's fury, clouds beginning to hurl sharp lances of icy snow. "What a damned grand day it is to die!"

THIRTY-THREE

There comes an overwhelming peace when a man finally stands upon the ground where he is prepared to die.

When all things are suddenly made right in his world . . . and in the world beyond.

Those five Blackfoot yelled at one another as they reached the rolling, snowy bottom ground along the Judith River. Close enough were these enemies that Scratch could see how they sneered and maybe even cackled to find themselves pursued by only three Crow horsemen. So sure of their numbers and their strength that they could rein up at any moment, whirl around, and overwhelm these three puny pursuers. Especially since they were sure to see that two of them were old men. A pair of tired old warriors, and the five of them were clearly strong, vital, and in the flower of their youth.

It did not matter to him what the hell the Blackfoot thought, or what the devil they did when all eight of them got close enough to fight. He kept his wind-weeping eye on that Red Coat, seeing now how the man clutched his left arm low against his hip. Wounded by the shot Bass gave him in the village after the Blackfoot killed Waits, but not wounded near bad enough that his pony couldn't lick it over this broken ground with the four others. No matter what those five warriors did when it came time for the close fighting, which way they turned or how they squared off against their pursuers, Titus vowed he would keep his eye on Red Coat, follow him to the death—and if Red Coat was the only one Bass could strangle this cold day . . . then all things would be made right in his world.

Scratch turned to Bear Who Sleeps. "The Red Coat is mine. He took my wife from me in camp."

The young man nodded solemnly. "I know. That one is yours." Then the Crow leaned forward slightly to peer around the white man and look directly at the Shoshone. "Friend," he said, a word that surprised both Bass and Slays in the Night, "I will go after these enemies on the left: the Painted Robe and the Green-Stripe Blanket."

Into a wild and feral smile, the Shoshone's old, wrinkled face beamed with happiness. "It is good! This day I will kill the Yellow Paint Elkskin and Buffalo Horn Headdress! *Keee-yiiii!*"

It was clear to see that the Blackfoot were running the horses toward the edge of an icy slough where the dead and hollow stalks of seven-foot-tall reeds stood shuddering in the freezing wind, the bottoms of every bush and clump of willow already collecting a delicate white ringlet of snow—a tiny, hard, icy snow. Not the gentle whisper of dry, downy flakes that normally fell on these northern plains, but a deadly, wind-driven pelting of pain. The stolen horses began to scatter off the narrow path they had been taking, starting to turn this way and that as the snow-crusted meadow widened against the long, narrow borders of willow, alder, and skeletal cottonwood, trees that seemingly stood alone against the lowering blue-black bulk of the clouds.

This had always been a beautiful valley, he remembered as he spotted the first of the snow-dusted beaver lodges. The industrious creatures had turned this meadow into a home fit for several families of the flat-tails. But now they and their tiny kits were holed up inside the warmth of their domed mud-and-branch lodges, staying dry, on shelves that kept them out of the freezing water, until spring finally broke winter's hold on this high and dangerous land once more in nature's never-ending cycle of giving life back after all had been taken away with the coming of a deep and mighty cold. Yes, this had always been a beautiful place, he reminded himself.

A fitting place to see this through to the end.

The Blackfoot wouldn't have much cover if they didn't make it to the foothills of those mountains still miles and miles away. He heard the first muffled gunshot from off to their left and turned quickly. Couldn't see any of the other raiders, nor the rest of the Crow pursuers. Another shot. The others must be drawing close enough to the raiders to bring things to a fight, he thought—but he kept his eye on Red Coat. And noticing how the gunshots unnerved some of the five enemies. No, these Blackfoot would not have much cover to hide in once they went afoot in this frozen swamp . . . but neither would their pursuers.

That's why Titus determined he would stay in the saddle as long as possible. He was nowhere near as quick and nimble on foot as his strong, young enemies would be. And he would have a decided advantage over the wounded man if he was able to run Red Coat down with his horse. Besides, he told himself as the five began to drift apart, no longer in a tight bunch, this painted pony beneath him might just serve as the finest shield of all for one or maybe two lead balls fired his way when things got close and deadly. When the guns of these enemies started to roar and their muzzles spewed jets of yellow fire back at their pursuers.

Closer and closer they got to the Blackfoot as the five continued to drift apart, two going to the right and Slays in the Night reining away with them. The other three he followed with Bear Who Sleeps. Red Coat turned to look over his shoulder, fear beginning to show in his eyes for the first time.

"You remember me, don't you?" he screamed at the warrior.

Red Coat stared a long moment at the white man, blinked.

"Yes! I'm the one going to kill you!"

As he turned back around, Red Coat shouted something to those who rode at his side. Buffalo Horn Headdress and Yellow Paint Elkskin were busy a moment pulling at something attached to the front part of their bodies. Figuring they were dragging pistols from their belts, he prepared to duck the moment they twisted around to fire at him . . . but then he watched the two companions with Red Coat bring their hands to their faces. They hadn't brought pistols!

In a moment they turned to peer back at their two pursuers, and Bass saw both had put whistles between their teeth. The sort of eagle wingbone whistle that many warriors wore from narrow thongs around their necks as they went into battle. Holding it between their lips as they charged into battle, blowing those shrill, high, keening notes of the majestic warbird, calling upon its spirit, invoking its courage and strength, perhaps praying that the cry of their whistle would turn an enemy's knees to water.

"Not today, boys," Titus muttered grimly. "Nothing gonna turn me away from this last fight."

The faintly shrill sounds of those whistles drifted back on a brutal gust of wind as winter's fury snarled past his ears with a mournful death howl—

Suddenly Buffalo Horn Headdress yanked back on his reins and brought his frightened pony around so savagely that the horse almost toppled with its rider into the soggy, icy bog of this grassy meadow, where beaver would thrive and a new generation flourish come the floods of spring. The young man's face was one of determination as he blew on his whistle, lowered his short-barreled English smoothbore at the two advancing enemies, then slammed the heels of his thick winter moccasins into his pony's sides.

"A brave one—this!" shouted Bear Who Sleeps.

"I only want Red Coat!" Titus screamed.

"Yes!" Bear Who Sleeps replied as he brought out his heavy flintlock pistol and raked back the hammer. "This coup is for me!"

"Shoot straight!" Titus roared at the warrior. "And your heart will be sure to follow!"

"My bones are the rocks of this earth," Bear Who Sleeps sang his high-pitched song, "and my eyes are doors to the sky! I will live always with those rocks and the sky!"

With a quick jab of the heels, Titus sharply reined his pinto to the right, away from the Crow, his eyes searching for the Shoshone and the other two Blackfoot. He found that Green-Stripe Blanket had dismounted and dropped to one knee, bringing up his rifle. But Slays in the Night was quick enough, good enough at that deadly range—firing before the Blackfoot could, tumbling the warrior onto his back as the Shoshone rode on over the dying man after that shot, pursuing Painted Robe on into the thick stands of reeds so tall they could almost hide a man on horseback.

Gunfire roared to his left, a little behind. Two shots so close together they could have been the two halves of a man's heartbeat. Twisting around, Bass watched Bear Who Sleeps bound backward onto the rear flank of his pony, his arms flung wide as he pitched off the horse into a shallow puddle of ice-rimed meadow water. Buffalo Horn Headdress immediately leaped his horse over the body of his enemy and reined around sharply, the pony's hooves sending up cockscombs of dirty spray at the edge of the shallow beaver pond. The eyes of the Blackfoot were trained on his next enemy as he suspended the empty firearm from the front of his saddle by a leather loop tied through its trigger guard. His other arm was already reaching behind his shoulder, pulling a bow and a handful of arrows from the wolfhide quiver strapped across his back.

Those intense, black-cherry eyes widened as Bass raced directly for him, bringing up his old flintlock as Buffalo Horn Headdress nocked an arrow against the twisted rawhide string and started to muscle it back. Scratch sensed the buck of his rifle as it fired—the half-inch-thick ball catching his enemy midchest. The bow and its lone arrow went spilling one way, the rest of the short arrows and the warrior toppled off the far side of the horse.

Yanking back on his reins, Bass skidded to a halt right over the body. The luster was gone from the eyes that peered up at him, the lips slowly releasing the wingbone whistle he had clamped between his teeth . . . mouthing something in silence. Then the lips moved no more.

Titus quickly jerked around, looked over his shoulder, and spotted the backs of the other two as they pushed their ponies behind the stolen horses up the long, low slope at the side of this beaver meadow, making for the saplings and stunted cedar. With a moment's hesitation, he reluctantly opened his left hand, watching the long-cherished flintlock tumble into the icy scum of black water.

"You been a good girl," he whispered, his eyes burning with remembrance and regret. " 'Ol' Make-'Em-Come' . . . you brung me all the way through the years 'thout ever lettin' me down. Appears I gotta do the rest of this on my own now."

Freeing a wild cry that raked his throat like the shards of a broken china mug some trader might use to dispense his watered-down whiskey, Titus Bass wheeled his wide-eyed, lathered pony and pounded his legs into its ribs—setting off after the last two. Stuffing the thick braid of buffalo-hair rein between his teeth, the old man yanked out both pistols from his belt.

A muffled shot rang out somewhere to his right. Must have been Slays in the Night, he figured. With a quick glance, he realized could not see anything of the others. Only the two left in front of him. They were all that mattered now. His old friend was finishing his business with these men who had stolen and killed what had mattered most to the Shoshone. Slays was having his finest moment—a redemption long coming to a man who had chosen the wrong path so many winters ago. A man who had climbed back onto his feet and owned up to his trespasses . . . stepping back from the brink of dishonor.

No matter now, Bass thought, Slays in the Night will die a warrior, an honorable man. His will be a life redeemed before his Creator, here in these glorious final heartbeats of a man's existence.

That's what it was. Redemption—

There! Yellow Paint Elkskin was leaning off his pony ungainly, suddenly lunging to the side, frantically grabbing a handful of Red Coat's sleeve as the warrior Bass had wounded back in the Crow camp slowly keeled to the side. Try as he might, Yellow Paint Elkskin could not prevent the wounded man from falling off his horse. Red Coat flopped to the snowy slope in a patch of cedar, rolled onto his back, and kicked his legs a little. Then lay still.

With that same awkwardness, Yellow Paint Elkskin wheeled his pony above his dying companion, then faced the oncoming enemy. The warrior slowly dismounted to kneel over Red Coat. As Bass thundered down on him the Blackfoot struggled with something at the front of Red Coat's blood-soaked sash. Yellow Paint Elkskin's arm became a blur as it shot up in an arc, a long yellow tongue of flame spewing from the weapon in the Indian's bare brown hand.

Bass sensed it slam into his chest, but not in a painful, gut-numbing way. Instead, as if the warrior had swung a long, stout limb of hickory at Titus as the white man rode past. Connecting with his breastbone so unmistakably solidly that its impact immediately made him weak to the soles of his moccasins. With a jerk he clamped down on the pistols with both cold hands, gritted his teeth around that braided rein, and did his best to lock his legs around the girth of his pony's rib cage. But instead it was as if some unseen hand reached out and had him by the nape of the neck, yanking him loose and flinging him off the back of the horse.

The air exploded from his lungs in an audible gush as he hit the hard, frozen snow and slid more than five feet, ultimately stopping against a clump of eight-foot-high willow growing at the edge of the frozen beaver pond. Frantically sucking in a breath, he blinked that one eye clear and tried to look down at his chest. It was hard to breathe. Pulling apart the folds of his blanket coat and the buffalo-hide vest, he saw it . . . and it took his breath away. A small black hole was seeping a little red. But not near enough, he cheered himself—

Then heard the warrior's shrill cry.

Rolling onto his left elbow, he flexed the fingers of both hands, found he had the pair of pistols still locked in them despite his fall from the pony . . . but discovered he had little strength to drag his legs under him. They were sluggish, almost like something once rigid or stiff now gone soggy and limp. They moved for him a little, and far too slowly as he attempted to rise. That war cry growing louder.

Bass managed to get turned slightly, recognizing the hard breathiness of the Blackfoot as the warrior bore down on him, a short war club held high overhead. Two blades, big ones, steel daggers, one protruding from each side of the club's head, swung high in the air, where they sliced their way through the swirling dance of the wind-driven snowflakes. All of a sudden his stomach wanted to lurch with the sour, thick taste of blood gumming up the back of his throat.

He knew he'd been shot in the lights. The way a man would bring down his family's supper. About the only way a man dropped as big a beast as a buffalo. Here he was . . . the old bull, he brooded. The old bull brought down by a shot to the lights.

But Titus forced back down what little contents his stomach held and squeezed his eyes shut an instant. Gasping for a breath as some blood and a little stomach bile gushed from his nostrils, the old mountain man pitched forward on hands and knees, coughing up red and yellow phlegm, managing to pivot onto one knee as the warrior loomed right in front of him.

His left hand bucked with the heavy powder charge in the pistol. On instinct he brought up the right hand at the target too, then caught himself for a heartbeat. Yellow Paint Elkskin was so close Bass could see his face, realize how young he was, less than half his own age . . . that smooth, flawless, unlined flesh suddenly turning gray as his moccasins slipped out from under him and he pitched backward with the force of the lead ball at such close range. Bass was showered with icy snow the man's spinning feet kicked up right in front of the trapper as the warrior crumpled backward with a grunt, hit the ground, then slowly kicked himself backward on the snow, using both of his legs in an ever-slowing cadence.

Turning at the sound of the hoofbeats, Scratch quickly reloaded the pistol with powder and ball as he prepared himself to find Slays in the Night, ready to tell his old friend that, sure, even though he'd been shot in the chest, it wasn't all that bad. He'd make it through to night . . . if Slays and the others could only get a fire going to warm him. Titus was just beginning to sense the deepening cold growing there in the very core of him—

But it was Green-Stripe Blanket bounding out of the timber, cutting to his right around the edge of the pond and the tall reeds, then suddenly reining up in a spray of icy snow and pond water. Bass blinked, spotting the smear of blood soaking the warrior's upper arm, as the Blackfoot wheeled his pony, called back up the hill.

Slowly, his head as unresponsive as a hundredweight pack of beaver hides, Scratch turned slightly . . . and found Painted Robe walking out of the scrub timber where Slays in the Night had followed the two. At the end of his left hand unmistakably hung the old Shoshone's full scalp, the long black-and-gray hair dragging the new crust of snow.

He was alone. Except for Pretty On Top and the others. But the sounds of their fighting came from so, so far away. He was alone, with this pistol, and his two knives, and the short-handled tomahawk that rubbed against the base of his spine. Alone with these last two Blackfoot. Yet both of them did not matter. Only one now. Painted Robe. Because that warrior carried an old friend's scalp.

The Blackfoot talked to one another. Not as if Bass could understand the two warriors, even really hear what they had to say in the shockingly cold air that seemed to cocoon around him all the more tightly, air so cold it was hard for him to catch his breath, nothing more than little gasps now. But—he watched their mouths moving as Green-Stripe Blanket urged his pony ahead a few more yards, then stopped halfway between the white man and the body of Yellow Paint Elkskin. As Titus's head began to weave and he felt the immense cold seeping down from his chest and into his belly, Green-Stripe Blanket nudged his horse into motion again, angling up the side of the hill slightly, moving out of Bass's vision now—gone to that left side where there was no seeing unless he managed to turn his head . . . that refused to budge.

Then he heard Painted Robe's moccasins crunch on the crusty snow and willed himself to look at that enemy. The warrior was yelling something to the unseen horseman. Then the Blackfoot started walking again, coming boldly around the upper end of the beaver meadow, where some of the stunted trees had been felled by the industrious flat-tails. One of them was still behind him, he remembered. And turned with a jerk that made his head swim.

But he found Green-Stripe Blanket had remained motionless, his pony standing uneasily over the bloodied body of Buffalo Horn Headdress. He yelled something at Painted Robe, then pointed off to the body of Red Coat.

Painted Robe cried angrily, shaking the Shoshone's scalp.

But Scratch's eye was drawn back to Green-Stripe Blanket as the warrior dropped to the ground. He tugged on the knot in that bright red sash that held the blanket around his waist and pulled a pistol from the sash as he freed the rein from his other mitten. That enemy was closer, Titus decided, and started to twist his upper body around so he could aim his last pistol at the nearer of his two enemies.

Yet while Green-Stripe Blanket stood only a matter of yards away, the warrior did not raise his pistol to fire. Instead he merely stared, his eyes glowing like coals there inside the hood made from the hide of a gray prairie wolf. Studying the white man.

I'm being given this chance, Scratch thought. This one last chance before he shoots—

The pistol bucked in his hand, and Green-Stripe Blanket visibly flinched as the ball passed harmlessly over his shoulder.

Damn, he thought as the realization that he had missed slapped him. Scratch crumpled forward onto his hands in the snow as he started to heave, his stomach spewing what little it held, blood and bile dripping from his lips and out of his nostrils too, steamy and warm on the frozen snow between his knees. He coughed, gagging some more—then recognized the sound of footsteps.

Turning his heavy head in that direction, he expected to find Green-Stripe Blanket come to finish him off with his pistol, but instead it was Painted Robe, carrying that long, black-and-gray scalp in one hand and a small-headed tomahawk in his right—the blade and some of the haft glistening with frozen blood. Fixing his gaze on that limp, bloody scalp, Titus wrenched himself backward, unsteadily rocking onto his knees until he managed to hold himself steady and reached around to the small of his back with his left hand, feeling for his own tomahawk. He needed it now that he held his last loaded firearm. With the heel of that hand clutching the tomahawk, Scratch shoved back the hammer to full cock and brought his wobbly arm up, the muzzle of the weapon weaving side to side across its target.

He'd already killed the bastard who killed his woman. And before he died he'd finish off the one who had scalped Slays in the Night. That done, it didn't matter what Green-Stripe Blanket did behind him. Hell, his mind rumbled with the thought, he was halfway to dead already. More'n that now . . . 'cause he was already halfway to dead when he put the Crow camp behind him and rode after these raiders, knowing in his marrow this was the last time he would ride away from his wife's people.

Real Bird had forewarned him, told the white man of that awful dream. But across the last three days there wasn't a one of the Crow warriors who remembered the old prophet's vision of doom for Titus Bass. There was simply too much misery and loss, too much blood someone must atone for, that any man who had long ago heard of Real Bird's vision would think to warn the old trapper that he best stay in the village with his children and protect the camp. But here the old rattle-shaker's dream was, come to pass—

He wearily pulled back on the trigger, heard the *klattttch* of the hammer as it fell against the frizzen. But the pistol didn't fire. Nothing more than a muffled *phfffft* of what little powder lay in the pan. For an instant he stared down at it, finding the black grains mixed with icy flecks of snow, realizing everything had been ruined when he tumbled off his horse into the trampled snow beside the frozen beaver pond—

The warrior's cry caused him to jerk up, but not in complete surprise. He had expected this.

Already Painted Robe was lunging his way . . . then suddenly stopped no more than five feet away and, for some crazed reason, stood staring down at the white man. His eyes wild, he yelled something to Green-Stripe Blanket, but

Bass did not care enough to worry about the one still behind him. He heard that wounded warrior trudging on the crusty snow, heard his steps as that unseen one, who wore the skullcap of a wolf tied around his head, circled to his left until he stood far back of Painted Robe's shoulder. That's when Painted Robe raised the scalp up at the end of his arm, held it straight out from his shoulder, shook it, and cursed. Finally he spit on the hair, a second time, then flung it aside into the beaver pond.

With his one good eye, Bass watched the scalplock sail through the snowy air, land among those stalks of dried, frozen rushes, tangled among them and suspended for a moment before it fell to the thin layer of dirty ice.

"You stupid, ignernt idjit," Titus growled, finding himself renewed as he spoke for the first time to these enemies. "You figger that's a Crow scalp, don'cha?"

Painted Robe's eyes narrowed as he shifted the tomahawk in his right hand.

With a snort of wild, unrestrained laughter, Titus pulled free the tomahawk from the back of his belt and roared, "Joke's on you, nigger! Joke's on you!"

As he was attempting to raise his tomahawk and heave himself onto one foot, Painted Robe snarled and lunged forward, the warrior's tomahawk cocking back in an arc as the Indian loomed over him. The handles of their weapons clattered together an instant before the two men collided. Bass spilled backward, Painted Robe atop him, the Blackfoot doing his best to swing the tomahawk at the end of his wrist. Suddenly Bass flung his head forward, slamming his forehead against the side of the warrior's jaw. Painted Robe hesitated.

And Scratch swung with his tomahawk, connecting with the back of the Indian's head, but only a glancing blow with the side of the blade, stunning the warrior.

With a pained grunt, the Blackfoot roped his left arm around the back of the white man's neck and yanked Bass's head off the ground as he raised the tomahawk in his right hand, preparing to slam it down into the trapper's face. But Titus shoved his open mouth right against the warrior's chin, clamping down with all he was worth, feeling his teeth grinding through the thin layer of flesh and muscle, tightening on bone.

He heard the man crying out, felt the Indian's hot breath there on his forehead as he chewed and clamped harder still, trying all the while to swing his own tomahawk with what strength he had left as the Blackfoot struggled, wriggled, thrashed—

Then Scratch felt it tear him in half.

As the white man released his grip on the Indian's chin, he cried out in shock. The lower half of his face smeared with blood, the warrior pulled back slightly. Like the bullet wound, Bass did not want to look. He knew already. Even though he had yet to feel the pain of it, he realized he had been dealt a second mortal wound. The terrible cold seemed to envelop his whole belly as he willed his left arm to squirm free from where it was imprisoned between their two bodies, so it could rise into the air clutching his tomahawk.

One of their voices screamed as he brought down the weapon in the last, desperate act of a doomed man, driving the bottom point of the blade into the crown at the back of the Blackfoot's head. Perhaps it was Green-Stripe Blanket who had cried out a warning to his friend. Bass wasn't for sure. He couldn't see the other warrior.

Or, it might have been Painted Robe himself who screamed as he saw the tomahawk on its way and could not get his head out of its path. Or, perhaps he yelled in surprise and pain the instant the sharp blade was being driven through his skull and into his brain. Bass felt the hot splatter of blood and brain. . . .

But none of that mattered now as Painted Robe collapsed backward, his legs tangled with the white man's as all strength drained out of the trapper. The Blackfoot spilled one way, Titus slowly sank onto his elbow, rolled onto his back away from the warrior, and let out a long raspy sigh.

Hard to breathe, growing harder still. His chest filling up with blood. Shot in the lights.

Gradually the fingers of his right hand crawled to his belly, feeling the amazing warmth, the gushing wetness, the bubbles of gut spewing from the deep, long, ghastly wound that had opened him up from side to side. Scratch closed his eyes, wishing he could have held Waits one more time. Wishing he could have spent just one more night lying against her before this last day had been given them both. Just one more night with her—

Sensing a presence, Scratch slowly opened his eyes, blinking his one good one until it focused on the hazy form that moved over him, then stopped. Green-Stripe Blanket stood frozen over the old man for a long, long time. Staring down at the white man. Then the Blackfoot's hand started down for the trapper's throat.

In a futile move, Bass seized the Indian's wrist, held it as tightly as he could while the Blackfoot used his other hand to pull himself free of the trapper's grip. It wasn't hard; almost all Scratch's strength was gone. His head flopped back into the bloody, trampled snow. Titus knew he was too weak to delay, much less stop, what was to come. But a strange calmness seeped through him as he realized death was now. Assured of it all the more when Green-Stripe Blanket reached around the back of the white man's head and seized hold of the collar of Bass's greasy warshirt.

Ain't you got a surprise comin'? Scratch thought as he was rolled onto his side. *Figger to tear off my hat to scalp me now . . . an' you're gonna find I awready been scalped!*

He felt his fur hat get torn off, then started to snort with this one last joke on his murderers when the Indian suddenly dropped to a knee so he could stare intently into Bass's face. The young warrior reached out tentatively, as if unsure of what he was about to do, then gently tugged the faded black silk bandanna off the old trapper's head. The Blackfoot's eyes widened . . . but not in fear or surprise. Instead, in something like . . . like recognition.

For a moment the Blackfoot's eyes grew big with wonder, even awe, as he looked this way, then that—as if afraid the Crow war party would come racing over the brow of the nearby hills and discover him . . . but eventually his dark eyes came back to rest on the white man's face once more. Not near as wide now, no longer filled with amazement. Strangely, they had grown soft.

Titus gagged, felt his riven stomach lurch as he did his best to turn his head aside, puking up a great glob of blood onto the Blackfoot's arm, the one that still gripped him by the back of his collar. Sensing how weak he was becoming, how much the temperature had fallen since he had ridden down on these five raiders, Scratch watched with dulled senses as the Indian scrambled onto his feet, turned, and with that hand still gripping the back of Bass's collar . . . started to drag the white man across the crusty snow.

Slowly, yard by yard, lunge by lunge, the young man got the old trapper turned. As the Blackfoot started up the long, shallow slope toward the stand of some saplings and taller timber, away from the rushes and willow, escaping the dirty ice of that frozen beaver pond, one of the white man's useless legs at a time slowly straightened out and trailed along behind him. He was helpless now. No matter what the Blackfoot decided to do with his body, it could not matter. He was good as dead already.

That dirty trench of new snow he was leaving behind told the story, smeared with gobs of his blood. How he struggled to maintain enough strength to hold in the long, warm, greasy coils of his own sundered gut, warm, steaming intestine that squirted out between his hands, escaping the pressure of his arms, spilling to his left side where Painted Robe had opened him like one of his grandpap's Christmas hogs . . . trailing beside him in the snow. Oh—how he didn't want his guts to be dragged through the bloody trench up this long, sagebrush-covered slope as the fat, frozen, fluffy flakes of snow collected on his coupled arms, steaming on the purplish coil of his warm gut that he could no longer contain.

With a grunt from them both, the Blackfoot stopped. Shifted his position, then yanked on the white man once more. Then again. Finally a last time. And eventually came around in front of the trapper, seized both of Bass's shoulders, and tugged him up into a sitting position.

He struggled to focus that one good eye on the warrior as the Blackfoot gently nudged him back now. Without protest, unable to fight, Titus sensed the trunk of the tree press between his shoulder blades. He let his head relax back against the rough bark and sighed. Listening to the sounds of the warrior as the Blackfoot moved off on the icy snow.

Titus coughed and spewed up some bloody phlegm. Nothing left in his belly to bring up but more blood. Hell, he didn't have a belly left to hold anything—

Suddenly the warrior was kneeling close again, unfurling the red capote as Bass watched the swimming of the colors and motion. Must be the murderer's coat, he thought. But why?

Green-Stripe Blanket gently spread the red capote over the white man's bloody body. He tugged it down Bass's legs and tucked it under them. Watching this ceremony with complete disbelief, Bass finally brought his one good eye again to the man's face. The smeared paint, the high cheekbones . . . like so many other brownskins he had fought and killed in all his seasons in this high and terrible land.

But this man's eyes were soft. Not like the chertlike eyes of Yellow Paint Elkskin, or Buffalo Horn Headdress. Not at all like Painted Robe's eyes filled with such hatred and fury.

"Old man," the Indian's lips said.

Bass thought he shook his head slightly, heavy as it was, befuddled that he understood the Blackfoot's language. And he tried to speak, but no sound came from his own tongue.

"Don't talk, old man," the warrior said, his words clear and distinct inside the white man's head again. As if the Blackfoot spoke a passable American. "Save your breath for what must come next. You must save your breath to start your walk on the wind."

"W-walk?" he finally uttered in a moist whisper. "Wind?"

With a nod, the Blackfoot stuffed a hand inside his blanket, reaching inside the sleeveless buffalo-hide vest he wore, where two of his fingers snagged the long, thin leather loop that was draped around his neck. Bending his head slightly, the warrior tugged the thong free of his otter-wrapped braids, on over the top of his head where he had tied a big handful of the hair at the front of his brow into a grease-crusted sprig that stood straight up, the sort of hairstyle a warrior would adapt when riding into battle, a symbol that any fighting man would understand: he was daring all his enemies to attempt to take his taunting scalplock.

With a tug, the Blackfoot finally pulled an object free from beneath the front of that buffalo-hide vest Bass could now make out was sewn from the reddish skin of a young buffalo calf. Straining, his vision fixed on what the warrior held out between them, the object just inches from the white man's eyes.

An eagle wingbone whistle, suspended from its thong and gently nudged by the icy wind that spat sharp snowy arrowpoints against their exposed flesh.

But . . . not just any eagle wingbone whistle. The half breath seized inside what Titus had left of his lungs. This . . . this whistle appeared familiar. Wrapped in porcupine quills of oxblood red and greasy yellow. A simple pattern of flattened, colored quills that he could not help but recognize.

Eventually his moist, swimming eye climbed to the warrior's face. Something like a smile seemed to cross that face as the Indian realized the old man was studying him. The Blackfoot reached up to his chin, yanked on the thong that tied the wolfhide cape on his head, and pulled it off.

"Do you know me now, old man?"

There it was again. That perfect white man's American talk he magically heard inside his head when the Blackfoot opened his mouth, moved his lips and tongue. Even though other, foreign sounds came out of the warrior's face, like the garbled tangle of some foreign language . . . what Bass heard inside his head was nonetheless American talk he understood perfectly.

"I-I don't know you," and he hacked up more of the thick blood congealing at the back of his throat. Finally he stared at the whistle, and whispered, "But . . . I know th-that."

"It was my brother's," the warrior said inside Bass's head. "You killed him many, many winters ago."

He stared at the whistle, realizing what the Blackfoot said must surely be true. That was where he had seen it before, having taken it off the dead man he had eventually buried in a tree, wrapped in a warrior's red blanket.

"I don't have a red blanket to bury you in," the young warrior apologized. "The way you buried my brother that day. All I have is this red coat that belonged to my friend who you killed."

Swallowing, Bass explained, "He killed my wife."

"Your woman?"

"In the village. He was the only one of you I really wanted. I am glad he is dead now."

"It is good you can wear his capote," the young warrior declared. "He honors you, a mighty warrior who killed him. You wear the color of war as you die, old man. Just the way you honored my brother many winters ago."

"One warrior always honors ano-another."

As the first tear slipped from the Blackfoot's eye, he said, "And you honored me that day too. Giving me my brother's war whistle, placing it between my lips to blow for him as he began to take his first steps on the wind."

He didn't know if he could talk anymore, it was getting so hard to breathe, just to keep his eyes open, "I-I . . ."

"Don't go to sleep yet," the Indian scolded. "You must walk this last road alone, but you must walk it before you sleep."

"C-can't—"

Scratch felt the Blackfoot slip the long leather loop around his neck, tug it down behind his long, curly hair, then gently straighten it out before he held up the whistle once more.

"Yes . . . you can. Because you are a warrior. You must do this before you start your last, long walk."

Then the young man brought his fingers up, gently parting the old trapper's lips, prying his teeth apart as Bass felt himself sinking into such unimaginable cold. Eventually the youngster managed to slip the end of the whistle between Scratch's teeth.

Leaning back at last, the Blackfoot brought his face down close to the old man's, his two dark-cherry eyes looking back and forth between the good eye and that milky, clouded one.

At long last the warrior whispered, "Now . . . it is time for you to blow for yourself. Blow to call on the First Maker, the guardian of all warriors. Blow to call upon He Who Will Listen To Our Final Prayers. Blow, you old warrior!"

He tried, but only a weak whisper of air escaped the end of the warrior's wingbone whistle.

"You must try harder, old man," the Blackfoot urged. "The day you were born, the First Maker blew His breath into your mouth, into your spirit the very moment you emerged from your mother's womb. Now it is time for you to blow out your last breath, to return it back to the First Maker . . . in the great circle of a warrior's life. That first breath He gave you, now you must send it back to Him with your final prayer, old warrior. One last breath and it will be finished."

He tried again. A little louder.

"That wasn't your last," the warrior explained. "The last will be strong. As strong and mighty as you have been a warrior all those seasons you have walked this earth. But now, you must begin a different journey. You will begin to walk on the wind for all time. So you must blow."

Leaning back, the Blackfoot rocked onto his haunches, then stood, looking down at the white man. "This is for you to do now, on your own. Make this last prayer of yours a good one, old warrior. The First Maker will hear what prayer rests in your heart as you blow with that final breath . . . and he will be there to walk beside you on the wind."

Bass sat there, leaning against the tree, blinking his pooling eyes as the young warrior turned slowly and trudged down the gentle slope. After a few steps, the young man whose life he had once saved, the young man whom Titus Bass had once sent back to his people . . . this Blackfoot warrior stopped—turned—and spoke one last time.

"Pray for what is most dear in your heart, Wind Walker."

THIRTY-FOUR

He watched the young warrior trudge down the snowy slope until he could not see the figure anymore for the swirling snow that swept in upon gusts of cold wind.

Cold.

How he wished he could spend one more warm night with her. Just holding her, not even taking her in a fevered, frantic rush. Just to cradle her against him one more night. To lie there feeling her heart beating against him, listening to the soft breathing of their children in their lodge until the sky at the top of the poles turned gray and a new day was a'born. What he wouldn't give to feel her arms around him one last night.

But it was too late now. So cold. Even his warm gut was starting to freeze in his hands.

The snow stung his eyes, sharp against his wet cheeks where his tears had fallen. So he closed them, wondering how he would ever have the strength to blow now that he was growing weaker and weaker. He didn't have enough will left in him—

With a soft rustle of movement, he felt them approach, brushing against him on both sides.

Slowly Titus opened his eyes, blinked to be sure. And saw them. The Little People. And gradually the realization of what that meant made his throat go dry.

One of them, almost completely covered with long, unkempt gray hair, leaned close to his face and whispered, "You see us, old friend?"

"Yes, I . . . I finally see you." He thought the words in his mind, his front teeth still clamped around the end of that whistle.

The Little Person smiled warmly, then peered down the old man's frame as he asked, "Do you remember what I told you long ago about when the time came that you would finally see us?"

Titus nodded, weakly.

"Do you feel pain?"

Bass nodded again.

The leader made a simple gesture, and his four companions came up to stand around the old man. They reached out with their tiny, hairy hands. Without warning, two of them slapped him on the soles of his feet, hard. One of the others gently laid his hands over the gaping belly wound, and the fourth spread his fingers over the bullet hole in his chest.

"Now—is there any pain?"

He shook his head, struck with wonder, bewildered by the magic. The immense, bone-numbing cold was still there, so icy he had never experienced anything close to it. But . . . no more did he suffer the pain.

"Then we have done all we can for you, old friend," the leader said softly as his four companions stepped behind him. "Do you remember what your Blackfoot helper said before he left you to do the rest on your own?"

He remembered.

"Good. We are going away too. Now you must do what remains for yourself. Close your eyes and make your prayer."

Without attempting to speak, he let his eyelids fall. And with his total being concentrated on struggling to draw one last, ragged, liquid breath deep within his shredded lungs. There it was! Such warmth that he wanted to sing out in victory, to cry out in joy. Lo, those many years, the countless seasons he had taken for granted this simple act of breathing. And only now, at the end, learning that the First Maker, his Creator who had given him his first breath as a newborn, was now asking him to utter one last prayer with his final breath.

"Pray for what is most dear in your heart, Wind Walker."

The young Blackfoot's words rang in his head.

And he felt that warmth from his chest rising into his throat, at the back of his tongue, one last gush of immense joy and gratitude for all that had been given him in his life, feeling the hot tears seeping between his eyelids he had clenched against the snowy, icy blasts of cold . . . that final prayer entered the whistle. Shrill and high.

An eagle's cry of victory as it leaped from the wingbone, into the air, rising . . . rising . . . rising through the terrible cold . . . far, far higher still.

For the longest time he sat there, the tears frozen on his cheeks, conscious of how the cold was gradually diminishing. Knowing that if he weren't already dead, he soon would be. After all, Titus reasoned, he no longer sensed the bone-jarring temperature, nor the insistent tug of the wind at his hair and flesh. Even the rock-hard trunk of the tree he leaned against no longer mattered—

Then, just when he wasn't so sure what had happened to him, Scratch sensed what felt like warm breath against his face, heard the gentle call of a Steller's jay as it rose in flight—so clear and distinct he could hear every flap of its wings.

Afraid his eyes would be frozen shut, Bass slowly opened them, but no more than slits because of the bright light illuminating the meadow before him. No winter scene . . . instead, what he saw was a sunlight benediction rained down upon a green, grassy beaver meadow ringed by jack pine and aspen, fragrant cedar and aromatic sage. Shadows dappled the far edge of that glen where sunlight shot through the leafy branches in a complex tapestry of color . . . enough to convince him it was no longer winter. He wasn't cold anymore. And suddenly he realized he wasn't alone.

At first he thought it was the Little People who had come to take away the pain from his dying, perhaps they who had created this dream for him. Because, he remembered with a sudden reckoning, that dream was in fact reality all along. If he had taken all those years in these high and majestic places to learn anything . . . it was that most simple fact that his dreams would always be more real than anything he had ever experienced.

Wanting to speak, Titus pushed his tongue against the wingbone whistle. But his lips were so dry they had fused together. So he reached up and gently pulled the whistle free. Licked his lips, and let the whistle lay against his chest. That's when he looked down and noticed the blood. He'd been wounded many times before—knives and lead balls and arrows too—but never before had he seen so much of his own blood. Wallowing in it by the time the young Blackfoot got him dragged up this slope, to this shady stand of trees overlooking the beaver meadow . . .

But, while the blood still soaked his shirt and leggings, brownish, blackened stains smeared up and down the middle of him, when he slowly raised his two arms away from his belly to inspect himself, there was no wound, no coil of torn and twisted gut. Bewildered, he moved the whistle aside and stared down at the chest wound. A blood-ringed hole in the middle of his buckskin shirt. But when he gently probed with a finger through that hole, he encountered no wound.

The Little People could tell him. There they were! Across the meadow in the streaks of sunlight and shadow streaming through those beckoning quakies. A beaver gave a warning slap with its tail, then slipped beneath the placid surface of the pond reflecting the aching blue of the sky overhead.

"I hear you!" he said, surprising himself with how strong his voice had become after being so weak, feeling so drained, so damned empty for so long. "C'mon out—I got a few more questions for you—"

But he cut off his call in midsentence as the shadow became figure and stepped into the edge of the light, moved down the emerald bank, and came to a stop at the grassy edge of the uncluttered pond.

"Titus!"

"Y-yes," he answered, his throat seizing in wonder as he recognized the man from the distant past. "That r-really you?"

"Cap'n Ebenezer Zane!" the man cried out, standing every bit as tall and bold as that day back in 1810 when he had waved aboard a gangly young lad from the Kentucky shore of the Ohio River, inviting him onto a flatboat loaded with goods bound for New Orleans, beckoning him to take that first leap into a lifetime of adventures where there would be no looking back.

"H-how you here . . .?"

"Don't you worry none 'bout that now, young Titus," Zane called. "I was sent to bring you along, son. It's your time now . . . time to come with us."

"Us?"

Zane turned slightly, took a step back to the line of quakies that whispered, quietly rattling with the warm breeze that barely ruffled the surface of the beaver pond. The old flatboat pilot made one simple gesture with his wrist.

Another tree's shadow blurred, taking shape as it inched into the sunlight. Striding down the hill to join Zane came Isaac Washburn, straight as a ramrod and fit as a freshly oiled square-jawed beaver trap.

"Hyar, ye boy! I see'd you made it to them Shinin' Mountains I tol't you of!" he called out with a wave across the meadow.

Titus rolled onto his hip, not sure if he could believe both of them being here. "I-I done it 'cause of what you told me, Gut," he said, his voice catching as he used the old mountaineer's handle. And felt the first of the warm tears begin to pool in his eyes.

"Nawww," Washburn protested with a bright smile that lit up his teeth the color of pin acorns, "you done it for your own self, Titus Bass. The way you was meant to all along."

He cleared the lump in his throat and called across the meadow, "You both come to fetch me, did you?"

"Me too," a new voice called as the shadow pulled itself away from the stand of aspen.

For a moment Titus sat right there, frozen and unable to move as he stared at Jack Hatcher, who stomped up between Washburn and Zane, looking hale and hearty and every bit as fit as that newly strung fiddle he raised up to the hollow of his shoulder.

"I come along to play us some of the ol' songs, Scratch," he cried out. "Ever' journey must have its music, ol't friend!"

"Never was much of a singer," Titus admitted as he started to rise to his feet.

"Neither was I," the new figure announced as it stepped into the meadow, hair the brilliant white of a newly born cloud. "But there was many a time I wished I could have sung, my heart was so filled with joy to find a friend like you."

"Asa? Jehoshaphat, if that ain't really you!"

McAfferty came up beside Hatcher, pounded Jack on the shoulder with his one hand, and said, "Maybe now's the time you play a li'l music for this'un been a long, long time gettin' into camp."

Drawing his ratty bow across the strings, Jack kicked off a light and merry tune, something Scratch knew he should recognize from long, long ago.

"If you won't sing," a new accent cried out as the shadow tore itself away from the copse of trees, "I sure will. You always told me it was my songs kept you from growing sore afraid on that trip we made down the mighty Columbia!"

The big man could be no one else. "J-Jarrell! I heard the ague laid you down."

Thornbrugh, the English-born former seaman who had finished out his life with the Hudson's Bay Company, came up to join the group, stomping his foot and clapping his hands. "This fiddler doesn't play so bad for being American!"

"C'mon, Titus!" Zane cheered.

Washburn waved him over, saying, "Come join the hurraw!"

As the notes from Hatcher's fiddle filled that meadow, more shadows now stepped away from the trees, taking form only when they emerged into the sunlight. His old friend Arapooesh, legendary chief of the Crow. And at his elbow came Whistler, Scratch's own father-in-law. At his side walked Whistler's tall and handsome son, Strikes In Camp. When the three warriors moved up, the white men opened their tiny crescent, enlarging it once more.

"W-Whistler!" he croaked, his voice breaking with sentiment, his eyes filling with tears. Seeing the man made him want to hope all the more. Oh, how he had prayed with that last and final breath.

"Yes, my son—you have a question?"

"Whistler, have . . . have you seen her?"

"Who is it you ask for?"

"W-Waits . . ." But suddenly he remembered that proper manners dictated that he wasn't supposed to speak the name of one who had died. "I'm sorry, I shouldn't use your names any longer—"

"That is not important now, *Pote Ani*," Whistler responded with amused kindness. "Who do you wish most to see?"

"My wife . . . the only woman I truly loved in all my life."

Strikes In Camp turned to his right and gestured to the line of quakies. A small figure stepped from the shadows, taking form as if emerging from beneath the surface of that beaver pond. Short, and towheaded, looking every bit like his mother—

"Lucas?" he cried as he finally lunged a step forward.

But instead of answering, the young child stopped right at that edge of the light, stretched out his little hand, reaching back into the shadows as Jack's fiddle sang so sweetly the notes of a gentle lullaby.

As Titus watched, slack-jawed and numbed with wonder, he saw her take shape, slipping her long-fingered hand between Lucas's little fingers. Into that edge of sunlight she came, dressed in a brilliant dress of doeskin, even more finely made than the one she had worn the day they gave their vows to one another. And cradled across her other arm . . .

In his heart Scratch knew.

And instantly started forward, stumbling at first, for his legs were so long without movement. Careening forward, he trudged faster and faster, skirting around the edge of that tranquil blue beaver pond.

Titus knew who Waits held in her arm as she walked beside the grinning boy, clutching Lucas's little hand, both of them slowly moving toward him while that crowd of old friends whooped and clapped, sang out their war song or some off-key ditty of an old tune their mam had soothed them to sleep with back in those days when there hadn't been a care in their world.

Titus shuddered to a stop the moment he glimpsed the infant's face, so like Waits-by-the-Water's: with her big round eyes and those high cheeks blushed with copper. Hair more brown than black, wavy too, like his father's.

As he stared dumbfounded at the babe, Lucas said in a whisper, "It's your li'l boy, Gran'papa. Now you an' me gonna teach him ever'thing . . . one day soon, ain't we?"

The old friends and compatriots were swallowing him up of a sudden, their hands reaching out to touch him at long last over the years, tousle his hair, slap him on the back, and pound him on the shoulder. Finally she took another step forward and reached him herself, laying her damp cheek against his breast.

"Your friends," she whispered to him, "they told me I wouldn't have to wait for you very long. They said you always kept your promise—especially the last promise you made to meet me here on the mountaintop."

His heart filling with joy as he wrapped his arms around her and raised his face to the sky, whispering his utter thanks . . . Titus knew he had made it to the mountaintop at last.

ABOUT THE AUTHOR

TERRY C. JOHNSTON was born the first day of 1947 on the plains of Kansas, and has lived all his life in the American West. His first novel, *Carry the Wind,* won the Medicine Pipe Bearer's Award from the Western Writers of America, and his subsequent books, among them *Dance on the Wind, Cry of the Hawk,* and *Long Winter Gone,* have appeared on bestseller lists throughout the country. He lives and writes in Big Sky country near Billings, Montana.

Each year Terry and his wife, Vanette, publish their annual "WinterSong" newsletter. Twice every summer they take readers on one-week tours of the rendezvous sites of the early Rocky Mountain Fur Trade, and to the battle sites of the Indian Wars.

Those wanting to write to the author, those requesting the annual "WinterSong" newsletter, or those desiring information on taking part in the author's summer historical tours can write to him at:

Terry C. Johnston
P. O. Box 50594
Billings, MT 59105

Or, you can find his website at:

http://www.imt.net/~tjohnston/

and can e-mail him at:

tjohnston@imt.net